THE MAMMOTH BOOK OF MODERN SCIENCE FICTION

Also available

The Mammoth Book of Classic Science Fiction—
Short Novels of the 1930s

The Mammoth Book of Golden Age Science Fiction—
Short Novels of the 1940s

The Mammoth Book of Vintage Science Fiction—
Short Novels of the 1950s

The Mammoth Book of New Age Science Fiction—
Short Novels of the 1960s

The Mammoth Book of Fantastic Science Fiction—
Short Novels of the 1970s

The Mammoth Book of Private Eye Stories

The Mammoth Book of Great Detective Stories

The Mammoth Book of Spy Thrillers

The Mammoth Book of True Murder

The Mammoth Book of True Crime

The Mammoth Book of True Crime 2

The Mammoth Book of Short Horror Novels

The Mammoth Book of True War Stories

The Mammoth Book of Modern War Stories

The Mammoth Book of the Western

The Mammoth Book of Ghost Stories

The Mammoth Book of Ghost Stories 2

The Mammoth Book of the Supernatural

The Mammoth Book of Astounding Puzzles

The Mammoth Book of Vampires

The Mammoth Book of Terror

The Mammoth Book of Killer Women

The Mammoth Book of

MODERN
SCIENCE FICTION

Short Novels of the 1980s

Presented by Isaac Asimov

Edited by

Charles G. Waugh and Martin H. Greenberg

Carroll & Graf Publishers, Inc.
New York

Carroll & Graf Publishers, Inc.
260 Fifth Avenue
New York
NY 10001

First published in Great Britain 1993

First Carroll & Graf edition 1993

ISBN 0-88184-959-6

Printed in Great Britain.

10 9 8 7 6 5 4 3 2 1

CONTENTS

ACKNOWLEDGEMENTS

"Slow Music" by James Tiptree, Jr.—Copyright © 1980 by James Tiptree, Jr. First appeared in *Interfaces*. Reprinted by permission of the author's Estate and the Estate's agent, Virginia Kidd.

"Le Croix (The Cross)" by Barry N. Malzberg—Copyright © 1980 by Barry N. Malzberg. First appeared in *Their Immortal Hearts*. Reprinted by permission of the author.

"Scorched Supper On New Niger" by Suzy McKee Charnas—Copyright © 1980 by Suzy McKee Charnas. First appeared in *New Voices III*. Reprinted by permission of the author.

"The Saturn Game" by Poul Anderson—Copyright © 1981 by Davis Publications, Inc. First appeared in ANALOG. Reprinted by permission of the Scott Meredith Literary Agency, Inc., 845 Third Avenue, New York, NY 10022.

"Hardfought" by Greg Bear—Copyright © 1982 by Davis Publications, Inc. First appeared in *Isaac Asimov's Science Fiction Magazine*. Reprinted by permission of the author.

"Swarmer, Skimmer" by Gregory Benford—Copyright © 1982 by Abbenford Associates. Reprinted by permission of the author.

"Sailing to Byzantium" by Robert Silverberg—Copyright © 1984, 1985 by Agberg, Ltd. Reprinted by permission of Agberg, Ltd.

"Trinity" by Nancy Kress—Copyright © 1984 by Davis Publications, Inc. First appeared in *Isaac Asimov's Science Fiction Magazine*. Reprinted by permission of the author.

"The Blind Geometer" by Kim Stanley Robinson—Copyright © 1987, 1989 by Kim Stanley Robinson. Reprinted by permission of the author.

"Surfacing" by Walter Jon Williams—Copyright © 1988 by Davis Publications, Inc. First appeared in *Isaac Asimov's Science Fiction Magazine*. Reprinted by permission of the author and his agent, Ralph M. Vicinanza.

SLOW MUSIC

James Tiptree, Jr.

> Caoilte tossing his burning hair
> and Niamh calling "Away, come away;
> Empty your heart of its mortal dream . . .
> We come between man and the deed of his hand,
> We come between him and the hope of his heart."
> —W.B. Yeats

LIGHT CAME ON AS JAKKO walked down the lawn past the house; elegantly concealed spots and floods which made the night into a great intimate room. Overhead the big conifers formed a furry nave drooping toward the black lake below the bluff ahead. This had been a beloved home he saw; every luxurious device was subdued to preserve the beauty of the forested shore. He walked on a carpet of violets and mosses, in his hand the map that had guided him here from the city.

It was the stillness before dawn. A long-winged night bird swirled in to catch a last moth in the dome of light. Before him shone a bright spear point. Jakko saw it was the phosphorescent tip of a mast against the stars. He went down velvety steps to find a small sailboat floating at the dock like a silver leaf reflected on a dark mirror.

In silence he stepped on board, touched the mast.

A gossamer sail spread its fan, the mooring parted soundlessly.

The dawn breeze barely filled the sail, but the craft moved smoothly out, leaving a glassy line of wake. Jakko half-poised to jump. He knew nothing of such playtoys, he should go back and find another boat. As he did so, the shore lights went out, leaving him in darkness. He turned and saw Regulus rising ahead where the channel must be. Still, this was not the craft for him. He tugged at the tiller and sail, meaning to turn it back.

But the little boat ran smoothly on, and then he noticed the lights of a small computer glowing by the mast. He relaxed; this was no toy, the boat was fully programmed and he could guess what the course must be. He stood examining the sky, a statue-man gliding across reflected night.

The eastern horizon changed, veiled its stars as he neared it. He could see the channel now, a silvery cut straight ahead between dark banks. The boat ran over glittering shallows where something splashed hugely, and headed into the shining lane. As it did so, all silver changed to lead and the stars were gone. Day was coming. A great pearl-colored blush spread upward before him, developed bands of lavender and rays of coral-gold fire melting to green iridescence overhead. The boat was now gliding on a ribbon of fiery light between black-silhouetted banks. Jakko looked back and saw dazzling cloud-cities heaped behind him in the west. The vast imminence of sunrise. He sighed aloud.

He understood that all this demonstration of glory was nothing but the effects of dust and vapor in the thin skin of air around a small planet, whereon he crawled wingless. No vastness brooded; the planet was merely turning with him into the rays of its mediocre primary. His family, everyone, knew that on the River he would encounter the Galaxy itself in glory. Suns beyond count, magnificence to which this was nothing. And yet—and yet to him this was not nothing. It was intimately his, man-sized. He made an ambiguous sound in his throat. He resented the trivialization of this beauty, and he resented being moved by it. So he passed along, idly holding the sail rope like a man leashing the living wind, his face troubled and very young.

The little craft ran on unerringly, threading the winding sheen of the canal. As the sun rose, Jakko began to hear a faint drone ahead. The sea surf. He thought of the persons who must have made this voyage before him: the ship's family, savoring their final days of mortality. A happy voyage, a picnic. The thought reminded him that he was hungry; the last groundcar's synthesizer had been faulty.

He tied the rope and searched. The boat had replenished its water, but there was only one food bar. Jakko lay down in the cushioned well and ate and drank comfortably, while the sky turned turquoise and then cobalt. Presently they emerged into an enormous lagoon and began to run south between low islands. Jakko trailed his hand and tasted brackish salt. When the boat turned east again and made for a seaward opening, he became doubly certain. The craft was programmed for the River, like almost everything else on the world he knew.

Sure enough, the tiny bark ran through an inlet and straight out into the chop beyond a long beach, extruded outriggers, and passed like a cork over the reef foam onto the deep green swells beyond. Here it pitched once and steadied; Jakko guessed it had thrust down a keel. Then it turned south and began to run along outside the reef, steady as a knife cut with the wind on its quarter. Going Riverward for sure. The nearest River-place was here called Vidalita or Beata, or sometimes Falaz, meaning "illusion." It was far south and inland. Jakko guessed they were making for a landing where a moveway met the sea. He had still time to think, to struggle with the trouble under his mind.

But as the sun turned the boat into a trim white-gold bird flying over green transparency, Jakko's eyes closed and he slept, protected by invisible deflectors from the bow-spray. Once he opened his eyes and saw a painted fish tearing along magically in the standing wave below his head. He smiled and slept again, dreaming of a great wave dying, a wave that was a many-headed beast. His face became sad and his lips moved soundlessly, as if repeating. "No . . . no . . ."

When he woke they were sailing quite close by a long bluff on his right. In the cliff ahead was a big white building or tower, only a little ruined. Suddenly he caught sight of a figure moving on the beach before it. A living human? He jumped up to look. He had not seen a strange human person in many years.

Yes—it was a live person, strangely colored gold and black. He waved wildly.

The person on the beach slowly raised an arm.

Alight with excitement, Jakko switched off the computer and grabbed the rudder and sail. The line of reef surf seemed open here. He turned the boat shoreward, riding on a big swell. But the wave left him. He veered erratically, and the surf behind broached into the boat, overturning it and throwing him out. He knew how to swim; he surfaced and struck out strongly for the shore, spluttering brine. Presently he was wading out onto the white beach, a short, strongly built, reddened young male person with pale hair and water-blue eyes.

The stranger was walking hesitantly toward him. Jakko saw it was a thin, dark-skinned girl wearing a curious netted hat. Her body was wrapped in orange silk and she carried heavy gloves in one hand. Three nervous moondogs followed her. He began turning water out of his shorts pockets as she came up.

"Your . . . boat," she said in the language of that time. Her voice was low and uncertain.

They both turned to look at the confused place by the reef where the sailboat floated half-submerged.

"I turned it off. The computer." His words came jerkily too, they were both unused to speech.

"It will come ashore down there." She pointed, still studying him in a wary, preoccupied way. She was much smaller than he. "Why did you turn? Aren't you going to the River?"

"No." He coughed. "Well, yes, in a way. My father wants me to say good-bye. They left while I was traveling."

"You're not . . . ready?"

"No. I don't—" He broke off. "Are you staying alone here?"

"Yes. I'm not going, either."

They stood awkwardly in the sea wind. Jakko noticed that the three moondogs were lined up single file, tiptoeing upwind toward him with their eyes closed, sniffing. They were not, of course, from the moon, but they looked it, being white and oddly shaped.

"It's a treat for them," the girl said. "Something different." Her voice was stronger now. After a pause she added, "You can stay here for a while if you want. I'll show you but I have to finish my work first."

"Thank you," he remembered to say.

As they climbed steps cut in the bluff Jakko asked. "What are you working at?"

"Oh, everything. Right now it's bees."

"Bees!" he marveled. "They made what—honey? I thought they were all gone."

"I have a lot of old things." She kept glancing at him intently as they climbed. "Are you quite healthy?"

"Oh yes. Why not? I'm all alpha so far as I know. Everybody is."

"Was," she corrected. "Here are my bee skeps."

They came around a low wall and stopped by five small wicker huts. A buzzing insect whizzed by Jakko's face, coming from some feathery shrubs. He saw that the bloom-tipped foliage was alive with the golden humming things. Recalling that they could sting, he stepped back.

"You better go around the other way." She pointed. "They might hurt a stranger." She pulled her veil down hiding her face. Just as he turned away, she added, "I thought you might impregnate me."

He wheeled back, not really able to react because of the distracting bees. "But isn't that terribly complicated?"

"I don't think so. I have the pills." She pulled on her gloves.

"Yes, the pills. I know." He frowned. "But you'd have to stay, I mean one just can't—"

"I know that. I have to do my bees now. We can talk later."

"Of course." He started away and suddenly turned back.

"Look!" He didn't know her name. "You, look!"

"What?" She was a strange little figure, black and orange with huge hands and a big veil-muffled head. "What?"

"I felt it. Just then, desire. Can't you see?"

They both gazed at his wet shorts.

"I guess not," he said finally. "But I felt it, I swear. Sexual desire."

She pushed back her veil, frowning. "It will stay, won't it? Or come back? This isn't a very good place. I mean, the bees. And it's no use without the pills."

"That's so."

He went away then, walking carefully because of the tension around his pubic bone. Like a keel, snug and tight. His whole body felt reorganized. It had been years since he'd felt flashes like that, not since he was fifteen at least. Most people never did. That was variously thought to be because of the River, or from their parents' surviving the Poison Centuries, or because the general alpha strain was so forebrain-dominant. It gave him an archaic, secret pride. Maybe he was a throwback.

He passed under cool archways, and found himself in a green, protected place behind the seaward wall. A garden, he saw, looking round surprised at clumps of large tied-up fruiting plants, peculiar trees with green balls at their tops, disorderly rows of rather unaesthetic greenery. Tentatively he identified tomatoes, peppers, a feathery leaf which he thought had an edible root. A utilitarian planting. His uncle had once amused the family by doing something of the sort, but not on this scale. Jakko shook his head.

In the center of the garden stood a round stone coping with a primitive apparatus on top. He walked over and looked down. Water, a bucket on a rope. Then he saw that there was also an ordinary tap. He opened it and drank, looking at the odd implements leaning on the coping. Earth tools. He did not really want to think about what the strange woman had said.

A shadow moved by his foot. The largest moondog had come quite close, inhaling dreamily. "Hello," he said to it. Some of these dogs could talk a little. This one opened its eyes wide but said nothing.

He stared about, wiping his mouth, feeling his clothes almost dry now in the hot sun. On three sides the garden was surrounded by arcades; above him on the ruined side was a square cracked masonry tower with no roof. A large place, whatever it was. He walked into the shade of the nearest arcade, which turned out to be littered with myriad disassembled or partly assembled objects: tools, containers, who knew what. Her "work"? The place felt strange, vibrant and busy. He realized he had entered only empty houses on his year-long journey. This one was alive, lived-in. Messy. It hummed like the bee skeps. He turned down a cool corridor, looking into rooms piled with more stuff. In one, three white animals he couldn't identify were asleep in a heap of cloth on a bed. They moved their ears at him like big pale shells but did not awaken.

He heard staccato noises and came out into another courtyard where plump white birds walked with jerking heads. "Chickens!" he decided, delighted by the irrational variety of this place. He went from there into a large room with windows on the sea, and heard a door close.

It was the woman, or girl, coming to him, holding her hat and gloves. Her hair was a dark curly cap, her head elegantly small; an effect he had always admired. He remembered something to say.

"I'm called Jakko. What's your name?"

"Jakko." She tasted the sound. "Hello, Jakko. I'm Peachthief." She smiled very briefly, entirely changing her face.

"Peachthief." On impulse he moved toward her, holding out his hands. She tucked her bundle under her arm and took both of his. They stood like that a moment, not quite looking at each other. Jakko felt excited. Not sexually, but more as if the air was electrically charged.

"Well." She took her hands away and began unwrapping a leafy wad. "I brought a honeycomb even if it isn't quite ready." She showed him a sticky-looking frame with two dead bees on it. "Come on."

She walked rapidly out into another corridor and entered a shiny room he thought might be a laboratory.

"My food room," she told him. Again Jakko was amazed. There stood a synthesizer, to be sure, but beside it were shelves full of pots and bags and jars and containers of all descriptions. Unknown implements lay about and there was a fireplace which had been partly sealed up. Bunches of plant parts hung from racks overhead. He identified some brownish ovoids in a bowl as eggs. From the chickens?

Peachthief was cleaning the honeycomb with a manually operated knife. "I use the wax for my loom, and for candles. Light."

"What's wrong with the lights?"

"Nothing." She turned around, gesturing emphatically with the knife. "Don't you understand? All these machines, they'll go. They won't run forever. They'll break or wear out or run down. There won't *be* any, anymore. Then we'll have to use natural things."

"But that won't be for centuries!" he protested. "Decades, anyhow. They're all still going, they'll last for us."

"For you," she said scornfully. "Not for me. I intend to stay. With my children." She turned her back on him and added in a friendlier voice, "Besides, the old things are aesthetic. I'll show you, when it gets dark."

"But you haven't any children! Have you?" He was purely astonished.

"Not yet." Her back was still turned.

"I'm hungry," he said, and went to work the synthesizer. He made it give him a bar with a hard filler; for some reason he wanted to crunch it in his teeth.

She finished with the honey and turned around. "Have you ever had a natural meal?"

"Oh yes," he said, chewing. "One of my uncles tried that. It was very nice," he added politely.

She looked at him sharply and smiled again, on—off. They went out of the food room. The afternoon was fading into great gold and orange streamers above the courtyard, colored like Peachthief's garment.

"You can sleep here." She opened a slatted door. The room was small and bare, with a window on the sea.

"There isn't any bed," he objected.

She opened a chest and took out a big wad of string. "Hang this end on that hook over there."

When she hung up the other end he saw it was a large mesh hammock.

"That's what I sleep in. They're comfortable. Try it."

He climbed in awkwardly. The thing came up around him like a bag. She gave a short sweet laugh as brief as her smile.

"No, you lie on the diagonal. Like this." She tugged his legs, sending a peculiar shudder through him. "That straightens it, see?"

It would probably be all right, he decided, struggling out. Peachthief was pointing to a covered pail.

"That's for your wastes. It goes on the garden, in the end."

He was appalled, but said nothing, letting her lead him out through a room with glass tanks in the walls to a big screened-in porch fronting the ocean. It was badly in need of cleaners. The sky was glorious with opalescent domes and spires, reflections of the sunset behind them, painting amazing colors on the sea.

"This is where I eat."

"What is this place?"

"It was a sea station last, I think. Station Juliet. They monitored the fish and the ocean traffic, and rescued people and so on."

He was distracted by noticing long convergent dove-blue rays like mysterious paths into the horizon; cloud shadows cast across the world. Beauty of the dust. Why must it move him so?

"—even a medical section," she was saying. "I really could have babies, I mean in case of trouble."

"You don't mean it." He felt only irritation now. "I don't feel any more desire," he told her.

She shrugged. "I don't either. We'll talk about it later on."

"Have you always lived here?"

"Oh, no." She began taking pots and dishes out of an insulated case. The three moondogs had joined them silently; she set bowls before them. They lapped, stealing glances at Jakko. They were, he knew, very strong despite their sticklike appearance.

"Let's sit here." She plumped down on one end of the lounge and began biting forcefully into a crusty thing like a slab of drybar. He noticed she had magnificent teeth. Her dark skin set them off beautifully, as it enhanced her eyes. He had never met anyone so different in every way from himself and his family. He vacillated between interest and a vague alarm.

"Try some of the honey." She handed him a container and spoon. It looked quite clean. He tasted it eagerly; honey was much spoken of in antique writings. At first he sensed nothing but a waxy sliding, but then an overpowering sweetness enveloped his tongue, quite unlike the sweets he was used to. It did not die away but seemed to run up his nose and almost into his ears, in a peculiar physical way. An *animal* food. He took some more, gingerly.

"I didn't offer you my bread. It needs some chemical, I don't know what. To make it lighter."

"Don't you have an access terminal?"

"Something's wrong with part of it," she said with her mouth full. "Maybe I don't work it right. We never had a big one like this, my tribe were travelers. They believed in sensory experiences." She nodded, licking her fingers. "They went to the River when I was fourteen."

"That's very young to be alone. My people waited till this year, my eighteenth birthday."

"I wasn't alone. I had two older cousins. But they wanted to take an aircar up north, to the part of the River called Rideout. I stayed here. I mean, we never stopped traveling, we never *lived* anywhere. I wanted to do like the plants, make roots."

"I could look at your program," he offered. "I've seen a lot of different models, I spent nearly a year in cities."

"What I need is a cow. Or a goat."

"Why?"

"For the milk. I need a pair, I guess."

Another animal thing; he winced a little. But it was pleasant, sitting here in the deep blue light beside her, hearing the surf plash quietly below.

"I saw quite a number of horses," he told her. "Don't they use milk?"

"I don't think horses are much good for milk." She sighed in an alert, busy way. He had the impression that her head was tremendously energic, humming with plans and intentions. Suddenly she looked up and began making a high squeaky noise between her front teeth, "Sssswwt! Sssswwwt!"

Startled, he saw a white flying thing swooping above them, and then two more. They whirled so wildly he ducked.

"That's right," she said to them. "Get busy."

"What are they?"

"My bats. They eat mosquitoes and insects." She squeaked again and the biggest bat was suddenly clinging to her hand, licking honey. It had a small, fiercely complicated face.

Jakko relaxed again. This place and its strange inhabitant were giving him remarkable memories for the River, anyway. He noticed a faint glow moving where the dark sky joined the darker sea.

"What's that?"

"Oh, the seatrain. It goes to the River landing."

"Are there people on it?"

"Not anymore. Look, I'll show you." She jumped up and was opening a console in the corner, when a sweet computer voice spoke into the air.

"Seatrain Foxtrot Niner calling Station Juliet! Come in, Station Juliet!"

"It hasn't done that for years," Peachthief said. She tripped tumblers. "Seatrain, this is Station Juliet, I hear you. Do you have a problem?"

"Affirmative. Passenger is engaging in nonstandard activities. He-slash-she does not conform to parameters. Request instructions."

Peachthief thought a minute. Then she grinned. "Is your passenger moving on four legs?"

"Affirmative! Affirmative!" Seatrain Foxtrot sounded relieved.

"Supply it with bowls of meat food and water on the floor and do not interfere with it. Juliet out."

She clicked off, and they watched the far web of lights go by on the horizon, carrying an animal.

"Probably a dog following the smell of people," Peachthief said. "I hope it gets off all right . . . We're quite a wide genetic spread," she went on in a different voice. "I mean, you're so light, and body type and all."

"I noticed that."

"It would give good heterosis. Vigor."

She was talking about being impregnated, about the fantasy child. He felt angry.

"Look, you don't know what you're saying. Don't you realize you'd have to stay and raise it for years? You'd be ethically and morally bound. And the River places are shrinking fast, you must know that. Maybe you'd be too late."

"Yes," she said somberly. "Now it's sucked everybody out it's going. But I still mean to stay."

"But you'd hate it, even if there's still time. My mother hated it, toward the end. She felt she had begun to deteriorate energically, that her life would be lessened. And me—what about me? I mean, I should stay, too."

"You'd only have to stay a month. For my ovulation. The male parent isn't ethically bound."

"Yes, but I think that's wrong. My father stayed. He never said he minded it, but he must have."

"You only have to do a month," she said sullenly. "I thought you weren't going on the River right now."

"I'm not. I just don't want to feel bound, I want to travel. To see more of the world, first. After I say goodbye."

She made an angry sound. "You have no insight. You're going, all right. You just don't want to admit it. You're going just like Mungo and Ferrocil."

"Who are they?"

"People who came by. Males, like you. Mungo was last year, I guess. He had an aircar. He said he was going to stay, he talked and talked. But two days later he went right on again. To the River. Ferrocil was earlier, he was walking through. Until he stole my bicycle."

A sudden note of fury in her voice startled him; she seemed to have some peculiar primitive relation to her bicycle, to her *things*.

"Did you want them to impregnate you, too?" Jakko noticed an odd intensity in his own voice as well.

"Oh, I was thinking about it, with Mungo." Suddenly she turned on him, her eyes wide open in the dimness like white-ringed jewels. "Look! Once and for all, I'm not going! I'm alive, I'm a human woman. I am going to stay on this earth and do human things. I'm going to make young ones to carry on the race, even if I have to die here. You can go on out, you—you pitiful shadows!"

Her voice rang in the dark room, jarring him down to his sleeping marrow. He sat silent as though some deep buried bell had tolled.

She was breathing hard. Then she moved, and to his surprise a small live flame sprang up between her cupped hands, making the room a cave.

"That's a candle. That's me. Now go ahead, make fun like Mungo did."

"I'm not making fun," he said, shocked. "It's just that I don't know what to think. Maybe you're right. I really . . . I really don't want to go, in one way," he said haltingly. "I love this earth, too. But it's all so fast. Let me . . ."

His voice trailed off.

"Tell me about your family," she said, quietly now.

"Oh, they studied. They tried every access you can imagine. Ancient languages, history, lore. My aunt made poems in English . . . The layers of the earth, the names of body cells and tissues, jewels, everything. Especially stars. They made us memorize star maps. So we'll know where we are, you know, for a while. At least the earthnames. My father kept saying, when you go on the River you can't come back and look anything up. All you have is what you remember. Of course you could ask others, but there'll be so much more, so much new . . ."

He fell silent, wondering for the millionth time: is it possible that I shall go out forever between the stars, in the great streaming company of strange sentiences?

"How many children were in your tribe?" Peachthief was asking.

"Six. I was the youngest."

"The others all went on the River?"

"I don't know. When I came back from the cities the whole family had gone on, but maybe they'll wait a while, too. My father left a letter asking me to come and say good-bye, and to bring him anything new I learned. They say you go slowly, you know. If I hurry there'll still be enough of his mind left there to tell him what I saw."

"What did you see? We were at a city once," Peachthief said dreamily. "But I was too young, I don't remember anything but people."

"The people are all gone now. Empty, every one. But everything works, the lights change, the moveways run. I didn't believe everybody was gone until I checked the central control offices. Oh, there were so many wonderful devices." He sighed. "The beauty, the complexity. Fantastic what people made." He sighed again, thinking of the wonderful technology, the creations abandoned, running down. "One strange thing. In the biggest city I saw, old Chio, almost every entertainment screen had the same tape running."

"What was it?"

"A girl, a young girl with long hair. Almost to her feet, I've never seen such hair. She was laying it out on a sort of table, with her head down. But no sound, I think the audio was broken. Then she poured a liquid all over very slowly. And then she lit it, she set fire to herself. It flamed and exploded and burned her all up. I think it was real." He shuddered. "I could see inside her mouth, her tongue going all black and twisted. It was horrible. Running over and over, everywhere. Stuck."

She made a revolted sound. "So you want to tell that to your father, to his ghost or whatever?"

"Yes. It's all new data, it could be important."

"Oh yes," she said scornfully. Then she grinned at him. "What about me? Am I new data, too? A woman who isn't going to the River? A woman who is going to stay here and make babies? Maybe I'm the last."

"That's very important," he said slowly, feeling a deep confusion in his gut. "But I can't believe, I mean, you—"

"*I mean it.*" She spoke with infinite conviction. "I'm going to live here and have babies by you or some other man if you won't stay, and teach them to live on the earth naturally."

Suddenly he believed her. A totally new emotion was rising up in him, carrying with it sunrises and nameless bonds with earth that hurt in a painless way; as though a rusted door was opening within him. Maybe this was what he had been groping for.

"I think—I think maybe I'll help you. Maybe I'll stay with you, for a while at least. Our—our children."

"You'll stay a month?" she asked wonderingly. "Really?"

"No, I mean I could stay longer. To make more and see them and help raise them, like Father did. After I come back from saying good-bye I'll really stay."

Her face changed. She bent to him and took his face between her slim dark hands.

"Jakko, listen. If you go to the River you'll never come back. No one ever does. I'll never see you again. We have to do it now, before you go."

"But a month is too long!" he protested. "My father's mind won't be there, I'm already terribly late."

She glared into his eyes a minute and then released him, stepping back with her brief sweet laugh. "Yes, and it's already late for bed. Come on."

She led him back to the room, carrying the candles, and he marveled anew at the clutter of strange activities she had assembled. "What's that?"

"My weaving room." Yawning, she reached in and held up a small, rough-looking cloth. "I made this."

It was ugly, he thought; ugly and pathetic. Why make such useless things? But he was too tired to argue.

She left him to cleanse himself perfunctorily by the well in the moonlit courtyard, after showing him another waste-place right in the garden. Other peoples' wastes smelled bad, he noticed sleepily. Maybe that was the cause of all the ancient wars.

In his room he tumbled into his hammock and fell asleep instantly. His dreams that night were chaotic: crowds, storms, jostling, and echoing through strange dimensions. His last image was of a great whirlwind that bore in its forehead a jewel that was a sleeping woman, curled like an embryo.

He waked in the pink light of dawn to find her brown face bending over him, smiling impishly. He had the impression she had been watching him, and jumped quickly out of the hammock.

"Lazy," she said. "I've found the sailboat. Hurry up and eat."

She handed him a wooden plate of bright natural fruits and led him out into the sunrise garden.

When they got down to the beach she led him south, and there was the little craft sliding to and fro, overturned in the shallows amid its tangle of sail. The keel was still protruding. They furled the sail in clumsily, and towed it out to deeper water to right it.

"I want this for the children," Peachthief kept repeating excitedly. "They can get fish, too. Oh how they'll love it!"

"Stand your weight on the keel and grab the siderail," Jakko told her, doing the same. He noticed that her silks had come loose from her breasts, which were high and wide-pointed, quite unlike those of his tribe. The sight distracted him, his thighs felt unwieldy, and he missed his handhold as the craft righted itself and ducked him. When he came up he saw Peachthief scrambling aboard like a cat, clinging tight to the mast.

"The sail! Pull the sail up," he shouted, and got another faceful of water. But she had heard him, the sail was trembling open like a great wing, silhouetting her shining dark body. For the first time Jakko noticed the boat's name, on the stern: *Gojack*. He smiled. An omen.

Gojack was starting to move smoothly away, toward the reef.

"The rudder!" he bellowed. "Turn the rudder and come back."

Peachthief moved to the tiller and pulled at it; he could see her strain. But *Gojack* continued to move away from him into the wind, faster and faster toward the surf. He remembered she had been handling the mast where the computer was.

"Stop the computer! Turn it off, turn it off!"

She couldn't possibly hear him. Jakko saw her in frantic activity, wrenching at the tiller, grabbing ropes, trying physically to push down the sail. Then she seemed to notice the computer, but evidently could not decipher it. Meanwhile *Gojack* fled steadily on and out, resuming its interrupted journey to the River. Jakko realized with horror that she would soon be in dangerous water; the surf was thundering on coral heads.

"Jump! Come back, jump off!" He was swimming after them as fast as he could, his progress agonizingly slow. He glimpsed her still wrestling with the boat, screaming something he couldn't hear.

"JUMP!"

And finally she did, but only to try jerking *Gojack* around by its mooring lines. The boat faltered and jibbed, but then went strongly on, towing the threshing girl.

"Let go! Let go!" A wave broke over his head.

When he could see again he found she had at last let go and was swimming aimlessly, watching *Gojack* crest the surf and wing away. At last she turned back toward shore, and Jakko swam to intercept her. He was gripped by an unknown emotion so strong it discoordinated him. As his feet touched bottom he realized it was rage.

She waded to him, her face contorted by weeping. "The children's boat," she wailed. "I lost the children's boat—"

"You're crazy," he shouted. "There aren't any children."

"I lost it—" She flung herself on his chest, crying. He thumped her back, her sides, repeating furiously, "Crazy! You're insane!"

She wailed louder, squirming against him, small and naked and frail. Suddenly he found himself flinging her down onto the wet sand, falling on top of her with his swollen sex crushed between their bellies. For a moment all was confusion, and then the shock of it sobered him. He raised to look under himself and Peachthief stared too, round-eyed.

"Do you w-want to, now?"

In that instant he wanted nothing more than to thrust himself into her, but a sandy wavelet splashed over them and he was suddenly aware of chafing wet cloth and Peachthief gagging brine. The magic waned. He got awkwardly to his knees.

"I thought you were going to be drowned," he told her, angry again.

"I wanted it so, for—for them . . ." She was still crying softly, looking up desolately at him. He understood she wasn't really meaning just the sailboat. A feeling of inexorable involvement spread through him. This mad little being had created some kind of energy vortex around her, into which he was being sucked along with animals, vegetables, chickens, crowds of unknown things; only *Gojack* had escaped her.

"I'll find it," she was muttering, wringing out her silks, staring beyond the reef at the tiny dwindling gleam. He looked down at her, so fanatic and so vulnerable, and his inner landscape tilted frighteningly, revealing some ancient-new dimension.

"I'll stay with you," he said hoarsely. He cleared his throat, hearing his voice shake. "I mean I'll really stay, I won't go to the River at all. We'll make them, our babies now."

She stared up at him openmouthed. "But your father! You promised!"

"My father stayed," he said painfully. "It's—it's right, I think."

She came close and grabbed his arms in her small hands.

"Oh, Jakko! But no, listen—*I'll go with you*. We can start a baby as we go, I'm sure of that. Then you can talk to your father and keep your promise and I'll be there to make sure you come back!"

"But you'd be—you'd be pregnant!" he cried in alarm. "You'd be in danger of taking an embryo on the River!"

She laughed proudly. "Can't you get it through your head that I will *not* go on the River? I'll just watch you and pull you out. I'll see you get back here. For a while, anyway," she added soberly. Then she brightened. "Hey, we'll see all kinds of things. Maybe I can find a cow or some goats on the way! Yes, yes! It's a perfect idea."

She faced him, glowing. Tentatively she brought her lips up to his, and they kissed inexpertly, tasting salt. He felt no desire, but only some deep resonance, like a confirmation in the earth. The three moondogs were watching mournfully.

"Now let's eat!" She began towing him toward the cliff steps. "We can start the pills right now. Oh, I have so much to do! But I'll fix everything, we'll leave tomorrow."

She was like a whirlwind. In the food room she pounced on a small gold-colored pillbox and opened it to show a mound of glowing green and red capsules.

"The red ones with the male symbol are for you."

She took a green one, and they swallowed solemnly, sharing a water mug. He noticed that the seal on the box had been broken, and thought of that stranger, Mungo, she had mentioned. How far had her plans gone with him? An unpleasant emotion he had never felt before rose in Jakko's stomach. He sensed that he was heading into more dubious realms of experience than he had quite contemplated, and took his foodbar and walked away through the arcades to cool down.

When he came upon her again she seemed to be incredibly busy, folding and filling and wrapping things, closing windows and tying doors open. Her intense relations with things again . . . He felt obscurely irritated and was pleased to have had a superior idea.

"We need a map," he told her. "Mine was in the boat."

"Oh, great idea. Look in the old control room, it's down those stairs. It's kind of scary." She began putting oil on her loom.

He went down a white ramp that became a tunnel stair-way, and came finally through a heavily armored portal to a circular room deep inside the rock, dimly illumined by portholes sunk in long shafts. From here he could hear the hum of the station energy source. As his eyes adjusted he made out a bank of sensor screens and one big console standing alone. It seemed to have been smashed open; some kind of sealant had been poured over the works.

He had seen a place like this before; he understood at once that from here had been controlled terrible ancient weapons that flew. Probably they still stood waiting in their hidden holes behind the station. But the master control was long dead. As he approached the console he saw that someone had scratched in the cooling sealant. He could make out only the words:—WAR NO MORE. Undoubtedly this was a shrine of the very old days.

He found a light switch that filled the place with cool glare, and began exploring side alleys. Antique gear, suits, cupboards full of masks and crumbling packets he couldn't identify. Among them was something useful—two cloth containers to carry stuff on one's back, only a little mildewed. But where were the maps?

Finally he found one on the control-room wall, right where he had come in. Someone had updated it with scrawled notations. With a tremor he realized how very old this must be; it dated from before the Rivers had touched earth. He could hardly grasp it.

Studying it, he saw that there was indeed a big landing dock not far south, and from there a moveway ran inland about a hundred kilometers to an airpark. If Peachthief could walk twenty-five kilometers they could make the landing by evening, and if the cars were still running the rest would be quick. All the moveways he'd seen had live cars on them. From the airpark a dotted line ran south-west across mountains to a big red circle with a cross in it, marked VIDA! That would be the River. They would just have to hope something on the airpark would fly, otherwise it would be a long climb.

His compass was still on his belt. He memorized the directions and went back upstairs. The courtyard was already saffron under great sunset flags.

Peachthief was squatting by the well, apparently having a conference with her animals. Jakko noticed some more white creatures he hadn't seen before, who seemed to live in an open hutch. They had long pinkish ears and mobile noses. Rabbits, or hares perhaps?

Two of the strange white animals he had seen sleeping were now under a bench, chirruping irritably at Peachthief.

"My raccoons," she told Jakko. "They're mad because I woke them up too soon." She said something in a high voice Jakko couldn't understand, and the biggest raccoon shook his head up and down in a supercilious way.

"The chickens will be all right," Peachthief said. "Lotor knows how to feed them, to get the eggs. And they can all work the water lever." The other raccoon nodded crossly, too.

"The rabbits are a terrible problem." Peachthief frowned. "You just haven't much sense, Eusebia," she said fondly, stroking the doe. "I'll have to fix something."

The big raccoon was warbling at her; Jakko thought he caught the word "dog-g-g."

"He wants to know who will settle their disputes with the dogs," Peachthief reported. At this, one of the moon-dogs came forward and said thickly, "We go-o." It was the first word Jakko had heard him speak.

"Oh, good!" Peachthief cried. "Well, that's that!" She bounced up and began pouring something from a bucket on a line of plants. The white raccoons ran off silently with a humping gait.

"I'm so glad you're coming, Tycho," she told the dog. "Especially if I have to come back alone with a baby inside. But they say you're very vigorous—at first, anyway."

"You aren't coming back alone," Jakko told her. She smiled a brilliant, noncommittal flash. He noticed she was dressed differently; her body didn't show so much, and she kept her gaze away from him in an almost timid way. But she became very excited when he showed her the backpacks.

"Oh, good. Now we won't have to roll the blankets around our waists. It gets cool at night, you know."

"Does it ever rain?"

"Not this time of year. What we mainly need is lighters and food and water. And a good knife each. Did you find the map?"

He showed it. "Can you walk, I mean really hike if we have to? Do you have shoes?"

"Oh yes. I walk a lot. Especially since Ferrocil stole my bike."

The venom in her tone amused him. The ferocity with which she provisioned her small habitat!

"Men build monuments, women build nests," he quoted from somewhere.

"I don't know what kind of monument Ferrocil built with my bicycle," she said tartly.

"You're a savage," he said, feeling a peculiar ache that came out as a chuckle.

"The race can use some savages. We better eat now and go to sleep so we can start early."

At supper in the sunset-filled porch they scarcely talked. Dreamily Jakko watched the white bats embroidering flight on the air. When he looked down at Peachthief he caught her gazing at him before she quickly lowered her eyes. It came to him that they might eat hundreds, thousands of meals here; maybe all his life. And there could be a child—children—running about. He had never seen small humans younger than himself. It was all too much to take in, unreal. He went back to watching the bats.

That night she accompanied him to his hammock and stood by, shy but stubborn, while he got settled. Then he suddenly felt her hands sliding on his body, toward his groin. At first he thought it was something clinical, but then he realized she meant sex. His blood began to pound.

"May I come in beside you? The hammock is quite strong."

"Yes," he said thickly, reaching for her arm.

But as her weight came in by him she said in a practical voice, "I have to start knotting a small hammock, first thing. Child-size."

It broke his mood.

"Look. I'm sorry, but I've changed my mind. You go on back to yours, we should get sleep now."

"All right." The weight lifted away.

With a peculiar mix of sadness and satisfaction he heard her light footsteps leaving him alone. That night he dreamed strange sensory crescendos, a tumescent earth and air; a woman who lay with her smiling lips in pale-green water, awaiting him, while thin black birds of sunrise stalked to the edge of the sea.

Next morning they ate by candles, and set out as the eastern sky was just turning rose-gray. The ancient white coral roadway was good walking. Peachthief swung right along beside him, her backpack riding smooth. The moondogs pattered soberly behind.

Jakko found himself absorbed in gazing at the brightening landscape. Jungle-covered hills rose away on their right, the sea lay below on their left, sheened and glittering with the coming sunrise. When a diamond chip of sun broke out of the horizon he almost shouted aloud for the brilliance of it; the palm trees beyond the road lit up like golden torches, the edges of every frond and stone were startlingly clear and jewel-like. For a moment he wondered if he could have taken some hallucinogen.

They paced on steadily in a dream of growing light and heat. The day wind came up, and torn white clouds began to blow over them, bringing momentary coolnesses. Their walking fell into the rhythm Jakko loved, broken only occasionally by crumbled places in the road. At such spots they would often be surprised to find the moondogs sitting waiting for them, having quietly left the road and circled ahead through the scrub on business of their own. Peachthief kept up sturdily, only once stopping to look back at the far white spark of Station Juliet, almost melted in the shimmering horizon.

"This is as far as I've gone south," she told him.

He drank some water and made her drink too, and they went on. The road began to wind, rising and falling gently. When he next glanced back the station was gone. The extraordinary luminous clarity of the world was still delighting him.

When noon came he judged they were well over halfway to the landing. They sat down on some rubble under the palms to eat and drink, and Peachthief fed the moondogs. Then she took out the fertility-pill box. They each took theirs in silence, oddly solemn. Then she grinned.

"I'll give you something for dessert."

She unhitched a crooked knife from her belt and went searching around in the rocks, to come back with a big yellow-brown palm nut. Jakko watched her attack it with rather alarming vigor; she husked it and then used a rock to drive the point home.

"Here." She handed it to him. "Drink out of that hole." He felt a sloshing inside; when he lifted it and drank it tasted hairy and gritty and nothing in particular. But sharp too, like the day. Peachthief was methodically striking the thing around and around its middle. Suddenly it fell apart, revealing vividly white meat. She pried out a piece.

"Eat this. It's full of protein."

The nutmeat was sweet and sharply organic.

"This is a coconut!" he suddenly remembered.

"Yes. I won't starve, coming back."

He refused to argue, but only got up to go on. Peachthief holstered her knife and followed, munching on a coconut piece. They went on so in silence a long time, letting the rhythm carry them. Once when a lizard waddled across the road Peachthief said to the moondog at her heels, "Tycho, you'll have to learn to catch and eat those one day soon." The moondogs all looked dubiously at the lizard but said nothing. Jakko felt shocked and pushed the thought away.

They were now walking with the sun westering slowly to their right. A flight of big orange birds with blue beaks flapped squawking out of a roadside tree, where they were apparently building some structure. Cloud shadows fled across the world, making blue and bronze reflections in the sea. Jakko still felt his sensory impressions almost painfully keen; a sunray made the surf line into a chain of diamonds, and the translucent green of the near shallows below them seemed to enchant his eyes. Every vista ached with light, as if to utter some silent meaning

He was walking in a trance, only aware that the road had been sound and level for some time, when Peachthief uttered a sharp cry.

"My bicycle! There's my bicycle!" She began to run; Jakko saw shiny metal sticking out of a narrow gulch in the roadway. When he came up to her she was pulling a machine out from beside the roadwall.

"The front wheel—Oh, he bent it! He must have been going too fast and wrecked it here. That Ferrocil! But I'll fix it, I'm sure I can fix it at the station. I'll push it back with me on the way home."

While she was mourning her machine Jakko looked around and over the low coping of the roadwall. Sheer cliff down there, with the sun just touching a rocky beach below. Something was stuck among the rocks—a tangle of whitish sticks, cloth, a round thing. Feeling his stomach knot, Jakko stared down at it, unwillingly discovering that the round thing had eyeholes, a U-shaped open mouth, blowing strands of hair. He had never seen a dead body before (nobody had), but he had seen pictures of human bones. Shakenly he realized what this had to be: Ferrocil. He must have been thrown over the coping when he hit that crack. Now he was dead, long dead. He would never go on the River. All that had been in that head was perished, gone forever.

Scarcely knowing what he was doing, Jakko grabbed Peachthief by the shoulders, saying roughly, "Come on! Come on!" When she resisted confusedly, he took her by the arm and began forcibly pulling her away from where she might look down. Her flesh felt burning hot and vibrant, the whole world was blasting colors and sounds and smells at him. Images of dead Ferrocil mingled with the piercing scent of some flowers on the roadway. Suddenly an idea struck him; he stopped.

"Listen. Are you sure those pills aren't hallucinaids? I've only had two and everything feels crazy."

"Three," Peachthief said abstractedly. She took his hand and pressed it on her back. "Do that again, run your hand down my back."

Bewildered, he obeyed. As his hand passed her silk shirt onto her thin shorts he felt her body move under it in a way that made him jerk away.

"Feel? Did you feel it? The lordotic reflex," she said proudly. "Female sexuality. It's starting."

"What do you mean, three?"

"You had three pills. I gave you one that first night, in the honey."

"*What*? But—but—" He struggled to voice the enormity of her violation, pure fury welling up in him. Choking, he lifted his hand and struck her buttocks the hardest blow he could, sending her staggering. It was the first time he had ever struck a person. A moondog growled, but he didn't care.

"Don't you ever—never—play a trick like—" He yanked at her shoulders, meaning to slap her face. His hand clutched a breast instead; he saw her hair blowing like dead Ferrocil's. A frightening sense of mortality combined with pride surged through him, lighting a fire in his loins. The deadness of Ferrocil suddenly seemed violently exciting. He, Jakko, was alive! Ignoring all sanity he flung himself on Peachthief, bearing her down on the road among the flowers. As he struggled to tear open their shorts he was dimly aware that she was helping him. His engorged penis was all reality; he fought past obstructions and then was suddenly, crookedly *in* her, fierce pleasure building. It exploded through him and then had burst out into her vitals, leaving him spent.

Blinking, fighting for clarity, he raised himself up and off her body. She lay wide-legged and disheveled, sobbing or gasping in a strange way, but smiling, too. Revulsion sent a sick taste in his throat.

"There's your baby," he said roughly. He found his canteen and drank. The three moondogs had retreated and were sitting in a row, staring solemnly.

"May I have some, please?" Her voice was very low; she sat

up, began fixing her clothes. He passed her the water and they got up.

"It's sundown," she said. "Should we camp here?"

"No!" Savagely he started on, not caring that she had to run to catch up. Was this the way the ancients lived? Whirled by violent passions, indecent, uncaring? His doing sex so close to the poor dead person seemed unbelievable. And the world was still assaulting all his senses; when she stumbled against him he could feel again the thrilling pull of her flesh, and shuddered. They walked in silence awhile; he sensed that she was more tired than he, but he wanted only to get as far away as possible.

"I'm not taking any more of those pills," he broke silence at last.

"But you have to! It takes a month to be sure."

"I don't care."

"But, ohhh—"

He said nothing more. They were walking across a twilit headland now. Suddenly the road turned, and they came out above a great bay.

The waters below were crowded with boats of all kinds, bobbing emptily where they had been abandoned. Some still had lights that made faint jewels in the opalescent air. Somewhere among them must be *Gojack*. The last light from the west gleamed on the rails of a moveway running down to the landing.

"Look, there's the seatrain." Peachthief pointed. "I hope the dog or whatever got ashore . . . I can find a sailboat down there, there's lots."

Jakko shrugged. Then he noticed movement among the shadows of the landing station and forgot his anger long enough to say, "See there! Is that a live man?"

They peered hard. Presently the figure crossed a light place, and they could see it was a person going slowly among the stalled waycars. He would stop with one awhile and then waver on.

"There's something wrong with him," Peachthief said.

Presently the stranger's shadow merged with a car, and they saw it begin to move. It went slowly at first, and then accelerated out to the center lanes, slid up the gleaming rails and passed beyond them to disappear into the western hills.

"The way's working!" Jakko exclaimed. "We'll camp up here and go over to the way station in the morning, it's closer."

He was feeling so pleased with the moveway that he talked easily with Peachthief over their foodbar dinner, telling her about the cities and asking her what places her tribe had seen. But when she wanted to put their blankets down together he said no, and took his away to a ledge farther up. The three moondogs lay down by her with their noses on their paws, facing him.

His mood turned to self-disgust again; remorse mingled with queasy surges of half-enjoyable animality. He put his arm over his head to shut out the brilliant moonlight and longed to forget everything, wishing the sky held only cold quiet stars. When he finally slept he didn't dream at all, but woke with ominous tollings in his inner ear. *The Horse is hungry*, deep voices chanted. *The Woman is bad*!

He roused Peachthief before sunrise. They ate and set off overland to the hill station; it was rough going until they stumbled onto an old limerock path. The moondogs ranged wide around them, appearing pleased. When they came out at the station shunt they found it crowded with cars.

The power pack of the first one was dead. So was the next, and the next. Jakko understood what the stranger at the landing had been doing; looking for a live car. The dead cars here stretched away out of sight up the siding; a miserable sight.

"We should go back to the landing," Peachthief said. "He found a good one there."

Jakko privately agreed, but irrationality smoldered in him. He squinted into the hazy distance.

"I'm going up to the switch end."

"But it's so far, we'll have to come all the way back—"

He only strode off; she followed. It was a long way, round a curve and over a rise, dead cars beside them all the way. They were almost at the main tracks when Jakko saw what he had been hoping for: a slight jolting motion in the line. New cars were still coming in ahead, butting the dead ones.

"Oh, fine!"

They went on down to the newest-arrived car and all climbed in, the moondogs taking up position on the opposite seat. When Jakko began to work the controls that would take them out to the main line, the car bleated an automatic alarm. A voder voice threatened to report him to Central. Despite its protests, Jakko swerved the car across the switches, where it fell silent and began to accelerate smoothly onto the outbound express lane.

"You really do know how to work these things," Peachthief said admiringly.

"You should learn."

"Why? They'll all be dead soon. I know how to bicycle."

He clamped his lips, thinking of Ferrocil's white bones. They fled on silently into the hills, passing a few more station jams. Jakko's perceptions still seemed too sharp, the sensory world too meaning-filled.

Presently they felt hungry, and found that the car's automatics were all working well. They had a protein drink and a pleasantly fruity bar, and Peachthief found bars for the dogs. The track was rising into mountains now; the car whirled smoothly through tunnels and came out in passes, offering wonderful views. Now and then they had glimpses of a great plain far ahead. The familiar knot of sadness gathered inside Jakko, stronger than usual. To think that all this wonderful system would run down and die in a jumble of rust . . . He had a fantasy of himself somehow maintaining it, but the memory of Peachthief's pathetic woven cloth mocked at him. Everything was a mistake, a terrible mistake. He wanted only to leave, to escape to rationality and peace. If she had drugged him he wasn't responsible for what he'd promised. He wasn't bound. Yet the sadness redoubled, wouldn't let him go.

When she got out the pillbox and offered it he shook his head violently. "No!"

"But you *promised—*"

"No. I hate what it does."

She stared at him in silence, swallowing hers defiantly. "Maybe there'll be some other men by the River," she said after a while. "We saw one."

He shrugged and pretended to fall asleep.

Just as he was really drowsing the car's warning alarm trilled and they braked smoothly to a halt.

"Oh, look ahead—the way's gone! What is it?"

"A rockslide. An avalanche from the mountains, I think."

They got out among other empty cars that were waiting their prescribed pause before returning. Beyond the last one the way ended in an endless tumble of rocks and shale. Jakko made out a faint footpath leading on.

"Well, we walk. Let's get the packs, and some food and water."

While they were back in the car working the synthesizer, Peachthief looked out the window and frowned. After Jakko finished she punched a different code and some brownish lumps rolled into her hand.

"What's that?"

"You'll see." She winked at him.

As they started on the trail a small herd of horses appeared, coming toward them. The two humans politely scrambled up out of their way. The lead horse was a large yellow male. When he came to Peachthief he stopped and thrust his big head up at her.

"Zhu-gar, zhu-gar," he said sloppily. At this all the other horses crowded up and began saying "zhu-ga, zu-cah," in varying degrees of clarity.

"This *I* know," said Peachthief to Jakko. She turned to the yellow stallion. "Take us on your backs around these rocks. Then we'll give you sugar."

"Zhu-gar," insisted the horse, looking mean.

"Yes, sugar. *After* you take us around the rocks to the rails."

The horse rolled his eyes unpleasantly, but he turned back down. There was some commotion, and two mares were pushed forward.

"Riding horseback is done by means of a saddle and bridle," protested Jakko.

"Also this way. Come on." Peachthief vaulted nimbly onto the back of the smaller mare.

Jakko reluctantly struggled onto the fat round back of the other mare. To his horror, as he got himself astride she put up her head and screamed shrilly.

"You'll get sugar, too," Peachthief told her. The animal subsided, and they started off along the rocky trail, single file. Jakko had to admit it was much faster than afoot, but he kept sliding backward.

"Hang onto her mane, that hairy place there," Peachthief called back to him, laughing. "I know how to run a few things too, see?"

When the path widened the yellow stallion trotted up alongside Peachthief.

"I thinking," he said importantly.

"Yes, what?"

"I push you down and eat zhugar now."

"All horses think that," Peachthief told him. "No good. It doesn't work."

The yellow horse dropped back, and Jakko heard him making horse-talk with an old gray-roan animal at the rear. Then he shouldered by to Peachthief again and said, "Why no good I push you down?"

"Two reasons," said Peachthief. "First, if you knock me down you'll never get any more sugar. All the humans will know you're bad and they won't ride on you anymore. So no more sugar, never again."

"No more hoomans," the big yellow horse said scornfully. "Hoomans finish."

"You're wrong there, too. There'll be a lot more humans. I am making them, see?" She patted her stomach.

The trail narrowed again and the yellow horse dropped back. When he could come alongside he sidled by Jakko's mare.

"I think I push you down now."

Peachthief turned around.

"You didn't hear my other reason," she called to him.

The horse grunted evilly.

"The other reason is that my three friends there will bite your stomach open if you try." She pointed up to where the three moondogs had appeared on a rock as if by magic, grinning toothily.

Jakko's mare screamed again even louder, and the gray roan in back made a haw-haw sound. The yellow horse lifted his tail and trotted forward to the head of the line, extruding manure as he passed Peachthief.

They went on around the great rockslide without further talk. Jakko was becoming increasingly uncomfortable; he would gladly have got off and gone slower on his own two legs. Now and then they broke into a jog-trot, which was so painful he longed to yell to Peachthief to make them stop. But he kept silent. As they rounded some huge boulders he was rewarded by a distant view of the unmistakable towers of an airpark, to their left on the plain below.

At long last the rockslide ended, quite near a station. They stopped among a line of stalled cars. Jakko slid off gratefully, remembering to say "Thank you" to the mare. Walking proved to be uncomfortable, too.

"See if there's a good car before I get off!" Peachthief yelled.

The second one he came to was live. He shouted at her.

Next moment he saw trouble among the horses. The big yellow beast charged in, neighing and kicking. Peachthief came darting out of the melée with the moondogs, and fell into the car beside him, laughing.

"I gave our mares all the sugar," she chuckled. Then she sobered. "I think mares *are* good for milk. I told them to come to the station with me when I come back. If that big bully will let them."

"How will they get in a car?" he asked stupidly.

"Why, I'll be walking, I can't run these things."

"But I'll be with you." He didn't feel convinced.

"What for, if you don't want to make babies? You won't be here."

"Well then, why are you coming with me?"

"I'm looking for a cow," she said scornfully. "Or a goat. Or a man."

They said no more until the car turned into the airpark station. Jakko counted over twenty apparently live ships floating at their towers. Many more hung sagging, and some towers had toppled. The field moveways were obviously dead.

"I think we have to find hats," he told Peachthief.

"Why?"

"So the service alarms won't go off when we walk around. Most places are like that."

"Oh."

In the office by the gates they found a pile of crew hats laid out, a thoughtful action by the last of the airpark people. A big hand-lettered sign said, ALL SHIPS ON STANDBY, MANUAL OVERRIDE. READ DIRECTIONS. Under it was a stack of dusty leaflets. They took one, put on their hats, and began to walk toward a pylon base with several ships floating at its tower. They had to duck under and around the web of dead moveways, and when they reached the station base there seemed to be no way in from the ground.

"We'll have to climb onto that moveway."

They found a narrow ladder and went up, helping the moondogs. The moveway portal was open, and they were soon in the normal passenger lounge. It was still lighted.

"Now if the lift only works."

Just as they were making for the lift shaft they were startled by a voice ringing out.

"Ho! Ho, Roland!"

"That's no voder," Peachthief whispered. "There's a live human here."

They turned back and saw that a strange person was lying half on and half off one of the lounges. As they came close their eyes opened wide: he looked frightful. His thin dirty white hair hung around a horribly creased caved-in face, and what they could see of his neck and arms was all mottled and decayed-looking. His jerkin and pants were frayed and stained and sagged in where flesh should be. Jakko thought of the cloth shreds around dead Ferrocil and shuddered.

The stranger was staring haggardly at them. In a faint voice he said, "When the chevalier Roland died he predicted that his body would be found a spear's throw ahead of all others and facing the enemy . . . If you happen to be real, could you perhaps give me some water?"

"Of course." Jakko unhooked his canteen and tried to hand it over, but the man's hands shook and fumbled so that Jakko had to hold it to his mouth, noticing a foul odor. The stranger sucked thirstily, spilling some. Behind him the moondogs inched closer, sniffing gingerly.

"What's *wrong* with him?" Peachthief whispered as Jakko stood back.

Jakko had been remembering his lessons. "He's just very, very old, I think."

"That's right." The stranger's voice was stronger. He stared at them with curious avidity. "I waited too long. Fibrillation." He put one feeble hand to his chest. "Fibrillating . . . rather a beautiful word, don't you think? My medicine ran out or I lost it . . . A small hot animal desynchronizing in my ribs."

"We'll help you get to the River right away!" Peachthief told him.

"Too late, my lords, too late. Besides, I can't walk and you can't possibly carry me."

"You can sit up, can't you?" Jakko asked. "There have to be some roll chairs around here, they had them for injured people." He went off to search the lounge office and found one almost at once.

When he brought it back the stranger was staring up at Peachthief, mumbling to himself in an archaic tongue of which Jakko only understood: ". . . *The breast of a grave girl makes a hill against sunrise.*" He tried to heave himself up to the chair but fell back, gasping. They had to lift and drag him in, Peachthief wrinkling her nose.

"Now if the lift only works."

It did. They were soon on the high departure deck, and the fourth portal-berth held a waiting ship. It was a small local ferry. They went through into the windowed main cabin, wheeling the old man, who had collapsed upon himself and was breathing very badly. The moondogs trooped from window to window, looking down. Jakko seated himself in the pilot chair.

"Read me out the instructions," he told Peachthief.

"One, place ship on internal guidance," she read. "Whatever that means. Oh, look, here's a diagram."

"Good."

It proved simple. They went together down the list, sealing the port, disengaging umbilicals, checking vane function, reading off the standby pressures in the gasbags above them, setting the reactor to warm up the drive motor and provide hot air for operational buoyancy.

While they were waiting, Peachthief asked the old man if he would like to be moved onto a window couch. He nodded urgently. When they got him to it he whispered, "See out!" They propped him up with chair pillows.

The ready-light was flashing. Jakko moved the controls, and the ship glided smoothly out and up. The computer was showing him wind speed, altitude, climb, and someone had marked all the verniers with the words COURSE SET—RIVER. Jakko lined everything up.

"Now it says, put it on automatic," Peachthief read. He did so.

The takeoff had excited the old man. He was straining to look down, muttering incomprehensibly. Jakko caught, "*The cool green hills of Earth* . . . Crap!" Suddenly he sang out loudly, "*There's a hell of a good universe next door—let's go!*" And fell back exhausted.

Peachthief stood over him worriedly. "I wish I could at least clean him up, but he's so weak."

The old man's eyes opened.

"*Nothing shall be whole and sound that has not been rent; for love hath built his mansion in the place of excrement.*" He began to sing crackedly, "Take me to the River, the bee-yew-tiful River, and wash all my sins a-away! . . . You think I'm crazy, girl, don't you?" he went on conversationally. "Never heard of William Yeats. Very high bit-rate, Yeats."

"I think I understand a little," Jakko told him. "One of my aunts did English literature."

"*Did* literature, eh?" The stranger wheezed, snorted. "And you two—going on the River to spend eternity together as energy matrices or something equally impressive and sexless . . . *Forever wilt thou love and she be fair.*" He grunted. "Always mistrusted Keats. No balls. He'd be right at home."

"We're not going on the River," Peachthief said. "At least, I'm not. I'm going to stay and make children."

The old man's ruined mouth fell open; he gazed up at her wildly.

"No!" he breathed. "Is it true? Have I stumbled on the lover and mother of man, the last?"

Peachthief nodded solemnly.

"What is your name, O Queen?"

"Peachthief."

"My God. Somebody still knows of Blake." He smiled tremulously, and his eyelids suddenly slid downward; he was asleep.

"He's breathing better. Let's explore."

The small ship held little but cargo space at the rear. When they came to the food-synthesizer cubby Jakko saw Peachthief pocket something.

"What's that?"

"A little spoon. It'll be just right for a child." She didn't look at him.

Back in the main cabin the sunset was flooding the earth below with level roseate light. They were crossing huge, oddly pockmarked meadows, the airship whispering along in silence except when a jet whistled briefly now and then for a course correction.

"Look—cows! Those must be cows," Peachthief exclaimed. "See the shadows."

Jakko made out small tan specks that were animals, with grotesque horned shadows stretching away.

"I'll have to find them when I come back. What *is* this place?"

"A big deathyard, I think. Where they put dead bodies. I never saw one this size. In some cities they had buildings just for dead people. Won't all that poison the cows?"

"Oh no, it makes good grass, I believe. The dogs will help me find them. Won't you, Tycho?" she asked the biggest moondog, who was looking down beside them.

On the eastern side of the cabin the full moon was rising into view. The old man's eyes opened, looking at it.

"More water, if you please," he croaked.

Peachthief gave him some, and then got him to swallow broth from the synthesizer. He seemed stronger, smiling at her with his mouthful of rotted teeth.

"Tell me, girl. If you're going to stay and make children, why are you going to the River?"

"He's going because he promised to talk to his father and I'm going along to see he comes back. And make the baby. Only now he won't take any more pills, I have to try to find another man."

"Ah yes, the pills. We used to call them Wakeups . . . They were necessary, after the population chemicals got around. Maybe they still are, for women. But I think it's mostly in the head. Why won't you take any more, boy? What's wrong with the old Adam?"

Peachthief started to answer but Jakko cut her off. "I can speak for myself. They upset me. They made me do bad, uncontrolled things, and feel, agh—" He broke off with a grimace.

"You seem curiously feisty, for one who values his calm above the continuance of the race."

"It's the pills, I tell you. They're—they're dehumanizing."

"De-humanizing," the old man mocked. "And what do you know of humanity, young one? . . . That's what I went to find, that's why I stayed so long among the old, old things from before the River came. I wanted to bring the knowledge of what humanity really was . . . I wanted to bring it all. It's simple, boy. *They died*." He drew a rasping breath. "Every one of them died. They lived knowing that nothing but loss and suffering and extinction lay ahead. And they cared, terribly . . . Oh, they made myths, but not many really believed them. *Death* was behind everything, waiting everywhere. Aging and death. No escape . . . Some of them went crazy, they fought and killed and enslaved each other by the millions, as if they could gain more life. Some of them gave up their precious lives for each other. They loved—and had to watch the ones they loved age and die. And in their pain and despair they built, they struggled, some of them sang. But above all, boy, they copulated! Fornicated, fucked, made love!"

He fell back, coughing, glaring at Jakko. Then, seeing that they scarcely understood his antique words, he went on more clearly. "Did sex, do you understand? Made children. It was their only weapon, you see. To send something of themselves into the future beyond their own deaths. Death was the engine of their lives, death fueled their sexuality. Death drove them at each other's throats and into each other's arms. Dying, they triumphed . . . *That* was human life. And now that mighty engine is long stilled, and you call this polite parade of immortal lemmings *humanity*? . . . Even the faintest warmth of that immemorial holocaust makes you flinch away?"

He collapsed, gasping horribly; spittle ran down his chin. One slit of eye still raked them.

Jakko stood silent, shaken by resonances from the old man's words, remembering dead Ferrocil, feeling some deep conduit of reality reaching for him out of the long-gone past. Peachthief's hand fell on his shoulder, sending a shudder through him. Slowly his own hand seemed to lift by itself and cover hers, holding her to him. They watched the old man so for a long moment. His face slowly composed, he spoke in a soft dry tone.

"I don't trust that River, you know . . . You think you're going to remain yourselves, don't you? Communicate with each other and with the essences of beings from other stars? . . . The latest news from Betelgeuse." He chuckled raspingly.

"That's the last thing people say when they're going," Jakko replied. "Everyone learns that. You float out, able to talk with real other beings. Free to move."

"What could better match our dreams?" He chuckled again. "I wonder . . . could that be the lure, just the input end of some cosmic sausage machine? . . ."

"What's that?" asked Peachthief.

"An old machine that ground different meats together until they came out as one substance . . . Maybe you'll find yourselves gradually mixed and minced and blended into some—some energic plasma . . . and then maybe squirted out again to impose the terrible gift of consciousness on some innocent race of crocodiles, or poached eggs . . . And so it begins all over again. Another random engine of the universe, giving and taking obliviously . . ." He coughed, no longer looking at them, and began to murmur in the archaic tongue, "*Ah, when the ghost begins to quicken, confusion of the deathbed over, is it sent . . . out naked on the roads as the books say, and stricken with the injustice of the stars for punishment?* The injustice of the stars . . ." He fell silent, and then whispered faintly, "Yet I too long to go."

"You will," Peachthief told him strongly.

"How . . . much longer?"

"We'll be there by dawn," Jakko said. "We'll carry you. I swear."

"A great gift," he said weakly. "But I fear . . . I shall give you a better." He mumbled on, a word Jakko didn't know; it sounded like "afrodisiack."

He seemed to lapse into sleep then. Peachthief went and got a damp, fragrant cloth from the cleanup and wiped his face gently. He opened one eye and grinned up at her.

"Madame Tasselass," he rasped. "Madame Tasselass, are you really going to save us?"

She smiled down, nodding her head determinedly, yes. He closed his eyes, looking more peaceful.

The ship was now fleeing through full moonlight, the cabin was so lit with azure and silver that they didn't think to turn on lights. Now and again the luminous mists of a low cloud veiled the windows and vanished again. Just as Jakko was about to propose eating, the old man took several gulping breaths and opened his eyes. His intestines made a bubbling sound.

Peachthief looked at him sharply and picked up one of his wrists. Then she frowned and bent over him, opening his filthy jerkin. She laid her ear to his chest, staring up at Jakko.

"He's not breathing, there's no heartbeat!" She groped inside his jerkin as if she could locate life, two tears rolling down her cheeks.

"He's dead—ohhh!" She groped deeper, then suddenly straightened up and gingerly clutched the cloth at the old man's crotch.

"What?"

"He's a woman!" She gave a sob and wheeled around to clutch Jakko, putting her forehead in his neck. "We n-never even knew her name . . ."

Jakko held her, looking at the dead man-woman, thinking, She never knew mine, either. At that moment the airship jolted, and gave a noise like a cable grinding or slipping before it flew smoothly on again.

Jakko had never in his life distrusted machinery, but now a sudden terror contracted his guts. This thing could fall! They could be made dead like Ferrocil, like this stranger, like the myriads in the deathyards below. Echoes of the old voice ranting about death boomed in his head, he had a sudden vision of Peachthief grown old and dying like that. After the Rivers went, dying alone. His eyes filled, and a deep turmoil erupted under his mind. He hugged Peachthief tighter. Suddenly he knew in a dreamlike way exactly what was about to happen. Only this time there was no frenzy; his body felt like warm living rock.

He stroked Peachthief to quiet her sobs, and led her over to the moonlit couch on the far side of the cabin. She was still sniffling, hugging him hard. He ran his hands firmly down her back, caressing her buttocks, feeling her body respond.

"Give me that pill," he said to her. "Now."

Looking at him huge-eyed in the blue moonlight, she pulled out the little box. He took out his and swallowed it deliberately, willing her to understand.

"Take off your clothes." He began stripping off his jerkin, proud of the hot, steady power in his sex. When she stripped and he saw again the glistening black bush at the base of her slim belly, and the silver-edged curves of her body, urgency took him, but still in a magical calm.

"Lie down."

"Wait a minute—" She was out of his hands like a fish, running across the cabin to where the dead body lay in darkness. Jakko saw she was trying to close the dead eyes that still gleamed from the shadows. He could wait; he had never imagined his body could feel like this. She laid the cloth over the stranger's face and came back to him, half shyly holding out her arms, sinking down spread-legged on the shining couch before him. The moonlight was so brilliant he could see the pink color of her sexual parts.

He came onto her gently, controlledly, breathing in an exciting animal odor from her flesh. This time his penis entered easily, an intense feeling of all-rightness.

But a moment later the fires of terror, pity, and defiance deep within him burst up into a flame of passionate brilliance in his coupled groin. The small body under his seemed no longer vulnerable but appetitive. He clutched, mouthed, drove deep into her, exulting. Death didn't die alone, he thought obscurely as the ancient patterns lurking in his vitals awoke. Death flew with them and flowed by beneath, but he asserted life upon the body of the woman, caught up in a great crescendo of unknown sensation, until a culminant spasm of almost painful pleasure rolled through him into her, relieving him from head to feet.

When he could talk, he thought to ask her, "Did you—" he didn't know the word. "Did it sort of explode you, like me?"

"Well, no." Her lips were by his ear. "Female sexuality is a little different. Maybe I'll show you, later . . . But I think it was good, for the baby."

He felt only a tiny irritation at her words, and let himself drift into sleep with his face in her warm-smelling hair. Dimly the understanding came to him that the great beast of his dreams, the race itself maybe, had roused and used them. So be it.

A cold thing pushing into his ear awakened him, and a hoarse voice said, "Ffoo-ood!" It was the moondogs.

"Oh my, I forgot to feed them!" Peachthief struggled nimbly out from under him.

Jakko found he was ravenous, too. The cabin was dark now, as the moon rose overhead. Peachthief located the switches, and made a soft light on their side of the cabin. They ate and drank heartily, looking down at the moonlit world. The deathyards were gone from below them now, they were flying over dark wooded foothills. When they lay down to sleep again they could feel the cabin angle upward slightly as the ship rose higher.

He was roused in the night by her body moving against him. She seemed to be rubbing her crotch.

"Give me your hand," she whispered in a panting voice. She began to make his hands do things to her, sometimes touching him too, her body arching and writhing, sleek with sweat. He found himself abruptly tumescent again, excited and pleased in a confused way. "Now, now!" she commanded, and he entered her, finding her interior violently alive. She seemed to be half-fighting him, half-devouring him. Pleasure built all through him, this time without the terror. He pressed in against her shuddering convulsions. "Yes—oh, yes!" she gasped, and a series of paroxysms swept through her, carrying him with her to explosive peace.

He held himself on and in her until her body and breathing calmed to relaxation, and they slipped naturally apart. It came to him that this sex activity seemed to have more possibilities, as a thing to do, than he had realized. His family had imparted to him nothing of all this. Perhaps they didn't know it. Or perhaps it was too alien to their calm philosophy.

"How do you know about all this?" he asked Peachthief sleepily.

"One of my aunts did literature, too." She chuckled in the darkness. "Different literature, I guess."

They slept almost as movelessly as the body flying with them on the other couch a world away.

A series of noisy bumpings wakened them. The windows were filled with pink mist flying by. The airship seemed to be sliding into a berth. Jakko looked down and saw shrubs and grass close below; it was a ground-berth on a hillside.

The computer panel lit up: RESET PROGRAM FOR BASE.

"No," said Jakko. "We'll need it going back." Peach-thief looked at him in a new, companionable way; he sensed that she believed him now. He turned all the drive controls to standby while she worked the food synthesizer. Presently he heard the hiss of the deflating lift bags, and went to where she was standing by the dead stranger.

"We'll take her, her body, out before we go back," Peachthief said. "Maybe the River will touch her somehow."

Jakko doubted it, but ate and drank his breakfast protein in silence.

When they went to use the wash-and-waste cubby he found he didn't want to clean all the residues of their contact off himself. Peachthief seemed to feel the same way; she washed only her face and hands. He looked at her slender, silk-clad belly. Was a child, his child, starting there? Desire flicked him again, but he remembered he had work to do. His promise to his father; get on with it. Sooner done, sooner back here.

"I love you," he said experimentally, and found the strange words had a startling trueness.

She smiled brilliantly at him, not just off-on. "I love you too, I think."

The floor-portal light was on. They pulled it up and uncovered a stepway leading to the ground. The moondogs poured down.

They followed, coming out into a blowing world of rosy mists. Clouds were streaming around them, the air was all in motion up the hillside toward the crest some distance ahead of the ship berth. The ground here was uneven and covered with short soft grass, as though animals had cropped it.

"All winds blow to the River," Jakko quoted.

They set off up the hill, followed by the moondogs, who stalked uneasily with pricked ears. Probably they didn't like not being able to smell what was ahead, Jakko thought. Peachthief was holding his hand very firmly as they went, as if determined to keep him out of any danger.

As they walked up onto the flat crest of the hilltop the mists suddenly cleared, and they found themselves looking down into a great shallow glittering sunlit valley. They both halted involuntarily to stare at the fantastic sight.

Before them lay a huge midden heap, kilometers of things upon things upon things, almost filling the valley floor. Objects of every description lay heaped there; Jakko could make out clothing, books, toys, jewelry, myriad artifacts and implements abandoned. These must be, he realized, the last things people had taken with them when they went on the River. In an outer ring not too far below them were tents, ground- and aircars, even wagons. Everything shone clean and gleaming as if the influence of the River had kept off decay.

He noticed that the nearest ring of encampments intersected other, apparently older and larger rings. There seemed to be no center to the pile.

"The River has moved, or shrunk," he said.

"Both, I think." Peachthief pointed to the right. "Look, there's an old war-place."

A big grass-covered mound dominated the hillcrest beside them. Jakko saw it had metal-rimmed slits in its sides. He remembered history: how there were still rulers of people when the River's tendrils first touched earth. Some of the rulers had tried to keep their subjects from the going-out places, posting guards around them and even putting killing devices in the ground. But the guards had gone themselves out on the River, or the River had swelled and taken them. And the people had driven beasts across the mined ground and surged after them into the stream of immortal life. In the end the rulers had gone too, or died out. Looking more carefully, Jakko could see that the green hill slopes were torn and pocked, as though ancient explosions had made craters everywhere.

Suddenly he remembered that he had to find his father in all this vast confusion.

"Where's the River now? My father's mind should reach there still, if I'm not too late."

"See that glittery slick look in the air down there? I'm sure that's a danger-place."

Down to their right, fairly close to the rim, was a strangely bright place. As he stared it became clearer: a great column of slightly golden or shining air. He scanned about, but saw nothing else like it all across the valley.

"If that's the only focus left, it's going away fast."

She nodded and then swallowed, her small face suddenly grim. She meant to live on here and die without the River, Jakko could see that. But he would be with her; he resolved it with all his heart. He squeezed her hand hard.

"If you have to talk to your father, we better walk around up here on the rim where it's safe," Peachthief said.

"No-oo," spoke up a moondog from behind them. The two humans turned and saw the three sitting in a row on the crest, staring slit-eyed at the valley.

"All right," Peachthief said. "You wait here. We'll be back soon."

She gripped Jakko's hand even tighter, and they started walking past the old war-mound, past the remains of ancient vehicles, past an antique pylon that leaned crazily. There were faint little trails in the short grass. Another war-mound loomed ahead; when they passed around it they found themselves suddenly among a small herd of white animals with long necks and no horns. The animals went on grazing quietly as the humans walked by. Jakko thought they might be mutated deer.

"Oh, look!" Peachthief let go his hand. "That's milk—see, her baby is sucking!"

Jakko saw that one of the animals had a knobby bag between its hind legs. A small one half-knelt down beside it, with its head up nuzzling the bag. A mother and her young.

Peachthief was walking cautiously toward them, making gentle greeting sounds. The mother animal looked at her calmly, evidently tame. The baby went on sucking, rolling its eyes. Peachthief reached them, petted the mother, and then bent down under to feel the bag. The animal sidestepped a pace, but stayed still. When Peachthief straightened up she was licking her hand.

"That's good milk! And they're just the right size, we can take them on the airship! On the waycars, even." She was beaming, glowing. Jakko felt an odd warm constriction in his chest. The intensity with which she furnished her little world, her future nest! *Their* nest . . .

"Come with us, come on," Peachthief was urging. She had her belt around the creature's neck to lead it. It came equably, the young one following in awkward galloping lunges.

"That baby is a male. Oh, this is *perfect*," Peachthief exclaimed. "Here, hold her a minute while I look at that one."

She handed Jakko the end of the belt and ran off. The beast eyed him levelly. Suddenly it drew its upper lip back and shot spittle at his face. He ducked, yelling for Peachthief to come back.

"I have to find my father first!"

"All right," she said, returning. "Oh, look at that!"

Downslope from them was an apparition—one of the white animals, but partly transparent, ghostly thin. It drifted vaguely, putting its head down now and then, but did not eat.

"It must have got partly caught in the River, it's half gone. Oh, Jakko, you can see how dangerous it is! I'm afraid, I'm afraid it'll catch you."

"It won't. I'll be very careful."

"I'm afraid so." But she let him lead her on, towing the animal alongside. As they passed the ghost-creature Peachthief called to it, "You can't live like that. You better go on out. Shoo, shoo!"

It turned and moved slowly out across the piles of litter, toward the shining place in the air.

They were coming closer to it now, stepping over more and more abandoned things. Peachthief looked sharply at everything; once she stooped to pick up a beautiful fleecy white square and stuff it in her pack. The hillcrest was merging with a long grassy slope, comparatively free of debris, that ran out toward the airy glittering column. They turned down it.

The River-focus became more and more awesome as they approached. They could trace it towering up and up now, twisting gently as it passed beyond the sky. A tendril of the immaterial stream of sidereal sentience that had embraced earth, a pathway to immortal life. The air inside looked no longer golden, but pale silver-gilt, like a great shaft of moonlight coming down through the morning sun. Objects at its base appeared very clear but shimmering, as if seen through cool crystal water.

Off to one side were tents. Jakko suddenly recognized one, and quickened his steps. Peachthief pulled back on his arm.

"Jakko, be careful!"

They slowed to a stop a hundred yards from the tenuous fringes of the River's effect. It was very still. Jakko peered intently. In the verges of the shimmer a staff was standing upright. From it hung a scarf of green and yellow silk.

"Look—that's my father's sign!"

"Oh Jakko, you *can't* go in there."

At the familiar-colored sign all the memories of his life with his family had come flooding back on Jakko. The gentle rationality, the solemn sense of preparation for going out from earth forever. Two different realities strove briefly within him. They had loved him, he realized that now. Especially his father . . . But not as he loved Peachthief, his awakened spirit shouted silently. I am of earth! Let the stars take care of their own. His resolve took deeper hold and won.

Gently he released himself from her grip.

"You wait here. Don't worry, it takes a long while for the change, you know that. Hours, days. I'll only be a minute, I'll come right back."

"Ohhh, it's crazy."

But she let him go and stood holding to the milk-animal while he went down the ridge and picked his way out across the midden heap toward the staff. As he neared it he could feel the air change around him, becoming alive and yet more still.

"Father! Paul! It's Jakko, your son. Can you still hear me?"

Nothing answered him. He took a step or two past the staff, repeating his call.

A resonant susurrus came in his head, as if unearthly reaches had opened to him. From infinity he heard without hearing his father's quiet voice.

You came.

A sense of calm welcome.

"The cities are all empty, Father. All the people have gone, everywhere."

Come.

"No!" He swallowed, fending off memory, fending off the lure of strangeness. "I think it's sad. It's wrong. I've found a woman. We're going to stay and make children."

The River is leaving, Jakko my son.

It was as if a star had called his name, but he said stubbornly, "I don't care. I'm staying with her. Good-bye, Father. Good-bye."

Grave regret touched him, and from beyond a host of silent voices murmured down the sky: *Come! Come away.*

"No!" he shouted, or tried to shout, but he could not still the rapt voices. And suddenly, gazing up, he felt the reality of the River, the overwhelming opening of the door to life everlasting among the stars. All his mortal fears, all his most secret dread of the waiting maw of death, all slid out of him and fell away, leaving him almost unbearably light and calmly joyful. He knew that he was being touched, that he could float out upon that immortal stream forever. But even as the longing took him, his human mind remembered that this was the start of the first stage, for which the River was called Beata. He thought of the ghost animal that had lingered too long. He must leave now, and quickly. With enormous effort he took one step backward, but could not turn.

"Jakko! Jakko! Come back!"

Someone was calling, screaming his name. He did turn then, and saw her on the little ridge. Nearby, yet so far. The ordinary sun of earth was brilliant on her and the two white beasts.

"Jakko! Jakko!" Her arms were outstretched, she was running toward him.

It was as if the whole beautiful earth was crying to him, calling to him to come back and take up the burden of life and death. He did not want it. But she must not come here, he knew that without remembering why. He began uncertainly to stumble toward her, seeing her now as his beloved woman, again as an unknown creature uttering strange cries.

"Lady Death," he muttered, not realizing he had ceased to move. She ran faster, tripped, almost fell in the heaps of stuff. The wrongness of her coming here roused him again; he took a few more steps, feeling his head clear a little.

"*Jakko*!" She reached him, clutched him, dragging him bodily forward from the verge.

At her touch the reality of his human life came back to him, his heart pounded human blood, all stars fled away. He started to run clumsily, half-carrying her with him up to the safety of the ridge. Finally they sank down gasping beside the animals, holding and kissing each other, their eyes wet.

"I thought you were lost, I thought I'd lost you," Peachthief sobbed.

"You saved me."

"H-here," she said. "We b-better have some food." She rummaged in her pack, nodding firmly as if the simple human act could defend against unearthly powers. Jakko discovered that he was quite hungry.

They ate and drank peacefully in the soft, flower-studded grass, while the white animals grazed around them. Peachthief studied the huge strewn valley floor, frowning as she munched.

"So many good useful things here. I'll come back someday, when the River's gone, and look around."

"I thought you only wanted natural things," he teased her.

"Some of these things will last. Look." She picked up a small implement. "It's an awl, for punching and sewing leather. You could make children's sandals."

Many of the people who came here must have lived quite simply, Jakko thought. It was true that there could be useful tools. And metal. Books, too. Directions for making things. He lay back dreamily, seeing a vision of himself in the far future, an accomplished artisan, teaching his children skills. It seemed deeply good.

"Oh, my milk-beast!" Peachthief broke in on his reverie. "Oh, no! You mustn't!" She jumped up.

Jakko sat up and saw that the white mother animal had strayed quite far down the grassy ridge. Peachthief trotted down after her, calling, "Come here! Stop!"

Perversely, the animal moved away, snatching mouthfuls of grass. Peachthief ran faster. The animal threw up its head and paced down off the ridge, among the litter piles.

"No! Oh, my milk! Come back here, come."

She went down after it, trying to move quietly and call more calmly.

Jakko had gotten up, alarmed.

"Come back! Don't go down there!"

"The babies' milk," she wailed at him, and made a dash at

the beast. But she missed and it drifted away just out of reach before her.

To his horror Jakko saw that the glittering column of the River had changed shape slightly, eddying out a veil of shimmering light close ahead of the beast.

"Turn back! Let it go!" he shouted, and began to run with all his might. "Peachthief—come back!"

But she would not turn, and his pounding legs could not catch up. The white beast was in the shimmer now; he saw it bound up onto a great sun- and moonlit heap of stuff. Peachthief's dark form went flying after it, uncaring, and the creature leaped away again. He saw her follow, and bitter fear grabbed at his heart. The very strength of her human life is betraying her to death, he thought; I have to get her physically, I will pull her out. He forced his legs faster, faster yet, not noticing that the air had changed around him, too.

She disappeared momentarily in a veil of glittering air, and then reappeared, still following the beast. Thankfully he saw her pause and stoop to pick something up. She was only walking now, he could catch her. But his own body was moving sluggishly, it took all his will to keep his legs thrusting him ahead.

"Peachthief! Love, come back!"

His voice seemed muffled in the silvery air. Dismayed, he realized that he too had slowed to a walk, and she was veiled again from his sight.

When he struggled through the radiance he saw her, moving very slowly after the wandering white beast. Her face was turned up, unearthly light was on her beauty. He knew she was feeling the rapture, the call of immortal life was on her. On him, too; he found he was barely stumbling forward, a terrible serenity flooding his heart. They must be passing into the very focus of the River, where it ran strongest.

"Love—" Mortal grief fought the invading transcendence. Ahead of him the girl faded slowly into the glimmering veils, still following her last earthly desire. He saw that humanity, all that he had loved of the glorious earth, was disappearing forever from reality. Why had it awakened, only to be lost? Spectral voices were near him, but he did not want specters. An agonizing lament for human life welled up in him, a last pang that he would carry with him through eternity. But its urgency fell away. Life incorporeal, immortal, was on him now; it had him as it had her. His flesh, his body was beginning to attenuate, to dematerialize out into the great current of sentience that flowed on its mysterious purposes among the stars.

Still the essence of his earthly self moved slowly after hers into the closing mists of infinity, carrying upon the River a configuration that had been a man striving forever after a loved dark girl, who followed a ghostly white milch deer.

LE CROIX (THE CROSS)

Barry N. Malzberg

Depersonalization takes over. As usual, he does not quite feel himself, which is for the best; the man that he knows could hardly manage these embarrassing circumstances. Adaptability, that is the key; swim in the fast waters. There is no other way that he, let alone I, could get through. "*Pardonnez tout ils,*" he says, feeling himself twirling upon the crucifix in the absent Roman breezes, a sensation not unlike flight, "*mais ils ne comprendre pas que ils fait.*"

Oh my, is that awful. He wishes that he could do better than that. Still, there is no one around, strictly speaking, to criticize and besides, he is merely following impulse which is the purpose of the program. Do what you will. "*Ah pere*, this is a bitch," he mutters.

The thief on his left, an utterly untrustworthy type, murmurs foreign curses, not in French, to the other thief; and the man, losing patience with his companions who certainly *look* as culpable as all hell, stares below. Casting his glance far down he can see the onlookers, not so many as one would think, far less than the texts would indicate but certainly enough (fair is fair and simple Mark had made an effort to get it right) to cast lots over his vestments. They should be starting that stuff just about now.

Ah, well. This too shall pass. He considers the sky, noting with interest that the formation of clouds against the dazzling sunlight must yield the aspect of stigmata. For everything a natural, logical explanation. It is a rational world back here after all. If a little on the monolithic side.

"I wonder how long this is going to go on," he says to make conversation. "It does seem to be taking a bloody long time."

"Long time?" the thief on the left says. "Until we die, that's how long, and not an instant sooner. It's easier," the thief says confidentially, "if you breathe in tight little gasps. Less pain. You're kind of grabbing for the air."

"Am I? Really?"

"Leave him alone," the other thief says. "Don't talk to him. Why give him advice?"

"Just trying to help a mate on the stations, that's all."

"Help *yourself*," the second thief grumbles. "That's the only possibility. If I had looked out for myself I wouldn't be in this mess."

"I quite agree," I say. "That's exactly my condition, *exactly*."

"Ah, stuff it, mate," the thief says.

It is really impossible to deal with these people. The texts imbue them with sentimental focus but truly they are swine. I can grasp Pilate's dilemma. Thinking of Pilate leads into another channel, but before I can truly consider the man's problems a pain of particular dimension slashes through me and there I am, there I am, suspended from the great cross groaning, all the syllables of thought trapped within.

"Ah," I murmur, "ah," he murmurs, "*ah monsieurs, c'est le plus*," but it is not, to be sure, it is not *le plus* at all. Do not be too quick to judge.

It goes on, in fact, for an unsatisfactorily extended and quite spiritually laden period of time. The lot-casting goes quickly and there is little to divert on the hillside; one can only take so much of that silly woman weeping before it loses all emotional impact. It becomes a long and screaming difficulty, a passage broken only by the careless deaths of the thieves who surrender in babble and finally, not an instant too soon, the man's brain bursts . . . but there is time, crucifixion being what it is, for slow diminution beyond that. Lessening color; black and grey. If there is one thing to be said about this process, it is exceedingly generous. One will be spared nothing.

Of course I had pointed out that I did not *want* to be spared anything. "Give me Jesus," I had asked and co-operating in their patient way they had given me Jesus. There is neither irony nor restraint to the process, which is exactly the way that it should be.

Even to the insult of the thieves abusing me.

Alive to the tenor of the strange and difficult times, I found myself moved to consider the question of religious knowledge versus fanaticism. Hard choices have to be made even in pursuit of self-indulgence. Both were dangerous to the technocratic state of 2219, of course, but of the two religion was considered the more risky because fanaticism could well be turned to the advantage of the institutions. (Then there were the countervailing arguments of course that they were partners, but these I chose to dismiss.) Sexuality was another pursuit possibly inimical to the state but it held no interest for me; the general Privacy and Social Taboo acts of the previous century had been taken very seriously by my subdivision and I inherited neither genetic nor socially-derived interest in sex for its own non-procreative sake.

Religion interested me more than fanaticism for a permanent program, but fanaticism was not without its temptations. "Religion after all imposes a certain rigor," I was instructed. "There is some kind of a rationalizing force and also the need to assimilate text. Then too there is the reliance upon another, higher power. One cannot fulfill ultimately narcissistic tendencies. On the other hand, fanaticism dwells wholly within the poles of self. You can destroy the systems, find immortality, lead a crushing revolt, discover immortality within the crevices. It is not to be neglected; it is also purgative and satisfying and removes much of that indecision and social alienation of which you have complained. No fanatic is truly lonely or at least he has learned to cherish his loneliness."

"I think I'd rather have the religious program," I said after due consideration. "The lives of the prophets, the question of the validity of the text, the matters of the passion attract me."

"You will find," they pointed out, "that much of the religious experience is misrepresented. It leads only to an increasing doubt for many, and most of the major religious figures were severely maladjusted. You would be surprised at how many were psychotics whose madness was retrospectively falsified by others for their own purpose."

"Still," I said, "there are levels of feeling worth investigating."

"That, of course, is your decision," they said, relenting. They were nothing if not cooperative; under the promulgated and revised acts of 2202, severely liberalizing board procedures, there have been many improvements of this illusory sort. "If you wish to pursue religion we will do nothing to stop you. It is your inheritance and our decree. We can only warn you that there is apt to be disappointment.

"Disappointment!" I said, allowing some affect for the first time to bloom perilously forth. "I am not interested in disappointment. This is of no concern to me whatsoever; what I am interested in is the truth. After all, and was it not said that it is the truth which will make ye—"

"Never in this lifetime," they cut me off, sadly, sadly, and sent me on my way with a proper program, a schedule of appointments with the technicians, the necessary literature to explain the effects that all of this would have upon my personal landscape, inevitable changes, the rules of dysfunction, little instances of psychotic break but all of it to be contained within the larger pattern. By the time I exit from the transverse I have used up the literature, and so I dispose of it, tearing it into wide strips, throwing the strips into the empty, sparkling air above the passage lanes, watching them catch the little filters of light for the moment before they flutter soundlessly to the metallic, glittering earth of this most unspeakable time.

I find myself at one point of the way the Grand Lubavitcher Rabbi of Bruck Linn administering counsel to all who would seek it. The Lubavitcher Sect of the Judaic religion was, I understand, a twenty- or twenty-first reconstitution of the older, stricter European forms which was composed of refugees who fled to Bruck Linn in the wake of one of the numerous purges of that crime. Now defunct, the Judaicists are, as I understand it, a sect characterized by a long history of ritual persecution from which they flourished, or at least the surviving remnants flourished, but then again the persecution might have been the most important part of the ritual. At this remove in time it is hard to tell. The hypnotics, as the literature and procedures have made utterly clear, work upon personal projections and do not claim historical accuracy, as historical accuracy exists for the historicists, if anyone, and often enough not for them. Times being what they are.

It is, in any case, interesting to be the Lubavitcher Rabbi in Bruck Linn, regardless of the origins of the sect or even of its historical reality; in frock coat and heavy beard I sit behind a desk in cramped quarters surrounded by murmuring advisors and render judgments one by one upon members of the congregation as they appear before me. Penalty for compelled intercourse during a period of uncleanliness is three months of abstention swiftly dealt out and despite explanations that the young bride had pleaded for comfort. The Book of Daniel, reinterpreted, does not signal the resumption of Holocaust within the coming month; the congregant is sent away relieved. Two rabbis appear with Talmudic dispute; one says that Zephaniah meant that all pagans and not all things were to be consumed utterly off the face of the Earth, but the other says that the edict of Zephaniah was literal and that one cannot subdivide "pagans" from "all things". I return to the text for clarification, remind them that Zephaniah no less than Second Isaiah or the sullen Ecclesiastes spoke in doubled perversities and advise that the literal interpretation would have made this conference unnecessary, therefore metaphor must apply. My advisors nod in approval at this and there are small claps of admiration. Bemused, the two rabbis leave. A woman asks for a ruling on *mikvah* for a pre-menstrual daughter who is nonetheless now fifteen years old, and I reserve decision. A conservative rabbi from Yawk comes to give humble request that I give a statement to the congregation for one of the minor festivals, and I decline pointing out that for the Lubavitcher fallen members of the Judaicists are more reprehensible than those who have never arrived. Once again my advisors applaud. There is a momentary break in the consultations and I am left to pace the study alone while advisors and questioners withdraw to give me time for contemplation.

It is interesting to be the Lubavitcher, although somewhat puzzling. One of the elements of which I was not aware was that in addition to the grander passions, the greater personages, I would also find myself enacting a number of smaller roles, the interstices of the religious life, as it were, and exactly as it was pointed out to me there is a great deal of rigor. Emotion does not seem to be part of this rabbi's persona; the question of Talmudic interpretation seems to be quite far from the thrashings of Calvary. Still, the indoctrinative techniques have done their job; I am able to make my way through these roles even as the others, on the basis of encoded knowledge; and although the superficialities I babble seem meaningless to me, they seem to please those who surround. I adjust my cuffs with a feeling of grandeur; Bruck Linn may not be all of the glistening spaces of Rome but it is a not inconsiderable part of the history, and within it I seem to wield a great deal of power. "Rabbi," an advisor says opening the door, "I am temerarious to interrupt your musings, but we have reached a crisis and your intervention is requested at this time."

"What crisis?" I say. "You know I must be allowed to meditate."

"Yes," he says. "Yes, we respect your meditations. It is wrong to impose. I should not—" and some edge of agony within his voice, some bleating aspect of his face touches me even as he is about to withdraw. I come from behind the desk saying, "What then, what?" and he says, "Rabbi, it was wrong to bother you, we should protect, we will respect," and now I am really concerned, from large hat to pointed shoe he is trembling and I push past him into the dense and smoky air of the vestibule where congregants, advisors, women and children are gathered. As they see me their faces one by one register intent and then they are pleading, their voices inchoate but massed. *Save us, Rabbi*, they are saying, *save us*, and I do not know what is going on here, an awkward position for a Talmudic judge to occupy, but I simply do not know; I push my way through the clinging throng pushing them aside, *Oh my God, Rabbi*, they are saying, *Oh my God*, and I go through the outer doors, look down the street and see the massed armaments, see the troops eight abreast moving in great columns toward the building, behind them the great engines of destruction, and in the sky, noise, *the holocaust, Rabbi*, someone says, *the holocaust has come, they will kill us*, and I feel disbelief. How can this be happening? There was no purge in Bruck Linn to the best of my recollection; there have never been any great purges on this part of the continent. Nevertheless here they are and behind me I can hear the children screaming. It is all that I can do to spread my arms and, toward them, toward the massed congregants and advisors behind, cry, "Stay calm, this is not happening; it is an aspect of the imagination, some misdirection of the machinery." Surely it must be that, some flaws in the fabric of my perceptions being fed through the machines and creating history out of context, and yet the thunder and smell of the armies is great in the air and I realize that they are heading directly toward this place, that they have from the beginning, and that there is nothing I can do to stop them.

"Be calm, be calm," I cry, "you are imagining this, indeed you are all imagining," but the words do not help, and as I look at the people, as they look at me, as the sounds of Holocaust overwhelm, I seem to fall through the situation leaving them to a worse fate—or perhaps it is a better, but it is only I who have exited, leaving the rest, these fragments of my imagination, to shore themselves against their ruins, and not a moment too soon, too soon.

Otherwise, life such as it is proceeds as always. I spend a portion of the time on the hypnotics and in the machinery, but there are commitments otherwise: to eat, to sleep, to participate in the minimal but always bizarre social activities of the complex; even, on occasion to copulate, which I accomplish in methodical fashion. The construction, I have been reminded, is only a portion of my life; responsibilities do not cease on its account. I maintain my cubicle, convey the usual depositions from level to level, busy myself in the perpetuation of microcosm. Only at odd times do I find myself thinking of the nature of the hypnotic experiences I have had, and then I try to push these recollections away. They are extremely painful and this subtext, as it were, is difficult to integrate into the outer span of my life. In due course I am assured that the fusion will be made, but in the meantime there is no way to hasten it. "You have changed, Harold," Edna says to me. Edna is my current companion. She is not named Edna, nor I Harold, but these are the names that they have assigned for our contemporary interaction, and Harold is as good as any; it is a name by which I would as soon be known. *Harold in Galilee. And I have spoken his name and it is Harold*. She leans toward me confidentially. "You are not the same person that you were."

"That is a common illusion provided by the treatments," I say. "I am exactly the same person. Nothing is any different than it was."

"Yes it is," she murmurs. "You may not realize how withdrawn and distracted you have become." She is a rather pretty woman and there are times, during our more or less mechanical transactions, when I have felt real surges of feeling for her, but they have only been incidental to the main purpose. In truth I can have no feeling for anyone but myself; I was told this a long time ago. She puts a hand on me intensely. "What are they doing to you?"

"Nothing," I say quite truthfully. "They are merely providing a means. Everything that is done I am doing myself; this is the principle of the treatment."

"You are deluded," she says and loops an arm around me, drags me into stinging but pleasurable embrace. Forehead to forehead we lay nestled amidst the bedclothes; I feel the tentative touch of her fingers. "Now," she says, moving her hand against me. "Do it now."

I push against her embrace. "No. It is impossible."

"Why?"

"During the treatments—"

"Nonsense," she says, "you are avoiding me. You are avoiding yourself. The treatments are anaesthetic, don't you see that? They are forcing you to avoid the terms of your life and you cannot do that." Her grasp is more insistent, at the beginning of pain. "Come on," she says. Insistent woman. Against myself, I feel a slow gathering.

"No," I mutter against her cheekbone, "it is impossible. I will not do it now."

"Fool."

"The chemicals. I am awash in chemicals; I remain in a sustaining dose all the time. I would upset all of the delicate balances—"

"You understand nothing," she says, but in an inversion of mood turns from me anyway, scurrying to a far point. "Have it as you will. Do you want me to leave?"

"Of course not."

"*Of course not*. You are so accommodating. Do you want me to entertain you then?"

"Whatever you will."

"You have changed utterly. You are not the same. These treatments have rendered you cataleptic. I had hopes for you, Harold; I want you to know that. I thought that there were elements of genuine perception, real thought. How was I to know that all of the time you merely wanted to escape into your fantasies?"

"What did you want me to do?" I say casually. "Overthrow the mentors?"

She shrugs. "Why not?" she says. "It would be something to keep us occupied."

"I'd rather overthrow myself."

"You know, Harold," she says and there is a clear, steady light of implication in her eye, "it is not impossible for me to like you; we could really come to understand one another, work together to deal with this crazy situation, but there is this one overwhelming problem, and do you know what that is?"

"Yes I do," I say wearily because this has happened before. "I surely do."

"Don't deprive me of the satisfaction," she says. "Harold, you are a fool."

"Well," I say shrugging, "in these perilous and difficult times, this madly technocratic age of 2219, when we have so become merely the machinery of our institutions, where any search for individuality must be accomplished by moving within rather than without, taking all of this into consideration and what with one thing being like every other thing in this increasingly homogeneous world, tell me, aren't we all?"

"Not like you," she says. "Harold, even in these perilous and difficult times, not like you at all."

On the great and empty desert he takes himself to see the form of Satan, manifest in the guise of an itinerant, wandering amidst the sands. Moving with an odd, off-center gait, rolling on limping leg, Satan seems eager for the encounter, and he is ready for it too, ready at last to wrestle the old, damned angel and be done with it, but Satan is taking his time—the cunning of the creature—and seems even reluctant to make the encounter. Perhaps he is merely being taunted. Once again he thinks of the odd discrepancy of persona; he is unable in this particular role to work within the first person but is instead a detached observer seeing all of it at a near and yet far remove, imprisoned within the perception, yet not able to affect it. An interesting phenomenon, perhaps he has some fear that to become the persona would be blasphemous. He must discuss this with the technicians sometime. Then again, maybe not. Maybe he will not discuss it with the technicians; it is none of their damned business, any of it, and besides, he has all that he can do to concentrate upon Satan, who in garb of bright hues and dull now comes upon him. "Are you prepared?" Satan says to him. "Are you prepared for the undertaking?"

He looks down at his sandals embedded in the dense and settled sands. "I am ready for the encounter," he says.

"Do you know the consequences?" Satan says. He has a curiously ingratiating voice, a warm and personal manner, an offhand ease which immediately grants a feeling of confidence, but then again this was to be expected. What belies the manner, however, is the face, the riven and broken features, the darting aspect of the eyes, the small crevices in which torment and desert sweat seem to lurk and which compel attention beyond the body which has been broken by the perpetration of many seeming injustices. Satan extends his arm. "Very well, then," Satan says, "let us wrestle."

"*Non disputandum*," he says. "I understood that first we were to talk and only after that to struggle."

"Latin is no protection here," Satan says firmly. "All tongues pay homage to me."

"*Mais non*," he says in his abominable French, "*voulez-vous je me porte bien*."

"Nor does humor exist in these dark spaces," Satan says. "From walking up and down upon the earth and to and fro I have learned the emptiness of present laughter. Come," he says, leaning forward, his arm extended, "let us wrestle now."

He reaches for that gnarled limb, then brings his hands back. The sun is pitiless overhead but like a painting; he does not feel the heat. His only physical sensation is of the dry and terrible odor seeping from his antagonist. "No," he says. "*Mais non, mon frere*. Not until we have had the opportunity to speak."

"There is nothing to speak about. There are no sophistries in this emptiness, merely contention."

Do not argue with Satan. He had been warned of this, had known it as his journey toward the darkness had begun, that there was no way in which the ancient and terrible enemy could be engaged with dialectic and yet, *non disputandum*, he has failed again. Not to do it. Not to try argument; it is time to wrestle and it might as well be done. He seizes the wrist and slowly he and the devil lock.

Coming to grips with that old antagonist it is to the man as if he has found not an enemy but only some long-removed aspect of himself, as if indeed, just as in sex or dreams, he is in the act of completing himself with this engagement. The stolidity of the form, the interlocking of limbs, gives him not a sense of horror, as he might have imagined, but rather comfort. It must have been this way. Their hands fit smoothly together. "Do you see?" Satan says winking and coming to close quarters. "You know that it must always have been meant this way. Touch me, my friend, touch me and find grace," and slowly, evenly, Satan begins to drag him forward.

He understands, he understands what is happening to him: Satan in another of his guises would seduce him with warmth when it is really a mask for evil. He should be fighting against the ancient and terrible enemy with renewed zeal for recognizing this, but it is hard, it is hard to do so when Satan is looking at him with such compassion, when the mesh of their bodies is so perfect. Never has he felt anyone has understood him this well; his secret and most terrible agonies seem to flutter, one by one, birdlike, across the features of the antagonist, and he could if he would sob out all of his agonies knowing that Satan could understand. Who ever would as well? It must have been the same for him. I do not believe, he wants to cry to the devil; I believe none of it; I am taken by strange, shrieking visions and messages in the night; I feel that I must take upon the host of Heaven, and yet these dreams which leave me empty and sick are, I know, madness. I hear the voice of God speaking unto me saying I am the Father, I am the incompleteness which you will fill and know that this must be madness, and yet I cannot deny that voice, can deny no aspect of it, which is what set me here upon the desert, but I am filled with fear, filled with loathing and trembling . . . he wants to cry all of this out to Satan, but he will not, he will not, and slowly he finds himself being drawn to the ground.

"Comfort," Satan says in the most confiding and compassionate of whispers, covering him now with his gnarled body so that the sun itself is obscured, all landscape dwindled to the small perception of shifting colors, "comfort: I understand, I am your dearest and closest friend. Who can ever understand you as I? Who would possibly know your anguish. Easy, be easeful," Satan says, and he begins to feel the pressure come across his chest. "So easy," Satan murmurs, "it will be so easy, for only I understand; we can dwell together," and breath begins to desert him. The devil is draining his respiration.

Understanding that, he understands much else: the nature of the engagement, the quality of deception, exactly what has been done to him. Just as Satan was the most beautiful and best-loved of all the angels, so in turn he would be Satan's bride in the act of death. It is the kiss that will convey the darkness, and seeing this, he has a flickering moment of transcendence: he thinks he knows now how he might be able to deal with this. Knowing the devil's meaning will enable him to contest, and yet it would be so easy—inevitable is the word—necessary—to yield to his antagonist and let it be done, let the old, cold, bold intruder have his will, thy will be done, and Satan's too, and the yielding is so close to him now he can feel himself leaning against the network of his being, the empty space where desire might have rested, in the interstices the lunge toward annihilation—*mais non*, he says, *mais non*, *je renounce*, *I will not do it*!—and forces himself against the figure, understanding finally the nature of this contest, what it must accomplish, in what mood it must be done and wearily, wearily, carrying all of consequence upon him he begins the first and final of all his contests with the devil.

It is a madly technocratic age, a madly technocratic age, and yet it is not cruel; the devices of our existence, we have been assured, exist only in order to perpetrate our being. Take away the technology and the planet would kill us; take away the institutions and the technology would collapse. There is no way in which we can continue to be supported without the technology and the institutions, and furthermore they are essentially benign. They are essentially benign. This is not rationalization or an attempt to conceal from myself and others the dreadful aspects of our mortality, the engines of our condition grinding us slowly away . . . no, this is a fixed and rational judgment which comes from a true assessment of this life.

It is true that a hundred years ago, in the decades of the great slaughters and even beyond, the institutions were characterized by vengeance, pusillanimity, murder and fear, but no more. In 2160 the oligarchy was finally toppled, the reordering began, and by 2189, the very year in which I was born, the slaughter was already glimpsed within a historical context. I was nurtured by a reasonable state in a reasonable fashion; if I needed love, I found it; sustenance was there in more forms than the purely physical. I grew within the bounds of the state; indeed, I matured to a full and reasonable compassion. Aware of the limits which were imposed, I did not resent them nor find them stifling.

There was space; there has been space for a long time now. Standing on the high parapet of the dormer, looking out on Inter-valley Six and the web of connecting arteries beneath the veil of dust, I can see the small lights of the many friendly cities nodding and winking in the darkness, the penetrating cast of light creating small spokes of fire moving upward in the night. Toward the west the great thrust of South. Harvest rears its bulk and spires, lending geometry to a landscape which would otherwise be endless, and I find reassurance in that presence just as I find reassurance in the act of being on the parapet itself. There was a time, and it was not so terribly long ago, that they would not have allowed residents to stand out on the parapet alone; the threat of suicide was constant, but in the last years the statistics have become increasingly favorable, and it is now within the means of all of us, if only we will to come out in the night for some air.

Edna is beside me. For once we are not talking; our relationship has become almost endlessly convoluted now, filled with despair, rationalization and dialogue, but in simple awe of the vision she too has stopped talking and it is comfortable, almost companionable standing with her thus, our hands touching lightly, smelling the strange little breezes of our technology. A long time ago people went out in pairs to places like this and had a kind of emotional connection by the solitude and the vision, but now emotions are resolved for more sensible arenas such as the hypnotics. Nevertheless, it is pleasant to stand with her thus. It would almost be possible for me at this moment to conceive some genuine attachment to her, except that I know better; it is not the union but its absence which tantalizes me at this moment, the knowledge that there is no connection which will ever mean as much to us as this landscape. The sensation is unbearably poignant although it does not match in poignance other moments I have had under the hypnotics. At length she turns toward me, her touch more tentative in the uneven light and says, "It hurts me too. It hurts all of us."

"I wasn't really thinking about pain."

"Nevertheless," she says. "Nevertheless. Pain is the constant for all of us. Some can bear it and others cannot. Some can face this on their own terms and others need artificial means of sustentation. There is nothing to be done about this."

"I don't *need* artificial means," I say. "I have elected—"

"Surely," she says. "Surely."

And they are not artificial, I want to add; the experiences under the hypnotics are as real, as personally viable, as much the blocks of personality formulation as anything which this confused and dim woman can offer, as anything which has passed between us. But that would only lead to another of our arguments and I feel empty of that need now. Deep below we can hear the uneven cries of the simulacrum animals let out at last for the nighttime zoo, the intermingled roars of tigers.

"Has it made any difference?" she says. "Any of it?"

"Any of what? I don't understand."

"The treatments. Your treatments."

Tantalizingly, I find myself on the verge of a comment which will anneal everything, but it slips away from me as is so often the case, and I say, "Of course they have made a difference."

"What have you gained?"

"*Pardonne? Pardonnez moi?*"

"Don't be obscure on me," she says. "That will get you nowhere. Tell me the truth."

I shrug. My habit of lapsing into weak French under stress is an old disability; nonetheless I find it difficult to handle. Most have been more understanding than Edna. "I don't know," I say. "I think so."

"I know. It's done nothing at all."

"Let's go inside now," I say. "It's beginning to chill here."

"You are exactly the same as you were. Only more withdrawn, more stupid. These treatments are supposed to heal?"

"No. Merely broaden. Healing comes from within."

"Broaden! You understand less than ever."

I put a hand to my face, feel the little webbing where years from now deep lines will be. "Let's go inside," I say again. "There's nothing more—"

"Why don't you face the truth? These treatments are not meant to help you; they are meant to make you more stupid so that you won't cause any trouble—"

I move away from her. "It doesn't matter," I say. "None of it matters. It is of no substance whatsoever. Why do you care for it to be otherwise?"

There is nothing for her to do but to follow me into the funnel. She would argue in position but my withdrawal has offered the most devastating answer of all: I simply do not care. The attitude is not simulated: on the most basic level I refuse to interact.

"You are a fool," she says, crowding against me for the plunge. "You do not understand what they are doing to you. You simply don't care."

"Quite right," I say. "Quite right. Absolutely. Not at all. That is the point now, isn't it?"

The light ceases and we plunge.

I am in an ashram surrounded by incense and the dull outlines of those who must be my followers. Clumped in the darkness they listen to me chant. It is a mantra which I appear to be singing in a high, cracked chant; it resembles the chanting of the Lubavitchers of Bruck Linn, although far more regularized in the vocal line, and limited in sound. *Om* or *ay* or *eeh*, the sounds are interchangeable and I am quite willing to accept the flow of it, not rationalize, not attempt to control those sounds but rather to let them issue according to my mood. It is peaceful and I am deeply locked within myself; the soft breathing of my followers lending resonance to the syllables which indeed seem to assume a more profound meaning, but at a certain point there is a commotion and the sound of doors crashing and then in the strophes of light I can see that the room has been invaded by what appear to be numerous members of the opposition. They are wearing their dull attack uniforms, even this if nothing else is perceptible in the light and from the glint of weaponry I can see that this is very serious. They move with an awful tread into the room, half a dozen of them, and then the portable incandescence is turned on and we are pinned there in frieze.

I know that it is going to be very bad; the acts of 2013 specifically proscribed exactly what is going on here and yet five years later the pogroms have dwindled to harassment, random isolated incursions. I did not think that in this abandoned church in the burned-out core of the devastated city they would ever move upon me, and yet it seems now that my luck has suddenly, convulsively run out, as I always knew that it would. Surely in some corner of the heart I must have known this; the *om* must have always been informed by doom; and yet it is one thing to consider demolition in a corner of the heart and another, quite another, to live it. *Ahbdul*, one of them says pointing, his finger enormous, dazzling, and as I lift my eyes to it I feel myself subsiding in the wickers of light, *Ahbdul, you are in violation of the codes and you have brought woe to all.*

In a moment, in one moment, they will plunge toward me. I know how it goes then, what will happen; they will strike at me with their weapons and bring me to a most painful position; they will obliterate consciousness and cause bloodstains; not of the least importance they will humiliate me before my small congregation, which has already witnessed enough humiliation—thank you very much—otherwise why would they have gathered here?—and yet I can tolerate all of that, I suppose. I have dreamed worse, not to say suffered many privations and indignities before opening this small, illegal sub-unit. In fact, none of this concerns me; what does, I must admit, is the fear that I will show weakness before my congregation. To be humiliated is one thing, but to show fear, beg for mercy, is quite another; I would hardly be able to deal with it. A religious man must put up a stiff front. A religious man whose cult is based upon the regular, monotonic articulation of ancient chants to seek for inner serenity can hardly be seen quivering and shrieking in front of those who have come for tranquillity. If tranquillity is all that I have to offer, I cannot give them pain.

Thinking this, I resolve, to be brave and draw myself to full stature or what there is left of it after all these years of controlled diet and deliberate physical mutilation. "You will not prevail," I say. "You cannot prevail against the force of the om," and with a signal I indicate to my congregation that I wish to resume the chant, humiliate them by my own transcendence, but they do not attend. Indeed they do not attend at all, so eager do so many of them appear to search out any means of exit open to them. A small alley has been left open by the massed opposition leading to one of the doors, and in their unseemly haste to clear the hall they ignore me. Religious disposition, it would seem, is a function of boredom: give people something really necessary to face in their lives and religion can be ignored, all except for the fanatics who consider religion itself important, of course; but they are disaster-ridden. Like flies these little insights buzz about, gnawing and striking small pieces of psychic flesh while the hall is emptied, the opposition standing there looking at me bleakly, but I find as usual that this insight does me no good whatsoever. It can, indeed, be said merely to magnify my sense of helplessness.

"Gentlemen," I say, raising a hand, "this is a futile business.

Join me in a chant." I kneel, my forehead near the floor, and begin to mumble, hoping that the intensity of this commitment will strike shame within them, convince them that they are dealing with someone so dangerously self-absorbed that all of their attacks would be futile, but even as I commence the syllables I am pulled to my feet by a man in a uniform which I do not recognize, obviously a late-comer to the room. He stares at me from a puffy, heart-shaped face and then raises his hand, strikes me skilfully across first one cheek and then the other. The collision of flesh is enormous; I feel as if I am spattering within. "Fool," he says, "why have you done this?"

"Why do you care? Why are you asking?"

He hits me again. No progression of the sacred blocks of personality; the levels of eminent reason have prepared me for this kind of pain. I realize that I am crying. "Give me a response," he says. "Don't withdraw, don't protest, don't argue; it will lead only to more blows and eventually the same results. Simply answer questions and it will go much easier for both of us. Knowing all of the penalties, knowing of the responsibilities for your acts and what would happen to you if you were discovered, why did you nonetheless persist? Didn't you understand? Didn't you know what danger you brought not only upon yourself but the fools you seduced? Now they too will have to pay."

He is choleric with rage, this man; his face seems to have inflated with blood and reason as he stands there and I begin to comprehend that he is suffering from more than situational stress. Looking at him I want to accentuate that sudden feeling of bonding, but there is every emotion but sympathy in that ruined face and suddenly he hits me again convulsively; this the most painful blow yet because it was not expected. I fall before him and begin to weep. It is not proper context for a martyr, but I never wanted it to be this way; I never imagined that there would be such blood in sacrifice. He puts one strong hand under an arm, drags me grunting to my feet, positions me in front of him as if I were a statue.

"Do you know what we're going to have to do now?" he says. "We're going to have to make an example of you, that's all, we're going to have to kill you. Why did you put us into this position?"

"I am not able to believe that you will do that," I say. I am struggling for tranquillity. "You wouldn't kill me, not here in the temple—"

"This is not a temple. It is a dirty cluttered room and you are an old fool who imagines it to be a church—"

"Om," I say. The word comes; I did not calculate. *"Om. Eeeh. Ay."*

"You would fight the state regardless. If the state believed in *om* you would cry for freedom of choice. If the state were stateless you would wish to form institutions within. There is no hope for you people, none at all; you would be aberrants in any culture at any time and you cannot understand this. You want to be isolated, persecuted, to die. It has nothing to do with religion."

"Eeh. Ay. Oooh. Ahh. Om."

"Enough," he says, "enough of this," and signals to the others at the rear; they come forward slowly, reluctantly, but with gathering speed at the approach, perhaps catching a whiff of death which comes from the syllables. "You wish a public death, you wish a martyrdom; then you will have it. Reports will be issued to all of the provinces. Icons will be constructed. Dispatches will even glorify. You will achieve everything that you were unable in life. But this will do you no good whatsoever."

The fear is tightly controlled now. Truly, the syllables work. I would not have granted them such efficacy and yet what I have advised my congregants all of this time turns out to be true. They paste over the sickness with the sweet contaminations of courage, grant purchase upon terror, make it possible for the most ignorant and cowardly of men, which must be myself, to face annihilation with constant grace. *"Om,"* I say. *"Eeh.* If it were to be done, then it must be done quickly."

"Ah," he says, "it is impossible. Nothing will be gained from this and yet you still will not face the truth. It would be so much easier if at least you would give up your bankrupt purchase, if you would understand that you are dying for no reason whatsoever and that it could have been no other way; it would make matters so much easier—"

"Ah," I say. "Oh."

"Ah, shit," the man with the heart-shaped face says and gives a signal to one of the supporters, who closes upon me, a small man in uniform with a highly calibered weapon and puts its cold surfaces against my temple. His hand shakes, imperceptibly to the vision, but I can feel that quiver against the ridged veins. It is remarkable how I have gained in courage and detachment; just a few moments ago it would have seemed impossible. Yet here I am, apparently, prepared to face what I feared the most with implacable ardor. "Now." the man says. "Do it now."

There is a pause. *Om* resonates through me; it will be that with which I will die, carrying me directly to the outermost curved part of the universe. I close my eyes, waiting for transport, but it does not come, and after a while I understand that it will not. Therefore I open my eyes, reasonable passage seeming to have been denied me. The positions are the same except that the leader has moved away some paces and the man carrying the gun has closed his eyes.

"Shoot him, you fool," the leader says. "Why haven't you shot him?"

"I am having difficulty—"

"Kill him, you bastard."

There is another long pause. I flutter my eyes. *Om* has receded. "I can't," the man with the gun says at last. "I can't put him down, just like that. This isn't what I was prepared to do. You didn't say that it would be this way. You promised—"

"Ah, shit," the heart-shaped man says again and comes toward us, breaks the connection with a swipe of his hand, knocking the gun arm down and the supporter goes scuttling away squealing. The leader looks at me with hatred, red-tinted veins alight. "You think you've proven something," he says. "Well, you've proven absolutely nothing. Weakness is weakness. I will have to do it myself."

I shrug. It is all that I can do to maintain my demeanor considering the exigencies but I have done it. Will; everything is will. *"Om,"* I murmur.

"Om," he says, *"om* yourself," and goes to the supporter; the supporter hands him the gun silently; the leader takes it in his left hand, flexes fingers, then puts it against my "temple." "All right," he says, "it could have been easier but instead it will be more complex. That does not matter, all that matters is consummation."

"Consummate," I say. *"Om."*

"I don't want to do this," he says with the most immense kindness. "I hope you understand. It's nothing personal; I have little against you; it's just a matter of assignment, of social roles." Unlike the others he seems to need to prepare himself for assassination through a massive act of disconnection. "Nothing personal," he says mildly, "I really don't want to."

I shrug. "I don't wait to die, particularly," I say. "Still, I seem able to face it." And this is the absolute truth. Calm percolates from the center of the corpus to the very brain stem; I seem awash in dispassion. Perhaps it is the knowledge that this is all a figment, that it is a dream and I will not die but awake again only to sterile enclosure and the busy hands of technicians. "Do it," I say. "Do it." Is this the secret of all the martyrs? That at the end, past flesh and panic, they knew when they would awaken and to what? Probably. On the other hand, maybe not. Like everything else it is difficult and complex. Still, it can be met with a reasonable amount of dignity, which is all that we can ask.

"Indeed," he says sadly, "indeed," and fires the gun into my temple killing me instantly and precipitating in one jagged bolt the great, religious riots and revivals of the early twenties. And not one moment too soon, Allah and the rest of them be praised.

Systematically I face examination in the cold room. It is a necessary part of the procedure. "The only hint of depersonalization other than at the end of the last segment," I say calmly, "has been during the Jesus episodes. I seem unable to occupy it within the first person but feel a profound disassociative reaction in which I am witnessing him as if from the outside, without controlling the actions."

The counselor nods. "Highly charged emotional material obviously," he says. "Disassociative reaction is common in such cases. At some point in your life you must have had a Jesus fixation."

"Not so," I say. "In fact I did not know who he was until I was introduced through the texts."

"Then it must have hit some responsive chord. I wouldn't be unduly concerned about this. As you integrate into the persona it will fall away and you will begin to actively participate."

"I feel no emotional reaction to the material at all. I mean, no more than to any of the others. It's inexplicable to me."

"I tell you," the counselor says with a touch of irritation, "that is of no concern. The process is self-reinforcing. What we are concerned about is your overall reactions, the gross medical signs, the question of organic balances. The psychic reactions will take care of themselves."

I look past him at the walls of the room which contain schematic portraits of the intervalley network. Interspersed are various documents certifying the authenticity of his observer's role. The absence of anything more abstract disturbs me; previously it never occurred to me how deprived our institutions seem to be of artistic effect, but now it does; the hypnotics must be working. There is a clear hunger within me for something more than a schematic response to our condition. "Are you listening to me?" he says. "Did you hear my question."

"I heard it."

"I am going to administer a gross verbal reaction test now, if you will pay attention."

"I assure you that is not necessary," I say. "I am in excellent contact."

"That is a judgment which we will make."

"Must you?"

"I'm afraid so," the counselor says. "We wish to guard against exactly that which you manifest, which strikes me as a rather hostile, detached response. We do not encourage this kind of side-effect, you see; we consider it a negative aspect of the treatment."

"I'm sorry to hear that."

"It is often necessary to terminate treatment in the face of such reactions, so I would take this very seriously."

"Why do you do this to us?" I say. I look at his bland, pleasant face, masked by the institutional sheen but nonetheless concealing, I am convinced, as passionate and confused a person as I might be, perhaps a little *more* passionate and confused since he has not had, after all, the benefit of the treatments. "Why can we simply not go through this on our own terms, take what we can take, miss the rest of it? Why must we be *monitored*?"

"The procedures—"

"Don't tell me of procedures," I say, leaning forward with a sudden intensity, aware that I am twitching at the joints and extremities in a new fashion, emotionally moved as rarely has been the case. Definitely the treatments are affecting me. "The real reason is that you're afraid that unless we're controlled we might really be changed, that we might begin to react in fashions that you couldn't predict, that we wouldn't be studying *religion* and *fanaticism* any more but would actually become religious fanatics and what would you do with us then?"

"Confine you," my confessor says flatly, "for your own protection. Which is exactly what we want to avoid by the process of what you call monitoring, which is merely certifying that you are in condition to continue the treatments without damage to yourself."

"Or to the state."

"Of course to the state. I work for it, you live within it; why should we not have the interests of the state at heart? The state need not be perceived as the enemy by you people, you know."

"I never perceived—"

"You can't make the state the repository of all your difficulties, the rationalizing force for your inadequacies. The state is a positive force in all of your lives and you have more personal freedom that any citizenry at any time in the history of the world."

"I never said that it wasn't—"

"In fact," the counselor says, rising, his face suffused now with what might be passion but then on the other hand might only be the consequence of improper diet, highly spiced intake, the slow closure of arteries, "we can get damned sick of you people and your attitudes. I'm no less human because I have a bureaucratic job, I want you to know; I have the same problems that you do. The only difference is that I'm trying to apply myself toward constructive purposes, whereas all you want to do is to tear things down." He wipes a hand across his streaming features, shrugs, sits again. "Sorry to overreact," he says. "It's just that a good deal of frustration builds up and it has to be expressed. This isn't easy for any of us, you know. We're not functionaries; we're people just as you are."

There seems nothing with which I can disagree. I consider certain religious virtues which would have to do with the absorption of provocation without malice and remain quietly in my chair, thinking of this and that and many other things having to do with the monitoring conducted by these institutions and what it might suggest about the nature of the interrelation, but thought more and more is repulsive to me; what I concentrate upon, what seems to matter is feeling, and it is feeling which I will cultivate. "Some questions," the counselor says in a more amiable tone. "Just a series of questions which I would like you to answer as briefly and straightforwardly as possible."

"Certainly," I say, echoing his calm. "*Très bonne, merci. Maintenant et pourquoi.*"

"*Pourquoi*?" he says with a glint in his eye and asks me how often I masturbate.

He looks at the man who has come from the tomb. Little sign of his entrapment is upon him; he looks merely as one might who had been in deep sleep for a couple of days. He touches him once gently upon the cheek to assure the pulse of light, then backs away. The crowd murmurs with awe. This is no small feat; here he has clearly outdone the loaves and the fishes. They will hardly be able to dismiss this one; it will cause great difficulty when the reports hit Rome. "How are you?" he says to Lazarus. "Have you been merely sleeping or did you perceive the darkness? What brings you back from those regions?"

Documentary sources indicate no speech from the risen man, of course. But documentary sources are notoriously undependable, and, besides, this is a free reconstruction as he has been so often advised. Perhaps Lazarus will have something to say after all; his eyes bulge with reason and his tongue seems about to burst forward with the liquid syllables of discovery. But only an incoherent babble emerges; the man says nothing.

He moves in closer, still holding the grip. "Were you sleeping?" he says, "or did you perceive?"

"*Ah*," Lazarus says. "*Eeeh. Om*."

He shrugs and dropping his hand moves away. If a miracle is to succeed, it must do so on its own terms; one must have a detached, almost airy attitude toward the miracles because at the slightest hint of uncertainty or effort they will dissipate. "Very well," he says, "be on your way. Return to your life."

The disciples surround him, all but Judas, of course, who as usual is somewhere in the city, probably making arrangements for betrayal. There is nothing to be done; he must suffer Judas exactly as Judas must suffer him, it is the condition of their pact. Peter puts a heavy hand on his shoulder. "What if the man cannot move, master?" he says, always practical. "What if he is unable to complete the journey from the grave."

"He will be able to."

Indeed Lazarus seems to have adopted a stiff gait which takes him slowly toward the crowd. The crowd is surprisingly sparse after all; it is not the throng indicated by scriptures, but instead might be only forty or fifty, many of whom are itinerants drawn to the scene in their wanderings. Scriptural sources were often only a foundation for the received knowledge, of course; the scribes had their own problems, their own needs to fill and retrospective falsification was part of their mission . . . still, he thinks, it is often embarrassing to see how hollow that rock is upon which the church was built. Oh well. "I think we had better leave now," Peter says.

"Oh?"

"Indeed," this man of practicality says. "It will make more of an impression, I think; it will lend more of an air of mystery and have greater lasting effect than if you were to stay around. A certain detachment must be cultivated."

"We will surround you, Master," little Mark says, "and leave together hiding your aspect from the populace. In this way you will seem to be attended at all times by a shield." He beckons to Luke, John, the others. "Come," Peter says, "nothing can be served by staying here longer. It would be best to move on."

He does admire the practicality, the disciples simply acting within the situation to bring the maximum interest, and yet reluctance tugs at him. He is really interested in Lazarus. He would like to see what happens next: will the man leave the area of the tomb or will he simply return to it? The rock has merely been pulled aside, the dark opening gapes; Lazarus could simply return to that comfort if he desired, and perhaps he does. Or perhaps not; it is hard to evaluate the responses of an individual toward death. The man is now shielded from view by the crowd which seems to be touching him, checking for the more obvious aspects of mortality. "Let us wait a moment," he says. "This is very interesting. Let's see what is happening here."

"It would not serve, Master," Peter says.

"It is not a matter of serving, merely one of observation. I am responsible for this man, after all; it is only reasonable that I would take an interest in his condition."

"No," Luke says. He scuttles over, a thin man with bulging, curiously piercing eyes. No wonder he wrote the most elaborate of the gospels—dictated, that is to say, all of the disciples being fundamentally illiterate. "That will not serve. It is important that we leave at once, Master."

"Why?"

"The mood of the crowd is uncertain; it could turn ugly at any time. There can be much contretemps over miracles, and the superstitious are turned toward fear. The very hills are filled with great portents—"

"Enough," Peter says. "You have a tendency for hyperbole, Luke; there is no danger here. But it would be better, from many standpoints if we were to leave; an air of mystery would serve best—"

"Oh, all right," I say. "*Je renouncée.*" It is, after all, best to adopt a pose of dignity and to give in to the wishes of the disciples, all of whom at least intermittently take this matter more seriously than I . . . they are, after all, in a position of greater vulnerability. I cast one last look at Lazarus, who is now leaning back against the suspended door of the tomb, elbows balanced precariously on stones, trying to assume an easeful posture for the group almost obscuring him. How exactly is one to cultivate a *je ne sais quoi* about death? It is something to consider; of course I will have ample time to consider the issue myself, but Lazarus could hardly yield much information on the subject. The man is speechless, highly inarticulate; one would have hoped that for a miracle such as this that I could have aroused someone less stupid, but nothing to be done. All of existence is tied together in one tapestry, take it all or leave it, no parts. Surrounded by my muttering disciples I walk toward the west, kicking up little stones and puffs of dust with my sandals.

It is disappointing, quite a letdown really, and I would like to discuss this, but not a one of them would want to hear it. I know that they already have sufficient difficulties having given up their lives for the duration of this mission and it would be an embarrassment for them to hear that I too do not quite know what I am doing. Or perhaps I do. It is hard to tell. In the distance I hear a vague collision of stone. I would not be surprised if Lazarus had gone back into the tomb. Of the tapestry of existence *je ne sais pas*.

As I copulate with Edna, images of martyrdom tumble through my mind, a stricken figure on the cross, stigmata ripped like lightning through the exposed sky, and it is all that I can do under the circumstances to perform, but thy will be done, the will must transcend, and so I force myself into a smaller and smaller corner of her, squeezing out the images with little birdcalls and carrying her whimpers through me. She coils and uncoils like a springy steel object and at long last obtains sexual release; I do so myself by reflex and then fall from her grunting. It is quite mechanical, but in a highly technological culture sexual union could only be such; otherwise it would be quite threatening to the apparatus of the state, or so, at least, I have deduced. She lies beside me, her face closed to all feeling, her fingers clawed around my wrist. I groan deep in my throat and compose for sleep, but it is apparent then that there will be no sleep because suddenly she is moving against me and then sitting upright in the bed, staring. Hands clasped behind my head, elbows jutting at an angle of eighty-five degrees I regard her bleakly. "I can't talk now," I say. "Please, if you must say something, let it be later. There's nothing right now."

"You mean you have to face your treatments in the morning and you need your rest so that you can be alert for the drugs. That's all you think about now, those treatments. Where are you living? Here or there? Come on, tell me."

"I don't want to talk, I told you."

"You've changed," she said. "They've destroyed you. You aren't what you used to be."

There comes a time in every relationship when one has approached terminus, when the expenditure of pain is not worth the pleasure input, where one can feel the raw edges of difference collide through the dissolved flesh of care. Looking at Edna I see that we have reached that point, that there is not much left, and that it will be impossible for me to see her again. This will be the end. After she leaves this time there will be no recurrence. It is this, more than anything else, which enables me to turn from her with equanimity, to confront the bold and staring face of the wall. "Goodnight," I say. "We won't talk about this any more."

"You can't avoid this. You can run from me but not from what has happened. You're not living here any more; you're living in the spaces of your own consciousness. Don't you realize that? You've turned inside; you've shut it out! These aren't experiences that you're having; they're dreams, and all of this is taking place inside you. I hate to see it happen; you're better than this; together we could have helped one another, worked to understand what our lives were, maybe even made progress—"

Too late. I stand. "You'd better leave now, Edna."

Arms folded across her little breasts, she juts her chin at me. "That won't solve anything at all. Getting rid of me won't change it."

"The only truth is the truth we create—within ourselves."

"I don't believe that. That's what they tell us, that's how you got started on these treatments, but it isn't so. There's an objective truth and it's outside of this and you're going to have to face it sooner or later. You're just going to have to realize—"

I look at her with enormous dispassion and my expression must be a blade which falls heavily across her rhetoric, chopping it, silencing her. At length, and when I know that she is ready to receive the necessary question, I pose it as calmly and flatly as I have ever done and its resonance fills the room, my heart, her eyes until there is nothing else but her flight, and at last that peace which I have promised myself.

"Why?" I say.

At Bruck Linn they do not start the pogrom after all, but instead seize me roughly and hurl me into detention. It seems that it was only this in which they were interested; they entered in such massive numbers only to make sure that they could scour the area for me if I were not at my appointed place. In detention I am given spartan but pleasant quarters within what appears to be their headquarters, and a plate of condiments on which to nibble, as well as the five sacred books of the Pentateuch, which, since they know I am a religious man, they have obviously given for the purposes of recreation. I look through them idly, munching on a piece of cake, but as always find the dead and sterile phrases insufficient on their own to provoke reaction, and it is almost with relief that I see them come into the room, obviously to explain themselves and advise what will happen next. It is high time. There are two of them, both splendidly uniformed, but one is apparently in the role of secretary; unspeaking, he sits in a corner with a recording device. The other has a blunt face and surprisingly expressive eyes. I would not have thought that they were permitted large wet blue eyes like this.

"You are giving us much difficulty," he says directly, sitting. "Too much and so we have had to arrange this rather dramatic interview. Our pardon for the melodrama but it could not, you see, be spared; we needed to seize and detain as quickly as possible, and we could not take a chance on riots."

"Certainly," I say rather grandly. "I am a world figure. My abduction would not be easy."

"It is not only that."

"But that in itself would be enough."

"No matter," he says. He looks at me intently. "We're going to have to abort the treatments," he says. "You are becoming obsessive."

"What?"

"It has leached out into your personal life and you are beginning to combine treatments and objective reality in a dangerous fashion. Therefore under the contract we are exercising our option to cut them off."

"I have no understanding of this," I say. "Treatments? I am the Lubavitcher Rabbi of Bruck Linn and I have been torn from the heart of my congregation in broad daylight by fascists who will tell me this? This is unspeakable. You speak madness."

"I am afraid," he says, and those expressive eyes are linked to mine, "that you are displaying precisely those symptoms which have made this necessary. You are not the Lubavitcher Rabbi, let alone of Brooklyn. You are Harold Thwaite of the twenty-third century; the Lubavitchers are a defunct, forgotten sect, and you are imagining all of this. You have reconceived your life; the partitions have broken; and we are therefore, for your own good, ceasing the treatments and placing you in temporary detention."

"This is an outrage," I say. "This is impossible. Pogrom? Pogroms I can understand, I can deal with them. But this madness is beyond me."

The uniformed man leans toward me and with the gentlest of fingers strokes my cheek. "It will go easier if you cooperate, Harold," he says. "I know how difficult this must be for you, the shock—"

"My followers will not be easy to deal with. You will have to cut them down with rifle fire. I am sure that you can do this, but the cost in blood and bodies will be very high, and in the long run you will not win. You will find a terrible outcome. We are God's chosen; we and only the Lubavitchers carry forth his living presence in this century, and you cannot tamper with that presence lacking the most serious consequences—"

And I see to my amazement and to my dismay that the interrogator, the one who has come to intimidate and defile, this man in the hard and terrible uniform of the state, appears to be weeping.

* * *

I part the Red Sea with a flourish of the cane but the fools nonetheless refuse to cross. "What is wrong with them?" I say to Aaron. "It's perfectly safe." I move further into the abyss between the waves and turn, but the throng remains on the shore staring with bleak expressions. Only Aaron is beside me. "I'm afraid they don't trust the evidence of sight," he says, "and also they don't trust you either; they feel that this is merely a scheme to lead them astray and as soon as they step over, the waters will close upon them."

"That is ridiculous," I say to him. "Would I take them this far, do so much, walk with the guidance of the Lord to betray the Children of Israel?"

Aaron shrugs, a bucolic sort. "What can I tell you?" he says. "There's no accounting for interpretation."

At the first great hammer to the temple it comes to me that they were all the time as serious as I. More serious, in fact. I was willing to trust the outcome of my rebellion to a higher power, whereas they, solid businessmen to the end, decided to make sure that the matter rested in their own hands.

Nevertheless, it hurts. I never knew that there was so much pain in it until they put me down at the mosque and oh my oh my oh my oh my no passion is worth any of the real blood streaming.

"You see now," the counselor says to me, "that you are clearly in need of help. There is no shame in it; there is precedent for this; it has all happened before. We know exactly how to treat the condition, so if you will merely lie quietly and cooperate, we should have you on your way before long. The fact that you are back in focus now, for instance, is a very promising sign. Just a few hours ago we despaired of this, but you are responding nicely."

I rear up on my elbows. "Let me out of here," I say. "I demand to be let out of here. You have no right to detain me in this fashion; I have a mission to perform, and I assure you that you will suffer greatly for what you have done. This is serious business; it is not to be trifled with. Detention will not solve your problems; you are in grave difficulty."

"I urge you to be calm."

"I am perfectly calm." I note that I appear to be lashed to the table by several painless but well contrived restraints, which pass across my torso, digging in only when I flail. It is a painless but humiliating business and I subside, grumbling. "Very well," I said. "You will find what happens when you adopt such measures, and that judgment will sit upon you throughout eternity."

The counselor sighs. He murmurs something about many of them at the beginning not being reasonable, and I do not remind him that this is exactly as Joseph had warned.

Tormented by the anguish on the Magdalene's face, the tears which leak unbidden down her cheeks, he says, "It is all right. The past does not matter; all that matters is what happens in the timeless present, the eternal future." He lifts a hand, strokes her cheeks, feeling its intensity; it is of a different sort from the more generalized tenderness he has felt through his earlier travels. "Come," he said. "You can join me."

She puts her hand against his. "You don't understand," she says. "This is not what I want."

"What?"

"Talk of paradise, of your father, of salvation; I don't understand any of it. I don't know what you think they want."

"I know what they want."

"You don't know anything," she says. "You are a kind man but of these people you know nothing." She smooths her garments with a free hand. "To them you are merely a diversion, an entertaining element in their lives, someone who amuses them, whereas you think in passionate terms. You will be deeply hurt."

"Of course."

"No," she says, "not in the way you think. Martyrdom will not hurt you; that is, after all, what you seek. It will be something else." Something else, he thinks. *Something else, I think*.

She is an attractive woman not without elements of sympathy, but staring at her I remember that she was, until very recently, a prostitute who committed perhaps even darker acts, and that it is an insolent thing which she, of all people, is doing in granting her Saviour such rebuke. "Come," I say to her. I should note that we have been having this dialogue by a river bank, the muddy waters of the river arching over the concealed stones, the little subterranean animals of the river whisking their way somewhere toward the north, the stunted trees of this time holding clumps of birds which eye us mournfully. "It is time to get back to the town."

"Why?"

"Because if we remain out here talking like this much longer some will misconceive. They will not understand why we have been gone so long."

"You are a strange, strange man."

"I am not a man. I am—"

"I would not take all of this so seriously," she says, and reaches toward me, a seductive impact in the brush of her hand, seductive clatter in her breath, and oh my Father it is a strange feeling indeed to see what passes between us then, and with halt and stuttering breath I hurl myself upright, thrust her away, and run toward Galilee. Behind me, it cannot be the sound of her laughter which trails. It cannot, it cannot.

"Fools," I say, my fingers hurtling through the sacred, impenetrable text, looking for the proper citation. "Can't you understand that you are living at the end of time? The chronologies of the Book of Daniel clearly indicate that the seven beasts emerge from the seven gates in the year 2222, the numbers aligned; it is this generation which will see the gathering of the light." They stare at me with interest but without conviction. "You had better attend," I say. "You have little time, little enough time to repent, and it will go easier for you if you do at the outset."

One of the congregants raises his hand and steps toward me. "Rabbi," he says, "you are suffering from a terrible misapprehension—"

"So are you all," I say with finality, "but misapprehension can itself become a kind of knowledge."

"This is not Bruck Linn and the Book of Daniel has nothing to do with what is happening."

"Fool," I say, lunging against my restraining cords, "you may conceive of a pogrom, but that cannot alter the truth. All of your murders will not stop the progress of apocalypse for a single moment."

"There is no apocalypse, rabbi," the congregant says, "and you are not a rabbi."

I scream with rage, lunging against the restraints once again and they back away with terror on their solemn faces. I grip Pentateuch firmly and hurl it at them, the pages opening like a bird's wing in flight, but it misses, spatters against an opposing wall, falls in spatters of light. "I have my duties," I say, "my obligations. You had better let me go out and deliver the summons to the world; keeping me here will not keep back the truth. It cannot be masked, and I assure you that it will go better for you if you cooperate."

"You are sick, rabbi," he says very gently. "You are a sick man. Thankfully you are getting the treatment that you so desperately need and you will be better."

"The great snake," I point out, "the great snake which lies coiled in guard of the gates is slowly rising; he is shaking off the sleep of ten thousand years—"

"To throw a holy book—"

"No books are holy. At the end of time, awaiting the pitiless and terrible judgment even the sacred texts fall away. All that is left is judgment, mercy, the high winds rising—"

"If you will relax, rabbi—"

"I want to walk to and fro upon the earth and up and down upon it!" I scream. "From all of these wanderings I will come to a fuller knowledge, crouching then at the end of time with the old antagonist to cast lots over the vestments of the saved and the damned alike, bargaining for their garments out of a better world—"

"If you will only be quiet—"

"The snake is quiet too," I say, "quiet and waiting for the time of judgment, but let me tell you that the silence which you will demand is the silence of the void—"

And so on and so forth, *je ne sais pas*. It is wearying to recount all of those admonitions which continue to rave through the spaces of the room at this time. If there is one thing to say about a Talmudic authority in heat, it is that once launched upon a point he can hardly pause; pauses would form interstices where the golem itself might worm. And of the golem, of course, little more need be said.

"Will you yield?" Satan says to me, putting me into an untenable position upon the sands. His face looms near mine like a lover's; he might be about to implant the most sustained and ominous of kisses. "Yield and it will go easier with you."

"No," I say, "never. I will not yield." The French has fled, likewise the depersonalization. I feel at one with the persona, which is a very good sign, surely a sign that I am moving closer to the accomplishment of my great mission. "You may torture me; you may bring all of your strength to bear; it is possible that you will bend and break me, but you will never hear renunciation." I grab purchase with my ankles, manage to open up a little bit of space, which of course I do not share with my ancient antagonist, and then with a sly wrench drag him toward me, defy his sense of balance and send him tumbling beside. He gasps, the exhalation of breath full as dead flowers in my face, and it is possible for me now to hurl myself all the way over him, pressing him into the sands. Gasping, he attempts to fling me, but as I collapse on top of him my knee strikes his horned and shaven head, administering a stunning blow and from the opening I see leaching the delicate, discolored blood of Satan. His eyes flutter to attention and then astonishment as I close upon him and my strength is legion. "Do you see?" I say to him. "Do you see now what you have done? You cannot win against the force of light," and I prepare myself to deliver the blow of vanquishment. Open to all touch he lies beneath me; his mouth opens.

"Stop!" he says weakly, and to my surprise I do so. There is no hurry, after all; he is completely within my power. "That's better," he says. His respiration is florid. "Stop this nonsense at once. Help me arise."

"No," I say, "absolutely not."

"You don't understand, you fool. This dispute was supposed to be purely dialectical; there was no need to raise arms—"

Ah, the cunning of Satan! Defeated on his own terms he would shift to others, but I have been warned against this too, I have been fully prepared for all the flounderings of the ancient enemy; there is nothing that he can do now to dissuade me, and so I laugh at him, secure in my own power and say, "Dialectical! No, it was a struggle unto the death; those were clearly the terms and you know that as well as I."

"No," he says, twitching his head. "No, absolutely not, you never saw this right. There was never the matter of murder; don't you realize that? We aren't antagonists at all! We are two aspects of the overwhelming one; our search was for fusion in these spaces, and that is what we are now prepared to do." His head sinks down; he is clearly exhausted. Still he continues muttering. "You fool," he says. "There is no way that one of us can vanquish the other. To kill either is to kill the self."

Sophistry! Sophistry! I am so sick of it; I intimate a life, a dark passageway through to the end lit only by the flickering and evil little candles of half-knowledge and witticism, casting ugly pictures on the stones, and the image enrages me; I cannot bear the thought of a life which will contain little more than small alterations of language or perception to make it bearable, reconsideration of a constant rather than changing the unbearable constant itself, but this is to what I have been condemned. Not only Satan, but I will have to live by rhetoric; there will be nothing else.

But at least, this first time on the desert, rhetoric will not have to prevail. Perhaps for the only time in my life I will have the opportunity to undertake the one purposive act, an act of circumstance rather than intellection.

And so, without wishing to withhold that moment any longer, I wheel fiercely upon Satan. "I've had enough of this shit," I say. "I've got to deal with it; I cannot go on like this forever; there has to be a time for confrontation." The words seem a bit confused, but my action is not; I plunge a foot into his face. It yields in a splatter of bone, and in that sudden rearrangement I look upon his truest form.

"Well," says Satan through flopping jaw. "Well, well." He puts a claw to a slipped cheekbone, "Well, I'll be damned."

"Oh, yes," I say, "but you don't have to take all of us with you."

His eyes, surprisingly mild, radiate, of all things, compassion. "You don't understand," he says. He falls to his knees like a great, stricken bird. "You don't understand anything at all."

"I do enough."

"I'm not here by choice," Satan murmurs. "I'm here because you *want* me. Do you think that this is easy? Being thrown out of Heaven and walking up and down the spaces of the earth, and to and fro upon it, and the plagues and the cattle and the boils? I've just been so *busy*, but it was you who brought me into being, or again—" Satan says, drawing up his knees to a less anguished posture, fluttering on the desert floor, "—is this merely rationalization? I am very good at sophistry, you know, but this isn't easy; there's a great deal of genuine *pain* in it. I have feelings too."

I stand, considering him. What he is saying is very complex and doubtless I should attend to it more closely (I sense that it would save me the most atrocious difficulty later on if only I would) but there is a low sense of accomplishment in having dealt with this assignment so effectively, and I do not want to lose it so easily. It may be one of the least equivocal moments in a life riven, as we all know, with conflicts. "I'm dying," Satan says. "Won't you at least reach out a hand to comfort me?"

The appeal is grotesque and yet I am moved. He is, after all, a creature of circumstance no less than any of us. I kneel beside him, trying not to show my revulsion at the smell of leaking mortality from him. Satan extends a hand. "Hold me," he says. "Hold me; you owe me at least that. You called me into being; you have to take responsibility for my vanquishment. Or are you denying complicity?

"No," I say, "I can hardly do that." I extend my hand. His claw, my fingers interlock.

"You see," Satan says gratefully, "you *know* at least that you're implicated. There may be some hope in that for all of us and now if you will permit me, I believe that I am going to die."

Grey and greenish blood spills from his mouth, his nasal passages, eyes and ears. It vaults into the desert and as I stare fascinated, he dies with quick muffled sighs not unlike the sounds of love. It is an enormous and dignified accomplishment not noted in all the Scripture, and I am held by the spectacle for more than a few moments.

But as his claw slips away, as touch is abandoned, I have a vision and in that vision I see what I should have known before going through all of this. I see what might have saved me all of this passage, which is to say that knowing he is dead there is a consequent wrench in my own corpus indicating an echoing, smaller death, and as I realize that he has told me the truth, that the divestment of Satan has resulted only in my own reduction, I stand in the desert stunned, knowing that none of this—and I am here to testify, gentlemen, I am here to testify!—is going to be as simple as I thought.

"Even the minor prophets have problems," I point out in the mosque. "The fact that I am not famous and that many of my judgments are vague does not mean that they are not deeply felt or that I will not suffer the fate of Isaiah. Jeremiah, Zephaniah, had their problems. Ezekiel had a limp and was tormented by self-hatred. Hosea had blood visions too."

They look at me bleakly, those fifteen. This is what my flock has dwindled into, and I should be grateful to have them, what with all of the efforts to discredit and those many threats of violence made toward those who would yet remain with me. They are quite stupid, the intelligent ones long since having responded to the pressure, but they are all I have, and I am grateful, I suppose, to have them. "Attend," I say. "The institutions cannot remain in this condition. Their oppression is already the source of its own decay; they panic, they can no longer control the uprising. The inheritors of these institutions are stupid; they do not know why they work or how, but just mechanically reiterate the processes for their own fulfillment, massacre to protect themselves, oppress because oppression is all they know of the machinery. But their time is limited; the wind is rising and the revolution will be heard," and so on and so forth, the usual rhetorical turns and flourishes done so skilfully that they occupy only the most fleeting part of my attention. Actually I am looking at the door. It is the door which I consider; from the left enter three men in the dress of the sect, but I have never seen them before and by some furtive, heightened expressions of their eyes I know that they have not come here on a merciful business.

They consult with one another against the wall and it is all that I can do to continue speaking. I must not show a lapse of rhetoric, I must not let them know that I suspect them, because all that I hold is the prospect of my inattention, but as my customary prose rolls and thunders I am already considering the way out of here. My alternatives are very limited. The windows are barred, the walls are blank behind me, the only exits are at the edge of the hall and what has happened to the guards? Did they not screen this group? Are they not supposed to protect me, or are they all part of the plot? "Be strong, be brave," I am telling my followers, but I do not feel strong or brave myself; I feel instead utterly perplexed and filled with a fear which is very close to self-loathing. Their conference concluded, the men scatter, one going for a seat in the center, the other two parting and sliding against the walls. They fumble inside their clothing; I am sure they have firearms.

I am sure that the assassins, on my trail for so very long, have at last stalked me to this point; but I am in a very unique and difficult position because, if I show any fear whatsoever, if I react to their presence, they will doubtless slay me in the mosque, causing the most unusual consternation to my followers assembled; but on the other hand, if I proceed through the speech and toward an orderly dismissal, all that will happen is that I will make the slaying more convenient and allow for less witnesses, to say nothing of giving them an easier escape. Anything I do, in short, is calculated to work against me, and yet I am a man who has always believed in dignity, the dignity of position, that is to say, taking a stand, following it through whatever the implications; and so I continue, my rhetoric perhaps a shade florid now, my sentences not as routinely parsed as I would wish but it is no go, no go at all; they have a different method, I see, as the seated one arises and moves briskly toward me. "This is not right," I say as he comes up to me, takes me by an elbow. "You could at least have let me finish; if I was willing to take this through, then you could have gone along with me." The congregants murmur.

"You'd better come with me, Harold," he says. "You need help."

"Take your hands off me."

"I'm afraid I'd best not do that," he says gently, gesturing toward the two in the back who begin to come toward me solemnly. "You see, what we have to do is to jolt you out of these little fugues, these essays in martyrdom, and it would be best if you cooperated; the more you cooperate, the quicker you see that it becomes evident that you are accepting reality, and therefore the more quickly you will be back to yourself. Come," he says, giving me a hearty little tug, "let's just bounce out of here now," and the others flank me fore and aft and quite forcefully I am propelled from the rostrum. To my surprise my congregants do not express dismay, nor are there scenes of riot or dislocation as I might have expected; on the contrary they look at me with bleak, passive interest, as I am shoved toward the door. It is almost, I think, as if they had expected me to come exactly to this state and they are glad that I am being taken off in this fashion.

"Can't you see," I say gesticulating to them, "can't you see what is happening here? They don't want you to know the truth, they don't want you to accept the truth of your lives; that's why they're taking me away from here, because I was helping you to face the truth."

"Come on, Harold," they murmur taking me away. "All of this has its place, but after a while it's just best to cooperate; just go along," and now they have me through the doors, not a single one of my congregants making the slightest attempt to fracture their progress. I shake a fist at them.

"For God's sake," I say, "don't any of you care, don't you know what's going on here?" and so on and so forth, the sounds of my rhetoric filling my ears, if hardly all the world, and outside I am plunged repeatedly into the brackish waters of Galilee, which to no one's surprise at all (or at least not to mine) hardly lend absolution.

"You'd better destroy them," I say in a conversational tone, settling myself more comfortably underneath the gourd. "They're a rotten bunch of people as you will note. Not a one of them has but a thought of their own pleasure, to say nothing of the sexual perversity."

"I may not," he says reasonably. He is always reasonable, which is a good thing if one is engaged in highly internalized dialogues. What would I do if he were to lose patience and scream? I could hardly deal with it. "After all, it's pretty drastic, and besides that, without life there is no possibility of repentance."

"Don't start that again," I say. "You sent me all of these miles, through heat and water, fire and pain to warn them of doom, and you would put both of us in a pretty ridiculous position, wouldn't you, if you didn't follow through? They'd never take me seriously again."

"You let *me* decide that, Jonah," he says, and there is no arguing with him when he gets into one of these moods, no possibility of argument whatsoever when he becomes stubborn, and so I say, "We'll see about this in the morning," much as if I were controlling the situation rather than he, which is not quite true of course, and slip into a thick doze populated with the images of sea and flying fish, but at the bottom of the sleep is pain, and when I bolt from it it is with terrible pain through the base of being, my head in anguish, my head as if it were carved open, and looking upward I see that the gourd which he had so kindly spread for me has shrivelled overnight, and I am now being assaulted by a monotonous eastern sun. "Art thou very angry?" he says companionably, lapsing into archaicism as is his wont.

"Of course I am very angry," I say, "You have allowed my gourd to die. And besides I want to know when you're going to get rid of these people. Looking down from this elevation I can see very distinctly that the city is still standing."

"Ah," he says as I scratch at my head, trying to clobber the sun away, "thou takest pity upon the gourd which was born in a night and died in a night; why should I not take pity upon forty thousand people who cannot discern their right hand from their left to say nothing of much cattle?"

"Sophistry," I say, "merely sophistry."

"Unfortunately," he says, "there is no room for your reply," and smites me wildly upon the head, causing me to stumble into the ground, Gomorrah still upright, and I am afflicted (and not for the first time I might add) with a perception of the absolute perversity of this creature who dwelleth within me. At all times.

The thieves have died, but I am still alive to the pain of the sun when I feel the nails slide free and I plunge a hundred feet into the arms of the soldiers. They cushion my fall, lave my body with strong liquids, murmur to me until slowly I come over the sill of consciousness to stare at them. Leaning over me is a face which looks familiar. "Forgive them," I say weakly, "forgive them, they know not what they do."

"They know what they do."

"*Jamais*," I say and to clarify, "never."

"You have not been crucified," he says. "You'd better accept that."

"Then this must be hell," I say, "and I still in it."

He slaps me across the face, a dull blow with much resonance. "You're just not being reasonable," he says. "You are not a reasonable man."

"Help me up there, then," I say. "It is not sufficient. Help me up there and crucify me again."

"Harold—"

"*Jesu*," I say admonishingly and close my eyes waiting for ascent and the perfect striations of the nails through the wrist: vaulting, stigmata.

The face looking at me is Edna's, but this is strange because Edna will not be born for several centuries yet, and what is even stranger than that is the fact that despite this I recognize her. How can this be? Nevertheless, one must learn to cope with dislocations of this sort if one is to be a satisfactory martyr. "They asked me to come here and speak to you," she says. "I don't know why I'm here. I don't think it will be of any use whatsoever. But I will talk to you. You have got to stop this nonsense now, do you hear me?"

"You could help by getting me out of here," I say, plucking at my clothing. "My appearance is disgusting and it is hardly possible for me to do the work when I am confined to a place like this. Or at least you could have them hurry and order up the crucifixion. Get it over with. There's no reason to go on this way; it's absolutely futile."

"That's what they want me to talk to you about. They seem to think that this is something that can be reasoned with. I keep on telling them that this is ridiculous; you're too far gone but they say to try so I will. They're as stupid as you. All of you are stupid; you've let the process take over and you don't even understand it. Face reality, Harold, and get out of this or it is going to go very badly—"

"*Jesu*," I remind her.

"Do you see?" she says to someone in the distance.

"It's absolutely hopeless. Nothing can come of this. I told you that it was a waste."

"Try," the voice says. "You have to try."

She leans toward me. Her face is sharp, her eyes glow fluorescent in the intensity. "Listen, Harold," she says. "You are not *Jesu* or anyone else—any of your religious figures. This is 2219 and you have been undergoing an administered hypnotic procedure enabling you to live through certain of your religious obsessions, but as is very rarely the case with others you have failed to come back all of the way at one point, and now they say you're in blocked transition or something. They're quite able to help you and to reverse the chemotherapeutic process, but in order to begin you have to accept these facts, that we are telling you the truth, that they are trying to help you. That isn't too much, is it? I mean, that isn't too much of an admission for you to make; and in return look at the wonderful life you'll have. Everything will be just as it was before, and you can remember how you loved it that way."

"Let me out of here," I say. "Where are my robes? Where are my disciples? Where are the sacred scrolls and the voice of the Lord? You cannot take all of this away; you will be dealt with very harshly."

"There are no sacred scrolls or followers. All of those people died a long time ago. This is your last chance, Harold; you'd better take it. Who knows what the alternative might be? Who knows what these people might be capable of doing?"

"Magdalene," I say reasonably, "simply because you're a whore does not mean that you always speak the truth. That is a sentimental fallacy."

Her face congests and she spits. I leave it rest there. A celebration. Stigmata.

Conveyed rapidly toward Calvary I get a quick glimpse of the sun appearing in strobes of light as they drive me with heavy kicks toward the goal. The yoke is easy at this time and burdens light; it is a speedy journey that I have made from the court to this place and it will be an easier one yet that I will make to Heaven. A few strokes of the hammer, some pain at the outset: blood, unconsciousness, ascension. Nothing will be easier than this, I think; the getting to this condition has far outweighed in difficulty this final stage. Struggling with the sacred texts has been boring, the miracles sheer propaganda; now at least I will find some consummative task worthy of my talents.

"Faster," they shout, "faster!" and I trot to their urging. *Vite, vite, vite* to that great mountain where I will show them at last that passion has as legitimate a place in this world as any of their policies and procedures and will last; I will convince them as I have already convinced myself a hell of a lot longer. *Brava passione*! *Brava*!

So they yank me from the restraints and toss me into the center of the huge room to meet the actors. There they all are, there they are: congregants, disciples, Romans, pagans, troopers, all of the paraphernalia and armament of my mission. Edna and the Magdalene are somewhere, but concealed; I have to take their presence on faith. I have had to take everything on faith, and at the end it destroys me; this is my lesson.

"Enough of this!" they cry. Or at least one of them says this; it is very difficult to be sure. The shout must come from an individual but then again it would appear to be a collective shout; they all feel this way. "This is your last chance, your very last chance to cooperate before it becomes very difficult."

"I don't know—"

"*Ne rien*," they cry. A great clout strikes, knocking me to the floor. It hurts like hell. *Attende bien*, I could have expected nothing less; I have waited for it so very long. Still, one tries to go on. I scramble for purchase, hurl myself upright. My capacity to absorb pain, oh happy surprise, seems limitless after all.

"Listen!" they say, not without a certain sympathy. "Listen, this is very serious business; it cannot go on; the matter of the treatments themselves is at stake. The treatment process is complex and expensive and there are complications, great difficulties—"

I confront them reasonably. I am a reasonable man. I always have been. "I will see you with my Father in Heaven," I say. "That is where I will see you and not a bloody moment sooner."

"Don't you understand? Don't you realize what you are doing? The penalties can be enormous. This must stay controlled; otherwise—"

"Otherwise," I say. "Otherwise you will lose your world and it is well worth losing. I have considered this. I have given it a great deal of thought. Martyrdom is not a posture, not at all; martyrdom springs from the heart. I am absolutely serious; it did not begin that way but that is the way it has ended. I will not yield. I will not apologize. I will not be moved. Thy will be done, *pater noster*, and besides, once you get going you can't just turn it off, if you have any respect, if you have any respect at all."

There is a sound like that of engines. They close upon me. I know exactly what they have in mind but am nonetheless relieved.

It would have had to be this way. "I will not yield," I say to them quietly. "I will not apologize. I will not be moved. This isn't folklore, you know; this is real pain and history."

They tear me apart.

I think of Satan now and am glad that we were able to have that little conversation in the desert the second time, to really get to know one another and to establish a relationship. He was quite right, of course, the old best-loved angel, and I wish I'd had the grace to acknowledge it at the time. We wanted him; we called him into it. It was better to have him outside than in that split and riven part of the self. Oh how I would like to embrace him now.

They leave me on the Cross for forty days and forty nights. On the forty-first the jackals from the south finally gnaw the wood to ash and it collapses. I am carried off, what is left of me, in their jaws and on to further adventures I cannot mention in bowels and partitions of the Earth.

SCORCHED SUPPER ON NEW NIGER

Suzy McKee Charnas

Bob W. Netchkay wanted my ship and I was damned if I was going to let him have it.

It was the last of the Steinway space fleet that my sister Nita and I had inherited from our aunt Juno. Aunt Juno had been a great tough lady of the old days and one hell of an administrator, far better alone than us two Steinway sisters together. I was young when she died, but smart enough to know that I was a hell of a pilot; so I hired an administrator to run the line for Nita and me.

Bob Netchkay administrated himself a large chunk of our income, made a bunch of deliberately bad deals, and secretly bought up all my outstanding notes after a disastrous trading season. I threw him out, but he walked away with six of my ships. I lost nine more on my own. Then my sister Nita married the bastard and took away with her all the remaining ships but one, my ship, the *Sealyham Eggbeater*.

And I'd mortgaged that to raise money for a high risk, high profit cargo in hopes of making a killing. But there were delays on Droslo, repairs to be made at Coyote Station, and the upshot was that Bob had gotten his hands on my mortgage. Now he was exercising his rights under it to call it early, while I was still racing for the one nearby dealer not trade-treatied to my competitors. His message was waiting for me when I woke that morning someplace between Rico and the Touchgate system.

Ripotee had checked in the message for me. He sat on the console chewing imaginary burrs out from between his paw pads. No comment from him. He was probably in one of those moods in which he seemed to feel that the best way to preserve his catlike air of mystery was keeping his mouth shut and acting felinely aloof.

I read my message, smacked the console, and bounced around the cabin yelling and hugging my hand. Then I said, "This is short range, from 'The Steinway Legal Department,' which means that creep Rily in Cabin D of our flagship—I mean the Netchkay pirate ship. They're close enough to intercept me before I can reach my buyer on Touchgate Center. Bob will get my ship and my cargo and find a way to keep both."

Ripotee yawned delicately, curling his pink tongue.

I wiped the console and cut every signal, in or out, that might help Bob to home in on me again. Then I set an automatic jig course to complicate his life. Fast evasive tactics would cost me heavily in fuel but still leave me enough to get to Red Joy Power Station, an outpost on Touchgate Six that was closer to me than my original buyer. Red Joy is an arm of Eastern Glory, the China combine that is one of the great long-hauling companies. I could make Red Joy before Bob caught me, dump my cargo with the Chinese for the best price they would give me, and nip out again.

The Chinese run an admirable line, knowing how to live well on little in these times of depression. They're arrogant in a falsely humble way, lack daring and imagination as Aunt Juno taught me to define those terms, and think very little of anything not Chinese. But they are honest and I could count on them to give me fair value for my cargo.

On the other hand, though the Steinway ships are shorthaulers, they are the only short haulers that can travel among star systems without having to hitch costly rides with long haulers like the Chinese. We are in competition, of a sort. The Chinese don't like competition on principle; so they don't much like Steinways.

Ripotee was observing the course readouts glowing on the wall. "Red Joy." he remarked, "used to be the trademark of underwear marketed in China in the days of Great Mao."

"At worst they would impound my ship," I said, "but they'd still pay me for what's in it."

Ripotee coughed. "About our cargo," he said. His tail thumped the top of the console. "I was mouse hunting this morning in the hold." I kept mice on the *Eggbeater* to eat up my crumbs and to keep Ripotee fit and amused. "All that pod is souring into oatmeal."

I sat there and spattered my instruments with tears.

Pod is one of the few really valuable alien trade items to have been found in the known universe. It integrates with any living system it's properly introduced to and realigns that system into a new balance that almost always turns out to be beneficial. People are willing to pay a lot for a pod treatment. But if pod gets contaminated with organic matter it integrates on its own and turns into "oatmeal," a sort of self-digested sludge which quickly becomes inert and very smelly and hard to clean up.

I hadn't had the time or the money to compartmentalize the hold of the *Eggbeater*. If some of the pod was soured, it was all soured.

"New Niger," Ripotee murmured. His eyes were sleepy blue slits, contemplating the wall charts. "We could reach New Niger faster than Netchkay could. They would buy the *Eggbeater* and fight Bob afterward to keep it."

I sat paralyzed with indecision. The New Nigerians certainly would buy the *Sealyham Eggbeater*, given the chance.

It was to keep my ship out of such hands as theirs that Bob was so anxious to take it over. All the other Steinways are later models, set to blow themselves up if strangers go poking around in their guts. This protects the Steinway secret: what Aunt Juno did to fit her short haul ships for travel between systems without hitching rides at the extortioners' rates that long haulers charge. An engineer could dig into my ship, though, and come out unscathed to report that Aunt Juno had simply modified the straight-and-tally system in a particular manner with half a dozen counter-clock Holbein pins, without disturbing the linkup with the stabilizers and the degreasing works. Everybody knows the general principles, but nobody outside of us Steinways knows the exact arrangement.

The Chinese, long haulers exclusively, wouldn't be interested. They would only take my ship to tuck it away out of commission so its secret couldn't be used by anybody else to cut down their income from giving hitches.

But the Africans of New Niger ran short haul ships and were long time competitors of the Steinway Line on the in-system short haul routes. They could use Aunt Juno's secret, if they had it, to bounce from system to system cheap, as we did, and wipe out our advantage.

Ripotee said, "Or you could just give up and let Netchkay have the ship. A lot of people would say you should. He's a good administrator." I took a swipe at him, but he eluded me with a graceful leap onto the food synthesizer, which burped happily and offered me a cup of steaming ersatz. "He's a North American," Ripotee continued, "a go-getter, who's trying to rebuild North American prestige—"

"To build himself, you mean, on my ships and my sister's treachery!"

"The Captain's always right," Ripotee said, "in her own ship."

I drank the ersatz and glared at the wall, ignoring for the moment the instruments blinking disaster warnings at me: Bob's ship was following my jig course already. If I was starting to pick him up, he would be picking me up too, first in signals and then in reality.

Among the instruments that gave the walls their baroque look of overdone detail I had stuck a snapshot of a New Nigerian captain I had encountered once, closely. What were the chances that somebody down there would know where Barnabas was these days? It would make a difference to know that I had one friend on New Niger.

My console jumped on, and there was a splintery image of Bob Netchkay's swarthy, handsome face. He looked grave and concerned, which made me fairly pant with hatred.

"You got my offer, Dee," he said in a honey voice.

If I turned off again he would think I was too upset to deal with him. I looked him in the eye and did not smile.

"Did you?" he pressed. He faced me full on, obscuring the predatory thrust of his beaky features.

"I know all about this final stage of your grab project, yes," I said.

He shook his head. "No, Dee, you don't understand. I'm thinking about the family now." He had changed his name to Steinway on marrying Nita, which was good for business but bad for my blood pressure. "I've talked this over with Nita and she agrees; the only way to handle it right is together, as a family."

I said, "I have no family."

Nita came and looked over his shoulder at me, her round, tanned face reproachful. I almost gagged: Nita, charter member of the New Lambchop League, sweet and slinky and one pace behind "her" man, pretending she knew nothing about business. She had dumped me as a partner for this ambitious buccaneer because he would play along with her frills and her protect-me-I'm-weak line. I think Aunt Juno had hoped to lead her in another direction by leaving half of the Steinway fleet to her. But Nita was part of the new swing back to "romance," a little lost lambchop, not an admiral of the spaceways.

"We're still sisters, Dee." She blinked her black eyes at me under her naked brows. She had undergone face stiffening years ago to create the supposedly alluring effect of enormous, liquid orbs in a mysterious mask.

"You may be somebody's sister," I snapped. "I'm not."

She whispered something to Bob.

He nodded. "I know. You see how bad things have gotten, Dee, when you get into a worse temper than ever at the sight of your own sister. Sometimes I think it's a chemical imbalance, that temper of yours, it's not natural. Nita has to go, she's got things to do. I just wanted you to know that anything I suggest has already been run past her, and she's in complete agreement. Isn't that right, Nita?"

Nita nodded, fluttered her tapered fingers in my direction, and whisked her svelte, body-suited figure out of the picture. Where she had been I saw something I recognized behind Bob's shoulder: one of those stretched guts from the Wailies of Tchan that's supposed to show images of the future if you expose it to anti-gravity. It had never shown Aunt Juno these two connivers running her flagship.

"Well?" I said. I sipped the cold dregs of my ersatz.

Bob lowered sincerely at me. "Look, Dee, I'm older than you and a lot more experienced at a lot of things, like running a successful trade business. And I'm very concerned about the future of the Steinway name. You and I have been at odds for a long time, but you don't really think I've gone to all this trouble just to junk the line, do you? I did what I had to do, that's all."

He stopped and glared past me; I turned. Ripotee had a hind foot stuck up in the air and was licking his crotch. He paused to say loudly, "I'm doing what I have to do too."

"Get that filth off the console!" Bob yelled. I chortled. He got control of himself and plowed on: "Already I've restored your family's reputation; Steinway is once again a name held in commercial respect. And I can do more.

"You don't realize; things are going to get rougher than you can imagine, and it won't be any game for a free-lance woman with nobody to back her up. Look around you: times are changing, it's a tougher and tougher short haul market, and women are pulling back into softer, older ways. What will you be out there, one of a handful of female freaks left over from the days of Juno and her type? Freaks don't get work, not when there are good, sound men around to take it away from them. You'll be a pauper.

"I don't want that. Nita doesn't want it. You don't want it. Give up and face facts."

He paused, the picture of a man carried away by his own eloquence. And a pleasure to look at too, if I hadn't been burning up with loathing for his very tripes. Even without the frame of curling black hair and high collar, the subtly padded shoulders and chest—the New Lambchops weren't the only ones looking back in time to more romantic eras—Bob was handsome, and very masculine looking in a hard, sharp-cut way.

He knew it and used it, posing there all earnest drama, to give me a minute to react, to cue him as to how all this was setting with me. I said, deadpan, "What's the deal?"

He looked pained. "Not a deal; a way for us all to come out all right. You give me the *Sealyham Eggbeater*, pull out of the business, take a holiday someplace, grow out your hair. In exchange for your ship I'll give you a one-third inalienable interest in the Steinway stock and a nice desk job for income. But I get to run things my own way without interference. You keep your mouth shut and let me do what I know how to do, and I take care of you and your sister."

I was so mad I could hardly work my jaw loose enough to utter a sound. "But I don't get to do what *I* know how to do which is to pilot a short haul ship. My answer is no."

I wiped the console and punched a new jig. Then I plugged in a tingle of electracalm and a light dose of antistress because I needed my head clear.

Ripotee lay stretched out along the sill of a viewport, curved within its curve, one paw hanging down. He liked to keep his distance when I was upset. His sapphire eyes rested on me, intent, unreadable. He had either found that he could not or decided that he would not learn to use his facial muscles for expressiveness on the human model. I couldn't interpret that masked, blunt-muzzled visage.

I said, "Ripotee, what do you know about New Niger?"

His tail started swinging, lashing. That was something he had never been able to control. He was excited, onto something.

"Jungle," he said. "Tall trees and vines and close underbrush. Good smells, earth and voidings and growth. Not like here."

"You've got cabin fever," I snorted. I was already setting up a fast but indirect course for Singlet, New Niger's main port. "Aren't your mice entertaining you enough any more?"

I reached out to pat his head, but he jerked away. He didn't say, Don't do that, though he could have. Sometimes he was pleased to show me the superfluity of that human invention, speech. We had been in space a longish while. Ripotee got just as irritable as anyone else—as me.

The autodrives took over at full speed on a wild zig-zag course. Strapping in tight, I signalled Ripotee, over the shout of the engines, to get into his harness. I tried to cut the graveys, but the switch stuck: it was going to be a rough ride. I felt reckless. Bob was close; if he tried to grab the *Eggbeater* now, he'd run a good chance of collision and of getting himself killed, if not all of us.

There was a lot of buffeting and slinging as the ship shunted from course to course. I kept my eyes on Ripotee, not wanting to see evidence of impossible strain, of damage, of imminent ruin on the dials that encrusted the walls. He lay flat in his nest of straps secured to a padded niche over the internal monitor banks, his claws bradded into the fibres. He was Siamese, fawn beneath and seal-brown on top, a slight shading of stripes on his upper legs, cheeks, and forehead. He had street blood in him, none of your overbred mincing and neurosis there. I hoped he wasn't about to come to a crashing end on account of my feud with Netchkay.

I am a natural pilot but not what they call a sheepherder, the kind who thrives on being alone in space. A good short haul ship can be managed by one operator and can carry more cargo that way, and I don't like crowding. So I had acquired Ripotee instead of a human partner.

He had been a gift as a kitten, along with a treatment contract on him for a place out in the Tic Tacs where they use pod infections to mutate animals upward—if humanizing their brains is actually a step in that direction. He came out of his pod fever with a good English vocabulary and a talent for being aggravating in pursuit of his own independence.

Even at his worst he was the companion I needed, a reminder of something besides the bright sterility of space and its stars. There wasn't anything else. We had yet to find alien life of true intelligence. Meanwhile, the few Earth animals that had survived the Oil Age were all the more important to us—to those of us who cared about such things, anyway.

The ship dropped hard, slewing around to a new heading. Straps bit my skin. I thought of the time when, after a brush with some name-proud settlers on Le Cloue, I had asked Ripotee, "Do you want to change your name? Maybe you don't like being called 'Ripotee?'" I was thinking that it was hard for him to pronounce it, as he had some trouble with t's.

He had said, "I don't care, I don't have to say it. I can say 'I,' just like a person. Anyway, Ripotee isn't my name; it's just your name for me."

Only later I wondered whether this proud statement covered not some private name he had for himself but the fact that he had no name except the one I had given him.

I could hardly draw breath to think with now, and I was very glad to have had no breakfast but that cup of ersatz.

Another hard swing, and I smelled rotting pod; a cargo seal must have broken and who knew what else. Ripotee let out a sudden wail—not pain, I hoped, just fear. I kept my eyes closed now. If he'd been shaken loose from his harness he could be slammed to death on the walls, just as I would be if I tried to go and help him.

One thing about Ripotee that neither of us nor his producers in the Tic Tacs knew was how long he had to live. He was approaching his first watermark, the eighth year, which if successfully passed normally qualifies a domestic cat for another seven or eight. In his case, we had no idea whether the pod infection had fitted him with a human life span to go with his amplified mind, or, given that, whether his physical small-animal frame would hold up to such extended usage. One thing was sure, enough of this battering around and he would end up just as punchy as any human pilot would.

I blacked out twice. Then everything smoothed down, and my power automatically cut as the landing beams locked on. A voice sang a peculiarly enriched English into my ears over the headset: looping vowels, a sonorous timbre—reminding me of Barnabas' voice. "Singlet Port. So now you will be boarded by a customs party. Please prepare to receive . . ."

Prepare to give up—but never to Bob.

Ripotee was first out on New Niger. I sprung the forward hatch and a group of people came in; he padded right past them, tail in the air, none of your hanging about sniffing to decide whether or not it was worth his time to go through the doorway. Normally he's as cautious as any cat, but he is also given to wild fits of berserker courage that are part existential meanness and part tomcat.

He paused in his progress only to lay a delicate line of red down the back of a reaching hand—just an eyeblink swipe of one paw, an exclamation from the victim, and Ripotee was off, belly stretched in an ecstatic arc of all-out effort above the landing pad. Well out of reach, he paused with his tail quirked up in its play mode, glanced back, and then bounded sideways out of sight behind a heap of cartons and drums.

I had to pay a quarantine fine on him, of course. They were very annoyed to have lost any organisms he might have brought in with him that could be useful in pod experiments. The fine was partly offset by some prime wrigglies they got out of me, leftovers from a visit to the swamps of Putt.

There were forms to fill out and a lot of "dash" to pay for hints on how to fill them out with the least chance of expensive mistakes. I stood in the security office, my head still fuzzy from the rough flight, and I wrote.

A young man with a long thin face like a deer's came and plucked me by the sleeve. He said in soft, accented English, "You are asked for, Missisi. Come with me please."

"Who?" I said, thinking damn it, Bob has landed, he's onto me already. I stalled. "I have these forms to finish—"

He looked at the official who had given me these books of papers and said, "Missisi Helen will see to it that everything is put right."

The official reached over, smiling, and eased the papers out from under my hand. "I did not know that Captain Steinway was a friend of Missisi Helen. Do not worry of your ship; it goes into our clean-out system because of the oatmeal."

My guide led me through corridors and once across a landing surface brilliant with sun. I wondered if this Missisi Helen was the famous Helen who had been trading from New Niger as far back as Aunt Juno's own times: a tough competitor.

We went to a hangar where a short hauler stood surrounded by half-unpacked bales and boxes and spilled fruit. For a barnyard flavor, chickens (the African lines would carry anything) ran among the feet of the passengers, who shouted and pawed through everything, looking, I supposed, for their own belongings mixed in with the scattered cargo. The mob, rumpled and steamy with their own noise and excitement, was all Black except for one skinny, shiny-bald White man in the stained white sari of a Holy Wholist missionary. He stood serenely above it all.

I picked my way along after my guide, trying not to wrinkle my nose; after all, I'd had no more opportunity for a thorough bath and fresh change of clothing than these folks had. To tell the truth, I felt nervous in that crush and scramble of people; there were so many, and I had lived without other humans for a long time.

A knot of argument suddenly burst, and a little woman in a long rose-colored dress stepped out to meet me, snapping angrily over her shoulder at a man who reached pleadingly to restrain her: "And I tell you, it is for you some of my cargo was dumped cheap at Lagos Port to make room for this, your cousin. I am surprised you did not want my very ancestor's bones thrown away so you could bring your whole family! You will pay back for my lost profits, or I will make you very sorry! Speak there to my secretary."

She faced me, one heavily braceleted arm cocked hand-on-hip, her bare, stubby feet planted wide. Her hair, a tight, springy pile of gray, was cut and shaped into an exaggerated part, like two steep hills on her head. She tipped her head back and looked down her curved, broad, delicate nose at me.

"Dee Steinway. You do not look at all like your aunt Juno."

"I favor my father's side."

"As well," she said. "Juno ran to fat in her later years. I knew her well; I am Helen Nwanyeruwa, head of Heaven Never Fail Short Hauling Limited. Why are you here, and why did Bob Netchkay land right behind you, waving pieces of paper under the noses of customs?"

Well, that was straight out, and it shook me up a little bit. Most trading people talk around things to see what all the orbits are before they set a plain course. I looked nervously at the intent faces surrounding us. I said, "He wants to take my ship."

She grimaced. "With papers; that means with laws."

"I'd rather sell the ship to you before he can slap those papers on me," I said.

"What ship?"

"Not just any ship. The Steinway *Eggbeater*."

Her eyes were very bright. "Then it is good I have set some friends of mine here to wrapping Bob Netchkay in many, many yards of bright red tape. If you knew how often I tried to get Juno to trade me a ship of hers—" She looked me up and down, scowling now. "I don't want to have to discuss this over Netchkay's papers; so, we must hide you. Hey!" She spoke rapidly in her own language to one of her attendants, who hurried away.

Helen watched the attendant engage in an animated conversation with the Holy Wholist. "See that missionary," she commented, "how he waves his arms, he is all rattled about, he outrages as if back in his own place now, not a foreign planet. I tell you, some of these White priest people think they are still in Nineteenth Century Africa when they throw their weights around. Ah, there, something is agreed; now tell me about this ship."

I started to tell her. Somewhere in the second paragraph, one and then the other of my legs were tapped and lifted as if I were a horse being shod. I looked down. My space boots had been deftly removed. Before I could object I was wrapped in an odorous garment which I recognized disgustedly as the yards and yards of the Holy Wholist's grubby sari. The Wholist himself was gone.

"A trade," said Helen calmly, adjusting a fold of this raggedy toga into a pretty tuck at my waist.

"What, my mag shoes for his clothes? Come on!" Space boots—mag shoes, we call them—are valuable in industry for walking on metal walls and such.

"Not so simple," she said, "but in the end, yes. He said he would take nothing for his sari but a permit to preach in the markets where we do not like such interferences. I know an official who has long wanted a certain emblem for the roof of his air car, for which he would surely give a preaching permit. And among my own family there is a young man upon whose air-sled there is fixed this same fancy metal emblem—"

"Which he was willing to swap for my mag shoes," I said. "But how did you work it all out so fast?"

"Why, I am a trader, what else?" Helen said. "Did your aunt never teach you not to interrupt your elders in the middle of a story?"

"Sorry," I muttered, got annoyed with myself for being so easily chastened, and added defiantly, "But I'm not going to shave my head as bare as the Wholist's for the sake of this fool disguise." I go baldheaded in space rather than fuss with hairnets and stiffeners and caps to keep long hair from swimming into my eyes in non-gravey. Approaching landfall, I always start it growing out again.

Helen shrugged. Then she whirled on her attendants and clapped her hands, shouting, "Is there no car to take these passengers to town?"

The passengers grabbed their things and were herded toward an ancient gas truck parked outside. The Heaven Never Fail Short Hauling Line seemed to deal in some very small consignments. The area was still littered with boxes and sacks. These were being haggled over by Helen's people and the drivers of air-sleds who loaded up and drove off.

Helen caught my arm and took me with her to a raised loading platform from which she could observe the exodus while she asked me about the *Sealyham Eggbeater*. She knew all the right questions to ask, about construction, running costs, capacity, maintenance record, logged travel history (and unlogged). When she heard of the long hauls that the little ship had made, she nodded shrewdly.

"So it has Juno's modifications; unshielded, as I have heard—it can be examined?"

"Yes."

"You do not know the specifications of the modifications yourself, do you?"

"I'm a pilot, not an engineer," I said huffily. It embarrasses me that I can't keep that sort of thing in my head.

She asked about the name of the ship.

I shrugged. "I don't know about '*Sealyham*', but '*Eggbeater*' dates from when the Kootenay Line ran ships shaped like eggs and it became a great fashion. Aunt Juno didn't want to spend money to modify our own ships, so we stuck with our webby, messy look and renamed all of them some kind of eggbeater."

Helen smiled and nodded. "Now I remember. At the time I

suggested taking slogans for her ships as we do here. You know my ships' names: *In God Starry Hand*; *No Rich Without Tears*; *Pearl of the Ocean Sky*. I have twenty-seven ships." She waved at the hangar floor. "You see how quickly my cargo is gone. I have a warehouse too but only small, and this is my one hangar. My goods move all the time, and my ships are moving them. Yams in the yam-house start no seedlings."

"Yams?" I said. I was beginning to feel a little feverish, probably from the antipoddies I'd taken before landing.

"You must scatter yams in the ground," Helen said impatiently. "In Old Africa. Yams don't grow here; we must import. But the saying is true everywhere, so my ships fly, my goods travel. I named the ships in old style pidgin talk from Africa, in honor of my beginnings—in my ancestors' lorry lines. All the lorries bore such fine slogans.

"My personal ship is *Let Them Say*. It means, I care nothing how people gossip on me, only how they work for me—"

She fell abruptly silent. Alarmed, I looked where she was looking. A machine was in the doorway I'd come in by, its scanner turning to sweep the hangar while its sensor arm patted about on the floor and door jambs.

Helen signaled to one of the freight sleds with a furious gesture. It lifted toward us. She tapped at her ear—that was when I noticed the speaker clipped there in the form of an earring—and said bitingly into a mike on her collar, "Robot sniffers are working this port, why were they not spotted, why was I not told?"

Jerked out of the spell of her exotic authority, I remembered my danger and I remembered Ripotee: "I had a companion, a cat—"

"It must find you, then. These machines come from the Steinway flagship."

I looked around frantically for some sign of Ripotee. "Don't you have to stay a little to make sure everything gets done right here?"

"My people will do for me. Sit down, that sniffer is turned this way."

With surprising strength, Helen yanked me onto the sled beside her; the sled, driven by a heavy girl in a bright blue jumper, slewed around and sped us swiftly out into the bright sunshine.

We headed toward a cluster of domes and spires some distance away. The sled skimmed over broad stubbly fields between high, shaggy green walls that were stands of trees and undergrowth: outposts of the jungle Ripotee had spoken of. Other sleds followed and preceded ours, most of them fully loaded.

"Where are we going?" I said.

"To market, of course."

I remembered that Helen was an old opponent in the market-places of the worlds, and it occurred to me that perhaps she was simply keeping me scarce until she could trade me in for a good profit. I checked the driver's instruments out of the corner of my eye, gauging the possibility of jumping for it and hiding out on my own in the jungle or something, just in case I had to. Helen must have seen me because she laughed and patted my knee.

"Ah, my runaway White girl, what are you looking for? Is it that you are suspicious of me now? Netchkay flashes his papers about, claiming that you are space-sick and need to be protected from yourself, or why would you flee from your own family to the home of the trade rivals of the great Steinway Line? You think I might sell you to Bob Netchkay.

"Foolish! I am your friend here, and not only because of Juno and her invention, which can make me very much richer; not even only for the sake of the Steinway Line as it was in its heyday, all those bright, sharp little ships running rings around the big men and their big plans. Yes; not only for these reasons am I your friend, but because women know how to help each other here. The knowledge comes in the blood, from so many generations that lived as many wives to one man. They all competed like Hell, but if the husband treated one wife badly, the others made complaint, and were sick, and scorched his food, until he behaved nicely again. So, here is Bob Netchkay being nasty with you; I will play co-wife, and for you I will scorch bad Bob's supper."

Now, why couldn't my own sister Nita take that line?

"That man is a fungus," I muttered.

"Now, that is the proper tone," Helen said approvingly, "for a missionary talking about one of another sect." Then she added with serene and perfect confidence, "As for Netchkay, I will shortly think what to do about him.

"First tell me just what you yourself want out of it."

"My ship back and some money to start flying." On a sudden inspiration I added, "My mag shoes were worth much more than this Holy Wholey rag I'm wearing. You have to count them in any deal between us."

She let that pass and leaned forward to snap out an order to our driver. "There is the market," she said to me, indicating a high translucent dome with landing pads hitched round it in a circle like a halo on a bald head.

I scowled. "I know you have business there, but what good is the market to me?"

"Bob Netchkay's robot sniffers cannot enter on your trail. No servos are permitted on the market floor. They are not agile enough for the crowds and always get trampled and pushed about until they break, and then they sit there in the way with their screamers on for assistance, driving everyone mad. In there you must play missionary a little. White missionaries are not remarkable here on New Niger; if those sniffers ask of you outside the market from people coming out, they will learn nothing.

"Sit still and be quiet till we land, I must listen to the trading reports."

She turned up the volume on the button communicator in her earring and ignored me. I studied her as we neared the market building. She didn't look old enough to have known Aunt Juno, but it never occurred to me to doubt that she had. I thought I saw in her the restless, swift energy of my aunt. In Helen it was keen ambition, right out there on the surface for all to see. Helen even had the same alert, eager poise of the head that Aunt Juno had so noticeably developed along with her progressive nearsightedness.

She shooed me out onto a ribbon lift which lowered me to the edge of the immense seethe and roar of the jam-packed market floor. She herself boarded a little floater. That way she could oversee the trading at her booths, darting like an insect from one end of the hall to the other.

I took up a position as deep within the crowd as I could elbow myself room. On my right a fat woman hawked chili-fruits from Novi Nussbaum; on my left squawking chickens were passed over the heads of the crowd to their purchasers. Women carrying loads on their heads strode between buyers and sellers, yelling at each other in the roughly defined aisles between stalls.

I shouted myself what I imagined might be the spiel of a Holy Wholist: "The sky of New Niger is the sky of Old Earth; our souls are pieces of one great eggshell enclosing the universe!" and similar rubbish. Some of the crowd stopped around me; about a dozen women, and two men with red eyes and the swaying stance of drunks.

Suddenly there was a shriek from the chili-fruit woman. Over a milling of excited marketers I could just glimpse her slapping among her wares with her shoe.

Helen's floater zipped in; she seized the shouting woman by the arm and spoke harshly into her ear, reducing her to silence. I managed to insinuate myself through the crowd, which was already beginning to disperse in search of more interesting matters.

Helen said to me in a venomous whisper, "Did you hear it? This woman says she saw moving, maybe, a sweetsucker among the chili-fruits. A sweetsucker, can you imagine, carried all the way from Novi Nussbaum with my cargo!"

The vendor, eyes cast down, muttered, "I saw it, I am telling you—sweetsucker or not. A long thing like what they call snake in Iboland, but hairy, and making a nasty sound," and she drew her lips back and made clicking sounds with her tongue and widely chomping teeth, like a kid who hasn't learned yet to chew with its mouth closed. It was just the sound Ripotee makes when he's eating.

Helen rounded on the woman again, snarling threats: "If you spread rumors of sweetsuckers drying up my Novi Nussbaum fruits, I will see you not only never sell for me again but find every market on New Niger closed to you!"

I bent down and hunted quietly around the stand, calling Ripotee's name. Not quietly enough: some friendly people at the next stall over turned to watch and saw my religious attire. Identifying my behavior as some exotic prayer ceremony, they cheerfully took up my call as a chant, clapping their hands: "Rip-o-tee! Rip-o-tee!"

Helen took me firmly by the wrist. "What are you doing?"

"This vending woman must have seen my cat."

"And by now many people in the market have your cat's name in their mouths, which is very foolish and not good for us. Netchkay is clever, and I just now get word that seeing he could not introduce his machines here to find if you are at the market, he has sent instead your own sister, Nita Steinway. She will know that cat's name if she hears it spoken, and she will look for you. So we must go at once, though it means I break my business early, which I do not like at all."

She propelled me onto the floater with her, hovering there a moment to give curt orders to the vending woman: "Go take these chili-fruits to put water in them and plump them up, so no one will believe this nonsense about sweetsuckers!" We rose straight for one of the roof hatches.

I said, "Helen, my cat—"

"Oh, your cat, this cat is driving me mad!" she cried, shooting us out onto one of the landing pads again and bustling me sharply into a waiting town skipper. It was an elegant model with hardwood and bright silver fittings inside. She drove it herself, shying us through the sky in aggressive swoops that made other skippers edge nervously out of our way.

"Now listen, is it this cat you want to talk about or diddling Bob Netchkay? If you are interested, I have arranged it; I have set engineers to copying the Steinway modification from your ship. When plans are drawn we will show them to Netchkay. If he wants them sold to every short hauler in the business, he can continue to worry you. If he agrees to leave you alone, he will have only one competitor with the secret of long-hauling in short haul ships: myself."

Chuckling, she sideslipped us past a steeple that had risen unexpectedly before us. "Oh, he will grind his teeth to powder, and I—I will be the one to carry on the true spirit of the Steinway Line."

I looked down at the bubble buildings we were skimming over, interspersed with what looked like not very satisfactorily transplanted palm trees, all brown and drooping. I felt lonesome and exposed in the hands of Helen Nwanyeruwa above that alien townscape.

We landed on the roof of a square, solid cement building. Helen shouted for attendants to come moor the skipper and for a guide to show me to my room. She said kindly, "Go there now, I have made a surprise for you. Maybe then you will stop wailing after this cat and enjoy my party tonight."

The surprise was Barnabas, sitting on the bed and grinning. He had grown a curl of beard along his jawline and wore not a captain's jumper but tan cord pants and a gown-like shirt of green and black.

"Barnabas!" I said. "What in the worlds—"

"Everybody here knows you and I have met and made connection before. New Niger is the market place of gossip."

"Better to make connection than to just talk about it," I said and began tossing off my clothes. I'd forgotten that peculiarly electrical expression of New Nigerian English; it set me off. I was suddenly so horny I could hardly see straight.

In space I forget; most of us do, though we like to keep up the legend of rampant pilots whooping it up in free fall. Actually, all that is inhibited out there, maybe by stress. But it comes back fast and furious when you are aground again.

Barnabas had the presence of mind to get up and shut the door. He knew right away what was happening and threw himself into it with a cheerful, warm gusto that had me almost in tears. I finally had to beg off because he was making me sore with all that driving, and he tumbled off me sideways, laughing: "Sorry, I didn't mean to hurt you, but it is long since I did this with a crew-cut woman!"

"It's the first thing I've done on New Niger that didn't feel all foreign and strange," I said. "Let's do it again, but this time I'll get on top."

Later on a small boy came padding in with his eyes downcast bringing us towels, and padded out again. Two towels.

Pilots tend to be a little prudish about these things, which are after all more important and isolated incidents for us than for your average planet-bunny with all his or her opportunities. "Don't you people know what servomechs are for?" I grumbled.

Barnabas was stroking my throat. "You have a beautiful neck, just like the belly of a snake. No, no, that is compliment! Don't mind the youngsters—Helen gives employment to many children of relatives. She is very rich, you know."

"How did he know there were two of us needing towels?"

"Everyone knows I was up here, and what else does a man do with a woman. They forget that I am a captain myself and might have business to talk with you. To people here, I am just a man, good only for fun and fathering . . ."

At his sudden glance of inquiry and concern I shook my head. "Lord no, Barnabas, I shot myself full of antipoddies before leaving the ship. Otherwise I'd be nailed to the toilet with the runs." All pilots use antis on landfall. You have to make a special effort to conceive.

"I have several children now," Barnabas said, and his voice took a bitter edge. "But unfortunately no ship. A falling out with my employer." He smiled wrily. "I am sorry for myself. What have you been doing, Deedee? I hear you have a lot of trouble with Bob Netchkay and your sister."

I explained. He grimaced and shook his head, half condemning, half admiring. "I told you long ago, that man is to be watched; he has plenty of brains and drive, and with your clever sister to help him he is making a great company to rival even the Chinese."

"He's a fungus," I said. I liked that word.

Barnabas laughed. "Let's not argue in the shower."

We stood in the wet corner under the fine spray shooting in from the walls and talked, rubbing and sponging each other and picking our hairs out of the drain. Then we toweled off, got back on the bed, and soon had to clean up all over again.

"Can you stay a while?" I asked, stroking the long muscles woven across his back. "You're doing me a lot of good, Barnabas."

"Me too," he said. "To be free of the worry, you know, of not making babies . . . They like a man to be fertile here." He shrugged and changed the subject. "Tell me about Ripotee. I was thinking of him just now; he used to complain that it was disgusting, us two together—"

"I think he was just jealous, not really overcome with horror at our inordinate hugenesses rolling around together. I tried taking a female cat aboard for him, but he couldn't stand her." I started to cry.

Barnabas hugged me and made soothing sounds into my frizz of new grown hair. I blubbed out how Ripotee had left the ship before I could do anything, even shoot him with antis. "He was in one of his crazy derring-do fits. He kept up with me as far as the market, but since then I don't know—Helen doesn't care. Maybe she's already heard that he's been caught and eaten. From what I've seen, no animals survive here except humans and chickens. People must be crazy for a taste of red meat—"

"Not cat meat, it is awful!" Barnabas exploded.

We curled up together and talked about Ripotee. I told Barnabas how it made me feel so peculiar to think back to the days when Ripotee had been a dumb cat that I could shove around and tickle and yell at, as people do with cats, without a thought. I'd teased him, called him all kinds of names, grabbed him up, and scrubbed him under the chin 'til he half-fainted with delight.

I didn't do things like that any more.

"Don't be put off," Barnabas said. "It is only his pride that keeps him from flopping down for a chin rub just as he used to do, and he would love for you to push him over and rub his chin anyway."

I shook my head. "He's changed since you knew him. I think it's all that reading. When he lies relaxed with his eyes half shut looking at nothing. I know he's not falling asleep any more; now he's brooding. Like a person."

Barnabas stood up and pulled on his shorts. "He is luckier than a person. If he were a mere man, he would be protesting always how all he needs are his mates, he must have good fellows to drink with and gossip and play cards."

"This afternoon you and I certainly proved that's a lie," I said smugly.

He didn't smile; he wrinkled his nose and sat down again, putting his arm around my shoulders. "But this is what they say here, and the women of New Niger can make it stick, too, I tell you. You know, Dee, I might have inherited wealth as you did, but my great grandfather was too ambitious. He was seduced by the big trade of international business like many other men in Nigeria. He jumped to put his money into the big boom of Europe and America, just as he had jumped right into Christianity and having only one wife at a time.

"So then the wars and the bad weather came and broke all the high finance, and him with it, among all the rest. He was left nothing but a worn out yam farm in an overcrowded, overworked corner of Iboland in the Eastern Region. Nobody had much of anything in Nigeria then, except some of the women traders with lorry fleets—the lorry mammies—and those who went even on foot from market to market, dealing haircombs and matches and sugar by the cube. They became the ones with funds to put into space travel.

"So here I am on the world they settled, trying to get rich myself. And who do you think is my boss, the one that is giving me trouble and keeping me grounded?"

"A woman," I guessed.

"A cousin of Helen's, and a woman, yes." He slipped on one of his plastic sandals. "The other men say, take it easy, relax and enjoy some drinking."

I felt less than completely sympathetic; I heard that angry, self-pitying tone again and didn't like it. I said lightly, "These women of New Niger are some tough ladies."

He answered with a grudging pride: "Listen, long ago, when your ancestor-mothers were chaining themselves to the gates of politicians' houses, my ancestor-mothers were rousing each other to riot against the English colonials' plan to take census of women and women's property. It was thought this would lead to special taxing of these women, for even then there were many wives who were farmers and petty traders on their own. They made what is still called the Women's War. Thousands rose up in different places to catch the chiefs the English had appointed and to sit on them—it means to frighten and belittle a man with angry, insulting songs and to spoil his property. They tore some public buildings to the ground. In all some fifty women were shot dead by the authorities, and many more were wounded—that is how frightened the government were. No tax was applied, and the English had a big inquiry in their parliament on how to rule Iboland.

"Helen herself is named for the woman who began the War. On being told in her own yard to count her goats and children, this woman shouted to the official who said it, 'Was your mother counted?' and seized him by the throat."

I could well believe it and said so.

Barnabas got up again.

"Where are you off to?" I said. Talking with him like this was almost like old times together in space.

"I must get ready for the party; you should too. Tonight Helen Nwanyeruwa holds a feast for the spirit of her ancestor the lorry mammy. Wealthy Missisi Helen had the ancestor-bones brought here on one of her ships; the spirit would not dare to displease her by staying behind."

He bent and rested both hands on my shoulders, looking intently into my face. "It is very good to see you, Deedee."

The outer surfaces of the house were illuminated so that the walled courtyard was brilliantly lit for the party. Family and guests milled around on the quickie grass, grown for the evening in an hour to cover where the plastic paving had been rolled back.

Wrapped in my Holy Wholist sari, worn properly this time with nothing underneath—it didn't bother me, I often go naked in my ship—I milled around with the best of them. As a missionary I was not expected to join the dancing, for which I was grateful. I felt nervous and shy and alien, and I wandered over toward where Helen sat on a huge couch beside the shrine she had had erected: a concrete stele with the image of a truck on it. On the way I passed a line of men and a line of women dancing opposite each other, and Barnabas stepped to my side out of the men's line. His skin was shiny with sweat. He caught me around the waist and murmured in my ear, "You and I do our own private dancing, Deedee, later on."

As we approached, Helen patted the slowflow plastic next to her, making room for me but not for Barnabas. He joined the crowd of retainers on her right.

Helen wore African clothing of sparkling silverweave and a piece of the same cloth tied around her head into an elaborate turban. Even her white plastic sandals couldn't spoil the effect. She was beautiful; by comparison, those around her who affected the fashionable billowing Victorian look of the new Romanticism seemed puny and laughable.

Sitting beside her wiry, tense body on the surface that slowly moulded to my shape, I felt protected by her feisty energy. Yet her boldness in having me up there in full view endangered me; suppose Bob had spies here? The drums thundered in the spaces of the courtyard. I gulped down the drink she handed me. It tasted like lemonade filtered through flannel.

I shivered. "Helen, what if—an enemy hears the drums and comes to your party?"

She looked at me out of the corner of her eye and said with haughty dismissiveness, "No enemy has been invited."

This was repeated among the others around us and brought much laughter. Of course she must have robot guards, computer security systems and so on, I thought; but I felt edgy.

Barnabas leaned toward us. "Even so, Missisi Helen, it might be wise to take extra care. I myself and a few friends have devised a special power hookup—"

Helen set down her drink and turned to him. "Don't worry yourself about these things, Barnabas; you will only get in the way. You are a good, strong young man, and Missisi Alicia tells me you have fathered a fine baby in her family. Go and drink from my private casks, over there, you and your friends. Go amuse yourselves."

Barnabas spun and forced his way out through the crowd toward the dancers—then swerved sharply back toward the bar.

"Why are you so hard on him?" I said.

"These boys get too big ideas of themselves, especially the young ones who have been out in space," Helen replied, reaching for a fresh drink from a tray offered her. "They begin thinking their fathers ran fleets of lorries too."

Everybody whooped over this. Helen was excited, feeding off the high spirits of those who fed off her own. She flung out her arm, pointing at a young man in the forefront of a huddle of others who had been looking our way on and off for quite a while. He resisted his friends' efforts to push him forward.

"You see that boy there," she said, pitching her voice so that everyone near the ancestor shrine must hear; "he has been chasing after that girl, my Anne, who is still nearly a baby, but he has not taken up his courage to speak to me about her. And he boasts that his father hunts lions with a spear in Old Africa, where there are fewer lions than here on New Niger." She snatched up a pebble and pitched it not to strike but to startle into squawking flight one of the ubiquitous chickens pecking for scraps around a food table. "See what kind of lions we have here! Just such as that boy's father hunts, just so fierce!"

At last, something familiar—the suitor who didn't suit Mother. "Anne is one of your daughters?"

"Oh no," Helen replied proudly, "one of my wives."

I didn't know what to say. Helen grinned at me, plainly pleased with the effect of her words.

"I have lots of wives," she added with great satisfaction. "It was always Ibo custom that a woman rich enough to support wives could marry so; and I am very rich. My Anne will find herself a young man who makes her happy for a while. No fear, in time she will bring me a child of that union to be brother or sister to the children of my own body and my other wives'."

She gave me an affectionate hug, chuckling. "Just as you look now, so shocked, that is how your aunt looked when I married my first wife. Even once I told her, 'Juno, you should have daughters to comfort your old age and inherit your goods. Do as I do, there must be some White way with many documents.' But she said, 'I only have time for one creation, and that is the Steinway Line.' Then she laughed because it was the kind of grand talk men use to impress each other; we both knew the petty trading would go on as always, while the men heroes choke on their grand schemes.

"I live by that petty trading, and I live well, as you see. Come make fast to my own good fortune, as in one of our African sayings: if a person is not successful at trading in the market, it would be cowardly to run away; instead she should change her merchandise.

"Give up wishing to be Admiral of a trading fleet, and say you will come work for my company, my bold White flyer."

I was looking at Barnabas. He danced, his shoulders rippling like water shunting down a long container, first to one end and then to the other. A bit wobbly, in fact; as he turned without seeing me I realized that it was not only the ecstasy of the dance that sealed his eyes. He was drunk. I was alone among strangers.

I shook my head.

"You are too stubborn," Helen said, giving me a thump in the side with her elbow. But she didn't look unhappy. Maybe she thought I was just making a move in a complicated bargaining game, and approved. If I were any good at that kind of thing, I wouldn't have been in this spot with Bob. It's not the dealing I love, it's the piloting. Helen didn't know me well enough yet to really understand that. "Well," she added, "you must do what suits you, and let them say!"

Somebody screamed, there was a swirling in the crowd as one of the food tables crashed down and a girl came flying toward us, shrieking. I leaped up, thinking, Netchkay has come, some one has been hurt because of him; but I was fuddled with drink and couldn't think what to do.

Helen strode to meet the screaming girl.

"It spoke to me, the spirit of your ancestor," the girl gibbered, twisting her head to stare wide-eyed over her shoulder at the tumbled ruin of the food table. "I was serving food, Missisi Helen, as you told me, and a little high voice said from someplace down low, behind me, 'A piece of light meat please, cut up small on a plate.' I looked in the dark by the wall, I saw eyes like red hot coins."

I hurried unsteadily over to where two servos were already sucking up the mess and getting in each other's way.

Behind me I heard the girl: "I was afraid, Missisi. The spirit repeated, so I put down food, but then some one passed behind me and I heard the spirit cry, 'Get off my tail!' and it vanished. Mary thinks she stepped on it—Oh, Missisi Helen, will Mary and me be cursed?"

I shoved one of the servos aside, looking for the poor, crushed remains of Ripotee.

I found nothing but a hole in the wall, low, rounded, and utterly puzzling. I rapped on the nearest servo, which was busy wiping at some sauce with the trailing end of my sari, apparently under the impression that this was a large, handy rag.

"What's this?" I said into the speaker of the servo, pointing at the hole. "Where does it lead to?"

"Madame or sir, it is hole for fowl," creaked the servo. "Madame or sir, it leads in for chickens seeking entry to this compound for the night and leads out for—"

"All right, all right," I said. While addressing me the tin fool had decided the sari was beyond salvage, and had begun ingesting it into its cannister body for disposal. I yanked.

The servo clicked disapprovingly and sheared off the swallowed portion of my garment with an interior blade. I made my way back through the crowd toward Helen, rearranging the remains of my clothing and swearing to myself.

"—Not possible that my ancestor has returned as *an animal*," Helen was saying in an ominous voice. "Felicity, remember this: I took you from your mother for a good bride price, I put you to school. I have adopted your children for my own. Now think what you are saying to me of my own ancestor here before all my guests."

Silence. I elbowed near enough to see just as the girl dropped suddenly full length on the ground, her hands spread flat beside her shoulders like some one doing the down part of a push-up.

The crowd gave a satisfied sigh; but Helen stamped her foot in exasperation and said, "We are not in Old Africa now, I will not have you prostrating to me. Just get up and ask my pardon nicely." She looked pleased though.

Felicity scrambled to her feet and whispered an apology. Helen came and linked her arm through mine, saying loudly, "If it was somebody's ancestor, it must go find food at the house of its proper descendants." In a lower voice she continued, "Monitors have been found under some of the spilled serving dishes; Netchkay will know you are here. You must leave for a mission church away from Singlet, just until my engineers have finished work on your ship. One of my freight sleds will take you. It goes at mid-morning tomorrow to tour the market towns. By the time you return—"

"Helen, listen, I can't just take off again like this. My cat is still hanging around here someplace—"

"Oh, cat, cat! You must get your mind to business now." She fiddled impatiently with her ear speaker. "Do you think I can keep track of all that happens here? I have a dozen wives to attend to. This is only an animal, after all."

"Ripotee is my friend."

"Then you must hope for the best for your friend, and meanwhile go and rest; you have a journey tomorrow."

And she walked away and stepped into the center of one of the lines of dancing women, stamping and whirling and flipping her head to the different parts of the complex beat, lithe as a girl.

When Barnabas came to my room, it was not to tumble into my bed.

I had fallen asleep, still in my sari, despite the music and voices from the courtyard. He shook me awake in the half-lit room—it was quiet now, near dawn—and whispered, "Dee—you can stop worrying about Ripotee. I have him safe for you, outside with a friend of mine who found him."

His breath smelled of liquor, but he seemed steady and alert, and I could have hugged him for the news he brought. I followed him downstairs. Some one murmured, from within another room with its door ajar, "Barnabas?" A woman's voice; and I thought, ha, he has other beds to sleep in at Helen's house than mine, no wonder he can visit as he likes.

I ran with him across the courtyard, holding up my hem to keep from tripping. As we passed out of the gateway, a long air car swept silently toward us and stopped. A door opened. I bent to look inside, and Barnabas grabbed both my arms from behind and thrust me forward into the interior, where not Ripotee but someone else waited. I tried to twist away, but Barnabas shoved in beside me, pinning me hard with his hip and shoulder. The other person was Nita, my sister.

While I was still caught in the first breathless explosion of shock and incredulous outrage, she slapped a little needle into my neck. She may be a lambchop, my sultry sister, but she is quick. Quicker than I am, who had never stopped to wonder in my sleepy daze why Barnabas hadn't just brought Ripotee up to me himself.

"—Too much in the needle," Barnabas was saying in underwater tones. I could feel breath on each cheek, and on one side was a tinge of wine odor: Barnabas. I was sitting wedged between them. It occurred to me that the antipoddies I had taken might have buffered the effect of the drug. I hoped so; and hoped that Barnabas, out of practice at the transition from space to land, would forget about the effects of antis.

"You've never fought with Dee," Nita said. "She's strong as a servo, and I'm not taking any chances." She fidgeted next to me, trying to get at something tucked into her clothing, doubtless another needle.

Barnabas said firmly, "If you give another needle, this is all finished. I will go back to Helen and tell everything. Mr. Netchkay and I made particular agreement that there would be no risk of harm to Dee."

A moment of frigid tenseness: good, good, fight or something. Shoot me again, Nita, it would be worth it, if only Barnabas would then go to Helen as he threatened.

She didn't, and he didn't. I smelled dust, smoke, and was that rocket fuel? The car stopped, and I slumped helplessly there until he hauled me out with a fair amount of grunting. True to her chosen style, Nita let Barnabas do the work: he was the man, after all. I was set down on a metal surface in what felt like an enclosed space. There was a nasty odor in the air.

Barnabas' hands moved mine to set them comfortably under my cheek, as if I lay sleeping. He whispered in my ear. I shut out the words, knowing what they would be: that he was sorry, that the only way he could go out as a pilot again was to work for a foreigner like Netchkay; that this was his only chance. That he would be sure nothing terrible happened to me. And so on.

I didn't blame him, exactly. I just felt sick and sorry. There isn't a captain alive who wouldn't understand the feeling of sitting on a planet for years, going soft in the head on a soft life, while good reflexes and knowledge soak away.

Nita was another story. I wondered if she hated me, if she meant to do me some hideous injury while I lay there defenseless.

"Please leave me alone with my sister, Captain," she said.

Barnabas made no more apologies to me; I heard his quiet steps recede.

Nita folded herself neatly, with poise, beside me. I didn't see her, but I knew, for her, there would be nothing so inelegant as a squat. Warm drops wet my cheek.

"You look awful," she groaned. "Dressed like a fanatic of some skinhead sect and smelling like a savage—Honestly, Dee, you are so crazy! Why don't you let us take care of you? Bob's not a bad man. He did take the Steinway Line, but he saved it from ruin, won't you credit him with that?"

She paused, snuffling forlornly. I wanted to cry myself. And in her accustomed manner, she was making it very hard for me to hate her. Nita never let anything happen the easy way for others, only for herself. It was very easy for her to betray me because she had fooled herself into believing she was doing the right thing.

"I hope there are no rats in here," she said miserably. "But I had to talk to you. Once Bob comes, it'll be all shouting and cursing and nobody getting in a sensible word.

"There's going to be a war. The independent short haul traders have had enough of being wrung dry by the Chinese long haulers, and Bob has finally gotten them together on a plan to take the Chinese long haul trade into American hands. So for a while there aren't going to be any nifty little short haul ships operating on their own, flitting around as they please, and calling themselves free-lancers—your way. It's going to be too dangerous. Everyone will have to choose a side and stick with it. But you've got no sense. You'll hold out on your own in some old ship and end getting blown up by us or the other side—and I'm not going to tolerate it."

She patted my fuzz of hair and pulled at my wrap, arranging me as a more modest heap on the floor. She blew her nose and added resentfully, "Bob says it's no more than you deserve, charging around the way you do. He should have known Aunt Juno, the awful example she set us—as if every girl could be like that, or should be! She may not have meant to get you killed, but that's just what it will turn out to be by leaving you space ships to run. She thought you were tough as a man, like her."

More sniffling. "She never thought much of me; but then I was always the realist."

Sure, if realism means you just coast along looking for somebody to notice how pretty you make yourself so they take the burden of your own life off your shoulders for you. I almost told her that, before reminding myself that my best chance was to fake being more knocked out by the drug than I was, so she wouldn't give me another shot. While I burned, she prattled on, fixing up my wayward life, and Aunt Juno's wayward life too for that matter, her own way.

"You and Bob and I would make a great team, once you got off your high horse and left the strategy to him. Bob's a natural leader. He'll do well, you'll see. But you have to come in with us, you have to stop fighting us and charging off in any crazy direction you feel like! Honestly, sometimes I think I must be the older one and you the younger.

"I haven't had even a minute to sit down and talk to you in more than four home years, do you realize that? I bet you don't even notice."

So she shot me after all, if only with guilt, an old lambchop trick. I was the older sister; it was all my fault, whatever "it" happened to be. BULLSHIT, I yelled silently. HELP, SOMEBODY!

"I'm warning you, Dee; if you insist on bucking Bob, I'll side with him. We'll see that you spend the war out of harm's way in nice, quiet seclusion somewhere, and so drugged up for your own good that you'll never get your pilot's license renewed again. Grounded forever. Think about it, Dee, please. This isn't just what you want and what I want any more. You've got to be realistic."

Then she leaned down and kissed me, my sister who knew how to set all my defense alarm systems roaring in a panic; and I swear the kiss was honest.

I was so glad when she got up and walked out that I nearly bawled with relief. A little while passed. I lay there trying to flex my sluggish muscles, thinking about being locked up, thinking about being grounded for good, so I shouldn't worry Nita or inconvenience Bob. I wondered if Barnabas would repent and go tell Helen what had happened; and what, if anything, Helen would or could do about me.

The place had a real stink to it, laced with the faint pungence of Barnabas' sweat and Nita's perfumes. Later on there was another smell: stinky cat breath, by the stars!

"Ripotee." I strained to see; by this time the drug had begun to wear off. There had to be some light in the place because there were the reflections in Ripotee's eyes, not a foot from my face:

just as Felicity had said, two burning red coins. I couldn't reach out to him, and he came no closer. "Are you hurt?" I cried.

"I'm fine, but hungry. At your party someone tramped on my tail before I could get anything to eat, and there's nothing here—they cleaned out my mice with the oatmeal."

What a pleasure it was to hear his voice—any voice, most particularly two voices, instead of Nita's sugary tones foretelling my ruin. I tried to sit up. My hand encountered a line of rivets in the wall beside me.

"What is this? Where has Bob had me locked up?"

Ripotee said, "We're in the hold of the *Sealyham Eggbeater*."

"Shit," I said. Now I recognized the smell, pod rot plus cleanzymes. So Bob had the *Eggbeater* and he had me, and he had Ripotee too now; which made me feel very stupid, very tired, and a little mean.

Ripotee elaborated. "Bob is outside. He took the flagship up last night. Now he's trying to buy clearance so he can take the *Eggbeater* up too, even though it's still officially in the cleaning process." He was angry. His tail kept slap-slapping the floor.

It annoyed me that he could see me in that darkness, and I couldn't see him. Sitting there blind, holding myself up against the wall, I said, "How was the jungle, Ripotee?"

"Hot," he said, "and tangled and full of bugs. Some of them are living in my ears. You smell of medicine."

"Drug. It's almost all worn off." I could hear his tail flailing away at the floor and the wall, and the faint click of his claws as he paced. I said, "Why did you stay away like that? I was worried to death about you."

"I just wanted to be on my own out there in the jungle, like the big cats used to be on Old Earth. It was lonesome. There was nobody there but chickens. I got mad and hungry and I ate some. People chased me." He coughed, minute explosions. I could see the blurry red discs of his eyes again. "I wanted to land here, but there isn't anything here for me; like there isn't anything here for you.

"What I really wanted," he added fiercely, "was a fight, as a matter of fact; another cat to fight with." This was solid ground. I knew how he loved to go tomming it at any landfall we made, coming home bloody and limping and high on adrenalin. I think he liked the instinctual speed and strength and ferocity of the contest, no chance to think, let alone talk. Which contradicted the last thing he'd said about the jungle, but he's just as capable of wanting two opposing things at the same time as I am.

"You just couldn't stand it that I was out there on my own," he raged, "you were scared I'd turn wild or something—a fish dropping back into the water will swim away and forget, that's all you thought I'd do. Well, even when my brain was just kitty brains it was bigger than that!"

"I was worried about you!" I yelled.

"Poor Ripotee, dumb Ripotee can't possibly manage on his own." He was pacing again. "In the jungle his ancestors ruled like kings, he needs his soft-bodied human to look after him and protect him! Go marry some rich man so you can retire from space and look after him!"

"Oh, Ripotee—"

"Don't talk to me!" His agitated voice wound right up into a real old fashioned Siamese yowl.

That yowl was heard; the hatch was swung open, letting in a sweep of light, and Bob stood framed against the afternoon outside. What a blast of energy it gave me to see that tall, strong, masterful silhouette: just what I needed to nerve me up for a fight.

"If it isn't the voice of the talking cat," he said. "I'd know it anywhere, damned unnatural noise. Nita's worried about the shot she gave you, Dee, but if you're trading mouse stories with the jumped-up lap-warmer you must be okay."

He didn't seem to have people with him, but I thought I heard voices outside; or was it only the cackling of the inescapable chickens of New Niger?

He read my admittedly obvious thoughts. "I have friends with me. Oh, yes, your friends are here too, I wouldn't lie to you, but there's nothing they can do for a foreigner in the face of trade federation papers—except obstruct and annoy me. When your friends run out of obstruction and annoyance, my friends will be free to come in here where you can't duck me again, and they'll be my witnesses and hold you down while I serve you with these papers."

One thing was certain, and that was that my friends couldn't help me as long as they were outside and I was trapped in here.

I said, "Go to Hell," while patting madly around on the floor in search of something, anything, to use as a weapon. All I had was the Holy Wholey sari; so I pulled that off and rested there on my knees with it in my hands, wondering how much Bob could see in the dimness of the hold.

I could see him fairly well. He was wearing one of those wide light capes popular in the upper ranks of federation office. It can disguise the fact that many of the members come from worlds where the human form has been pretty heavily engeneticked to fit alien environments. Bob let his hang loose to the floor so that anyone could see what a fine, straight figure of a man he was. And he was, too. Nita has good taste—in appearances.

Myself, I have good taste in disasters, which was what led me to be crouching naked in front of my enemy, nothing but a bunch of wrinkled cloth in my fists, nothing at all in my head.

Ripotee minced over and rubbed against Bob's ankle. I held my breath. He said, "Something to tell you, Uncle Bob," using the twee little voice and baby talk that Bob always wanted from him.

With his head up so that he could keep an eye on me, Bob sank onto his haunches. He wasn't dumb enough to try to pick Ripotee up, something that even I seldom did and never without an invitation. He hunkered there in the doorway, one hand braced on the floor, the other hooked into his belt; a dashing figure even on his hams.

Ripotee said, "I want to go away with you, Uncle Bob; will you take me, for a secret? A secret about the Steinway modification?"

Bob bent a little lower, bringing his dark Byronic curls closer to Ripotee's narrow face.

Ripotee did what a fighting tom does; he shot up so high on his hind legs that he stood for an instant on the tip of his extended tail, and he let go a left and right too swift to see. Bob screamed and reared up, both hands clapped to his face, and Ripotee leaped between his legs and out of the hatchway.

Holding my garment stretched out in front of me I flung myself at the light, bowling Bob out onto the ground with me, entangled in folds of cloth. I am not a giant, regardless of Ripotee's opinion, but I am solid and I landed on top, knees and elbows first.

People came rushing over and pried us apart, lifting me to my feet and trying to wrap me up. I think some thought Bob had gotten my clothes off me for some nefarious purpose and were somewhat miffed by my own lack of concern. As I said, I float around naked in space a lot, and I carried it off pretty coolly.

When Bob panted that he was all right, his eyes hadn't been

touched, I thought, thank gods. It was enough to be able to laugh freely at the sight he made, scrubbing at his blood-smeared face with his prettily embroidered cuffs.

At my side Helen said rapidly, "He has a federation warrant to suspend your license and immobilize you pending mental exam. It applies at once, as you are not a citizen here."

Shaking bright drops onto the soiled white cloth heaped on the ground at his feet, Bob groped for the paper held out by one of his minions.

I spoke first. "Helen, you'd make any girl a wonderful husband. Will you marry me?"

Helen swooped down on a chicken that was scrabbling around by our feet. She bit off its head and spit it out, held up the fluttering corpse and sprinkled us both with blood. Then she tossed the bird away, threw her arms around my waist, and announced loudly, "Robert Wilkie Netchkay Steinway—that is your name on those papers?—you and your people are invited to my house tonight to celebrate this wedding I have just made here with Dee Steinway. It is sudden, but here in New Niger we have very hot blood and we do things suddenly. I myself am surprised to find that I have married again.

"As for your papers, they cannot be executed on a woman of New Niger. Try going through the local courts if you wish. You will find many of my relatives there hard at work; just as I have numbers of cousins and grown children working also here at Singlet Port, where you docked your big ship illegally yesterday."

"Docked illegally?" snapped Bob. "Your own port people let me in and let me out again."

"Someone made a mistake," said Helen blandly. "Your flagship was too big for our facilities. Some damage has been done and certain other traders were prevented from landing and have suffered losses on that account. There will be a large fine, I fear.

"If you do not come tonight," she added, "I will be very insulted, and so too will all my hard-working relatives. Also you would miss a fine trade we are arranging for you, to make you happy at our celebration."

As we walked away amid Helen's voluble crowd of supporters, I looked back; there was the *Eggbeater*, freshly plated and rewired, ports open to let in the air. There was Bob, trying to push Nita off him as she clung and wailed.

And there was Ripotee, trotting along behind us, a few feathers stuck to his whiskers.

As the bride, I didn't have anything to do at the wedding feast but dance around. Helen and a few of her kindred skilled in law and business sat at a table with Bob, Nita, a mess of papers, and a records terminal. They talked while platters of food were brought, notably the speciality of the evening. Yams Wriggly, an Oriental dish; the wrigglies came from a Red Joy tariff delegation. Bob himself didn't eat much; his face looked as if whatever they served him was burnt.

I danced, badly, with Ripotee clinging to my shoulders. We threw the whole line of dancers off.

Our guests from the flagship got up to leave rather early, seen out personally by their host and the beaming bride. Bob looked at me coolly, with an unbloodied eye—he'd had fast, first rate treatment of the scratches and showed not a mark—and said, "If you ever grow up, Dee, you'll be welcome at home."

I laughed in his face.

He was trembling ever so slightly—with pure rage, I sincerely hoped. As he turned and started to steer Nita away with him in an iron grip, she burst into tears and cried, "Oh, Dee, what will become of your life? My sister has turned into a naked savage—"

I was wearing my jumper, as a matter of fact, trimmed with bright patterns that a couple of Helen's junior wives had applied to the chest, back, and bottom. But I suppose Nita was still seeing me as I had burst from the ship that afternoon, bare and blood-spattered.

Other guests began leaving, hurried out by Helen's loud, laughing complaints that she was being ruined by two parties on successive nights.

She drew me over to the long table where she and Bob and Nita had feasted. Ripotee jumped down from my shoulder.

"I'm going off for a walk. Don't get worried about me this time. I'll meet you in the morning at the, ah, hole for fowl."

Helen called sharply after him, "Food will be left out for you. Please confine your eating to *cold* chicken."

She turned to me. "Here are your ship papers and your debt agreements. Netchkay paid his fine with your ship, since that was the only currency the port would accept; and I did a bit of dealing so that the ownership papers end in my hands—and now in yours."

I was pretty well bowled over by this; and I found that now that we had done it, diddled Bob and saved my neck, it wasn't going to be so simple just to accept my salvation at the hands of an old trading rival. I was suddenly worried about some hidden twist, some pitfall, in the already odd situation in which I had landed myself.

Into the awkward silence—awkward for me, though Helen was grinning triumphantly—came noise from an adjoining courtyard, where many of the guests seemed to have congregated on their way out. Singing, it was, and loud laughter.

"They are sitting on Barnabas," Helen said with relish.

"Helen, let him go work for Netchkay if that's what he wants. He's earned it."

"His just desserts!" She laughed. "White people are terrible to work for. Oh, yes, I worked for your Aunt Juno once, on the computer records of the Steinway Line—making sure they were fit for the eyes of certain officials. I learned a lot working for Juno, but she would not learn much from me, or even about me—she was so surprised when I went my own way, to make my own fleet! Perhaps she thought I would spend my life as a faithful retainer!"

I took a deep breath. "Look, Helen, I like to hear about Aunt Juno, but things can't be left like this between you and me. You paid no bride wealth for me, and maybe I can't bring you any children to add to your family, and I'll never learn local ways enough to be comfortable or to be a credit to you—"

Helen threw back her head and screamed with laughter. She slapped my arms, she hugged me. "Oh, you child you!" she crowed, dashing tears of mirth from her eyes. "Listen, you silly White girl; what do you think, we get married like that? A marriage is an alliance of families, planned long in advance. The bride comes and works for years first in the husband's house, so the husband's family can see is she worth marrying. We are not impulsive like you people, and we do not marry with chicken blood! But, that is what a man like Bob Netchkay would believe."

"Then I'm not—?"

"You are not. Nor am I so foolish as to marry a foreigner, bringing nothing but trouble and misunderstanding on all sides."

"But then it's all pure gift," I said, getting up from the table. "I can't accept, Helen—my freedom, my ship—"

"Sit down, sit, sit, sit," she said, pulling me back down beside her. "You forget, there are still the plans for the Steinway modifications, which are worth a great deal to me.

"Also I act in memory of certain debts to your Aunt Juno; and because you are a woman and not a puny weed like that sister of yours; and to black the eye of my rival Netchkay in front of everyone; and also for the pleasure of doing a small something for a White girl, whose race was once so useful in helping my people to get up.

"But I could also say, Dee, that I hope to make you just enough beholden to me so that you will bend your pride—not much, only small-small—and a Steinway will fly her ship for me out there in space that she loves better than any world."

I leaned forward and made wet circles on the plastic table with the bottom of my glass. An image of Aunt Juno came into my mind—a plump dynamo of a woman with her hair piled high on her head to make her look taller; and pretty, pretty even after her neck thickened and obliterated her shapely little chin, and age began to freckle her hands. She had come tripping into my shop class in the Learning Center where I was raised, and batting her long lashes above a dazzling smile that left the teaching team charmed and humbled, she had summoned me away with her because she believed I could become a pilot.

Helen murmured, "Do you know, I myself never fly. All my dealings are made from here, from landfall. In Iboland it was taboo forever for women to climb up above the level of any man's head, it brought sickness. Now we are bolder, we have discarded such notions, we climb easily to the top floors of tall buildings and nobody falls ill. But I am old fashioned, and I am still not comfortable climbing into black space among the stars."

I said, "I'll fly for you."

And so I have done ever since, with brief visits to my "family" on New Niger. I think sometimes how sharp Ripotee was to see that there was no living there for either of us. But I don't tell him; he thinks well enough of himself as it is.

THE SATURN GAME

Poul Anderson

1

If we are to understand what happened, which is vital if we are to avoid repeated and worse tragedies in the future, we must begin by dismissing all accusations. Nobody was negligent; no action was foolish. For who could have predicted the eventuality, or recognized its nature, until too late? Rather should we appreciate the spirit with which those people struggled against disaster, inward and outward, after they knew. The fact is that thresholds exist throughout reality, and that things on their far sides are altogether different from things on their hither sides. The *Chronos* crossed more than an abyss, it crossed a threshold of human experience.

—Francis L. Minamoto, *Death Under Saturn: A Dissenting View* (Apollo University Communications, Leyburg, Luna, 2057)

"The City of Ice is now on my horizon," *Kendrick says. Its towers gleam blue.* "My griffin spreads his wings to glide." *Wind whistles among those great, rainbow-shimmering pinions. His cloak blows back from his shoulders; the air strikes through his ring-mail and sheathes him in cold.* "I lean over and peer after you." *The spear in his left hand counterbalances him. Its head flickers palely with the moonlight that Wayland Smith hammered into the steel.*

"Yes, I see the griffin," *Ricia tells him,* "high and far, like a comet above the courtyard walls. I run out from under the portico for a better look. A guard tries to stop me, grabs my sleeve, but I tear the spider silk apart and dash forth into the open." *The elven castle wavers as if its sculptured ice were turning to smoke. Passionately, she cries,* "Is it in truth you, my darling?"

"Hold, there!" *warns Alvarlan from his cave of arcana ten thousand leagues away.* "I send your mind the message that if the King suspects this is Sir Kendrick of the Isles, he will raise a dragon against him, or spirit you off beyond any chance of rescue. Go back, Princess of Maranoa. Pretend you decide that it is only an eagle. I will cast a belief-spell on your words."

"I stay far aloft," *Kendrick says.* "Save he use a scrying stone, the Elf King will not be aware this beast has a rider. From here I'll spy out city and castle." *And then—? He knows not. He knows simply that he must set her free or die in the quest. How long will it take him, how many more nights will she lie in the King's embrace?*

"I thought you were supposed to spy out Iapetus," Mark Danzig interrupted.

His dry tone startled the three others into alertness. Jean Broberg flushed with embarrassment, Colin Scobie with irritation; Luis Garcilaso shrugged, grinned, and turned his gaze to the pilot console before which he sat harnessed. For a moment silence filled the cabin, and shadows, and radiance from the universe.

To help observation, all lights were out except a few dim glows from the instruments. The sunward ports were lidded. Elsewhere thronged stars, so many and so brilliant that they well-nigh drowned the blackness which held them. The Milky Way was a torrent of silver. One port framed Saturn at half phase, dayside pale gold and rich bands amidst the jewelry of its rings, nightside wanly ashimmer with starlight upon clouds, as big to the sight as Earth over Luna.

Forward was Iapetus. The spacecraft rotated while orbiting the moon, to maintain a steady optical field. It had crossed the dawn line, presently at the middle of the inward-facing hemisphere. Thus it had left bare, crater-pocked land behind it in the dark, and was passing above sunlit glacier country. Whiteness dazzled, glittered in sparks and shards of color, reached fantastic shapes heavenward; cirques, crevasses, caverns brimmed with blue.

"I'm sorry," Jean Broberg whispered. "It's too beautiful, unbelievably beautiful, and . . . almost like the place where our game had brought us. Took us by surprise—"

"Huh!" Mark Danzig said. "You had a pretty good idea of what to expect, therefore you made your play go in the direction of something that resembled it. Don't tell me any different. I've watched these acts for eight years."

Colin Scobie made a savage gesture. Spin and gravity were too slight to give noticeable weight, and his movement sent him flying through the air, across the crowded cabin. He checked himself by a handhold just short of the chemist. "Are you calling Jean a liar?" he growled.

Most times he was cheerful, in a bluff fashion. Perhaps because of that, he suddenly appeared menacing. He was a big, sandy-haired man in his mid-thirties; a coverall did not disguise the muscles beneath, and the scowl on his face brought forth its ruggedness.

"Please!" Broberg exclaimed. "Not a quarrel, Colin."

The geologist glanced back at her. She was slender and fine-featured. At her age of forty-two, despite longevity treatment, the reddish-brown hair that fell to her shoulders was becoming streaked with white, and lines were engraved around large gray eyes.

"Mark is right," she sighed. "We're here to do science, not daydream." She reached forth to touch Scobie's arm, smiling shyly. "You're still full of your Kendrick persona, aren't you? Gallant, protective—" She stopped. Her voice had quickened with more than a hint of Ricia. She covered her lips and flushed again. A tear broke free and sparkled off on air currents. She forced a laugh. "But I'm just physicist Broberg, wife of astronomer Tom, mother of Johnnie and Billy."

Her glance went Saturnward, as if seeking the ship where her family waited. She might have spied it, too, as a star that moved among stars by the solar sail. However, that was now furled, and naked vision could not find even such huge hulls as *Chronos* possessed, across millions of kilometers.

Luis Garcilaso asked from his pilot's chair: "What harm if we carry on our little *commedia dell' arte*?" His Arizona drawl soothed the ear. "We won't be landin' for a while yet, and everything's on automatic till then." He was small, swarthy, and deft, still in his twenties.

Danzig twisted his leathery countenance into a frown. At sixty, thanks to his habits as well as to longevity, he kept springiness in a lank frame; he could joke about wrinkles and encroaching baldness. In this hour, he set humor aside.

"Do you mean you don't know what's the matter?" His beak of a nose pecked at a scanner screen which magnified the moonscape. "Almight God! That's a new world we're about to touch down on—tiny, but a world, and strange in ways we can't guess. Nothing's been here before us except one unmanned flyby and one unmanned lander that soon quit sending. We can't rely on meters and cameras alone. We've got to use our eyes and brains."

He addressed Scobie. "You should realize that in your bones, Colin, if nobody else aboard does. You've worked on Luna as well as Earth. In spite of all the settlements, in spite of all the study that's been done, did you never hit any nasty surprises?"

The burly man had recovered his temper. Into his own voice came a softness that recalled the serenity of the Idaho mountains from which he hailed. "True," he admitted. "There's no such thing as having too much information when you're off Earth, or enough information, for that matter." He paused. "Nevertheless, timidity can be as dangerous as rashness—not that you're timid, Mark," he added in haste. "Why, you and Rachel could've been in a nice O'Neill on a nice pension—"

Danzig relaxed and smiled. "This was a challenge, if I may sound pompous. Just the same, we want to get home when we're finished here. We should be in time for the Bar Mitzvah of a great-grandson or two. Which requires staying alive."

"My point is," Scobie said, "if you let yourself get buffaloed, you may end up in a worse bind than—Oh, never mind. You're probably right, and we should not have begun fantasizing. The spectacle sort of grabbed us. It won't happen again."

Yet when Scobie's eyes looked anew on the glacier, they had not quite the dispassion of a scientist in them. Nor did Broberg's or Garcilaso's. Danzig slammed fist into palm. "The game, the damned childish game," he muttered, too low for his companions to hear. "Was nothing saner possible for them?"

2

Was nothing saner possible for them? Perhaps not.

If we are to answer the question, we should first review some history. When early industrial operations in space offered the hope of rescuing civilization, and Earth, from ruin, then greater knowledge of sister planets, prior to their development, became a clear necessity. The effort started with Mars, the least hostile. No natural law forbade sending small manned spacecraft yonder. What did was the absurdity of using as much fuel, time, and effort as were required, in order that three or four persons might spend a few days in a single locality.

Construction of the *J. Peter Vajk* took longer and cost more, but paid off when it, virtually a colony, spread its immense solar sail and took a thousand people to their goal in half a year and in comparative comfort. The payoff grew overwhelming when they, from orbit, launched Earthward the beneficiated minerals of Phobos that they did not need for their own purposes. Those purposes, of course, turned on the truly thorough, long-term study of Mars, and included landings of auxiliary craft, for ever-lengthier stays, all over the surface.

Sufficient to remind you of this much; no need to detail the triumphs of the same basic concept throughout the inner Solar System, as far as Jupiter. The tragedy of the *Vladimir* became a reason to try again for Mercury, and, in a left-handed, political way, pushed the Britannic-American consortium into its *Chronos* project.

They named the ship better than they knew. Sailing time to Saturn was eight years.

Not only the scientists must be healthy, lively-minded people. Crewfolk, technicians, medics, constables, teachers, clergy, entertainers—every element of an entire community must be. Each must command more than a single skill, for emergency backup, and keep those skills alive by regular, tedious rehearsal. The environment was limited and austere; communication with home was soon a matter of beamcasts; cosmopolitans found themselves in what amounted to an isolated village. What were they to *do*?

Assigned tasks. Civic projects, especially work on improving the interior of the vessel. Research, or writing a book, or the study of a subject, or sports, or hobby clubs, or service and handicraft enterprises, or more private interactions, or—There was a wide choice of television tapes, but Central Control made sets usable for only three hours in twenty-four. You dared not get into the habit of passivity.

Individuals grumbled, squabbled, formed and dissolved cliques, formed and dissolved marriages or less explicit relationships, begot and raised occasional children, worshipped, mocked, learned, yearned, and for the most part found reasonable satisfaction in life. But for some, including a large proportion of the gifted, what made the difference between this and misery were their psychodramas.

—Minamoto

Dawn crept past the ice, out onto the rock. It was a light both dim and harsh, yet sufficient to give Garcilaso the last data he wanted for descent.

The hiss of the motor died away. A thump shivered through the hull, landing jacks leveled it, and stillness fell. The crew did not speak for a while. They were staring out at Iapetus.

Immediately around them was desolation like that which reigns in much of the Solar System. A darkling plain curved visibly away to a horizon that, at man-height, was a bare three kilometers distant; higher up in the cabin, you could see farther, but that only sharpened the sense of being on a minute ball awhirl among the stars. The ground was thinly covered with cosmic dust and gravel; here and there a minor crater or an upthrust mass lifted out of the regolith to cast long, knife-edged, utterly black shadows. Light reflections lessened the number of visible stars, turning heaven into a bowlful of night. Halfway between the zenith and the south, half-Saturn and its rings made the vista beautiful.

Likewise did the glacier—or the glaciers? Nobody was sure. The sole knowledge was that, seen from afar, Iapetus gleamed bright as the western end of its orbit and grew dull at the eastern end, because one side was covered with whitish material while the other side was not; the dividing line passed nearly beneath the planet which it eternally faced. The probes from *Chronos* had reported the layer was thick, with puzzling spectra that varied from place to place, and little more about it.

In this hour, four humans gazed across pitted emptiness and saw wonder rear over the world-rim. From north to south went ramparts, battlements, spires, depths, peaks, cliffs, their shapes and shadings an infinity of fantasies. On the right Saturn cast soft amber, but that was nearly lost in the glare from the east, where a sun dwarfed almost to stellar size nonetheless blazed too fierce to look at, just above the summit. There the silvery sheen exploded in brilliance, diamond-glitter of shattered light, chill blues and greens; dazzled to tears, eyes saw the vision glimmer and waver, as if it boarded on dreamland, or on Faerie. But despite all delicate intricacies, underneath was a sense of chill and of brutal mass: here dwelt also the Frost Giants.

Broberg was the first to breathe forth a word. "The City of Ice."

"Magic," said Garcilaso as low. "My spirit could lose itself forever, wanderin' yonder. I'm not sure I'd mind. My cave is nothin' like this, nothin'—"

"Wait a minute!" snapped Danzig in alarm.

"Oh, yes. Curb the imagination, please." Though Scobie was quick to utter sobrieties, they sounded drier than needful. "We know from probe transmissions the scarp is, well, Grand Canyon-like. Sure, it's more spectacular than we realized, which I suppose makes it still more of a mystery." He turned to Broberg. "I've never seen ice or snow as sculptured as this. Have you, Jean? You've mentioned visiting a lot of mountain and winter scenery when you were a girl in Canada."

The physicist shook her head. "No. Never. It doesn't seem possible. What could have done it? There's no weather here . . . is there?"

"Perhaps the same phenomenon is responsible that laid a hemisphere bare," Danzig suggested.

"Or that covered a hemisphere," Scobie said. "An object seventeen hundred kilometers across shouldn't have gases, frozen or otherwise. Unless it's a ball of such stuff clear through, like a comet, which we know it's not." As if to demonstrate, he unclipped a pair of pliers from a nearby tool rack, tossed it, and caught it on its slow way down. His own ninety kilos of mass weighed about seven. For that, the satellite must be essentially rocky.

Garcilaso registered impatience. "Let's stop tradin' facts and theories we already know about, and start findin' answers."

Rapture welled in Broberg. "Yes, let's get out. Over *there*."

"Hold on," protested Danzig as Garcilaso and Scobie nodded eagerly. "You can't be serious. Caution, step-by-step advance—"

"No, it's too wonderful for that," Broberg's tone shivered.

"Yeah, to hell with fiddlin' around," Garcilaso said. "We need at least a preliminary scout right away."

The furrows deepened in Danzig's visage. "You mean you too, Luis? But you're our pilot!"

"On the ground I'm general assistant, chief cook, and bottle washer to you scientists. Do you think I want to sit idle, with somethin' like that to explore?" Garcilaso calmed his voice. "Besides, if I should come to grief, any of you can fly back, given a bit of radio talk from *Chronos* and a final approach under remote control."

"It's quite reasonable, Mark," Scobie argued. "Contrary to doctrine, true; but doctrine was made for us, not vice versa. A short distance, low gravity, and we'll be on the lookout for hazards. The point is, until we have some notion of what that ice is like, we don't know what the devil to pay attention to in this vicinity, either. No, first we'll take a quick jaunt. When we return, then we'll plan."

Danzig stiffened. "May I remind you, if anything goes wrong, help is at least a hundred hours away? An auxiliary like this can't boost any higher if it's to get back, and it'd take longer than that to disengage the big boats from Saturn and Titan."

Scobie reddened at the implied insult. "And may I remind you: on the ground I am the captain. I say an immediate reconnaissance is safe and desirable. Stay behind if you want—In fact, yes, you must. Doctrine is right in saying the vessel mustn't be deserted."

Danzig studied him for several seconds before murmuring, "Luis goes, though, is that it?"

"Yes!" cried Garcilaso so that the cabin rang.

Broberg patted Danzig's limp hand. "It's okay, Mark," she said gently. "We'll bring back samples for you to study. After that, I wouldn't be surprised but what the best ideas about procedure will be yours."

He shook his head. Suddenly he looked very tired. "No," he replied in a monotone, "that won't happen. You see, I'm only a hardnosed industrial chemist who saw this expedition as a chance to do interesting research. The whole way through space, I kept myself busy with ordinary affairs, including, you remember, a couple of inventions I'd wanted the leisure to develop. You three, you're younger, you're romantics—"

"Aw, come off it, Mark." Scobie tried to laugh. "Maybe Jean

and Luis are, a little, but me, I'm about as otherworldly as a plate of haggis."

"You played the game, year after year, until at last the game started playing you. That's what's going on this minute, no matter how you rationalize your motives." Danzig's gaze on the geologist, who was his friend, lost the defiance that had been in it and turned wistful. "You might try recalling Delia Ames."

Scobie bristled. "What about her? The business was hers and mine, nobody else's."

"Except afterward she cried on Rachel's shoulder, and Rachel doesn't keep secrets from me. Don't worry, I'm not about to blab. Anyhow, Delia got over it. But if you'd recollect objectively, you'd see what had happened to you, already three years ago."

Scobie set his jaw. Danzig smiled in the left corner of his mouth. "No, I suppose you can't," he went on. "I admit I had no idea either, till now, how far the process had gone. At least keep your fantasies in the background while you're outside, will you? Can you?"

In half a decade of travel, Scobie's apartment had become idiosyncratically his—perhaps more so than was usual, since he remained a bachelor who seldom had women visitors for longer than a few nightwatches at a time. Much of the furniture he had made himself; the agrosections of *Chronos* produced wood, hide, and fiber as well as food and fresh air. His handiwork ran to massiveness and archaic carved decorations. Most of what he wanted to read he screened from the data banks, of course, but a shelf held a few old books—Childe's border ballads, an eighteenth-century family Bible (despite his agnosticism), a copy of *The Machinery of Freedom*, which had nearly disintegrated but displayed the signature of the author, and other valued miscellany. Above them stood a model of a sailboat in which he had cruised Northern European waters, and a trophy he had won in handball aboard this ship. On the bulkheads hung his fencing sabers and numerous pictures—of parents and siblings, of wilderness areas he had tramped on Earth, of castles and mountains and heaths in Scotland where he had often been too, of his geological team on Luna, of Thomas Jefferson and, imagined, Robert the Bruce.

On a certain evenwatch he had, though, been seated before his telescreen. Lights were turned low in order that he might fully savor the image. Auxiliary craft were out in a joint exercise, and a couple of their personnel used the opportunity to beam back views of what they saw.

That was splendor. Starful space made a chalice for *Chronos*. The two huge, majestically counter-rotating cylinders, the entire complex of linkages, ports, locks, shields, collectors, transmitters, docks, all became Japanesely exquisite at a distance of several hundred kilometers. It was the solar sail which filled most of the screen, like a turning golden sun-wheel; yet remote vision could also appreciate its spiderweb intricacy, soaring and subtle curvatures, even the less-than-gossamer thinness. A mightier work than the Pyramids, a finer work than a refashioned chromosome, the ship moved on toward a Saturn which had become the second-brightest beacon in the firmament.

The doorchime hauled Scobie out of his exultation. As he started across the deck, he stubbed his toe on a table leg. Coriolis force caused that. It was slight, when a hull this size spun to give a full gee of weight, and a thing to which he had long since adapted; but now and then he got so interested in something that Terrestrial habits returned. He swore at his absentmindedness, good-naturedly, since he anticipated a pleasurable time.

When he opened the door, Delia Ames entered in a single stride. At once she closed it behind her and stood braced against it. She was a tall blond woman who did electronics maintenance and kept up a number of outside activities. "Hey!" Scobie said. "What's wrong? You look like"—he tried for levity—"something my cat would've dragged in, if we had any mice or beached fish aboard."

She drew a ragged breath. Her Australian accent thickened till he had trouble understanding: "I . . . today . . . I happened to be at the same cafeteria table as George Harding—"

Unease tingled through Scobie. Harding worked in Ames's department but had much more in common with him. In the game group to which they both belonged, Harding likewise took a vaguely ancestral role, N'Kuma the Lionslayer.

"What happened?" Scobie asked.

Woe stared back at him. "He mentioned . . . you and he and the rest . . . you'd be taking your next holiday together . . . to carry on your . . . your bloody act uninterrupted."

"Well, yes. Work at the new park over in Starboard Hull will be suspended till enough metal's been recycled for the water pipes.

The area will be vacant, and my gang has arranged to spend a week's worth of days—"

"But you and I were going to Lake Armstrong!"

"Uh, wait, that was just a notion we talked about, no definite plan yet, and this is such an unusual chance—Later, sweetheart. I'm sorry." He took her hands. They felt cold. He essayed a smile. "Now, c'mon, we were going to cook a festive dinner together and afterward spend a, shall we say, quiet evening at home. But for a start, this absolutely gorgeous presentation on the screen—"

She jersked free of him. The gesture seemed to calm her. "No, thanks," she said, flat-voiced. "Not when you'd rather be with that Broberg woman. I only came by to tell you in person I'm getting out of the way of you two."

"*Huh*?" He stepped back. "What the flaming hell do you mean?"

"You know jolly well."

"I don't! She, I, she's happily married, got two kids, she's older than me, we're friends, sure, but there's never been a thing between us that wasn't in the open and on the level—" Scobie swallowed. "You suppose maybe I'm in love with her?"

Ames looked away. Her fingers writhed together. "I'm not about to go on being a mere convenience to you, Colin. You have plenty of those. Myself, I'd hoped—But I was wrong, and I'm going to cut my losses before they get worse."

"But . . . Dee, I swear I haven't fallen for anybody else, and I . . . I swear you're more than a body to me, you're a fine person—" She stood mute and withdrawn. Scobie gnawed his lip before he could tell her. "Okay, I admit it, the main reason I volunteered for this trip was I'd lost out in a love affair on Earth. Not that the project doesn't interest me, but I've come to realize what a big chunk out of my life it is. You, more than any other woman, Dee, you've gotten me to feel better about the situation."

She grimaced. "But not as much as your psychodrama has, right?"

"Hey, you must think I'm obsessed with the game. I'm not. It's fun and—oh, maybe 'fun' is too weak a word—but anyhow, it's just little bunches of people getting together fairly regularly to play. Like my fencing, or a chess club, or, or anything."

She squared her shoulders. "Well, then," she asked, "will you cancel the date you've made and spend your holiday with me?"

"I, uh, I can't do that. Not at this stage. Kendrick isn't off on the periphery of current events, he's closely involved with everybody else. If I didn't show, it'd spoil things for the rest."

Her glance steadied upon him. "Very well. A promise is a promise, or so I imagined. But afterward—Don't be afraid. I'm not trying to trap you. That would be no good, would it? However, if I maintain this liaison of ours, will you phase yourself out of your game?"

"I can't—" Anger seized him. "No, God damn it!" he roared.

"Then goodbye, Colin," she said, and departed. He stared for minutes at the door she had shut behind her.

Unlike the large Titan- and Saturn-vicinity explorers, landers on the airless moons were simply modified Luna-to-space shuttles, reliable, but with limited capabilities. When the blocky shape had dropped below the horizon, Garcilaso said into his radio: "We've lost sight of the boat, Mark. I must say it improves the view." One of the relay microsatellites which had been sown in orbit passed his words on.

"Better start blazing your trail, then," Danzig reminded.

"My, my, you *are* a fussbudget, aren't you?" Nevertheless Garcilaso unholstered the squirt gun at his hip and splashed a vividly fluorescent circle of paint on the ground. He would do it at eyeball intervals until his party reached the glacier. Except where dust lay thick over the regolith, footprints were faint under the feeble gravity, and absent when a walker crossed continuous rock.

Walker? No, leaper. The three bounded exultant, little hindered by spacesuits, life support units, tool and ration packs. The naked land fled from their haste, and ever higher, ever clearer and more glorious to see, loomed the ice ahead of them.

There was no describing it, not really. You could speak of lower slopes and palisades above, to a mean height of perhaps a hundred meters, with spires towering farther still. You could speak of gracefully curved tiers going up those braes, of lacy parapets and fluted crags and arched openings to caves filled with wonders, of mysterious blues in the depths and greens where light streamed through translucencies, of gem-sparkle across whiteness where radiance and shadow wove mandalas—and none of it would convey anything more than Scobie's earlier, altogether inadequate comparison to the Grand Canyon.

"Stop," he said for the dozenth time. "I want to take a few pictures."

"Will anybody understand them who hasn't been here?" whispered Broberg.

"Probably not," said Garcilaso in the same hushed tone. "Maybe no one but us ever will."

"What do you mean by that?" demanded Danzig's voice.

"Never mind," snapped Scobie.

"I think I know," the chemist said. "Yes, it is a great piece of scenery, but you're letting it hypnotize you."

"If you don't cut out that drivel," Scobie warned, "we'll cut you out of the circuit. Damn it, we've got work to do. Get off our backs."

Danzig gusted a sigh. "Sorry. Uh, are you finding any clues to the nature of that—that thing?"

Scobie focused his camera. "Well," he said, partly mollified, "the different shades and textures, and no doubt the different shapes, seem to confirm what the reflection spectra from the flyby suggested. The composition is a mixture, or a jumble, or both, of several materials, and varies from place to place. Water ice is obvious, but I feel sure of carbon dioxide too, and I'd bet on ammonia, methane, and presumably lesser amounts of other stuff."

"Methane? Could that stay solid at ambient temperatures, in a vacuum?"

"We'll have to find out for sure. However, I'd guess that most of the time it's cold enough, at least for methane strata that occur down inside where there's pressure on them."

Within the vitryl globe of her helmet, Broberg's features showed delight. "Wait!" she cried. "I have an idea—about what happened to the probe that landed." She drew a breath. "It came down almost at the foot of the glacier, you recall. Our view of the site from space seemed to indicate that an avalanche buried it, but we couldn't understand how that might have been triggered. Well, suppose a methane layer at exactly the wrong location melted. Heat radiation from the jets may have warmed it, and later the radar beam used to map contours added the last few degrees necessary. The stratum flowed, and down came everything that had rested on top of it."

"Plausible," Scobie said. "Congratulations, Jean."

"Nobody thought of the possibility in advance?" Garcilaso scoffed. "What kind of scientists have we got along?"

"The kind who were being overwhelmed by work after we reached Saturn, and still more by data input," Scobie answered. "The universe is bigger than you or anybody can realize, hot-shot."

"Oh. Sure. No offense." Garcilaso's glance returned to the ice. "Yes, we'll never run out of mysteries, will we?"

"Never." Broberg's eyes glowed enormous. "At the heart of things will always be magic. The Elf King rules—"

Scobie returned his camera to its pouch. "Stow the gab and move on," he ordered curtly.

His gaze locked for an instant with Broberg's. In the weird, mingled light, it could be seen that she went pale, then red, before she sprang off beside him.

Ricia had gone alone into Moonwood on Midsummer Eve. The King found her there and took her unto him as she had hoped. Ecstasy became terror when he afterward bore her off; yet her captivity in the City of Ice brought her many more such hours, and beauties and marvels unknown among mortals. Alvarlan, her mentor, sent his spirit in quest of her, and was himself beguiled by what he found. It was an effort of will for him to tell Sir Kendrick of the Isles where she was, albeit he pledged his help in freeing her.

N'Kuma the Lionslayer, Bela of Eastmarch, Karina Far West, Lady Aurelia, Olav Harpmaster had none of them been present when this happened.

The glacier (a wrong name for something that might have no counterpart in the Solar System) lifted off the plain abruptly as a wall. Standing there, the three could no longer see the heights. They could, though, see that the slope which curved steeply upward to a filigree-topped edge was not smooth. Shadows lay blue in countless small craters. The sun had climbed just sufficiently high to beget them; an Iapetan day is more than seventy-nine of Earth's.

Danzig's question crackled in their earphones: "Now are you satisfied? Will you come back before a fresh landslide catches you?"

"It won't," Scobie replied. "We aren't a vehicle, and the local configuration has clearly been stable for centuries or better. Besides, what's the point of a manned expedition if nobody investigates anything?"

"I'll see if I can climb," Garcilaso offered.

"No, wait," Scobie commanded. "I've had experience with mountains and snowpacks, for whatever that may be worth. Let me work out a route for us first."

"You're going onto that stuff, the whole gaggle of you?" exploded Danzig. "Have you completely lost your minds?"

Scobie's brow and lips tightened. "Mark, I warn you again, if you don't get your emotions under control we'll cut you off. We'll hike on a ways if I decide it's safe."

He paced back and forth, in floating low-weight fashion, while he surveyed the jökull. Layers and blocks of distinct substances were plain to see, like separate ashlars laid by an elvish mason—where they were not so huge that a giant must have been at work. The craterlets might be sentry posts on this lowest embankment of the City's defenses . . .

Garcilaso, most vivacious of men, stood motionless and let his vision lose itself in the sight. Broberg knelt down to examine the ground, but her own gaze kept wandering aloft.

Finally she beckoned. "Colin, come over here, please," she said. "I believe I've made a discovery."

Scobie joined her. As she rose, she scooped a handful of fine black particles off the shards on which she stood and let it trickle from her glove. "I suspect this is the reason the boundary of the ice is sharp," she told him.

"What is?" Danzig inquired from afar. He got no answer.

"I noticed more and more dust as we went along," Broberg continued. "If it fell on patches and lumps of frozen stuff, isolated from the main mass, and covered them, it would absorb solar heat till they melted or, likelier, sublimed. Even water molecules would escape to space, in this weak gravity. The main mass was too big for that; square-cube law. Dust grains there would simply melt their way down a short distance, then be covered as surrounding material collapsed on them, and the process would stop."

"H'm." Scobie raised a hand to stroke his chin, encountered his helmet, and sketched a grin at himself. "Sounds reasonable. But where did so much dust come from—and the ice, for that matter?"

"I think—" Her voice dropped until he could barely hear, and her look went the way of Garcilaso's. His remained upon her face, profiled against stars. "I think this bears out your comet hypothesis,

Colin. A comet struck Iapetus. It came from the direction it did because it got so near Saturn that it was forced to swing in a hairpin bend around the planet. It was enormous; the ice of it covered almost a hemisphere, in spite of much more being vaporized and lost. The dust is partly from it, partly generated by the impact."

He clasped her armored shoulder. "*Your* theory, Jean. I was not the first to propose a comet, but you're the first to corroborate with details."

She didn't appear to notice, except that she murmured further. "Dust can account for the erosion that made those lovely formations, too. It caused differential melting and sublimation on the surface, according to the patterns it happened to fall in and the mixes of ices it clung to, until it was washed away or encysted. The craters, these small ones and the major ones we've observed from above, they have a separate but similar origin. Meteorites—"

"Whoa, there," he objected. "Any sizable meteorite would release enough energy to steam off most of the entire field."

"I know. Which shows the comet collision was recent, less than a thousand years ago, or we wouldn't be seeing this miracle today. Nothing big has since happened to strike, yet. I'm thinking of little stones, cosmic sand, in prograde orbits around Saturn so that they hit with low relative speed. Most simply make dimples in the ice. Lying there, however, they collect solar heat because they're dark, and re-radiate it to melt away their surroundings, till they sink beneath. The concavities they leave reflect incident radiation from side to side, and thus continue to grow. The pothole effect. And again, because the different ices have different properties, you don't get perfectly smooth craters, but those fantastic bowls we saw before we landed."

"By God!" Scobie hugged her. "You're a genius."

Helmet against helmet, she smiled and said, "No. It's obvious, once you've seen for yourself." She was quiet for a bit while still they held each other. "Scientific intuition is a funny thing, I admit," she went on at last. "Considering the problem, I was hardly aware of my logical mind. What I thought was—the City of Ice, made with starstones out of that which a god called down from heaven—"

"Jesus Maria!" Garcilaso spun about to stare at them.

Scobie released the woman. "We'll go after confirmation," he said unsteadily. "To the large crater we spotted a few klicks inward. The surface appears quite safe to walk on."

"I called that crater the Elf King's Dance Hall," Broberg mused, as if a dream were coming back to her.

"Have a care." Garcilaso's laugh rattled. "Heap big medicine yonder. The King is only an inheritor; it was giants who built these walls, for the gods."

"Well, I've got to find a way in, don't I?" Scobie responded.

"Indeed," *Alvarlan says*. "I cannot guide you from this point. My spirit can only see through mortal eyes. I can but lend you my counsel, until we have neared the gates."

"Are you sleepwalking in that fairy tale of yours?" Danzig yelled. "Come back before you get yourselves killed!"

"Will you dry up?" Scobie snarled. "It's nothing but a style of talk we've got between us. If you can't understand that, you've got less use of your brain than we do."

"Listen, won't you? I didn't say you're crazy. You don't have delusions or anything like that. I do say you've steered your fantasies toward this kind of place, and now the reality has reinforced them till you're under a compulsion you don't recognize. Would you go ahead so recklessly anywhere else in the universe? Think!"

"That does it. We'll resume contact after you've had time to improve your manners." Scobie snapped off his main radio switch. The circuits that stayed active served for close-by communication but had no power to reach an orbital relay. His companions did likewise.

The three faced the awesomeness before them. "You can help me find the Princess when we are inside, Alvarlan," *Kendrick says*.

"That I can and will," *the sorcerer vows*.

"I wait for you, most steadfast of my lovers," *Ricia croons*.

Alone in the spacecraft, Danzig well-nigh sobbed, "Oh, damn that game forever!" The sound fell away into emptiness.

3

To condemn psychodrama, even in its enhanced form, would be to condemn human nature.

It begins in childhood. Play is necessary to an immature mammal, a means of learning to handle the body, the perceptions, and the outside world. The young human plays, must play, with its brain too. The more intelligent the child, the more its imagination needs exercise. There are degrees of activity, from the passive watching of a show on a screen, onward through reading, daydreaming, storytelling, and psychodrama . . . for which the child has no such fancy name.

We cannot give this behavior any single description, for the shape and course it takes depends on an endless number of variables. Sex, age, culture, and companions are only the most obvious. For example, in pre-electronic North America little girls would often play "house" while little boys played "cowboys and Indians" or "cops and robbers," whereas nowadays a mixed group of their descendants might play "dolphins" or "astronauts and aliens." In essence, a small band forms, and each individual makes up a character to portray or borrows one from fiction. Simple props may be employed, such as toy weapons, or a chance object—a stick, for instance—may be declared something else such as a metal detector, or a thing may be quite imaginary, as the scenery almost always is. The children then act out a drama which they compose as they go along. When they cannot physically perform a certain action, they describe it. ("I jump real high, like you can do on Mars, an' come out over the edge o' that ol' Valles Marineris, an' take that bandit by surprise.") A large cast of characters, especially villains, frequently comes into existence by fiat.

The most imaginative member of the troupe dominates the game and the evolution of the story line, though in a rather subtle fashion, through offering the most vivid possibilities. The rest, however, are brighter than average; psychodrama in this highly developed form does not appeal to everybody.

For those to whom it does, the effects are beneficial and lifelong. Besides increasing their creativity through use, it lets them try out a play version of different adult roles and experiences. Thereby they begin to acquire insight into adulthood.

Such playacting ends when adolescence commences, if not earlier—but only in that form, and not necessarily forever in it. Grown-ups have many dream-games. This is plain to see in lodges, for example, with their titles, costumes, and ceremonies; but does it not likewise animate all pageantry, every ritual? To what extent are our heroisms, sacrifices, and self-aggrandizements the acting out of personae that we maintain? Some thinkers have attempted to trace this element through every aspect of society.

Here, though, we are concerned with overt psychodrama among

adults. In Western civilization it first appeared on a noticeable scale during the middle twentieth century. Psychiatrists found it a powerful diagnostic and therapeutic technique. Among ordinary folk, war and fantasy games, many of which involved identification with imaginary or historical characters, became increasingly popular. In part this was doubtless a retreat from the restrictions and menaces of that unhappy period, but likely in larger part it was a revolt of the mind against the inactive entertainment, notably television, which had come to dominate recreation.

The Chaos ended those activities. Everybody knows about their revival in recent times—for healthier reasons, one hopes. By projecting three-dimensional scenes and appropriate sounds from a data bank—or, better yet, by having a computer produce them to order—players gained a sense of reality that intensified their mental and emotional commitment. Yet in those games that went on for episode after episode, year after real-time year, whenever two or more members of a group could get together to play, they found themselves less and less dependent on such appurtenances. It seemed that, through practice, they had regained the vivid imaginations of their childhoods, and could make anything, or airy nothing itself, into the objects and the worlds they desired.

I have deemed it necessary thus to repeat the obvious in order that we may see it in perspective. The news beamed from Saturn has brought widespread revulsion. (Why? What buried fears have been touched? This is subject matter for potentially important research.) Overnight, adult psychodrama has become unpopular; it may become extinct. That would, in many ways, be a worse tragedy than what has occurred yonder. There is no reason to suppose that the game ever harmed any mentally sound person on Earth; on the contrary. Beyond doubt, it has helped astronauts stay sane and alert on long, difficult missions. If it has no more medical use, that is because psychotherapy has become a branch of applied biochemistry.

And this last fact, the modern world's death of experience with madness, is at the root of what happened. Although he could not have foreseen the exact outcome, a twentieth-century psychiatrist might have warned against spending eight years, an unprecedented stretch of time, in as strange an environment as the *Chronos*. Strange it certainly has been, despite all efforts—limited, totally man-controlled, devoid of countless cues for which our evolution on

Earth has fashioned us. Extraterrestrial colonists have, thus far, had available to them any number of simulations and compensations, of which close, full contact with home and frequent opportunities to visit there are probably the most significant. Sailing time to Jupiter was long, but half of that to Saturn. Moreover, because they were earlier, scientists in the *Zeus* had much research to occupy them en route, which it would be pointless for later travelers to duplicate; by then, the interplanetary medium between the two giants held few surprises.

Contemporary psychologists were aware of this. They understood that the persons most adversely affected would be the most intelligent, imaginative, and dynamic—those who were supposed to make the very discoveries at Saturn which were the purpose of the undertaking. Being less familiar than their predecessors with the labyrinth that lies, Minotaur-haunted, beneath every human consciousness, the psychologists expected purely benign consequences of whatever psychodramas the crew engendered.

—Minamoto

Assignments to teams had not been made in advance of departure. It was sensible to let professional capabilities reveal themselves and grow on the voyage, while personal relationships did the same. Eventually such factors would help in deciding what individuals should train for what tasks. Long-term participation in a group of players normally forged bonds of friendship that were desirable, if the members were otherwise qualified.

In real life, Scobie always observed strict propriety toward Broberg. She was attractive, but she was monogamous, and he had no wish to alienate her. Besides, he liked her husband. (Tom did not partake of the game. As an astronomer, he had plenty to keep his attention happily engaged.) They had played for a couple of years, and their group had acquired as many characters as it could accommodate in a narrative whose milieu and people were becoming complex, before Scobie and Broberg spoke of anything intimate.

By then, the story they enacted was doing so, and maybe it was not altogether by chance that they met when both had several idle hours. This was in the weightless recreation area at the spin axis. They tumbled through aerobatics, shouting and laughing, until they were pleasantly tired, went to the clubhouse, turned in their wingsuits, and showered. They had not seen each other nude before; neither commented, but he did not hide his enjoyment of the sight, while she colored and averted her glance as tactfully as she was able. Afterward, their clothes resumed, they decided on a drink before they went home, and sought the lounge.

Since evenwatch was approaching nightwatch, they had the place to themselves. At the bar, he thumbed a chit for Scotch, she for Pinot Chardonnay. The machine obliged them and they carried their refreshments out onto the balcony. Seated at a table, they looked across immensity. The clubhouse was built into the support frame on a Lunar gravity level. Above them they saw the sky wherein they had been as birds; its reach did not seem any more hemmed in by far-spaced, spidery girders than it was by a few drifting clouds. Beyond, and straight ahead, decks opposite were a commingling of masses and shapes which the scant illumination at this hour turned into mystery. Among those shadows the humans made out woods, brooks, pools, turned hoary or agleam by the light of stars which filled the skyview strips. Right and left, the hull stretched off beyond sight, a dark in which such lamps as there were appeared lost.

The air was cool, slightly jasmine-scented, drenched with silence. Underneath and throughout, subliminally, throbbed the myriad pulses of the ship.

"Magnificent," Broberg said low, gazing outward. "What a surprise."

"Eh?" asked Scobie.

"I've only been here before in daywatch. I didn't anticipate a simple rotation of the reflectors would make it wonderful."

"Oh, I wouldn't sneer at the daytime view. Mighty impressive."

"Yes, but—but then you see too plainly that everything is man-made, nothing is wild or unknown or free. The sun blots out the stars; it's as though no universe existed beyond this shell we're in. Tonight is like being in Maranoa," *the kingdom of which Ricia is Princess, a kingdom of ancient things and ways, wildernesses, enchantments.*

"H'm, yeah, sometimes I feel trapped myself," Scobie admitted. "I thought I had a journey's worth of geological data to study, but my project isn't going anywhere very interesting."

"Same for me." Broberg straightened where she sat, turned to him, and smiled a trifle. The dusk softened her features, made them look young. "Not that we're entitled to self-pity. Here we are, safe and comfortable till we reach Saturn. After that we should never lack for excitement, or for material to work with on the way home."

"True." Scobie raised his glass. "Well, skoal. Hope I'm not mispronouncing that."

"How should I know?" she laughed. "My maiden name was Almyer."

"That's right, you've adopted Tom's surname. I wasn't thinking. Though that is rather unusual these days, hey?"

She spread her hands. "My family was well-to-do, but they were—are—Jerusalem Catholics. Strict about certain things; archaistic, you might say." She lifted her wine and sipped. "Oh, yes, I've left the Church, but in several ways the Church will never leave me."

"I see. Not to pry, but, uh, this does account for some traits of yours I couldn't help wondering about."

She regarded him over the rim of her glass. "Like what?"

"Well, you've got a lot of life in you, vigor, a sense of fun, but you're also—what's the word?—uncommonly domestic. You've told me you were a quiet faculty member of Yukon University till you married Tom." Scobie grinned. "Since you two kindly invited me to your last anniversary party, and I know your present age, I deduced that you were thirty then." Unmentioned was the likelihood that she had still been a virgin. "Nevertheless—oh, forget it. I said I don't want to pry."

"Go ahead, Colin," she urged. "That line from Burns sticks in my mind, since you introduced me to his poetry. 'To see ourselves as others see us!' Since it looks as if we may visit the same moon—"

Scobie took a hefty dollop of Scotch. "Aw, nothing much," he said, unwontedly diffident. "If you must know, well, I have the impression that being in love wasn't the single good reason you had for marrying Tom. He'd already been accepted for this expedition, and given your personal qualifications, that would get you in too. In short, you'd grown tired of routine respectability and here was how you could kick over the traces. Am I right?"

"Yes." Her gaze dwelt on him. "You're more perceptive than I supposed."

"No, not really. A roughneck rockhound. But Ricia's made it

plain to see that you're more than a demure wife, mother, and scientist—" She parted her lips. He raised a palm. "No, please, let me finish. I know it's bad manners to claim somebody's persona is a wish fulfilment, and I'm not doing that. Of course you don't want to be a free-roving, free-loving female scamp, any more than I want to ride around cutting down assorted enemies. Still, if you'd been born and raised in the world of our game, I feel sure you'd be a lot like Ricia. And that potential is part of you, Jean." He tossed off his drink. "If I've said too much, please excuse me. Want a refill?"

"I'd better not, but don't let me stop you."

"You won't." He rose and bounded off.

When he returned, he saw that she had been observing him through the vitryl door. As he sat down, she smiled, leaned a bit across the table, and told him softly: "I'm glad you said what you did. Now I can declare what a complicated man Kendrick reveals you to be."

"What?" Scobie asked in honest surprise. "Come on! He's a sword-and-shield tramp, a fellow who likes to travel, same as me; and in my teens I was a brawler, same as him."

"He may lack polish, but he's a chivalrous knight, a compassionate overlord, a knower of sagas and traditions, an appreciator of poetry and music, a bit of a bard . . . Ricia misses him. When will he get back from his latest quest?"

"I'm bound home this minute. N'Kuma and I gave those pirates the slip and landed at Haverness two days ago. After we buried the swag, he wanted to visit Béla and Karina and join them in whatever they've been up to, so we bade goodbye for the time being." Scobie and Harding had lately taken a few hours to conclude that adventure of theirs. The rest of the group had been mundanely occupied for some while.

Broberg's eyes widened. "From Haverness to the Isles? But I'm in Castle Devaranda, right in between."

"I hoped you'd be."

"I can't wait to hear your story."

"I'm pushing on after dark. The moon is bright and I've got a pair of remounts I bought with a few gold pieces from the loot." *The dust rolls white beneath drumming hoofs. Where a horseshoe strikes a flint pebble, sparks fly ardent. Kendrick scowls.* "You, aren't you with . . . what's his name? . . . Joran the Red? I don't like him."

"I sent him packing a month ago. He got the idea that sharing my bed gave him authority over me. It was never anything but a romp. I stand alone on the Gerfalcon Tower, looking south over moonlit fields, and wonder how you fare. The road flows toward me like a gray river. Do I see a rider come at a gallop, far and far away?"

After many months of play, no image on a screen was necessary. *Pennons on the night wind stream athwart the stars.* "I arrive. I sound my horn to rouse the gatekeepers."

"How I do remember those merry notes—"

That same night, Kendrick and Ricia become lovers. Experienced in the game and careful of its etiquette, Scobie and Broberg uttered no details about the union; they did not touch each other and maintained only fleeting eye contact; the ultimate goodnights were very decorous. After all, this was a story they composed about two fictitious characters in a world that never was.

The lower slopes of the jökull rose in tiers which were themselves deeply concave; *the humans walked around their rims and admired the extravagant formations beneath. Names sprang onto lips: the Frost Garden, the Ghost Bridge, the Snow Queen's Throne, while Kendrick advances into the City, and Ricia awaits him at the Dance Hall, and the spirit of Alvarlan carries word between them so that it is as if already she too travels beside her knight.*

Nevertheless they proceeded warily, vigilant for signs of danger, especially whenever a change of texture or hue or anything else in the surface underfoot betokened a change in its nature.

Above the highest ledge reared a cliff too sheer to scale, Iapetan gravity or no, *the fortress wall.* However, from orbit the crew had spied a gouge in the vicinity, forming a pass, doubtless plowed by a small meteorite *in the war between the gods and the magicians, when stones chanted down from the sky wrought havoc so accursed that none dared afterward rebuild.* That was an eerie climb, hemmed in by heights which glimmered in the blue twilight they cast, heaven narrowed to a belt between them where stars seemed to blaze doubly brilliant.

"There must be guards at the opening," *Kendrick says.*

"A single guard," *answers the mind-whisper of Alvarlan,* "but he is a dragon. If you did battle with him, the noise and flame would bring every warrior here upon you. Fear not. I'll slip into his burnin' brain and weave him such a dream that he'll never see you."

"The King might sense the spell," *says Ricia through him*. "Since you'll be parted from us anyway while you ride the soul of that beast, Alvarlan, I'll seek him out and distract him."

Kendrick grimaces, knowing full well what means are hers to do that. She has told him how she longs for freedom and her knight; she has also hinted that elven lovemaking transcends the human. Does she wish for a final time before her rescue? . . . Well, Ricia and Kendrick have neither plighted nor practiced single troth. Assuredly Colin Scobie had not. He jerked forth a grin and continued through the silence that had fallen on all three.

They came out on top of the glacial mass and looked around them. Scobie whistled. Garcilaso stammered, "I-I-Jesus Christ!" Broberg smote her hands together.

Below them the precipice fell to the ledges, whose sculpturing took on a wholly new, eldritch aspect, gleam and shadow, until it ended at the plain. Seen from here aloft, the curvature of the moon made toes strain downward in boots, as if to cling fast and not be spun off among the stars which surrounded, rather than shone above, its ball. The spacecraft stood minute on dark, pocked stone, like a cenotaph raised to loneliness.

Eastward the ice reached beyond an edge of sight which was much closer. ("Yonder could be the rim of the world," Garcilaso said, and *Ricia replies*, "Yes, the City is nigh to there.") Bowls of different sizes, hillocks, crags, no two of them eroded the same way, turned its otherwise level stretch into a surreal maze. An arabesque openwork ridge which stood at the explorers' goal overtopped the horizon. Everything that was illuminated lay gently aglow. Radiant though the sun was, it cast the light of only, perhaps, five thousand full Lunas upon Earth. Southward, Saturn's great semidisc gave about one-half more Lunar shining; but in that direction, the wilderness sheened pale amber.

Scobie shook himself. "Well, shall we go?" His prosaic question jarred the others; Garcilaso frowned and Broberg winced.

She recovered. "Yes, hasten," *Ricia says*. "I am by myself once more. Are you out of the dragon, Alvarlan?"

"Aye," *the wizard informs her*. "Kendrick is safely behind a ruined palace. Tell us how best to reach you."

"You are at the time-gnawed Crown House. Before you lies the Street of the Shieldsmiths—"

Scobie's brows knitted. "It is noonday, when elves do not fare abroad," *Kendrick says* remindingly, commandingly. "I do not wish to encounter any of them. No fights, no complications. We are going to fetch you and escape, without further trouble."

Broberg and Garcilaso showed disappointment, but understood him. A game broke down when a person refused to accept something that a fellow player tried to put in. Often the narrative threads were not mended and picked up for many days. Broberg sighed.

"Follow the street to its end at a forum where a snow fountain springs," *Ricia directs*. "Cross, and continue on Aleph Zain Boulevard. You will know it by a gateway in the form of a skull with open jaws. If anywhere you see a rainbow flicker in the air, stand motionless until it has gone by, for it will be an auroral wolf . . ."

At a low-gravity lope, the distance took some thirty minutes to cover. In the later part, the three were forced to detour by great banks of an ice so fine-grained that it slid about under their bootsoles and tried to swallow them. Several of these lay at irregular intervals around their destination.

There the travelers stood again for a time in the grip of awe.

The bowl at their feet must reach down almost to bedrock, a hundred meters, and was twice as wide. On this rim lifted the wall they had seen from the cliff, an arc fifty meters long and high, nowhere thicker than five meters, pierced by intricate scrollwork, greenly agleam where it was not translucent. It was the uppermost edge of a stratum which made serrations down the crater. Other outcrops and ravines were more dreamlike yet . . . was that a unicorn's head, was that a colonnade of caryatids, was that an icicle bower . . .? The depths were a lake of cold blue shadow.

"You have come, Kendrick, beloved!" *cries Ricia, and casts herself into his arms.*

"Quiet," *warns the sending of Alvarlan the wise*. "Rouse not our immortal enemies."

"Yes, we must get back." Scobie blinked. "Judas priest, what possessed us? Fun is fun, but we sure have come a lot farther and faster than was smart, haven't we?"

"Let us stay for a little while," Broberg pleaded. "This is such a miracle—the Elf King's Dance Hall, which the Lord of the Dance built for him—"

"Remember, if we stay we'll be caught, and your captivity may be forever." Scobie thumbed his main radio switch. "Hello, Mark? Do you read me?"

Neither Broberg nor Garcilaso made that move. They did not hear Danzig's voice: "Oh, yes! I've been hunkered over the set gnawing my knuckles. How are you?"

"All right. We're at the big hole and will be heading back as soon as I've gotten a few pictures."

"They haven't made words to tell how relieved I am. From a scientific standpoint, was it worth the risk?"

Scobie gasped. He stared before him.

"Colin?" Danzig called. "You still there?"

"Yes. Yes."

"I asked what observations of any importance you made."

"I don't know," Scobie mumbled. "I can't remember. None of it after we started climbing seems real."

"Better you return right away," Danzig said grimly. "Forget about photographs."

"Correct." Scobie addressed his companions: "Forward march."

"I can't," *Alvarlan answers*. "A wanderin' spell has caught my spirit in tendrils of smoke."

"I know where a fire dagger is kept," *Ricia says*. "I'll try to steal it."

Broberg moved ahead, as though to descend into the crater. Tiny ice grains trickled over the verge from beneath her boots. She could easily lose her footing and slide down.

"No, wait," *Kendrick shouts to her*. "No need. My spearhead is of moon alloy. It can cut—"

The glacier shuddered. The ridge cracked asunder and fell in shards. The area on which the humans stood split free and toppled into the bowl. An avalanche poured after. High-flung crystals caught sunlight, glittered prismatic in challenge to the stars, descended slowly and lay quiet.

Except for shock waves through solids, everything had happened in the absolute silence of space.

Heartbeat by heartbeat, Scobie crawled back to his senses. He found himself held down, immobilized, in darkness and pain. His armor had saved, was still saving his life; he had been stunned but escaped a real concussion. Yet every breath hurt abominably. A rib or two on the left side seemed broken; a monstrous impact must have dented metal. And he was buried under more weight than he could move.

"Hello," he coughed. "Does anybody read me?" The single reply was the throb of his blood. If his radio still worked—which it should, being built into the suit—the mass around him screened him off.

It also sucked heat at an unknown but appalling rate. He felt no cold because the electrical system drew energy from his fuel cell as fast as needed to keep him warm and to recycle his air chemically. As a normal thing, when he lost heat through the slow process of radiation—and, a trifle, through kerofoam-lined bootsoles—the latter demand was much the greater. Now conduction was at work on every square centimeter. He had a spare unit in the equipment on his back, but no means of getting at it.

Unless—He barked forth a chuckle. Straining, he felt the stuff that entombed him yield the least bit under the pressure of arms and legs. And his helmet rang slightly with noise, a rustle, a gurgle. This wasn't water ice that imprisoned him, but stuff with a much lower freezing point. He was melting it, subliming it, making room for himself.

If he lay passive, he would sink, while frozenness above slid down to keep him in his grave. He might evoke superb new formations, but he would not see them. Instead, he must use the small capability given him to work his way upward, scrabble, get a purchase on matter that was not yet a flow, burrow to the stars.

He began.

Agony soon racked him. Breath rasped in and out of lungs aflame. His strength drained away and trembling took its place, and he could not tell whether he ascended or slipped back. Blind, half-suffocated, Scobie made mole claws of his hands and dug.

It was too much to endure. He fled from it—

His strong enchantments failing, the Elf King brought down his towers of fear in wreck. If the spirit of Alvarlan returned to its body, the wizard would brood upon things he had seen, and understand what they meant, and such knowledge would give mortals a terrible power against Faerie. Waking from sleep, the King scryed Kendrick about to release that fetch. There was no time to do more than break the spell which upheld the

Dance Hall. It was largely built of mist and starshine, but enough blocks quarried from the cold side of Ginnungagap were in it that when they crashed they should kill the knight. Ricia would perish too, and in his quicksilver intellect the King regretted that. Nevertheless he spoke the necessary word.

He did not comprehend how much abuse flesh and bone can bear. Sir Kendrick fights his way clear of the ruins, to seek and save his lady. While he does, he heartens himself with thoughts of adventures past and future—

—and suddenly the blindness broke apart and Saturn stood lambent within rings.

Scobie belly flopped onto the surface and lay shuddering.

He must rise, no matter how his injuries screamed, lest he melt himself a new burial place. He lurched to his feet and glared around.

Little but outcroppings and scars was left of the sculpture. For the most part, the crater had become a smooth-sided whiteness under heaven. Scarcity of shadows made distances hard to gauge, but Scobie guessed the new depth was about seventy-five meters. And empty, empty.

"Mark, do you hear?" he cried.

"That you, Colin?" rang in his earpieces. "Name of mercy, what's happened? I heard you call out, and saw a cloud rise and sink . . . then nothing for more than an hour. Are you okay?"

"I am, sort of. I don't see Jean or Luis. A landslide took us by surprise and buried us. Hold on while I search."

When he stood upright, Scobie's ribs hurt less. He could move about rather handily if he took care. The two types of standard analgesic in his kit were alike useless, one too weak to give noticeable relief, one so strong that it would turn him sluggish. Casting to and fro, he soon found what he expected, a concavity in the tumbled snowlike material, slightly aboil.

Also a standard part of his gear was a trenching tool. Scobie set pain aside and dug. A helmet appeared. Broberg's head was within it. She too had been tunneling out.

"Jean!"

"Kendrick!" She crept free and they embraced, suit to suit. "Oh, Colin."

"How are you?" rattled from him.

"Alive," she answered. "No serious harm done, I think. A lot to be said for low gravity . . . You? Luis?" Blood was clotted in a streak beneath her nose, and a bruise on her forehead was turning purple, but she stood firmly and spoke clearly.

"I'm functional. Haven't found Luis yet. Help me look. First, though, we'd better check out our equipment."

She hugged arms around chest, as if that would do any good here. "I'm chilled," she admitted.

Scobie pointed at a telltale. "No wonder. Your fuel cell's down to its last couple of ergs. Mine isn't in a lot better shape. Let's change."

They didn't waste time removing their backpacks, but reached into each other's. Tossing the spent units to the ground, where vapors and holes immediately appeared and then froze, they plugged the fresh ones into their suits. "Turn your thermostat down," Scobie advised. "We won't find shelter soon. Physical activity will help us keep warm."

"And require faster air recycling," Broberg reminded.

"Yeah. But for the moment, at least, we can conserve the energy in the cells. Okay, next let's check for strains, potential leaks, any kind of damage or loss. Hurry. Luis is still down there."

Inspection was a routine made automatic by years of drill. While her fingers searched across the man's spacesuit, Broberg let her eyes wander. "The Dance Hall is gone," *Ricia murmurs*. "I think the King smashed it to prevent our escape."

"Me too. If he finds out we're alive, and seeking for Alvarlan's soul—Hey, wait! None of that!"

Danzig's voice quavered. "How're you doing?"

"We're in fair shape, seems like," Scobie replied. "My corselet took a beating but didn't split or anything. Now to find Luis . . . Jean, suppose you spiral right, I left, across the crater floor."

It took a while, for the seething which marked Garcilaso's burial was minuscule. Scobie started to dig. Broberg watched how he moved, heard how he breathed, and said, "Give me that tool. Just where are you bunged up, anyway?"

He admitted his condition and stepped back. Crusty chunks flew from Broberg's toil. She progressed fast, since whatever kind of ice lay at this point was, luckily, friable, and under Iapetan gravity she could cut a hole with almost vertical sides.

"I'll make myself useful," Scobie said, "namely, find us a way out."

When he started up the nearest slope, it shivered. All at once he was borne back in a tide that made rustly noises through his armor, while a fog of dry white motes blinded him. Painfully, he scratched himself free at the bottom and tried elsewhere. In the end he could report to Danzig: "I'm afraid there is no easy route. When the rim collapsed where we stood, it did more than produce a shock which wrecked the delicate formations throughout the crater. It let tons of stuff pour down from the surface—a particular sort of ice that, under local conditions, is like fine sand. The walls are covered by it. Most places, it lies meters deep over more stable material. We'd slide faster than we could climb, where the layer is thin; where it's thick, we'd sink."

Danzig sighed. "I guess I get to take a nice, healthy hike."

"I assume you've called for help."

"Of course. They'll have two boats here in about a hundred hours. The best they can manage. You knew that already."

"Uh-huh. And our fuel cells are good for perhaps fifty hours."

"Oh, well not to worry about that. I'll bring extras and toss them to you, if you're stuck till the rescue party arrives. M-m-m . . . maybe I'd better rig a slingshot or something first."

"You might have a problem locating us. This isn't a true crater, it's a glorified pothole, the lip of it flush with the top of the glacier. The landmark we guided ourselves by, that fancy ridge, is gone."

"No big deal. I've got a bearing on you from the directional antenna, remember. A magnetic compass may be no use here, but I can keep myself oriented by the heavens. Saturn scarcely moves in this sky, and the sun and the stars don't move fast."

"Damn! You're right. I wasn't thinking. Got Luis on my mind, if nothing else." Scobie looked across the bleakness toward Broberg. Perforce she was taking a short rest, stoop-shouldered above her excavation. His earpieces brought him the harsh sound in her windpipe.

He must maintain what strength was left him, against later need. He sipped from his water nipple, pushed a bite of food through his chowlock, pretended an appetite. "I may as well try reconstructing what happened," he said. "Okay, Mark, you were right, we got crazy reckless. The game—Eight years was too long to play the game, in an environment that gave us too few reminders of reality. But who could have foreseen it? My God, warn *Chronos*! I happen to know that one of the Titan teams started playing an expedition to the merfolk under the Crimson Ocean—on account of the red mists—deliberately, like us, before they set off . . ."

Scobie gulped. "Well," he slogged on, "I don't suppose we'll ever know exactly what went wrong here. But plain to see, the configuration was only metastable. On Earth, too, avalanches can be fatally easy to touch off. I'd guess at a methane layer underneath the surface. It turned a little slushy when temperatures rose after dawn, but that didn't matter in low gravity and vacuum—till we came along. Heat, vibration—Anyhow, the stratum slid out from under us, which triggered a general collapse. Does that guess seem reasonable?"

"Yes, to an amateur like me," Danzig said. "I admire how you can stay academic under these circumstances."

"I'm being practical," Scobie retorted. "Luis may need medical attention earlier than those boats can come for him. If so, how do we get him to ours?"

Danzig's voice turned stark. "Any ideas?"

"I'm fumbling my way toward that. Look, the bowl still has the same basic form. The whole shebang didn't cave in. That implies hard material, water ice and actual rock. In fact, I see a few remaining promontories, jutting out above the sandlike stuff. As for what *it* is—maybe an ammonia-carbon dioxide combination, maybe more exotic—that'll be for you to discover later. Right now . . . my geological instruments should help me trace where the solid masses are least deeply covered. We all have trenching tools, so we can try to shovel a path clear, along a zigzag of least effort. That may bring more garbage slipping down on us from above, but that in turn may expedite our progress. Where the uncovered shelves are too steep or slippery to climb, we can chip footholds. Slow and tough work; and we may run into a bluff higher than we can jump, or something like that."

"I can help," Danzig proposed. "While I waited to hear from you, I inventoried our stock of spare cable, cord, equipment I can cannibalize for wire, clothes and bedding I can cut into strips—whatever might be knotted together to make a rope. We won't need much tensile strength. Well, I estimate I can get about forty meters. According to your description, that's about half the slope length of that trap you're in. If you can climb halfway up while I trek there, I can haul you the rest of the way."

"Thanks, Mark," Scobie said, "although—"

"Luis!" shrieked in his helmet. "Colin, come fast, help me, this is dreadful!"

Regardless of the pain, except for a curse or two, Scobie sped to Broberg's aid.

Garcilaso was not quite unconscious. In that lay much of the horror. They heard him mumble, "—Hell, the King threw my soul into Hell. I can't find my way out, I'm lost. If only Hell weren't so cold—" They could not see his face; the inside of his helmet was crusted with frost. Deeper and longer buried than the others, badly hurt in addition, he would have died shortly after his fuel cell was exhausted. Broberg had uncovered him barely in time, if that.

Crouched in the shaft she had dug, she rolled him over onto his belly. His limbs flopped about and he babbled, "A demon attacks me. I'm blind here but I feel the wind of its wings," in a blurred monotone. She unplugged the energy unit and tossed it aloft, saying, "We should return this to the ship if we can."

Above, Scobie gave the object a morbid stare. It didn't even retain the warmth to make a little vapor, like his and hers, but lay quite inert. Its case was a metal box, thirty centimeters by fifteen by six, featureless except for two plug-in prongs on one of the broad sides. Controls built into the spacesuit circuits allowed you to start and stop the chemical reactions within and regulate their rate manually; but as a rule you left that chore to your thermostat and aerostat. Now those reactions had run their course. Until it was recharged, the cell was merely a lump.

Scobie leaned over to watch Broberg, some ten meters below him. She had extracted the reserve unit from Garcilaso's gear, inserted it properly at the small of his back, and secured it by clips on the bottom of his packframe. "Let's have your contribution, Colin," she said. Scobie dropped the meter of heavy-gauge insulated wire which was standard issue on extravehicular missions, in case you needed to make a special electrical connection or a repair. She joined it by Western Union splices to the two she already had, made a loop at the end and, awkwardly reaching over her left shoulder, secured the opposite end by a hitch to the top of her packframe. The triple strand bobbed above her like an antenna.

Stooping, she gathered Garcilaso in her arms. The Iapetan weight of him and his apparatus was under ten kilos, of her and hers about the same. Theoretically she could jump straight out of the hole with her burden. In practice, her spacesuit was too hampering; constant-volume joints allowed considerable freedom of movement, but not as much as bare skin, especially when circum-Saturnian temperatures required extra insulation. Besides, if she could have reached the top, she could not have stayed. Soft ice would have crumbled beneath her fingers and she would have tumbled back down.

"Here goes," she said. "This had better be right the first time, Colin. I don't think Luis can take much jouncing."

"Kendrick, Ricia, where are you?" Garcilaso moaned. "Are you in Hell too?"

Scobie dug his heels into the ground near the edge and crouched ready. The loop in the wire rose to view. His right hand grabbed hold. He threw himself backward, lest he slide forward, and felt the mass he had captured slam to a halt. Anguish exploded in his rib cage. Somehow he dragged his burden to safety before he fainted.

He came out of that in a minute. "I'm okay," he rasped at the anxious voices of Broberg and Danzig. "Only let me rest a while."

The physicist nodded and knelt to minister to the pilot. She stripped his packframe in order that he might lie flat on it, head and legs supported by the packs themselves. That would prevent significant heat loss by convection and cut loss by conduction. Still, his fuel cell would be drained faster than if he were on his feet, and first it had a terrible energy deficit to make up.

"The ice is clearing away inside his helmet," she reported. "Merciful Mary, the blood! Seems to be from the scalp, though; it isn't running anymore. His occiput must have been slammed against the vitryl. We ought to wear padded caps in these rigs. Yes, I know accidents like this haven't happened before, but—" She unclipped the flashlight at her waist, stooped, and shone it downward. "His eyes are open. The pupils—yes, a severe concussion, and likely a skull fracture, which may be hemorrhaging into the brain. I'm surprised he isn't vomiting. Did the cold prevent that? Will he start soon? He could choke on his own vomit, in there where nobody can lay a hand on him."

Scobie's pain had subsided to a bearable intensity. He rose, went over to look, whistled, and said, "I judge he's doomed unless we get him to the boat and give him proper care soon. Which isn't possible."

"Oh, Luis." Tears ran silently down Broberg's cheeks.

"You think he can't last till I bring my rope and we carry him back?" Danzig asked.

"'Fraid not," Scobie replied. "I've taken paramedical courses, and in fact I've seen a case like this before. How come you know the symptoms, Jean?"

"I read a lot," she said dully.

"They weep, the dead children weep," Garcilaso muttered.

Danzig sighed. "Okay, then. I'll fly over to you."

"*Huh*?" burst from Scobie, and from Broberg: "Have you also gone insane?"

"No, listen," Danzig said fast. "I'm no skilled pilot, but I have the same basic training in this type of craft that everybody does who might ride in one. It's expendable; the rescue vessels can bring us back. There'd be no significant gain if I landed close to the glacier—I'd still have to make that rope and so forth—and we know from what happened to the probe that there would be a real hazard. Better I make straight for your crater."

"Coming down on a surface that the jets will vaporize out from under you?" Scobie snorted. "I bet Luis would consider that a hairy stunt. You, my friend, would crack up."

"Nu?" They could almost see the shrug. "A crash from low altitude, in this gravity, shouldn't do more than rattle my teeth. The blast will cut a hole clear to bedrock. True, the surrounding ice will collapse in around the hull and trap it. You may need to dig to reach the airlock, though I suspect thermal radiation from the cabin will keep the upper parts of the structure free. Even if the craft topples and strikes sidewise—in which case, it'll sink down into a deflating cushion—even if it did that on bare rock, it shouldn't be seriously damaged. It's designed to withstand heavier impacts." Danzig hesitated. "Of course, could be this would endanger you. I'm confident I won't fry you with the jets, assuming I descend near the middle and you're as far offside as you can get. Maybe, though, maybe I'd cause a . . . an ice quake that'll kill you. No sense in losing two more lives."

"Or three, Mark," Broberg said low. "In spite of your brave words, you could come to grief yourself."

"Oh, well, I'm an oldish man. I'm fond of living, yes, but you guys have a whole lot more years due you. Look, suppose the worst, suppose I don't just make a messy landing but wreck the boat utterly. Then Luis dies, but he would anyway. You two, however, would have access to the stores aboard, including those extra fuel cells. I'm willing to run what I consider to be a small risk of my own neck, for the sake of giving Luis a chance at survival."

"Um-m-m," went Scobie, deep in his throat. A hand strayed in search of his chin, while his gaze roved around the glimmer of the bowl.

"I repeat," Danzig proceeded, "if you think this might jeopardize you in any way, we scrub it. No heroics, please. Luis would surely agree, better three people safe and one dead than four stuck with a high probability of death."

"Let me think." Scobie was mute for minutes before he said: "No, I don't believe we'd get in too much trouble here. As I remarked earlier, the vicinity has had its avalanche and must be in a reasonably stable configuration. True, ice will volatilize. In the case of deposits with low boiling points, that could happen explosively and cause tremors. But the vapor will carry heat away so fast that only material in your immediate area should change state. I daresay that the fine-grained stuff will get shaken down the slopes, but it's got too low a density to do serious harm; for the most part, it should simply act like a brief snowstorm. The floor will make adjustments, of course, which may be rather violent. However, we can be above it—do you see that shelf of rock over yonder, Jean, at jumping height? It has to be part of a buried hill; solid. That's our place to wait . . . Okay, Mark, it's go as far as we're concerned. I can't be absolutely certain, but who ever is about anything? It seems like a good bet."

"What are we overlooking?" Broberg wondered. She glanced down at Luis, who lay at her feet. "While we considered all the possibilities, Luis might die. Yes, fly if you want to, Mark, and God bless you."

But when she and Scobie had brought Garcilaso to the ledge, she gestured from Saturn to Polaris and: "I will sing a spell, I will cast what small magic is mine, in aid of the Dragon Lord, that he may deliver Alvarlan's soul from Hell," *says Ricia.*

4

No reasonable person will blame any interplanetary explorer for miscalculations about the actual environment, especially when *some* decision has to be made, in haste and under stress. Occasional errors are inevitable. If we knew exactly what to expect throughout the Solar System, we would have no reason to explore it.

—Minamoto

The boat lifted. Cosmic dust smoked away from its jets. A hundred and fifty meters aloft, thrust lessened and it stood still on a pillar of fire.

Within the cabin was little noise, a low hiss and a bone-deep but nearly inaudible rumble. Sweat studded Danzig's features, clung glistening to his beard stubble, soaked his coverall and made it reek. He was about to undertake a maneuver as difficult as a rendezvous, and without guidance.

Gingerly, he advanced a vernier. A side jet woke. The boat lurched toward a nose dive. Danzig's hands jerked across the console. He must adjust the forces that held his vessel on high and those that pushed it horizontally, to get a resultant that would carry him eastward at a slow, steady pace. The vectors would change instant by instant, as they do when a human walks. The control computer, linked to the sensors, handled much of the balancing act, but not the crucial part. He must tell it what he wanted it to do.

His handling was inexpert. He had realized it would be. More altitude would have given him more margin for error, but deprive him of cues that his eyes found on the terrain beneath and the horizon ahead. Besides, when he reached the glacier he would perforce fly low to find his goal. He would be too busy for the precise celestial navigation he could have practiced afoot.

Seeking to correct his error, he overcompensated, and the boat pitched in a different direction. He punched for "hold steady" and the computer took over. Motionless again, he took a minute to catch his breath, regain his nerve, rehearse in his mind. Biting his lip, he tried afresh. This time he did not quite approach disaster. Jets aflicker, the boat staggered drunkenly over the moonscape.

The ice cliff loomed nearer and nearer. He saw its fragile loveliness and regretted that he must cut a swathe of ruin. Yet what did any natural wonder mean unless a conscious mind was there to know it? He passed the lowest slope. It vanished in billows of steam.

Onward. Beyond the boiling, right and left and ahead, the Faerie architecture crumbled. He crossed the palisade. Now he was a bare fifty meters above the surface, and the clouds reached vengefully close before they disappeared into vacuum. He squinted through the port and made the scanner sweep a magnified overview across its screen, a search for his destination.

A white volcano erupted. The outburst engulfed him. Suddenly he was flying blind. Shocks belled through the hull when upflung stones hit. Frost sheathed the craft; the scanner screen went as blank as the ports. Danzig should have ordered ascent, but he was inexperienced. A human in danger has less of an instinct to jump than to run. He tried to scuttle sideways. Without exterior vision to aid him, he sent the vessel tumbling end over end. By the time he saw his mistake, less than a second, it was too late. He was out of control. The computer might have retrieved the situation after a while, but the glacier was too close. The boat crashed.

"Hello, Mark?" Scobie cried. "Mark, do you read me? Where are you, for Christ's sake?"

Silence replied. He gave Broberg a look which lingered. "Everything seemed to be in order," he said, "till we heard a shout, and a lot of racket, and nothing. He should've reached us by now. Instead, he's run into trouble. I hope it wasn't lethal."

"What can we do?" she asked redundantly. They needed talk, any talk, for Garcilaso lay beside them and his delirious voice was dwindling fast.

"If we don't get fresh fuel cells within the next forty or fifty hours, we'll all be at the end of our particular trail. The boat should be someplace near. We'll have to get out of this hole under our own power, seems like. Wait here with Luis and I'll scratch around for a possible route."

Scobie started downward. Broberg crouched by the pilot.

"—alone forever in the dark —" she heard.

"No, Alvarlan." She embraced him. Most likely he could not feel that, but she could. "Alvarlan, hearken to me. This is Ricia. I hear in my mind how your spirit calls. Let me help. Let me lead you back to the light."

"Have a care," advised Scobie. "We're too damn close to rehypnotizing ourselves as it is."

"But I might, I just might get through to Luis and . . . comfort him . . . Alvarlan, Kendrick and I escaped. He's seeking a way home for us. I'm seeking you. Alvarlan, here is my hand, come take it."

On the crater floor, Scobie shook his head, clicked his tongue, and unlimbered his equipment. Binoculars would help him locate the most promising areas. Devices that ranged from a metal rod to a portable geosonar would give him a more exact idea of what sort of footing lay buried under what depth of unclimbable sand-ice. Admittedly the scope of such probes was very limited. He did not have time to shovel tons of material aside in order that he could mount higher and test further. He would simply have to get some preliminary results, make an educated guess at which path up the side of the bowl would prove negotiable, and trust he was right.

He shut Broberg and Garcilaso out of his consciousness as much as he was able, and commenced work.

An hour later, he was ignoring pain while clearing a strip across a layer of rock. He thought a berg of good, hard frozen water lay ahead, but wanted to make sure.

"Jean! Colin! Do you read?"

Scobie straightened and stood rigid. Dimly he heard Broberg: "If I can't do anything else, Alvarlan, let me pray for your soul's repose."

"Mark!" ripped from Scobie. "You okay? What the hell happened?"

"Yeah, I wasn't too badly knocked around," Danzig said, "and the boat's habitable, though I'm afraid it'll never fly again. How are you? Luis?"

"Sinking fast. All right, let's hear the news."

Danzig described his misfortune. "I wobbled off in an unknown direction for an unknown distance. It can't have been extremely far, since the time was short before I hit. Evidently I plowed into a large, um, snowbank, which softened the impact but blocked radio transmission. It's evaporated from the cabin area now, and formations in the offing . . . I'm not sure what damage the jacks and the stern jets suffered. The boat's on its side at about a forty-five-degree angle, presumably with rock beneath. But the after part is still buried in less whiffable stuff—water and CO_2 ices, I think—that's reached temperature equilibrium. The jets must be clogged with it. If I tried to blast, I'd destroy the whole works."

Scobie nodded. "You would, for sure."

Danzig's voice broke. "Oh, God, Colin! What have I done? I wanted to help Luis, but I may have killed you and Jean."

Scobie's lips tightened. "Let's not start crying before we're hurt. True, this has been quite a run of bad luck. But neither you nor I nor anybody could have known that you'd touch off a bomb underneath yourself."

"What was it? Have you any notion? Nothing of the sort ever occurred at rendezvous with a comet. And you believe the glacier is a wrecked comet, don't you?"

"Uh-huh, except that conditions have obviously modified it. The impact produced heat, shock, turbulence. Molecules got scrambled. Plasmas must have been momentarily present. Mixtures, compounds, clathrates, alloys—stuff formed that never existed in free space. We can learn a lot of chemistry here."

"That's why I came along . . . Well, then, I crossed a deposit of some substance or substances that the jets caused to sublime with tremendous force. A certain kind of vapor refroze when it encountered the hull. I had to defrost the ports from inside after the snow had cooked off them."

"Where are you in relation to us?"

"I told you, I don't know. And I'm not sure I can determine it. The crash crumpled the direction-finding antenna. Let me go outside for a better look."

"Do that," Scobie said. "I'll keep busy meanwhile."

He did, until a ghastly rattling noise and Broberg's wail brought him at full speed back to the rock.

Scobie switched off Garcilaso's fuel cell. "This may make the difference that carries us through," he said low. "Think of it as a gift. Thanks, Luis."

Broberg let go of the pilot and rose from her knees. She straightened the limbs that had threshed about in the death struggle and crossed his hands on his breast. There was nothing she could do about the fallen jaw or the eyes that glared at heaven. Taking him out of this suit, here, would have worsened his appearance. Nor could she wipe the tears off her own face. She could merely try to stop their flow. "Goodbye, Luis," she whispered.

Turning to Scobie, she asked, "Can you give me a new job? Please."

"Come along," he directed. "I'll explain what I have in mind about making our way to the surface."

They were midway across the bowl when Danzig called. He had not let his comrade's dying slow his efforts, nor said much while it happened. Once, most softly, he had offered Kaddish.

"No luck," he reported like a machine. "I've traversed the largest circle I could while keeping the boat in sight, and found only weird, frozen shapes. I can't be a huge distance from you, or I'd see an identifiably different sky, on this miserable little ball. You're probably within a twenty or thirty kilometer radius of me. But that covers a bunch of territory."

"Right," Scobie said. "Chances are you can't find us in the time we've got. Return to the boat."

"Hey, wait," Danzig protested. "I can spiral onward, marking my trail. I might come across you."

"It'll be more useful if you return," Scobie told him. "Assuming we climb out, we should be able to hike to you, but we'll need a beacon. What occurs to me is the ice itself. A small energy release, if it's concentrated, should release a large plume of methane or something similarly volatile. The gas will cool as it expands, recondense around dust particles that have been carried along—it'll steam—and the cloud ought to get high enough, before it evaporates again, to be visible from here."

"Gotcha!" A tinge of excitement livened Danzig's words. "I'll go straight to it. Make tests, find a spot where I can get the showiest result, and . . . how about I rig a thermite bomb? No, that might be too hot. Well, I'll develop a gadget."

"Keep us posted."

"But I, I don't think we'll care to chatter idly," Broberg ventured.

"No, we'll be working our tails off, you and I," Scobie agreed.

"Uh, wait," said Danzig. "What if you find you can't get clear to the top? You implied that's a distinct possibility."

"Well, then it'll be time for more radical procedures, whatever they turn out to be," Scobie responded. "Frankly, at this moment my head is too full of . . . of Luis, and of choosing an optimum escape route, for much thought about anything else."

"M-m, yeah, I guess we've got an ample supply of trouble without borrowing more. Tell you what, though. After my beacon's ready to fire off, I'll make that rope we talked of. You might find you prefer having it to clean clothes and sheets when you arrive." Danzig was silent for seconds before he ended: "God damn it, you *will* arrive."

Scobie chose a point on the north side for his and Broberg's attempt. Two rock shelves jutted forth, near the floor and several meters higher, indicating that stone reached at least that far. Beyond, in a staggered pattern, were similar outcroppings of hard ices. Between them, and onward from the uppermost, which was scarcely more than halfway to the rim, was nothing but the featureless, footingless slope of powder crystals. Its angle of repose gave a steepness that made the surface doubly treacherous. The question, unanswerable save by experience, was how deeply it covered layers on which humans could climb, and whether such layers extended the entire distance aloft.

At the spot, Scobie signaled a half. "Take it easy, Jean," he said. "I'll go ahead and commence digging."

"Why don't we go together? I have my own tool, you know."

"Because I can't tell how so large a bank of that pseudoquicksand will behave. It might react to the disturbance by causing a gigantic slide."

She bridled. Her haggard countenance registered mutiny. "Why not me first, then? Do you suppose I always wait passive for Kendrick to save me?"

"As a matter of fact," he rapped, "I'll begin because my rib is giving me billy hell, which is eating away what strength I've got left. If we run into trouble, you can better come to my help than I to yours."

Broberg bent her neck. "Oh, I'm sorry. I must be in a fairly bad state myself, if I let false pride interfere with our business." Her look went toward Saturn, around which *Chronos* orbited, bearing her husband and children.

"You're forgiven." Scobie bunched his legs and sprang the five meters to the lower ledge. The next one up was slightly too far for such a jump, when he had no room for a running start.

Stooping, he scraped his trenching tool against the bottom of the declivity that sparkled before him, and shoveled. Grains poured from above, a billionfold, to cover what he cleared. He worked like a robot possessed. Each spadeful was nearly weightless, but the number of spadefuls was nearly endless. He did not bring the entire bowlside down on himself as he had half feared half hoped. (If that didn't kill him, it would save a lot of toil.) A dry torrent went right and left over his ankles. Yet at last somewhat more of the underlying rock began to show.

From beneath, Broberg listened to him breathe. It sounded rough, often broken by a gasp or a curse. In his spacesuit, in the raw, wan sunshine, he resembled a knight who, in despite of wounds, did battle against a monster.

"All right," he called at last. "I think I've learned what to expect and how we should operate. It'll take the two of us."

"Yes . . . oh, yes, my Kendrick."

The hours passed. Ever so slowly, the sun climbed and the stars wheeled and Saturn waned.

Most places, the humans labored side by side. They did not require more than the narrowest of lanes, but unless they cut it wide to begin with, the banks to right and left would promptly slip down and bury it. Sometimes the conformation underneath allowed a single person at a time to work. Then the other could rest. Soon it was Scobie who must oftenest take advantage of that. Sometimes they both stopped briefly, for food and drink and reclining on their packs.

Rock yielded to water ice. Where this rose very sharply, the couple knew it, because the sand-ice that they undercut would come down in a mass. After the first such incident, when they were nearly swept away, Scobie always drove his geologist's hammer into each new stratum. At any sign of danger, he would seize its handle and Broberg would cast an arm around his waist. Their other hands clutched their trenching tools. Anchored, but forced to strain every muscle, they would stand while the flood poured around them, knee-high, once even chesthigh, seeking to bury them irretrievably deep in its quasi-fluid substance. Afterward they would confront a bare stretch. It was generally too steep to climb unaided, and they chipped footholds.

Weariness was another tide to which they dared not yield. At best, their progress was dismayingly slow. They needed little heat input to keep warm, except when they took a rest, but their lungs put a furious demand on air recyclers. Garcilaso's fuel cell, which they had brought along, could give a single person extra hours of life, though depleted as it was after coping with his hypothermia, the time would be insufficient for rescue by the teams from *Chronos*. Unspoken was the idea of taking turns with it. That would put them in wretched shape, chilled and stifling, but at least they would leave the universe together.

Thus it was hardly a surprise that their minds fled from pain, soreness, exhaustion, stench, despair. Without that respite, they could not have gone on as long as they did.

At ease for a few minutes, their backs against a blue-shimmering parapet which they must scale, they gazed across the bowl, where Garcilaso's suited body gleamed like a remote pyre, and up the curve opposite Saturn. The planet shone lambent amber, softly banded, the rings a coronet which a shadow band across their arc seemed to make all the brighter. That radiance overcame sight of most nearby stars, but elsewhere they arrayed themselves multitudinous, in splendor, around the silver road which the galaxy clove between them.

"How right a tomb for Alvarlan," *Ricia says in a dreamer's murmur*.

"Has he died, then?" *Kendrick asks*.

"You do not know?"

"I have been too busied. After we won free of the ruins and I left you to recover while I went scouting, I encountered a troop of warriors. I escaped, but must needs return to you by devious, hidden ways." *Kendrick strokes Ricia's sunny hair*. "Besides, dearest dear, it has ever been you, not I, who had the gift of hearing spirits."

"Brave darling . . . Yes, it is a glory to me that I was able to call his soul out of Hell. It sought his body, but that was old and frail and could not survive the knowledge it now had. Yet Alvarlan passed peacefully, and before he did, for his last magic he made himself a tomb from whose ceiling starlight will eternally shine."

"May he sleep well. But for us there is no sleep. Not yet. We have far to travel."

"Aye. But already we have left the wreckage behind. Look! Everywhere around in this meadow, anemones peep through the grass. A lark sings above."

"These lands are not always calm. We may well have more adventures ahead of us. But we shall meet them with high hearts."

Kendrick and Ricia rise to continue their journey.

* * *

Cramped on a meager ledge, Scobie and Broberg shoveled for an hour without broadening it much. The sand-ice slid from above as fast as they could cast it down. "We'd better quit this as a bad job," the man finally decided. "The best we've done is flatten the slope ahead of us a tiny bit. No telling how far inward the shelf goes before there's a solid layer on top. Maybe there isn't any."

"What shall we do instead?" Broberg asked in the same worn tone.

He jerked a thumb. "Scramble back to the level beneath and try a different direction. But first we absolutely require a break."

They spread kerofoam pads and sat. After a while during which they merely stared, stunned by fatigue, Broberg spoke.

"I go to the brook," *Ricia relates*. "It chimes under arches of green boughs. Light falls between them to sparkle on it. I kneel and drink. The water is cold, pure, sweet. When I raise my eyes, I see the figure of a young woman, naked, her tresses the color of leaves. A wood nymph. She smiles."

"Yes, I see her too," *Kendrick joins in*. "I approach carefully, not to frighten her off. She asks our names and errands. We explain that we are lost. She tells us how to find an oracle which may give us counsel."

They depart to find it.

Flesh could no longer stave off sleep. "Give us a yell in an hour, will you, Mark?" Scobie requested.

"Sure," Danzig said, "but will that be enough?"

"It's the most we can afford, after the setbacks we've had. We've come less than a third of the way."

"If I haven't talked to you," Danzig said slowly, "it's not because I've been hard at work, though I have been. It's that I figured you two were having a plenty bad time without me nagging you. However—do you think it's wise to fantasize the way you have been?"

A flush crept across Broberg's cheeks and down toward her bosom. "You listened, Mark?"

Well, yes, of course. You might have an urgent word for me at any minute."

"Why? What could you do? A game is a personal affair."

"Uh, yes, yes—"

Ricia and Kendrick have made love whenever they can. The accounts were never explicit, but the words were often passionate.

"We'll keep you tuned in when we need you, like for an alarm clock," Broberg clipped. "Otherwise we'll cut the circuit."

"But—Look, I never meant to—"

"I know." Scobie sighed. "You're a nice guy and I daresay we're overreacting. Still, that's the way it's got to be. Call us when I told you."

Deep within the grotto, the Pythoness sways on her throne, in the ebb and flow of her oracular dream. As nearly as Ricia and Kendrick can understand what she chants, she tells them to fare westward on the Stag Path until they meet a one-eyed graybeard who will give them further guidance; but they must be wary in his presence, for he is easily angered. They make obeisance and depart. On their way out, they pass the offering they brought. Since they had little with them other than garments and his weapons, the Princess gave the shrine her golden hair. The knight insists that, close-cropped, she remains beautiful.

"Hey, whoops, we've cleared us an easy twenty meters," Scobie said, albeit in a voice which weariness had hammered flat. *At first, the journey through the land of Nacre is a delight.*

His oath afterward had no more life in it. "Another blind alley, seems like." *The old man in the blue cloak and wide-brimmed hat was indeed wrathful when Ricia refused him her favors and Kendrick's spear struck his own aside. Cunningly, he has pretended to make peace and told them what road they should next take. But at the end of it are trolls. The wayfarers elude them and double back.*

"My brain's stumbling around in a fog." Scobie groaned. "My busted rib isn't exactly helping, either. If I don't get another nap I'll keep on making misjudgments till we run out of time."

"By all means, Colin," Broberg said. "I'll stand watch and rouse you in an hour."

"What?" he asked in dim surprise. "Why not join me and have Mark call us as he did before?"

She grimaced. "No need to bother him. I'm tired, yes, but not sleepy."

He lacked wit or strength to argue. "Okay," he said. He stretched his insulating pad on the ice, and toppled out of awareness.

Broberg settled herself next to him. They were halfway to the heights, but they had been struggling, with occasional breaks, for more than twenty hours, and progress grew harder and trickier even as they themselves grew weaker and more stupefied. If ever they reached the top and spied Danzig's signal, they would have something like a couple of hours' stiff travel to shelter.

Saturn, sun, stars shone through vitryl. Broberg smiled down at Scobie's face. He was no Greek god. Sweat, grime, unshavenness, the manifold marks of exhaustion were upon him, but—For that matter, she was scarcely an image of glamour herself.

Princess Ricia sits by her knight, where he slumbers in the dwarf's cottage, and strums a harp the dwarf lent her before he went off to his mine, and sings a lullaby to sweeten the dreams of Kendrick. When it is done, she passes her lips lightly across his, and drifts into the same gentle sleep.

Scobie woke a piece at a time. "Ricia, beloved," *Kendrick whispers, and feels after her. He will summon her up with kisses—*

He scrambled to his feet. "Judas priest!" She lay unmoving. He heard her breath in his earplugs, before the roaring of his pulse drowned it. The sun glared farther aloft, he could see it had moved, and Saturn's crescent had thinned more, forming sharp horns at its ends. He forced his eyes toward the watch on his left wrist.

"Ten hours," he choked.

He knelt and shook his companion. "Come, for Christ's sake!" Her lashes fluttered. When she saw the horror on his visage, drowsiness fled from her.

"Oh, no," she said. "Please, no."

Scobie climbed stiffly erect and flicked his main radio switch. "Mark, do you receive?"

"Colin!" Danzig chattered. "Thank God! I was going out of my head from worry."

"You're not off that hook, my friend. We just finished a ten-hour snooze."

"What? How far did you get first?"

"To about forty meters' elevation. The going looks tougher ahead than in back. I'm afraid we won't make it."

"Don't *say* that, Colin," Danzig begged.

"My fault," Broberg declared. She stood rigid, fists doubled, her features a mask. Her tone was steely. "He was worn out, had to have a nap. I offered to wake him, but fell asleep myself."

"Not your fault, Jean," Scobie began.

She interrupted: "Yes. Mine. Perhaps I can make it good. Take my fuel cell. I'll still have deprived you of my help, of course, but you might survive and reach the boat anyway."

He seized her hands. They did not unclench. "If you imagine I could do that—"

"If you don't, we're both finished," she said unbendingly. "I'd rather go out with a clear conscience."

"And what about my conscience?" he shouted. Checking himself, he wet his lips and said fast: "Besides, you're not to blame. Sleep slugged you. If I'd been thinking, I'd have realized it was bound to do so, and contacted Mark. The fact that you didn't either shows how far gone you were yourself. And . . . you've got Tom and the kids waiting for you. Take my cell." He paused. "And my blessing."

"Shall Ricia forsake her true knight?"

"Wait, hold on, listen," Danzig called. "Look, this is terrible, but—oh, hell, excuse me, but I've got to remind you that dramatics only clutter the action. From what descriptions you've sent, I don't see how either of you can possibly proceed solo. Together, you might yet. At least you're rested—sore in the muscles, no doubt, but clearer in the head. The climb before you may prove easier than you think. Try!"

Scobie and Broberg regarded each other for a whole minute. A thawing went through her, and warmed him. Finally they smiled and embraced. "Yeah, right," he growled. "We're off. But first a bite to eat. I'm plain, old-fashioned hungry. Aren't you?" She nodded.

"That's the spirit," Danzig encouraged them. "Uh, may I make another suggestion? I am just a spectator, which is pretty hellish but does give me an overall view. Drop that game of yours."

Scobie and Broberg tautened.

"It's the real culprit," Danzig pleaded. "Weariness alone wouldn't have clouded your judgment. You'd never have cut me off, and—But weariness and shock and grief did lower your defenses to the point where the damned game took you over. You weren't yourselves when you fell asleep. You were those dream-world characters. They had no reason not to cork off!"

Broberg shook her head violently. "Mark," said Scobie, "you are correct about being a spectator. That means there are some things you don't understand. Why subject yourself to the torture of listening in, hour after hour? We'll call you back from time to time, naturally. Take care." He broke the circuit.

"He's wrong," Broberg insisted.

Scobie shrugged. "Right or wrong, what difference? We won't pass out again in the time we have left. The game didn't handicap us as we traveled. In fact, it helped, by making the situation feel less gruesome."

"Aye. Let us break our fast and set forth anew on our pilgrimage."

The struggle grew stiffer. "Belike the White Witch has cast a spell on this road," *says Ricia*.

"She shall not daunt us," *vows Kendrick*.

"No, never while we fare side by side, you and I, noblest of men."

A slide overcame them and swept them back a dozen meters. They lodged against a crag. After the flow had passed by, they lifted their bruised bodies and limped in search of a different approach. The place where the geologist's hammer lay was no longer accessible.

"What shattered the bridge?" *asks Ricia*.

"A giant," *answers Kendrick*. "I saw him as I fell into the river. He lunged at me, and we fought in the shallows until he fled. He bore away my sword in his thigh."

"You have your spear that Wayland forged," *Ricia says*, "and always you have my heart."

They stopped on the last small outcrop they uncovered. It proved to be not a shelf but a pinnacle of water ice. Around it glittered sand-ice, again quiescent. Ahead was a slope thirty meters in length, and then the rim, and stars.

The distance might as well have been thirty light-years. Whoever tried to cross would immediately sink to an unknown depth.

There was no point in crawling back down the bared side of the pinnacle. Broberg had clung to it for an hour while she chipped niches to climb by with her knife. Scobie's condition had not allowed him to help. If they sought to return, they could easily slip, fall, and be engulfed. If they avoided that, they would never find a new path. Less than two hours' worth of energy was left in their fuel cells. Attempting to push onward while swapping Garcilaso's back and forth would be an exercise in futility.

They settled themselves, legs dangling over the abyss, and held hands.

"I do not think the orcs can burst the iron door of this tower," *Kendrick says*, "but they will besiege us until we starve to death."

"You never yielded up your hope ere now, my knight," *replies Ricia, and kisses his temple*. "Shall we search about? These walls are unutterably ancient. Who knows what relics of wizardry lie forgotten within? A pair of phoenix-feather cloaks, that will bear us laughing through the sky to our home—?"

"I fear not, my darling. Our weird is upon us." *Kendrick touches the spear that leans agleam against the battlement*. "Sad and gray will the world be without you. We can but meet our doom bravely."

"Happily, since we are together." *Ricia's gamine smile breaks forth*. "I did notice that a certain room holds a bed. Shall we try it?"

Kendrick frowns. "Rather should we seek to set our minds and souls in order."

She tugs his elbow. "Later, yes. Besides—who knows?—when we dust off the blanket, we may find it is a Tarnkappe that will take us invisible through the enemy."

"You dream."

Fear stirs behind her eyes. "What if I do?" *Her words tremble*. "I can dream us free if you will help."

Scobie's fist smote the ice. "No!" he croaked. "I'll die in the world that is."

Ricia shrinks from him. He sees terror invade her. "You, you rave, beloved," *she stammers*.

He twisted about and caught her by the arms. "Don't you want to remember Tom and your boys?"

"Who—?"

Kendrick slumps. "I don't know. I have forgotten too."

She leans against him, there on the windy height. A hawk circles above. "The residuum of an evil enchantment, surely. Oh, my heart, my life, cast it from you! Help me find the means to save us." *Yet her entreaty is uneven, and through it speaks dread*.

Kendrick straightens. He lays hand on Wayland's spear, and it is as though strength flows thence, into him. "A spell in truth," *he says. His tone gathers force*. "I will not abide in its darkness, nor suffer it to blind and deafen you, my lady." *His gaze takes hold of hers, which cannot break away*. "There is but a single road to our freedom. It goes through the gates of death."

She waits, mute and shuddering.

"Whatever we do, we must die, Ricia. Let us fare hence as our own folk."

"You see before you the means of your deliverance. It is sharp, I am strong, you will feel no pain."

She bares her bosom. "Then quickly, Kendrick, before I am lost!"

He drives the weapon home. "I love you," he says. *She sinks at his feet*. "I follow you, my darling," *he says, withdrawing the steel, bracing the shaft against stone, and lunging forward. He falls beside her*. "Now we are free."

"That was . . . a nightmare." Broberg sounded barely awake.

Scobie's voice shook. "Necessary, I think, for both of us." He gazed straight before him, letting Saturn fill his eyes with dazzle. "Else we'd have stayed . . . insane? Maybe not, by definition. But we'd not have been in reality either."

"It would have been easier," she mumbled. "We'd never have known we were dying."

"Would you have preferred that?"

Broberg shivered. The slackness in her countenance gave place to the same tension that was in his. "Oh, no," she said, quite softly but in the manner of full consciousness. "No, you were right, of course. Thank you for your courage."

"You've always had as much guts as anybody, Jean. You just have more imagination than me." Scobie's hand chopped empty space in a gesture of dismissal. "Okay, we should call poor Mark and let him know. But first—" His words lost the cadence he had laid on them. "First—"

Her glove clasped his. "What, Colin?"

"Let's decide about that third unit—Luis's," he said with difficulty, still confronting the great ringed planet. "Your decision, actually, though we can discuss the matter if you want. I will not hog it for the sake of a few more hours. Nor will I share it; that would be a nasty way for us both to go out. However, I suggest you use it."

"To sit beside your frozen corpse?" she replied. "No. I wouldn't even feel the warmth, not in my bones—"

She turned toward him so fast that she nearly fell off the pinnacle. He caught her. "*Warmth*," she screamed, shrill as the cry of a hawk on the wing. "Colin, we'll take our bones home!"

"In point of fact," said Danzig, "I've climbed onto the hull. That's high enough for me to see over those ridges and needles. I've got a view of the entire horizon."

"Good," grunted Scobie. "Be prepared to survey a complete circle quick. This depends on a lot of factors we can't predict. The beacon will certainly not be anything like as big as what you had arranged. It may be thin and short-lived. And, of course, it may rise too low for sighting at your distance." He cleared his throat. "In that case, we two have bought the farm. But we'll have made a hell of a try, which feels great by itself."

He hefted the fuel cell, Garcilaso's gift. A piece of heavy wire, insulation stripped off, joined the prongs. Without a regulator, the unit poured its maximum power through the short circuit. Already the strand glowed.

"Are you sure you don't want me to do it, Colin?" Broberg asked. "Your rib—"

He made a lopsided grin. "I'm nonetheless better designed by nature for throwing things," he said. "Allow me that much male arrogance. The bright idea was yours."

"It should have been obvious from the first," she said. "I think it would have been, if we weren't bewildered in our dream."

"M-m, often the simple answers are the hardest to find. Besides, we had to get this far or it wouldn't have worked, and the game helped mightily . . . Are you set, Mark? Heave ho!"

Scobie cast the cell as if it were a baseball, hard and far through the Iapetan gravity field. Spinning, its incandescent wire wove a sorcerous web across vision. It landed somewhere beyond the rim, on the glacier's back.

Frozen gases vaporized, whirled aloft, briefly recondensed before they were lost. A geyser stood white against the stars.

"I see you!" Danzig yelped. "I see your beacon, I've got my bearing, I'll be on my way! With rope and extra energy units and everything!"

Scobie sagged to the ground and clutched at his left side. Broberg knelt and held him, as if either of them could lay hand on his pain. No large matter. He would not hurt much longer.

"How high would you guess the plume goes?" Danzig inquired, calmer.

"About a hundred meters," Broberg replied after study.

"Oh, damn, these gloves do make it awkward punching the calculator . . . Well, to judge by what I observe of it, I'm between ten and fifteen klicks off. Give me an hour or a tad more to get there and find your exact location. Okay?"

Broberg checked gauges. "Yes, by a hair. We'll turn our thermostats down and sit very quietly to reduce oxygen demand. We'll get cold, but we'll survive."

"I may be quicker," Danzig said. "That was a worst-case estimate. All right, I'm off. No more conversation till we meet. I won't take any foolish chances, but I will need my wind for making speed."

Faintly, those who waited heard him breathe, heard his hastening, footfalls. The geyser died.

They sat, arms around waists, and regarded the glory which encompassed them. After a silence, the man said: "Well, I suppose this means the end of the game. For everybody."

"It must certainly be brought under strict control," the woman answered. "I wonder, though, if they will abandon it altogether—out here."

"If they must, they can."

"Yes. We did, you and I, didn't we?"

They turned face to face, beneath that star-beswarmed, Saturn-ruled sky. Nothing tempered the sunlight that revealed them to each other, she a middle-aged wife, he a man ordinary except for his aloneness. They would never play again. They could not.

A puzzled compassion was in her smile. "Dear friend—" she began.

His uplifted palm warded her from further speech. "Best we don't talk unless it's essential," he said. "That'll save a little oxygen, and we can stay a little warmer. Shall we try to sleep?"

Her eyes widened and darkened. "I dare not," she confessed. "Not till enough time has gone past. Now, I might dream."

HARDFOUGHT

Greg Bear

Humans called it the Medusa. Its long twisted ribbons of gas strayed across fifty parsecs, glowing blue, yellow, and carmine. Its central core was a ghoulish green flecked with watery black. Half a dozen protostars circled the core, and as many more dim conglomerates pooled in dimples in the nebula's magnetic field. The Medusa was a huge womb of stars—and disputed territory.

Whenever Prufrax looked at it in displays or through the ship's ports, it seemed malevolent, like a zealous mother showing an ominous face to protect her children. Prufrax had never had a mother, but she had seen them in some of the fibs.

At five, Prufrax was old enough to know the *Mellangee's* mission and her role in it. She had already been through four ship-years of indoctrination. Until her first battle she would be educated in both the Know and the Tell. She would be exercised and trained in the Mocks; in sleep she would dream of penetrating the huge red-and-white Senexi seedships and finding the brood mind. "Zap, Zap," she went with her lips, silent so the tellman wouldn't think her thoughts were straying.

The tellman peered at her from his position in the center of the spherical classroom. Her mates stared straight at the center, all focusing somewhere around the tellman's spiderlike teaching desk, waiting for the trouble, some fidgeting. "How many branch individuals in the Senexi brood mind?" he asked. He looked around the classroom. Peered face by face. Focused on her again. "Pru?"

"Five," she said. Her arms ached. She had been pumped full of moans the wake before. She was already three meters tall, in elfstate, with her long, thin limbs not nearly adequately fleshed out and her fingers still crisscrossed with the surgery done to adapt them to the gloves.

"What will you find in the brood mind?" the tellman pursued, his impassive face stretched across a hammerhead as wide as his shoulders. Some of the fems thought tellmen were attractive. Not many—and Pru was not one of them.

"Yoke," she said.

"What is the brood-mind yoke?"

"Fibs."

"More specifically? And it really isn't all fib, you know."

"Info. Senexi data."

"What will you do?"

"Zap," she said, smiling.

"Why, Pru?"

"Yoke has team gens-memory. Zap yoke, spill the life of the team's five branch inds."

"Zap the brood, Pru?"

"No," she said solemnly. That was a new instruction, only in effect since her class's inception. "Hold the brood for the supreme overs." The tellman did not say what would be done with the Senexi broods. That was not her concern.

"Fine," said the tellman. "You tell well, for someone who's always half-journeying."

Brainwalk, Prufrax thought. Tellman was fancy with the words, but to Pru, what she was prone to do during Tell was brainwalk, seeking out her future. She was already five, soon six. Old. Some saw Senexi by the time they were four.

"Zap, Zap," she went with her lips.

Aryz skidded through the thin layer of liquid ammonia on his broadest pod, considering his new assignment. He knew the Medusa by another name, one that conveyed all the time and effort the Senexi had invested in it. The protostar nebula held few mysteries for him. He and his four branch-mates, who along with the all-important brood mind comprised one of the six teams aboard the seedship, had patrolled the nebula for ninety-three orbits, each orbit—including the timeless periods outside status geometry—taking some one hundred and thirty human years. They had woven in and out of the tendrils of gas, charting the infalling masses and exploring the rocky accretion disks of stars entering the main sequence. With each measure and update, the brood minds refined their view of the nebula as it would be a hundred generations hence, when the Senexi plan would finally mature.

The Senexi were nearly as old as the galaxy. They had achieved spaceflight during the time of the starglobe, when the galaxy had been a sphere. They had not been a quick or brilliant race. Each great achievement had taken thousands of generations, and not just because of their material handicaps. In those times, elements heavier than helium had been rare, found only around stars that had greedily absorbed huge amounts of primeval hydrogen, burned fierce and blue and exploded early, permeating the ill-defined galactic arms with carbon and nitrogen, lithium and oxygen. Elements heavier than iron had been almost nonexistent. The biologies of cold gas-giant worlds had developed with a much smaller palette of chemical combinations in producing the offspring of the primary Population II stars.

Aryz, even with the limited perspective of a branch ind, was aware that, on the whole, the humans opposing the seedship were more adaptable, more vital. But they were not more experienced. The Senexi with their billions of years had often matched them. And Aryz's perspective was expanding with each day of his new assignment.

In the early generations of the struggle, Senexi mental stasis and cultural inflexibility had made them avoid contact with the Population I species. They had never begun a program of extermination of the younger, newly life-forming worlds; the task would have been monumental and probably useless. So when spacefaring cultures developed, the Senexi had retreated, falling back into the redoubts of old stars even before engaging with the new kinds. They had retreated for three generations, about thirty thousand human years, raising their broods on cold nestworlds around red dwarfs, conserving, holding back for the inevitable conflicts.

As the Senexi had anticipated, the younger Population I races had found need of even the aging groves of the galaxy's first stars.

They had moved in savagely, voraciously, with all the strength and mutability of organisms evolved from a richer soup of elements. Biology had, in some ways, evolved in its own right and superseded the Senexi.

Aryz raised the upper globe of his body, with its five silicate eyes arranged in a cross along the forward surface. He had memory of those times, and times long before, though his team hadn't existed then. The brood mind carried memories selected from the total store of nearly twelve billion years' experience; an awesome amount of knowledge, even to a Senexi. He pushed himself forward with his rear pods.

Through the brood mind Aryz could share the memories of a hundred thousand past generations, yet the brood mind itself was younger than its branch of individuals. For a time in their youth, in their liquid-dwelling larval form, the branch inds carried their own sacs of data, each a fragment of the total necessary for complete memory. The branch inds swam through ammonia seas and wafted through thick warm gaseous zones, protoplasmic blobs three to four meters in diameter—developing their personalities under the weight of the past—and not even a complete past. No wonder they were inflexible, Aryz thought. Most branch inds were aware enough to see that—especially when they were allowed to compare histories with the Population I species, as he was doing—but there was nothing to be done. They were content the way they were. To change would be unspeakably repugnant. Extinction was preferable . . . almost.

But now they were pressed hard. The brood mind had begun a number of experiments. Aryz's team had been selected from the seedship's contingent to oversee the experiments, and Aryz had been chosen as the chief investigator. Two orbits past, they had captured six human embryos in a breeding device, as well as a highly coveted memory storage center. Most Senexi engagements had been with humans for the past three or four generations. Just as the Senexi dominated Population II species, humans were ascendant among their kind.

Experiments with the human embryos had already been conducted. Some had been allowed to develop normally; others had been tampered with, for reasons Aryz was not aware of. The tamperings had not been very successful.

The newer experiments, Aryz suspected, were going to take a

different direction, and the seedship's actions now focused on him; he believed he would be given complete authority over the human shapes. Most branch inds would have dissipated under such a burden, but not Aryz. He found the human shapes rather interesting, in their own horrible way. They might, after all, be the key to Senexi survival.

The moans were toughening her elfstate. She lay in pain for a wake, not daring to close her eyes; her mind was changing and she feared sleep would be the end of her. Her nightmares were not easily separated from life; some, in fact, were sharper.

Too often in sleep she found herself in a Senexi trap, struggling uselessly, being pulled in deeper, her hatred wasted against such power. . . .

When she came out of the rigor, Prufrax was given leave by the subordinate tellman. She took to the *Mellangee's* greenroads, walking stiffly in the shallow gravity. Her hands itched. Her mind seemed almost empty after the turmoil of the past few wakes. She had never felt so calm and clear. She hated the Senexi double now; once for their innate evil, twice for what they had made her overs put her through to be able to fight them. Logic did not matter. She was calm, assured. She was growing more mature wake by wake. Fight-budding, the tellman called it, hate coming out like blooms, synthesizing the sunlight of his teaching into pure fight.

The greenroads rose temporarily beyond the labyrinth shields and armor of the ship. Simple transparent plastic and steel geodesic surfaces formed a lacework over the gardens, admitting radiation necessary to the vegetation growing along the paths. No machines scooted one forth and inboard here. It was necessary to walk. Walking was luxury and privilege.

Prufrax looked down on the greens to each side of the paths without much comprehension. They were *beautiful*. Yes, one should say that, think that, but what did it mean? Pleasing? She wasn't sure what being pleased meant, outside of thinking Zap. She sniffed a flower that, the signs explained, bloomed only in the light of young stars not yet fusing. They were near such a star now, and the greenroads were shiny black and electric green with the blossoms. Lamps had been set out for other plants unsuited to such darkened conditions. Some technic allowed suns to appear in selected plastic panels when viewed from certain angles. Clever, the technicals.

She much preferred the looks of a technical to a tellman, but she was common in that. Technicals required brainflex, tellmen cargo capacity. Technicals were strong and ran strong machines, like in the adventure fibs, where technicals were often the protags. She wished a technical were on the greenroads with her. The moans had the effect of making her receptive—what she saw, looking in mirrors, was a certain shine in her eyes—but there was no chance of a breeding liaison. She was quite unreproductive in this moment of elfstate. Other kinds of meetings were not unusual.

She looked up and saw a figure at least a hundred meters away, sitting on an allowed patch near the path. She walked casually, as gracefully as possible with the stiffness. Not a technical, she saw soon, but she was not disappointed. Too calm.

"Over," he said as she approached.

"Under," she replied. But not by much—he was probably six or seven ship years old and not easily classifiable.

"Such a fine elfstate," he commented. His hair was black. He was shorter than she, but something in his build reminded her of the glovers. She accepted his compliment with a nod and pointed to a spot near him. He motioned for her to sit, and she did so with a whuff, massaging her knees.

"Moans?" he asked.

"Bad stretch," she said.

"You're a glover." He was looking at the fading scars on her hands.

"Can't tell what you are," she said.

"Noncombat," he said. "Tuner of the mandates."

She knew very little about the mandates, except that law decreed every ship carry one, and few of the crew were ever allowed to peep. "Noncombat, hm?" she mused. She didn't despise him for that; one never felt strong negatives for a crew member. She didn't feel much of anything. Too calm.

"Been working on ours this wake," he said. "Too hard, I guess. Told to walk." Overzealousness in work was considered an erotic trait aboard the *Mellangee*. Still, she didn't feel too receptive toward him.

"Glovers walk after a rough growing," she said.

He nodded. "My name's Clevo."

"Prufrax."

"Combat soon?"

"Hoping. Waiting forever."

"I know. Just been allowed access to the mandate for a half-dozen wakes. All new to me. Very happy."

"Can you talk about it?" she asked. Information about the ship not accessible in certain rates was excellent barter.

"Not sure," he said, frowning. "I've been told caution."

"Well, I'm listening."

He could come from glover stock, she thought, but probably not from technical. He wasn't very muscular, but he wasn't as tall as a glover, or as thin, either.

"If you'll tell me about gloves."

With a smile she held up her hands and wriggled the short, stumpy fingers. "Sure."

The brood mind floated weightless in its tank, held in place by buffered carbon rods. Metal was at a premium aboard the Senexi ships, more out of tradition than actual material limitations. From what Aryz could tell, the Senexi used metals sparingly for the same reason—and he strained to recall the small dribbles of information about the human past he had extracted from the memory store—for the same reason **that the Romans of old Earth regarded farming as the only truly noble occupation—**

Farming being the raising of *plants* for food and raw materials. *Plants* were analogous to the freeth Senexi ate in their larval youth, but the freeth were not green and sedentary.

There was always a certain fascination in stretching his mind to encompass human concepts. He had had so little time to delve deeply—and that was good, of course, for he had been set to answer specific questions, not mire himself in the whole range of human filth.

He floated before the brood mind, all these thoughts coursing through his tissues. He had no central nervous system, no truly differentiated organs except those that dealt with the outside world—limbs, eyes, permea. The brood mind, however, was all central nervous system, a thinly buffered sac of viscous fluids about ten meters wide.

"Have you investigated the human memory device yet?" the brood mind asked.

"I have."

"Is communication with the human shapes possible for us?"

"We have already created interfaces for dealing with their machines. Yes, it seems likely we can communicate."

"Does it occur to you that in our long war with humans, we have made no attempt to communicate before?"

This was a complicated question. It called for several qualities that Aryz, as a branch ind, wasn't supposed to have. Inquisitiveness, for one. Branch inds did not ask questions. They exhibited initiative only as offshoots of the brood mind.

He found, much to his dismay, that the question had occurred to him. "We have never captured a human memory store before," he said, by way of incomplete answer. "We could not have communicated without such an extensive source of information."

"Yet, as you say, even in the past we have been able to use human machines."

"The problem is vastly more complex."

The brood mind paused. "Do you think the teams have been prohibited from communicating with humans?"

Aryz felt the closest thing to anguish possible for a branch ind. Was he being considered unworthy? Accused of conduct inappropriate to a branch ind? His loyalty to the brood mind was unshakable. "Yes."

"And what might our reasons be?"

"Avoidance of pollution."

"Correct. We can no more communicate with them and remain untainted than we can walk on their worlds, breathe their atmosphere." Again, silence. Aryz lapsed into a mode of inactivity. When the brood mind readdressed him, he was instantly aware.

"Do you know how you are different?" it asked.

"I am not . . ." Again, hesitation. Lying to the brood mind was impossible for him. What snared him was semantics, a complication in the radiated signals between them. He had not been aware that he was different; the brood mind's questions suggested he might be. But he could not possibly face up to the fact and analyze it all in one short time. He signaled his distress.

"You are useful to the team," the brood mind said. Aryz calmed instantly. His thoughts became sluggish, receptive. There was a possibility of redemption. But how was he different? "You are to attempt communication with the shapes yourself. You will not engage in any discourse with your fellows while you are so involved." He was banned. "And after completion of this mission and transfer of certain facts to me, you will dissipate."

Aryz struggled with the complexity of the orders. "How am I different, worthy of such a commission?"

The surface of the brood mind was as still as an undisturbed pool. The indistinct black smudges that marked its radiative organs circulated slowly within the interior, then returned, one above the other, to focus on him. "You will grow a new branch ind. It will not have your flaws, but, then again, it will not be useful to me should such a situation come a second time. Your dissipation will be a relief, but it will be regretted."

"How am I different?"

"I think you know already," the brood mind said. "When the time comes, you will feed the new branch ind all your memories but those of human contact. If you do not survive to that stage of its growth, you will pick your fellow who will perform that function for you."

A small pinkish spot appeared on the back of Aryz's globe. He floated forward and placed his largest permeum against the brood mind's cool surface. The key and command were passed, and his body became capable of reproduction. Then the signal of dismissal was given. He left the chamber.

Flowing through the thin stream of liquid ammonia lining the corridor, he felt ambiguously stimulated. His was a position of privilege and anathema. He had been blessed—and condemned. Had any other branch ind experienced such a thing?

Then he knew the brood mind was correct. He was different from his fellows. None of them would have asked such questions. None of them could have survived the suggestion of communicating with human shapes. If this task hadn't been given to him, he would have had to dissipate away.

The pink spot grew larger, then began to make greyish flakes. It broke through the skin, and casually, almost without thinking, Aryz scraped it off against a bulkhead. It clung, made a radio-frequency emanation something like a sigh, and began absorbing nutrients from the ammonia.

Aryz went to inspect the shapes.

She was intrigued by Clevo, but the kind of interest she felt was new to her. She was not particularly receptive. Rather, she felt a mental gnawing as if she were hungry or had been injected with some kind of brain moans. What Clevo told her about the mandates opened up a topic she had never considered before. How did all things come to be—and how did she figure in them?

The mandates were quite small, Clevo explained, each little more than a cubic meter in volume. Within them was the entire history and culture of the human species, as accurate as possible, culled from all existing sources. The mandate in each ship was updated whenever the ship returned to a contact station. It was not likely the *Mellangee* would return to a contact station during their lifetimes, with the crew leading such short lives on the average.

Clevo had been assigned small tasks—checking data and adding ship records—that had allowed him to sample bits of the mandate. "It's mandated that we have records," he explained, "and what we have, you see, is *man-data*." He smiled. "That's a joke," he said. "Sort of."

Prufrax nodded solemnly. "So where do we come from?"

"Earth, of course," Clevo said. "Everyone knows that."

"I mean, where do we come from—you and I, the crew."

"Breeding division. Why ask? You know."

"Yes." She frowned, concentrating. "I mean, we don't come from the same place as the Senexi. The same way."

"No, that's foolishness."

She saw that it was foolishness—the Senexi were different all around. What was she struggling to ask? "Is their fib like our own?"

"Fib? History's not a fib. Not most of it, anyway. Fibs are for unreal. History is overfib."

She knew, in a vague way, that fibs were unreal. She didn't like to have their comfort demeaned, though. "Fibs are fun," she said. "They teach Zap."

"I suppose," Clevo said dubiously. "Being noncombat, I don't see Zap fibs."

Fibs without Zap were almost unthinkable to her. "Such dull," she said.

"Well, of course you'd say that. I might find Zap fibs dull—think of that?"

"We're different," she said. "Like Senexi are different."

Clevo's jaw hung over. "No way. We're crew. We're human. Senexi are . . ." He shook his head as if fed bitters.

"No, I mean . . ." She paused, uncertain whether she was entering unallowed territory. "You and I, we're fed different, given different moans. But in a big way we're different from Senexi. They aren't made, nor act, as you and I. But . . ." Again it was difficult to express. She was irritated. "I don't want to talk to you anymore."

A tellman walked down the path, not familiar to Prufrax. He held out his hand for Clevo, and Clevo grasped it. "It's amazing," the tellman said, "how you two gravitate to each other. Go, elfstate," he addressed Prufrax. "You're on the wrong greenroad."

She never saw the young researcher again. With glover training underway, the itches he aroused soon faded, and Zap resumed its overplace.

The Senexi had ways of knowing humans were near. As information came in about fleets and individual cruisers less than one percent nebula diameter distant, the seedship seemed warmer, less hospitable. Everything was UV with anxiety, and the new branch ind on the wall had to be shielded by a special silicate cup to prevent distortion. The brood mind grew a corniculum automatically, though the toughened outer membrane would be of little help if the seedship was breached.

Aryz had buried his personal confusion under a load of work. He had penetrated the human memory store deeply enough to find instruction on its use. It called itself a *mandate* (the human word came through the interface as a correlated series of radiated symbols), and even the simple preliminary directions were difficult for Aryz. It was like swimming in another family's private sea, though of course infinitely more alien; how could he connect with experiences never had, problems and needs never encountered by his kind?

He could speak some of the human languages in several radio frequencies, but he hadn't yet decided how he was going to produce modulated sound for the human shapes. It was a disturbing prospect. What would he vibrate? A permeum could vibrate subtly—such signals were used when branch inds joined to form the brood mind—but he doubted his control would ever be subtle enough. Sooner expect a human to communicate with a Senexi by controlling the radiations of its nervous system! The humans had distinct organs within their breathing passages that produced the vibrations; perhaps those structures could be mimicked. But he hadn't yet studied the dead shapes in much detail.

He observed the new branch ind once or twice each watch period. Never before had he seen an induced replacement. The normal process was for two brood minds to exchange plasm and form new team buds, then to exchange and nurture the buds. The buds were later cast free to swim as individual larvae. While the larvae often swam through the liquid and gas atmosphere of a Senexi world for thousands, even tens of thousands of kilometers, inevitably they returned to gather with the other buds of their team. Replacements were selected from a separately created pool of "generic" buds only if one or more originals had been destroyed during their wanderings. The destruction of a complete team meant reproductive failure.

In a mature team, only when a branch ind was destroyed did the brood mind induce a replacement. In essence, then, Aryz was already considered dead.

Yet he was still useful. That amused him, if the Senexi emotion could be called amusement. Restricting himself from his fellows was difficult, but he filled the time by immersing himself, through the interface, in the mandate.

The humans were also connected with the mandate through their surrogate parent, and in this manner they were quiescent.

He reported infrequently to the brood mind. Until he had established communication, there was little to report.

And throughout his turmoil, like the others he could sense a fight was coming. It could determine the success or failure of all their work in the nebula. In the grand scheme, failure here might not be crucial. But the Senexi had taken the long view too often in the past. Their age and experience—their calmness—were working against them. How else to explain the decision to communicate with human shapes? Where would such efforts lead? If he succeeded.

And he knew himself well enough to doubt he would fail.

He could feel an affinity for them already, peering at them through the thick glass wall in their isolated chamber, his skin paling at the thought of their heat, their poisonous chemistry. A diseased affinity. He hated himself for it. And reveled in it. It was what made him particularly useful to the team. If he was defective, and this was the only way he could serve, then so be it.

The other branch inds observed his passings from a distance, making no judgments. Aryz was dead, though he worked and moved. His sacrifice had been fearful. Yet he would not be a hero. His kind could never be emulated.

It was a horrible time, a horrible conflict.

She floated in language, learned it in a trice; there were no distractions. She floated in history and picked up as much as she could, for the source seemed inexhaustible. She tried to distinguish between eyes-open—the barren, pale grey-brown chamber with the thick green wall, beyond which floated a murky roundness—and eyes-shut, when she dropped back into language and history with no fixed foundation.

Eyes-open, she saw the Mam with its comforting limbs and its soft voice, its tubes and extrusions of food and its hissings and removal of waste. Through Mam's wires she learned. Mam also tended another like herself, and another, and one more unlike any of them, more like the shape beyond the green wall.

She was very young, and it was all a mystery.

At least she knew her name. And what she was supposed to do. She took small comfort in that.

They fitted Prufrax with her gloves, and she went into the practice chamber, dragged by her gloves almost, for she hadn't yet knitted her plug-in nerves in the right index digit and her pace control was uncertain.

There, for six wakes straight, she flew with the other glovers back and forth across the dark spaces like elfstate comets. Constellations and nebula aspects flashed at random on the distant walls, and she oriented to them like a night-flying bird. Her glovemates were Ornin, an especially slender male, and Ban, a red-haired female, and the special-projects sisters Ya, Trice, and Damu, new from the breeding division.

When she let the gloves have their way, she was freer than she had ever felt before. Did the gloves really control? The question wasn't important. Control was somewhere uncentered, behind her eyes and beyond her fingers, as if she were drawn on a beautiful silver wire where it was best to go. Doing what was best to do. She barely saw the field that flowed from the grip of the thick, solid gloves or felt its caressing, life-sustaining influence. Truly, she hardly saw or felt anything but situations, targets, opportunities, the success or failure of the Zap. Failure was an acute pain. She was never reprimanded for failure; the reprimand was in her blood, and she felt as if she wanted to die. But then the opportunity would improve, the Zap would succeed, and everything around her—stars, Senexi seedship, the *Mellangee*, everything—seemed part of a beautiful dream all her own.

She was intense in the Mocks.

Their initial practice over, the entry play began.

One by one, the special-projects sisters took their hyperbolic formation. Their glove fields threw out extensions, and they combined force. In they went, the mock Senexi seedship brilliant red and white and UV and radio and hateful before them. Their tails swept through the seedship's outer shields and swirled like long silk hair laid on water; they absorbed fantastic energies, grew brighter like violent little stars against the seedship outline. They were engaged in the drawing of the shields, and sure as topology, the spirals of force had to have a dimple on the opposite side that would iris wide enough to let in glovers. The sisters twisted the forces, and Prufrax could see the dimple stretching out under them—

The exercise ended. The elfstate glovers were cast into sudden dark. Prufrax came out of the mock unprepared, her mind still bent on the Zap. The lack of orientation drove her as mad as a moth suddenly flipped from night to day. She careened until gently mitted and channeled. She flowed down a tube, the field slowly neutralizing, and came to a halt still gloved, her body jerking and tingling.

"What the breed happened?" she screamed, her hands beginning to hurt.

"Energy conserve," a mechanical voice answered. Behind Prufrax, the other elfstate glovers lined up in the catch tube, all but the special-projects sisters. Ya, Trice, and Damu had been taken out of the exercise early and replaced by simulations. There was no way their functions could be mocked. They entered the tube ungloved and helped their comrades adjust to the overness of the real.

As they left the mock chamber, another batch of glovers, even younger and fresher in elfstate, passed them. Ya held her hands up, and they saluted in return. "Breed more every day," Prufrax grumbled. She worried about having so many crew she'd never be able to conduct a satisfactory Zap herself. Where would the honor of being a glover go if everyone was a glover?

She wriggled into her cramped bunk, feeling exhilarated and irritated. She replayed the mocks and added in the missing Zap, then stared gloomily at her small, narrow feet.

Out there the Senexi waited. Perhaps they were in the same state as she—ready to fight, testy at being reined in. She pondered her ignorance, her inability to judge whether such things were even possible among the enemy. She thought of the researcher, Clevo. "Blank," she murmured. "Blank, blank." Such thoughts were unnecessary, and humanizing Senexi was unworthy of a glover.

Aryz looked at the instrument, stretched a pod into it, and willed. Vocal human language came out the other end, thin and squeaky in the helium atmosphere. The sound disgusted and thrilled him. He removed the instrument from the gelatinous strands of the engineering wall and pushed it into his interior through a stretched permeum. He took a thick draft of ammonia and slid to the human shapes chamber again.

He pushed through the narrow port into the observation room. Adjusting his eyes to the heat and bright light beyond the transparent wall, he saw the round mutated shape first—the result of their unsuccessful experiments. He swung his sphere around and looked at the others.

For a time he couldn't decide which was uglier—the mutated shape or the normals. Then he thought of what it would be like to have humans tamper with Senexi and try to make them into human forms. . . . He looked at the round human and shrunk as if from sudden heat. Aryz had had nothing to do with the experiments. For that, at least, he was grateful.

Apparently, even before fertilization, human buds—eggs—were adapted for specific roles. The healthy human shapes appeared sufficiently different—discounting *sexual* characteristics—to indicate some variation in function. They were four-podded, two-opticked, with auditory apparatus and olfactory organs mounted on the *head*, along with one permeum, the *mouth*. At least, he thought, they were hairless, unlike some of the other Population I species Aryz had learned about in the mandate.

Aryz placed the tip of the vocalizer against a sound-transmitting plate and spoke.

"Zello," came the sound within the chamber. The mutated shape looked up. It lay on the floor, great bloated stomach backed by four almost useless pods. It usually made high-pitched sounds continuously. Now it stopped and listened, straining on the tube that connected it to the breed-supervising device.

"Hello," replied the male. It sat on a ledge across the chamber, having unhooked itself.

The machine that served as surrogate parent and instructor stood in one corner, an awkward parody of a human, with limbs too long and head too small. Aryz could see the unwillingness of the designing engineers to examine human anatomy too closely.

"I am called—" Aryz said, his name emerging as a meaningless stretch of white noise. He would have to do better than that. He compressed and adapted the frequencies. "I am called Aryz."

"Hello," the young female said.

"What are your names?" He knew that well enough, having listened many times to their conversations.

"Prufrax," the female said. "I'm a glover."

The human shapes contained very little genetic memory. As a kind of brood marker, Aryz supposed, they had been equipped with their name, occupation, and the rudiments of environmental knowledge. This seemed to have been artificially imposed; in their natural state, very likely, they were born almost blank. He could not, however, be certain, since human reproductive chemistry was extraordinarily subtle and complicated.

"I'm a teacher, Prufrax," Aryz said. The logic structure of the language continued to be painful to him.

"I don't understand you," the female replied.

"You teach me, I teach you."

"We have the Mam," the male said, pointing to the machine. "She teaches us." The Mam, as they called it, was hooked into the mandate. Withholding that from the humans—the only equivalent, in essence, to the Senexi sac of memory—would have been unthinkable. It was bad enough that humans didn't come naturally equipped with their own share of knowledge.

"Do you know where you are?" Aryz asked.

"Where we live," Prufrax said. "Eyes-open."

Aryz opened a port to show them the stars and a portion of the nebula. "Can you tell where you are by looking out the window?"

"Among the lights," Prufrax said.

Humans, then, did not instinctively know their positions by star patterns as other Population I species did.

"Don't talk to it," the male said. "Mam talks to us." Aryz consulted the mandate for some understanding of the name they had given to the breed-supervising machine. Mam, it explained, was probably a natural expression for womb-carrying parent. Aryz severed the machine's power.

"Mam is no longer functional," he said. He would have the engineering wall put together another less identifiable machine to link them to the mandate and to their nutrition. He wanted them to associate comfort and completeness with nothing but himself.

The machine slumped, and the female shape pulled herself free of the hookup. She started to cry, a reaction quite mysterious to Aryz. His link with the mandate had not been intimate enough to answer questions about the wailing and moisture from the eyes. After a time the male and female lay down and became dormant.

The mutated shape made more soft sounds and tried to approach the transparent wall. It held up its thin arms as if beseeching. The others would have nothing to do with it; now it wished to go with him. Perhaps the biologists had partially succeeded in their attempt at transformation; perhaps it was more Senexi than human.

Aryz quickly backed out through the port, into the cool and security of the corridor beyond.

It was an endless orbital dance, this detection and matching of course, moving away and swinging back, deceiving and revealing, between the *Mellangee* and the Senexi seedship. It was inevitable that the human ship should close in; human ships were faster, knew better the higher geometries.

Filled with her skill and knowledge, Prufrax waited, feeling like a ripe fruit about to fall from the tree. At this point in their training, just before the application, elfstates were very receptive. She was allowed to take a lover, and they were assigned small separate quarters near the outer greenroads.

The contact was satisfactory, as far as it went. Her mate was an older glover named Kumnax, and as they lay back in the cubicle, soothed by air-dance fibs, he told her stories about past battles, special tactics, how to survive.

"Survive?" she asked, puzzled.

"Of course." His long brown face was intent on the view of the greenroads through the cubicle's small window.

"I don't understand," she said.

"Most glovers don't make it," he said patiently.

"I will."

He turned to her. "You're six," he said. "You're very young. I'm ten. I've seen. You're about to be applied for the first time, you're full of confidence. But most glovers won't make it. They breed thousands of us. We're expendable. We're based on the best glovers of the past, but even the best don't survive."

"I will," Prufrax repeated, her jaw set.

"You always say that," he murmured.

Prufrax stared at him for a moment.

"Last time I knew you," he said, "you kept saying that. And here you are, fresh again."

"What last time?"

"Master Kumnax," a mechanical voice interrupted.

He stood, looking down at her. "We glovers always have big mouths. They don't like us knowing, but once we know, what can they do about it?"

"You are in violation," the voice said. "Please report to S."

"But now, if you last, you'll know more than the tellman tells."

"I don't understand," Prufrax said slowly, precisely, looking him straight in the eye.

"I've paid my debt," Kumnax said. "We glovers stick. Now I'm going to go get my punishment." He left the cubicle. Prufrax didn't see him again before her first application.

The seedship buried itself in a heating protostar, raising shields against the infalling ice and stone. The nebula had congealed out of a particularly rich cluster of exploded fourth-and fifth-generation stars, thick with planets, the detritus of which now fell on Aryz's ship like hail.

Aryz had never been so isolated. No other branch ind addressed him; he never even saw them now. He made his reports to the brood mind, but even there the reception was warmer and warmer, until he could barely endure to communicate. Consequently—and he realized this was part of the plan—he came closer to his charges, the human shapes. He felt more sympathy for them. He discovered that even between human and Senexi there could be a bridge and need—the need to be useful.

The brood mind was interested in one question: how successfully could they be planted aboard a human ship? Would they be accepted until they could carry out their sabotage, or would they be detected? Already Senexi instructions were being coded into their teachings.

"I think they will be accepted in the confusion of an engagement," Aryz answered. He had long since guessed the general outlines of the brood mind's plans. Communication with the human shapes was for one purpose only: to use them as decoys, insurgents. They were weapons. Knowledge of human activity and behavior was not an end in itself; seeing what was happening to him, Aryz fully understood why the brood mind wanted such study to proceed no further.

He would lose them soon, he thought, and his work would be over. He would be much too human-tainted. He would end, and his replacement would start a new existence, very little different from Aryz—but, he reasoned, adjusted. The replacement would not have Aryz's peculiarity.

He approached his last meeting with the brood mind, preparing himself for his final work, for the ending. In the cold liquid-filled chamber, the great red-and-white sac waited, the center of his team, his existence. He adored it. There was no way he could criticize its action.

Yet—

"We are being sought," the brood mind radiated. "Are the shapes ready?"

"Yes," Aryz said. "The new teaching is firm. They believe they are fully human." And, except for the new teaching, they were. "They defy sometimes." He said nothing about the mutated shape. It would not be used. If they won this encounter, it would probably be placed with Aryz's body in a fusion torch for complete purging.

"Then prepare them," the brood mind said. "They will be delivered to the vector for positioning and transfer."

Darkness and waiting. Prufrax nested in her delivery tube like a freshly chambered round. Through her gloves she caught distant communications, murmurs that resembled voices down hollow pipes. The *Mellangee* was coming to full readiness.

Huge as her ship was, Prufrax knew that it would be dwarfed by the seedship. She could recall some hazy details about the seedship's structure, but most of that information was stored securely away from interference by her conscious mind. She wasn't even positive what the tactic would be. In the mocks, that at least had been clear. Now such information either had not been delivered or had waited in inaccessible memory, to be brought forward by the appropriate triggers.

More information would be fed to her just before the launch, but she knew the general procedure. The seedship was deep in a protostar, hiding behind the distortion of geometry and the complete hash of electromagnetic energy. The *Mellangee* would approach, collide if need be. Penetrate. Release. Find. Zap. Her fingers ached. Sometime before the launch she would also be fed her final moans—the tempers—and she would be primed to leave elfstate. She would be a mature glover. She would be a woman.

If she returned

will return

she could become part of the breed, her receptivity would end in ecstasy rather than mild warmth, she would contribute second state, naturally born glovers. For a moment she was content with the thought. That was a high honor.

Her fingers ached worse.

The tempers came, moans tiding in, then the battle data. As it passed into her subconscious, she caught a flash of—

Rocks and ice, a thick cloud of dust and gas glowing red but seeming dark, no stars, no constellation guides this time. The beacon came on. That would be her only way to orient once the gloves stopped inertial and locked onto the target.

The seedship
was like
a shadow within a shadow
twenty-two kilometers across, yet
carrying
only six
teams

LAUNCH *She flies*!

Data: the *Mellangee* has buried herself in the seedship, ploughed deep into the interior like a carnivore's muzzle looking for vitals.

Instruction: a swarm of seeks is dashing through the seedship, looking for the brood minds, for the brood chambers, for branch inds. The glovers will follow.

Prufrax sees herself clearly now. She is the great avenging

comet, bringer of omen and doom, like a knife moving through the glass and ice and thin, cold helium as if they weren't there, the chambered round fired and tearing at hundreds of kilometers an hour through the Senexi vessel, following the seeks.

The seedship cannot withdraw into higher geometries now.

It is pinned by the *Mellangee*. It is hers.

Information floods her, pleases her immensely. She swoops down orange-and-grey corridors, buffeting against the walls like a ricocheting bullet. Almost immediately she comes across a branch ind, sliding through the ammonia film against the outrushing wind, trying to reach an armored cubicle. Her first Zap is too easy, not satisfying, nothing like what she thought. In her wake the branch ind becomes scattered globules of plasma. She plunges deeper.

Aryz delivers his human charges to the vectors that will launch them. They are equipped with simulations of the human weapons, their hands encased in the hideous grey gloves.

The seedship is in deadly peril; the battle has almost been lost at one stroke. The seedship cannot remain whole. It must self-destruct, taking the human ship with it, leaving only a fragment with as many teams as can escape.

The vectors launch the human shapes. Aryz tries to determine which part of the ship will be elected to survive; he must not be there. His job is over, and he must die.

The glovers fan out through the seedship's central hollow, demolishing the great cold drive engines, bypassing the shielded fusion flare and the reprocessing plant, destroying machinery built before their Earth was formed.

The special-projects sisters take the lead. Suddenly they are confused. They have found a brood mind, but it is not heavily protected. They surround it, prepare for the Zap—

It is sacrificing itself, drawing them in to an easy kill and away from another portion of the seedship. Power is concentrating elsewhere. Sensing that, they kill quickly and move on.

Aryz's brood mind prepares for escape. It begins to wrap itself in flux bind as it moves through the ship toward the frozen fragment. Already three of its five branch inds are dead; it can feel other brood minds dying. Aryz's bud replacement has been killed as well.

Following Aryz's training, the human shapes rush into corridors away from the main action. The special-projects sisters encounter the decoy male, allow it to fly with them . . . until it aims its weapons. One Zap almost takes out Trice. The others fire on the shape immediately. He goes to his death weeping, confused from the very moment of his launch.

The fragment in which the brood mind will take refuge encompasses the chamber where the humans had been nurtured, where the mandate is still stored. All the other brood minds are dead, Aryz realizes; the humans have swept down on them so quickly. What shall he do?

Somewhere, far off, he feels the distressed pulse of another branch ind dying. He probes the remains of the seedship. He is the last. He cannot dissipate now; he must ensure the brood mind's survival.

Prufrax, darting through the crumbling seedship, searching for more opportunities, comes across an injured glover. She calls for a mediseek and pushes on.

The brood mind settles into the fragment. Its support system is damaged; it is entering the time-isolated state, the flux bind, more rapidly than it should. The seals of foamed electric ice cannot quite close off the fragment before Ya, Trice, and Damu slip in. They frantically call for bind-cutters and preservers; they have instructions to capture the last brood mind, if possible.

But a trap falls upon Ya, and snarling fields tear her from her gloves. She is flung down a dark disintegrating shaft, red cracks opening all around as the seedship's integrity fails. She trails silver dust and freezes, hits a barricade, shatters.

The ice seals continue to close. Trice is caught between them and pushes out frantically, blundering into the region of the intensifying flux bind. Her gloves break into hard bits, and she is melded into an ice wall like an insect trapped on the surface of a winter lake.

Damu sees that the brood mind is entering the final phase of flux bind. After that they will not be able to touch it. She begins a desperate Zap and is too late.

Aryz directs the subsidiary energy of the flux against her. Her Zap deflects from the bind region, she is caught in an interference pattern and vibrates until her tiniest particles stop their knotted whirlpool spins and she simply becomes space and searing light.

The brood mind, however, has been damaged. It is losing information from one portion of its anatomy. Desperate for storage, it looks for places to hold the information before the flux bind's last wave.

Aryz directs an interface onto the brood mind's surface. The silvery pools of time-binding flicker around them both. The brood mind's damaged sections transfer their data into the last available storage device—the human mandate.

Now it contains both human and Senexi information.

The silvery pools unite, and Aryz backs away. No longer can he sense the brood mind. It is out of reach but not yet safe. He must propel the fragment from the remains of the seedship. Then he must wrap the fragment in its own flux bind, cocoon it in physics to protect it from the last ravages of the humans.

Aryz carefully navigates his way through the few remaining corridors. The helium atmosphere has almost completely dissipated, even there. He strains to remember all the procedures. Soon the seedship will explode, destroying the human ship. By then they must be gone.

Angry red, Prufrax follows his barely sensed form, watching him behind barricades of ice, approaching the moment of a most satisfying Zap. She gives her gloves their way and finds a shape behind her, wearing gloves that are not gloves, not like her own, but capable of grasping her in tensed fields, blocking the Zap, dragging them together. The fragment separates, heat pours in from the protostar cloud. They are swirled in their vortex of power, twin locked comets—one red, one sullen grey.

"Who are you?" Prufrax screams as they close in on each other in the fields. Their environments meld. They grapple. In the confusion, the darkening, they are drawn out of the cloud with the fragment, and she sees the other's face.

Her own.

The seedship self-destructs. The fragment is propelled from the protostar, above the plane of what will become planets in their orbits, away from the crippled and dying *Mellangee*.

Desperate, Prufrax uses all her strength to drill into the fragment. Helium blows past them, and bits of dead branch inds.

Aryz catches the pair immediately in the shapes chamber, rearranging the fragment's structure to enclose them with the mutant shape and mandate. For the moment he has time enough to concentrate on them. They are dangerous. They are almost equal to each other, but his shape is weakening faster than the true glover. They float, bouncing from wall to wall in the chamber, forcing the mutant to crawl into a corner and howl with fear.

There may be value in saving the one and capturing the other. Involved as they are, the two can be carefully dissected from their fields and induced into a crude kind of sleep before the glover has a chance to free her weapons. He can dispose of the gloves—fake and real—and hook them both to the Mam, reattach the mutant shape as well. Perhaps something can be learned from the failure of the experiment.

The dissection and capture occur faster than the planning. His movement slows under the spreading flux bind. His last action, after attaching the humans to the Mam, is to make sure the brood mind's flux bind is properly nested within that of the ship.

The fragment drops into simpler geometries.

It is as if they never existed.

The battle was over. There were no victors. Aryz became aware of the passage of time, shook away the sluggishness, and crawled through painfully dry corridors to set the environmental equipment going again. Throughout the fragment, machines struggled back to activity.

How many generations? The constellations were unrecognizable. He made star traces and found familiar spectra and types, but advanced in age. There had been a malfunction in the overall flux bind. He couldn't find the nebula where the battle had occurred. In its place were comfortably middle-aged stars surrounded by young planets.

Aryz came down from the makeshift observatory. He slid through the fragment, established the limits of his new home, and found the solid mirror surface of the brood mind's cocoon. It was still locked in flux bind, and he knew of no way to free it. In time the bind would probably wear off—but that might require life spans. The seedship was gone. They had lost the brood chamber, and with it the stock.

He was the last branch ind of his team. Not that it mattered now; there was nothing he could initiate without a brood mind. If the flux bind was permanent—as sometimes happened during malfunction—then he might as well be dead.

He closed his thoughts around him and was almost completely submerged when he sensed an alarm from the shapes chamber. The interface with the mandate had turned itself off; the new version of the Mam was malfunctioning. He tried to repair the equipment, but without the engineer's wall he was almost helpless. The best he could do was rig a temporary nutrition supply through the old human-form Mam. When he was done, he looked at the captive and the two shapes, then at the legless, armless Mam that served as their link to the interface and life itself.

She had spent her whole life in a room barely eight by ten meters, and not much taller than her own height. With her had been Grayd and the silent round creature whose name—if it had any—they had never learned. For a time there had been Mam, then another kind of Mam not nearly as satisfactory. She was hardly aware that her entire existence had been miserable, cramped, in one way or another incomplete.

Separated from them by a transparent partition, another round shape had periodically made itself known by voice or gesture.

Grayd had kept her sane. They had engaged in conspiracy. Removing themselves from the interface—what she called "eyes-shut"—they had held on to each other, tried to make sense out of what they knew instinctively, what was fed them through the interface, and what the being beyond the partition told them.

First they knew their names, and they knew that they were glovers. They knew that glovers were fighters. When Aryz passed instruction through the interface of how to fight, they had accepted it eagerly but uneasily. It didn't seem to jibe with instructions locked deep within their instincts.

Five years under such conditions had made her introspective. She expected nothing, sought little beyond experience in the eyes-shut. Eyes-open with Grayd seemed scarcely more than a dream. They usually managed to ignore the peculiar round creature in the chamber with them; it spent nearly all its time hooked to the mandate and the Mam.

Of one thing only was she completely sure. Her name was Prufrax. She said it in eyes-open and eyes-shut, her only certainty.

Not long before the battle, she had been in a condition resembling dreamless sleep, like a robot being given instructions. The part of Prufrax that had taken on personality during eyes-shut and eyes-open for five years had been superseded by the fight instructions Aryz had programmed. She had flown as glovers must fly (though the gloves didn't seem quite right). She had fought, grappling (she thought) with herself, but who could be certain of anything?

She had long since decided that reality was not to be sought too avidly. After the battle she fell back into the mandate—into eyes-shut—all too willingly.

And what matter? If eyes-open was even less comprehensible than eyes-shut, why did she have the nagging feeling eyes-open was so compelling, so necessary? She tried to forget.

But a change had come to eyes-shut, too. Before the battle, the information had been selected. Now she could wander through the mandate at will. She seemed to smell the new information, completely unfamiliar, like a whiff of ocean. She hardly knew where to begin. She stumbled across:

—that all vessels will carry one, no matter what their size or class, just as every individual carries the map of a species. The mandate shall contain all the information of our kind, including accurate and uncensored history, for if we have learned anything, it is that censored and untrue accounts distort the eyes of the leaders. Leaders must have access to the truth. It is their responsibility. Whatever is told those who work under the leaders, for whatever reasons must not be believed by the leaders. Unders are told lies. Leaders must seek and be provided with accounts as accurate as possible, or we will be weakened and fall—

What wonderful dreams the *leaders* must have had. And they possessed some intrinsic gift called *truth*, through the use of the *mandate*. Prufrax could hardly believe that. As she made her tentative explorations through the new fields of eyes-shut, she began to link the word *mandate* with what she experienced. That was where she was.

And she alone. Once, she had explored with Grayd. Now there was no sign of Grayd.

She learned quickly. Soon she walked along a beach on Earth, then a beach on a world called Myriadne, and other beaches, fading in and out. By running through the entries rapidly, she came up with a blurred *eidos* and so learned what a beach was in the abstract. It was a boundary between one kind of eyes-shut and another, between water and land, neither of which had any corollary in eyes-open.

Some beaches had sand. Some had clouds—the *eidos* of clouds was quite attractive. And one—

had herself running scared, screaming.

She called out, but the figure vanished. Prufrax stood on a beach under a greenish-yellow star, on a world called Kyrene, feeling lonelier than ever.

She explored farther, hoping to find Grayd, if not the figure that looked like herself. Grayd wouldn't flee from her. Grayd would—

The round thing confronted her, its helpless limbs twitching. Now it was her turn to run, terrified. Never before had she met the round creature in eyes-shut. It was mobile; it had a purpose. Over land, clouds, trees, rocks, wind, air, equations, and an edge of physics she fled. The farther she went, the more distant from the round one with hands and small head, the less afraid she was.

She never found Grayd.

The memory of the battle was fresh and painful. She remembered the ache of her hands, clumsily removed from the gloves. Her environment had collapsed and been replaced by something indistinct. Prufrax had fallen into a deep slumber and had dreamed.

The dreams were totally unfamiliar to her. If there was a left-turning in her arc of sleep, she dreamed of philosophies and languages and other things she couldn't relate to. A right-turning led to histories and sciences so incomprehensible as to be nightmares.

It was a most unpleasant sleep, and she was not at all sorry to find she wasn't really asleep.

The crucial moment came when she discovered how to slow her turnings and the changes of dream subject. She entered a pleasant place of which she had no knowledge but which did not seem threatening. There was a vast expanse of water, but it didn't terrify her. She couldn't even identify it as water until she scooped up a handful. Beyond the water was a floor of shifting particles. Above both was an open expanse, not black but obviously space, drawing her eyes into intense pale blue-green. And there was that figure she had encountered in the seedship. Herself. The figure pursued. She fled.

Right over the boundary into Senexi information. She knew then that what she was seeing couldn't possibly come from within herself. She was receiving data from another source. Perhaps she had been taken captive. It was possible she was now being forcibly debriefed. The tellman had discussed such possibilities, but none of the glovers had been taught how to defend themselves in specific situations. Instead it had been stated—in terms that brooked no second thought—that selfdestruction was the only answer. So she tried to kill herself.

She sat in the freezing cold of a red-and-white room, her feet meeting but not touching a fluid covering on the floor. The information didn't fit her senses—it seemed blurred, inappropriate. Unlike the other data, this didn't allow participation or motion. Everything was locked solid.

She couldn't find an effective means of killing herself. She resolved to close her eyes and simply will herself into dissolution. But closing her eyes only moved her into a deeper or shallower level of deception—other categories, subjects, visions. She couldn't sleep, wasn't tired, couldn't die.

Like a leaf on a stream, she drifted. Her thoughts untangled, and she imagined herself floating on the water called ocean. She kept her eyes open. It was quite by accident that she encountered:

Instruction. Welcome to the introductory use of the mandate. As a noncombat processor, your duties are to maintain the mandate, provide essential information for your overs, and, if necessary, protect or destroy the mandate. The mandate is your immediate over. If it requires maintenance, you will oblige. Once linked with the mandate, as you are now, you may explore any aspect of the information by requesting delivery. To request delivery, indicate the core of your subject—

Prufrax! she shouted silently. What is Prufrax?

A voice with different tone immediately took over.

Ah, now that's quite a story. I was her biographer, the organizer of her life tapes (ref. GEORGE MACKNAX), and knew her well in the last years of her life. She was born in the Ferment 26468. Here are selected life tapes. Choose emphasis. Analyses follow.

—Hey! Who are you? There's someone here with me . . .

—Shh! Listen. Look at her. Who is she?

They looked, listened to the information.

—Why, she's *me* . . . sort of.

—She's *us*.

She stood two and a half meters tall. Her hair was black and thick, though cut short; her limbs well-muscled though drawn out by the training and hormonal treatments. She was seventeen years old, one of the few birds born in the solar system, and for the time being she had a chip on her shoulder. Everywhere she went, the birds asked about her mother, Jayax. "You better than her?"

Of course not! Who could be? But she was good; the instructors said so. She was just about through training, and whether she graduated to hawk or remained bird she would do her job well. Asking Prufrax about her mother was likely to make her set her mouth tight and glare.

On Mercior, the Grounds took up four thousand hectares and had its own port. The Grounds was divided into Land, Space, and Thought, and training in each area was mandatory for fledges, those birds embarking on hawk training. Prufrax was fledge three. She had passed Land—though she loathed downbound fighting—and was two years into Space. The tough part, everyone said, was not passing Space, but lasting through four years of Thought after the action in nearorbit and planetary.

Prufrax was not the introspective type. She could be studious when it suited her. She was a quick study at weapon maths, physics came easy when it had a direct application, but theory of service and polinstruc—which she had sampled only in prebird courses—bored her.

Since she had been a little girl, no more than five—

—Five! Five what?

and had seen her mother's ships and fightsuits and fibs, she had known she would never be happy until she had ventured far out and put a seedship in her sights, had convinced a Senexi of the overness of end—

—The Zap! She's talking the Zap!

—What's that?

—You're me, you should know.

—I'm not you, we're not her.

The Zap, said the mandate, and the data shifted.

"Tomorrow you receive your first implants. These will allow you to coordinate with the zero-angle phase engines and find your targets much more rapidly than you ever could with simple biologic. The implants, of course, will be delivered through your noses—minor irritation and sinus trouble, no more—into your limbic system. Later in your training, hookups and digital adapts will be installed as well. Are there any questions?"

"Yes, sir." Prufrax stood at the top of the spherical classroom, causing the hawk instructor to swivel his platform. "I'm having problems with the zero-angle phase maths. Reduction of the momenta of the real."

Other fledge threes piped up that they, too, had had trouble with those maths. The hawk instructor sighed. "We don't want to install cheaters in all of you. It's bad enough needing implants to supplement biologic. Individual learning is much more desirable. Do you request cheaters?" That was a challenge. They all responded negatively, but Prufrax had a secret smile. She knew the subject. She just took delight in having the maths explained again. She could reinforce an already thorough understanding. Others not so well versed would benefit. She wasn't wasting time. She was in the pleasure of her weapon—the weapon she would be using against the Senexi.

"Zero-angle phase is the temporary reduction of the momenta of the real." Equations and plexes appeared before each student as the instructor went on. "Nested unreals can conflict if a barrier is placed between the participator princip and the assumption of the real. The effectiveness of the participator can be determined by a convenience model we call the angle of phase. Zero-angle phase is achieved by an opaque probability field according to modified Fourier of the separation of real waves. This can also be caused by the reflection of the beam—an effective counter to zero-angle phase, since the beam is always compoundable and the compound is always time-reversed. Here are the true gedanks—"

—Zero-angle phase. She's learning the Zap.

—She hates them a lot, doesn't she?

—The Senexi? They're Senexi.

—I think . . . eyes-open is the world of the Senexi. What does that mean?

—That we're prisoners. You were caught before me.

—Oh.

The news came as she was in recovery from the implant. Seedships had violated human space again, dropping cuckoos on thirty-five worlds. The worlds had been young colonies, and the cuckoos had wiped out all life, then tried to reseed with Senexi forms. The overs had reacted by sterilizing the planet's surfaces. No victory, loss to both sides. It was as if the Senexi were so malevolent they didn't care about success, only about destruction.

She hated them. She could imagine nothing worse.

Prufrax was twenty-three. In a year she would be qualified to hawk on a cruiser/raider. She would demonstrate her hatred.

Aryz felt himself slipping into endthought, the mind set that always preceded a branch ind's self-destruction. What was there for him to do? The fragment had survived, but at what cost, to what purpose? Nothing had been accomplished. The nebula had been lost, or he supposed it had. He would likely never know the actual outcome.

He felt a vague irritation at the lack of a spectrum of responses. Without a purpose, a branch ind was nothing more than excess plasm.

He looked in on the captive and the shapes, all hooked to the mandate, and wondered what he would do with them. How would humans react to the situation he was in? More vigorously, probably. They would fight on. They always had. Even without leaders, with no discernible purpose, even in defeat. What gave them such stamina? Were they superior, more deserving? If they were better, then was it right for the Senexi to oppose their triumph?

Aryz drew himself tall and rigid with confusion. He had studied them too long. They had truly infected him. But here at least was a hint of purpose. A question needed to be answered.

He made preparations. There were signs the brood mind's flux bind was not permanent, was in fact unwinding quite rapidly. When it emerged, Aryz would present it with a judgment, an answer.

He realized, none too clearly, that by Senexi standards he was now a raving lunatic.

He would hook himself into the mandate, improve the somewhat isolating interface he had used previously to search for selected answers. He, the captive, and the shapes would be immersed in human history together. They would be like young suckling on a Population I mother-animal—just the opposite of the Senexi process, where young fed nourishment and information into the brood mind.

The mandate would nourish, or poison. Or both.

—Did she love?

—What—you mean, did she receive?

—No, did she—we—I—give?

—I don't know what you mean.

—I wonder if *she* would know what I mean . . .

Love, said the mandate, and the data proceeded.

Prufrax was twenty-nine. She had been assigned to a cruiser in a new program where superior but untested fighters were put into thick action with no preliminary. The program was designed to see how well the Grounds prepared fighters; some thought it foolhardy, but Prufrax found it perfectly satisfactory.

The cruiser was a million-ton raider, with a hawk contingent of fifty-three and eighty regular crew. She would be in a second-wave attack, following the initial hardfought.

She was scared. That was good; fright improved basic biologic, if properly managed. The cruiser would make a raid into Senexi space and retaliate for past cuckoo-seeding programs. They would come up against thornships and seedships, likely.

The fighting was going to be fierce.

The raider made its final denial of the overness of the real and pip-squeezed into an arduous, nasty sponge space. It drew itself together again and emerged far above the galactic plane.

Prufrax sat in the hawks wardroom and looked at the simulated rotating snowball of stars. Red-coded numerals flashed along the borders of known Senexi territory, signifying old stars, dark hulks of stars, the whole ghostly home region where they had first come to power when the terrestrial sun had been a mist-wrapped youngster. A green arrow showed the position of the raider.

She drank sponge-space supplements with the others but felt isolated because of her firstness, her fear. Everyone seemed so calm. Most were fours or fives—on their fourth or fifth battle call. There were ten ones and an upper scatter of experienced hawks with nine to twenty-five battles behind them. There were no thirties. Thirties were rare in combat; the few that survived so many engagements were plucked off active and retired to PR service under the polinstructors. They often ended up in fibs, acting poorly, looking unhappy.

Still, when she had been more naive, Prufrax's heroes had been a man-and-woman thirty team she had watched in fib after fib—Kumnax and Arol. They had been better actors than most.

Day in, day out, they drilled in their fightsuits. While the crew bustled, hawks were put through implant learning, what slang was already calling the Know, as opposed to the Tell, of classroom teaching. Getting background, just enough to tickle her curiosity, not enough to stimulate morbid interest.

—There it is again. Feel?

—I know it. Yes. The round one, part of eyes-open . . .

—Senexi?

—No, brother without name.

—Your . . . brother?

—No . . . I don't know.

—Can it hurt us?

—It never has. It's trying to talk to us.

—Leave us alone!

—It's going.

Still, there were items of information she had never received before, items privileged only to the fighters, to assist them in their work. Older hawks talked about the past, when data had been freely available. Stories circulated in the wardroom about the Senexi, and she managed to piece together something of their origins and growth.

Senexi worlds, according to a twenty, had originally been large, cold masses of gas circling bright young suns nearly metal-free. Their gas-giant planets had orbited the suns at hundreds of millions of kilometers and had been dusted by the shrouds of neighboring dead stars; the essential elements carbon, nitrogen, silicon, and fluorine had gathered in sufficient quantities on some of the planets to allow Population II biology.

In cold ammonia seas, lipids had combined in complex chains. A primal kind of life had arisen and flourished. Across millions of years, early Senexi forms had evolved. Compared with evolution on Earth, the process at first had moved quite rapidly. The mechanisms of procreation and evolution had been complex in action, simple in chemistry.

There had been no competition between life forms of different genetic bases. On Earth, much time had been spent selecting between the plethora of possible ways to pass on genetic knowledge.

And among the early Senexi, outside of predation there had been no death. Death had come about much later, self-imposed for social reasons. Huge colonies of protoplasmic individuals had gradually resolved into the team-forms now familiar.

Soon information was transferred through the budding of branch inds; cultures quickly developed to protect the integrity of larvae, to allow them to regroup and form a new brood mind. Technologies had been limited to the rare heavy materials available, but the Senexi had expanded for a time with very little technology. They were well adapted to their environment, with few predators and no need to hunt, absorbing stray nutrients from the atmosphere and from layers of liquid ammonia. With perceptions attuned to the radio and microwave frequencies, they had before long turned groups of branch inds into radio telescope chains, piercing the heavy atmosphere and probing the universe in great detail, especially the very active center of the young galaxy. Huge jets of matter, streaming from other galaxies and emitting high-energy radiation, had provided laboratories for their vicarious observations. Physics was a primitive science to them.

Since little or no knowledge was lost in breeding cycles, cultural growth was rapid at times; since the dead weight of knowledge was often heavy, cultural growth often slowed to a crawl.

Using water, as a building material, developing techniques that humans still understood imperfectly, they prepared for travel away from their birthworlds.

Prufrax wondered, as she listened to the older hawks, how humans had come to know all this. Had Senexi been captured and questioned? Was it all theory? Did anyone really know—anyone she could ask?

—She's weak.

—Why weak?

—Some knowledge is best for glovers to ignore. Some questions are best left to the supreme overs.

—Have you thought that in here, you can answer her questions, our questions?

—No. No. Learn about me—us—first.

In the hour before engagement, Prufrax tried to find a place alone. On the raider this wasn't difficult. The ship's size was overwhelming for the number of hawks and crew aboard. There were many areas where she could put on an environs and walk or drift in silence, surrounded by the dark shapes of equipment wrapped in plexerv. There was so much about ship operations she didn't understand, hadn't been taught. Why carry so much excess equipment, weapons—far more than they'd need even for replacements? She could think of possibilities—superiors on Mercior wanting their cruisers to have flexible mission capabilities, for one—but her ignorance troubled her less than *why* she was ignorant. Why was it necessary to keep fighters in the dark on so many subjects?

She pulled herself through the cold G-less tunnels, feeling slightly awked by the loneness, the quiet. One tunnel angled outboard, toward the hull of the cruiser. She hesitated, peering into its length with her environs beacon, when a beep warned her she was near another crew member. She was startled to think someone else might be as curious as she. The other hawks and crew, for the most part, had long outgrown their need to wander and regarded it as birdish. Prufrax was used to being different—she had always perceived herself, with some pride, as a bit of a freak. She scooted expertly up the tunnel, spreading her arms and tucking her legs as she would in a fightsuit.

The tunnel was filled with a faint milky green mist, absorbing her environs beam. It couldn't be much more than a couple of hundred meters long, however, and it was quite straight. The signal beeped louder.

Ahead she could make out a dismantled weapons blister. That explained the fog: a plexerv aerosol diffused in the low pressure. Sitting in the blister was a man, his environs glowing a pale violet. He had deopaqued a section of the blister and was staring out at the stars. He swiveled as she approached and looked her over dispassionately. He seemed to be a hawk—he had fightform, tall, thin with brown hair above hull-white skin, large eyes with pupils so dark she might have been looking through his head into space beyond.

"Under," she said as their environs met and merged.

"Over. What are you doing here?"

"I was about to ask you the same."

"You should be getting ready for the fight," he admonished.

"I am. I need to be alone for a while."

"Yes." He turned back to the stars. "I used to do that, too."

"You don't fight now?"

He shook his head. "Retired. I'm a researcher."

She tried not to look impressed. Crossing rates was almost impossible. A bitalent was unusual in the service.

"What kind of research?" she asked.

"I'm here to correlate enemy finds."

"Won't find much of anything, after we're done with the zero phase."

It would have been polite for him to say, "Power to that," or offer some other encouragement. He said nothing.

"Why would you want to research them?"

"To fight an enemy properly, you have to know what they are. Ignorance is defeat."

"You research tactics?"

"Not exactly."

"What, then?"

"You'll be in a tough hardfought this wake. Make you a proposition. You fight well, observe, come to me and tell me what you see. Then I'll answer your questions."

"Brief you before my immediate overs?"

"I have the authority," he said. No one had ever lied to her; she didn't even suspect he would. "You're eager?"

"Very."

"You'll be doing what?"

"Engaging Senexi fighters, then hunting down branch inds and brood minds."

"How many fighters going in?"

"Twelve."

"Big target, eh?"

She nodded.

"While you're there, ask yourself—what are they fighting for? Understand?"

"I—"

"Ask, what are they fighting for. Just that. Then come back to me."

"What's your name?"

"Not important," he said. "Now go."

She returned to the prep center as the sponge-space warning tones began. Overhawks went among the fighters in the lineup, checking gear and giveaway body points for mental orientation. Prufrax submitted to the molded sensor mask being slipped over her face. "Ready!" the overhawk said. "Hardfought!" He clapped her on the shoulder. "Good luck."

"Thank you, sir." She bent down and slid into her fightsuit. Along the launch line, eleven other hawks did the same. The overs and other crew left the chamber, and twelve red beams delineated the launch tube. The fightsuits automatically lifted and aligned on their individual beams. Fields swirled around them like silvery tissue in moving water, then settled and hardened into cold scintillating walls, pulsing as the launch energy built up.

The tactic came to her. The ship's sensors became part of her information net. She saw the Senexi thornship—twelve kilometers in diameter, cuckoos lacing its outer hull like maggots on red fruit, snakes waiting to take them on.

She was terrified and exultant, so worked up that her body temperature was climbing. The fightsuit adjusted her balance.

At the count of ten and nine, she switched from biologic to cyber. The implant—after absorbing much of her thought processes for weeks—became Prufrax.

For a time there seemed to be two of her. Biologic continued, and in that region she could even relax a bit, as if watching a fib.

With almost dreamlike slowness, in the electronic time of cyber, her fightsuit followed the beam. She saw the stars and oriented herself to the cruiser's beacon, using both for reference, plunging in the sword-flower formation to assault the thornship. The cuckoos retreated in the vast red hull like worms withdrawing into an apple. Then hundreds of tiny black pinpoints appeared in the closest quadrant to the sword flower.

Snakes shot out, each piloted by a Senexi branch ind. "Hardfought!" she told herself in biologic before that portion gave over completely to cyber.

Why were we flung out of dark
through ice and fire, a shower
of sparks? a puzzle;
Perhaps to build hell.

We strike here, there;
Set brief glows, fall through
and cross round again.

By our dimming, we see what
Beatitude we have.
In the circle, kindling
together, we form an
exhausted Empyrean.

We feel the rush of
igniting winds but still
grow dull and wan.

New rage flames, new light,
dropping like sun through muddy
ice and night and fall
Close, spinning blue and bright.
In time they, too,
Tire. Redden.
We join, compare pasts
cool in huddled paths,
turn grey.

And again.
We are a companion flow
of ash, in the slurry,
out and down.
We sleep.

Rivers form above and below.
Above, iron snakes twist,
clang and slice, chime,
helium eyes watching, seeing
Snowflake hawks,
signaling adamant muscles and
energy teeth. What hunger
compels our venom spit?

It flies, strikes the crystal
flight, making mist grey-green
with ammonia rain.

Sleeping, we glide,
and to each side
unseen shores wait
with the moans of an
unseen tide.

—She wrote that. We. One of her—our—poems.
—Poem?
—A kind of fib, I think.

—I don't see what it says.
—Sure you do! She's talking hardfought.
—The Zap? Is that all?
—No, I don't think so.
—Do you understand it?
—Not all . . .

She lay back in the bunk, legs crossed, eyes closed, feeling the receding dominance of the implant—the overness of cyber—and the almost pleasant ache in her back. She had survived her first. The thornship had retired, severely damaged, its surface seared and scored so heavily it would never release cuckoos again.

It would become a hulk, a decoy. Out of action. *Satisfaction/out of action/Satisfaction* . . .

Still, with eight of the twelve fighters lost, she didn't quite feel the exuberance of the rhyme. The snakes had fought very well. Bravely, she might say. They lured, sacrificed, cooperated, demonstrating teamwork as fine as that in her own group. Strategy was what made the cruiser's raid successful. A superior approach, an excellent tactic. And perhaps even surprise, though the final analysis hadn't been posted yet.

Without those advantages, they might have all died.

She opened her eyes and stared at the pattern of blinking lights in the ceiling panel, lights with their secret codes that repeated every second, so that whenever she looked at them, the implant deep inside was debriefed, reinstructed. Only when she fought would she know what she was now seeing.

She returned to the tunnel as quickly as she was able. She floated up toward the blister and found him there, surrounded by packs of information from the last hardfought. She waited until he turned his attention to her.

"Well?" he said.

"I asked myself what they are fighting for. And I'm very angry."

"Why?"

"Because I don't know. I *can't* know. They're Senexi."

"Did they fight well?"

"We lost eight. Eight." She cleared her throat.

"Did they fight well?" he repeated, an edge in his voice.

"Better than I was ever told they could."

"Did they die?"

"Enough of them."

"How many did you kill?"

"I don't know." But she did. Eight.

"You killed eight," he said, pointing to the packs. "I'm analyzing the battle now."

"You're behind what we read, what gets posted?" she asked.

"Partly," he said. "You're a good hawk."

"I knew I would be," she said, her tone quiet, simple.

"Since they fought bravely—"

"How can Senexi be brave?" she asked sharply.

"Since," he repeated, "they fought bravely, why?"

"They want to live, to do their . . . work. Just like me."

"No," he said. She was confused, moving between extremes in her mind, first resisting, then giving in too much. "They're Senexi. They're not like us."

"What's your name?" she asked, dodging the issue.

"Clevo."

Her glory hadn't even begun yet, and already she was well into her fall.

Aryz made his connection and felt the brood mind's emergency cache of knowledge in the mandate grow up around him like ice crystals on glass. He stood in a static scene. The transition from living memory to human machine memory had resulted in either a coding of data or a reduction of detail; either way, the memory was cold, not dynamic. It would have to be compared, recorrelated, if that would ever be possible.

How much human data had had to be dumped to make space for this?

He cautiously advanced into the human memory, calling up topics almost at random. In the short time he had been away, so much of what he had learned seemed to have faded or become scrambled. Branch inds were supposed to have permanent memory; human data, for one reason or another, didn't take. It required so much effort just to begin to understand the different modes of thought.

He backed away from sociological data, trying to remain within physics and mathematics. There he could make conversations to fit his understanding without too much strain.

Then something unexpected happened. He felt the brush of

another mind, a gentle inquiry from a source made even stranger by the hint of familiarity. It made what passed for a Senexi greeting, but not in the proper form, using what one branchind of a team would radiate to a fellow; a gross breach, since it was obviously not from his team or even from his family. Aryz tried to withdraw. How was it possible for minds to meet in the mandate? As he retreated, he pushed into a broad region of incomprehensible data. It had none of the characteristics of the other human regions he had examined.

—This is for machines, the other said.—Not all cultural data is limited to biologic. You are in the area where programs and cyber designs are stored. They are really accessible only to a machine hooked into the mandate.

—What is your family? Aryz asked, the first step-question in the sequence Senexi used for urgent identity requests.

—I have no family. I am not a branch ind. No access to active brood minds. I have learned from the mandate.

—Then what are you?

—I don't know, exactly. Not unlike you.

Aryz understood what he was dealing with. It was the mind of the mutated shape, the one that had remained in the chamber, beseeching when he approached the transparent barrier.

—I must go now, the shape said. Aryz was alone again in the incomprehensible jumble. He moved slowly, carefully, into the Senexi sector, calling up subjects familiar to him. If he could encounter one shape, doubtless he could encounter the others—perhaps even the captive.

The idea was dreadful—and fascinating. So far as he knew, such intimacy between Senexi and human had never happened before. Yet there was something very Senexi-like in the method, as if branch inds attached to the brood mind were to brush mentalities while searching in the ageless memories.

The dread subsided. There was little worse that could happen to him, with his fellows dead, his brood mind in flux bind, his purpose uncertain.

What Aryz was feeling, for the first time, was a small measure of *freedom*.

The story of the original Prufrax continued.

In the early stages she visited Clevo with a barely concealed anger.

His method was aggravating, his goals never precisely spelled out. What did he want with her, if anything?

And she with him? Their meetings were clandestine, though not precisely forbidden. She was a hawk, one now with considerable personal liberty between exercises and engagements. There were no monitors in the closed-off reaches of the cruiser, and they could do whatever they wished. The two met in areas close to the ship's hull, usually in weapons blisters that could be opened to reveal the stars; there they talked.

Prufrax was not accustomed to prolonged conversation. Hawks were not raised to be voluble, nor were they selected for their curiosity. Yet the exhawk Clevo talked a great deal and was the most curious person she had met, herself included and she regarded herself as uncharacteristically curious.

Often he was infuriating, especially when he played the "leading game," as she called it. Leading her from one question to the next like an instructor, but without the trappings of any clarity of purpose. "What do you think of your mother?"

"Does that matter?"

"Not to me."

"Then why ask?"

"Because you matter."

Prufrax shrugged. "She was a fine mother. She bore me with a well-chosen heritage. She raised me as a hawk candidate. She told me her stories."

"Any hawk I know would envy you for listening at Jay-ax's knee."

"I was hardly at her knee."

"A speech tactic."

"Yes, well, she was important to me."

"She was a preferred single?"

"Yes."

"So you have no father."

"She selected without reference to individuals."

"Then you are really not that much different from a Senexi."

She bristled and started to push away. "There! You insult me again."

"Not at all. I've been asking one question all this time, and you haven't even heard. How well do you know the enemy?"

"Well enough to destroy them." She couldn't believe that was the only question he'd been asking. His speech tactics were very odd.

"Yes, to win battles, perhaps. But who will win the war?"

"It'll be a long war," she said softly, floating a few meters from him. He rotated in the blister, blocking out a blurred string of stars. The cruiser was preparing to shift out of status geometry again. "They fight well."

"They fight with conviction. Do you believe them to be evil?"

"They destroy us."

"We destroy them."

"So the question," she said, smiling at her cleverness, "is who began to destroy?"

"Not at all," Clevo said. "I suspect there's no longer a clear answer to that. Our leaders have obviously decided the question isn't important. No. We are the new, they are the old. The old must be superseded. It's a conflict born in the essential difference between Senexi and humans."

"That's the only way we're different? They're old, we're not so old? I don't understand."

"Nor do I, entirely."

"Well, finally!"

"The Senexi," Clevo continued, unperturbed, "long ago needed only gas-giant planets like their homeworlds. They lived in peace for billions of years before our world was formed. But as they moved from star to star, they learned uses for other types of worlds. We were most interested in rocky Earth-like planets. Gradually, we found uses for gas giants, too. By the time we met, both of us encroached on the other's territory. Their technology is so improbable, so unlike ours, that when we first encountered them, we thought they must come from another geometry."

"Where did you learn all this?" Prufrax squinted at him suspiciously.

"I'm no longer a hawk," he said, "but I was too valuable just to discard. My experience was too broad, my abilities too useful. So I was placed in research. It seems a safe place for me. Little contact with my comrades." He looked directly at her. "We must try to know our enemy, at least a little."

"That's dangerous," Prufrax said, almost instinctively.

"Yes, it is. What you know, you cannot hate."

"We must hate," she said. "It makes us strong. Senexi hate."

"They might," he said. "But, sometime, wouldn't you like to . . . sit down and talk with one, after a battle? Talk with a fighter? Learn its tactic, how it bested you in one move, compare—"

"No!" Prufrax shoved off rapidly down the tube. "We're shifting now. We have to get ready."

—She's smart. She's leaving him. He's crazy.

—Why do you think that?

—He would stop the fight, end the Zap.

—But he was a hawk.

—And hawks became glovers, I guess. But glovers go wrong, too. Like you.

—?

—Did you know they used you? How you were used?

—That's all blurred now.

—She's doomed if she stays around him. Who's that?

—Someone is listening with us.

—Recognize?

—No, gone now.

The next battle was bad enough to fall into the hellfought. Prufrax was in her fightsuit, legs drawn up as if about to kick off. The cruiser exited sponge space and plunged into combat before sponge-space supplements could reach full effectiveness. She was dizzy, disoriented. The overhawks could only hope that a switch from biologic to cyber would cure the problem.

She didn't know what they were attacking. Tactic was flooding the implant, but she was only receiving the wash of that; she hadn't merged yet. She sensed that things were confused. That bothered her. Overs did not feel confusion.

The cruiser was taking damage. She could sense at least that, and she wanted to scream in frustration. Then she was ordered to merge with the implant. Biologic became cyber. She was in the Know.

The cruiser had reintegrated above a gas-giant planet. They were seventy-nine thousand kilometers from the upper atmosphere. The damage had come from ice mines—chunks of Senexi-treated water ice, altered to stay in sponge space until a human vessel integrated nearby. Then they emerged, packed with momentum and all the residual instability of an unsuccessful exit into status geometry. Unsuccessful for a ship, that is—very successful for a weapon.

The ice mines had given up the overness of the real within range of the cruiser and had blasted out whole sections of the hull. The launch lanes had not been damaged. The fighter lined up on their beams and were peppered out into space spreading in the classic sword flower.

The planet was a cold nest. Over didn't know what the atmosphere contained, but Senexi activity had been high in the star system, concentrating on this world. Over had decided to take a chance. Fighters headed for the atmosphere. The cruise began planting singularity eggs. The eggs went ahead of the fighters, great black grainy ovoids that seemed to leave a trail of shadow—the wake of a birthing disruption in status geometry that could turn a gas giant into a short-lived sun.

Their time was limited. The fighters would group on entry sleds and descend to the liquid water regions where Senexi commonly kept their upwelling power plants. The fighter would first destroy any plants, loop into the liquid ammonia region to search for hidden cuckoos, then see what was so important about the world.

She and five other fighters mounted the sled. Growing closer, the hazy clear regions of the atmosphere sparkled with Senexi sensors. Spiderweb beams shot from the six sleds to down the sensors. Buffet began. Scream, heat, then a second flower from the sled at a depth of two hundred kilometers. The sled slowed and held station. It would be their only way back. The fightsuits couldn't pull out of such a large gravity well.

She descended deeper. The pale, bloated beacon of the red star was dropping below the second cloudtops, limning the strata in orange and purple. At the liquid ammonia level she was instructed to key in permanent memory of all she was seeing. She wasn't "seeing" much, but other sensors were recording a great deal, all of it duly processed in her implant. "There's life here," she told herself. Indigenous life. Just another example of Senexi disregard for basic decency: they were interfering with a world developing its own complex biology.

The temperature rose to ammonia vapor levels, then to liquid water. The pressure on the fightsuit was enormous, and she was draining her stores much more rapidly than expected. At this level the atmosphere was particularly thick with organics.

Senexi snakes rose from below, passed them in altitude, then doubled back to engage. Prufrax was designated the deep diver; the others from her sled would stay at this level in her defense. As she fell, another sled group moved in behind her to double the cover.

She searched for the characteristic radiation curve of an upwelling plant. At the lower boundary of the liquid water level, below which her suit could not safely descend, she found it.

The Senexi were tapping the gas giant's convection from greater depths than usual. Above the plant, almost indetectable, was another object with an uncharacteristic curve. They were separated by ten kilometers. The power plant was feeding its higher companion with tight energy beams.

She slowed. Two other fighters, disengaged from the brief skirmish above, took positions as backups a few dozen kilometers higher than she. Her implant searched for an appropriate tactic. She would avoid the zero-angle phase for the moment, go in for reconnaissance. She could feel sound pouring from the plant and its companion—rhythmic, not waste noise, but deliberate. And homing in on that sound were waves of large vermiform organisms, like chains of gas-filled sausage. They were dozens of meters long, two meters at their greatest thickness, shaped vaguely like the Senexi snake fighters. The vermiforms were native, and they were being lured into the uppermost floating structure. None were emerging. Her backups spread apart, descending, and drew up along her flanks.

She made her decision almost immediately. She could see a pattern in the approach of the natives. If she fell into the pattern, she might be able to enter the structure unnoticed.

—It's a grinder. She doesn't recognize it.

—What's a grinder?

—She should make the Zap! It's an ugly thing; Senexi use them all the time. Net a planet with grinders, like a cuckoo, but for larger operations.

The creatures were being passed through separator fields. Their organics fell from the bottom of the construct, raw material for new growth—Senexi growth. Their heavier elements were stored for later harvest.

With Prufrax in their midst, the vermiforms flew into the separator. The interior was hundreds of meters wide, lead-white walls with flat grey machinery floating in a dust haze, full of hollow noise, the distant bleats of vermiforms being slaughtered. Prufrax tried to retreat, but she was caught in a selector field. Her suit bucked and she was whirled violently, then thrown into a repository for examination. She had been screened from the separator; her plan to record, then destroy, the structure had been foiled by an automatic filter.

"Information sufficient." Command logic programmed into the implant before launch was now taking over. "Zero-angle phase both plant and adjunct." She was drifting in the repository, still slightly stunned. Something was fading. Cyber was hissing in and out; the over logic-commands were being scrambled. Her implant was malfunctioning and was returning control to biologic. The selector fields had played havoc with all cyber functions, down to the processors in her weapons.

Cautiously she examined the down systems one by one, determining what she could and could not do. This took as much as thirty seconds—an astronomical time on the implant's scale.

She still could use the phase weapon. If she was judicious and didn't waste her power, she could cut her way out of the repository, maneuver and work with her escorts to destroy both the plant and the separator. By the time they returned to the sleds, her implant might have rerouted itself and made sufficient repairs to handle defense. She had no way of knowing what was waiting for her if—when—she escaped, but that was the least of her concerns for the moment.

She tightened the setting of the phase beam and swung her fightsuit around, knocking a cluster of junk ice and silty phosphorescent dust. She activated the beam. When she had a hole large enough to pass through, she edged the suit forward, beamed through more walls and obstacles, and kicked herself out of the repository into free fall. She swiveled and laid down a pattern of wide-angle beams, at the same time relaying a message on her situation to the escorts.

The escorts were not in sight. The separator was beginning to break up, spraying debris through the almost-opaque atmosphere. The rhythmic sound ceased, and the crowds of vermiforms began to disperse.

She stopped her fall and thrust herself several kilometers higher—directly into a formation of Senexi snakes. She had barely enough power to reach the sled, much less fight and turn her beams on the upwelling plant.

Her cyber was still down.

The sled signal was weak. She had no time to calculate its

direction from the inertial guidance cyber. Besides, all cyber was unreliable after passing through the separator.

Why do they fight so well? Clevo's question clogged her thoughts. Cursing, she tried to blank and keep all her faculties available for running the fightsuit. *When evenly matched, you cannot win against your enemy unless you understand them. And if you truly understand, why are you fighting and not talking?* Clevo had never told her that—not in so many words. But it was part of a string of logic all her own.

Be more than an automaton with a narrow range of choices. Never underestimate the enemy. Those were old Grounds dicta, not entirely lost in the new training, but only emphasized by Clevo.

If they fight as well as you, perhaps in some ways they fight-think like you do. Use that.

Isolated, with her power draining rapidly, she had no choice. They might disregard her if she posed no danger. She cut her thrust and went into a diving spin. Clearly she was on her way to a high-pressure grave. They would sense her power levels, perhaps even pick up the lack of field activity if she let her shields drop. She dropped the shields. If they let her fall and didn't try to complete the kill—if they concentrated on active fighters above—she had enough power to drop into the water vapor regions, far below the plant, and silently ride a thermal into range. With luck, she could get close enough to lay a web of zero-angle phase and take out the plant.

She had minutes in which to agonize over her plan. Falling, buffeted by winds that could knock her kilometers out of range, she spun like a vagrant flake of snow.

She couldn't even expend the energy to learn if they were scanning her, checking out her potential.

Perhaps she underestimated them. Perhaps they would be that much more thorough and take her out just to be sure. Perhaps they had unwritten rules of conduct like the ones she was using, taking hunches into account. Hunches were discouraged in Grounds training—much less reliable than cyber.

She fell. Temperature increased. Pressure on her suit began to constrict her air supply. She used fighter trancing to cut back on her breathing.

Fell.

And broke the trance. Pushed through the dense smoke of exhaustion. Planned the beam web. Counted her reserves. Nudged into an updraft beneath the plant. The thermal carried her, a silent piece of paper in a storm, drifting back and forth beneath the objective. The huge field intakes pulsed above, lightning outlining their invisible extension. She held back on the beam.

Nearly faded out. Her suit interior was almost unbearably hot.

She was only vaguely aware of laying down the pattern. The beams vanished in the murk. The thermal pushed her through a layer of haze, and she saw the plant, riding high above clear-atmosphere turbulence. The zero-angle phase had pushed through the field intakes, into their source nodes and the plant body, surrounding it with bright blue Tcherenkov. First the surface began to break up, then the middle layers, and finally key supports. Chunks vibrated away with the internal fury of their molecular, then atomic, then particle disruption. Paraphrasing Grounds description of beam action, the plant became less and less convinced of its reality. "Matter dreams," an instructor had said a decade before. "Dreams it is real, maintains the dream by shifting rules with constant results. Disturb the dreams, the shifting of the rules results in inconstant results. Things cannot hold."

She slid away from the updraft, found another, wondered idly how far she would be lifted. Curiosity at the last. Let's just see, she told herself; a final experiment.

Now she was cold. The implant was flickering, showing signs of reorganization. She didn't use it. No sense expanding the amount of time until death. No sense—at all.

The sled, maneuvered by one remaining fighter, glided up beneath her almost unnoticed.

Aryz waited in the stillness of a Senexi memory, his thinking temporarily reduced to a faint susurrus. What he waited for was not clear.

—Come.

The form of address was wrong, but he recognized the voice. His thoughts stirred, and he followed the nebulous presence out of Senexi territory.

—Know your enemy.

Prufrax . . . the name of one of the human shapes sent out against their own kind. He could sense her presence in the mandate, locked into a memory store. He touched on the store and caught the essentials—the grinder, the updraft plant, the fight from Prufrax's viewpoint.

—Know how your enemy knows you.

He sensed a second presence, similar to that of Prufrax. It took him some time to realize that the human captive was another form of the shape, a reproduction of the . . .

Both were reproductions of the female whose image was in the memory store. Aryz was not impressed by threes—Senexi mysticism, what had ever existed of it, had been preoccupied with fives and sixes—but the coincidence was striking.

—Know how your enemy *sees* you.

He saw the grinder processing organics—the vermiform natives—in preparation for a widespread seeding of deuterium gatherers. The operation had evidently been conducted for some time; the vermiform populations were greatly reduced from their usual numbers. Vermiforms were a common type-species on gas giants of the sort depicted. The mutated shape nudged him into a particular channel of the memory, that which carried the original Prufrax's emotions. She had reacted with *disgust* to the Senexi procedure. It was a reaction not unlike what Aryz might feel when coming across something forbidden in Senexi behavior. Yet eradication was perfectly natural, analogous to the human cleansing of *food* before *eating*.

—It's in the memory. The vermiforms are intelligent. They have their own kind of civilization. Human action on this world prevented their complete extinction by the Senexi.

—So what matter they were *intelligent*? Aryz responded. They did not behave or think like Senexi, or like any species Senexi find compatible. They were therefore not desirable. Like humans.

—You would make humans extinct?

—We would protect ourselves from them.

—Who damages whom most?

Aryz didn't respond. The line of questioning was incomprehensible. Instead he flowed into the memory of Prufrax, propelled by another aspect of complete freedom, confusion.

The implant was replaced. Prufrax's damaged limbs and skin were repaired or regenerated quickly, and within four wakes, under intense treatment usually reserved only for overs, she regained all her reflexes and speed. She requested liberty of the cruiser while it returned for repairs. Her request was granted.

She first sought Clevo in the designated research area. He wasn't there, but a message was, passed on to her by a smiling young crew member. She read it quickly:

"You're free and out of action. Study for a while, then come find me. The old place hasn't been damaged. It's less private, but still good. Study! I've marked highlights."

She frowned at the message, then handed it to the crew member, who duly erased it and returned to his duties. She wanted to talk with Clevo, not study.

But she followed his instructions. She searched out highlighted entries in the ship's memory store. It was not nearly as dull as she had expected. In fact, by following the highlights, she felt she was learning more about Clevo and about the questions he asked.

Old literature was not nearly as graphic as fibs, but it was different enough to involve her for a time. She tried to create imitations of what she read, but erased them. Nonfib stories were harder than she suspected. She read about punishment, duty; she read about places called heaven and hell, from a writer who had died tens of thousands of years before. With ed supplement guidance, she was able to comprehend most of what she read. Plugging the store into her implant, she was able to absorb hundreds of volumes in an hour.

Some of the stores were losing definition. They hadn't been used in decades, perhaps centuries.

Halfway through, she grew impatient. She left the research area. Operating on another hunch, she didn't go to the blister as directed, but straight to memory central, two decks inboard the research area. She saw Clevo there, plugged into a data pillar, deep in some aspect of ship history. He noticed her approach, unplugged, and swiveled on his chair. "Congratulations," he said, smiling at her.

"Hardfought," she acknowledged, smiling.

"Better than that, perhaps," he said.

She looked at him quizzically. "What do you mean, better?"

"I've been doing some illicit tapping on over channels."

"So?"

—He is *dangerous*!

"You've been recommended."

"For what?"

"Not for hero status, not yet. You'll have a good many more

fights before that. And you probably won't enjoy it when you get there. You won't be a fighter then."

Prufrax stood silently before him.

"You may have a valuable genetic assortment. Overs think you behaved remarkably well under impossible conditions."

"Did I?"

He nodded. "Your type may be preserved."

"Which means?"

"There's a program being planned. They want to take the best fighters and reproduce them—clone them—to make uniform topgrade squadrons. It was rumored in my time—you haven't heard?"

She shook her head.

"It's not new. It's been done, off and on, for tens of thousands of years. This time they believe they can make it work."

"You were a fighter, once," she said. "Did they preserve your type?"

Clevo nodded. "I had something that interested them, but not, I think, as a fighter."

Prufrax looked down at her stubby-fingered hands. "It was grim," she said. "You know what we found?"

"An extermination plant."

"You want me to understand them better. Well, I can't. I refuse. How could they do such things?" She looked disgusted and answered her own question. "Because they're Senexi."

"Humans," Clevo said, "have done much the same, sometimes worse."

"No!"

—No!

"Yes," he said firmly. He sighed. "We've wiped Senexi worlds, and we've even wiped worlds with intelligent species like our own. Nobody is innocent. Not in this universe."

"We were never taught that."

"It wouldn't have made you a better hawk. But it might make a better human of you, to know. Greater depth of character. Do you want to be more aware?"

"You mean, study more?"

He nodded.

"What makes you think *you* can teach me?"

"Because you thought about what I asked you. About how Senexi thought. And you survived where some other hawk might not have. The overs think it's in your genes. It might be. But it's also in your head."

"Why not tell the overs?"

"I have," he said. He shrugged. "I'm too valuable to them, otherwise I'd have been busted again, a long time ago."

"They wouldn't want me to learn from you?"

"I don't know," Clevo said. "I suppose they're aware you're talking to me. They could stop it if they wanted. They may be smarter than I give them credit for." He shrugged again. "Of course they're smart. We just disagree at times."

"And if I learn from you?"

"Not from me, actually. From the past. From history, what other people have thought. I'm really not any more capable than you . . . but I know history, small portions of it. I won't teach you so much, as guide."

"I did use your questions," Prufrax said. "But will I ever need to use them—think that way—again?"

Clevo nodded. "Of course."

—You're quiet.

—She's giving in to him.

—She gave in a long time ago.

—She should be afraid.

—Were you—we—ever really afraid of a challenge?

—No.

—Not Senexi, not forbidden knowledge.

—Someone listens with us. Feel—

Clevo first led her through the history of past wars, judging that was appropriate considering her occupation. She was attentive enough, though her mind wandered; sometimes he was didactic, but she found that didn't bother her much. At no time did his attitude change as they pushed through the tangle of the past. Rather her perception of his attitude changed. Her perception of herself changed.

She saw that in all wars, the first stage was to dehumanize the enemy, reduce the enemy to a lower level so that he might be killed without compunction. When the enemy was not human to begin with, the task was easier. As wars progressed, this tactic frequently led to an underestimation of the enemy, with disastrous consequences. "We aren't exactly underestimating the Senexi,"

Clevo said. "The overs are too smart for that. But we refuse to understand them, and that could make the war last indefinitely."

"Then why don't the overs see that?"

"Because we're being locked into a pattern. We've been fighting for so long, we've begun to lose ourselves. And it's getting worse." He assumed his didactic tone, and she knew he was reciting something he'd formulated years before and repeated to himself a thousand times. "There is no war so important that to win it, we must destroy our minds."

She didn't agree with that; losing the war with the Senexi would mean extinction, as she understood things.

Most often they met in the single unused weapons blister that had not been damaged. They met when the ship was basking in the real between sponge-space jaunts. He brought memory stores with him in portable modules, and they read, listened, experienced together. She never placed a great deal of importance in the things she learned; her interest was focused on Clevo. Still, she learned.

The rest of her time she spent training. She was aware of a growing isolation from the hawks, which she attributed to her uncertain rank status. Was her genotype going to be preserved or not? The decision hadn't been made. The more she learned, the less she wanted to be singled out for honor. Attracting that sort of attention might be dangerous, she thought. Dangerous to whom, or what, she could not say.

Clevo showed her how hero images had been used to indoctrinate birds and hawks in a standard of behavior that was ideal, not realistic. The results were not always good; some tragic blunders had been made by fighters trying to be more than anyone possibly could or refusing to be flexible.

The war was certainly not a fib. Yet more and more the overs seemed to be treating it as one. Unable to bring about strategic victories against the Senexi, the overs had settled in for a long war of attrition and were apparently bent on adapting all human societies to the effort.

"There are overs we never hear of, who make decisions that shape our entire lives. Soon they'll determine whether or not we're even born, if they don't already."

"That sounds paranoid," she said, trying out a new word and concept she had only recently learned.

"Maybe so."

"Besides, it's been like that for ages—not knowing all our overs."

"But it's getting worse," Clevo said. He showed her the projections he had made. In time, if trends continued unchanged, fighters and all other combatants would be treated more and more mechanically, until they became the machines the overs wished them to be.

—No.

—Quiet. How does he feel toward her?

It was inevitable that as she learned under his tutelage, he began to feel responsible for her changes. She was an excellent fighter. He could never be sure that what he was doing might reduce her effectiveness. And yet he had fought well—despite similar changes—until his billet switch. It had been the overs who had decided he would be more effective, less disruptive, elsewhere.

Bitterness over that decision was part of his motive. The overs had done a foolish thing, putting a fighter into research. Fighters were tenacious. If the truth was to be hidden, then fighters were the ones likely to ferret it out. And pass it on. There was a code among fighters, seldom revealed to their immediate overs, much less to the supreme overs parsecs distant in their strategospheres. What one fighter learned that could be of help to another had to be passed on, even under penalty. Clevo was simply following that unwritten rule.

Passing on the fact that, at one time, things had been different. That war changed people, governments, societies, and that societies could effect an enormous change on their constituents, especially now—change in their lives, their thinking. Things could become even more structured. Freedom of fight was a drug, an illusion —

—No!

I used to perpetuate a state of hatred.

"Then why do they keep all the data in stores?" she asked. "I mean, you study the data, everything becomes obvious."

"There are still important people who think we may want to find our way back someday. They're afraid we'll lose our roots, but —"

His face suddenly became peaceful. She reached out to touch him, and he jerked slightly, turning toward her in the blister. "What is it?" she asked.

"It's not organized. We're going to lose the information. Ship overs are going to restrict access more and more. Eventually it'll decay, like some already has in these stores. I've been planning for some time to put it all in a single unit —"

—*He* built the mandate!

"and have the overs place one on every ship, with researchers to tend it. Formalize the loose scheme still in effect, but dying. Right now I'm working on the fringes. At least I'm allowed to work. But soon I'll have enough evidence that they won't be able to argue. Evidence of what happens to societies that try to obscure their histories. They go quite mad. The overs are still rational enough to listen; maybe I'll push it through." He looked out the transparent blister. The stars were smudging to one side as the cruiser began probing for entrances to sponge space. "We'd better get back."

"Where are you going to be when we return? We'll all be transferred."

"That's some time removed. Why do you want to know?"

"I'd like to learn more."

He smiled. "That's not your only reason."

"I don't need someone to tell me what my reasons are," she said testily.

"We're so reluctant," he said. She looked at him sharply, irritated and puzzled. "I mean," he continued, "we're hawks. Comrades. Hawks couple like *that*." He snapped his fingers. "But you and I sneak around it all the time."

Prufrax kept her face blank.

"Aren't you receptive toward me?" he asked, his tone almost teasing.

"You're so damned superior. Stuffy," she snapped.

"Aren't you?"

"It's just that's not all," she said, her tone softening.

"Indeed," he said in a barely audible whisper.

In the distance they heard the alarms.

—It was never any different.

—What?

—Things were never any different before me.

—Don't be silly. It's all here.

—If Clevo made the mandate, then he put it here. It isn't true.

—Why are you upset?

—I don't like hearing that everything I believe is a . . . fib.

—I've never known the difference, I suppose. Eyes-open was never all that real to me. This isn't real, you aren't . . . this is eyes-shut. So why be upset? You and I . . . we aren't even whole people. I feel you. You wish the Zap, you fight, not much else. I'm just a shadow, even compared to you. But she is whole. She loves him. She's less a victim than either of us. So something has to have changed.

—You're saying things have gotten worse.

—If the mandate is a lie, that's all I am. You refuse to accept. I *have* to accept, or I'm even less than a shadow.

—I don't refuse to accept. It's just hard.

—You started it. You thought about love.

—You did!

—Do you know what love is?

—Reception.

They first made love in the weapons blister. It came as no surprise; if anything, they approached it so cautiously they were clumsy. She had become more and more receptive, and he had dropped his guard. It had been quick, almost frantic, far from the orchestrated and drawn-out ballet the hawks prided themselves for. There was no pretense. No need to play the roles of artists interacting. They were depending on each other. The pleasure they exchanged was nothing compared to the emotions involved.

"We're not very good with each other," Prufrax said.

Clevo shrugged. "That's because we're shy."

"Shy?"

He explained. In the past—at various times in the past, because such differences had come and gone many times—making love had been more than a physical exchange or even an expression of comradeship. It had been the acknowledgment of a bond between people.

She listened, half-believing. Like everything else she had heard, that kind of love seemed strange, distasteful. What if one hawk was lost, and the other continued to love? It interfered with the hardfought, certainly. But she was also fascinated. Shyness—the fear of one's presentation to another. The hesitation to present truth, or the inward confusion of truth at the awareness that another might be important, more important than one thought possible. That such emotions might have existed at one time, and seem so alien now, only emphasized the distance of the past, as Clevo had tried to tell her. And that she felt those emotions only confirmed she was not as far from that past as, for dignity's sake, she might have wished.

Complex emotion was not encouraged either at the Grounds or among hawks on station. Complex emotion degraded complex performance. The simple and direct was desirable.

"But all we seem to do is talk—until now," Prufrax said, holding his hand and examining his fingers one by one. They were very little different from her own, though extended a bit from hawk fingers to give greater versatility with key instruction.

"Talking is the most human thing we can do."

She laughed. "I know what you are," she said, moving up until her eyes were even with his chest. "You're stuffy. You aren't the party type."

"Where'd you learn about parties?"

"You gave me literature to read, I read it. You're an instructor at heart. You make love by telling." She felt peculiar, almost afraid, and looked up at his face. "Not that I don't enjoy your lovemaking, like this. Physical."

"You receive well," he said. "Both ways."

"What we're saying," she whispered, "is not truth-speaking. It's amenity." She turned into the stroke of his hand through her hair. "Amenity is supposed to be decadent. That fellow who wrote about heaven and hell. He would call it a sin."

"Amenity is the recognition that somebody may see or feel differently than you do. It's the recognition of individuals. You and I, we're part of the end of all that."

"Even if you convince the overs?"

He nodded. "They want to repeat success without risk. New individuals are risky, so they duplicate past success. There will be more and more people, fewer individuals. More of you and me, less of others. The fewer individuals, the fewer stories to tell. The less history. We're part of the death of history."

She floated next to him, trying to blank her mind as she had before, to drive out the nagging awareness he was right. She thought she understood the social structure around her. Things seemed new. She said as much.

"It's a path we're taking," Clevo said. "Not a place we're at."

—It's a place *we're* at. How different are *we*?

—But there's so much history in here. How can it be over for us?

—I've been thinking. Do we know the last event recorded in the mandate?

—Don't, we're drifting from Prufrax now . . .

Aryz felt himself drifting with them. They swept over countless millennia, then swept back the other way. And it became evident that as much change had been wrapped in one year of the distant past as in a thousand years of the closing entries in the mandate. Clevo's voice seemed to follow them, though they were far from his period, far from Prufrax's record.

"Tyranny is the death of history. We fought the Senexi until we became like them. No change, youth at an end, old age coming upon us. There is no important change, merely elaborations in the pattern."

—How many times have we been here, then? How many times have we died?

Aryz wasn't sure, now. *Was* this the first time humans had been captured? Had he been told everything by the brood mind? Did the Senexi have no *history*, whatever that was —

The accumulated lives of living, thinking beings. Their actions, thoughts, passions, hopes.

The mandate answered even his confused, nonhuman requests. He could understand action, thought, but not passion or hope. Perhaps without those there was no *history*.

—You have no history, the mutated shape told him. There have been millions like you, even millions like the brood mind. What is the last event recorded in the brood mind that is not duplicated a thousand times over, so close they can be melded together for convenience?

—You understand that? Aryz asked the shape.

—Yes.

—How do you understand—because we made you between human and Senexi?

—Not only that.

The requests of the twins, captive and shape were moving them back once more into the past, through the dim grey millennia of repeating ages. History began to manifest again, differences in the record.

On the way back to Mercior, four skirmishes were fought. Prufrax did well in each. She carried something special with her, a thought she didn't even tell Clevo, and she carried the same thought with her through their last days at the Grounds.

Taking advantage of hawk liberty, she opted a posthard-fought residence just outside the Grounds, in the relatively uncrowded Daughter of Cities zone. She wouldn't be returned to fight until several issues had been decided—her status most important among them.

Clevo began making his appeal to the middle overs. He was given Grounds duty to finish his proposals. They could stay together for the time being.

The residence was sixteen square meters in area, not elegant—*natural*, as rentOpts described it. Clevo called it a "garret," inaccurately as she discovered when she looked it up in his memory blocs, but perhaps he was describing the tone.

On the last day she lay in the crook of Clevo's arm. They had done a few hours of nature sleep. He hadn't come out yet, and she looked up at his face, reached up with a hand to feel his arm.

It was different from the arms of others she had been receptive toward. It was unique. The thought amused her. There had never been a reception like theirs. This was the beginning. And if both were to be duplicated, this love, this reception, would be repeated an infinite number of times. Clevo meeting Prufrax, teaching her, opening her eyes.

Somehow, even though repetition contributed to the death of history, she was pleased. This was the secret thought she carried into fight. Each time she would survive, wherever she was, however many duplications down the line. She would receive Clevo, and he would teach her. If not now—if one or the other died—then in the future. The death of history might be a good thing. Love could go on forever.

She had lost even a rudimentary apprehension of death, even with present pleasure to live for. Her functions had sharpened. She would please him by doing all the things he could not. And if he was to enter that state she frequently found him in, that state of introspection, of reliving his own battles and envying her activity, then that wasn't bad. All they did to each other was good.

—*Was* good

—*Was*

She slipped from his arm and left the narrow sleeping quarter, pushing through the smoke-colored air curtain to the lounge. Two hawks and an over she had never seen before were sitting there. They looked up at her.

"Under," Prufrax said.

"Over," the woman returned. She was dressed in tan and green, Grounds colors, not ship.

"May I assist?"

"Yes."

"My duty, then?"

The over beckoned her closer. "You have been receiving a researcher."

"Yes," Prufrax said. The meetings could not have been a secret on the ship, and certainly not their quartering near the Grounds. "Has that been against duty?"

"No." The over eyed Prufrax sharply, observing her perfected fightform, the easy grace with which she stood, naked, in the middle of the small compartment. "But a decision has been reached. Your status is decided now."

She felt a shiver.

"Prufrax," said the elder hawk. She recognized him from fibs, and his companion: Kumnax and Arol. Once her heroes. "You have been accorded an honor, just as your partner has. You have a valuable genetic assortment—"

She barely heard the rest. They told her she would return to fight, until they deemed she had had enough experience and background to be brought into the polinstruc division. Then her fighting would be over. She would serve better as an example, a hero.

Clevo emerged from the air curtain. "Duty," the over said. "The residence is disbanded. Both of you will have separate quarters, separate duties."

They left. Prufrax held out her hand, but Clevo didn't take it. "No use," he said.

Suddenly she was filled with anger. "You'll give it up? Did I expect too much? *How strongly*?"

"Perhaps even more strongly than you," he said. "I knew the order was coming down. And still I didn't leave. That may hurt my chances with the supreme overs."

"Then at least I'm worth more than your breeding history?"

"Now you are history. History the way they make it."

"I feel like I'm dying," she said, amazement in her voice. "What is that, Clevo? What did you do to me?"

"I'm in pain, too," he said.

"You're hurt?"

"I'm confused."

"I don't believe that," she said, her anger rising again. "You knew, and you didn't do anything?"

"That would have been counter to duty. We'll be worse off if we fight it."

"So what good is your great, exalted history?"

"History is what you have," Clevo said. "I only record."

—Why did they separate them?

—I don't know. You didn't like him, anyway.

—Yes, but now . . .

—See? You're her. We're her. But shadows. She was whole.

—I don't understand.

—We don't. Look what happens to her. They took what was best out of her. Prufrax

went into battle eighteen more times before dying as heroes often do, dying in the midst of what she did best. The question of what made her better before the separation—for she definitely was not as fine a fighter after—has not been settled. Answers fall into an extinct classification of knowledge, and there are few left to interpret, none accessible to this device.

—So she went out and fought and died. They never even made fibs about her. This killed her?

—I don't think so. She fought well enough. She died like other hawks died.

—And she might have lived otherwise.

—How can I know that, any more than you?

—They—we—met again, you know. I met a Clevo once, on my ship. They didn't let me stay with him long.

—How did you react to him?

—There was so little time, I don't know.

—Let's ask . . .

In thousands of duty stations, it was inevitable that some of Prufrax's visions would come true, that they should meet now and then. Clevos were numerous, as were Prufraxes. Every ship carried complements of several of each. Though Prufrax was never quite as successful as the original, she was a fine type. She—

—She was never quite as successful. They took away her edge. They didn't even know it!

—They must have known.

—Then they didn't want to win!

—We don't know that. Maybe there were more important considerations.

—Yes, like killing history.

Aryz shuddered in his warming body, dizzy as if about to bud, then regained control. He had been pulled from the mandate, called to his own duty.

He examined the shapes and the human captive. There was something different about them. How long had they been immersed in the mandate? He checked quickly, frantically, before answering the call. The reconstructed Mam had malfunctioned. None of them had been nourished. They were thin, pale, cooling.

Even the bloated mutant shape was dying; lost, like the others, in the mandate.

He turned his attention away. Everything was confusion. Was he human or Senexi now? Had he fallen so low as to understand them? He went to the origin of the call, the ruins of the temporary brood chamber. The corridors were caked with ammonia ice, burning his pod as he slipped over them. The brood mind had come out of flux bind. The emergency support systems hadn't worked well; the brood mind was damaged.

"Where have you been?" it asked.

"I assumed I would not be needed until your return from the flux bind."

"You have not been watching!"

"Was there any need? We are so advanced in time, all our actions are obsolete. The nebula is collapsed, the issue is decided."

"We do not know that. We are being pursued."

Aryz turned to the sensor wall—what was left of it—and saw that they were, indeed, being pursued. He had been lax.

"It is not your fault," the brood mind said. "You have been set a task that tainted you and ruined your function. You will dissipate."

Aryz hesitated. He had become so different, so tainted, that he actually *hesitated* at a direct command from the brood mind. But it was damaged. Without him, without what he had learned, what could it do? It wasn't reasoning correctly.

"There are facts you must know, important facts—"

Aryz felt a wave of revulsion, uncomprehending fear, and something not unlike human anger radiate from the brood mind. Whatever he had learned and however he had changed, he could not withstand that wave.

Willingly, and yet against his will—it didn't matter—he felt himself liquefying. His pod slumped beneath him, and he fell over, landing on a pool of frozen ammonia. It burned, but he did not attempt to lift himself. Before he ended, he saw with surprising clarity what it was to be a branch ind, or a brood mind, or a human. Such a valuable insight, and it leaked out of his permea and froze on the ammonia.

The brood mind regained what control it could of the fragment. But there were no defenses worthy of the name. Calm, preparing for its own dissipation, it waited for the pursuit to conclude.

The Mam set off an alarm. The interface with the mandate was severed. Weak, barely able to crawl, the humans looked at each other in horror and slid to opposite corners of the chamber.

They were confused: which of them was the captive, which the decoy shape? It didn't seem important. They were both bone-thin, filthy with their own excrement. They turned with one motion to stare at the bloated mutant. It sat in its corner, tiny head incongruous on the huge thorax, tiny arms and legs barely functional even when healthy. It smiled wanly at them.

"We felt you," one of the Prufraxes said. "You were with us in there." Her voice was a soft croak.

"That was my place," it replied. "My own place."

"What function, what name?"

"I'm . . . I know that. I'm a researcher. In there. I knew myself in there."

They squinted at the shape. The head. Something familiar, even now. "You're a Clevo . . ."

There was noise all around them, cutting off the shape's weak words. As they watched, their chamber was sectioned like an orange, and the wedges peeled open. The illumination ceased. Cold enveloped them.

A naked human female, surrounded by tiny versions of herself, like an angel circled by fairy kin, floated into the chamber. She was thin as a snake. She wore nothing but silver rings on her wrists and a narrow torque around her waist. She glowed blue-green in the dark.

The two Prufraxes moved their lips weakly but made no sound in the near vacuum. *Who are you?*

She surveyed them without expression, then held out her arms as if to fly. She wore no gloves, but she was of their type.

As she had done countless times before on finding such Senexi experiments—though this seemed older than most—she lifted one arm higher. The blue-green intensified, spread in waves to the mangled walls, surrounded the freezing, dying shapes. Perfect, angelic, she left the debris behind to cast its fitful glow and fade.

They had destroyed every portion of the fragment but one. They left it behind unharmed.

Then they continued, millions of them thick like mist, working the spaces between the stars, their only master the overness of the real.

They needed no other masters. They would never malfunction.

The mandate drifted in the dark and cold, its memory going on, but its only life the rapidly fading tracks where minds had once passed through it. The trails writhed briefly, almost as if alive, but only following the quantum rules of diminishing energy states. Finally, a small memory was illuminated.

Prufrax's last poem, explained the mandate reflexively.

How the fires grow! Peace passes
All memory lost.
Somehow we always miss that single door
Dooming ourselves to circle.

Ashes to stars, lies to souls,
Let's spin round the sinks and holes.

Kill the good, eat the young.
Forever and more
You and I are never done.

The track faded into nothing. Around the mandate, the universe grew old very quickly.

SWARMER, SKIMMER

Gregory Benford

1

Warren watched the Manamix going down. The ocean was in her and would smother the engines soon, swamping her into silence. Her lights still glowed in the mist and rain.

She lay on her starboard side, down by the head, and the swell took her solidly with a dull hammering. The strands that the Swarmers cast had laced across her decks and wrapped around the gun emplacements and over the men who had tended them.

The long green and yellow strands still licked up the sides and over the deck, seeking and sticking. They were spun out from the swollen belly pouches of the Swarmers. Their green bodies clustered in the dark water at the bows.

A long finger of tropical lightning cracked. It lit the wedge of space between the close black storm clouds and the rain-pocked, wrinkled skin of the sea. The big aliens glistened in the glare.

Warren treaded water and floated. He tried to make no noise. A strand floated nearby and a wave brushed him against it but there was no sting. The Swarmer it came from was probably dead and drifting down now. But there were many more in the crashing surf near the ship and he could hear screams from the other crewmen who had gone over the side with him.

The port davits on the top deck dangled, trailing ropes, and the lifeboats hung from them unevenly, useless. Warren had tried to get one down but the winch and cabling fouled and he had finally gone over the side like the rest.

Her running lights winked and then came on steady again. The strands made a tangled net over the decks now. Once they stunned a man, the sticky yellow nerve sap stopped coming and they lost their sting. As he watched, bobbing in the waves, one of the big aliens amidships rolled and brought in its strand and pulled a body over the railing. The man was dead and when the body hit the water there was some quick fighting over it.

Wisps of steam curled from the engine-room hatch. He thought he could hear the whine of the diesels. Her port screw was clear and spinning like a metal flower. In the hull plates he could see the ragged holes punched by the packs of Swarmers. She was filling fast now.

Warren knew the jets the Filipinos had promised the captain would never get out this far. It was a driving, splintering storm and to drop the canisters of poison that would kill the Swarmers would take low and dangerous flying. The Filipinos would not risk it.

She went without warning. The swell came over her bows and the funnel slanted down fast. The black water poured into her and into the high hoods of her ventilators and the running lights started to go out. The dark gully of her forward promenade and bay filled and steam came gushing up from the hatches like a giant thing exhaling.

He braced himself for it, thinking of the engine he had tended, and the sudden deep booming came as the sea reached in and her boilers blew. She slid in fast. Lightning crackled and was reflected in a thousand shattered mirrors of the sea. The waters accepted her and the last he saw was a huge rush of steam as great chords boomed in her hull.

In the quiet afterward, calls and then screams came to him, carried on the gusts. There had been so many men going off the aft deck the Swarmers had missed him. Now they had coiled their strands back in and would find him soon. He began to kick, floating on his back, trying not to splash.

Something brushed his leg. He went limp.

It came again.

He pressed the fear back, far away from him. The thing was

down there in the blackness, seeing only by its phosphorescent stripes along the jawline. If it caught some movement—

A wave rolled him over. He floated face down and did nothing about it. A wave rocked him and then another and his face came out for an instant and he took a gasp of air. Slowly he let the current turn him to the left until a slit of his mouth broke clear and he could suck in small gulps of air.

The cool touch came at a foot. A hip. He waited. He let the air bubble out of him slowly when his chest started to burn so that he would have empty lungs when he broke surface. A slick skin rubbed against him. His throat began to go tight. His head went under again and he felt himself in the black without weight and saw a dim glimmering, a wash of silvery light like stars—and he realized he was staring at the Swarmer's grinning phosphorescent jaw.

The fire in his throat and chest was steady and he struggled to keep them from going into spasm. The grin of gray light came closer. Something cold touched his chest, nuzzled him, pushed—

A wave broke hard over him and he tumbled and was in the open, face up, gasping, ears ringing. The wave was deep and he took two quick breaths before the water closed over him again.

He opened his eyes in the dark water. Nothing. No light anywhere. He could not risk a kick to take him to the air. He waited to bob up again, and did, and this time saw something riding down the wave near him. A lifeboat.

He made a slow easy stroke toward it. Nothing touched him. If the Swarmer had already eaten it might just have been curious. Maybe it was not making its turn and coming back.

A wave, a stroke, a wave—He stretched and caught the trailing aft line. He wrenched himself up and sprawled aboard, rattling the oars in the gunwale. Quietly he paddled toward the weakening shouts. Then the current took him to starboard. He did not use the oars in the locks because they would clank and the sound would carry. He pulled toward the sounds but they faded. A fog came behind the rain.

There was a foot of water in the boat and the planking was splintered where a Swarmer tried to stove it in. A case of supplies was still clamped in the gunwale.

Awhile later he sighted a smudge of yellow. It was the woman, Rosa, clinging to a life jacket she had got on wrong. He had been staying down in the boat to keep hidden from the Swarmers but without thinking about it he pulled her aboard.

She was a journalist he had seen before on the *Manamix*. She was covering the voyage for Brazilian TV and wanted to take this fast run down from Taiwan to Manila. She had said she wanted to see a Swarm beaten off and her camera crew was on deck all day bothering the crew.

She sat aft and huddled down and then after a time started to talk. He covered her mouth. Her eyes rolled from side to side, searching the water. Warren paddled slowly. He wore jeans and a long-sleeved shirt, and even soaked they kept off the night chill. The fog was thick. They heard some distant splashes and once a rifle shot. The fog blotted out the sounds.

They ate some of the provisions when it got light enough to see. Warren felt the planking for seepage and he could tell it was getting worse.

A warm dawn broke over them. Wreckage drifted nearby. There were uprooted trees, probably carried out to sea by the storm. The rain had started just as the first packs struck the bows. That had made it harder to hit them with the automatic rifles on deck and Warren was pretty sure the Swarmers knew that.

There was smashed planking from other boats near them, an empty box, some thin twine, life jackets, bottles. No one had ever seen Swarmers show interest in debris in the water, only prey. The things had no tools. Certainly they had not made the ships that dropped into the atmosphere and seeded the oceans. Those craft would have been worth looking at but they had broken up on the seas and sunk before anyone could get to them.

The wreckage would not attract Swarmers but they might be following the current to find survivors. Warren knew no school of Swarmers was nearby because they always broke surface while in a Swarm and you could see the mass of them from a long way off. There were always the lone Swarmers that some people thought were scouts, though. Nobody really knew what they did but they were just as dangerous as the others.

He could not steer well enough to pick up wreckage. The boat was taking on more water and he did not think they had much time. They needed the drifting wood and he had to swim for it. Five times he went in the water and each time he had to push the fear away from him and swim as smoothly and quietly as he could until finally the fear came strongly and he could not do it anymore.

He skinned the bark from two big logs, using the knife from the provisions case, and made lashings. The boat was shipping water now as it rolled in the swell. He and Rosa cut and lashed and built. When they had a frame of logs they broke up the boat and used some of the planks for decking. The boat sank before they could save most of it but they got the case onto the raft.

He pried nails out of some of the driftwood. By now his vision was blurring in the bright sunlight and he was clumsy. They cleared a space in the frame to lie on and Rosa fell asleep while he was pounding in the last board. Each task he had now was at the end of a tunnel and he peered through it at his hands doing the job and they were dumb and thick as though he was wearing gloves. He secured the case and other loose pieces and hooked his right arm over a limb to keep from falling overboard. He fell asleep face down.

2

The next day as he got more driftwood and lashed it into the raft there was a slow, burning, pointless kind of anger in him. He could have stayed on land and lived off the dole. He had known the risks when he signed on as engineer.

It had been six years since the first signs of the aliens. With each year more ships had gone down, hulled in deep water and beyond protection from the air. The small craft, fishermen and the like, had been first to go. That did not change things much. Then the Swarmers multiplied and cargo vessels started going down. Trade across open seas was impossible.

The oceanographers and biologists said they were starting to understand the Swarmer mating and attack modes by that time. It was slow work. Studying them on the open water was dangerous. When they were captured they hammered themselves against the walls of their containers until the jutting bone of their foreheads shattered and drove splinters into their brains.

Then the Swarmers began taking bigger ships. They found a way to mass together and hull even the big supertankers.

By then the oceanographers were dying, too, in their reinforced-hull research ships. The Swarmers could sink anything then and no one could explain how they had learned to modify their tactics. The things did not have particularly large brains.

There were reports of strange-looking Swarmers, of strays from the schools, of massed Swarmers who could take a ship down in minutes. Then came photographs of a totally new form, the Skimmers, who leaped and dove deep and were smaller than the Swarmers. The specimens had been killed by probots at depths below 200 fathoms, where Swarmers had never been seen.

The automatic stations and hunters were the only way men could study the Swarmers by that time. Large cargo vessels could not sail safely. Oil did not move from the Antarctic or China or the Americas. Wheat stayed in the farm nations. The intricate world economy ground down.

Warren had been out of work and stranded in the chaos of Tokyo. His wife had left him years before, so he had no particular place to go. When the *Manamix* advertised that it had special plates in her hull and deck defenses, he signed into a berth. The pay was good and there was no other sea work anyway. He could have run on the skimships that raced across the Taiwan Straits or to Korea, but those craft did not need engineers. If their engines ever went out they were finished before any repair could get done because the loud motors always drew the Swarmers in their wake.

Warren was an engineer and he wanted to stick to what he knew. He had worked hard for the rating. The heavy plates in the fore and aft holds had looked strong to him. But they had buckled inside of half an hour.

Rosa held up well at first. They never saw any other survivors of the *Manamix*. They snagged more wreckage and logs and lashed it together. Floating with the wood they found a coil of wire and an aluminum railing. He pounded the railing into nails and they made a lean-to for protection from the sun.

They were drifting northwest at first. Then the current shifted and took them east. He wondered if a search pattern could allow for that and find them.

One night he took Rosa with a power and confidence he had not felt since years before, with his wife. It surprised him.

They ate the cans of provisions. He used some scraps for bait and caught a few fish but they were small. She knew a way to make the twine tight and springy. He used it to make a bow and arrow and it was accurate enough to shoot fish if they came close.

Their water began to run out. Rosa kept their stores under the lean-to and at seven days Warren found the water was almost gone. She had been drinking more than her share.

"I had to," she said, backing away from him at a crouch. "I can't stand it, I . . . I get so bad. And the sun, it's too hot, I just . . ."

He wanted to stop but he could not and he hit her several times. There was no satisfaction in it.

Through the afternoon Rosa cringed at a corner of the raft and Warren lay under the lean-to and thought. In the cool, orderly limits of the problem he found a kind of rest. He squatted on a plank and rocked with the swell and inside, where he had come to live more and more these past years, the world was not just the gurgle and rush of waves and the bleaching raw edge of salt and sun. Inside there were the books and the diagrams and things he had known. He struggled to put them together.

Chemistry. He cut a small slit in the rubber stopper of a water can and lowered it into the sea on a long fishing line.

The deeper water was cold. He pulled the can up and put it inside a bigger can. It steamed like a champagne bucket. Water beaded on the outside of the small can. The big can held the drops. It was free of salt but there was not much.

Nine days out the water was gone. Rosa cried. Warren tried to find a way to make the condensing better but they did not have many cans. The yield was no more than a mouthful a day.

In the late afternoon of that day Rosa suddenly hit him and started shouting filthy names. She said he was a sailor and should get them water and get them to land and when they finally did get picked up she would tell everybody how bad a sailor he was and how they had nearly died because he did not know how to find the land.

He let her run down and stayed away from her. If she scratched him with her long fingernails the wound would heal badly and there was no point in taking a risk. They had not taken any fish on the lines for a long time now and they were getting weaker. The effort of hauling up the cans from below made his arms tremble.

The next day the sea ran high. The raft groaned, rising sluggishly and plunging hard. Waves washed them again and again so it was impossible to sleep or even rest. At dusk Warren discovered jelly seahorses as big as a thumbnail riding in the foam that lapped over the raft. He stared at them and tried to remember what he had learned of biology.

If they started drinking anything with a high salt content the end would come fast. But they had to have something. He put a few on his tongue, tentatively, and waited until they melted. They were salty and fishy but seemed less salty than sea water. The cool moisture seemed right and his throat welcomed it. He spoke to Rosa and showed her and they gathered handfuls of the seahorses until nightfall.

On the eleventh day there were no seahorses and the sun pounded at them. Rosa had made hats for them, using cloth from the wreckage. That helped with the worst of the day but to get through the hours Warren had to sit with closed eyes under the lean-to, carefully working through the clear hallways of his mind.

The temptation to drink sea water was festering in him, flooding the clean places inside him where he had withdrawn. He kept before him the chain of things to keep himself intact.

If he drank sea water he would take in a quantity of dissolved salt. The body did not need much salt so it had to get rid of most of what he took in. The kidneys would sponge up the salt from his blood and secrete it. But doing that took pure water, at least a pint a day.

The waves churned before him and he felt the rocking of the deck and he made it into a chant.

Drink a pint of sea water a day. The body turns it into about twenty cubic centimeters of pure water.

But the kidneys need more than that to process the salt. They react. They take water from the body tissues.

The body dries out. The tongue turns black. Nausea. Fever. Death.

He sat there for hours, reciting it, polishing it down to a few key words, making it perfect. He told it to Rosa and she did not understand but that was all right.

In the long afternoon he squinted against the glare and the world became one of sounds. The rattling of their cans came to him against the murmur of the sea and the hollow slap of waves against the underside of the raft. Then there was a deep thump. He peered to starboard. A rippling in the water. Rosa sat up. He gestured for silence. The planks and logs creaked and worked against each other and the thump came again.

He had heard dolphins knocking under the raft before and this was not their playful string of taps. Warren crawled out from the lean-to and into the yellow sunlight and a big green form broke surface and rolled belly-over, goggling at them with a bulging eye. Its mouth was like a slash in the blunt face. The teeth were narrow and sharp.

Rosa cried in terror and the Swarmer seemed to hear her. It circled the raft, following her awkward scuttling. She screamed and moved faster but the big thing flicked its tail and kept alongside her.

His concentration narrowed to an absolute problem that took in the Swarmer and its circling and the closed geometry of the raft. If they let it come in when it chose, it would lunge against the raft and catch them off balance and have a good chance of tumbling them into the water or breaking up the raft.

The green form turned and dove deep under the raft.

"Rosa!" He tore off his shirt. "Here! Wave it in the water on the side." He dipped the shirt, crouching at the edge. "Like this."

She hung back. "I . . . but . . . no, I . . ."

"Damn it! I'll stop it before it gets to you."

She gaped at him and the Swarmer broke water on the far side of the raft. It rolled ponderously, as if it was having trouble understanding how to attack a thing so much smaller than a ship, and attack it alone.

Rosa took the shirt hesitantly. He encouraged her and she bent over and swished a tip of it in the surf. "Good."

Warren brought out the crude arrow he had made with a centimeter-thick slat from the *Manamix* lifeboat. He had tapered it down and driven a nail in the head. He tucked the arrow into the rubber strip of his bow and tested it. The arrow had a line on it and did not fly very straight. Not much good for fish.

He slitted his eyes against the glare and looked out at the shallow troughs. The sea warped and rippled where the thing had just disappeared. Warren sensed that it had judged them now and was gliding back in the blue shadows under the raft, coming around for its final pass. It would not see the shirt until it turned and that would bring it up and near the corner where Warren now stood, between its path and Rosa. He drew the arrow back in a smooth motion, sighting, straining, sighting—

Rosa saw the dim shape first. She flicked the rag out of the water with a jerk. Warren saw something dart up, seeming to come up out of the floor of the ocean itself, catching the refracted bands of light from the waves.

Rosa screamed and stepped back. The snout broke water and the mouth like a cut was leering at them, and Warren let go the arrow *thunk* and followed it forward, scrabbling on all fours. The thing had the arrow in under the gills and the big flaps of green flesh bulged and flared open in spasms as it rolled to the side.

Warren snatched at the arrow line and missed. "Grab the end!" he called. The arrow was enough to stun the Swarmer but that was all. The thing was stunned with the nail driven deep in it but Warren wanted more of it now, more than just the killing of it, and he splashed partway off the raft to reach the snout and drag it in. He got a slippery grip on a big blue ventral fin. The mouth snapped. It thrashed and Warren used the motion to haul it toward the raft. He swung himself, the wood cutting into his hip, and levered the body partway onto the deck. Rosa took a fin and pulled. He used the pitch of the deck and his weight to flip the thing over on its side. It arched its back, twisting to gain leverage to thrash back over the side. Warren had his knife out and as the thing slid away from him he drove the blade in, slipping it through soft tissue at the side and riding up against the spine. Warren slashed down the body, feeling the Swarmer convulse in agony. Then it straightened and seemed to get smaller.

The two stood back and looked at the scaly green body, three meters long. Its weight made the raft dip in the swell.

Something sticky was beginning to drain from the long cut. Warren fetched a can and scooped up the stuff. It was a thin, pale yellow fluid. He did not hear Rosa's whimpering, stumbling approach as he lifted the can to his lips.

He caught the cool, slightly acrid taste of it for an instant. He opened his mouth wider to take it in. She struck the can from his hands. It clattered on the deck.

His punch drove her to her knees. "Why?" he yelled. "What do you care—"

"Wrong," she sputtered out. "Ugly. They're not . . . not *normal* . . . to . . . to eat."

"You want to drink? Want to live?"

She shook her head, blinking. "Na . . . ah, yeah, but . . . not that. Maybe . . ."

He looked at her coldly and she moved away. The carcass was

dripping. He wedged it against a log and propped cans under it. He drank the first filled can, and the second.

The dorsal and ventral fins sagged in death. In the water he had seen them spread wide as wings. The bulging brain case and the goggle eyes seemed out of place, even in the strange face with its squeezed look. The rest of the body was sleek like the large fish. He had heard somebody say that evolution forced the same slim contours on any fast thing that lived in an ocean, even on submarines.

The Swarmer had scaly patches around the forefins and at each ventral fin. The skin looked like it was getting thick and hard. Warren did not remember seeing that in the photographs of dead ones but then the articles and movies had not said anything about the Swarmer scouts either until a year ago. They kept changing.

Rosa crouched under the lean-to. Once, when he drank, she spat out some word he could not understand.

The third can he set down on the boards halfway between them. He cut into the body and found the soft pulpy places where it was vulnerable to an arrow. He learned the veins and arteries and ropes of muscle. There were big spaces in the head that had something to do with hearing. In the belly pouch the strand was shriveled and laced with a kind of blue muscle. Around the fins where the skin became scaly there were little bones and cartilage that did not seem to have any use.

Rosa edged closer as he worked. The heat weighed on her. She licked her lips until they were raw and finally she drank.

He kept track of the days by making a cut each morning in a tree limb. The ritual sawing became crucial, part of the struggle. The itching salt spray and the hammering of the sun blurred distinctions. In the simple counting he found there was some order, the beauty of number that existed outside the steady rub of the sea's green sameness.

Between the two of them they made the killing of the Swarmers a ritual as well. The scouts came at random intervals now, with never more than three days of waiting until the next thumping probes at the planking. Then Rosa would stoop and wave the shirt in the water. The thing would make a pass to look and then turn to strike, coming by the jutting corner, and Warren would drive the arrow into the soft place.

Rosa would crouch under the shelter then and mumble to herself and wait for him to gut it and bleed the watery pouches of fin fluid and finally take the sour syrup from behind the eyes.

With each fresh kill he learned more. They cut up some cloth and made small bags to hold the richer parts of the carcass and then chewed it for each drop. Sometimes it made them sick. After that he twisted chunks of the flesh in a cloth bag and let the drops air in the sun. That was not so bad. They ate the big slabs of flesh but it was the fluid they needed most.

With each kill Rosa became more distant. She sat dreamily swaying at the center of their plank island, humming and singing to herself, coiling inward. Warren worked and thought.

On the twenty-first day of drifting she woke him. He came up reluctantly from the vague, shifting sleep. She was shouting.

Darting away into the bleak dawn was something lean and blue. It leaped into the air and plunged with a shower of foam and then almost in the same instant was flying out of the steep wall of a wave, turning in the gleaming fresh sun.

"A Skimmer," he murmured. It was the first he had ever seen.

Rosa cried out. Warren stared out into the hills and valleys of moving water, blinking, following her finger. A gray cylinder the size of his hand floated ten meters away.

He picked up the tree limb they used for marking the days. His hands were puffed up now from the constant damp and the bark of the limb scraped them. No green shapes moved below. He rocked with the swell, waiting at the edge of the raft for a random current to bring the gray thing closer.

A long time passed. It bobbed sluggishly and came no closer. Warren leaned against the pitch of the deck and stretched for it. The limb was short at least a meter.

He swayed back, relaxing, letting the clenching in his muscles ease away. His arms trembled. He could swim to it in a few quick strokes, turn and get back in a few—

No. If he let go he would be sucked into the same endless caverns that Rosa was wandering. He had to hold on. And take no risks.

He stepped back. The thing to do was wait and see if—

White spray exploded in front of him. The lean form shot up into the air and Warren rolled back away from it. He came up with the knife held close to him.

But the Skimmer arced away from the raft. It cut back into a wave and was gone for an instant and then burst up and caught the cylinder in its slanting mouth. In the air it rolled and snapped its head. The cylinder clunked onto the raft. The Skimmer leaped again, blue-white, and was gone into the endlessly shifting faces of green marble.

Rosa was huddled in the shelter. Warren picked up the cylinder carefully. It was smooth and regular but something about it told him it had not been made with tools. There were small flaws in the soft, foamy gray, like the blotches on a tomato. At one end it puckered as though a tassel had fallen away.

He rubbed it, pulled at it, turned the ends—It split with a moist pop. Inside there curled a thick sheet of the same softly resistant gray stuff. He unrolled it.

ECHTON XMENAPU DE AN LANSDORFKOPPEN SW BY W ABLE SAGON MXIL VESSE L ANSAGEN MANLATS WIR UNS? FTH ASBØLENGS ERTY EARTHN PROFUILEN CO NISHI NAGARE KALLEN KOPFT EARTHN UMI

He studied the combinations and tried to fit them together so there was some logic to it. It was no code, he guessed. Some of the words were German and there was some English and Japanese, but most of it was either meaningless or no language he knew. VESSE L might be *vessel*. ANSAGEN—to say? He wished he remembered more of the German he had picked up in the merchant marine.

The words were in a clear typeface like a newspaper and were burned into the sheet.

He could make no more of it. Rosa did not want to look at the sheet. When he made her, she shook her head, no, she could not pick out any new words.

A Swarmer came later that day. Rosa did not back away fast enough and the big shape shot up out of the water. It bit down hard on the shirt as Warren's arrow took it and the impact made the blunt head snap back. Rosa was not ready for it and she stumbled forward and into the sea. The Swarmer tried to flip away. Warren caught her as she went into the water. The alien lunged at her but he heaved her back onto the deck. He had dropped the bow. The Swarmer rolled. The bow washed overboard and then the tail fins caught the edge of the raft and it twisted and came tumbling aboard. Warren hit it with the tree limb. It kept thrashing but the blows stunned it. He waited for the right angle and then slipped the knife in deep, away from the snapping jaws, and the thing went still.

Rosa helped with the cutting up. She started talking suddenly while he looked for the bow. He was intent on seeing if it was floating nearby and at first did not notice that she was not just muttering. He spotted the bow and managed to fetch it in. Rosa was discussing the Swarmers, calmly and in a matter-of-fact voice he had not heard from her before.

"The important thing, *ja*, is to not let one get away," she concluded.

"Guess so," Warren said.

"They know about the raft, the Swarm comes."

"If they can find us, yeah."

"They send out these scouts. The pack, it will follow where the lone ones tell it."

"We'll get 'em."

"Forever? No. Only solution is land."

"None I've seen. We're drifting west, could be—"

"I thought you are sailor."

"Was."

"Then sail us to land."

"Not that easy," Warren said, and went on to tell her how hard it was to get any control of a raft, and anyway he didn't know where they were, what the landfalls were out here. She sniffed contemptuously at this news. "Find an island," she repeated several times. Warren argued, not because he had any clear reason, but because he knew how to survive here and a vague fear came when he thought about the land. Rosa was speaking freely and easily now and she thought fast, sure of herself. Finally he broke off and set to work storing away the slabs of Swarmer meat. The talk confused him.

The next day a Skimmer came and leaped near the raft and there was another cylinder. It swam away, a blur of silvery motion. He read the sheet.

GEFAHRLICH GROSS HIRO ADFIN SOLID MNX 8 SHIO NISHI. KURO NAGARE. ANAXLE UNS NORMEN 286 W SCATTER PORTLINE ZERO NAGARE. NISHI.

He could not make any sense of it. Rosa worked on it, not much interested, and shrugged. He tried to scratch marks on the sheets, thinking that he could send them something, ask questions. The sheet would not take an impression.

A Swarmer surfaced to the west the next day. Rosa shrieked. It circled them twice and came in fast toward Rosa's lure. Warren shot at it and hit too far back. The tip buried itself uselessly in a spot where he knew there was only fatty tissue. The Swarmer lunged at Rosa. She was ready though, falling back from the edge, and it missed. Warren yanked on the line and freed the arrow. The Swarmer flinched as the arrow came out and rolled off the raft. It sank and was gone.

"Don't let it get away!" Rosa cried.

"It's not coming up."

"You hit it in the wrong place."

"Went in pretty deep, though. Might die before it can get back to the pack."

"You think so?"

Warren didn't but he said, "Might."

"You, you have *got* to find us an island. *Now*."

"I still think we're safe here."

"Incredible! You are no kind of sailor at all and you are afraid to admit it. Afraid to say you don't know how to find land."

"Bullshit. I—" but she interrupted him with a flood of words he couldn't keep up with. He heard her out, nodding finally, not knowing himself why he wanted to stay on the raft, on the sea. It just *felt* better, was all, and he did not know how to tell her that.

When the argument was finally over, he went back to thinking about the second message. Some of it was German and he knew a little of that, but not those particular words. He had never learned any Japanese even though he had lived in Tokyo.

The next morning at dawn he woke suddenly and thought there was something near the raft. The swell was smooth and orange as the sun caught it. On the glassy horizon he saw nothing. He was very hungry and he remembered the Swarmer from yesterday. He had used the meat from the first kills to bait their lines but nothing bit. He wondered if that was because the fish would not take Swarmer meat or if there were no fish down there to have. The aliens had been changing the food chain in the oceans, he had read about that.

Then he saw the gray dot floating far away. The raft was

drifting toward it and in a few minutes he snagged it. The message said:

> CONSQUE KPOF AMN SOLID. DA ØLEN MACHEN SMALL YOUTH SCHLECHT UNS. DERINGER CHANGE DA. UNS B WSW. SAGEN ARBEIT BEI MOUTH. SHIMA CIRCLE STEIN NONGO NONGO UMI DRASVITCH YOU.

He peered at the words and squatted on the deck and felt the long dragging minutes go by. If he could—

"Warren! Wa—Warren!" Rosa called. He followed her gesture.

A blur on the horizon. It dipped and rose among the ragged waves. Warren breathed deeply. "Land."

Rosa's eyes swelled and she barked out a sharp cackling laughter. Her lips went white with the laughing and she cried, "Yeah! Yeah! Land!" and shook her fists in the air.

Warren blinked and measured with his eyes the current and the angle the brown smudge ahead made with their course. They would not reach it by drifting.

He worked quickly.

He took the tree limb and knocked away the supports of the lean-to. In the center of the raft he knelt and measured out the distances with hands and fingers and worked a hole in between two planks. He could wedge the limb into it. He made a collar out of strips of bark. The limb was crooked but it made a vertical beam.

He took the plywood sheet of the lean-to and lashed it to the limb. With the knife he dug stays in the plywood. The wire that held the logs in place in the deck would have been good to use but he could not risk unlashing them. He used the last of their twine instead, passing it through the stays in the plywood and making them into trailing lines. The plywood was standing up now like a sail catching the wind; and by pulling the twine he could tack. The raft took the waves badly but by turning the plywood sheet he could take the strain off the weak places where the logs and boards met.

The wind backed into the east in late morning. They could not make much headway and the land was still a dark strip on the horizon. Warren broke off a big piece of wood at the raft corner. He hacked at it with the knife. A Swarmer surfaced nearby and Rosa started her screeching. He hit her and watched the Swarmer but he never stopped whittling at the wood in his lap. The Swarmer circled once and then turned and swam away to the south.

He finished with the wood. He made a housing for it with the rest of the bark strips. It sat badly at the end of the raft but the broad part dug into the water and by leaning against the top of it he could hold the angle. He got Rosa to hold two blocks of wood against the shaft for leverage and that way the thing worked something like a rudder. The raft turned to the south, toward the land.

Noon passed. Warren fought the wind and the rudder and tried to estimate the distance and the time left. If dark came before they reached it the current would take them past the land and they would never be able to beat back against the wind to find it again. He had been so long away from firm ground that he felt a need for it that was worse than his hunger. The pitch of the deck took the energy out of you day and night, you could not sleep for holding on to the deck when the sea got high, and you would do anything for something solid under you, for just—

Solid.

The message had said *solid*. Did that mean land? *Gefahrlich gross* something something *solid*. *Gefahrlich* had some kind of feel to it, something about bad or dangerous, he thought. *Gross* was *big*. Dangerous big blank blank land? Then some Japanese and other things and then *scatter portline zero*. *Scatter*. Make to go away?

Warren sweated and thought. Rosa brought him an old piece of Swarmer but he could not eat it. He thought about the words and saw there was some key to them, some beauty in it.

The rudder creaked against the wooden chocks. The land was a speck of brown now and he was pretty sure it was an island. The wind picked up. It was coming on to late afternoon.

Rosa moved around the raft when he did not need her, humming to herself, the Swarmers forgotten, eating from the pieces of meat still left. He did not try to stop her. She was eating out of turn but he needed all his thought now for the problem.

They were coming in on the northern shore. He would bring them in at a graze, to have a look before beaching. The current fought against them but the plywood was enough to sweep them to the south.

South? What was there . . .

WSW. West south west?

UNS B WSW.

Uns was *we* in German, he was pretty sure of that. We be WSW? On the WSW part of the land? The island? Or WSW of the island? We—the Skimmers.

He noticed Rosa squatting in the bow of the raft, eager, her weight dipping the boards into the blue-green swell and bringing hissing foam over the planks. It slowed them but she did not seem to see that. He opened his mouth to yell at her and then closed it. If they went slow, he would have more time.

The Skimmers were all he had out here and they had tried to tell him. . . .

Portline. *Port* was left. A line to the left? They were coming in from the northeast as near as he could judge. Veering left would take them around and to the southwest. Or WSW.

The island seemed to grow fast now as the sun set behind it. Warren squinted against the glare on the waves. There was something between them and the island. At the top of a wave he strained to see and could make out a darker line against pale sand. White rolls of surf broke on it.

A reef. The island was going to be harder to reach. He would have to bring the raft in easy and search for a passage. Either that or smash up on it and swim the lagoon, if there was no way through the circle of coral around—

Circle stein nongo. He did not know what *stein* was, something to drink out of or something, but the rest might say *don't go in the circle*.

Warren slammed the tiller over full. It groaned and the collar nearly buckled but he held it, throwing his shoulder into it.

Rosa grunted and glared at him. The raft tacked to port. He pulled the twine and brought the plywood further into the wind.

Small youth schlecht uns. The Swarmers were bigger than the Skimmers but they might mean smaller in some other way. Smaller development? Smaller brain? *Schlecht uns*. Something about *us* and the Swarmers. If they were younger than the Skimmers, maybe their development was still to come. Something told him that *schlecht* was a word like *gefahrlich* but what the difference was he did not know. *Swarmers dangerous us*? There was nothing in the words to show action, to show who *us* was. Did *us* include Warren?

Rosa stumbled toward him. The swell was coming abaft now and she clutched at him for support. "Wha'? Land! Go!"

He rubbed his eyes and focused on her face but it looked different in the waning light. He saw that in all the days they had been together he had never known her. The face was just a face. There had never been enough words between them to make the face into something else. He . . .

The wind shifted and he shrugged away the distraction and worked the twine. He studied the dark green mass ahead. It was thickly wooded and there were bare patches and a beach. The white curves of breaking surf were clear now. The thick brown reef—

Things moved on the beach.

At first he thought they were driftwood, logs swept in by a storm. Then he saw one move and then another and they were green bodies in the sand. They crawled inland. A few had made it to the line of trees.

Small youth. Young ones who were still developing.

He numbly watched the island draw near. Dimly he felt Rosa pounding on his chest and shoulder. "Steer us in! You hear me? Make this thing—"

"Wha—what?"

"You afraid of the rocks, that it?" she spit out something in Spanish or Portuguese, something angry and full of scorn. Her eyes bulged unnaturally. "No *man* would—"

"Shut up." His lips felt thick. They were rushing by the island now, drawn by the fast currents.

"You fool, we're going to *miss*."

"Look . . . look at it. The Skimmers, they're telling us not to go there. You'll see . . ."

"See what?"

"The things. On the beach.

She followed his pointing. She peered at it, shook her head, and said fiercely, "So? Nothing there but logs."

Warren squinted and saw logs covered with green moss. The surf broke over some of them and they rolled in the swell, looking like they were crawling.

"I . . . I don't . . ." he began.

Rosa shook her head impatiently. "Huh!" She bent down and found a large board that was working loose. Grunting, she pried it up. Warren peered at the beach and saw stubs on the logs, stubs where there had once been fins. They began to work against the sand again. The logs stirred.

"You can stay here and die," Rosa said clearly. "Me, *no*." The reef swept by only meters away. Waves slapped and muttered against its flanks. The gray shelves of coral dipped beneath the water. Its shadowy mass below thinned and a clear sandy spot appeared. A passage. Shallow, but maybe enough . . .

"Wait . . ." Warren looked toward the beach again. *If he was wrong* . . . The logs had fleshy stubs now that pushed at the sand, crawling up the beach. What he had seen as knotholes were something else. Sores? He strained to see . . . .

Rosa dived into the break in the reef. She hit cleanly and wallowed onto the board. Resolutely she stroked through the water, battling the swells of waves refracted into the opening.

"Wait! I think the Swarmers are—" She could not hear him over the slopping of waves on the reef.

He remembered distantly the long days . . . the Skimmers . . . "Wait!" he called. Rosa was through the passage and into the calm beyond. "Wait!" She went on.

Where he had seen logs he now saw something bloated and grotesque, sick. He shook his head. His vision cleared—*or did it?* he wondered—and how he could not tell what waited for Rosa on the glimmering sand.

He lost sight of her as the raft followed deflected currents around the island. The trade wind was coming fresh. He felt it on his skin like a reminder, and the sunset sat hard and bright on the west. Automatically he tacked out free of the reef and turned WSW. When he looked back in the soft twilight it was hard to see the forms struggling like huge lungfish up onto their new home. Under the slanted light the wind broke the sea into oily facets that became a field of mirrors reflecting shattered images of the burnt orange sky and the raft. He peered at the mirrors.

The logs on the beach . . . He felt the tug of the twine and made a change in heading to steady a yaw.

He gathered speed. When the thin scream came out of the dusk behind him he did not turn around.

3

The wind had backed into the northeast and was coming up strong again. Warren watched the sullen clouds moving in. He shook his head. It was still hard for him to leave his sleep.

It was three days now since he had passed the island. He had thought much about the thing with Rosa. When his head was clear he was certain that he had made no mistake. He had let her do what she wanted and if she had not understood it was because he could not find a way to tell her. It was the sea itself which taught and the Skimmers too, and you had to listen. Rosa had listened only to herself and her belly.

On the second day past the island the air had become thick and a storm came down from the north. He had thought it was a squall until the deck began to pitch at steep angles and a piece broke away with a groan. Then he had lashed himself to the log and tried to pull the plywood sheet down. He could reach it but the collar he had made out of his belt was slippery with rain. He pulled at the cracked leather. He thought of using the knife to cut the sheet free but then the belt would be no good. He twisted at the stiff knot and then the first big wave broke into foam over the deck and he lost it. The waves came fast then and he could not get to his feet. When he looked up it was dark overhead and the plywood was wrenched away from the mast. The wind battered it against the mast and the collar at the top hung free. A big wave slapped him and when next he saw the sheet it had splintered. A piece fell to the deck and Warren groped for it and slipped on the worn planking. A wave carried the piece over the side. The boards of the deck worked against each other and there was more splintering among them. Warren held on to the log. The second collar on the mast broke and the sheet slammed into the deck near him. He reached for it with one hand and felt something cut into his arm. The deck pitched. The plywood sheet fell backward and then slid and was over the side before he could try to get to it.

The storm lasted through the night. It washed away the shelter and the supplies. He clung to the log and the lashing around his waist cut into him in the night. Warren let the water wash freely over the cuts, the salt stinging across his back and over his belly, because it would heal faster that way. He tried to sleep. Toward dawn he dozed and woke only when he sensed a shift in the currents. The wind had backed into the northeast. Chop still washed across the deck and a third of the raft had broken away, but the sea was lessening as dawn came on. Warren woke slowly, not wanting to let go of the dreams.

There was nothing left but the mast, some poles he had lashed to the center log, and his knife and arrow. From a pole and a meter of twine he made a gaff with the knife. The twine had frayed. It was slow work and the twine slipped in his raw fingers. The bark of the log had cut them in the night. The sun rose quickly and a heat came into the air that worked at the cuts in him and made them sweat. He could feel that the night had tired him and he knew he would have to get food to keep his head clear. The Skimmers would come to him again he knew, and if there was a message he would have to understand it.

He made the knife fast to the pole with the twine but it was not strong and he did not want to risk using it unless he had to. A green patch of seaweed came nearby and he hooked it. He meant to use it for bait if he could but as he shook it out small shrimps fell to the planking. They jumped and kicked like sand fleas, and without thinking Warren pinched off their heads with his fingernails and ate them. The shells and tails crunched in his teeth and filled his mouth with a salty moist tang.

He kept a few for bait even though they were small. The twine was too heavy for a good line but he used it as he had before, in the first days after the *Manamix* went down when he had tried with some of their food as bait and had never caught anything. He was a sailor but he did not know how to fish. He set three trailing lines and sat to wait, wishing he had the shelter to stop the sun. The current moved well now and the chop was down. Warren hefted the gaff and hoped for a Swarmer to come. He thought of them as moving appetites, senseless alone but dangerous if enough came at once and butted the raft.

He bent over and looked steadily at a ripple of water about twenty meters from the raft. Something moved. Shifting prisms of green light descended into the dark waters. He thought about a lure. With Rosa it had been simple, a movement to draw them in and a quick shot. Warren turned, looking for something to rig to coax with, and he saw the trailing line on the left strengthen and then the line hissed and water jumped from it.

He reached to take some of the weight off and play in the line. It snapped. To the right something leaped from the water. The slim blue form whacked its tail noisily three times. Another sailed aloft on the other side of the raft as the first crashed back in a loud white splash. A third leaped and shone silver-blue in the sun and another and another and they were jumping to all sides at once, breaking free of the flat sea, their heads tilted sideways to see the raft. Warren had never seen Skimmers in schools and the way they rippled the water with their quick rushes. They were not like the Swarmers in their grace and the way they glided in the air for longer than seemed right until you looked closely at the two aft tails that beat the water and gave the look of almost walking.

Warren stood and stared. The acrobatic swivel of the Skimmers at the peak of their arc was swift and deft, a dash of zest. Their markings ran downward toward the tail. There were purplings and then three fine white stripes that fanned into the aft tails. There was no hole in the gut like the place where the Swarmers spun out their strands. Warren guessed the smallest of them was three meters long. Bigger than most marlin or sharks. Their thin mouths parted at the top of the arc and sharp narrow teeth showed white against the slick blue sky.

It was easy to see why his clumsy fishing had never hooked any big fish. These creatures and the Swarmers had teeth for a reason. There were many of them in the oceans now and they had to feed on something.

They leaped and leaped and leaped again. Their forefins wriggled in flight. The fins separated into bony ridges at their edge and rippled quickly. Each ridge made a stubby projection. The rear fins were the same. They smacked the water powerfully and filled the air with so much spray that he could see a rainbow in one of the fine white clouds.

Just as suddenly they were gone.

Warren waited for them to return. After a while he licked his lips and sat down. He began to think of water without wanting to. He had to catch a Swarmer. He wondered if the Skimmers drove them away.

In the afternoon he saw a rippling to the east but it passed going north. The high hard glare of the sun weighed on him. Nothing tugged at his lines. The mast traced an ellipse in the sky as the waves came.

A white dab of light caught his eye. It was a blotch on the flat plane of the sea. It came steadily closer. He squinted.

Canvas. Under it was a blue form tugging at a corner. Warren hauled it aboard and the alien leaped high, showering him, the bony head slanted to bring one of the big elliptical white eyes toward the figure on the deck. The Skimmer plunged, leaped again, and swam away fast, taking short leaps. Warren studied the soggy bleached canvas. It looked like a tarp used to cover the gun emplacements on the *Manamix* but he could not be sure. There were copper-rimmed holes along one edge. He used them to hoist it up the mast, lashing it with wire and punching new holes to fasten the boom. He did not have enough lines to get it right but the canvas filled with the quickening breeze of late afternoon.

He watched the bulging canvas and patiently did not think about his thirst. A splash of spray startled him. A Skimmer—the same one?—was leaping next to the raft. He licked his swollen lips and thought for a moment of fetching the gaff and then put the idea away. He watched the Skimmer arc and plunge and then speed away. It went a few tens of meters and then leaped high and turned and came back. It splashed him and then left and did the same thing again. Warren frowned. The Skimmer was heading southwest. It cut a straight line in the shifting waters.

To keep that heading he would need a tiller. He tore up a plank at the raft edge and lashed a pole to it. Fashioning a collar that would seat in the deck was harder. He finally wrapped strips of bark firmly into a hole he had punched with the gaff. They held for a while and he had to keep replacing them. The tiller was weak and he could not turn it quickly for fear of breaking the lashing. It was impossible to perform any serious maneuver like coming about if the wind shifted, but the sunset breeze usually held steady and anyway he could haul down the canvas if the wind changed too much. He nodded. It would be enough.

He brought the bow around on the path the Skimmer was marking. The current tugged him sideways and he could feel it through the tiller but the raft steadied and began to make a gurgle where it swept against the drift. The canvas filled.

The clouds were fattening again and he hoped there would not be another storm. The raft was weaker. The boards creaked with the rise and fall of each wave. He would not last an hour if he had to cling to a log in the water. He could feel a heavy fatigue settle in him.

The sea was calming, going flat. He scratched his skin where the salt had caked and stung. He slitted his eyes and looked toward the sunset. Banks of clouds were reflected in the ocean that now at sunset was like a lake. Waves made the image of the clouds into stacked bars of light. Pale cloud, then three washes of blue, then rods of cloud again. The reflection made light seem bony, broken into beams and angles. Square custard wedges floated on the glassy skin. He looked up into the empty sky, above the orange ball of sun, and saw a thin streak of white. At first he tried to figure out how this illusion was made but there was nothing in optics that would give a line of light that stood up into the sky rather than lying in it. It was no jet or rocket trail.

After describing it to himself this way Warren knew what it had to be. The Skyhook. He had forgotten the project, had not heard it mentioned in years. He supposed they were still building it. The strand started far out in orbit and lowered toward the earth as men added to it. It would be more years before the tip touched the air and began the worst part of the job. If they could lower it through the miles of air and pin it to the ground, the thing would make a kind of elevator. People and machines would ride up it and into orbit and the rockets would not streak the sky anymore. Warren had thought years ago about trying to get a job working on the Skyhook but he knew only how engines worked and they did not use any of that up there, nothing that needed air to burn. It was a fine thing where it caught the sun like a spider thread. He watched it until it turned red against the black and then faded as the night came on.

4

He woke in the morning with the first glow of light. His left arm was crooked around the tiller to hold it even though he had moored it with a wire. The first thing he checked was the heading. It had drifted some and he sat up to correct it and then found that his left arm was cramped. He shook it. It would not loosen so he gave it a few minutes to come right while he unlashed the tiller and brought them around to the right bearing. He was pretty sure he knew the setting even though he could feel that the current had changed. The raft cut across the shallow waves more at this new angle. Foam broke over the deck and the swell was deeper, the planking groaned, but he held to it.

The left arm would not uncramp. The cold of the night and sleeping on it had done this. He hoped the warmth later would loosen the muscles though he knew it was probably because his body was not getting enough food or the right food. The arm would just have to come loose on its own. He massaged it. The muscles jumped under his right hand and after a while he could feel a tingling all down the arm although that was probably from rubbing the salt in, he knew.

There was nothing on his lines. He drew in the bait but it had been nibbled away. He kept himself busy gathering seaweed with the gaff and resetting the lines with the weed but he knew it was not much use and he was trying to keep his mind off the thirst. It had been bad since he woke up and was getting worse as the sun rose. He searched for the Skyhook to take his mind off his throat and the raw puffed-up feel in his mouth but he could not see it.

He checked the bearing whenever he remembered it but there was a buzzing in his head that made it hard to tell how much time had passed. He thought about the Swarmers and how much he wanted one. The Skimmers were different but they had left him here now and he was not sure how much longer he could hold the bearing or even remember what the bearing was. The steady hollow slap of the waves against the underside of the raft soothed him and he closed his eyes against the sun.

He did not know how long he slept but when he woke his face burned and his left arm had come free. He lay there feeling it and noticed a new kind of buzzing. He looked around for an insect even though he had not seen any for many days and then cocked his head up and heard the sound coming out of the sky. Miles away a dot drifted across a cloud. The airplane was small and running on props, not jets. Warren got to his feet with effort and waved his arms. He was sure they would see him because there was nothing else in the sea and he would stick out if he could just keep standing. He waved and the plane kept going straight and he thought he could see under it something jumping in the water after its shadow had passed. Then the plane was a speck and he lost the sound of it and finally stopped waving his arms although it had not really come to him yet that they had not seen him. He sat down heavily. He was panting from the waving and then without noticing it for a while he began crying.

After a time he checked the bearing again, squinting at the sun and judging the current. He sat and watched and did not think.

The splash and thump startled him out of a fever dream.

The Skimmer darted away, plunging into a wave and out the other side with a turning twist of its aft fins.

A cylinder like the others rolled across the deck. He scrambled to catch it. The rolled sheet inside was ragged and uneven.

WAKTPL OGO SHIMA
WSW WSW CIRCLE ALAPMTO GUNJO
GEHEN WSW WSW
SCHLECT SCHLECT YOUTH UNSSTOP NONGO
LUCK LOTS

Now instead of NONGO there was OGO. Did they think this was the opposite? Again WSW and again CIRCLE. Another island? The misspelled SCHLECHT, if that was what it was, and repeated. A warning? What point could there be in that when he had not seen a Swarmer in days? If UNS was the German *we*, then UNSSTOP might be *we stop*. The line might mean *bad youth we stop not go*. And it might not. But GEHEN WSW WSW meant *go west south west* or else everything else made no sense at all and he had been wrong ever since the island. There was Japanese in it too but he had never crewed on a ship where it was spoken and he didn't know any. SHIMA. He remembered the city, Hiroshima, and wondered if *shima* was *town* or *river* or something geographical. He shook his head. The last line made him smile. The Skimmers must have been in contact with something well enough to know a salute at the end was a human gesture. Or was that what they meant? The cold thought struck him that this might be *goodbye*. Or, looking at it another way, that they were telling him he needed lots of luck. He shook his head again.

That night he dreamed about the eyes and blood and fin-fluid of the Swarmers, about swimming in it and dousing his head in it and about water that was clear and fresh. When he woke the sun was already high and hot. The sail billowed west. He got the heading close to what he could remember and then crawled into the shadow of the sail, as he had done the days before. He had kept his clothes on all the time on the raft and they were rags now. They kept off the sun still but were caked with salt and rubbed at the cuts and stung when he moved. At his neck and on his hands were black patches where the skin had peeled away and then burned again. He had worn a kind of hat he made before from Swarmer skin and bone and it was good shade but it had gone overboard in the storm.

Warren thought about the message but could make no more sense of it. He scratched his beard and found it had a crust of salt in it like hoarfrost. The salt was in his eyebrows too and he leaned over the side face down in the water and scrubbed it away. He peered downward at the descending blades of green light and the dark shadow of the raft tapering away like a steep pyramid into the shifting murky darkness. He thought he saw something moving down there but he could not be sure.

He was getting weak now. He caught some more seaweed and used it as bait on the lines. The effort left him trembling. He set the heading and sat in the shade.

He woke with a jerk and there was splashing near the raft. Skimmers. They leaped into the noonday glare and beyond them was a brown haze. He blinked and it was an island. The wind had picked up and the canvas pulled full-bellied toward the land.

He sat numb and tired at the tiller and brought the raft in toward the island, running fast before the wind and cutting the waves and sending foam over the deck. There was a lagoon. Surf broke on the coral reefs hooking around the island. The land looked to be about a kilometer across, wooded hills and glaring white beaches. The Skimmers moved off to the left and Warren saw a pale space in the lagoon that looked like a passage. He slammed the tiller over full and the raft yawed and bucked against the waves that were coming harder now. The deck groaned and the canvas luffed but the raft came into the pocket of the pale space and then the waves took it through powerfully and fast. Beyond the crashing of surf on the coral he sailed close to the wind to keep away from the dark blotches in the shallows and then turned toward shore. The Skimmers were gone now, but he did not notice until the raft snagged on a sandbar and he looked around, judging the distance to the beach. He was weak and it would be stupid to risk anything this close. He stood up with a grunt and jumped heavily on the free side of the raft. It slewed and then broke free of the sandbar and the wind blew it fifty meters more. He got his tools and stood on the raft, hesitating as if leaving it after all this time was hard to imagine and then he swore at himself and stepped off. He swam slowly until his feet hit sand and then took slow steps up to the beach, careful to keep his balance, so he did not see the man come out of the palms.

Warren pitched forward onto the sand and tried to get up. The sand felt hard and hot against him. He stood again with pains in his legs and the man was standing nearby, Chinese or maybe Filipino.

He said something to Warren and Warren asked him a question and they stared at each other. Warren waited for an answer and when he saw there was not going to be one he held out his right hand, palm up. In the silence they shook hands.

5

For a day he was weak and could not walk far. The Chinese brought him cold food in tin cans and coconut milk. They talked at each other but neither one knew a single word the other did, and soon they stopped. The Chinese pointed to himself and said "Gijan" or something close to it so Warren called him that.

It looked as though Gijan had drifted to the island in a small lifeboat. He wore clothes like gray pajamas and had two cases of canned food.

Warren slept deeply and woke to a distant booming. He stumbled down to the beach, looking around for Gijan. The Chinese was standing waist-deep in the lagoon and he pointed a pistol into the water and fired, making a loud bang but not kicking up much spray. Warren watched as slim white fish floated up, stunned. Gijan picked them from the water and put them in a palm frond he carried. He came ashore smiling and held out one of the fish to Warren. Its eyes bulged.

"Raw?" Warren shook his head. But Gijan had no matches.

Warren pointed to the pistol. Gijan took the medium-caliber automatic and hefted it and looked at him. "No. I mean, give me a shell." He realized it was pointless talking. He made a gesture of things coming out of the muzzle and Gijan caught it and fished a cartridge out of his pockets. Gijan took the fish up on the sand as they started flopping in the palm frond, waking up from the stunning. Warren gathered dry brush and twigs and mixed them and dug a pit for the mixture with his hands. He still had his knife and some wire. He forced open the cartridge with them. He mixed the gunpowder with the wood. He had been watching Gijan the night before and the man was not using fire, just eating out of cans. Warren found some hardwood and rubbed the wire along it quickly while Gijan watched, frowning at first. The fish were dead and gleamed in the sun. Warren was damned if he was going to eat raw fish now that he was on land. He rubbed the wire harder, bracing the wood between his knees and drawing the wire quickly.

back and forth. He felt it get warm in his hands. When he was sweating and the wire was both burning and biting into his hands he knelt beside the wood and pressed the searing wire into it. The powder fizzled and sputtered for a moment and then with a rush it caught, the twigs snapped, and the fire made its own pale yellow glow in the sun. Gijan smiled.

Warren had felt a dislike of Gijan's using the gun to get the fish. He thought about it as he and Gijan roasted them on sticks, but the thought went away as he started eating them and the rich crisp flavor burst in his mouth. He ate four of them in a row without stopping to drink any of the coconut milk Gijan had in tin cans. The hunger came on him suddenly as if he had just remembered food and it did not go away until he finished six fish and ate half of the coconut meat. Then he thought again about using the gun that way but it did not seem so bad now.

Gijan tried to describe something by using his hands and drawing pictures in the sand. A ship, sinking. Gijan in a boat. The sun coming into the sky seven times. Then the island. Boat broken up on the coral, but Gijan swimming beside it and getting it to shore, half sunken.

Warren nodded and drew his own story. He did not show the Swarmers or the Skimmers except at the shipwreck because he did not know how to tell the man what it was like and also he was not sure how Gijan would like the idea of eating Swarmer. Warren was not sure why this hesitation came into his head but he decided to stick with it and not tell Gijan too much about how he survived.

In the afternoon Warren made a hat for himself and walked around the island. It was flat most of the way near the beach with a steep outcropping of brown rock where the ridgeline of the island ran down into the sea. There were palms and scrub brush and sea grass and dry stream beds. He found a big rocky flat space on the southern flank of the island and squinted at it awhile. Then he went back and brought Gijan to it and made gestures of picking out some of the pale rocks and carrying them. The man caught the idea on the second try. Warren scratched out SOS in the sand and showed it to him. Gijan frowned, puzzled. He made his own sign with a stick and Warren could not understand it. There were four lines like the out-line of a house and a cross bar. Warren thumped the sand next to the SOS and said "Yes!" and thumped it again. He was pretty sure SOS was an international symbol but the other man simply stared at him. The silence got longer. There was tension in the air. Warren could not understand where it had come from. He did not move. After a moment Gijan shrugged and went off to collect more of the light-colored rocks.

They laid them out across the stony clearing, letters fifty meters tall. Warren suspected the airplane he had seen was searching for survivors of Gijan's ship, which had gone down nearby, and not the *Manamix*. It was funny Gijan had not thought of making a signal but then he did not think of making a fire either.

The next morning Warren drew pictures of fishing and found that Gijan had not tried it. Warren guessed the man was simply waiting to be picked up and was a little afraid of the big silent island and even more of the empty sea. Gijan's hands were softer than Warren's and he guessed maybe the man had been mainly a desk worker. When the canned food ran out Gijan would have tried fishing but not before. So far all he had done was climb a few palms and knock down coconuts. The palms were stunned here though and there was not much milk in the coconuts. They would need water.

Warren worked the metal in the leftover cans and made fishhooks. Gijan saw what he was doing and went away into the north part of the island.

Warren was surveying the lagoon, looking for deep spots near the shore, when he found the raft moored in a narrow cove. Gijan must have found it drifting and tied it there. The boards looked worn and weak and the whole thing—cracked tiller, bleached canvas, rusted wire lashings—carried the feel of an old useless wreck. Warren studied it for a while and then turned away.

Gijan found him at a rough shelf of rock that stuck out over the lagoon. Gijan was carrying a box Warren had not seen. He put the box down and gestured to it, smiling slightly, proud. Warren looked inside. There was a tangle of fishing line inside, some hooks, a rod, a diving mask, fins, a manual in Chinese or something like it, a screw-driver, and some odds and ends. Warren looked at the man and wished he knew how to ask a question. The box was the same kind that the canned food was in, so Warren guessed Gijan had brought all this in the boat.

They went down to the beach and Gijan drew some more pictures and that was the story that came out of it. He did not draw anything about hiding the box away but Warren could guess that he had. Gijan must have seen the raft coming, and in a hurry, afraid, he would snatch up what he could and hide it. Then when he saw that Warren was no trouble he came out and brought the food. He left the rest behind just to be careful. He was still being careful when he used the pistol to fish. Maybe that was a way to show Warren he had it without making any threats.

Warren smiled broadly and shook his hand and insisted on carrying the box back to their camp. Land crabs skittered away from their feet as they walked, two men with a strange silence between them.

Warren fished in the afternoon. The canned goods would not last long with two of them eating and Warren was more hungry than he could ever remember. His body was waking up after being half dead and it wanted food and water, more water than they could get out of the coconuts. He would have to do something about that. He thought about it while he fished, using worms from the shady parts of the island, and then he saw moving shadows in the lagoon. They were big fish but they twisted on their turns in a way he remembered. He watched and they did not break water but he was sure.

He began to notice the thirst again after he had caught two fish. He left a line with bait and went inland and knocked down three coconuts but they did not yield much of the sweet milk. He took the fish back to camp where Gijan was keeping the fire going. Warren sat and watched him gut the fish, not making a good job of it. He felt the way he had in the first days on the raft. New facts, new problems. This island was just a bigger raft with more to take from but you had to learn the ways first.

Gijan's odd box of equipment had some rubber hose that had sheared off some missing piece of equipment. Warren stared at the collection in the box for a while. He began idly making a cover for one of the large tin cans, fitting pieces of metal together. Crimping them over the lip of the can and around the edge of the hose he found that they made a pretty fair seal. He made a holder for the can, working patiently. Gijan watched him with interest. Warren sent him to get sea water in a big can. He rigged the hose to pass through a series of smaller cans. With the sea water he filled the big can and sealed the tight cover and put it on the fire. The men watched the water boil and then steam came out of the hose. Gijan saw the idea and put sea water into the small cans. It cooled the hose so that in the end the thin steam faded into a dribble of fresh water. They smiled at each other and watched the slow drip. By late afternoon they had their first drink. It was brackish but not bad.

Warren used gestures and sketches in the sand to ask Gijan about the assortment of equipment. Had he been on a research vessel? A fast skimship?

Gijan drew the profile of an ordinary freighter, even adding the loading booms. Gijan pointed at Warren so he drew an outline of the *Manamix*. With pantomime and gestures and imitating sounds they got across their trades. Warren worked with machines and Gijan was some kind of trader. Gijan drew a lopsided map of the Pacific and pointed to a speck not big enough or in the right place to be any island Warren knew about. Gijan sketched in nets and motor boats and Warren guessed they had been using a freighter to try for tuna. It sounded stupid. Until now he had not thought about the islands isolated for years now and how they would get food. You could not support a population by fishing from the shore. Most crops were thin in the sandy soil. So he guessed Gijan's island had armored a freighter and sent it out with nets, desperate. If it was a big enough island they might have an airplane and some fuel left and maybe that was the one he saw.

Gijan showed him the stuff in the box again. It was pretty banged up and salt-rusted and Warren guessed it had been left years ago when the freighter was still working. In the years when the Swarmers were spreading Warren had had a gun like everybody else in the crew, not in his own duffle where somebody might find it, but in a locker of spare engine parts. Now that he thought about it a lifeboat was a better place to stow a weapon, down in with some old gear nobody would want. When you needed a gun you would be on deck already and you could get to it easy.

He looked at Gijan's pinched face and tried to read it but the man's eyes were blank, just watching with a puzzled frown. It was hard to tell what Gijan meant by some of his drawings and Warren got tired of the whole thing.

They ate coconuts at sundown. The green ones were like jelly inside. Gijan had a way of opening them using a stake wedged into the hardpacked ground. The stake was sharp and Gijan slammed the coconut down on it until the green husk split away. The hard-shelled ones had the tough white meat inside but not much milk. The palms were bent over in the trade winds and were short. Warren counted them up and down the beach and estimated how long the two men would take to strip the island. Less than a month.

Afterward Warren went down to the beach and waded out. A current tugged at his ankles and he followed with his eyes the crinkling of the pale water where a deep current ran. It swept around the island toward the passage in the coral, the basin of the lagoon pouring out into the ocean under the night tide. Combers snarled white against the dark wedge of the coral ring and beyond was the jagged black horizon.

They would have to get fish from the lagoon and lines from shore would not be enough. But that was only one of the reasons to go out again.

In the dim moonlight he went back, past the fire where Gijan sat watching the hissing distiller and then into the scrub. Uphill he found a tree and stripped bark from it. He cut it into chips and mashed them on a rock. He was tired by the time he got a sour-smelling soup going on the fire. Gijan watched. Warren did not feel like trying to tell the man what he was doing. Warren tended the simmering and fell asleep and woke when Gijan bent over him to taste the can's thick mash. Gijan made a face. Warren roughly yanked the can away, burning his own fingers. He shook his head abruptly and set the can where it would come to a rolling boil. Gijan moved off. Warren ignored him and fell back into sleep.

This night mosquitoes found them. Warren woke and slapped his forehead and each time in the fading orange firelight his hand was covered by a mass of squashed red-brown. Gijan grunted and complained. Toward morning they trudged back into the scrub and the mosquitoes left them and they curled up on the ground to sleep until the sun came through the canopy of fronds above.

The lines he had left overnight were empty. The fishing was bound to be bad when you had no chance to play the line. They had more coconuts for breakfast and Warren checked the cooling mash he had made. It was thick and it stained wood a deep black. He put it aside without thinking much about how he could use it.

In the cool of the morning he repaired the raft. The slow working of the tide had loosened the lashings and some of the boards were rotting. It would do for the lagoon, but as he worked he thought of the Swarmers crawling ashore at the last island. The big things had been slow and clumsy and with Gijan's pistol the men would have an advantage, but there were only two of them. They could not cover the whole island. If the Swarmers came, the raft might be the only escape they had.

He brought the fishing gear aboard and cast off. Gijan saw him and came running down the hard white sand. Warren waved. Gijan was excited and jabbering and his eyes rolled back and forth from Warren to the break in the reef. He pulled out his pistol and waved it in the air. Warren ran up the worn canvas sail and swung the boom around so that the raft peeled away from the passage and made headway along the beach, around the island. When he looked back Gijan was aiming the pistol at him. Warren frowned. He could not understand the man but after a moment when Gijan saw that he was running steady in the lagoon the pistol came down. Warren saw the man put the thing back in his pocket and then he set to work laying his lines. He kept enough wind in the sail to straighten the pull and move the bait so it would look like it was swimming.

Maybe he should have drawn a sketch for Gijan. Warren thought about it a moment and then shrugged. An aft line jerked as something hit it and Warren forgot Gijan and his pistol and played in the catch.

He took four big fish in the morning. One had the striped back and silvery belly of a bonito and the others he did not recognize. He and Gijan ate two and stripped and salted the others and in the afternoon he went out again. Standing on the raft he could see the shadows of the big fish as they came into the lagoon. A Skimmer darted in the distance and he stayed away from it, afraid it would come for the trailing lines. After a while he remembered that they had never hit the lines in the ocean so he did not veer the raft when the Skimmer leaped high nearby, rolling over in that strange way. Gijan was standing on the glaring white beach, he noticed, watching. Another leap, splashing foam, and then a tube rattled on the boards of the raft.

SHIMA STONES CROSSING SAFE YOUTH
world nest unssprachen
shigano you sprachen
youth umi hiro safe nagare circle uns shio wait
wait you
luck

Warren came ashore with it and Gijan reached for the slick sheet. The man moved suddenly and Warren stepped back, bracing himself. The two stood still for a moment looking at each other, Gijan's face compressed and intent. Then in a controlled way Gijan relaxed, making a careless gesture with his hands, and helped moor the raft. Warren moved the tube and sheet from one hand to the other and finally, feeling awkward handed them to Gijan. The man read the words slowly, lips pressed together. "Shima," he said. "Shio. Nagare. Umi." He shook his head and looked at Warren, his lips forming the words again silently.

They drew pictures in the sand. For *shima* Gijan sketched the island and for *umi* the sea around it. In the lagoon he drew wavy lines in the water and said several times, "Nagare." Across the island he drew a line and then made swooping motions of bigness and said, "Hiro."

Warren murmured, "Wide island? Hiro shima?" but aside from blinking Gijan gave no sign that he understood. Warren showed him a rock for *stone* and drew the Earth for *world* but he was not sure if that was what the words on the sheet meant jammed in with the others. What did the dark **W** of *world* mean?

The men spoke haltingly to each other over the booming of the reef. The clusters of words would not yield to a sensible plan and even if it had, Warren was not sure he could tell Gijan his part of it, the English smattering of words, or that Gijan could get across to him the foreign ones. He felt in Gijan a restless energy now, an impatience with the crabbed jumble of language. *Wait wait you* and then *luck*. It seemed to Warren he had been waiting a long time now and even though this message had more English and was clearer there was no way for the Skimmers to know what language Warren understood, not unless he told them. Frowning over a diagram Gijan was drawing in the floury sand, he saw suddenly why he had made the bark mash last night.

It took hours to write a message on the back of the sheet. A bamboo quill stabbed the surface and if you held it right it did not puncture. The sour black ink dripped and ran but by pinning the sheet flat in the sun he got it to dry without a lot of blurring.

> SPEAK ENGLISH. WILL YOUTH COME HERE? ARE WE SAFE FROM YOUTH ON ISLAND? SHIMA IS ISLAND IN ENGLISH. WHERE ARE YOU FROM? CAN WE HELP YOU? WE ARE FRIENDLY.
>
> LUCK

Gijan could not understand any of it or at least he gave no sign. Warren took the raft out again at dusk as the wind backed into the north and ebbed into fitful breezes. The sail luffed and he had trouble bringing the raft out of the running lagoon currents and toward the spot where flickering shadows played on the white expanse of a sandbar. A Skimmer leaped and turned as he came near. He held the boom to catch the last gusts of sunset wind and when the shadows were under the raft he threw the tube into the water. It bobbed and began to drift out toward the passage to the sea as Warren waited, watching the shadows, wondering if they had seen it, knowing he could not catch the tube now with the raft before it reached the reef, and then a quick flurry of motion below churned the pale sand and a form came up, turning, then ripping the smooth water as it leaped. The Skimmer flexed in air and hung for an instant, rolling, before it fell with a smack and was gone in an upwash of bright foam. The tube was gone.

That night the mosquitoes came again and drove them onto the rocky ground near the center of the island. In the morning their hands were blood-streaked where they had slapped their faces and legs in the night and caught the fat mosquitoes partway through the feeding.

In the morning Warren went out again and laid his lines as early as possible. Near the sandbar there were many fish. One of them hit a line and when Warren pulled it in the thing had deep-set eyes, a small mouth like a parrot's beak, slimy gills and hard blue scales. He pressed at the flesh and a dent stayed in it for a while, the way it did if you squeezed the legs of a man with leprosy or dropsy. The thing smelled bad as it lay on the planks and the sun warmed it so he threw it back, pretty sure it was poisonous. It floated and a Skimmer leaped near it and then took the thing and was gone. Warren could see more Skimmers moving below. They were feeding on the poison fish.

He caught two skipjack tuna and brought them ashore for Gijan to clean. The man was watching him steadily from the beach and Warren did not like it. The thing between him and the Skimmers was his and he did not want any more of the stupid drawing and hand-waving of trying to explain it to Gijan.

He went into the palm grove where the fire crackled and got the diving mask he had seen in Gijan's box. It was made for a smaller head but with the rubber strap drown tight he could ride it up against the bridge of his nose and make it fit. As he came back down to the beach, Gijan said something but Warren went on to the raft and cast off, bearing in the southerly wind out toward the sandbar. He grounded the raft on the bar to hold it steady.

He lay on the raft and peered down at the moving shapes. They were at least twenty fathoms down and they had finished off the poison fish. Seven Skimmers hovered over a dark patch, rippling their forefins where the bony ridges stuck out like thick fingers. Sunlight caught a glint from the thing they were working on and suddenly a gout of gray mist came up from it and broke into bubbles. It was steam. He lay halfway over the side of the raft and watched the regular puffs of steam billow up from the machine. Without thinking of the danger he slipped overboard and dove, swimming hard, pushing as deep as he could despite the tightness and burning in his chest. The Skimmers moved as they saw him and the machine became clearer. It was like a pile of junk, pieces of a ship's hull and deck collars and fittings of all sizes. Four batteries were mounted on one side and rust-caked cables led from them into the machine. There were other fragments and bits of worked metal and some of it he was sure had not been made by men. Knobs of something yellow grew here and there and in the wavering, rippling green light there was something about the form and shape of the thing that Warren recognized as right and yet he knew he had never seen anything like it before. There is a logic to a piece of equipment that comes out of the job it has to do and he felt that this machine was well shaped. Then his lungs at last burned too much and he fought upward, all thought leaving him as he let the air burst from him and followed the silvery bubbles up toward the shifting slanting blades of yellow-green sun.

6

In the lagoon the water shaded from pale blue at the beach to emerald in the deep channel where the currents ran with the tides. Beyond the snarling reef the sea was a hard gray.

Warren worked for five days in the slow dark waters near the sandbar. He double-anchored the raft so the deck was steady and he could write well on it with the bark mash and then dry the sheets the Skimmers brought up to him.

Their first reply was not much better than the earlier messages but he printed out in capital letters a simple answer and gradually they learned what he could not follow. Their next message had more English in it and less Japanese and German and fewer of the odd words made up out of parts of languages. There were longer stretches in it, too, more like sentences now than string of nouns.

The Skimmers did not seem to think of things acting but instead of things just being, so they put down names of objects in long rows as though the things named would react on each other, each making the other clearer and more specific and what the things did would be obvious because of the relations between them. It was a hard way to learn to think and Warren was not sure he knew what the impacted knots of words meant most of the time. Sometimes the chains of words said nothing to him and the blue forms below would flick across the bonewhite sand in elaborate looping arabesques, turning over and over with their ventral fins flared, in designs that escaped him. When the sun was low at morning or at dusk he could not tell the Skimmers from their shadows and the gliding long forms merged with their dark echoes on the sand in a kind of slow elliptical dance. He lay halfway off the raft and watched them when he was tired from the messages, and peered through the mask, and something in their quick darting glide would come through to him. He would try then to ask a simple question. He would write it out and dry it and throw it into the lagoon. Sometimes that was enough to cut through the jammed lines of endless nouns they had offered him and he would see a small thought that hung between the words in a space each word allowed but did not define. It was as if the words packed together still left a hole between them and the job was to see the hole instead of the blurred lumpy things that made the edges of the hole. That was a part of what it was like to think about the long strings of letters and to watch the skimming grace they had down in the dusky emerald green. There was more to it than that but he could not sort it out.

He went ashore at dusk each day. The catch from the trailing lines was good in the morning and went away in the afternoon. Maybe it had something to do with the Skimmers. The easy morning catch left him most of the day to study the many sheets they brought up to him and to work on his own halting answers.

Gijan stood on the beach most of the day and watched. He did not show the pistol again when Warren went out. He kept the fire and the distiller going and they ate well. Warren brought the finished sheets ashore and kept them in Gijan's box but he could not tell the man much of what was in them, at first because lines in the sand and gestures were not enough and later because Warren did not know himself how to tell it.

Gijan did not seem to mind not knowing. He tended the fire and knocked down coconuts and split them and gutted the catch and after a while asked nothing more. At times he would leave the beach for hours and Warren guessed he was collecting wood or some of the pungent edible leaves they had at supper.

To Warren the knowing was all there was and he was glad Gijan would do the work and not bother him. At noon beneath the high hard dazzle of the sky he ate little because he wanted to keep his head clear. At night though he filled himself with the hot moist fish and tin-flavored water. He woke to a biting early sun. The mosquitoes still stung but he did not mind it so much now.

On the third day like this he began to write down for himself a kind of patchwork of what he thought they meant. He knew as soon as he read it over that it was not right. He had never been any good with words. When he was married he did not write letters to his wife when he shipped out even if he was gone half a year. But this writing was a way of getting it down and he liked the act of scratching out the blunt lines on the backs of the Skimmer sheets.

In the long times before, the early forms went easy in the ***World****, then rose up leaping out of the bottom of the* ***World****, to the land, made the tools we knew, struck the fire, made* *the fire-hardened sand we could see through so that we could cup the light. The clouds open, we can see lights, learn the dots above, we see lights we cannot reach, even the highest jumper of us cannot touch the lights that move. We cup the light, scoop it up, and find the lights in the sky are small and hot, but there is one light that we cup to us and find it is a stone in the sky, we think other lights are stones in the sky but far away, we see no other place like the* **World***, we swim at the bottom of everything, in the* **World***, the place where stones want to fall, but the flow takes the stones in the sky, makes them circle us, circle forever like the hunters in the* **World** *before they close for the killing, so the stones cannot strike us in the nest of us, the* **World** *of the people. We thought that ours was the only* **World** *and that all else was cold stone or burning stone. And as we cupped the light not thinking of it we saw the cold stone in the sky grow a light which went on, then off, then on, again and again, moving now strangely in the sky and then growing more stones, moving, stones falling into the* **World***, stones smaller than the big sky stone, hitting killing bringing big animals that stink, eating every piece of the* **World** *that comes before them, taking some of us in them, big stones making big animals that are not alive but swallow, keeping us in them in water, sour water that brings pain, we live there, light coming from land that is not land,* **World** *that is not the* **World***, no waves no land but there is the glowing stone on all sides that we cannot climb, no land for the youth to crawl to, long time passing, we sing over and over the soon-birthing but it does not come, the song does not make it stir out of this red* **World***, this small* **World** *that one of us can cross in the time of a single singing. The youth change their song slowly then more and then more, their song goes away from us, they sing strangely but do not crawl, hot red things bubble in the small* **World** *where we live and the youth drink it. The smooth stone on all sides makes this* **World** *glow with light that never grows and never dims, we keep some of our tools and can feel the time going, many songs pass, we do not let the youth sing or crawl but then they do not know us and sing their own noise, drinking in the foul currents of the big animal we inhabit, the smooth stone oozing light, always rumbling, the currents not right, we move thickly,* *lose our tides, the red currents suck and bring food sweet and bitter, wrong, through long times the walls humming and no waves for us to fly through and splash white. Then the smooth stone grows slowly hot, cracks open, some of us die, the song dims among us, bitter blue currents drive us down, more of us fall from the song, long cold sounds stab us, and more fall, from the sour streams come now waves, fresh streams, we taste, sing weakly, speak, it is a* **W***orld like the one* **W***orld, the smooth stone on all sides is gone, we break water. There are waves cutting white, sharp, we find salt foods, leap into hot airs, waves hard fast, we cup the light and see big stone in sky, far stones moving across the many stones, like our* **W***orld but not of our* **W***orld. The song is weak, we seek to cross this* **W***orld but cannot, we know we will lose ourselves in this* **W***orld if our song is stretched farther. But the youth have a strange song and they go out. They find food, they find big animals in the waves and bigger animals that crush the waves, they strike at them in the way we once did long times past, throw their webs to bring down the crushers of waves. These crushers are not the big animals we knew in the* **W***orld and when the youth drag them down closer to the center they are not ripe, do not burst with fruit, are fiery to the mouth and kill some youth without releasing the pods that would drive the youth to the land, drive them to the air to suck, drive the change to make the youth into the form that would be us. These things that float and crush the waves we fear and flee but the youth eat of them and yet do not go to the land to crawl, we lose the song with them forever, they fly the waves no more, they take the big animals that walk above the waves, the youth have become able to kill the bitter wave-walkers, they feast on the things in them. We see from a distance that it is you the youth eat, even if you are sick and death-causing, you are killed in the skins that carry you walking the waves. The youth do not sing, they split your skins, they grow and eat all that comes before them. Now you are gone like us, nearly chewed. We come to here, we drive the youth away, the act chews us but does not finish us. We find you in the skins you love and we cannot sing with you. We find you one and in one you can sing, together you are deaf. You are the twenty-fourth we have sung with on the waves.*

Your kind cannot hear unless you are one and cannot sing to each other but many of the others who sang with us are now chewed but we can keep the youth away for a time we grow weak the youth run with sores and leave stink in the currents foul where they go we smell them the **World** *that was false* **World** *made them this way not as they were when we knew them in the* **World** *that was ours. They can not sing but know of the places where you sing to each other and some now go there with their sores they may be chewed by you but there are many many of them they ache now for the skins-that-sink but they are madness they are coming and they chew you others last.*

Each night after it got too dark for Warren to write in the yellow firelight they would move inland. The mosquitoes stayed near the beach and there were a lot of other insects, too. Warren listened to fish in the lagoon leaping for the insects and the splashing as the Skimmers took the fish in turn. He could see their phosphorescent wakes in the water.

They smeared themselves with mud to keep off the mosquitoes but it did not keep off the ticks that dropped from the trees. There was no iodine in Gijan's box of random items. Putting a drop of iodine on the tick's tail was the best treatment and second best was burning them off. Each morning the men inspected each other and there were always a few black dots where the ticks burrowed in. An ember from the fire pressed against the tick's hind-quarters made it let go and then Warren could pull the tick out with his fingernails. He knew that if the head came off in the skin it would rot and the whole area would become a boil. He noticed that Gijan got few ticks and he wondered if it had anything to do with the oriental skin.

The next morning he got a good catch and when he brought it in he was sore from the days of work on the raft. After eating the fish he went for more coconuts. The softer fronds were good too for rubbing the skin to take away the sting of mosquito bites and to get the salt out. Finding good coconuts was harder now and he worked his way across the island, up the ridgeline and down to a swampy part on the southern side. There were edible leaves there and he chewed some slowly as he made his way back, thinking. He was nearly across a bare stretch of soil when he saw it was the place they had laid out the SOS. The light-colored rocks were there but they were scattered. The SOS was broken up.

Gijan was looking in the storage box when Warren came back into the camp. "Hey!" he called. Gijan looked at him, calm and steady, and then stood up, taking his time.

Warren pointed back to the south and glared at the man and then bent down and drew the SOS in the sand. He rubbed it out and pointed at Gijan.

Warren had expected the man to give him a blank look or a puzzled expression. Instead, Gijan put a hand in a pocket.

Then Gijan said quite clearly, "It does not matter."

Warren stood absolutely still. Gijan pulled the pistol casually out of his pocket but he did not aim it at anything.

Warren said carefully, "Why?"

"Why deceive you? So that you would go on with your—" he paused—"your good work. You have made remarkable progress."

"The Skimmers."

"Yes."

"And the SOS . . ."

"I did not want anyone to spot the island who should not."

"Who would that be?"

"Several. The Japanese. The Americans. There are reports of Soviet interest."

"So you are—"

"Chinese, of course."

"Of course."

"I would like to know how you wrote that summary. I read the direct messages you got from them, read them many times. I could not see in them very much."

"There's more to it than what they wrote."

"You are sure that you brought all their messages ashore?"

"Sure. I kept them all."

"How do you discover things that are not in the messages?"

"I don't think I can tell you that."

"Cannot? Or will not?"

"Can't."

Gijan became pensive, studying Warren. Finally he said, "I cannot pass judgment on that. Others will have to decide that, others who know more than I do." He paused. "Were you truly in a shipwreck?"

"Yeah."

"Remarkable that you survived. I thought you would die when I saw you first. You are a sailor?"

"Engine man. What're you?"

"Soldier. A kind of soldier."

"Funny kind, seems to me."

"This is not the duty I would have chosen. I sit on this terrible place and try to talk to those things."

"Uh huh. Any luck?"

"Nothing. They do not answer me. The tools I was given do not work. Kinds of flashlights. Sound makers. Things floating in the water. I was told they are drawn to these things."

"What would happen if they did answer?"

"My job is over then."

"Well, I guess I've put you out of work. We're still going to need something to eat, though." He gestured at the raft and turned toward it and Gijan leveled the pistol.

"You can rest," the man said. "It will not be long."

7

In mid-afternoon six delta-planes came in low, made a pass and arced up, one at a time, to land in V-mode. They came down in the rocky area to the south and a few minutes after the shrieking engines shut down three squads of fast, lean-looking infantry came double-timing onto the beach.

Warren watched them from the shade where he sat within clear view of Gijan. The man had made him carry the radio and power supply from its concealment in the scrub and onto the beach, where he could talk down the planes. Gijan shouted at the men and they backed away from the beach where the Skimmers might see them. A squad took Warren and marched him south, saying nothing. At the landing site men and forklifts were unloading and building and no one looked at him twice. The squad took him to a small building set down on rocky soil and locked him inside.

It was light durablock construction, three meters square with three windows with heavy wire mesh over them. There was a squat wooden chair, a thin sleeping pad on the floor, and a fifty-watt glow plate in the ceiling that did not work. Warren tasted the water in a gallon jug and found it tepid and metallic. There was a bucket to use as a toilet.

He could not see much through the windows but the clang and rumble of unloading went on. Darkness came. A motor started up nearby and he tried to tell if it was going or coming until he realized it was turning over at a steady rpm. He touched the wall switch and the soft glow above came on so he guessed the generator had started. In the dim light everything in the room stood out bleak and cold.

Later a muscular soldier came with a tin plate of vegetable stew. Warren ate it slowly, tasting the boiled onions and carrots and spinach and tomatoes, holding back his sudden appetite so that he got each taste separately. He licked the pan clean and drank some water and rather than sit and think fruitlessly he laid down and slept.

At dawn the same guard came again with more of the stew, cold this time. Warren had not finished it when the guard came back and took it away and yanked him to his feet. The soldier quick-marched him across a compound in the pale morning light. He memorized the sizes and distances of the buildings as well as he could. The guard took him to the biggest building in the compound, a prefab that was camouflage-speckled for the jungle. The front room was an office with Gijan sitting in one of the four flimsy chairs and a tall man, Chinese or Japanese, standing beside a plywood desk.

"You know Underofficer Gijan? Good. Sit." The tall man moved quickly to offer Warren a chair. He turned and sat behind the desk and Warren watched him. Each motion of the man had a kind of sliding quality to it, as though he was keeping his body centered and balanced at all times to take a new angle of defense or attack if needed.

"Please relax," the man said. Warren noticed that he was sitting on the edge of the chair. He settled back in it, using the moment to locate the guard in a far corner to his right, an unreachable two meters away.

"What is your name?"

"Warren."

"You have only one name?" the man asked, smiling.

"Your men didn't introduce themselves either. I didn't think I had to be formal."

"I am sure you understand the circumstances, Warren. In any case, my name is Tseng Wong. Since we are using only single names, call me Tseng." His words came out separately like smooth round objects forming in the still air.

"I can see that conditions have been hard on you."

"Not so bad."

Tseng pursed his lips. "The evidence given by your little—" he searched for the word—"spasm in the face, is enough to show me—"

"What spasm?"

"Perhaps you do not notice it any longer. The left side, a tightening in the eyes and the mouth."

"I don't have anything like that."

Tseng looked at Gijan, just a quick glance, and then back at Warren. There was something in it Warren did not like and he found himself focusing his attention on his own face, waiting to see if there was anything wrong with it he had not noticed. Maybe he—

"Well, we shall let it pass. A casual remark, that is all. I did not come to criticize you but to, first, ask for your help, and second, to get you off this terrible island."

"You coulda got me off here days ago. Gijan had the radio."

"His task came first. You are fascinated by the same problem, are you, Warren?"

"Seems to me my big problem is you people."

"I believe your long exposure out here has distorted your judgment, Warren. I also believe you overestimate your ability to survive for long on this island. With Under-officer Gijan the two of you did well enough but in the long run I—" Tseng stopped when he saw the slight upward turn of Warren's mouth that was clearly a look of disdain.

"I saw that case of rations Gijan had stashed back in the brush," Warren said. "None of you know nothing about living out here."

Tseng stood up, tall and straight, and leaned against the back wall of the office. It gave him a more casual look but put him so that Warren had to look up to talk to him.

"I will do you the courtesy of speaking frankly. My government—and several others, we believe—has suspected for some time that there are two distinct populations among the aliens. One—the Swarmers—is capable of mass actions, almost instinctive actions, which are quite effective against ships. The others, the Skimmers, are far more intelligent. They are also verbal. Yet they did not respond to our research vessels. They ignored attempts to communicate."

Warren said, "You still have ships?"

For the first time Gijan spoke. "No. I was on one of the last that went down. They got us off with helicopters, and then—"

"No need to go into that," Tseng cut him off smoothly.

"It was the Swarmers who sank you. Not Skimmers," Warren said. It was not a question.

"Skimmer intelligence was really only an hypothesis," Tseng said, "until we had reports that they had sought out single men or women. Usually people adrift, though sometimes even at the shore."

"Safer for them," Warren said.

"Apparently. They avoid the Swarmers. They avoid ships. Isolated contact is all that is left to them. It was really quite stupid of us not to have thought of that earlier."

"Yeah."

Tseng smiled slightly. "Everything is of course clearer in, as you say, the rearview mirror."

"Uh huh."

"It seems they learned the bits of German and Japanese and English from different individual encounters. The words were passed among the Skimmers so that each new contact had more available vocabulary."

"But they didn't know the words were from different languages," Gijan added.

"Maybe they only got one," Warren said.

"So we gather," Tseng said. "I have read your, ah, summary. Yours is the most advanced contact so far."

"A lot of it doesn't make much sense," Warren said. He knew Tseng was drawing him into the conversation but it did not matter. Tseng would have to give information to get some.

"The earlier contacts confirm part of your summary."

"Uh huh."

"They said that Swarmers can go ashore."

"Uh huh."

"How do you know that?"

"It's in the stuff I wrote. The stuff Gijan stole."

Gijan said sharply, "You showed it to me."

Warren looked at him without expression and Gijan stared back and after a moment looked away.

"Let us not bother with that. We are all working on the same problem, after all."

"Okay," Warren said. He had managed to get the talk away from how he knew about the Swarmers going on the land. Tseng was good at talking, a lot better than Warren, so he would have to keep the man away from some things. He volunteered, "I guess going up on the shore is part of their, uh, evolution."

"You mean their development?"

"They said something, the last day I saw them, about a deathlight. A deathlight coming on the land and only the Swarmers could live through it."

"Light from their star?"

"Guess so. It comes sometimes and that's why the Skimmers don't go up onto the land."

Tseng stood and began pacing against the back wall. Warren wondered if he knew that Swarmers had already gone inland on an island near here. Tseng gave no sign of it and said out of his concentration, "That agrees with the earlier survivors' reports. We think that means their star is irregular. It flares in the UV. The Swarmers have simple nervous systems, smaller brains. They can survive a high UV flux."

"For about two of their planet's years, the Skimmers said," Warren murmured. "But you're wrong—the Swarmers aren't dumb."

"They have heads of mostly bone."

"That's for killing the big animals, the ones that float on the surface of their sea. Something like whales, I guess. Maybe they stay at the top to use the UV or something."

"The Swarmers ram them, throw those webs over them? Sink them?"

"Yeah. Just what they did to our ships."

"Target confusion. They think ships are animals."

"The Swarmers, they drag the floaters under, eat some kind of pods inside 'em. That's what triggers their going up on the land."

"If we could find a way to prevent their confusing our ships with—"

Gijan said, "But they are going to the land now. They are in the next mode."

"Uh huh." Warren studied the two men, tried to guess if they knew anything he could use. "Look, what're they doing when they get ashore?"

Tseng looked at him sharply. "What do the Skimmers say?"

"Far as I can tell, the Swarmers aren't dumb, not once they get on land. They make the machines and stuff for the Skimmers. They're really the same kind of animal. They grow hands and feet and the Skimmers have some way to tell them—singing—how to build stuff, make batteries, tools, that stuff."

Tseng stared at Warren for a long moment. "A break in the evolutionary ladder? Life trying to get out of the oceans, but turned back by the solar flares?" Tseng leaned forward and rested his knuckles on the gray plywood. He had a strange weight and force about him. And a desperate need.

Warren said, "Maybe it started out with the Swarmers crawling up on the beaches to lay eggs or something. Good odds they'd be back in the water before a flare came. Then the Skimmers invented tools and saw they needed things on the land, needed to make fire or something. So they got the Swarmers, the younger form of their species, to help. Maybe—"

"The high UV speeded up their evolutionary rate. Perhaps the Swarmers became more intelligent, in their last phase, on land, where the intelligence would be useful in making the tools. Um, yes."

Tseng gave Gijan an intense glance. "Possible. But I think there is more than that. These creatures are here for some purpose beyond this charming little piece of natural history we have been told. Or sold."

Tseng turned back to Warren. "We have our partially successful procedures of communication, as you have probably guessed. I have been ordered to carry out systematic methods of approach." He was brisk and sure, as though he had digested Warren's information and found a way to classify it. "Yours will be among them. But it is an idiosyncratic technique and I doubt we could teach it to our field men. Underofficer Gijan, for example." The contempt in his voice for Gijan was obvious. "Meanwhile, I will call upon you for help if we need it, Warren."

"Uh huh."

Tseng took a map of the ocean from his desk drawer and flipped it across to Warren. "I trust this will be of help in writing your report."

"Report?"

"An account of your interactions with the aliens. I must file it with my superior. I am sure it will be in your own interests to make it as accurate as possible." He made a smile without any emotion behind it. "If you can fix the point where your ship went down, we might even be able to find some other survivors."

Warren could see there was nothing in this last promise. He thought and then said, "Mr. Wong, I wondered if I could, you know, rest a little. And when the guard there brings me my food, I'd like a long time to eat it. My stomach, being out on the ocean so long, it can't take your food unless I kind of take it easy."

"Of course, of course." Tseng smiled with genuine emotion this time. Warren could see that he was glad to be dispensing favors and that the act made him sure he had judged the situation and had it right.

"Sure do appreciate that, Mr. Wong," he said, getting the right tone into the words so that the man would classify him and file him away and forget him.

8

He worked for two days on the report. The guard gave him a pad of paper and a short stubby little pen and Tseng told him to write it in English. Warren smiled at that. They thought any seaman had to speak a couple of languages but he had never any trouble getting around with one and a few words picked up from others. You learned more from watching people than from listening to all their talk anyway.

He had never been any good at writing and a lot of the things about the Skimmers he could not get down. He worked on the writing in his cell, listening all the time for the sound of new motors or big things moving. It was hard to tell anything about what the teams were doing. He was glad he could rest in the shadows of the cell and think, eating the food they brought him as quickly as he could while still getting the taste of it.

The same chinless guard he had from the first came once a day to take him down to the shore. Warren carried the waste bucket. The guard would not let him take the time to bury the waste and instead made him throw it into the surf. The guard stayed back in the sea-grape bushes while Warren went down to the lagoon. The man was probably under orders not to show himself on the beach, Warren guessed. On the windward side of the island there was a lot of dry grass and some gullies. Dried-up streambeds ran down into little half-moon beaches and Warren could see the teams had moored catboats and other small craft there. Some of the troops had pitched tents far back in the gullies but most of them were empty. The guard marched him back that way. On one of the sandy crescents Warren's raft was beached, dragged up above the tide line but not weighted down or moored.

Coming back on the second day some sooty terns were hanging in the wind, calling with long low cries. Some were nested in the rocks up at the windward and others in the grass of the lee. The terns would fall off the wind and swoop down over the heads of the men gathering the eggs out of the rocky nests. The birds cawed and dipped down through the wind but the men did not look up.

The next morning the chinless soldier came too soon after the breakfast tin and Warren had to straighten his sleeping pad in a hurry. The guard never came into the shadowy cell because of the smell from the bucket which Warren kept next to the door. The man had discovered that Warren knew no Chinese and so instead of giving orders he shoved Warren in whatever direction he wanted. This time they went north.

Tseng was surveying a work team at a point halfway up the ridge at the middle of the island. He nodded to Warren and signaled that the guard should remain nearby. "Your report?"

"Nearly done with it."

"Good. I will translate it myself. Be sure it is legible."

"I printed it out."

"Just as do the Skimmers."

"Yeah."

"We duplicated your methods, you know, and dropped several messages into the lagoon." From here on the ridge moving shadows were plain against the sand. The soft green of the lagoon was like a ring and beyond it was the hard blue that went to the horizon. "No reply."

"How'd you deliver them?"

"Three men, two armed for safety. After so many incidents they are afraid to go out unprotected."

"They go in that?" Warren pointed to a skiff beached below them.

"Yes. I'm going to supplement their work with a set of acoustics. They should be—yes, here we are." A buzz came from the south and a motorboat came up the lagoon leaving a white wake. It cut in among the shoals and sandbars and a big reel on the back of it was spinning in the sun, throwing quick darts of yellow into Warren's eyes.

"We will have a complete acoustic bed. A very promising method."

"You make any sense out of that?"

Tseng shaded his eyes against the glare and turned to smile at Warren. "Their high-frequency 'songs' are their basic method of communication. We already have much experience with the dolphins. We can converse freely with them. Only on simpleminded subjects, of course. Much of what we know about Swarmer and Skimmer movements comes from the dolphins."

Warren said sharply, "Look, why fool with that stuff. Let me go out and I'll ask them what you want."

Tseng nodded. "Eventually I might. But you must understand that the Skimmers have reasons of their own for not telling you everything that is important."

"Such as?"

"Here." Tseng snapped his fingers at an aide standing nearby. The soldier brought over a document pouch. Tseng took out a set of photographs and handed them to Warren. The top one was a color shot of a woman's stomach and breasts. There were small bumps on them, white mounds on the tan skin. One lump was in her left nipple.

Warren went on to the next, and the next. The lumps got bigger and whiter. "They are quite painful," Tseng said distantly. "Some kind of larva burrows into a sweatsore and in a day this begins. The larva is biggest near the skin, armed with sharp yellow spines. The worm turns as it feeds. Spines grate against the nerves. The victim feels sudden, deep pain. Within another day the victim is hysterical and tries to claw the larva out. These are small larvae. There are reports of larger ones."

In one photograph the open sores were bleeding and dripping a white pus. "Like a tick," Warren said. "Burn it out. Use iodine. Or cover it with tape so it can't get air."

Tseng sighed. "Any such attack and the larva releases something, we are unsure what, into the victim's bloodsteam. It paralyzes the victim so he cannot treat himself further."

"Well, if you—"

"The larva apparently does not breathe. It takes oxygen directly from the host. If anything dislodges the spines, once they are hooked in, the larva releases the paralyzer and something else, something that carries a kind of egg so that other larvae can grow elsewhere. All this in minutes."

Warren shook his head. "Never heard of any tick or bug like that."

"They come from the Swarmers. When they are ashore."

Warren watched the motorboat methodically crisscrossing the lagoon, the reel spinning. He shook his head.

"Something to do with their mating? Don't know. The Skimmers—"

"They said nothing about it. Interesting, eh?"

"Maybe they don't know."

"It seems unlikely."

"So you're listening for what?"

"Contact between the Skimmers and the Swarmers. Some knowledge of how they interact."

"Can't you treat this bug, get rid of it?"

"Possibly. The European medical centers are at work now. But there are other diseases. They are spreading rapidly from contact points near Ning-po and Macau."

"Maybe you can block them off."

"The things are everywhere. They come ashore and the larvae are carried by the birds, by animals—somehow. That is why we burn our reserves of fuel to come this far."

"To the islands?"

"Only in isolation do they make contact. The reported incidents are from the Pacific basin. That is why there are Japanese aircraft near here, Soviet, American—you are an American, aren't you?"

"No."

"Oh? Somehow I thought—but never mind. The other powers are desperate. They do not know what is happening and they envy our lead in information. You will notice the installation to the south?"

Tseng gestured. Warren saw at the rocky tip of the island a fan of slender shapes knifing up at the sky. "Anti-air missiles. We would not want anyone else to exploit this opportunity."

"Uh huh."

The motorboat droned, working its way up the eastern shore. Warren studied the island, noticing where the tents were pitched and where the men moved in work teams and where the scrub jungle cut off visibility.

"If you're smart you won't use a motor in the lagoon."

"The men will not go out without some way of returning quickly. I understand their fear. I have seen—"

An aide approached. He spoke quickly and Tseng answered with anxiety creeping into his voice. Warren watched the motorboat cross near the sandbar and saw the shadows dart and twist and turn, swift black shapes in the watery green light.

That night he felt a dark hammering thing above him that wove and wove, rippling the sunlight, swimming badly, and dropped metal that settled on him, heavy and foul. The steady dead rasp from above cut and burned and he turned on his side. Then he was above the motor and saw the fuel line backfilled and heard the sluggish rumble as they blew the lines out and heard the plugs not running right either. That was it: nothing ran right. Humans were great talkers but down here, lofting in the salty murk, he could see that they worked their mouths a lot but said damned little to each other. In Tokyo he'd never learned a word of Japanese, and here Gijan had played a mute without Warren's minding, and now the Chinese were trying to talk to Skimmers—who wanted something they couldn't say either—and each life form had its own private language. He turned over again and felt his wife sleeping against him warm and moist and then on top of him the way she liked. She was heavy too, like the falling spreading metal the hammering machine laid in the lagoon, heavy and yet soft, and her hair lay silky on his face and in his eyes. In shadows her face was intersecting planes, lean and white the way he had always liked, and he took her hair in his mouth and tasted it. The salt and musk was like her sex below. He touched the canted planes of her and remembered that she had fallen away from him when more than anything he had wanted her weight. And her hair swinging across his face and the taste of it.

When he woke the pad was damp with sweat. He felt in the

blackness for the table turned over on its side to conceal the far wall. This reassuring flat plane of wood gave him back the present so he did not have to think about the past. But he remembered the hammering from above and the falling cold metal and knew how much they hated what was happening to them out in the lagoon.

Before dawn his cell rattled and there was a booming that rolled down from the sky. He woke and looked out the windows through the heavy wire mesh. High up in the black, luminous things tumbled and exploded into auras of blue and crimson and then gutted into nothing. Distant hollow boomings came long after the lights were gone and then the sounds faded into the crashing on the reef.

In the morning the chinless soldier came again and took the tin dish that Warren had rubbed clean. The soldier did not like this job and he cuffed Warren twice to show him where to walk. First they went to the beach with the waste bucket, which had more in it now because Warren's body no longer absorbed almost everything he was fed. From the beach he watched the small motor ketches and cats that stayed near the shore while they laid something into the water, dropping boxes off the stern where they would lie on the bottom and, Warren was sure, send back reports on the passing sounds and movements.

The guard took him north and inland, just out of view of the reef. Tseng was there with a crowd and they were all watching the green water from far back among the trees.

"See them?" Tseng said to Warren when he had worked his way through the group of men and women. Warren looked out past the brilliant white sand that stung the eyes and saw silver-blue forms leaping.

"What's . . . why are they doing that?" he asked.

"We are returning their acoustic signals to them. As a kind of test."

"Not smart."

"Oh?" Tseng turned with interest. "Why?"

"I can't really tell you but—"

"It is a technique of progression. We give them back their songs. We see how they react. The dolphins eventually did well with this approach."

"These aren't dolphins."

"So. Yes." Tseng seemed to lose interest in the splashing forms in the lagoon. He turned, hands placed neatly behind his back, and led Warren through the group of advisers around them. "But you must admit they are giving a kind of response."

Warren swore. "Would you talk to somebody if they kept poking you in the eye?"

"Not a good analogy."

"Yeah?"

"Still . . ." Tseng slowed, peering out through the brush and palm trees at the glistening water. "You are the only one who got the material about how they came here. Getting scooped up and going on a long voyage and then being dumped into the ocean—you got that. I had not heard it before.

"It does make a certain kind of sense. Fish like that—they might make printed messages, yes. They have shown they can put together our own wreckage and make a kind of electrostatic printing press—underwater, even. But to build a rocket? A ship that goes between stars? No."

"Somebody brought them."

"I am beginning to believe that. But why? To spread these diseases?"

"I dunno. Let me go out and—"

"Later, when we are more sure. Yes, then. But tomorrow we have more tests."

"Have you counted the number of them out there?"

"No. They are hard to keep track of. I—"

"There are a lot less of 'em now. I can see. You know what happens when you drive them away?"

"Warren, you will get your turn." Tseng put a restraining hand on his sleeve. "I know you have had a hard time here and on that raft but believe me, we are able to—"

Gijan approached, carrying some pieces of paper. He rattled off something in Chinese and Tseng nodded. "I am afraid we are being interrupted once more. Those incidents last night—you saw them?—have involved us, a research party, in—Well, the Americans have been humiliated again. Their missiles we knocked down with ease."

"You're sure that stuff was theirs?"

"They are the ones complaining—isn't the conclusion obvious? I believe they and perhaps too their lackeys, the Japanese, have discovered how much progress we are making. They would very much like to turn the Swarmers and their larvae to their own nationalistic advantage. These messages—" he waved the pack of them—"are more diplomatic notices. The Japanese have given my government an ultimatum of sorts. I am sure even you understand that this is part of a larger game. Of course China does not wish to use the Swarmers against other powers, even if we did understand the creatures."

"I don't know about that."

"But I thought you were American." Tseng smiled without mirth.

"No."

"I see. I think it is perhaps time to have Underofficer Gijan take you back to your little room, then."

The guard took Warren down the center of the island, along a path worn smooth in the last few days by the troops. They passed a dozen technicians working on acoustic equipment and playing back the high-pitched squeals of Skimmer song. The troops were making entries on computer screens and chattering to each other, breaking down the problem into bits that could be cross-referenced and reassembled to make patterns that people could understand. It would have to be good because they wanted to eavesdrop. But the way the Skimmers talked to the Swarmers might not be anything like the songs the Skimmers sang among themselves.

It made no sense that the Skimmers had much control over the Swarmers, Warren thought to himself as he marched down the dirt path. No sense at all. Something had brought them all to Earth and given the Swarmers some disease and the answer lay in thinking about that fact, not playing stupid games with machines in the water.

The troops were spread out more now, he saw. There were nests of high-caliber cannon strung out along the ridge and down near the beaches men were digging in where they could set up a cross fire over the natural clearings.

The men and women he passed were talking among themselves now, not silent and efficient the way they had been at first. They looked at him with suspicion. He guessed the missile attack in the night had made them nervous and even the hot work of clearing fields of fire in the heavy humidity did not take it out of them.

Coming down the rocky ridgeline Warren slipped on a stone and fell. The guard hit him to get him to hurry. Warren went on and saw ahead one of the bushes with leaves he knew he could eat and when he went by it he pulled some off and started to stuff them into his pockets for later. The guard shouted and hit him in the back with the butt of his rifle and Warren went down suddenly, banging his knee on a big tree root. The guard kicked him in the ribs and Warren saw the man was jumpy and bored at the same time. That was dangerous. He carefully got up and moved along the path, limping from the dull pain spreading in his knee. The guard pushed him into his cell and kicked him again. Warren fell and lay there, not moving, waiting, and the guard finally grunted and slammed the door.

Noon came and went and he got no food. He ate the leaves. He did not blame the Chinese for the way they treated him. The great powers all acted the same, independent of what they said their politics were, and it was easier to think of them as big machines that did what they were designed to do rather than as bunches of people.

Night came. Warren had gotten used to not thinking about food when he was on the raft and he was just as glad the guard did not bring food. Eventually the squat chinless soldier would come all the way into the cell and look behind the table which was overturned and would see the dirt mounds. Warren lay on the rocky ground that was the floor and wondered if he would dream of his wife again. It was a good dream because it took away all the pain they both had caused and left only her smells and taste. But when he dozed off he was in the deep place where clanking came from above, a metallic sound that blended with the dull buzzing he had heard all that afternoon from the motorboat in the lagoon, the sounds washing together until he realized they were the same but the loud clanking one was the way the Skimmers heard it. It was hard to think with the ringing hammering sound in his head and he tried to swim up and break water to get away from it. The clanking went on and then was a roar, louder, and he woke up suddenly and felt the sides of the cell tremble with the sound. Two abrupt crashes came down out of the sky and then sudden blue light.

Warren looked out through the mesh on the windows and saw women running. There was no moon but in the starlight he could see they were carrying rifles. A sudden rattling came from the north and west and then answering fire from up on the ridge.

He used the flickering light from the windows to find the map Tseng had given him. He pulled back the sleeping pad to expose the hole he had dug and without hesitation crawled in. He knew the feel of it well and in the complete dark found the stone at the end he used. He had estimated that there was only a foot of dirt left above. Using the pan to scrape away the last few feet of dirt had left him with a feel for how strong the earth was above but when he hit it with the stone it did not give. There was not much room to swing and three more solid hits did not even shake loose clods of it. Warren was sweating in the closeness of the tunnel and the dirt stuck to his face as he chipped away at the hard soil over him. It was hardpacked and filled with rocks that struck him in the face and rolled onto his chest. His arm started to ache and then tire but he did not stop. He switched the stone to his left hand and felt a softness give above and then was hitting nothing. The stone broke the crust and he could see stars.

He studied the area carefully: A soldier ran by carrying a tripod for an automatic rifle. The sharp cracking fire still came from north and west.

There was a spark of light high up and Warren snapped his head away to keep his night vision. Then the glare was gone and a hollow roar rolled over the camp. Mortars, not far away. He struggled up out of the tunnel and ran for the trees nearby. Halfway there his knee folded under him and he cursed it silently as he went down. It was worse than he had thought from the fall, and lying on the hard cell floor had made it go stiff. He got up and limped to the trees, each moment feeling a spot between his shoulder blades where the slug would come if any of the running men in the camp behind him saw the shadow making its painful way. The slug did not come but a flare went up as he reached a clump of bushes. He threw himself into them and rolled over so he could see the clearing. The flare had taken away most of his night vision. He waited for it to come back and smelled the wind. There was something heavy and musky in it. It was the easterly trade, blowing steady, which meant the tide was getting ready to shift and it was past midnight. Coming from the east the wind should not have picked up the smell of the fire fight so the musky smell was something else. Warren knew the taste but could not remember what it was and what it might mean about the tide. He squinted, moving back into the bush, and saw a man in the camp coming straight toward him.

The figure stopped at the door of Warren's cell. It fumbled at the door and a banging of automatic-weapons fire came from the other side of camp. The man jumped back and yelled to someone and then went back to trying to unlock the door. Warren glanced into the distance where sudden flashes lit the camp in pale orange light. The firing got heavier, and when he looked back at the cell there were two men there and the first one was opening the door. Warren crawled out of the dry bushes, moving when a burst of machine-gun fire covered any sound he might make. He got to a thin stand of trees and turned. A flare went up, burning yellow. It was the chinless soldier. He had the door open and Gijan was coming out, waving a hand, pointing north. They shouted at each other for a moment. Warren edged back further into the trees. He was about fifty meters away now and could see each man unshoulder the slim rifles they carried. They held them at the ready. Gijan pointed again and the two men separated, moving apart about thirty meters. They were going to search. They turned and walked into the brush. Gijan came straight at Warren.

It would be easy to give himself up now. Wait for a flare and come forward with his hands held high. He had counted on getting further away than this before anyone came after him. Now in the dark and with the fighting going there was a good chance they were jumpy and would shoot him if they saw some movement. But as he thought this Warren moved back, sinking into the shadows. He had faced worse than this on the raft. He limped away, going by feel in the shadows.

He reached a line of palms and moved along them toward the north. He was still about five hundred meters from the beach but there was a big clearing in the way so he angled in toward the ridge. Muffled thuds from the west told him that the Chinese were using mortars against whoever was coming into the beaches. Five spaced screeches cut through the deep sounds of distant battle.

Warren guessed the Japanese or the Americans had decided to take the island and try to speak to the Skimmers themselves. Maybe they would try their own machines and codes.

They might know about him, though. The Chinese wanted to keep him or else Gijan would not have come with the soldier. Warren stumbled and slammed his knee into a tree. He paused, panting and trying to see if the men were within sight. With a moment to think he saw that Gijan might want to kill him to keep him out of the hands of the others. He could not be sure that giving himself up was safe anymore.

The five shrill notes came again and he recognized them as an emergency signal blown on a whistle. They were from close by, Gijan was calling for help. With the Chinese fighting other troops on the other side of the island, Gijan might not get a quick answer. But help would come and then they would box him in.

Warren turned toward the beach. He moved as fast as he could without making a lot of noise. His knee went out from under him again and as he got up he realized he was not going to give them much trouble. They had him bracketed already; they had good knees, and help was coming. He could not outrun them. The only chance he had was to circle around and ambush one of them, ambush an armed, well-trained man, using his bare hands. Then get away before the other one found out.

He picked up a rock and put it in his pocket. It banged against his leg with each step. A rustling came from behind him and he hurried and stumbled at the edge of a gully.

A shout. He jumped down into the gully. As he landed there was a sharp crack and something zipped by overhead. It chunked into a tree on the other bank. Warren knew there was no point in going back now.

He trotted down the deepening water-carved wash. It was too narrow for two men. He tried to think how Gijan would figure it. The smartest thing was to wait for the other troops and then comb the area.

But Warren might reach the beach by then. Better to send one man down the gully and another through the trees, to cut him off.

Warren went what felt like a hundred meters before he stopped to listen. The crack of a twig snapping came from far back in the blackness. To the left? He could not be sure. The gully was rocky and it slowed him down. There were some good places to hide in the shadows and then try to hit the following man as he came by. Better than in the scrub above, anyway. But by then the other man would have gotten between him and the beach.

A pebble rattled faintly behind him. He stopped. The hard clay of the gully was three meters high here and steep. He found some thick roots sticking out and carefully pulled himself up. He stuck his head above the edge and looked around. Nothing moving. He crawled over the lip and a rock came loose under his foot. He lunged and caught it. A stabbing pain came in his knee and he bit his tongue to keep from making a noise.

The scrub was thicker here. He rolled into a stand of trees, keeping down and out of the starlight. Twigs snagged at his clothes.

There was an even chance the man would come on this side of the gully. If he didn't Warren could slip off to the north. But Gijan had probably guessed where he was headed and he would not have much of a lead when he reached the beach. On the open sand he would be exposed, easy to pick off.

Warren crawled into the dark patches under the trees and waited, rubbing his leg. The wind smelled bad here, damp and heavy. He wondered if the tide had changed.

He leaned his head on his hands to rest and felt a muscle jump in his face. It startled him. He could not feel it unless he put his hand to it. So Tseng had been right and he did have a spasm without knowing it. Warren frowned. He did not know what to think about that. It was a fact he would have to understand. For now, though, he put the thought away from him and watched the darkness.

He pulled the rock out of his pocket and hefted it and a pale form moved in the trees forty meters inland. It was a short soldier, the chinless one. Warren crouched low to follow. The pain that shot through his knee reminded him of how the chinless man had kicked him but the memory did not make him feel anything about what he was going to do. He moved forward.

In the dry brush he kept as quiet as he could. The dull claps and crashes that came over the ridge were muffled now, just when he needed them to be loud. Under the trees it was quieter, and he was surprised to hear the rasping of the soldier breathing. The man moved slowly, rifle at the ready, the weapon looking big in the starlight. The man kept in the starlight and watched the shadows. That was smart.

The breathing got louder. Warren moved, favoring his knee. He would have to jump up fast and take the soldier from behind.

The figure came closer. Suddenly Warren saw that the man wore a helmet. To use the rock now he would have to hit him in the face. That made the odds a lot worse. But he would have to try.

The man stopped, turned, looked around. Warren froze and waited. The head turned away and Warren eased forward, closing, the pain shooting in his knee. The leg would try to give way when he came up for the rush. He would watch for that and force it to hold. The air was still and heavy under the trees and the smell was worse, something from the beach. The soldier's was the only visible movement.

In the quilted pattern of shadows and light it was hard to follow the silhouette. Warren put his hand out and gathered his feet under him and felt something wet and slick ahead and suddenly knew that the slow rasping laboring breath did not come from the chinless soldier but from something between them. He felt the ground and brought his hand up to his face and smelled the strong reek he had tasted on the wind. Ahead in the faint light that fell between two palms he saw the long form struggling, pulling itself forward on blunt legs. It sucked in the air with each step. It was thick and heavy and the skin was a gunmetal gray, pocked with inch-wide round holes. Warren felt a whirring in the air and something brushed against his face, lingered, and was gone. Another whirring followed, so quiet he could barely hear it. The stubby fin-legs of the Swarmer went mechanically forward and back, dragging its bloated body. In the starlight he could see the glistening where fluid seeped from the moist holes.

the young run with sores

Another small whirring sound came and he saw from one of the dark openings a thing as big as a finger spring out, slick with moisture, and spread its wings. It beat against the thick and reeking air and then lifted its heavy body, coming free of its hole, wings fluttering. It lifted into the air and hovered, seeking. It darted away, missing Warren, passing on into the night. He did not move. The Swarmer pulled itself forward. Its dry rattling gasps caught the attention of the soldier and the man turned and took a step. The Swarmer gathered itself and kicked with its hind leg. It reached the man's leg and the massive head turned to take the calf between its jaws. It seized and twisted and Warren heard the sharp intake of breath before the soldier went down. He screamed and the Swarmer turned itself and rolled over the man. The long blunt head came up and nuzzled down into the belly of the man and the sharp shrill scream cut off suddenly. Warren stood, the smell stronger now, and watched the two forms struggle on the open sand. The man pawed for his rifle where it had fallen and the thick leg of the Swarmer pinned his arm. They rolled to the side. The thing wallowed on him, covering him with a slick sheen, cutting off the low moans he made. Warren ran toward them and picked up the rifle. He backed away, thumbing off the safety. The man went limp and the air rushed out of him as the alien settled into place. Its head turned toward Warren and held there for a moment and then it turned back and dipped down to the belly of the man. It began feeding.

The soldier was dead. Gijan had heard the screams and would be here soon. There was no point in shooting the Swarmer and giving Gijan a sound to follow. Warren turned and limped away from the licking and chewing sounds.

He walked silently through brush, hobbling. The rifle had a bayonet on the muzzle. If a Swarmer came at him he would use that instead of firing. He stayed in the open, watching the shadows.

Abruptly from behind him came a loud hammering of automatic fire. Warren dodged to the side and then realized that no bullets were thumping into the trees near him. It was Gijan, killing the Swarmer a hundred meters or more away.

Warren was sure the Chinese did not know the Swarmers were crawling ashore or else they would have come after him in a group. Now Gijan would be shaken and uncertain. But in a few minutes he would recover and know what he had to do. Gijan would run to the beach, moving faster than Warren could, and try to cut him off.

Warren heard a light humming. He looked up between the trees where the sound came and could see nothing against the stars.

the World that was false World made them this way not as they were when we knew them in the World that was ours they cannot sing but know of the places where you sing to each other and some now go there with their sores they may be chewed by you but there are many many

Something smacked into his throat. It was wet and it attached itself with a sudden clenching thrust like a ball of needles. Warren snatched at it. He stopped an inch short of grabbing at the thing when he caught the musty sea stench full in his nostrils. The moist lump dripped something down his throat. He brought the rifle up quickly and pointed the bayonet at his throat and jabbed, aiming by instinct in the dark. He felt the tip go into the thing and turned the blade so it scraped, pulling the wet centimeter-long larva out. It came away before the spines had sunk in. Blood seeped out and trickled down his throat. He sopped it up with his sleeve and held the bayonet up in the starlight. The thing was white as a maggot and twisted feebly on the blade. One wing fluttered. The other was gone. The skin of it peeled back some more and the wing fell off. He stuck the blade into the sand to clean it and stepped on the thing that moved in spasms on the ground. Something still stuck on his neck. He scraped it off. The other wing was on the blade and some thin dark needles. He wiped them on the sand and with a sudden rushing fear slammed his heel down on them again and again.

He was breathing hard by the time he reached the beach. The fear had gone away when he had concentrated on staying away from the shadows, not thinking about what could be in them. The stabbing pain in his knee helped. He listened for the deep rasping and the humming and tasted the wind for their smell.

He hobbled out from the last line of palms and onto the white glow of the beach beneath the stars. He could see maybe fifty meters and there were no dark forms struggling up from the water. To the north he could hear faint shouts. That did not bother him because he did not have far to go. He stumbled toward the shouts, ignoring the quick rippling flashes of yellow light from a mortar barrage and the long *crump* that came after them. There were motorboats moored in the shallows with the big reels in the stern but no one in them. He took an oar out of one.

He came around the last horn of a crescent beach and saw ahead the dark blotch of the raft far up on the sand. He threw his rifle aboard and began dragging the raft toward the water. Big combers boomed on the reef.

He got it into the shallows and rolled aboard without looking back. He pushed off with the oar and kept pushing until he felt the current catch him. Speed, now. Speed.

The tide had just turned. It was slow but it would pick up in a few minutes and take him toward the pass in the reef. When he was sure of that he sat down and felt for the rifle. Sitting, he would be harder to see and he could steady the rifle against his good knee. His throat had nearly stopped bleeding but his shirt was heavy with blood. He wondered if the flying things would smell it and find him. The Skimmers had never said anything about the things like maggots with wings and he was sure now it was because they did not know about it. There was no reason the Swarmers would have evolved a thing like that to help them live on the land. And with the

Skimmers driven from the lagoon by the men there was nothing to keep the Swarmers from bringing the things ashore.

He saw something move on the land and he lay down on the raft and Gijan came out onto the sand, running. Gijan stopped and looked straight out at Warren and then turned and ran north. Warren picked up his rifle. Gijan was carrying his weapon at the ready. Was the man trying to cut him off but keep him alive? Then he should have run south, toward the motorboats. But there might be boats to the north, too. Maybe Gijan had heard the shouts in that direction and was running for help.

Warren thumbed off the safety and put the rifle on automatic fire. He would know what to do if Gijan would tell him by some action what he intended to do. If he could just shout to the man, ask him—But maybe Gijan had not seen him after all. And the man might lie even if he answered.

Suddenly the running figure dropped his rifle and slapped at his neck and then fell heavily on the sand. He twisted and brought both hands to his neck and struggled for a moment. Then he brought something out from his neck and threw it into the water and made a sound of fear. Gijan lurched up and staggered. He still clutched his neck with one hand but turned and looked for his weapon. He seemed dazed. His head came up and his gaze swept past Warren and then came back again. Gijan had seen the raft for sure this time.

Warren wished he could read the man's face. Gijan hesitated only a moment. Then he picked up his weapon and turned to the north. He took some steps and Warren relaxed, and then there was something about the way Gijan moved his arm. Warren aimed quickly, with no pause for conscious thought, and Gijan was bringing the rifle around. It made a bright yellow flash, firing on automatic, as Gijan swept the muzzle, fanning, and Warren fired a burst. It took Gijan high in the shoulder and then in the chest, spinning him.

Warren slowly put down the rifle, panting. He had not thought at all about killing Gijan but had just done it, not stopping for the instant of balancing the equation and seeing if it had to be that way, and that was what had saved him.

He peered shoreward again. Voices, near. There was some sea still running against the ebb but now the tide was taking hold and carrying him out. The pass was a dark patch in the snarling white of the combers. He had to get away fast now because the men to the north would be coming toward the gunfire. Hoisting the sail would just give them a target. He had to wait for the slow steady draw to take him through.

Something thumped against the bottom of the raft. It came again. Warren stood and cradled the rifle. The boards worked against each other as they came into the chop near the pass. A big dark thing broke water and rolled hugely. Eyes looked at him and legs that had grown from fins kicked against the current. The Swarmer turned and wallowed in the wash from the passage and then sank, the great head turning toward shore.

Warren used the oar to turn the raft free of the rocks. The surf broke to each side and the deep bands of current sucked the raft through with a sudden rush. Behind him Warren heard a cry, lonely and harsh and full of surprise. The warring rumbled beyond the ridge and was lost in the crashing of the waves running hard before an east wind and he went out into the dark ocean, the raft rising fast and plunging as it came into the full sea swell.

A sharp crack. A motorboat was coming fast behind. Warren lay flat on the raft and groped for his rifle.

They would get him out here for sure. He aimed at the place where the pilot would be but in the fast chop he knew he would miss. There came a short, stuttering bark of automatic-weapons fire.

The raft slewed to port and the boat turned to follow. Warren crawled to the edge of the raft, ready to slip overboard when they got too close. It would be better than getting cut down, even with the Swarmers in the water.

The boat whined and bounced on the swell, bearing down. He lifted the rifle to take aim and knew the odds were damn long against him. He saw a muzzle flash and the deck spat splinters at him where the shots hit. Warren squeezed carefully and narrowed his eyes to frame the target and saw something leap suddenly across the bow of the boat. It was big and another followed, landing in front of the pilot and wriggling back over the windshield in one motion. It crashed into the men there. Shouts. A blue-white shape flicked a man overboard and knocked another sprawling. The boat veered to starboard. From this angle Warren could see the pilot holding to the wheel and crouched to avoid the flicking tail of the Skimmer.

A hammering of the automatic weapon. The Skimmer jumped

and slashed at the man with its tail. Warren leaped up and rocked against the swell to improve his aim. He got off two quick shots at the man. The figure staggered and the Skimmer struck him solidly and he pitched over the side. The pilot glanced back and saw he was alone. The Skimmer stopped thrashing and went still. Warren did not give the man time to think. He fired at the dark splotch at the wheel until it was gone.

Distant shouts came from shore but no sounds of another boat. The boat drifted away. Warren thought of the Skimmer who lay dead in it. He tried to reach the boat, but the currents separated them further. In moments it was gone in the darkness and the island itself faded into a mere looming shadow on the sea.

9

At noon the next day three jets split the sky with their roaring and passed over the south. All morning the sky had been streaked with the trails of craft that flew high and made no sound. He had rounded the island in the night and run up his worn sail and then run before the wind to get distance. He had the map from Tseng and the fishing lines were still on the raft with their hooks so he could try for something. The rifle had no rounds left in its clip but with the bayonet it made a good gaff. He had a strike in the morning from a small tuna. It had got away when he hauled it in. But there would be more now that the Swarmers were going to land and would not be taking the fish.

The Skimmers came in the afternoon. They leaped in crystal showers that glinted in the raw sunlight.

In the night there was a sudden distant glare of orange light reflected off clouds near the horizon. It became a glow and the color seeped out of it, and then it was gone. Afterward a rolling hammer blow of sound came. Later there were more huge bursts of light, faint and far away.

High up, silvery specks coasted smoothly across the dark. One by one they vanished in bright firefly glows—yellow, blue, orange. Satellite warfare. Soon they were gone.

At dawn he woke and searched the sky and found the thin silver thread that reached up into the dark bowl overhead.

But now it curled about itself. Warren looked down the sky

toward the dawn and found another pale streak far below, where nothing should be. The Skyhook was broken. Part of it was turning upward while the other fell. Somebody had blown it in two.

For long moments he watched the faint band fall. Finally he lost it in the glare as the sun rose. There had been men and women working on the lower tip of the Skyhook, and he tried to imagine what it was to fall hopeless that far and that long and then to burn quick and high in the air like a shooting star.

His knee had swollen up now and he could not stand so he laid in the shade of the sail. The wound in his neck had a crusted blue scab and did not hurt so much. He thought it would be all right. He would ask the Skimmers about the larvae that flew but he was sure that they were not natural to the Swarmers. Something had changed the Swarmers so that the Skimmers did not know them anymore.

He remembered the sheets he had written on, the tangled sentences and thoughts, things he had not been able to understand. He had known that the Skimmers hated the machines that intruded into the water. They had learned that through the long years of voyaging, when they had been in ships, carried like cargo, moved and fed and poked at by things that hummed and jerked and yet had no true life, things they had never seen before: machines. Computers and robots that could span the stars. A civilization of nothing but devices and remorseless logic. Things that had evolved, because the same laws of selection operated on them as did on living matter. Things that came out of those laws and would kill to survive, to protect themselves from any enemy. And life, arising from nothing at all, flowering and blooming wherever chemicals met and sunlight boomed through a blanket of gas—life was constant competition. The machines must have come from long-dead civilizations whose computer nets survived, but in time the machines would come to fear the rivalry of life that burst forth from every possible corner of the galaxy. And fear would, by evolution's logic, kindle something that could stir the machines to action when necessary, something like hatred.

In the long years of their voyage, that would become clear to the ripe cargo the machines carried. So the Swarmers and Skimmers had come to hate them in return. And when they saw the simple, noisy machines of men, they hated those, too.

He fished through the day without success.

That night there were more orange flashes to the west.

Then, in the hours before dawn, things moved in the sky. Shapes glided through the black, catching the sunlight as they moved out of the earth's shadow. They were in close orbit, moving fast, the orbits repeating in less than an hour. They were huge and irregular, their surfaces grainy and blotched. For Warren to be able to see the features on them, they had to be far bigger than the ships that had brought the Swarmers and Skimmers.

No defenses rose to meet these shapes. There were no military satellites left, no high-energy lasers, no particle-beam weapons. The ships absorbed the sunlight and gave back a strange glowing gray. As Warren watched they began to split. Chunks broke away and fell, separating again and again as they streaked across the sky.

With dawn came three Skimmers.

They stayed deep. Warren leaned over and put his head in the water. He let his eyes adjust until he could see the quick, darting movements they made. There was something in the elaborate twistings that recalled some passages from the lagoon. He watched them and when he thought he understood, he lay back on the raft and thought.

The gray ships were bigger than the earlier ones, but they had the same aim. To set one kind of life against another. To cause a war that looked to men like a simple fight with aliens from the sea.

So the men had done the same things they always did when they were in groups. The Swarmers were a threat, but there were always humans who would use the situation against each other, to get the advantage, and somehow the thing had gotten away from them, and in these last nights the terrible weapons had at last been used. And they had killed the Skyhook, too.

Nuclear war, once ignited, was a runaway instability. Life at this stage of development was vulnerable to it. The machines probably knew that. They understood that the humans, carried away by passions, would miss the fact that the Swarmers and Skimmers were only a piece of a bigger puzzle. That somewhere something wanted life to cancel other life and for each form to pull the other down. An efficient way to eliminate competitors.

But this morning, watching the intricate turns of the Skimmers, seeing it in a blurred way through the water that would always separate him from them, he had understood new things. The gray ships were hurling themselves into the sea, far from the battles raging on the continents.

The Skimmers knew these machines, had lived for generations in them. **The gray things float deep beneath the waves,** the Skimmers had said. **They mine the sea; their factories clank; we can hear them for great distances. They make copies of themselves. The Swarmers are gone to the land and the gray things think they are safe.**

He caught some small fish in the afternoon and used them to bait the lines. He got two hits immediately and brought them in. The meat was tough and strong-flavored. The sea was gathering itself again after the long time of the Swarmers, blossoming, growing, the schools of fish returning. He was sure he could live here now.

They think they are safe. They think there is only us, trapped in this new *W*orld. We cannot make tools. But we know the waters and the machines do not, cannot know them, cannot taste the essence of them.

He watched the long rolling waves, squinting. The Skimmers had spoken of other men and women who had learned to live on the sea. Remnants. They would have little to work with, just the wreckage of the mainlands where the death was spreading, and of old ships, but with the Skimmers they could fashion things.

To reach the land the gray machines would have to come up finally. They would be prepared to take the solid ground. They would not be ready for life that had lasted and fought battles and lost them and endured and fought again because it did not know it was defeated, and went on silently, still peering forward and by instinct seeking other life, and still waiting when the gray things began to move again, still powerful and still asking as life always does, and still dangerous and still coming.

He finished the fish he had caught and lay there letting the sun warm him. As dusk came he could see more of the gray shapes in orbit but they did not fill him with the fear he had known before. He was tired. He fell asleep early. He lay face down on the worn deck, rolling gently with the steady swell. He did not wake at first when a Skimmer leaped near the raft. He was dreaming of his wife.

SAILING TO BYZANTIUM

Robert Silverberg

At dawn he arose and stepped out onto the patio for his first look at Alexandria, the one city he had not yet seen. That year the five cities were Chang-an, Asgard, New Chicago, Timbuctoo, Alexandria: the usual mix of eras, cultures, realities. He and Gioia, making the long flight from Asgard in the distant north the night before, had arrived late, well after sundown, and gone straight to bed. Now, by the gentle apricot-hued morning light, the fierce spires and battlements of Asgard seemed merely something he had dreamed.

The rumor was that Asgard's moment was finished, anyway. In a little while, he had heard, they were going to tear it down and replace it, elsewhere, with Mohenjo-daro. Though there were never more than five cities, they changed constantly. He could remember a time when they had had Rome of the Caesars instead of Chang-an, and Rio de Janeiro rather than Alexandria. These people saw no point in keeping anything very long.

It was not easy for him to adjust to the sultry intensity of Alexandria after the frozen splendors of Asgard. The wind, coming off the water, was brisk and torrid both at once. Soft turquoise wavelets lapped at the jetties. Strong presences assailed his senses: the hot heavy sky, the stinging scent of the red lowland sand borne on the breeze, the sullen swampy aroma of the nearby sea. Everything trembled and glimmered in the early light. Their hotel was beautifully situated, high on the northern slope of the huge artificial mound known as the Paneium that was sacred to the goat-footed god. From here they had a total view of the city: the wide noble boulevards, the soaring obelisks and monuments, the palace of Hadrian just below the hill, the stately and awesome Library, the temple of Poseidon, the teeming marketplace, the royal lodge that Mark Antony had built after his defeat at Actium. And of course the Lighthouse, the wondrous many-windowed Lighthouse, the seventh wonder of the world, that immense pile of marble and limestone and reddish-purple Aswan granite rising in majesty at the end of its mile-long causeway. Black smoke from the beacon-fire at its summit curled lazily into the sky. The city was awakening. Some temporaries in short white kilts appeared and began to trim the dense dark hedges that bordered the great public buildings. A few citizens wearing loose robes of vaguely Grecian style were strolling in the streets.

There were ghosts and chimeras and phantasies everywhere about. Two slim elegant centaurs, a male and a female, grazed on a hillside. A burly thick-thighed swordsman appeared on the porch of the temple of Poseidon holding a Gorgon's severed head; he waved it in a wide arc, grinning broadly. In the street below the hotel gate three small pink sphinxes, no bigger than housecats, stretched and yawned and began to prowl the curbside. A larger one, lion-sized, watched warily from an alleyway: their mother, surely. Even at this distance he could hear her loud purring.

Shading his eyes, he peered far out past the Lighthouse and across the water. He hoped to see the dim shores of Crete or Cyprus to the north, or perhaps the great dark curve of Anatolia. *Carry me toward that great Byzantium*, he thought. *Where all is ancient, singing at the oars*. But he beheld only the endless empty sea, sun-bright and blinding though the morning was only just beginning. Nothing was ever where he expected it to be. The continents did not seem to be in their proper places any longer. Gioia, taking him aloft long ago in her little flitterflitter, had shown him that. The tip of South America was canted far out into the Pacific; Africa was weirdly foreshortened; a broad tongue of ocean separated Europe and Asia. Austrialia did not appear to exist at all. Perhaps they had dug it up and used it for other things. There was no trace of the world he once had known. This was the fiftieth century. "The fiftieth century after *what*?" he had asked several times, but no one seemed to know, or else they did not care to say.

"Is Alexandria very beautiful?" Gioia called from within.

"Come out and see."

Naked and sleepy-looking, she padded out onto the white-tiled patio and nestled up beside him. She fit neatly under his arm. "Oh, yes, yes!" she said softly. "So very beautiful, isn't it? Look, there, the palaces, the Library, the Lighthouse! Where will we go first? The Lighthouse, I think. Yes? And then the marketplace—I want to see the Egyptian magicians—and the stadium, the races—will they be having races today, do you think? Oh, Charles, I want to see everything!"

"Everything? All on the first day?"

"All on the first day, yes," she said. "Everything."

"But we have plenty of time, Gioia."

"Do we?"

He smiled and drew her tight against his side.

"Time enough," he said gently.

He loved her for her impatience, for her bright bubbling eagerness. Gioia was not much like the rest in that regard, though she seemed identical in all other ways. She was short, supple, slender, dark-eyed, olive-skinned, narrow-hipped with wide shoulders and flat muscles. They were all like that, each one indistinguishable from the rest, like a horde of millions of brothers and sisters—a world of small, lithe, child-like Mediterraneans, built for juggling, for bull-dancing, for sweet white wine at midday and rough red wine at night. They had the same slim bodies, the same broad mouths, the same great glossy eyes. He had never seen anyone who appeared to be younger than twelve or older than twenty. Gioia was somehow a little different, although he did not quite know how; but he knew that it was for that imperceptible but significant difference that he loved her. And probably that was why she loved him also.

He let his gaze drift from west to east, from the Gate of the Moon down broad Canopus Street and out to the harbor, and off to the tomb of Cleopatra at the tip of long slender Cape Lochias. Everything was here and all of it perfect, the obelisks, the statues and marble colonnades, the courtyards and shrines and groves, great Alexander himself in his coffin of crystal and gold: a splendid gleaming pagan city. But there were oddities—an unmistakable mosque near the public gardens, and what seemed to be a Christian church not far from the Library. And those ships in the harbor, with all those red sails and bristling masts—surely they were medieval, and late medieval at that. He had seen such anachronisms in other places before. Doubtless these people found them amusing. Life was a game for them. They played at it unceasingly. Rome, Alexandria, Timbuctoo—why not? Create an Asgard of translucent bridges and shimmering ice-girt palaces, then grow weary of it and take it away? Replace it with Mohenjo-daro? Why not? It seemed to him a great pity to destroy those lofty Nordic feasting-halls for the sake of building a squat, brutal, sun-baked city of brown brick; but these people did not look at things the way he did. Their cities were only temporary. Someone in Asgard had said that Timbuctoo would be the next to go, with Byzantium rising in its place. Well, why not? Why not? They could have anything they liked. This was the fiftieth century, after all. The only rule was that there could be no more than five cities at once. "Limits," Gioia had informed him solemnly when they first began to travel together, "are very important." But she did not know why, or did not care to say.

He stared once more toward the sea.

He imagined a newborn city congealing suddenly out of mists, far across the water: shining towers, great domed palaces, golden mosaics. That would be no great effort for them. They could just summon it forth whole out of time, the Emperor on his throne and the Emperor's drunken soldiery roistering in the streets, the brazen clangor of the cathedral gong rolling through the Grand Bazaar, dolphins leaping beyond the shoreside pavilions. Why not? They had Timbuctoo. They had Alexandria. Do you crave Constantinople? Then behold Constantinople! Or Avalon, or Lyonesse, or Atlantis. They could have anything they liked. It is pure Schopenhauer here: the world as will and imagination. Yes! These slender dark-eyed people journeying tirelessly from miracle to miracle. Why not Byzantium next? Yes! Why not? *That is no country for old men*, he thought. *The young in one another's arms, the birds in the trees—yes*! Yes! Anything they liked. They even had him. Suddenly he felt frightened. Questions he had not asked for a long time burst through into his consciousness. *Who am I? Why am I here? Who is this woman beside me*?

"You're so quiet all of a sudden, Charles," said Gioia, who could not abide silence for very long. "Will you talk to me? I want you to talk to me. Tell me what you're looking for out there."

He shrugged. "Nothing."

"Nothing?"

"Nothing in particular."

"I could see you seeing something."

"Byzantium," he said. "I was imagining that I could look straight across the water to Byzantium. I was trying to get a glimpse of the walls of Constantinople."

"Oh, but you wouldn't be able to see as far as that from here. Not really."

"I know."

"And anyway Byzantium doesn't exist."

"Not yet. But it will. Its time comes later on."

"Does it?" she said. "Do you know that for a fact?"

"On good authority. I heard it in Asgard," he told her. "But even if I hadn't, Byzantium would be inevitable, don't you think? Its time would have to come. How could we not do Byzantium, Gioia? We certainly will do Byzantium, sooner or later. I know we will. It's only a matter of time. And we have all the time in the world."

A shadow crossed her face. "Do we? Do we?"

He knew very little about himself, but he knew that he was not one of them. That he knew. He knew that his name was Charles Phillips and that before he had come to live among these people he had lived in the year 1984, when there had been such things as computers and television sets and baseball and jet planes, and the world was full of cities, not merely five but thousands of them, New York and London and Johannesburg and Paris and Liverpool and Bangkok and San Francisco and Buenos Aires and a multitude of others, all at the same time. There had been four and a half billion people in the world then; now he doubted that there were as many as four and a half million. Nearly everything had changed beyond comprehension. The moon still seemed the same, and the sun; but at night he searched in vain for familiar constellations. He had no idea how they had brought him from then to now, or why. It did no good to ask. No one had any answers for him; no one so much as appeared to understand what it was that he was trying to learn. After a time he had stopped asking; after a time he had almost entirely ceased wanting to know.

He and Gioia were climbing the Lighthouse. She scampered ahead, in a hurry as always, and he came along behind her in his more stolid fashion. Scores of other tourists, mostly in groups of two or three, were making their way up the wide flagstone ramps, laughing, calling to one another. Some of them, seeing him, stopped a moment, stared, pointed. He was used to that. He was so much taller than any of them; he was plainly not one of them. When they pointed at him he smiled. Sometimes he nodded a little acknowledgment.

He could not find much of interest in the lowest level, a massive square structure two hundred feet high built of huge marble blocks: within its cool musty arcades were hundreds of small dark rooms, the offices of the Lighthouse's keepers and mechanics, the barracks of the garrison, the stables for the three hundred donkeys that carried the fuel to the lantern far above. None of that appeared inviting to him. He forged onward without halting until he emerged on the balcony that led to the next level. Here the Lighthouse grew narrower and became octagonal: its face granite now and handsomely fluted, rose in a stunning sweep above him.

Gioia was waiting for him there. "This is for you," she said, holding out a nugget of meat on a wooden skewer. "Roast lamb. Absolutely delicious. I had one while I was waiting for you." She gave him a cup of some cool green sherbet also, and darted off to buy a pomegranate. Dozens of temporaries were roaming the balcony, selling refreshments of all kinds.

He nibbled at the meat. It was charred outside, nicely pink and moist within. While he ate, one of the temporaries came up to him and peered blandly into his face. It was a stocky swarthy male wearing nothing but a strip of red and yellow cloth about its waist. "I sell meat," it said. "Very fine roast lamb, only five drachmas."

Phillips indicated the piece he was eating. "I already have some," he said.

"It is excellent meat, very tender. It has been soaked for three days in the juices of—"

"Please," Phillips said. "I don't want to buy any meat. Do you mind moving along?"

The temporaries had confused and baffled him at first, and there was still much about them that was unclear to him. They were not machines—they looked like creatures of flesh and blood—but they did not seem to be human beings, either, and no one treated them as if they were. He supposed they were artifical constructs, products of a technology so consummate that it was invisible. Some appeared to be more intelligent than others, but all of them behaved as if they had no more autonomy than characters in a play, which was essentially what they were. There were untold numbers of them in each of the five cities, playing all manner of roles: shepherds and swineherds, street-sweepers, merchants, boatmen, vendors of grilled meats and cool drinks, hagglers in the marketplace, schoolchildren, charioteers, policemen, grooms, gladiators, monks, artisans, whores and cutpurses, sailors—whatever was needed to sustain the illusion of a thriving, populous urban center. The dark-eyed people, Gioia's people, never performed work. There were not enough of them to keep a city's functions going, and in any case they were strictly tourists, wandering with the wind, moving from city to city as the whim took them, Chang-an to New Chicago, New Chicago to Timbuctoo, Timbuctoo to Asgard, Asgard to Alexandria, onward, ever onward.

The temporary would not leave him alone. Phillips walked away and it followed him, cornering him against the balcony wall. When Gioia returned a few minutes later, lips prettily stained with pomegranate juice, the temporary was still hovering about him, trying with lunatic persistence to sell him a skewer of lamb. It stood much too close to him, almost nose to nose, great sad cowlike eyes peering intently into his as it extolled with mournful mooing urgency the quality of its wares. It seemed to him that he had had trouble like this with temporaries on one or two earlier occasions. Gioia touched the creature's elbow lightly and said, in a short sharp tone Phillips had never heard her use before, "He isn't interested. Get away from him." It went at once. To Phillips she said, "You have to be firm with them."

"I was trying. It wouldn't listen to me."

"You ordered it to go away, and it refused?"

"I asked it to go away. Politely. Too politely, maybe."

"Even so," she said. "It should have obeyed a human, regardless."

"Maybe it didn't think I was human," Phillips suggested. "Because of the way I look. My height, the color of my eyes. It might have thought I was some kind of temporary myself."

"No," Gioia said, frowning. "A temporary won't solicit another temporary. But it won't ever disobey a citizen, either. There's a very clear boundary. There isn't ever any confusion. I can't understand why it went on bothering you." He was surprised at how troubled she seemed: far more so, he thought, than the incident warranted. A stupid device, perhaps miscalibrated in some way, overenthusiastically pushing its wares—what of it? What of it? Gioia, after a moment, appeared to come to the same conclusion. Shrugging, she said, "It's defective, I suppose. Probably such things are more common than we suspect, don't you think?" There was something forced about her tone that bothered him. She smiled and handed him her pomegranate. "Here. Have a bite, Charles. It's wonderfully sweet. They used to be extinct, you know. Shall we go on upward?"

The octagonal midsection of the Lighthouse must have been several hundred feet in height, a grim claustrophobic tube almost entirely filled by the two broad spiraling ramps that wound around the huge building's central well. The ascent was slow: a donkey team was a little way ahead of them on the ramp, plodding along laden with bundles of kindling for the lantern. But at last, just as Phillips was growing winded and dizzy, he and Gioia came out onto the second balcony, the one marking the transition between the octagonal section and the Lighthouse's uppermost storey, which was cylindrical and very slender.

She leaned far out over the balustrade. "Oh, Charles, look at the view! Look at it!"

It was amazing. From one side they could see the entire city, and swampy Lake Mareotis and the dusty Egyptian plain beyond it, and from the other they peered far out into the gray and choppy Mediterranean. He gestured toward the innumerable reefs and shallows that infested the waters leading to the harbor entrance. "No wonder they needed a lighthouse here," he said. "Without some kind of gigantic landmark they'd never have found their way in from the open sea."

A blast of sound, a ferocious snort, erupted just above him. He looked up, startled. Immense statues of trumpet-wielding Tritons jutted from the comers of the Lighthouse at this level; that great blurting sound had come from the nearest of them. A signal, he thought. A warning to the ships negotiating that troubled passage. The sound was produced by some kind of steam-powered mechanism, he realized, operated by a team of sweating temporaries clustered about bonfires at the base of each Triton.

Once again he found himself swept away by admiration for the clever way these people carried out their reproductions of antiquity. Or *were* they reproductions, he wondered? He still did not understand how they brought their cities into being. For all he knew, this place was the authentic Alexandria itself, pulled forward out of its proper time just as he himself had been. Perhaps this was the true and original Lighthouse, and not a copy. He had no idea which was the case, nor which would be the greater miracle.

"How do we get to the top?" Gioia asked.

"Over there, I think. That doorway."

The spiraling donkey-ramps ended here. The loads of lantern fuel went higher via a dumb-waiter in the central shaft. Visitors continued by way of a cramped staircase, so narrow at its upper end that it was impossible to turn around while climbing. Gioia, tireless, sprinted ahead. He clung to the rail and labored up and up, keeping count of the tiny window-slits to ease the boredom of the ascent. The count was nearing a hundred when finally he stumbled into the vestibule of the beacon chamber. A dozen or so visitors were crowded into it. Gioia was at the far side, by the wall that was open to the sea.

It seemed to him he could feel the building swaying in the winds, up here. How high were they? Five hundred feet, six hundred, seven? The beacon chamber was tall and narrow, divided by a catwalk into upper and lower sections. Down below, relays of temporaries carried wood from the dumb-waiter and tossed it on the blazing fire. He felt its intense heat from where he stood, at the rim of the platform on which the giant mirror of polished metal was hung. Tongues of flame leaped upward and danced before the mirror, which hurled its dazzling beam far out to sea. Smoke rose through a vent. At the very top was a colossal statue of Poseidon, austere, ferocious, looming above the lantern.

Gioia sidled along the catwalk until she was at his side. "The guide was talking before you came," she said, pointing. "Do you see that place over there, under the mirror? Someone standing there and looking into the mirror gets a view of ships at sea that can't be seen from here by the naked eye. The mirror magnifies things."

"Do you believe that?"

She nodded toward the guide. "It said so. And it also told us that if you look in a certain way, you can see right across the water into the city of Constantinople."

She is like a child, he thought. They all are. He said, "You told me yourself this morning that it isn't possible to see that far. Besides, Constantinople doesn't exist right now."

"It will," she replied. "*You* said that to me, this very morning. And when it does, it'll be reflected in the Lighthouse mirror. That's the truth. I'm absolutely certain of it." She swung about abruptly toward the entrance of the beacon chamber. "Oh, look Charles! Here come Nissandra and Aramayne! And there's Hawk! There's Stengard!" Gioia laughed and waved and called out names. "Oh, everyone's here! *Everyone!*"

They came jostling into the room, so many newcomers that some of those who had been there were forced to scramble down the steps on the far side. Gioia moved among them, hugging, kissing. Phillips could scarcely tell one from another—it was hard for him even to tell which were the men and which were the women, dressed as they all were in the same sort of loose robes—but he recognized some of the names. These were her special friends, her set, with whom she had journeyed from city to city on an endless round of gaiety in the old days before he had come into her life. He had met a few of them before, in Asgard, in Rio, in Rome. The beacon-chamber guide, a squat wide-shouldered old temporary wearing a laurel wreath on its bald head, reappeared and began its potted speech, but no one listened to it; they were all too busy greeting one another, embracing, giggling. Some of them edged their way over to Phillips and reached up, standing on tiptoes, to touch their fingertips to his cheek in that odd hello of theirs. "Charles," they said gravely, making two syllables out of the name, as these people often did. "So good to see you again. Such a pleasure. You and Gioia—such a handsome couple. So well suited to each other."

Was that so? He supposed it was.

The chamber hummed with chatter. The guide could not be heard at all. Stengard and Nissandra had visited New Chicago for the water-dancing—Aramayne bore tales of a feast in Chang-an that had gone on for *days*—Hawk and Hekna had been to Timbuctoo to see the arrival of the salt caravan, and were going back there soon—a final party soon to celebrate the end of Asgard that absolutely should not be missed—the plans for the new city, Mohenjo-daro—we have reservations for the opening, we wouldn't pass it up for anything—and, yes, they were definitely going to do Constantinople after that, the planners were already deep into their Byzantium research—so good to see you, you look so beautiful all the time—have you been to the Library yet? The zoo? To the temple of Serapis?—

To Phillips they said, "What do you think of our Alexandria, Charles? Of course you must have known it well in your day. Does it look the way you remember it?" They were always asking things like that. They did not seem to comprehend that the Alexandria of the Lighthouse and the Library was long lost and legendary by his time. To them, he suspected, all the places they had brought back into existence were more or less contemporary. Rome of the Caesars, Alexandria of the Ptolemies, Venice of the Doges, Chang-an of the T'angs, Asgard of the Aesir, none any less real than the next nor any less unreal, each one simply a facet of the distant past, the fantastic immemorial past, a plum plucked from that dark backward and abysm of time. They had no contexts for separating one era from another. To them all the past was one borderless timeless realm. Why then should he not have seen the Lighthouse before, he who had leaped into this era from the New York of 1984? He had never been able to explain it to them. Julius Caesar and Hannibal, Helen of Troy and Charlemagne, Rome of the gladiators and New York of the Yankees and Mets, Gilgamesh and Tristan and Othello and Robin Hood and George Washington and Queen Victoria—to them, all equally real and unreal, none of them any more than bright figures moving about on a painted canvas. The past, the past, the elusive and fluid past—to them it was a single place of infinite accessibility and infinite connectivity. Of course, they would think he had seen the Lighthouse before. He knew better than to try again to explain things. "No," he said simply. "This is my first time in Alexandria."

They stayed there all winter long, and possibly some of the spring. Alexandria was not a place where one was sharply aware of the change of seasons, nor did the passage of time itself make itself very evident when one was living one's entire life as a tourist.

During the day there was always something new to see. The zoological garden, for instance: a wondrous park, miraculously green and lush in this hot dry climate, where astounding animals roamed in enclosures so generous that they did not seem like enclosures at all. Here were camels, rhinoceroses, gazelles, ostriches, lions, wild asses; and here too, casually adjacent to those familiar African beasts, were hippogriffs, unicorns, basilisks, and fire-snorting dragons with rainbow scales. Had the original zoo of Alexandria had dragons and unicorns? Phillips doubted it. But this one did; evidently it was no harder for the backstage craftsmen to manufacture mythic beasts than it was for them to turn out camels and gazelles. To Gioia and her friends all of them were equally mythical, anyway. They were just as awed by the rhinoceros as by the hippogriff. One was no more strange—nor any less—than the other. So far as Phillips had been able to discover, none of the mammals or birds of his era had survived into this one except for a few cats and dogs, though many had been reconstructed.

And then the Library! All those lost treasures, reclaimed from the jaws of time! Stupendous columned marble walls, airy high-vaulted reading-rooms, dark coiling stacks stretching away into infinity. The ivory handles of seven hundred thousand papyrus scrolls bristling on the shelves. Scholars and librarians gliding quietly about, smiling faint scholarly smiles but plainly preoccupied with serious matters of the mind. They were all temporaries, Phillips realized. Mere props, part of the illusion. But were the scrolls illusions too? "Here we have the complete dramas of Sophocles," said the guide with a blithe wave of its hand, indicating shelf upon shelf of texts. Only seven of his hundred twenty-three plays had survived the successive burnings of the library in ancient times by Romans, Christians, Arabs: were the lost ones here, the *Triptolemus*, the *Nausicaa*, the *Jason*, and all the rest? And would he find here too, miraculously restored to being, the other vanished treasures of ancient literature—the memoirs of Odysseus, Cato's history of Rome, Thucydides' life of Pericles, the missing volumes of Livy? But when he asked if he might explore the stacks, the guide smiled apologetically and said that all the librarians were busy just now. Another time, perhaps? Perhaps, said the guide. It made no difference, Phillips decided. Even if these people somehow had brought back those lost masterpieces of antiquity, how would he read them? He knew no Greek.

The life of the city buzzed and throbbed about him. It was a dazzlingly beautiful place: the vast bay thick with sails, the great avenues running rigidly east-west, north-south, the sunlight rebounding almost audibly from the bright walls of the palaces of kings and gods. They have done this very well, Phillips thought: very well indeed. In the marketplace, hard-eyed traders squabbled in half a dozen mysterious languages over the price of ebony, Arabian incense, jade, panther-skins. Gioia bought a dram of pale musky Egyptian perfume in a delicate tapering glass flask. Magicians and jugglers and scribes called out stridently to passersby, begging for a few moments of attention and a handful of coins for their labor. Strapping slaves, black and tawny and some that might have been Chinese, were put up for auction, made to flex their muscles, to bare their teeth, to bare their breasts and thighs to prospective buyers. In the gymnasium naked athletes hurled javelins and discuses, and wrestled with terrifying zeal. Gioia's friend Stengard came rushing up with a gift for her, a golden necklace that would not have embarrassed Cleopatra. An hour later she had lost it, or perhaps had given it away while Phillips was looking elsewhere. She bought another, even finer, the next day. Anyone could have all the money he wanted, simply by asking: it was as easy to come by as air, for these people.

Being here was much like going to the movies, Phillips told himself. A different show every day: not much plot, but the special effects were magnificent and the detail-work could hardly have been surpassed. A megamovie, a vast entertainment that went on all the time and was being played out by the whole population of Earth. And it was all so effortless, so spontaneous: just as when he had gone to a movie he had never troubled to think about the myriad technicians behind the scenes, the cameramen and the costume designers and the set-builders and the electricians and the model-makers and the boom operators, so too here he chose not to question the means by which Alexandria had been set before him. It felt real. It *was* real. When he drank the strong red wine it gave him a pleasant buzz. If he leaped from the beacon chamber of the Lighthouse he suspected he would die, though perhaps he would not stay dead for long: doubtless they had some way of restoring him as often as was necessary. Death did not seem to be a factor in these people's lives.

By day they saw sights. By night he and Gioia went to parties, in their hotel, in seaside villas, in the palaces of the high nobility. The usual people were there all the time, Hawk and Hekna, Aramayne, Stengard and Shelimir, Nissandra, Asoka, Afonso, Protay. At the parties there were five or ten temporaries for every citizen, some as mere servants, others as entertainers or even surrogate guests, mingling freely and a little daringly. But everyone knew, all the time, who was a citizen and who just a temporary. Phillips began to think his own status lay somewhere between. Certainly they treated him with a courtesy that no one ever would give a temporary, and yet there was a condescension to their manner that told him not simply that he was not one of them but that he was someone or something of an altogether different order of existence. That he was Gioia's lover gave him some standing in their eyes, but not a great deal: obviously he was always going to be an outsider, a primitive, ancient and quaint. For that matter he noticed that Gioia herself, though unquestionably a member of the set, seemed to be regarded as something of an outsider, like a tradesman's great-granddaughter in a gathering of Plantagenets. She did not always find out about the best parties in time to attend; her friends did not always reciprocate her effusive greetings with the same degree of warmth; sometimes he noticed her straining to hear some bit of gossip that was not quite being shared with her. Was it because she had taken him as her lover? Or was it the other way around: that she had chosen to be his lover precisely because she was *not* a full member of their caste?

Being a primitive gave him, at least, something to talk about at their parties. "Tell us about war," they said. "Tell us about elections. About money. About disease." They wanted to know everything, though they did not seem to pay close attention: their eyes were quick to glaze. Still, they asked. He described traffic jams to them, and politics, and deodorants, and vitamin pills. He told them about cigarettes, newspapers, subways, telephone directories, credit cards, and basketball.

"Which was your city?" they asked. New York, he told them. "And when was it? The seventh century, did you say?" The twentieth, he told them. They exchanged glances and nodded. "We will have to do it," they said. "The World Trade Center, the Empire State Building, the Citicorp Center, the Cathedral of St. John the Divine: how fascinating! Yankee Stadium. The Verrazzano Bridge. We will do it all. But first must come Mohenjo-daro. And then, I think, Constantinople. Did your city have many people?" Seven million, he said. Just in the five boroughs alone. They nodded, smiling amiably, unfazed by the number.

Seven million, seventy million—it was all the same to them, he sensed. They would just bring forth the temporaries in whatever quantity was required. He wondered how well they would carry the job off. He was no real judge of Alexandrias and Asgards, after all. Here they could have unicorns and hippogriffs in the zoo, and live sphinxes prowling in the gutters, and it did not trouble him. Their fanciful Alexandria was as good as history's, or better. But how sad, how disillusioning it would be, if the New York that they conjured up had Greenwich Village uptown and Times Square in the Bronx, and the New Yorkers, gentle and polite, spoke with the honeyed accents of Savannah or New Orleans. Well, that was nothing he needed to brood about just now. Very likely they were only being courteous when they spoke of doing his New York. They had all the vastness of the past to choose from: Nineveh, Memphis of the Pharaohs, the London of Victoria or Shakespeare or Richard the Third, Florence of the Medici, the Paris of Abelard and Heloise or the Paris of Louis XIV, Moctezuma's Tenochtitlan and Atahuallpa's Cuzco; Damascus, St. Petersburg, Babylon, Troy. And then there were all the cities like New Chicago, out of time that was time yet unborn to him but ancient history to them. In such richness, such an infinity of choices, even mighty New York might have to wait a long while for its turn. Would he still be among them by the time they got around to it? By then, perhaps, they might have become bored with him and returned him to his own proper era. Or possibly he simply have grown old and died. Even here, he supposed, he would eventually die, though no one else ever seemed to. He did not know. He realized that in fact he did not know anything.

The north wind blew all day long. Vast flocks of ibises appeared over the city, fleeing the heat of the interior, and screeched across the sky with their black necks and scrawny legs extended. The sacred birds, descending by the thousands, scuttered about in every crossroad, pouncing on spiders and beetles, on mice, on the debris of the meat-shops and the bakeries. They were beautiful but annoyingly ubiquitous, and they splashed their dung over the marble building; each morning squadrons of temporaries carefully washed it off. Gioia said little to him now. She seemed cool, withdrawn, depressed; and there was something almost intangible about her, as though she were gradually becoming transparent. He felt it would be an intrusion upon her privacy to ask her what was wrong. Perhaps it was only restlessness. She became religious, and presented costly offerings at the temples of Serapis, Isis, Poseidon, Pan. She went to the necropolis west of the city to lay wreaths on the tombs in the catacombs. In a single day she climbed the Lighthouse three times without any sign of fatigue. One afternoon he returned from a visit to the Library and found her naked on the patio; she had anointed herself all over with some aromatic green salve. Abruptly she said, "I think it's time to leave Alexandria, don't you?"

She wanted to go to Mohenjo-daro, but Mohenjo-daro was not yet ready for visitors. Instead they flew eastward to Chang-an, which they had not seen in years. It was Phillips' suggestion: he hoped that the cosmopolitan gaudiness of the old T'ang capital would lift her mood.

They were to be guests of the Emperor this time: an unusual privilege, which ordinarily had to be applied for far in advance, but Phillips had told some of Gioia's highly placed friends that she was unhappy, and they had quickly arranged everything. Three endlessly bowing functionaries in flowing yellow robes and purple sashes met them at the Gate of Brilliant Virtue in the city's south wall and conducted them to their pavilion, close by the imperial palace and the Forbidden Garden. It was a light, airy place, thin walls of plastered brick braced by graceful columns of some dark, aromatic wood. Fountains played on the roof of green and yellow tiles, creating an unending cool rainfall of recirculating water. The balustrades were of carved marble, the door-fittings were of gold.

There was a suite of private rooms for him, and another for her, though they would share the handsome damask-draped bedroom at the heart of the pavilion. As soon as they arrived Gioia announced that she must go to her rooms to bathe and dress. "There will be a formal reception for us at the palace tonight," she said. "They say the imperial receptions are splendid beyond anything you could imagine. I want to be at my best." The Emperor and all his ministers, she told him, would receive them in the Hall of the Supreme Ultimate; there would be a banquet for a thousand people; Persian dancers would perform, and the celebrated jugglers of Chung-nan. Afterward everyone would be conducted into the fantastic landscape of the Forbidden Garden to view the dragon-races and the fireworks.

He went to his own rooms. Two delicate little maid-servants undressed him and bathed him with fragrant sponges. The pavilion came equipped with eleven temporaries who were to be their servants: soft-voiced unobtrusive cat-like Chinese, done with perfect verisimilitude, straight black hair, glowing skin, epicanthic folds. Phillips often wondered what happened to a city's temporaries when the city's time was over. Were the towering Norse heros of Asgard being recycled at this moment into wiry dark-skinned Dravidians for Mohenjo-daro? When Timbuctoo's day was done, would its brightly robed black warriors be converted into supple Byzantines to stock the arcades of Constantinople? Or did they simply discard the old temporaries like so many excess props, stash them in warehouses somewhere, and turn out the appropriate quantities of the new model? He did not know; and once when he had asked Gioia about it she had grown uncomfortable and vague. She did not like him to probe for information, and he suspected it was because she had very little to give. These people did not seem to question the workings of their own world; his curiosities were very twentieth-century of him, he was frequently told, in that gently patronizing way of theirs. As his two little maids patted him with their sponges he thought of asking them where they had served before Chang-an. Rio? Rome? Haroun al-Raschid's Baghdad? But these fragile girls, he knew, would only giggle and retreat if he tried to question them. Interrogating temporaries was not only improper, but pointless: it was like interrogating one's luggage.

When he was bathed and robed in rich red silks he wandered the pavilion for a little while admiring the tinkling pendants of green jade dangling on the portico, the lustrous auburn pillars, the rainbow hues of the intricately interwoven girders and brackets that supported the roof. Then, wearying of his solitude, he approached the bamboo curtain at the entrance to Gioia's suite. A porter and one of the maids stood just within. They indicated that he should not enter; but he scowled at them and they melted from him like snowflakes. A trail of incense led him through the pavilion to Gioia's innermost dressing-room. There he halted, just outside the door.

Gioia sat naked with her back to him at an ornate dressing-table of some rare flame-colored wood inlaid with bands of orange and green procelain. She was studying herself intently in a mirror of polished bronze held by one of her maids: picking through her scalp with her fingernails, as a woman might do who was searching out her gray hairs.

But that seemed strange. Gray hair, on Gioia? On a citizen? A temporary might display some appearance of aging, perhaps, but surely not a citizen. Citizens remained forever young. Gioia looked like a girl. Her face was smooth and unlined, her flesh was firm, her hair was dark: that was true of all of them, every citizen he had ever seen. And yet there was no mistaking what Gioia was doing. She found a hair, frowned, drew it taut, nodded, plucked it. Another. Another. She pressed the tip of her finger to her cheek as if testing it for resilience. She tugged at the skin below her eyes, pulling it downward. Such familiar little gestures of vanity; but so odd here, he thought, in this world of the perpetually young. Gioia, worried about growing old? Had he simply failed to notice the signs of age on her? Or was it that she worked hard behind his back at concealing them? Perhaps that was it. Was he wrong about the citizens, then? Did they age even as the people of less blessed eras had always a done, but simply have better ways of hiding it? How old was she, anyway? Thirty? Sixty? Three hundred?

Gioia appeared satisfied now. She waved the mirror away; she rose; she beckoned for her banquet robes. Phillips, still standing unnoticed by the door, studied her with admiration: the small round buttocks, almost but not quite boyish, the elegant line of her spine, the surprising breadth of her shoulders. No, he thought, she is not aging at all. Her body is still like a girl's. She looks as young as on the day they first had met, however long ago that was—he could not say; it was hard to keep track of time here; but he was sure some years had passed since they had come together. Those gray hairs, those wrinkles and sags for which she had searched just now with such desperate intensity, must all be imaginary, mere artifacts of vanity. Even in this remote future epoch, then, vanity was not extinct. He wondered why she was so concerned with the fear of aging. And affectation? Did all these timeless people take some perverse pleasure in fretting over the possibility that they might be growing old? Or was it some private fear of Gioia's, another symptom of the mysterious depression that had come over her in Alexandria?

Not wanting her to think that he had been spying on her, when all he had really intended was to pay her a visit, he slipped silently away to dress for the evening. She came to him an hour later, gorgeously robed, saddled from chin to ankles in a brocade of brilliant colors shot through with threads of gold, face painted, hair drawn up tightly and fastened with ivory combs: very much the lady of the court. His servants had made him splendid also, a lustrous black surplice embroidered with golden dragons over a sweeping floor-length gown of shining white silk, a necklace and pendant of red coral, a five-cornered gray felt hat that rose in tower upon tower like a ziggurat. Gioia, grinning, touched her fingertips to his cheek. "You look marvelous!" she told him. "Like a grand mandarin!"

"And you like an empress," he said. "Like some distant land: Persia, India. Here to pay a ceremonial visit on the son of Heaven." An excess of love suffused his spirit, and, catching her lightly by the wrist, he drew her toward him, as close as he could manage it considering how elaborate their costumes were. But as he bent forward and downward, meaning to brush his lips lightly and affectionately against the tip of her nose, he perceived an unexpected strangeness, an anomaly: The coating of white paint that was her makeup seemed oddly to magnify rather than mask the contours of her skin, highlighting and revealing details he had never observed before. He saw a pattern of fine lines radiating from the corners of her eyes, and the unmistakable beginning of a quirk-mark in her cheek just to the left of her mouth, and perhaps the faint indentation of frown-lines in her flawless forehead. A shiver traveled along the nape of his neck. So it was not affectation, then, that had had her studying her mirror so fiercely. Age was in truth beginning to stake its claim on her, despite all that he had come to believe about these people's agelessness. But a moment later he was not so sure. Gioia turned and slid gently half a step back from him—she must have found his stare disturbing—and the lines he had thought he had seen were gone. He searched for them and saw only girlish smoothness once again. A trick of the light? A figment of an overwrought imagination? He was baffled.

"Come," she said. "We mustn't keep the Emperor waiting."

Five mustachioed warriors in armor of white quilting and seven musicians playing cymbals and pipes escorted them to the Hall of the Supreme Ultimate. There they found the full court arrayed: princes and ministers, high officials, yellow-robed monks, a swarm of imperial concubines. In a place of honor to the right of the royal thrones, which rose like gilded scaffolds high above all else, was a little group of stern-faced men in foreign costumes, the ambassadors of Rome and Byzantium, of Arabia and Syria, of Korea, Japan, Tibet, Turkestan. Incense smouldered in enameled braziers. A poet sang a delicate twanging melody, accompanying himself on a small harp. Then the Emperor and Empress entered: two tiny aged people. Like waxen images, moving with infinite slowness, taking steps no greater than a child's. There was the sound of trumpets as they ascended their thrones. When the little Emperor was seated—he looked like a doll up there, ancient, faded, shrunken, yet still somehow a figure of extraordinary power—he stretched forth both his hands, and enormous gongs began to sound. It was a scene of astonishing splendor, grand and overpowering.

These are all temporaries, Phillips realized suddenly. He saw only a handful of citizens—eight, ten, possible as many as a dozen—scattered here and there about the vast room. He knew them their eyes, dark, liquid, knowing. They were watching not only the imperial spectacle but also Gioia and him; and Gioia, smiling secretly, nodding almost imperceptibly to them, was acknowledging their presence and their interest. But those few were the only ones in here who were autonomous living beings. All the rest—the entire splendid court, the great mandarins and paladins, the officials, the giggling concubines, the haughty and resplendent ambassadors, the aged Emperor and Empress themselves, were simply part of the scenery. Had the world ever seen entertainment on so grand a scale before? All this pomp, all this pageantry, conjured up each night for the amusement of a dozen or so viewers?

At the banquet the little group of citizens sat together at a table apart, a round onyx slab draped with translucent green silk. There turned out to be seventeen of them in all, including Gioia; Gioia appeared to know all of them, though none, so far as he could tell, was a member of her set that he had met before. She did not attempt introductions. Nor was conversation at all possible during the meal: there was a constant astounding roaring din in the room. There orchestras played at once and there were troupes of strolling musicians also, and a steady stream of monks and their attendants marched back and forth between the tables loudly chanting sutras and waving censers to the deafening accompaniment of drums and gongs. The Emperor did not descend from his throne to join the banquet; he seemed to be asleep, though now and then he waved his hand in time to the music. Gigantic half-naked brown slaves with broad cheekbones and mouths like gaping pockets brought forth the food, peacock tongues and breast of phoenix heaped on mounds of glowing saffron-colored rice, served on frail alabaster plates. For chopsticks they were given slender rods of dark jade. The wine, served in glistening crystal beakers, was thick and sweet, with an aftertaste of raisins, and no beaker was allowed to remain empty for more than a moment.

Phillips felt himself growing dizzy: when the Persian dancers emerged he could not tell whether there were five of them or fifty, and as they performed their intricate whirling routines it semed to him that their slender muslin-veiled forms were blurring and merging one into another. He felt frightened by their proficiency, and wanted to look away, but he could not. The Chung-nan jugglers that followed them were equally skilful, equally alarming, filling the air with scythes, flaming torches, live animals, rare porcelain vases, pink jade hatchets, silver bells, gilded cups, wagon-wheels, bronze vessels, and never missing a catch. The citizens applauded politely but did not seem impressed. After the jugglers, the dancers returned, performing this time on stilts; the waiters brought platters of steaming meat of a pale lavender color, unfamiliar in taste and texture: filet of camel, perhaps, or haunch of hippopotamus, or possibly some choice chop from a young dragon. There was more wine. Feebly Phillips tried to wave it away, but the servitors were implacable. This was a drier sort, greenish-gold, austere, sharp on the tongue. With it came a silver dish, chilled to a polar coldness, that held shaved ice flavored with some potent smoky-flavored brandy. The jugglers were doing a second turn, he noticed. He thought he was going to be ill. He looked helplessly toward Gioia, who seemed sober but fiercely animated, almost manic, her eyes blazing like rubies. She touched his cheek fondly.

A cool draft blew through the hall: they had opened one entire wall, revealing the garden, the night, the stars. Just outside was a colossal wheel of oiled paper stretched on wooden struts. They must have erected it in the past hour: it stood a hundred fifty feet high or even more, and on it hung lanterns by the thousands, glimmering like giant fireflies. The guests began to leave the hall. Phillips let himself be swept along into the garden, where under a yellow moon strange crook-armed trees with dense black needles looked ominously. Gioia slipped her arm through his. They went down to a lake of bubbling crimson fluid and watched scarlet flamingo-like birds ten feet tall fastidiously spearing angry-eyed turquoise eels. They stood in awe before a fat-bellied Buddha of gleaming blue tilework, seventy feet high. A horse with a golden mane came prancing by, striking showers of brilliant red sparks wherever its hooves touched the ground. In a grove of lemon trees that seemed to have the power to wave their slender limbs about, Phillips came upon the Emperor, standing by himself and rocking gently back and forth. The old man seized Phillips by the hand and pressed something into his palm, closing his fingers tight about it; when he opened his fist a few moments later he found his palm full of gray irregular pearls. Gioia took them from him and cast them into the air, and they burst like exploding firecrackers, giving off splashes of colored light. A little later, Phillips realized that he was no longer wearing his surplice or his white silken undergown. Gioia was naked too, and she drew him gently down into a carpet of moist blue moss, where they made love until dawn, fiercely at first, then slowly, languidly, dreamily. At sunrise he looked at her tenderly and saw that something was wrong.

"Gioia?" he said doubtfully.

She smiled. "Ah, no. Gioia is with Fenimon tonight. I am Belilala."

"With—Fenimon."

"They are old friends. She had not seen him in years."

"Ah. I see. And you are—?"

"Belilala," she said again, touching her fingertips to his cheek.

It was not unusual, Belilala said. It happened all the time; the only unusual thing was that it had not happened to him before now. Couples formed, traveled together for a while, drifted apart, eventually reunited. It did not mean that Gioia had left him forever. It meant only that just now she chose to be with Fenimon. Gioia would return. In the meanwhile he would not be alone. "You and I met in New Chicago," Belilala told him. "And then we saw each other again in Timbuctoo. Have you forgotten? Oh, yes, I see that you have forgotten!" She laughed prettily; she did not seem at all offended.

She looked enough like Gioia to be her sister. But, then, all the citizens looked more or less alike to him. And apart from their physical resemblance, so he quickly came to realize, Belilala and Gioia were not really very similar . . . There was a calmness, a deep reservior of serenity, in Belilala that Gioia, eager and volatile and ever impatient, did not seem to have. Strolling the swarming streets of Chang-an with Belilala, he did not perceive in her any of Gioia'a restless feverish need always to know what lay beyond, and beyond, and beyond even that. When they toured the Hsing-ch'ing Palace, Belilala did not after five minutes begin—as Gioia surely would have done—to seek directions to the Fountain of Hsuan-tsung or the Wild Goose Pagoda. Curiosity did not consume Belilala as it did Gioia. Plainly she believed that there would always be enough time for her to see everything she cared to see. There were some days when Belilala chose not to go out at all, but was content merely to remain at their pavilion playing a solitary game with flat porcelain counters, or viewing the flowers of the garden.

He found, oddly, that he enjoyed the respite from Gioia's intense world-swallowing appetities; and yet he longed for her to return. Belilala—beautiful, gentle, tranquil, patient—was too perfect for him. She seemed unreal in her gleaming impeccability, much like one of those Sung celadon vases that appear too flawless to have been thrown and glazed by human hands. There was something a little soulless about her: an immaculate finish outside, emptiness within. Belilala might almost have been a temporary, he thought, though he knew she was not. He could explore the pavilions and palaces of Chang-an with her, he could make graceful conversation with her while they dined, he could certainly enjoy coupling with her; but he could not love her or even contemplate the possibility. It was hard to imagine Belilala worriedly studying herself in a mirror for wrinkles and gray hairs. Belilala would never be any older than she was at this moment; nor could Belilala ever have been any younger. Perfection does not move along an axis of time. But the perfection of Belilala's glossy surface made her inner being impenetrable to him. Gioia was more vulnerable, more obviously flawed—her restlessness, her moodiness, her vanity, her fears—and therefore she was more accessible to his own highly imperfect twentieth-century sensibility.

Occasionally he saw Gioia as he roamed the city, or thought he did. He had a glimpse of her among the miracle-vendors in the Persian Bazaar, and outside the Zoroastrian temple, and again by the goldfish pond in the Serpentine Park. But he was never quite sure that the woman he saw was really Gioia, and he never could get close enough to her to be certain: she had a way of vanishing as he approached, like some mysterious Lorelei luring him onward and onward in a hopeless chase. After a while he came to realize that he was not going to find her until she was ready to be found.

He lost track of time. Weeks, months, years? He had no idea. In this city of exotic luxury, mystery, and magic all was in constant flux and transition and the days had a fitful, unstable quality. Buildings and even whole streets were torn down of an afternoon and re-erected, within days, far away. Grand new pagodas sprouted like toadstools in the night. Citizens came in from Asgard, Alexandria, Timbuctoo, New Chicago, stayed for a time, disappeared, returned. There was a constant round of court receptions, banquets, theatrical events, each one much like the one before. The festivals in honor of past emperors and empresses might have given some form to the year, but they seemed to occur in a random way, the ceremony marking the death of T'ai Tsung coming around twice the same year, so it seemed to him, once in a season of snow and again in high summer, and the one honoring the ascension of the Empress Wu being held twice in a single season. Perhaps he had misunderstood something. But he knew it was no use asking anyone.

One day Belilala said unexpectedly, "Shall we go to Mohenjo-daro?"

"I didn't know it was ready for visitors," he replied.

"Oh, yes. For quite some time now."

He hesitated. This had caught him unprepared. Cautiously he said, "Gioia and I were going to go there together, you know."

Belilala smiled amiably, as though the topic under discussion were nothing more than the choice of that evening's restaurant.

"Were you?" she asked.

"It was all arranged while we were still in Alexandria. To go with you instead—I don't know what to tell you, Belilala." Phillips sensed that he was growing terribly flustered. "You know that I'd like to go. With you. But on the other hand I can't help feeling that I shouldn't go there until I'm back with Gioia again. If I ever am." How foolish this sounds, he thought. How clumsy, how adolescent. He found that he was having trouble looking straight at her. Uneasily he said, with a kind of desperation in his voice, "I did promise her—there was a commitment, you understand—a firm agreement that we would go to Mohenjo-daro together—"

"Oh, but Gioia's already there!" said Belilala in the most casual way.

He gaped as though she had punched him.

"*What*?"

"She was one of the first to go, after it opened. Months and months ago. You didn't know?" she asked, sounding surprised, but not very. "You really didn't know?"

That astonished him. He felt bewildered, betrayed, furious. His cheeks grew hot, his mouth gaped. He shook his head again and again, trying to clear it of confusion. It was a moment before he could speak. "Already there?" he said at last. "Without waiting for me? After we had talked about going there together—after we had agreed—"

Belilala laughed. "But how could she resist seeing the newest city? You know how impatient Gioia is!"

"Yes. Yes."

He was stunned. He could barely think.

"Just like all short-timers," Belilala said. "She rushes here, she rushes there. She must have it all, now, now, right away, at once, instantly. You ought never expect her to wait for you for anything for very long: the fit seizes her, and off she goes. Surely you must know that about her by now."

"A short-timer?" He had not heard that term before.

"Yes. You knew that. You must have known that." Belilala flashed her sweetest smile. She showed no sign of comprehending his distress. With a brisk wave of her hand she said, "Well, then, shall we go, you and I? To Mohenjo-daro?"

"Of course," Phillips said bleakly.

"When would you like to leave?"

"Tonight," he said. He paused a moment. "What's a short-timer, Belilala?"

Color came to her cheeks. "Isn't it obvious?" she asked.

Had there ever been a more hideous place on the face of the earth than the city of Mohenjo-daro? Phillips found it difficult to imagine one. Nor could he understand why, out of all the cities that had ever been, these people had chosen to restore this one to existence. More than ever they seemed alien to him, unfathomable, imcomprehensible.

From the terrace atop the many-towered citadel he peered down into grim claustrophobic Mohenjo-daro and shivered. The stark, bleak city looked like nothing so much as some prehistoric prison colony. In the manner of an uneasy tortoise it huddled, squat and compact, against the gray monotonous Indus River plain: miles of dark burnt-brick walls enclosing miles of terrifyingly orderly streets, laid out in an awesome, monstrous gridiron pattern of maniacal rigidity. The houses themselves were dismal and forbidding too, clusters of brick cells gathered about small airless courtyards. There were no windows, only small doors that opened not onto the main boulevards but onto the tiny mysterious lanes that ran between the buildings. Who had designed this horrifying metropolis? What harsh, sour souls they must have had, these frightening and frightened folk, creating for themselves in the lush fertile plains of India such a Supreme Soviet of a city!

"How lovely it is," Belilala murmured. "How fascinating!"

He stared at her in amazement.

"Fascinating? Yes," he said. "I suppose so. The same way that the smile of a cobra is fascinating."

"What's a cobra?"

"Poisonous predatory serpent," Phillips told her. "Probably extinct. Or formerly extinct, more likely. It wouldn't surprise me if you people had re-created a few and turned them loose in Mohenjo to make things livelier."

"You sound angry, Charles."

"Do I? That's not how I feel."

"How do you feel, then?"

"I don't know," he said after a long moment's pause. He shrugged. "Lost, I suppose. Very far from home."

"Poor Charles."

"Standing here in this ghastly barracks of a city, listening to you tell me how beautiful it is, I've never felt more alone in my life."

"You miss Gioia very much, don't you?"

He gave her another startled look.

"Gioia had nothing to do with it. She's probably been having ecstasies over the loveliness of Mohenjo just like you. Just like all of you. I suppose I'm the only one who can't find the beauty, the charm. I'm the only one who looks out there and sees only horror, and then wonders why nobody else sees it, why in fact people would set up a place like this for *entertainment*, for *pleasure*—"

Her eyes were gleaming. "Oh, you are angry! You really are!"

"Does that fascinate you too?" he snapped. "A demonstration of genuine primitive emotion? A typical quaint twentieth-century outburst?" He paced the rampart in short quick anguished steps. "Ah. Ah. I think I understand it now, Belilala. Of course: I'm part of your circus, the star of the sideshow. I'm the first experiment in setting up the next stage of it, in fact." Her eyes were wide. The sudden harshness and violence in his voice seemed to be alarming and exciting her at the same time. That angered him even more. Fiercely he went on, "Bringing whole cities back out of time was fun for a while, but it lacks a certain authenticity, eh? For some reason you couldn't bring the inhabitants too; you couldn't just grab a few million prehistorics out of Egypt or Greece or India and dump them down in this era, I suppose because you might have too much trouble controlling them, or because you'd have the problem of disposing of them once you were bored with them. So you had to settle for creating temporaries to populate your ancient cities. But now you've got me. I'm something more real than a temporary, and that's a terrific novelty for you, and novelty is the thing you people crave more than anything else: maybe the *only* thing you crave. And here I am, complicated, unpredictable, edgy, capable of anger, fear, sadness, love, and all those other formerly extinct things. Why settle for picturesque architecture when you can observe picturesque emotion, too? What fun I must be for all of you! And if you decide that I was really interesting, maybe you'll ship me back where I came from and check out a few other ancient types—a Roman gladiator, maybe, or a Renaissance pope, or even a Neanderthal or two—

"Charles," she said tenderly. "Oh, Charles, Charles, Charles, how lonely you must be, how lost, how troubled! Will you ever forgive me? Will you ever forgive us all?"

Once more he was astounded by her. She sounded entirely sincere, altogether sympathetic. Was she? Was she, really? He was not sure he had ever had a sign of genuine caring from any of them before, not even Gioia. Nor could he bring himself to trust Belilala now. He was afraid of her, afraid of all of them, of their brittleness, their slyness, their elegance. He wished he could go to her and have her take him in her arms; but he felt too much the shaggy prehistoric just now to be able to risk asking that comfort of her.

He turned away and began to walk around the rim of the citadel's massive wall.

"Charles?"

"Let me alone for a little while," he said.

He walked on. His forehead throbbed and there was a pounding in his chest. All stress systems going full blast, he thought: secret glands dumping gallons of inflammatory substances into his bloodstream. The heat, the inner confusion, the repellent look of this place—

Try to understand, he thought. Relax. Look about you. Try to enjoy your holiday in Mohenjo-daro.

He leaned warily outward, over the edge of the wall. He had never seen a wall like this; it must be forty feet thick at the base, he guessed, perhaps even more, and every brick perfectly shaped, meticulously set. Beyond the great rampart, marshes ran almost to the edge of the city, although close by the wall the swamps had been dammed and drained for agriculture. He saw lithe brown farmers down there, busy with their wheat and barley and peas. Cattle and buffaloes grazed a little farther out. The air was heavy, dank, humid. All was still. From somewhere close at hand came the sound of a droning, whining stringed instrument and a steady insistent chanting.

Gradually a sort of peace pervaded him. His anger subsided. He felt himself beginning to grow calm again. He looked back at the city, the rigid interlocking streets, the maze of inner lanes, the millions of courses of precise brickwork.

It is a miracle, he told himself, that this city is here in this place and at this time. And it is a miracle that I am here to see it.

Caught for a moment by the magic within the bleakness, he thought he began to understand Belilaia's awe and delight, and he wished now that he had not spoken to her so sharply. The city was alive. Whether it was the actual Mohenjo-daro of thousands upon thousands of years ago, ripped from the past by some wondrous hook, or simply a cunning reproduction, did not matter at all. Real or not, this was the true Mohenjo-daro. It had been dead and now, for the moment, it was alive again. These people, these *citizens*, might be trivial, but reconstructing Mohenjo-daro was no trivial achievement. And that the city that had been reconstructed was oppressive and sinister-looking was unimportant. No one was compelled to live in Mohenjo-daro any more. Its time had come and gone, long ago; those little dark-skinned peasants and craftsmen and merchants down there were mere temporaries, mere inanimate things, conjured up like zombies to enhance the illusion. They did not need his pity. Nor did he need to pity himself. He knew that he should be grateful for the chance to behold these things. Some day, when this dream had ended and his hosts had returned him to the world of subways and computers and income tax and television networks, he would think of Mohenjo-daro as he had once beheld it, lofty walls of tightly woven dark brick under a heavy sky, and he would remember only its beauty.

Glancing back, he searched for Belilala and could not for a moment find her. Then he caught sight of her carefully descending a narrow staircase that angled down the inner face of the citadel wall.

"Belilala!" he called.

She paused and looked his way, shading her eyes from the sun with her hand. "Are you all right?"

"Where are you going?"

"To the baths," she said. "Do you want to come?"

He nodded. "Yes. Wait for me, will you? I'll be right there." He began to run toward her along the top of the wall.

The baths were attached to the citadel: a great open tank the size of a large swimming pool, lined with bricks set on edge in gypsum mortar and waterproofed with asphalt, and eight smaller tanks just north of it in a kind of covered arcade. He supposed that in ancient times the whole complex had had some ritual purpose, the large tank used by common folk and the small chambers set aside for the private ablutions of priests or nobles. Now the baths were maintained, it seemed, entirely for the pleasure of visiting citizens. As Phillips came up the passageway that led to the main bath he saw fifteen or twenty of them lolling in the water or padding languidly about, while temporaries of the dark-skinned Mohenjo-daro type served them drinks and pungent little morsels of spiced meat as though this were some sort of luxury resort. Which was, he realized, exactly what it was. The temporaries wore white cotton loincloths; the citizens were naked. In his former life he had encountered that sort of casual public nudity a few times on visits to California and the south of France, and it had made him mildly uneasy. But he was growing accustomed to it here.

The changing-rooms were tiny brick cubicles connected by rows of closely placed steps to the courtyard that surrounded the central tank. They entered one and Belilala swiftly slipped out of the loose cotton robe that she had worn since their arrival that morning. With arms folded she stood leaning against the wall, waiting for him. After a moment he dropped his own robe and followed her outside. He felt a little giddy, sauntering around naked in the open like this.

On the way to the main bathing area they passed the private baths. None of them seemed to be occupied. They were elegantly constructed chambers, with finely jointed brick floors and carefully designed runnels to drain excess water into the passageway that led to the primary drain. Phillips was struck with admiration for the cleverness of the prehistoric engineers. He peered into this chamber and that to see how the conduits and ventilating ducts were arranged, and when he came to the last room in the sequence he was surprised and embarrassed to discover that it was in use. A brawny grinning man, big-muscled, deep-chested, with exuberantly flowing shoulder-length red hair and a flamboyant, sharply tapering beard, was thrashing about merrily with two women in the small tank. Phillips had a quick glimpse of a lively tangle of arms, legs, breasts, buttocks.

"Sorry," he muttered. His cheeks reddened. Quickly he ducked out, blurting apologies as he went. "Didn't realize the room was occupied—no wish to intrude—"

Belilala had proceeded on down the passageway. Phillips hurried after her. From behind him came peals of cheerful raucous booming laughter and high-pitched giggling and the sound of splashing water. Probably they had not even noticed him.

He paused a moment, puzzled, playing back in his mind that one startling glimpse. Something was not right. Those women, he was fairly sure, were citizens: little slender elfin dark-haired girlish creatures, the standard model. But the man? That great curling sweep of red hair? Not a citizen. Citizens did not affect shoulder-length hair. And *red*? Nor had he ever seen a citizen so burly, so powerfully muscular. Or one with a beard. But he could hardly be a temporary, either. Phillips could conceive no reason why there would be so Anglo-Saxon-looking a temporary at Mohenjo-daro; and it was unthinkable for a temporary to be frolicking like that with citizens, anyway.

"Charles?"

He looked up ahead. Belilala stood at the end of the passageway, outlined in a nimbus of brilliant sunlight. "Charles?" she said again. "Did you lose your way?"

"I'm right here behind you," he said. "I'm coming."

"Who did you meet in there?"

"A man with a beard."

"With a what?"

"A beard," he said. "Red hair growing on his face. I wonder who he is."

"Nobody I know," said Belilala. "The only one I know with hair on his face is you. And yours is black, and you shave it off every day." She laughed. "Come along, now! I see some friends by the pool!"

He caught up with her and they went hand in hand out into the courtyard. Immediately a waiter glided up to them, an obsequious little temporary with a tray of drinks. Phillips waved it away and headed for the pool. He felt terribly exposed: he imagined that the citizens disporting themselves here were staring intently at him, studying his hairy primitive body as though he were some mythical crature, a Minotaur, a werewolf, summoned up for their amusement. Belilala drifted off to talk to someone and he slipped into the water, grateful for the concealment it offered. It was deep, warm, comforting. With swift powerful strokes he breast-stroked from one end to the other.

A citizen perched elegantly on the pool's rim smiled at him. "Ah, so you've come at last, Charles!" Char-less. Two syllables. Someone from Gioia's set: Stengard, Hawk, Aramayne? He could not remember which one. They were all so much alike.

Phillips returned the man's smile in a half-hearted, tentative way. He searched for something to say and finally asked, "Have you been here long?"

"Weeks. Perhaps months. What a splendid achievement this city is, eh, Charles? Such utter unity of mood—such a total statement of a uniquely single-minded esthetic—"

"Yes. Single-minded is the word," Phillips said drily.

"Gioia's word, actually. Gioia's phrase. I was merely quoting."

Gioia. He felt as if he had been stabbed.

"You've spoken to Gioia lately?" he said.

"Actually, no. It was Hekna who saw her. You do remember Hekna, eh?" He nodded toward two naked women standing on the brick platform that bordered the pool, chatting, delicately nibbling morsels of meat. They could have been twins. "There is Hekna, with your Belilala," Hekna, yes. So this must be Hawk, Phillips thought, unless there has been some recent shift of couples. "How sweet she is, your Belilala," Hawk said. "Gioia chose very wisely when she picked her for you."

Another stab: a much deeper one. "Is that how it was?" he said. "Gioia *picked* Belilala for me?"

"Why, of course!" Hawk seemed surprised. It went without saying, evidently. "What did you think? That Gioia would merely go off and leave you to fend for yourself?"

"Hardly. Not Gioia."

"She's very tender, very gentle, isn't she?"

"You mean Belilala? Yes, very," said Phillips carefully. "A dear woman, a wonderful woman. But of course I hope to get together with Gioia again soon." He paused. "They say she's been in Mohenjo-daro almost since it opened."

"She was here, yes."

"*Was*?"

"Oh, you know Gioia," Hawk said lightly. "She's moved along by now, naturally."

Phillips leaned forward. "Naturally," he said. Tension thickened his voice. "Where has she gone this time?"

"Timbuctoo, I think. Or New Chicago. I forget which one it was. She was telling us that she hoped to be in Timbuctoo for the closing-down party. But then Fenimon had some pressing reason for going to New Chicago. I can't remember what they decided to do." Hawk gestured sadly. "Either way, a pity that she left Mohenjo before the new visitor came. She had such a rewarding time with you, after all: I'm sure she'd have found much to learn from him also."

The unfamiliar term twanged an alarm deep in Phillips' consciousness. "*Visitor*?" he said, angling his head sharply toward Hawk. "What visitor do you mean?"

"You haven't met him yet? Oh, of course, you've only just arrived."

Phillips moistened his lips. "I think I may have seen him. Long red hair? Beard like this?"

"That's the one! Willoughby, he's called. He's—what?—a Viking, a pirate, something like that. Tremendous vigor and force. Remarkable person. We should have many more visitors, I think.

They're far superior to temporaries, everyone agrees. Talking with a temporary is a little like talking to one's self, wouldn't you say? They give you no significant illumination. But a visitor—someone like this Willoughby—or like you, Charles—a visitor can be truly enlightening, a visitor can transform one's view of reality—"

"Excuse me," Phillips said. A throbbing began behind his forehead. "Perhaps we can continue this conversation later, yes?" He put the flats of his hands against the hot brick of the platform and hoisted himself swiftly from the pool. "At dinner, maybe—or afterward—yes? All right?" He set off at a quick half-trot back toward the passageway that led to the private baths.

As he entered the roofed part of the structure his throat grew dry, his breath suddenly came short. He padded quickly up the hall and peered into the little bath-chamber. The bearded man was still there, sitting up in the tank, breast-high above the water, with one arm around each of the women. His eyes gleamed with fiery intensity in the dimness. He was grinning in marvelous self-satisfaction; he seemed to brim with intensity, confidence, gusto.

Let him be what I think he is, Phillip prayed. I have been alone among these people long enough.

"May I come in?" he asked.

"Aye, fellow!" cried the man in the tub thunderously. "By my troth, come ye in, and bring your lass as well! God's teeth, I wot there's room aplenty for more folk in this tub than we!"

At that great uproarious outcry Phillips felt a powerful surge of joy. What a joyous rowdy voice! How rich, how lusty, how totally uncitizen-like!

And those oddly archaic words! *God's teeth*? *By my troth*? What sort of talk was that? What else but the good pure sonorous Elizabethan diction! Certainly it had something of the roll and fervor of Shakespeare about it. And spoken with—an Irish brogue, was it? No, not quite: it was English, but English spoken in no manner Phillips had ever heard.

Citizens did not speak that way. But a *visitor* might.

So it was true. Relief flooded Phillips' soul. Not alone, then! Another relict of a former age—another wanderer—a companion in chaos, a brother in adversity—a fellow voyager, tossed even farther than he had been by the tempests of time—

The bearded man grinned heartily and beckoned to Phillips with a toss of his head. "Well, join us, join us, man! 'Tis good to see an English face again, amidst all these Moors and rogue Portugals! But what have ye done with thy lass? One can never have enough wenches, d'ye not agree?"

The force and vigor of him were extraordinary: almost too much so. He roared, he bellowed, he boomed. He was so very much what he ought to be that he seemed more a character out of some old pirate movie than anything else, so blustering, so real, that he seemed unreal. A stage-Elizabethan, larger than life, a boisterous young Falstaff without the belly.

Hoarsely, Phillips said, "Who are you?"

"Why, Ned Willoughby's son Francis am I, of Plymouth. Late of the service of Her Most Protestant Majesty, but most foully abducted by the powers of darkness and cast away among these blackamoor Hindus, or whatever they be. And thyself?"

"Charles Phillips." After a moment's uncertainty he added, "I'm from New York."

"*New* York? What place is that? In faith, man, I know it not!"

"A city in America."

"A city in America, forsooth! What a fine fancy that is! In America, you say, and not on the Moon, or perchance underneath the sea?" To the women Willoughby said, "D'ye hear him? He comes from a city in America! With the face of an Englishman, though not the manner of one, and not quite the proper sort of speech. A city in America! A *city*. God's blood, what will I hear next?"

Phillips trembled. Awe was beginning to take hold of him. This man had walked the streets of Shakespeare's London, perhaps. He had clinked canisters with Marlowe or Essex or Walter Raleigh; he had watched the ships of the Armada wallowing in the Channel. It strained Phillips' spirit to think of it. This strange dream in which he found himself was compounding its strangeness now. He felt like a weary swimmer assailed by heavy surf, winded, dazed. The hot close atmosphere of the baths was driving him toward vertigo. There could be no doubt of it any longer. He was not the only primitive—the only *visitor*—who was wandering loose in this fiftieth century. They were conducting other experiments as well. He gripped the sides of the door to steady himself and said, "When you speak of Her Most

Protestant Majesty, it's Elizabeth the First you mean, is that not so?"

"Elizabeth, aye! As to the First, that is true enough, but why trouble to name her thus? There is but one. First and Last, I do trow, and God save her, there is no other!

Phillips studied the other man warily. He knew that he must proceed with care. A misstep at this point and he would forfeit any chance that Willoughby would take him seriously. How much metaphysical bewilderment, after all, could this man absorb? What did he know, what had anyone of his time known, of past and present and future and the notion that one might somehow move from one to the other as readily as one would go from Surrey to Kent? That was a twentieth-century idea, late nineteenth at best, a fantastical speculation that very likely no one had even considered before Wells had sent his time traveler off to stare at the reddened sun of the earth's last twilight. Willoughby's world was a world of Protestants and Catholics, of kings and queens, of tiny sailing vessels, of swords at the hip and ex-carts on the road: that world seemed to Phillips far more alien and distant than was this world of citizens and temporaries. The risk that Willoughby would not begin to understand him was great.

But this man and he were natural allies against a world they had never made. Phillips chose to take the risk.

"Elizabeth the First is the queen you serve," he said. "There will be another of her name in England, in due time. Has already been, in fact."

Willoughby shook his head like a puzzled lion. "Another Elizabeth, d'ye say?"

"A second one, and not much like the first. Long after your Virgin Queen, this one. She will reign in what you think of as the days to come. That I know without doubt."

The Englishman peered at him and frowned. "You see the future? Are you a soothsayer, then? A necromancer, mayhap? Or one of the very demons that brought me to this place?"

"Not at all," Phillips said gently. "Only a lost soul, like yourself." He stepped into the little room and crouched by the side of the tank. The two citizen-women were staring at him in bland fascination. He ignored them. To Willoughby he said, "Do you have any idea where you are?"

* * *

The Englishman had guessed, rightly enough, that he was in India: "I do believe these little brown Moorish folk are of the Hindu sort," he said. But that was as far as his comprehension of what had befallen him could go.

It had not occurred to him that he was no longer living in the sixteenth century. And of course he did not begin to suspect that this strange and somber brick city in which he found himself was a wanderer out of an era even more remote than his own. Was there any way, Phillip wondered, of explaining that to him?

He had been here only three days. He thought it was devils that had carried him off. "While I slept did they come for me," he said. "Mephistophilis Sathanas his henchmen seized me—God alone can say why—and swept me in a moment out to this torrid realm from England, where I had reposed among friends and family. For I was between one voyage and the next, you must understand, awaiting Drake and his ship—you know Drake, the glorious Francis? God's blood, there's a mariner for ye! We were to go to the Main again, he and I, but instead here I be in this other place—" Willoughby leaned close and said, "I ask you, soothsayer, how can it be, that a man go to sleep in Plymouth and wake up in India? It is passing strange, is it not?"

"That it is," Phillips said.

"But he that is in the dance must needs dance on, though he do but hop, eh? So do I believe." He gestured toward the two citizen-women. "And therefore to console myself in this pagan land I have found me some sport among these little Portugal women—"

"Portugal?" said Phillips.

"Why, what else can they be, but Portugals? Is it not the Portugals who control all these coasts of India? See, the people are of two sorts here, the blackamoors and the others, the fair-skinned ones, the lords and masters who lie here in these baths. If they be not Hindus, and I think they are not, then Portugals is what they must be." He laughed and pulled the women against himself and rubbed his hands over their breasts as though they were fruits on a vine. "Is that not what you are, you little naked shameless Papist wenches? A pair of Portugals, eh?"

They giggled, but did not answer.

"No," Phillips said. "This is India, but not the India you think you know. And these women are not Portuguese."

"Not Portuguese?" Willoughby said, baffled.

"No more so than you. I'm quite certain of that."

Willoughby stroked his beard. "I do admit I found them very odd, for Portugals. I have heard not a syllable of their Portugee speech on their lips. And it is strange also that they run naked as Adam and Eve in these baths, and allow me free plunder of their women, which is not the way of Portugals at home, God wot. But I thought me, this is India, they choose to live in another fashion here—"

"No," Phillips said. "I tell you, these are not Portuguese, nor any other people of Europe who are known to you."

"Prithee, who are they, then?"

Do it delicately, now, Phillips warned himself. *Delicately.*

He said, "It is not far wrong to think of them as spirits of some kind—demons, even. Or sorcerers who have magicked us out of our proper places in the world." He paused, groping for some means to share with Willoughby, in a way that Willoughby might grasp, this mystery that had enfolded them. He drew a deep breath. "They've taken us not only across the sea," he said, "but across the years as well. We have both been hauled, you and I, far into the days that are to come."

Willoughby gave him a look of blank bewilderment.

"Days that are to come? Times yet unborn, d'ye mean? Why, I comprehend none of that!"

"Try to understand. We're both castaways in the same boat, man! But there's no way we can help each other if I can't make you see—"

Shaking his head, Willoughby muttered, "In faith, good friend, I find your words the merest folly. Today is today, and tomorrow is tomorrow, and how can a man step from one to t'other until tomorrow be turned into today?"

"I have no idea," said Phillips. Struggle was apparent on Willoughby's face; but plainly he could perceive no more than the haziest outline of what Phillips was driving at, if that much. "But this I know," he went on, "that your world and all that was in it is dead and gone. And so is mine, though I was born four hundred years after you, in the time of the second Elizabeth."

Willoughby snorted scornfully. "Four hundred—"

"You must believe me!"

"Nay! Nay!"

"It's the truth. Your time is only history to me. And mine and yours are history to *them*—ancient history. They call us visitors, but what we are is captives." Phillips felt himself quivering in the intensity of his effort. He was aware how insane this must sound to Willoughby. It was beginning to sound insane to him. "They've stolen us out of our proper times—seizing us like gypsies in the night—"

"Fie, man! You rave with lunacy!"

Phillips shook his head. He reached out and seized Willoughby tightly by the wrist. "I beg you, listen to me!" The citizen-women were watching closely, whispering to one another behind their hands, laughing. "Ask them!" Phillips cried. "Make them tell you what century this is! The sixteenth, do you think? Ask them!"

"What century could it be, but the sixteenth of our Lord?"

"They will tell you it is the fiftieth."

Willoughby looked at him pityingly. "Man, man, what a sorry thing thou art! The fiftieth, indeed!" He laughed. "Fellow, listen to me, now. There is but one Elizabeth, safe upon her throne in Westminster. This is India. The year is Anno 1591. Come, let us you and I steal a ship from these Portugals, and make our way back to England, and peradventure you may get from there to your America—"

"There is no England."

"Ah, can you say that and not be mad?"

"The cities and nations we knew are gone. These people live like magicians, Francis." There was no use holding anything back now, Phillips thought leadenly. He knew that he had lost. "They conjure up places of long ago, and build them here and there to suit their fancy, and when they are bored with them they destroy them, and start anew. There is no England. Europe is empty, featureless, void. Do you know what cities there are? There are only five in all the world. There is Alexandria of Egypt. There is Timbuctoo in Africa. There is New Chicago in America. There is a great city in China—in Cathay, I suppose you would say. And there is this place, which they call Mohenjo-daro, and which is far more ancient than Greece, than Rome, than Babylon."

Quietly Willoughby said, "Nay. This is mere absurdity. You say we are in some far tomorrow, and then you tell me we are dwelling in some city of long ago."

"A conjuration, only," Phillips said in desperation. "A likeness of that city. Which these folk have fashioned somehow for their own amusement. Just as we are here, you and I: to amuse them. Only to amuse them."

"You are completely mad."

"Come with me, then. Talk with the citizens by the great pool. Ask them what year this is; ask them about England; ask them how you came to be here." Once again Phillips grasped Willoughby's wrist. "We should be allies. If we work together, perhaps we can discover some way to get ourselves out of this place, and—"

"Let me be, fellow."

"Please—"

"Let me be!" roared Willoughby, and pulled his arm free. His eyes were stark with rage. Rising in the tank, he looked about furiously as though searching for a weapon. The citizen-women shrank back away from him, though at the same time they seemed captivated by the big man's fierce outburst. "Go to, get you to Bedlam! Let me be, madman! Let me be!"

Dismally Phillips roamed the dusty unpaved streets of Mohenjo-daro alone for hours. His failure with Willoughby had left him bleak-spirited and somber: he had hoped to stand back to back with the Elizabethan against the citizens, but he saw now that that was not to be. He had bungled things; or, more likely, it had been impossible ever to bring Willoughby to see the truth of their predicament.

In the stifling heat he went at random through the confusing congested lanes of flat-roofed, windowless houses and blank, featureless walls until he emerged into a broad marketplace. The life of the city swirled madly around him: the pseudo-life, rather, the intricate interactions of the thousands of temporaries who were nothing more than wind-up dolls set in motion to provide the illusion that pre-Vedic India was still a going concern. Here vendors sold beautiful little carved stone seals portraying tigers and monkeys and strange humped cattle, and women bargained vociferously with craftsmen for ornaments of ivory, gold, copper and bronze. Weary-looking women squatted behind immense mounds of newly made pottery, pinkish-red with black designs. No one paid any attention to him. He was the outsider here, neither citizen nor temporary. They belonged.

He went on, passing the huge granaries where workmen ceaselessly unloaded carts of wheat and others pounded grain on great circular brick platforms. He drifted into a public restaurant thronging with joyless silent people standing elbow to elbow at small brick counters, and was given a flat round piece of bread, a sort of tortilla or chapatti, in which was stuffed some spiced mincemeat that stung his lips like fire. Then he moved onward, down a wide, shallow, timbered staircase into the lower part of the city, where the peasantry lived in cell-like rooms packed together as though in hives.

It was an oppressive city, but not a squalid one. The intensity of the concern with sanitation amazed him: wells and fountains and public privies everywhere, and brick drains running from each building, leading to covered cesspools. There was none of the open sewage and pestilent gutters that he knew still could be found in the India of his own time. He wondered whether ancient Mohenjo-daro had in truth been so fastidious. Perhaps the citizens had redesigned the city to suit their own ideals of cleanliness. No: most likely what he saw was authentic, he decided, a function of the same obsessive discipline that had given the city its rigidity of form. If Mohenjo-daro had been a verminous filthy hole, the citizens probably would have re-created it just that way, and loved it for its fascinating, reeking filth.

Not that he had ever noticed an excessive concern with authenticity on the part of the citizens; and Mohenjo-daro, like all the other restored cities he had visited, was full of the usual casual anachronisms. Phillips saw images of Shiva and Krishna here and there on the walls of buildings he took to be temples, and the benign face of the mother-goddess Kali loomed in the plazas. Surely those deities had arisen in India long after the collapse of the Mohenjo-daro civilization. Were the citizens indifferent to such matters of chronology? Or did they take a certain naughty pleasure in mixing the eras—a mosque and a church in Greek Alexandria, Hindu gods in prehistoric Mohenjo-daro? Perhaps their records of the past had become contaminated with errors over the thousands of years. He would not have been surprised to see banners bearing portraits of Gandhi and Nehru being carried in procession through the streets. And there were phantasms and chimeras at large here again too, as if the citizens were untroubled by the boundary between history and myth: little fat elephant-headed Ganeshas blithely plunging their trunks into water-fountains, a six-armed, three-headed woman sunning herself on a brick terrace. Why not? Surely that was the motto of these people: *Why not, why not, why not*? They could do as they pleased, and they did. Yet Gioia had said to him, long ago, "Limits are very important." In what, Phillips wondered, did they limit themselves, other than in the number of their cities? Was there a quota, perhaps, on the number of "visitors" they allowed themselves to kidnap from the past. Until today he had thought he was the only one; now he knew there was at least one other; possibly there were more elsewhere, a step or two ahead or behind him, making the circuit with the citizens who traveled endlessly from New Chicago to Chang-an to Alexandria. We should join forces, he thought, and compel them to send us back to our rightful eras. *Compel*? How? File a class-action suit, maybe? Demonstrate in the streets? Sadly he thought of his failure to make common cause with Willoughby. We are natural allies, he thought. Together perhaps we might have won some compassion from these people. But to Willoughby it must be literally unthinkable that Good Queen Bess and her subject were sealed away on the far side of a barrier hundreds of centuries thick. He would prefer to believe that England was just a few months' voyage away around the Cape of Good Hope, and that all he need do was commandeer a ship and set sail for home. Poor Willoughby: probably he would never see his home again.

The thought came to Phillips suddenly:

Neither will you.

And then, after it:

If you could go home, would you really want to?

One of the first things he had realized here was that he knew almost nothing substantial about his former existence. His mind was well stocked with details on life in twentieth-century New York, to be sure; but of himself he could not say much more than that he was Charles Phillips and had come from 1984. Profession? Age? Parents' names? Did he have a wife? Children? A cat, a dog, hobbies? No data: none. Possibly the citizens had stripped such things from him when they brought him here to spare him from the pain of separation. They might be capable of that kindness. Knowing so little of what he had lost, could he truly say that he yearned for it? Willoughby seemed to remember much more of his former life, and longed for it all the more. He was spared that. Why not stay here, and go on and on from city to city, sightseeing all of time past as the citizens conjured it back into being? Why not? Why not? The chances were that he had no choice about it, anyway.

He made his way back up toward the citadel and to the baths once more. He felt a little like a ghost haunting a city of ghosts.

Belilala seemed unaware that he had been gone for most of the day. She sat by herself on the terrace of the baths, placidly sipping some thick milky beverage that had been sprinkled with a dark spice. He shook his head when she offered him some.

"Do you remember I mentioned that I saw a man with red hair and a beard this morning?" Phillips asked. "He's a visitor. Hawk told me that."

"Is he?" Belilala asked.

"From a time about four hundred years before mine. I talked with him. He thinks he was brought here by demons." Phillips gave her a searching look. "I'm a visitor too, isn't that so?"

"Of course, love."

"And how was *I* brought here? By demons also?"

Belilala smiled indifferently. "You'd have to ask someone else. Hawk, perhaps. I haven't looked into these things very deeply."

"I see. Are there many visitors here, do you know?"

A languid shrug. "Not many, no, not really. I've only heard of three or four besides you. There may be others by now, I suppose." She rested her hand lightly on his. "Are you having a good time in Mohenjo, Charles?"

He let her question pass as though he had not heard it.

"I asked Hawk about Gioia," he said.

"Oh?"

"He told me that she's no longer here, that she's gone on to Timbuctoo or New Chicago, he wasn't sure which."

"That's quite likely. As everybody knows, Gioia rarely stays in the same place very long."

Phillips nodded. "You said the other day that Gioia is a short-timer. That means she's going to grow old and die, doesn't it?"

"I thought you understood that, Charles."

"Whereas you will not age? Nor Hawk, nor Stengard, nor any of the rest of your set?"

"We will live as long as we wish," she said. "But we will not age, no."

"What makes a person a short-timer?"

"They're born that way, I think. Some missing gene, some extra gene—I don't actually know. It's extremely uncommon. Nothing can be done to help them. It's very slow, the aging. But it can't be halted."

Phillips nodded. "That must be very disagreeable," he said. "To find yourself one of the few people growing old in a world where everyone stays young. No wonder Gioia is so impatient. No wonder she runs around from place to place. No wonder she attached herself so quickly to the barbaric hairy visitor from the twentieth century, who comes from a time when *everybody* was a short-timer. She and I have something in common, wouldn't you say?"

"In a manner of speaking, yes."

"We understand aging. We understand death. Tell me: is Gioia likely to die very soon, Belilala?"

"Soon? Soon?" She gave him a wide-eyed child-like stare. "What is soon? How can I say? What you think of as soon and what I think of as soon are not the same thing, Charles." Then her manner changed: she seemed to be hearing what he was saying for the first time. Softly she said. "No, no, Charles. I don't think she will die very soon."

"When she left me in Chang-an, was it because she had become bored with me?"

Belilala shook her head. "She was simply restless. It had nothing to do with you. She was never bored with you."

"Then I'm going to go looking for her. Wherever she may be, Timbuctoo, New Chicago, I'll find her. Gioia and I belong together."

"Perhaps you do," said Belilala. "Yes. Yes, I think you really do." She sounded altogether unperturbed, unrejected, unbereft. "By all means Charles. Go to her. Follow her. Find her. Wherever she may be."

They had already begun dismantling Timbuctoo when Phillips got there. While he was still high overhead, his flitterflitter hovering above the dusty tawny plain where the River Niger met the sands of the Sahara, a surge of keen excitement rose in him as he looked down at the square gray flat-roofed mud and brick buildings of the great desert capital. But when he landed he found gleaming metal-skinned robots swarming everywhere, a horde of them scuttling about like giant shining insects, pulling the place apart.

He had not known about the robots before. So that was how all these miracles were carried out, Phillips realized: an army of obliging machines. He imagined them bustling up out of the earth whenever their services were needed, emerging from some sterile subterranean storehouse to put together Venice or Thebes or Knossos or Houston or whatever place was required, down to the finest detail, and then at some later time returning to undo everything that they had fashioned. He watched them now, diligently pulling down the adobe walls, demolishing the heavy metal-studded gates, bulldozing the amazing labyrinth of alleyways and thoroughfares, sweeping away the market. On his last visit to Timbuctoo that market had been crowded with a horde of veiled Tuaregs and swaggering Moors, black Sudanese, shrewd-faced Syrian traders, all of them busily dickering for camels, horses, donkeys, slabs of salt, huge green melons, silver bracelets, splendid vellum Korans. They were all gone now, that picturesque crowd of swarthy temporaries. Nor were there any citizens to be seen. The dust of destruction choked the air. One of the robots came up to Phillips and said in a dry crackling insect-voice, "You ought not to be here. This city is closed."

He stared at the flashing, buzzing band of scanners and sensors across the creature's glittering tapered snout. "I'm trying to find someone, a citizen who may have been here recently. Her name is—"

"This city is closed," the robot repeated inexorably.

They would not let him stay as much as an hour. There is no food here, the robot said, no water, no shelter. This is not a place any longer. You may not stay. You may not stay. You may not stay.

This is not a place any longer.

Perhaps he could find her in New Chicago, then. He took to the air again, soaring northward and westward over the vast emptiness. The land below him curved away into the hazy horizon, bare, sterile. What had they done with the vestiges of the world that had gone before? Had they turned their gleaming metal beetles loose to clean everything away? Were there no ruins of genuine antiquity anywhere? No scrap of Rome, no shard of Jerusalem, no stump of Fifth Avenue? It was all so barren down there: an empty stage, waiting for its next set to be built. He flew on a great arc across the jutting hump of Africa and on into what he supposed was southern Europe: the little vehicle did all the work, leaving him to doze or stare as he wished. Now and again he saw another flitterflitter pass by, far away, a dark distant winged teardrop outlined against the hard clarity of the sky. He wished there was some way of making radio contact with them, but he had no idea how to go about it. Not that he had anything he wanted to say; he wanted only to hear a human voice. He was utterly isolated. He might just as well have been the last living man on Earth. He closed his eyes and thought of Gioia.

"Like this?" Phillips asked. In an ivory-paneled oval room sixty stories above the softly glowing streets of New Chicago he touched a small cool plastic cannister to his upper lip and pressed the stud at its base. He heard a foaming sound, and then blue vapor rose to his nostrils.

"Yes," Cantilena said. "That's right."

He detected a faint aroma of cinnamon, cloves, and something that might almost have been broiled lobster. Then a spasm of dizziness hit him and visions rushed through his head: Gothic cathedrals, the Pyramids, Central Park under fresh snow, the harsh brick warrens of Mohenjo-daro, and fifty thousand other places all at once, a wild rollercoaster ride through space and time. It seemed to go on for centuries. But finally his head cleared and he looked about, blinking, realizing that the whole thing had taken only a moment. Cantilena still stood at his elbow. The other citizens in the room—fifteen, twenty of them—had scarcely moved. The strange little man with the celadon skin over by the far wall continued to stare at him.

"Well?" Cantilena asked. "What did you think?"

"Incredible."

"And very authentic. It's an actual New Chicagoan drug. The exact formula. Would you like another?"

"Not just yet," Phillips said uneasily. He swayed and had to struggle for his balance. Sniffing that stuff might not have been such a wise idea, he thought.

He had been in New Chicago a week, or perhaps it was two, and he was still suffering from the peculiar disorientation that that city always aroused in him. This was the fourth time he had come here, and it had been the same every time. New Chicago was the only one of the reconstructed cities of this world that in its original incarnation had existed *after* his own era. To him it was an outpost of the incomprehensible future; to the citizens it was a quaint simulacrum of the archaeological past. That paradox left him aswirl with impossible confusions and tensions.

What had happened to *old* Chicago was of course impossible for him to discover. Vanished without a trace, that was clear: No Water Tower, no Marina City, no Hancock Center, no Tribune building, not a fragment, not an atom. But it was hopeless to ask any of the million-plus inhabitants of New Chicago about their city's predecessor. They were only temporaries; they knew no more than they had to know, and all that they had to know was how to go through the motions of whatever it was that they did by way of creating the illusion that this was a real city. They had no need of knowing ancient history.

Nor was he likely to find out anything from a citizen, of course. Citizens did not seem to bother much about scholarly matters. Phillips had no reason to think that the world was anything other than an amusement park to them. Somewhere, certainly, there had to be those who specialized in the serious study of the lost civilizations of the past—for how, otherwise, would these uncanny reconstructed cities be brought into being? "The planners," he had once heard Nissandra or Aramayne say, "are already deep into their Byzantium research." But who were the planners? He had no idea. For all he knew, they were the robots. Perhaps the robots were the real masters of this whole era, who created the cities not primarily for the sake of amusing the citizens but in their own diligent attempt to comprehend the life of the world that had passed away. A wild speculation, yes; but not without some plausibility, he thought.

He felt oppressed by the party gaiety all about him. "I need some air," he said to Cantilena, and headed toward the window. It was the merest crescent, but a breeze came through. He looked out at the strange city below.

New Chicago had nothing in common with the old one but its name. They had built it, at least, along the western edge of a large inland lake that might even be Lake Michigan, although when he had flown over it had seemed broader and less elongated that the lake he remembered. The city itself was a lacy fantasy of slender pastel-hued buildings rising at odd angles and linked by a webwork of gently undulating aerial bridges. The streets were long parentheses that touched the lake at their northern and southern ends and arched gracefully westward in the middle. Between each of the great boulevards ran a track for public transportation—sleek aquamarine bubble-vehicles gliding on soundless wheels—and flanking each of the tracks were lush strips of park. It was beautiful, astonishingly so, but insubstantial. The whole thing seemed to have been contrived from sunbeams and silk.

A soft voice beside him said, "Are you becoming ill?"

Phillips glanced around. The celadon man stood beside him: a compact, precise person, vaguely Oriental in appearance. His skin was of a curious gray-green hue like no skin Phillips had ever seen, and it was extraordinarily smooth in texture, as though he were made of fine porcelain.

He shook his head. "Just a little queasy," he said. "This city always scrambles me."

"I suppose it can be disconcerting," the little man replied. His tone was furry and veiled, the inflection strange. There was something feline about him. He seemed sinewy, unyielding, almost menacing. "Visitor, are you?"

Phillips studied him for a moment. "Yes," he said.

"So am I, of course."

"Are you?"

"Indeed." The little man smiled. "What's your locus? Twentieth? Twenty-first at the latest, I'd say."

"I'm from 1984. 1984 A.D."

Another smile, a self-satisfied one. "Not a bad guess, then." A brisk tilt of the head. "Y'ang-Yeovil."

"Pardon me?" Phillips said.

"Y'ang-Yeovil. It is my name. Formerly Colonel Y'ang-Yeovil of the Third Septentriad."

"Is that on another planet?" asked Phillips, feeling a bit dazed.

"Oh, no, not at all," Y'ang-Yeovil said pleasantly. "This very world, I assure you. I am quite of human origin. Citizen of the Republic of Upper Han, native of the city of Port Ssu. And you—forgive me—your name—?"

"I'm sorry. Phillips. Charles Phillips. From New York City once upon a time."

"Ah, New York!" Y'ang-Yeovil's face lit with a glimmer of recognition that quickly faded. "New York—New York—it was very famous, that I know—"

This is strange, Phillips thought. He felt greater compassion for poor bewildered Francis Willoughby now. This man comes from a time so far beyond my own that he barely knows of New York—he must be a contemporary of the real New Chicago, in fact; I wonder whether he finds this version authentic—and yet to the citizens this Y'ang-Yeovil too is just a primitive, a curio out of antiquity—

"New York was the largest city of the United States of America," Phillips said.

"Of course. Yes. Very famous."

"But virtually forgotten by the time the Republic of Upper Han came into existence, I gather."

Y'ang-Yeovil said, looking uncomfortable, "There were disturbances between your time and mine. But by no means should you take from my words the impression that your city was—"

Sudden laughter resounded across the room. Five or six newcomers had arrived at the party. Phillips stared, gasped, gaped. Surely that was Stengard—and Aramayne beside him—and that other woman, half-hidden behind them—

"If you'll pardon me a moment—" Phillips said, turning abruptly away from Y'ang-Yeovil. "Please excuse me. Someone just coming in—a person I've been trying to find ever since—"

He hurried toward her.

"Gioia?" he called. "Gioia, it's me! Wait! Wait!"

Stengard was in the way. Aramayne, turning to take a handful of the little vapor-sniffers from Cantilena, blocked him also. Phillips pushed through them as though they were not there. Gioia, halfway out the door, halted and looked toward him like a frightened deer.

"Don't go," he said. He took her hand in his.

He was startled by her appearance. How long had it been since their strange parting on that night of mysteries in Chang-an? A year? A year and a half? So he believed. Or had he lost all track of time? Were his perceptions of the passing of the months in this world that unreliable? She seemed at least ten or fifteen years older. Maybe she really was; maybe the years had been passing for him here as in a dream, and he had never known it. She looked strained, faded, worn. Out of a thinner and strangely altered face her eyes blazed at him almost defiantly, as though saying, *See? See how ugly I have become?*

He said, "I've been hunting for you for—I don't know how long it's been, Gioia. In Mohenjo, in Timbuctoo, now here. I want to be with you again."

"It isn't possible."

"Belilala explained everything to me in Mohenjo. I know that you're a short-timer—I know what that means, Gioia. But what of it? So you're beginning to age a little. So what? So you'll only have three or four hundred years, instead of forever. Don't you think I know what it means to be a short-timer? I'm just a simple ancient man of the twentieth century, remember? Sixty, seventy, eighty years is all we would get. You and I suffer from the same malady, Gioia. That's what drew you to me in the first place. I'm certain of that. That's why we belong with each other now. However much time we have, we can spend the rest of it together, don't you see?"

"You're the one who doesn't see, Charles," she said softly.

"Maybe. Maybe I still don't understand a damned thing about this place. Except that you and I—that I love you—that I think you love me—"

"I love you, yes. But you don't understand. It's precisely because I love you that you and I—you and I can't—"

With a despairing sigh she slid her hand free of his grasp. He reached for her again, but she shook him off and backed up quickly into the corridor.

"Gioia?"

"Please," she said. "No. I would never have come here if I knew you were here. Don't come after me. Please. Please."

She turned and fled.

He stood looking after her for a long moment. Cantilena and Aramayne appeared, and smiled at him as if nothing at all had happened. Cantilena offered him a vial of some sparkling amber fluid. He refused with a brusque gesture. Where do I go now, he wondered? What do I do? He wandered back into the party.

Y'ang-Yeovil glided to his side. "You are in great distress," the little man murmured.

Phillips glared. "Let me be."

"Perhaps I could be of some help."

"There's no help possible," said Phillips. He swung about and plucked one of the vials from a tray and gulped its contents. It made him feel as if there were two of him, standing on either side of Y'ang-Yeovil. He gulped another. Now there were four of him.

"I'm in love with a citizen," he blurted. It seemed to him that he was speaking in chorus.

"Love. Ah. And does she love you?"

"So I thought. So I think. But she's a short-timer. Do you know what that means? She's not immortal like the others. She ages. She's beginning to look old. And so she's been running away from me. She doesn't want me to see her changing. She thinks it'll disgust me, I suppose. I tried to remind her just now that I'm not immortal either, that she and I could grow old together, but she—"

"Oh, no," Y'ang-Yeovil said quietly. "Why do you think you will age? Have you grown any older in all the time you have been here?"

Phillips was nonplussed. "Of course I have. I—I—"

"Have you?" Y'ang-Yeovil smiled. "Here. Look at yourself." He did something intricate with his fingers and a shimmering zone of mirror-like light appeared between them. Phillips stared at his reflection. A youthful face stared back at him. It was true, then. He had simply not thought about it. How many years had he spent in this world? The time had simply slipped by: a great deal of time, though he could not calculate how much. They did not seem to keep close count of it here, nor had he. But it must have been many years, he thought. All that endless travel up and down the globe—so many cities had come and gone—Rio, Rome Asgard, those were the first three that came to mind—and there were others; he could hardly remember every one. Years. His face had no changed at all. Time had worked its harshness on Gioia, yes, but not on him.

"I don't understand," he said. "Why am I not aging?"

"Because you are not real," said Y'ang-Yeovil. "Are you unaware of that?"

Phillips blinked. "Not—real?"

"Did you think you were lifted bodily out of your own time?" the little man asked. "Ah, no, no, there is no way for them to do such a thing. We are not actual time travelers: not you, not I, not any of the visitors. I thought you were aware of that. But perhaps your era is too early for proper understanding of these things. We are very cleverly done, my friend. We are ingenious constructs, marvelously stuffed with the thoughts and attitudes and events of our own times. We are their finest achievement, you know: far more complex even than one of these cities. We are a step beyond the temporaries—more than a step, a great deal more. They do only what they are instructed to do, and their range is very narrow. They are nothing but machines, really. Whereas we are autonomous. We move about by our own will; we think, we talk, we even, so it seems, fall in love. But we will not age. How could we age? We are not real. We are mere artificial webworks of mental responses. We are mere illusions, done so well that we deceive even ourselves. You did not know that? Indeed, you did not know?"

He was airborne, touching destination buttons at random. Somehow he found himself heading back toward Timbuctoo. *This city is closed. This is not a place any longer.* It did not matter to him. Why should anything matter?

Fury and a choking sense of despair rose within him. I am software, Phillips thought. I am nothing but software.

Not real. Very cleverly done. An ingenious construct. A mere illusion. No trace of Timbuctoo was visible from the air. He landed anyway. The gray sandy earth was smooth, unturned, as though there had never been anything there. A few robots were still about, handling whatever final chores were required in the shutting-down of a city. Two of them scuttled up to him. Huge bland gleaming silver-skinned insects, not friendly.

"There is no city here," they said. "This is not a permissible place."

"Permissible by whom?"

"There is no reason for you to be here."

"There's no reason for me to be anywhere," Phillips said. The robots stirred, made uneasy humming sounds and ominous clicks, waved their antennae about. They seem troubled, he thought. They seem to dislike my attitude. Perhaps I run some risk of being taken off to the home for unruly software for debugging. "I'm leaving now," he told them. "Thank you. Thank you very much." He backed away from them and climbed into his flitterflitter. He touched more destination buttons.

We move about by our own will. We think, we talk, we even fall in love.

He landed in Chang-an. This time there was no reception committee waiting for him at the Gate of Brilliant Virtue. The city seemed larger and more resplendent: new pagodas, new palaces.

It felt like winter: a chilly cutting wind was blowing. The sky was cloudless and dazzlingly bright. At the steps of the Silver Terrace he encountered Francis Willoughby, a great hulking figure in magnificent brocaded robes, with two dainty little temporaries, pretty as jade statuettes, engulfed in his arms. "Miracles and wonders! The silly lunatic fellow is here too!" Willoughby roared. "Look, look, we are come to far Cathay, you and I!"

We are nowhere, Phillips thought. We are mere illusions, done so well that we deceive even ourselves.

To Willoughby he said, "You look like an emperor in those robes, Francis."

"Aye, like Prester John!" Willoughby cried. "Like Tamburlaine himself! Aye, am I not majestic?" He slapped Phillips gaily on the shoulder, a rough playful poke that spun him halfway about, coughing and wheezing. "We flew in the air, as the eagles do, as the demons do, as the angels do! Soared like angels! Like angels!" He came close, looming over Phillips. "I would have gone to England, but the wench Belilala said there was an enchantment on me that would keep me from England just now; and so we voyaged to Cathay. Tell me this, fellow, will you go witness for me when we see England again? Swear that all that has befallen us did in truth befall? For I fear they will say I am as mad as Marco Polo, when I tell them of flying to Cathay."

"One madman backing another?" Phillips asked. "What can I tell you? You still think you'll reach England, do you?" Rage rose to the surface in him, bubbling hot. "Ah, Francis, Francis, do you know your Shakespeare? Did you go to the plays? We aren't real. *We aren't real*. We are such stuff as dreams are made of, the two of us. That's all we are. O brave new world! What England? Where? There's no England. There's no Francis Willoughby. There's no Charles Phillips. What we are is—"

"Let him be, Charles," a cool voice cut in.

He turned. Belilala, in the robes of an empress, coming down the steps of the Silver Terrace.

"I know the truth," he said bitterly. "Y'ang-Yeovil told me. The visitor from the twenty-fifth century. I saw him in New Chicago."

"Did you see Gioia there too?" Belilala asked.

"Briefly. She looks much older."

"Yes. I know. She was here recently."

"And has gone on, I suppose?"

"To Mohenjo again, yes. Go after her, Charles. Leave poor Francis alone. I told her to wait for you. I told her that she needs you, and you need her."

"Very kind of you. But what good is it, Belilala? I don't even exist. And she's going to die."

"You exist. How can you doubt that you exist? You feel, don't you? You suffer. You love. You love Gioia: is that not so? And you are loved by Gioia. Would Gioia love what is not real?"

"You think she loves me?"

"I know she does. Go to her, Charles. Go. I told her to wait for you in Mohenjo."

Phillips nodded numbly. What was there to lose?

"Go to her," said Belilala again. "Now."

"Yes," Phillips said. "I'll go now." He turned to Willoughby. "If ever we meet in London, friend, I'll testify for you. Fear nothing. All will be well, Francis."

He left them and set his course for Mohenjo-daro, half expecting to find the robots already tearing it down. Mohenjo-daro was still there, no lovelier than before. He went to the baths, thinking he might find Gioia there. She was not; but he came upon Nissandra, Stengard, Fenimon. "She has gone to Alexandria," Fenimon told him. "She wants to see it one last time, before they close it."

"They're almost ready to open Constantinople," Stengard explained. "The capital of Byzantium, you know, the great city by the Golden Horn. They'll take Alexandria away, you understand, when Byzantium opens. They say it's going to be marvelous. We'll see you there for the opening, naturally?"

"Naturally," Phillips said.

He flew to Alexandria. He felt lost and weary. All this is hopeless folly, He told himself. I am nothing but a puppet jerking about on its strings. But somewhere above the shining breast of the Arabian Sea the deeper implications of something that Belilala had said to him started to sink in, and he felt his bitterness, his rage, his despair, all suddenly beginning to leave him. *You exist. How can you doubt that you exist? Would Gioia love what is not real?* Of course. Of course. Y'ang-Yeovil had been wrong: visitors were something more than mere illusions. Indeed Y'ang-Yeovil had voiced the truth of their condition without understanding what he was really saying: *We think, we talk, we fall in love*. Yes. That was the heart of the situation. The visitors might be artificial, but they were not unreal. Belilala had been trying to tell him that just the other night. *You suffer. You love. You love Gioia. Would Gioia love what is not real?* Surely he was real, or at any rate real enough. What he was was something strange, something that would probably have been all but incomprehensible to the twentieth-century people whom he had been designed to simulate. But that did not mean that he was unreal. Did one have to be of woman born to be real? No. No. No. His kind of reality was a sufficient reality. He had no need to be ashamed of it. And, understanding that, he understood that Gioia did not need to grow old and die. There was a way by which she could be saved, if only she would embrace it. If only she would.

When he landed in Alexandria he went immediately to the hotel on the slopes of the Paneium where they had stayed on their first visit, so very long ago; and there she was, sitting quietly on a patio with a view of the harbor and the Lighthouse. There was something calm and resigned about the way she sat. She had given up. She did not even have the strength to flee from him any longer.

"Gioia," he said gently.

She looked older than she had in New Chicago. Her face was drawn and sallow and her eyes seemed sunken; and she was not even bothering these days to deal with the white strands that stood out in stark contrast against the darkness of her hair. He sat down beside her and put his hand over hers, and looked out toward the obelisks, the palaces, the temples, the lighthouse. At length he said, "I know what I really am, now."

"Do you, Charles?" She sounded very far away.

"In my era we called it software. All I am is a set of commands, responses, cross-references, operating some sort of artificial body. It's infinitely better software than we could have imagined. But we were only just beginning to learn, after all. They pumped me full of twentieth-century reflexes. The right moods, the right appetites, the right irrationalities, the right sort of combativeness. *Somebody* knows a lot about what it was like to be a twentieth-century man. They did a good job with Willoughby, too, all that Elizabethan rhetoric and swagger. And I suppose they got Y'ang-Yeovil right. *He* seems to think so: who better to judge? The twenty-fifth century, the Republic of Upper Han, people with gray-green skin, half Chinese and half Martian for all I know.

Somebody knows. Somebody here is very good at programming, Gioia."

She was not looking at him.

"I feel frightened, Charles," she said in that same distant way.

"Of me? Of the things I'm saying?"

"No, not of you. Don't you see what has happened to me?"

"I see you. There are changes."

"I lived a long time wondering when the changes would begin. I thought maybe they wouldn't, not really. Who wants to believe they'll get old? But it started when we were in Alexandria that first time. In Chang-an it got much worse. And now—now—"

He said abruptly, "Stengard tells me they'll be opening Constantinople very soon."

"So?"

"Don't you want to be there when it opens?"

"I'm becoming old and ugly, Charles."

"We'll go to Constantinople together. We'll leave tomorrow, eh? What do you say? We'll charter a boat. It's a quick little hop, right across the Mediterranean. Sailing to Byzantium! There was a poem, you know, in my time. Not forgotten, I guess, because they've programmed it into me. All these thousands of years, and someone still remembers old Yeats. *The young in one another's arms, birds in the trees*. Come with me to Byzantium, Gioia."

She shrugged. "Looking like this? Getting more hideous every hour? While *they* stay young forever? While *you*—" She faltered; her voice cracked; she fell silent.

"Finish the sentence, Gioia."

"Please. Let me alone."

"You were going to say, 'While *you* stay young forever too, Charles,' isn't that it? You knew all along that I was never going to change. I didn't know that, but you did."

"Yes, I knew. I pretended that it wasn't true—that as I aged, you'd age too. It was very foolish of me. In Chang-an, when I first began to see the real signs of it—that was when I realized I couldn't stay with you any longer. Because I'd look at you, always young, always remaining the same age, and I'd look at myself, and—" She gestured, palms upward. "So I gave you to Belilala and ran away."

"All so unnecessary, Gioia."

"I didn't think it was."

"But you don't have to grow old. Not if you don't want to!"

"Don't be cruel, Charles," she said tonelessly. "There's no way of escaping what I have."

"But there is," he said.

"You know nothing about these things."

"Not very much, no," he said. "But I see how it can be done. Maybe it's a primitive simple-minded twentieth-century sort of solution, but I think it ought to work. I've been playing with the idea ever since I left Mohenjo. Tell me this, Gioia: Why can't you go to them, to the programmers, to the artificers, the planners, whoever they are, the ones who create the cities and the temporaries and the visitors. And have yourself made into something like me!"

She looked up, startled. "What are you saying?"

"They can cobble up a twentieth-century man out of nothing more than fragmentary records and make him plausible, can't they? Or an Elizabethan, or anyone else of any era at all, and he's authentic, he's convincing. So why couldn't they do an even better job with you? Produce a Gioia so real that even Gioia can't tell the difference? But a Gioia that will never age—a Gioia-construct, a Gioia-program, a visitor-Gioia! Why not? Tell me why not, Gioia."

She was trembling. "I've never heard of doing any such thing!"

"But don't you think it's possible?"

"How would I know?"

"Of course it's possible. If they can create visitors, they can take a citizen and duplicate her in such a way that—"

"It's never been done. I'm sure of it. I can't imagine any citizen agreeing to any such thing. To give up the body—to let yourself be turned into—into—"

She shook her head, but it seemed to be a gesture of astonishment as much as of negation.

He said, "Sure. To give up the body. Your natural body, your aging, shrinking, deteriorating short-timer body. What's so awful about that?"

She was very pale. "This is craziness, Charles. I don't want to talk about it any more."

"It doesn't sound crazy to me."

"You can't possibly understand."

"Can't I? I can certainly understand being afraid to die. I don't have a lot of trouble understanding what it's like to be one of the few aging people in a world where nobody grows old. What I can't understand is why you aren't even willing to consider the possibility that—"

"No," she said. "I tell you, it's crazy. They'd laugh at me."

"Who?"

"All of my friends. Hawk, Stengard, Aramayne—" Once again she would not look at him. "They can be very cruel, without even realizing it. They despise anything that seems ungraceful to them, anything sweaty and desperate and cowardly. Citizens don't do sweaty things, Charles. And that's how this will seem. Assuming it can be done at all. They'll be terribly patronising. Oh, they'll be sweet to me, yes, dear Gioia, how wonderful for you, Gioia, but when I turn my back they'll laugh. They'll say the most wicked things about me. I couldn't bear that."

"They can afford to laugh," Phillips said. "It's easy to be brave and cool about dying when you know you're going to live forever. How very fine for them; but why should you be the only one to grow old and die? And they won't laugh, anyway. They're not as cruel as you think. Shallow, maybe, but not cruel. They'll be glad that you've found a way to save yourself. At the very least, they won't have to feel guilty about you any longer, and that's bound to please them. You can—"

"Stop it," she said.

She rose, walked to the railing of the patio, stared out toward the sea. He came up behind her. Red sails in the harbor, sunlight glittering along the sides of the Lighthouse, the palaces of the Ptolemies stark white against the sky. Lightly he rested his hand on her shoulder. She twitched as if to pull away from him, but remained where she was.

"Then I have another idea," he said quietly. "If you won't go to the planners, *I* will. Reprogram me, I'll say. Fix things so that I start to age at the same rate you do. It'll be more authentic, anyway, if I'm supposed to be playing the part of a twentieth-century man. Over the years I'll very gradually get some lines in my face, my hair will turn gray, I'll walk a little more slowly—we'll grow old together, Gioia. To hell with your lovely immortal friends. We'll have each other. We won't need them."

She swung around. Her eyes were wide with horror.

"Are you serious, Charles?"

"Of course."

"No," she murmured. "No. Everything you've said to me today is monstrous nonsense. Don't you realize that?"

He reached for her hand and enclosed her fingertips in his. "All I'm trying to do is find some way for you and me to—"

"Don't say any more," she said. "Please." Quickly, as though drawing back from a suddenly flaring flame, she tugged her fingers free of his and put her hand behind her. Though his face was just inches from hers he felt an immense chasm opening between them. They stared at one another for a moment; then she moved deftly to his left, darted around him, and ran from the patio.

Stunned, he watched her go, down the long marble corridor and out of sight. It was folly to give pursuit, he thought. She was lost to him: that was clear, that was beyond any question. She was terrified of him. Why cause her even more anguish? But somehow he found himself running through the halls of the hotel, along the winding garden path, into the cool green groves of the Paneium. He thought he saw her on the portico of Hadrian's palace, but when he got there the echoing stone halls were empty. To a temporary that was sweeping the steps he said, "Did you see a woman come this way?" A blank sullen stare was his only answer.

Phillips cursed and turned away.

"Gioia?" he called. "Wait! Come back!"

Was that her, going into the Library? He rushed past the startled mumbling librarians and sped through the stacks, peering beyond the mounds of double-handled scrolls into the shadowy corridors. "Gioia? *Gioia*!" It was a desecration, bellowing like that in this quiet place. He scarcely cared.

Emerging by a side door, he loped down to the harbor. The Lighthouse! Terror enfolded him. She might already be a hundred steps up that ramp, heading for the parapet from which she meant to fling herself into the sea. Scattering citizens and temporaries as if they were straws, he ran within. Up he went, never pausing for breath, though his synthetic lungs were screaming for respite, his ingeniously designed heart was desperately pounding. On the first balcony he imagined he caught a glimpse of her, but he circled it without finding her. Onward, upward. He went to the top, to the beacon chamber itself: no Gioia. Had she jumped? Had she gone down one ramp while he was ascending the other? He clung to the rim and looked out, down, searching the base of the Lighthouse, the rocks offshore, the causeway. No Gioia. I will find her somewhere, he thought. I will keep going until I find her. He went running down the ramp, calling her name. He reached ground level and sprinted back toward the center of town. Where next? The temple of Poseidon? The tomb of Cleopatra?

He paused in the middle of Canopus Street, groggy and dazed.

"Charles?" she said.

"Where are you?"

"Right here. Beside you." She seemed to materialize from the air. Her face was unflushed, her robe bore no trace of perspiration. Had he been chasing a phantom through the city? She came to him and took his hand and said, softly, tenderly, "Were you really serious, about having them make you age?"

"If there's no other way, yes."

"The other way is so frightening, Charles."

"Is it?"

"You can't understand how much."

"More frightening than growing old? Than dying?"

"I don't know," she said. "I suppose not. The only thing I'm sure of is that I don't want you to get old, Charles."

"But I won't have to. Will I?" He stared at her.

"No," she said. "You won't have to. Neither of us will."

Phillips smiled. "We should get away from here," he said after a while. "Let's go across to Byzantium, yes, Gioia? We'll show up in Constantinople for the opening. Your friends will be there. We'll tell them what you've decided to do. They'll know how to arrange it. Someone will."

"It sounds so strange," said Gioia. "To turn myself into—into a visitor. A visitor in my own world?"

"That's what you've always been, though."

"I suppose. In a way. But at least I've been *real* up to now."

"Whereas I'm not?"

"Are you, Charles?"

"Yes. Just as real as you. I was angry at first, when I found out the truth about myself. But I came to accept it. Somewhere between Mohenjo and here, I came to see that it was all right to be what I am: that I perceive things, I form ideas, I draw conclusions. I am very well designed, Gioia. I can't tell the difference between being what I am and being completely alive, and to me that's being real enough. I think, I feel, I experience joy and pain. I'm as real as

I need to be. And you will be too. You'll never stop being Gioia, you know. It's only your body that you'll cast away, the body that played such a terrible joke on you anyway." He brushed her cheek with his hand. "It was all said for us before, long ago:

Once out of nature I shall never take
My bodily form from any natural thing,
But such a form as Grecian goldsmiths make
Of hammered gold and gold enamelling
To keep a drowsy Emperor awake—"

"Is that the same poem?" she asked.

"The same poem, yes. The ancient poem that isn't quite forgotten yet."

"Finish it, Charles."

—"Or set upon a golden bough to sing
To lords and ladies of Byzantium
Of what is past, or passing, or to come."

"How beautiful. What does it mean?"

"That it isn't necessary to be mortal. That we can allow ourselves to be gathered into the artifice of eternity, that we can be transformed, that we can move on beyond the flesh. Yeats didn't mean it in quite the way I do—he wouldn't have begun to comprehend what we're talking about, not a word of it—and yet, and yet—the underlying truth is the same. Live, Gioia! With me!" He turned to her and saw color coming into her pallid cheeks. "It does make sense, what I'm suggesting, doesn't it? You'll attempt it, won't you? Whoever makes the visitors can be induced to remake you. Right? What do you think: can they, Gioia?"

She nodded in a barely perceptible way. "I think so," she said faintly. "It's very strange. But I think it ought to be possible. Why not, Charles? Why not?"

"Yes," he said. "Why not?"

In the morning they hired a vessel in the harbor, a low sleek pirogue with a blood-red sail, skippered by a rascally-looking temporary whose smile was irresistible. Phillips shaded his eyes and peered northward across the sea. He thought he could almost make out the shape of the great city sprawling on its seven hills, Constantine's New Rome beside the Golden Horn, the mighty dome of Hagia Sophia, the somber walls of the citadel, the palaces and churches, the Hippodrome, Christ in glory rising above all else in brilliant mosaic streaming with light.

"Byzantium," Phillips said. "Take us there the shortest and quickest way."

"It is my pleasure," said the boatman with unexpected grace.

Gioia smiled. He had not seen her looking so vibrantly alive since the night of the imperial feast in Chang-an. He reached for her hand—her slender fingers were quivering lightly—and helped her into the boat.

TRINITY

Nancy Kress

"Lord, I believe; help Thou mine unbelief!"
—Mark 9:24

At first I didn't recognize Devrie.

Devrie—I didn't recognize *Devrie*. Astonished at myself, I studied the wasted figure standing in the middle of the bare reception room: arms like wires, clavicle sharply outlined, head shaved, dressed in that ugly long tent of light-weight gray. God knew what her legs looked like under it. Then she smiled, and it was Devrie.

"You look like shit."

"Hello. Seena. Come on in."

"I am in."

"Barely. It's not catching, you know."

"Stupidity fortunately isn't," I said and closed the door behind me. The small room was too hot; Devrie would need the heat, of course, with almost no fat left to insulate her bones and organs. Next to her I felt huge, although I am not. Huge, hairy, sloppy-breasted.

"Thank you for not wearing bright colors. They do affect me."

"Anything for a sister," I said, mocking the childhood formula, the old sentiment. But Devrie was too quick to think it was only mockery; in that, at least, she had not changed.

She clutched my arm and her fingers felt like chains, or talons.

"You found him. Seena, you found him."

"I found him."

"Tell me," she whispered.

"Sit down first, before you fall over. God, Devrie, don't you eat at all?"

"*Tell me.*" she said. So I did.

Devrie Caroline Konig had admitted herself to the Institute of the Biological Hope on the Caribbean island of Dominica eleven months ago, in Late November of 2017, when her age was 23 years and 4 months. I am precise about this because it is all I can be sure of. I need the precision. The Institute of the Biological Hope is not precise; it is a mongrel, part research laboratory in brain sciences, part monastery, part school for training in the discipline of the mind. That made my baby sister guinea pig, postulant, freshman. She had always been those things, but, until now, sequentially. Apparently so had many other people, for when eccentric Nobel Prize winner James Arthur Bohentin had founded his Institute, he had been able to fund it, although precariously. But in that it did not differ from most private scientific research centers.

Or most monasteries.

I wanted Devrie out of the Institute of Biological Hope.

"It's located on Dominica," I had said sensibly—what an ass I had been—to an unwasted Devrie a year ago, "because the research procedures there fall outside United States laws concerning the safety of research subjects. Doesn't that *tell* you something, Devrie? Doesn't that at least give you pause? In New York, it would be illegal to do to anyone what Bohentin does to his people."

"Do you know him?" she had asked.

"I have met him. Once."

"What is he like?"

"Like stone."

Devrie shrugged, and smiled. "All the participants in the Institute are willing. Eager."

"That doesn't make it ethical for Bohentin to destroy them. Ethical or legal."

"It's legal on Dominica. And in thinking you know better than the participants what they should risk their own lives for, aren't you playing God?"

"Better me than some untrained fanatic who offers himself up like an exalted Viking hero, expecting Valhalla."

"You're an intellectual snob, Seena."

"I never denied it."

"Are you sure you aren't really objecting not to the Institute's dangers but to its purpose? Isn't the 'Hope' part what really bothers you?"

"I don't think scientific method and pseudo-religious mush mix, no. I never did. I don't think it leads to a perception of God."

"The holotank tapes indicate it leads to a perception of *something* the brain hasn't encountered before," Devrie said, and for a moment I was silent.

I was once, almost, a biologist. I was aware of the legitimate studies that formed the basis for Bohentin's megalomania: the brain wave changes that accompany anorexia nervosa, sensory deprivation, biological feedback, and neurotransmitter stimulants. I have read the historical accounts, some merely pathetic but some disturbingly not, of the Christian mystics who achieved rapture through the mortification of the flesh and the Eastern mystics who achieved anesthesia through the control of the mind, of the faith healers who succeeded, of the carcinomas shrunk through trained will. I knew of the research of focused clairvoyance during orgasm, and of what happens when neurotransmitter number and speed are increased chemically.

And I knew all that was known about the twin trance.

Fifteen years earlier, as a doctoral student in biology, I had spent one summer replicating Sunderwirth's pioneering study of drug-enhanced telepathy in identical twins. My results were positive, except that within six months all eight of my research subjects had died. So had Sunderwirth's. Twin-trance research became the cloning controversy of the new decade, with the same panicky cycle of public outcry, legal restrictions, religious misunderstandings, fear, and demagoguery. When I received the phone call that the last of my subjects was dead—cardiac arrest, no history of heart disease, forty-three Goddamn years old—I locked myself in my apartment, with the lights off and my father's papers clutched in my hand, for three days. Then I resigned from the neurology department and became an entomologist. There is no pain in classifying dead insects.

"There is something *there*," Devrie had repeated. She was holding the letter sent to our father, whom someone at the Institute had not heard was dead. "It says the holotank tapes—"

"So there's something there," I said. "So the tanks are picking up some strange radiation. Why call it 'God'?"

"Why not call it God?"

"Why not call it Rover? Even if I grant you that the tape pattern looks like a presence—which I don't—you have no way of knowing that Bohentin's phantom isn't, say, some totally ungodlike alien being."

"But neither do I know that it *is*."

"Devrie—"

She had smiled and put her hands on my shoulders. She had—has, has always had—a very sweet smile. "Seena. *Think*. If the Institute can prove rationally that God exists—can prove it to the intellectual mind, the doubting Thomases who need something concrete to study . . . faith that doesn't need to be taken on faith . . ."

She wore her mystical face, a glowing softness that made me want to shake the silliness out of her. Instead I made some clever riposte, some sarcasm I no longer remember, and reached out to ruffle her hair. Big-sisterly, patronizing, thinking I could deflate her rapturous interest with the pinprick of ridicule. God, I was an ass. It hurts to remember how big an ass I was.

A month and a half later Devrie committed herself and half her considerable inheritance to the Institute of the Biological Hope.

"Tell me," Devrie whispered. The Institute had no windows; outside I had seen grass, palm trees, butterflies in the sunshine, but inside here in the bare gray room there was nowhere to look but at her face.

"He's a student in a Master's program at a third-rate college in New Hampshire. He was adopted when he was two, nearly three, in March of 1997. Before that he was in a government-run children's home. In Boston, of course. The adopting family, as far as I can discover, never was told he was anything but one more toddler given up by somebody for adoption."

"Wait a minute," Devrie said. "I need . . . a minute."

She had turned paler, and her hands trembled. I had recited the information as if it were no more than an exhibit listing at my museum. Of course she was rattled. I wanted her rattled. I wanted her out.

Lowering herself to the floor, Devrie sat cross-legged and closed her eyes. Concentration spread over her face, but a concentration so serene it barely deserved that name. Her breathing slowed, her color freshened, and when she opened her eyes, they had the rested energy of a person who has just slept eight hours in mountain air. Her face even looked plumper, and an EEG, I guessed, would show damn near alpha waves. In her year at the Institute she must have mastered quite an array of biofeedback techniques to do that, so fast and with such a malnourished body.

"Very impressive," I said sourly.

"Seena—have you seen him?"

"No. All this is from sealed records."

"How did you get into the records?"

"Medical and governmental friends."

"Who?"

"What do you care, as long as I found out what you wanted to know?"

She was silent. I knew she would never ask me if I had obtained her information legally or illegally; it would not occur to her to ask. Devrie, being Devrie, would assume it had all been generously offered by my modest museum connections and our dead father's immodest research connections. She would be wrong.

"How old is he now?"

"Twenty-four years last month. They must have used your two-month tissue sample."

"Do you think Daddy knew where the . . . baby went?"

"Yes. Look at the timing—the child was normal and healthy, yet he wasn't adopted until he was nearly three. The researchers kept track of him, all right, they kept all six clones in a government-controlled home where they could monitor their development as long as humanely possible. The same-sex clones were released for adoption after a year, but they hung onto the cross-sex ones until they reached an age where they would become harder to adopt. They undoubtedly wanted to study *them* as long as they could. And even after the kids were released for adoption, the researchers held off publishing until April, 1998, remember. By the time the storm broke, the babies were out of its path, and anonymous."

"And the last," Devrie said.

"And the last," I agreed, although of course the researchers hadn't foreseen *that*. So few in the scientific community had foreseen that. Offense against God and man, Satan's work, natter natter. Watching my father's suddenly stooped shoulders and stricken eyes, I had thought how ugly public revulsion could be and had nobly resolved—how had I thought of it then? So long ago—resolved to snatch the banner of pure science from my fallen father's hand. Another time that I had been an ass. Five years later, when it had been my turn to feel the ugly scorching of public revulsion, I had broken, left neurological research, and fled down the road that led to the Museum of Natural History, where I was the curator of ants fossilized in amber and moths pinned securely under permaplex.

"The other four clones," Devrie said, "the ones from that university in California that published almost simultaneously with Daddy—"

"I don't know. I didn't even try to ask. It was hard enough in Cambridge."

"Me," Devrie said wonderingly. "He's *me*."

"Oh, for—Devrie, he's your twin. No more than that. No—actually less than that. He shares your genetic material exactly as an identical twin would, except for the Y chromosome, but he shares none of the congenital or environmental influences that shaped your personality. There's no mystical replication of spirit in cloning. He's merely a twin who got born eleven months late!"

She looked at me with luminous amusement. I didn't like the look. On that fleshless face, the skin stretched so taut that the delicate bones beneath were as visible as the veins of a moth wing, her amusement looked ironic. Yet Devrie was never ironic. Gentle, passionate, trusting, a little stupid, she was not capable of irony. It was beyond her, just as it was beyond her to wonder why I, who had fought her entering the Institute of the Biological Hope, had brought her this information now. Her amusement was one-layered, and trusting.

God's fools, the Middle Ages had called them.

"Devrie," I said, and heard my own voice unexpectedly break, "leave here. It's physically not safe. What are you down to, ten percent body fat? Eight? Look at yourself, you can't hold body heat, your palms are dry, you can't move quickly without getting dizzy. Hypotension. What's your heartbeat? Do you still menstruate? It's insane."

She went on smiling at me. God's fools don't need menstruation. "Come with me, Seena. I want to show you the Institute."

"I don't want to see it."

"Yes. This visit you should see it."

"Why this visit?"

"Because you *are* going to help me get my clone to come here, aren't you? Or else why did you go to all the trouble of locating him?"

I didn't answer. She still didn't see it.

Devrie said, "'Anything for a sister.' But you were always more like a mother to me than a sister." She took my hand and pulled herself off the floor. So had I pulled her up to take her first steps, the day after our mother died in a plane crash at Orly. Now Devrie's hand felt cold. I imprisoned it and counted the pulse.

"Bradycardia."

But she wasn't listening.

The Institute was a shock. I had anticipated the laboratories: monotonous gray walls, dim light, heavy soundproofing, minimal fixtures in the ones used for sensory dampening; high-contrast textures and colors, strobe lights, quite good sound equipment in those for sensory arousal. There was much that Devrie, as subject rather than researcher, didn't have authority to show me, but I deduced much from what I did see. The dormitories, divided by sex, were on the sensory-dampening side. The subjects slept in small cells, ascetic and chaste, that reminded me of an abandoned Carmelite convent I had once toured in Belgium. That was the shock: the physical plant felt scientific, but the atmosphere did not.

There hung in the gray corridors a wordless peace, a feeling so palpable I could feel it clogging my lungs. No. "Peace" was the wrong word. Say "peace" and the picture is pastoral, lazy sunshine and dreaming woods. This was not like that at all. The research subjects—students? postulants?—lounged in the corridors outside closed labs, waiting for the next step in their routine. Both men and women were anorectic, both wore gray bodysuits or caftans, both were fined down to an otherworldly ethereality when seen from a distance and a malnourished asexuality when seen up close. They talked among themselves in low voices, sitting with backs against the wall or stretched full-length on the carpeted floor, and on all their faces I saw the same luminous patience, the same certainty of being very near to something exciting that they nonetheless could wait for calmly, as long as necessary.

"They look," I said to Devrie, "as if they're waiting to take an exam they already know they'll ace."

She smiled. "Do you think so? I always think of us as travelers waiting for a plane, boarding passes stamped for Eternity."

She was actually serious. But she didn't in fact wear the same expression as the others; hers was far more intense. If they were travelers, she wanted to pilot.

The lab door opened and the students brought themselves to their feet. Despite their languid movements, they looked sharp: sharp protruding clavicles, bony chins, angular unpadded elbows that could chisel stone.

"This is my hour for biofeedback manipulation of drug effects," Devrie said. "Please come watch."

"I'd sooner watch you whip yourself in a twelfth-century monastery."

Devrie's eye widened, then again lightened with that luminous amusement. "It's for the same end, isn't it? But they had such unsystematic means. Poor struggling God-searchers. I wonder how many of them made it."

I wanted to strike her. "*Devrie—*"

"If not biofeedback, what would you like to see?"

"You out of here."

"What else?"

There was only one thing: the holotanks. I struggled with the temptation, and lost. The two tanks stood in the middle of a roomy lab carpeted with thick gray matting and completely enclosed in a Faraday cage. That Devrie had a key to the lab was my first clue that my errand for her had been known, and discussed, by someone higher in the Institute. Research subjects do not carry keys to the most delicate brain-perception equipment in the world. For this equipment Bohentin had received his Nobel.

The two tanks, independent systems, stood as high as my shoulder. The ones I had used fifteen years ago had been smaller.

Each of these was a cube, opaque on its bottom half, which held the sensing apparatus, computerized simulators, and recording equipment; clear on its top half, which was filled with the transparent fluid out of whose molecules the simulations would form. A separate sim would form for each subject, as the machine sorted and mapped all the electromagnetic radiation received and processed by each brain. *All* that each brain perceived, not only the visuals; the holograph equipment was capable of picking up all wavelengths that the brain did, and of displaying their brain-processed analogues as three-dimensional images floating in a clear womb. When all other possible sources of radiation were filtered out except for the emanations from the two subjects themselves, what the sims showed was what kinds of activity were coming from—and hence going on in—the other's brain. That was why it worked best with identical twins in twin trance: no structural brain differences to adjust for. In a rawer version of this holotank, a rawer version of myself had pioneered the recording of twin trances. The UCIC, we had called in then: What you see, I see.

What I had seen was eight autopsy reports.

"We're so *close*," Devrie said. "Mona and Marlene—" she waved a hand toward the corridor, but Mona and Marlene, whichever two they had been, had gone—"had taken KX3, that's the drug that—"

"I know what it is," I said, too harshly. KX3 reacts with one of the hormones overproduced in an anorectic body. The combination is readily absorbed by body fat, but in a body without fat, much of it is absorbed by the brain.

Devrie continued, her hand tight on my arm. "Mona and Marlene were controlling the neural reactions with biofeed-back, pushing the twin trance higher and higher, working it. Dr. Bohentin was monitoring the holotanks. The sims were incredibly detailed—everything each twin perceived in the perceptions of the other, in all wavelengths. Mona and Marlene forced their neurotransmission level even higher and then, in the tanks—" Devrie's face glowed, the mystic-rapture look—"a completely third sim formed. Completely separate. A third *presence*."

I stared at her.

"It was recorded in *both* tanks. It was shadowy, yes, but it was *there*. A third presence that can't be perceived except through another human's electromagnetic presence, and then only with every drug and trained reaction and arousal mode and the twin trance all pushing the brain into a supraheightened state. A third presence!"

"Isotropic radiation. Bohentin fluffed the pre-screening program and the computer hadn't cleared the background microradiation—" I said, but even as I spoke I knew how stupid that was. Bohentin didn't make mistakes like that, and isotropic radiation simulates nowhere close to the way a presence does. Devrie didn't even bother to answer me.

This, then, was what the rumors had been about, the rumors leaking for the last year out of the Institute and through the scientific community, mostly still scoffed at, not yet picked up by the popular press. This. A verifiable, replicable third presence being picked up by holography. Against all reason, a long shiver went over me from neck to that cold place at the base of the spine.

"There's more," Devrie said feverishly. "They *felt* it. Mona and Marlene. Both said afterwards that they could feel it, a huge presence filled with light, but they couldn't quite reach it. Damn—they couldn't reach it, Seena! They weren't playing off each other enough, weren't close enough. Weren't, despite the twin trance, *melded* enough."

"Sex," I said.

"They tried it. The subjects are all basically heterosexual. They inhibit."

"So go find some homosexual God-yearning anorectic incestuous twins!"

Devrie looked at me straight. "I need him. Here. He *is* me."

I exploded, right there in the holotank lab. No one came running in to find out if the shouting was dangerous to the tanks, which was my second clue that the Institute knew very well why Devrie had brought me there. "Damn it to hell, he's a human being, not some chemical you can just order up because you need it for an experiment! You don't have the right to expect him to come here, you didn't even have the right to tell anyone that he exists, but that didn't stop you, did it? There are still anti-bioengineering groups out there in the real world, religious split-brains who—how *dare* you put him in any danger? How dare you even presume he'd be interested in this insane mush?"

"He'll come," Devrie said. She had not changed expression.

"How the hell do you know?"

"He's me. And I want God. He will, too."

I scowled at her. A fragment of one of her poems, a thing she had written when she was fifteen, came to me: "Two human species/Never one—/One aching for God/One never." But she had been fifteen then. I had assumed that the sentiment, as adolescent as the poetry, would pass.

I said, "What does Bohentin think of this idea of importing your clone?"

For the first time she hesitated. Bohentin, then, was dubious. "He thinks it's rather a long shot."

"You could phrase it that way."

"But *I* know he'll want to come. Some things you just know, Seena, beyond rationality. And besides—" she hesitated again, and then went on, "I have left half my inheritance from Daddy, and the income on the trust from Mummy."

"Devrie. God, Devrie—you'd *buy* him?"

For the first time she looked angry. "The money would be just to get him here, to see what is involved. Once he sees, he'll want this as much as I do, at any price! What price can you put on God? I'm not 'buying' his life—I'm offering him the way to *find* life. What good is breathing, existing, if there's no purpose to it? Don't you realize how many centuries, in how many ways, people have looked for that light-filled presence and never been able to be *sure*? And now we're almost there, Seena, I've seen it for myself—*almost there*. With verifiable, scientifically-controlled means. Not subjective faith this time—scientific data, the same as for any other actual phenomenon. This research stands now where research into the atom stood fifty years ago. Can you touch a quark? But it's there! And my clone can be a part of it, can *be* it, how can you talk about the money buying him under circumstances like that!"

I said slowly, "How do you know that whatever you're so close to is God?" But that was sophomoric, of course, and she was ready for it. She smiled warmly.

"What does it matter what we call it? Pick another label if it will make you more comfortable."

I took a piece of paper from my pocket. "His name is Keith Torellen. He lives in Indian Falls, New Hampshire. Address and mailnet number here. Good luck, Devrie." I turned to go.

"Seena! *I* can't go!"

She couldn't, of course. That was the point. She barely had the strength in that starved, drug-battered body to get through the day, let alone to New Hampshire. She needed the sensory-controlled environment, the artificial heat, the chemical monitoring. "Then send someone from the Institute. Perhaps Bohentin will go."

"Bo*hen*tin!" she said, and I knew that was impossible; Bohentin had to remain officially ignorant of this sort of recruiting. Too many U.S. laws were involved. In addition, Bohentin had no persuasive skills; people as persons and not neurologies did not interest him. They were too far above chemicals and too far below God.

Devrie looked at me with a kind of level fury. "This is really why you found him, isn't it? So I would have to stop the drug program long enough to leave here and go get him. You think that once I've gone back out into the world either the build-up effects in the brain will be interrupted or else the spell will be broken and I'll have doubts about coming back here!"

"Will you listen to yourself? 'Out in the world.' You sound like some archaic nun in a cloistered order!"

"You always did ridicule anything you couldn't understand," Devrie said icily, turned her back on me, and stared at the empty holotanks. She didn't turn when I left the lab, closing the door behind me. She was still facing the tanks, her spiny back rigid, the piece of paper with Keith Torellen's address clutched in fingers delicate as glass.

In New York the museum simmered with excitement. An unexpected endowment had enabled us to buy the contents of a small, very old museum located in a part of Madagascar not completely destroyed by the African Horror. Crate after crate of moths began arriving in New York, some of them collected in the days when naturalists-gentlemen shot jungle moths from the trees using dust shot. Some species had been extinct since the Horror and thus were rare; some were the brief mutations from the bad years afterward and thus were even rarer. The museum staff uncrated and exclaimed.

"Look at this one," said a young man, holding it out to me. Not on my own staff, he was one of the specialists on loan to us—DeFabio or DeFazio, something like that. He was very handsome. I looked at the moth he showed me, all pale wings outstretched and pinned to black silk. "A perfect Thysania Africana. *Perfect.*"

"Yes."

"You'll have to loan us the whole exhibit, in a few years."

"Yes," I said again. He heard the tone in my voice and glanced up quickly. But not quickly enough—my face was all professional interest when his gaze reached it. Still, the professional interest had not fooled him; he had heard the perfunctory note. Frowning, he turned back to the moths.

By day I directed the museum efficiently enough. But in the evenings, home alone in my apartment, I found myself wandering from room to room, touching objects, unable to settle to work at the oversize teak desk that had been my father's, to the reports and journals that had not. His had dealt with the living, mine with the ancient dead—but I had known that for years. The fogginess of my evenings bothered me.

"Faith should not mean fogginess."

Who had said that? Father, of course, to Devrie, when she had joined the dying Catholic Church. She had been thirteen years old. Skinny, defiant, she had stood clutching a black rosary from God knows where, daring him from scared dark eyes to forbid her. Of course he had not, thinking, I suppose, that Heaven, like any other childhood fever, was best left alone to burn out its course.

Devrie had been received into the Church in an overdecorated chapel, wearing an overdecorated dress of white lace and carrying a candle. Three years later she had left, dressed in a magenta body suit and holding the keys to Father's safe, which his executor had left unlocked after the funeral. The will had, of course, made me Devrie's guardian. In the three years Devrie had been going to Mass, I had discovered that I was sterile, divorced my second husband, finished my work in entomology, accepted my first position with a museum, and entered a drastically premature menopause.

That is not a flip nor random list.

After the funeral, I sat in the dark in my father's study, in his maroon leather chair and at his teak desk. Both felt oversize. All the lights were off. Outside it rained; I heard the steady beat of water on the window, and the wind. The dark room was cold. In my palm I held one of my father's research awards, a small abstract sculpture of a double helix, done by Harold Landau himself. It was very heavy. I couldn't think what Landau had used, to make it so heavy. I couldn't think, with all the noise from the rain. My father was dead, and I would never bear a child.

Devrie came into the room, leaving the lights off but bringing with her an incandescent rectangle from the doorway. At sixteen she was lovely, with long brown hair in the masses of curls again newly fashionable. She sat on a low stool beside me, all that hair falling around her, her face white in the gloom. She had been crying.

"He's gone. He's really gone. I don't believe it yet."

"No."

She peered at me. Something in my face, or my voice, must have alerted her; when she spoke again it was in that voice people use when they think your grief is understandably greater than theirs. A smooth dark voice, like a wave.

"You still have me, Seena. We still have each other." I said nothing.

"I've always thought of you more as my mother than my sister, anyway. You took the place of Mother. You've been a mother to at least *me*."

She smiled and squeezed my hand. I looked at her face—so young, so pretty—and I wanted to hit her. I didn't want to be her mother; I wanted to be her. All her choices lay ahead of her, and it seemed to me that self-indulgent night as if mine were finished. I could have struck her.

"Seena—"

"Leave me alone! Can't you ever leave me alone? All my life you've been dragging behind me; why don't *you* die and finally leave me alone!"

We make ourselves pay for small sins more than large ones. The more trivial the thrust, the longer we're haunted by memory of the wound.

I believe that.

Indian Falls was out of another time: slow, quiet, safe. The Avis counter at the airport rented not personal guards but cars, and the only shiny store on Main Street sold wilderness equipment. I suspected that the small state college, like the town, traded mostly on trees and trails. That Keith Torellen was trying to take an academic degree *here* told me more about his adopting family than if I had hired a professional information service.

The house where he lived was shabby, paint peeling and steps none too sturdy. I climbed them slowly, thinking once again what I wanted to find out.

Devrie would answer none of my messages on the mailnet. Nor would she accept my phone calls. She was shutting me out, in retaliation for my refusing to fetch Torellen for her. But Devrie would discover that she could not shut me out as easily as that; we were sisters. I wanted to know if she had contacted Torellen herself, or had sent someone from the Institute to do so.

If neither, then my visit here would be brief and anonymous; I would leave Keith Torellen to his protected ignorance and shabby town. But if he *had* seen Devrie, I wanted to discover if and what he had agreed to do for her. It might even be possible that he could be of use in convincing Devrie of the stupidity of what she was doing. If he could be used for that, I would use him.

Something else: I was curious. This boy was my brother—nephew? no, brother—as well as the result of my father's rational mind. Curiosity prickled over me. I rang the bell.

It was answered by the landlady, who said that Keith was not home, would not be home until late, was "in rehearsal."

"Rehearsal?"

"Over to the college. He's a student and they're putting on a play."

I said nothing, thinking.

"I don't remember the name of the play," the landlady said. She was a large woman in a faded garment, dress or robe. "But Keith says it's going to be real good. It starts this weekend." She laughed. "But you probably already know all that! George, my husband George, he says I'm forever telling people things they already know!"

"How would I know?"

She winked at me. "Don't you think I got eyes? Sister, or cousin? No, let me guess—older sister. Too much alike for cousins."

"Thank you," I said. "You've been very helpful."

"Not sister!" She clapped her hand over her mouth, her eyes shiny with amusement. "You're checking up on him, ain't you? You're his mother! I should of seen it right off!"

I turned to negotiate the porch steps.

"They rehearse in the new building, Mrs. Torellen," she called after me. "Just ask anybody you see to point you in the right direction."

"Thank you," I said carefully.

Rehearsal was nearly over. Evidently it was a dress rehearsal; the actors were in period costume and the director did not interrupt. I did not recognize the period or the play. Devrie had been interested in theater; I was not. Quietly I took a seat in the darkened back row and waited for the pretending to end.

Despite wig and greasepaint, I had no trouble picking out Keith Torellen. He moved like Devrie: quick, light movements, slightly pigeon-toed. He had her height and, given the differences of a male body, her slenderness. Sitting a theater's length away, I might have been seeing a male Devrie.

But seen up close, his face was mine.

Despite the landlady, it was a shock. He came towards me across the theater lobby, from where I had sent for him, and I saw the moment he too struck the resemblance. He stopped dead, and we stared at each other. Take Devrie's genes, spread them over a face with the greater bone surface, larger features, and coarser skin texture of a man—and the result was my face. Keith had scrubbed off his make-up and removed his wig, exposing brown curly hair the same shade Devrie's had been. But his face was mine.

A strange emotion, unnamed and hot, seared through me.

"Who are *you*? Who the hell *are* you?"

So no one had come from the Institute after all. Not Devrie, not any one.

"You're one of them, aren't you?" he said; it was almost a whisper. "One of my real family?"

Still gripped by the unexpected force of emotion, still dumb, I said nothing. Keith took one step toward me. Suspicion played over his face—Devrie would not have been suspicious—and vanished, replaced by a slow painful flush of color.

"You are. You *are* one. Are you . . . are you my mother?"

I put out a hand against a stone post. The lobby was all stone and glass. Why were all theater lobbies stone and glass? Architects had so little damn imagination, so little sense of the bizarre.

"No! I am not your mother!"

He touched my arm. "Hey, are you okay? You don't look good. Do you need to sit down?"

His concern was unexpected, and touching. I thought that he shared Devrie's genetic personality and that Devrie had always been hypersensitive to the body. But this was not Devrie. His hand on my arm was stronger, firmer, warmer than Devrie's. I felt giddy, disoriented. This was not Devrie.

"A mistake," I said unsteadily. "This was a mistake. I should not have come. I'm sorry. My name is Dr. Seena Konig and I am a . . . relative of yours, but I think this is a mistake. I have your address and I promise that I'll write about your family, but now I think I should go." Write some benign lie, leave him in ignorance. This was a mistake.

But he looked stricken, and his hand tightened on my arm. "You can't! I've been searching for my biological family for two years! You can't just go!"

We were beginning to attract attention in the theater lobby. Hurrying students eyed us sideways. I thought irrelevantly how different they looked from the "students" at the Institute, and with that thought regained my composure. This was a student, a boy—"you can't!" a boyish protest, and boyish panic in his voice—and not the man-Devrie-me he had seemed a foolish moment ago. He was nearly twenty years my junior. I smiled at him and removed his hand from my arm.

"Is there somewhere we can have coffee?"

"Yes. Dr. . . ."

"Seena," I said. "Call me Seena."

Over coffee, I made him talk first. He watched me anxiously over the rim of his cup, as if I might vanish, and I listened to the words behind the words. His adopting family was the kind that hoped to visit the Grand Canyon but not Europe, go to movies but not opera, aspire to college but not to graduate work, buy wilderness equipment but not wilderness. Ordinary people. Not religious, not rich, not unusual. Keith was the only child. He loved them.

"But at the same time I never really felt I belonged," he said, and looked away from me. It was the most personal thing he had knowingly revealed, and I saw that he regretted it. Devrie would not have. More private, then, and less trusting. And I sensed in him a grittiness, a tougher awareness of the world's hardness, than Devrie had ever had—or needed to have. I made my decision. Having disturbed him thus far, I owed him the truth—but not the whole truth.

"Now you tell me," Keith said, pushing away his cup. "Who were my parents? Our parents? Are you my sister?"

"Yes."

"Our parents?"

"Both are dead. Our father was Dr. Richard Konig. He was a scientist. He—" But Keith had recognized the name. His readings in biology or history must have been more extensive than I would have expected. His eyes widened, and I suddenly wished I had been more oblique.

"Richard Konig. He's one of those scientists that were involved in that bioengineering scandal—"

"How did you learn about that? It's all over and done with. Years ago."

"Journalism class. We studied how the press handled it, especially the sensationalism surrounding the cloning thing twenty years—"

I saw the moment it hit him. He groped for his coffee cup, clutched the handle, didn't raise it. It was empty anyway. And then what I said next shocked me as much as anything I have ever done.

"It was Devrie," I said, and heard my own vicious pleasure, "*Devrie* was the one who wanted me to tell you!"

But of course he didn't know who Devrie was. He went on staring at me, panic in his young eyes, and I sat frozen. That tone I heard in my own voice when I said "Devrie," that vicious pleasure that it was she and not I who was hurting him . . .

"Cloning," Keith said. "Konig was in trouble for claiming to have done illegal cloning. Of humans." His voice held so much dread that I fought off my own dread and tried to hold my voice steady to his need.

"It's illegal now, but not then. And the public badly misunderstood. All that sensationalism—you were right to use that word, Keith—covered up the fact that there is nothing abnormal about producing a fetus from another diploid cell. In the womb, identical twins—"

"Am I a clone?"

"Keith—"

"*Am I a clone?*"

Carefully I studied him. This was not what I had intended, but although the fear was still in his eyes, the panic had gone.

And curiosity—Devrie's curiosity, and her eagerness—they were there as well. This boy would not strike me, nor stalk out of the restaurant, nor go into psychic shock.

"Yes. You are."

He sat quietly, his gaze turned inward. A long moment passed in silence.

"Your cell?"

"No. My—our sister's. Our sister Devrie."

Another long silence. He did not panic. Then he said softly, "Tell me."

Devrie's phrase.

"There isn't much to tell, Keith. If you've seen the media accounts, you know the story, and also what was made of it. The issue then becomes how you feel about what you saw. Do you believe that cloning is meddling with things man should best leave alone?"

"No. I don't."

I let out my breath, although I hadn't known I'd been holding it. "It's actually no more than delayed twinning, followed by surrogate implantation. A zygote—"

"I know all that," he said with some harshness, and held up his hand to silence me. I didn't think he knew that he did it. The harshness did not sound like Devrie. To my ears, it sounded like myself. He sat thinking, remote and troubled, and I did not try to touch him.

Finally he said, "Do my parents know?"

He meant his adoptive parents. "No."

"Why are you telling me now? Why did you come?"

"Devrie asked me to."

"She needs something, right? A kidney? Something like that?"

I had not foreseen that question. He did not move in a class where spare organs are easily purchasable. "No. Not a kidney, not any kind of biological donation." A voice in my mind jeered at that, but I was not going to give him any clues that would lead to Devrie. "She just wanted me to find you."

"Why didn't she find me herself? She's my age, right?"

"Yes. She's ill just now and couldn't come."

"Is she dying?"

"No!"

Again he sat quietly, finally saying, "No one could tell me

anything. For two years I've been searching for my mother, and not one of the adoptee-search agencies could find a single trace. Not one. Now I see why. Who covered the trail so well?"

"My father."

"I want to meet Devrie."

I said evenly, "That might not be possible."

"Why not?"

"She's in a foreign hospital. Out of the country. I'm sorry."

"When does she come home?"

"No one is sure."

"What disease does she have?"

She's sick for God, I thought, but aloud I said, not thinking it through, "A brain disease."

Instantly, I saw my own cruelty. Keith paled, and I cried, "No, no, nothing you could have as well! Truly, Keith, it's not—she took a bad fall. From her hunter."

"Her hunter," he said. For the first time, his gaze flickered over my clothing and jewelry. But would he even recognize how expensive they were? I doubted it. He wore a synthetic, deep-pile jacket with a tear at one shoulder and a cheap wool hat, dark blue, shapeless with age. From long experience I recognized his gaze: uneasy, furtive, the expression of a man glimpsing the financial gulf between what he had assumed were equals. But it wouldn't matter. Adopted children have no legal claim on the estates of their biological parents. I had checked.

Keith said uneasily, "Do you have a picture of Devrie?"

"No," I lied.

"Why did she want you to find me? You still haven't said." I shrugged. "The same reason, I suppose, that you looked for your biological family. The pull of blood."

"Then she wants me to write to her."

"Write to me instead."

He frowned. "Why? Why not to Devrie?"

What to say to that? I hadn't bargained on so much intensity from him. "Write in care of me, and I'll forward it to Devrie."

"Why not to her directly?"

"Her doctors might not think it advisable," I said coldly, and he backed off—either from the mention of doctors or from the coldness.

"Then give me your address, Seena. Please."

I did. I could see no harm in his writing me. It might even be pleasant. Coming home from the museum, another wintry day among the exhibits, to find on the mailnet a letter I could answer when and how I chose, without being taken by surprise. I liked the idea.

But no more difficult questions now. I stood. "I have to leave, Keith."

He looked alarmed. "So soon?"

"Yes."

"But why?"

"I have to return to work."

He stood, too. He was taller than Devrie. "Seena," he said, all earnestness, "just a few more questions. How did you find me?"

"Medical connections."

"Yours?"

"Our father's. I'm not a scientist." Evidently his journalism class had not studied twin-trance sensationalism.

"What do you do?"

"Museum curator. Arthropods."

"What does Devrie do?"

"She's too ill to work, I must go, Keith."

"One more. Do I look like Devrie as well as you?"

"It would be wise, Keith, if you were careful whom you spoke with about all of this. I hadn't intended to say so much."

"I'm not going to tell my parents. Not about being—not about all of it."

"I think that's best, yes."

"Do I look like Devrie as well as you?"

A little of my first, strange emotion returned with his intensity. "A little, yes. But more like me. Sex variance is a tricky thing."

Unexpectedly, he held my coat for me. As I slipped into it, he said from behind, "Thank you, Seena," and let his hands rest on my shoulders.

I did not turn around. I felt my face flame, and self-disgust flooded through me, followed by a desire to laugh. It was all so transparent. This man was an attractive stranger, was Devrie, was youth, was myself, was the work not of my father's loins but of his mind. Of course I was aroused by him. Freud outlasts cloning: a note for a research study, I told myself grimly, and inwardly I did laugh.

But that didn't help either.

In New York, winter came early. Cold winds whipped whitecaps on harbor and river, and the trees in the Park stood bare even before October had ended. The crumbling outer boroughs of the shrinking city crumbled a little more and talked of the days when New York had been important. Manhattan battened down for snow, hired the seasonal increases in personal guards, and talked of Albuquerque. Each night museum security hunted up and evicted the drifters trying to sleep behind exhibits, drifters as chilled and pale as the moths under permaplex, and, it seemed to me, as detached from the blood of their own age. All of New York seemed detached to me that October, and cold. Often I stood in front of the cases of Noctuidae, staring at them for so long that my staff began to glance at each other covertly. I would catch their glances when I jerked free of my trance. No one asked me about it.

Still no message came from Devrie. When I contacted the Institute on the mailnet, she did not call back.

No letter from Keith Torellen.

Then one night, after I had worked late and was hurrying through the chilly gloom towards my building, he was there, bulking from the shadows so quickly that the guard I had taken for the walk from the museum sprang forward in attack position.

"No! It's all right! I know him!"

The guard retreated, without expression. Keith stared after him, and then at me, his face unreadable.

"Keith, what are you doing here? Come inside!"

He followed me into the lobby without a word. Nor did he say anything during the metal scanning and ID procedure. I took him up to my apartment, studying him in the elevator. He wore the same jacket and cheap wool hat as in Indian Falls, his hair wanted cutting, and the tip of his nose was red from waiting in the cold. How long had he waited there? He badly needed a shave.

In the apartment he scanned the rugs, the paintings, my grandmother's ridiculously ornate, ugly silver, and turned his back on them to face me.

"Seena. I want to know where Devrie is."

"Why? Keith, what has happened?"

"Nothing has happened," he said, removing his jacket but not laying it anywhere. "Only that I've left school and spent two days hitching here. It's no good, Seena. To say that cloning is just like twinning: it's no good. I want to see Devrie."

His voice was hard. Bulking in my living room, unshaven, that hat pulled down over his ears, he looked older and less malleable than the last time I had seen him. Alarm—not physical fear, I was not afraid of him, but a subtler and deeper fear—sounded through me.

"Why do you want to see Devrie?"

"Because she cheated me."

"Of *what*, for God's sake?"

"Can I have a drink? Or a smoke?"

I poured him a Scotch. If he drank, he might talk. I had to know what he wanted, why such a desperate air clung to him, how to keep him from Devrie. I had never seen *her* like this. She was strong-willed, but always with a blitheness, a trust that eventually her will would prevail. Desperate forcefulness of the sort in Keith's manner was not her style. But of course Devrie had always had silent money to back her will; perhaps money could buy trust as well as style.

Keith drank off his Scotch and held out his glass for another. "It was freezing out there. They wouldn't let me in the lobby to wait for you."

"Of course not."

"You didn't tell me your family was rich."

I was a little taken aback at his bluntness, but at the same time it pleased me; I don't know why.

"You didn't ask."

"That's shit, Seena."

"Keith. Why are you here?"

"I told you. I want to see Devrie."

"What is it you've decided she cheated you of? Money?"

He looked so honestly surprised that again I was startled, this time by his resemblance to Devrie. She too would not have thought of financial considerations first, if there were emotional ones possible. One moment Keith was Devrie, one moment he was not. Now he scowled with sudden anger.

"Is that what you think—that fortune hunting brought me hitching from New Hampshire? God, Seena, I didn't even know how much you had until this very—I still don't know!"

I said levelly, "Then what is it you're feeling so cheated of?"

Now he was rattled. Again that quick, half-furtive scan of my apartment, pausing a millisecond too long at the Caravaggio, subtly lit by its frame. When his gaze returned to mine it was troubled, a little defensive. Ready to justify. Of course I had put him on the defensive deliberately, but the calculation of my trick did not prepare me for the staggering naivete of his explanation. Once more it was Devrie complete, reducing the impersonal greatness of science to a personal and emotional loss.

"Ever since I knew that I was adopted, at five or six years old, I wondered about my biological family. Nothing strange in that—I think all adoptees do. I used to make up stories, kid stuff, about how they were really royalty, or lunar colonists, or survivors of the African Horror. Exotic things. I thought especially about my mother, imagining this whole scene of her holding me once before she released me for adoption, crying over me, loving me so much she could barely let me go but had to for some reason. Sentimental shit." He laughed, trying to make light of what was not, and drank off his Scotch to avoid my gaze.

"But Devrie—the fact of her—destroyed all that. I never had a mother who hated to give me up. I never had a mother at all. What I had was a cell cut from Devrie's fingertip or someplace, something discardable, and she doesn't even know what I look like. But she's damn well going to."

"Why?" I said evenly. "What could you expect to gain from her knowing what you look like?"

But he didn't answer me directly. "The first moment I saw you, Seena, in the theater at school, I thought *you* were my mother."

"I know you did."

"And you hated the idea. Why?"

I thought of the child I would never bear, the marriage, like so many other things of sweet promise, gone sour. But selfpity is a fool's game. "None of your business."

"Isn't it? Didn't you hate the idea because of the way I was made? Coldly. An experiment. Weren't you a little bit insulted at being called the mother of a discardable cell from Devrie's fingertip?"

"What the hell have you been reading? An experiment—what is any child but an experiment? A random egg, a random sperm. Don't talk like one of those anti-science religious splitbrains!"

He studied me levelly. Then he said, "Is Devrie religious? Is that why you're so afraid of her?"

I got to my feet, and pointed at the sideboard. "Help yourself to another drink if you wish. I want to wash my hands. I've been handling specimens all afternoon." Stupid, clumsy lie—nobody would believe such a lie.

In the bathroom I leaned against the closed door, shut my eyes, and willed myself to calm. Why should I be so disturbed by the angry lashing-out of a confused boy? I was handy to lash out against; my father, whom Keith was really angry at, was not. It was all so predictable, so earnestly adolescent, that even over the hurting in my chest I smiled. But the smile, which should have reduced Keith's ranting to the tantrum of a child—there, there, when you grow up you'll find out that no one really knows who he is—did not diminish Keith. His losses were real—mother, father, natural place in the natural sequence of life and birth. And suddenly, with a clutch at the pit of my stomach, I knew why I had told him all that I had about his origins. It was not from any ethic of fidelity to "the truth." I had told him he was clone because I, too, had had real losses—research, marriage, motherhood—and Devrie could never have shared them with me. Luminous, mystical Devrie, too occupied with God to be much hurt by man. *Leave me alone*! *Can't you ever leave me alone*! *All my life you've been dragging behind me—why don't you die and finally leave me alone*! And Devrie had smiled tolerantly, patted my head, and left me alone, closing the door softly so as not to disturb my grief. My words had not hurt her. I could not hurt her.

But I could hurt Keith—the other Devrie—and I had. That was why he disturbed me all out of proportion. That was the bond. My face, my pain, my fault.

Through my fault, through my fault, through my most grievous fault. But what nonsense. I was not a believer, and the comforts of superstitious absolution could not touch me. What shit. Like all nonbelievers, I stood alone.

It came to me then that there was something absurd in thinking all this while leaning against a bathroom door. Grimly absurd, but absurd. The toilet as confessional. I ran the cold water, splashed some on my face and left. How long had I left Keith alone in the living room?

When I returned, he was standing by the mailnet. He had

punched in the command to replay my outgoing postal messages, and displayed on the monitor was Devrie's address at the Institute of the Biological Hope.

"What is it?" Keith said. "A hospital?"

I didn't answer him.

"I can find out, Seena. Knowing this much, I can find out. Tell me."

Tell me. "Not a hospital. It's a research laboratory. Devrie is a voluntary subject."

"Research on what? I will find out, Seena."

"Brain perception."

"Perception of what?"

"Perception of *God*," I said, torn among weariness, anger and a sudden gritty exasperation, irritating as sand. Why not just leave him to Devrie's persuasions, and her to mystic starvation? But I knew I would not. I still, despite all of it, wanted her out of there.

Keith frowned, "What do you mean, 'perception of God'?"

I told him. I made it sound as ridiculous as possible, and as dangerous. I described the anorexia, the massive use of largely untested drugs that would have made the Institute illegal in the United States, the skepticism of most of the scientific community, the psychoses and death that had followed twintrance research fifteen years earlier. Keith did not remember that—he had been eight years old—and I did not tell him that I had been one of the researchers. I did not tell him about the tapes of the shadowy third presence in Bohentin's holotanks. In every way I could, with every verbal subtlety at my use, I made the Institute sound crackpot, and dangerous, and ugly. As I spoke, I watched Keith's face, and sometimes it was mine, and sometimes the expression altered it into Devrie's. I saw bewilderment at her having chosen to enter the Institute but not what I had hoped to see. Not scorn, not disgust.

When I had finished, he said, "But why did she think that *I* might want to enter such a place as a twin subject?"

I had saved this for last. "Money. She'd buy you."

His hand, holding his third Scotch, went rigid. "Buy me."

"It's the most accurate way to put it."

"What the hell made her think—" he mastered himself, not

without effort. Not all the discussion of bodily risk had affected him as much as this mention of Devrie's money. He had a poor man's touchy pride. "She thinks of me as something to be *bought*."

I was carefully quiet.

"Damn her," he said. "*Damn* her." Then roughly, "And I was actually considering—"

I caught my breath. "Considering the Institute? After what I've just told you? How in hell could you? And you said, I remember, that your background was not religious!"

"It's not. But I . . . I've wondered." And in the sudden turn of his head away from me so that I wouldn't see the sudden rapt hopelessness in his eyes, in the defiant set of shoulders, I read more than in his banal words, and more than he could know. Devrie's look, Devrie's wishfulness, feeding on air. The weariness and anger, checked before, flooded me again and I lashed out at him.

"Then go ahead and fly to Dominica to enter the Institute yourself!"

He said nothing. But from something—his expression as he stared into his glass, the shifting of his body—I suddenly knew that he could not afford the trip.

I said, "So you fancy yourself as a believer?"

"No. A believer manqué." From the way he said it, I knew that he had said it before, perhaps often, and that the phrase stirred some hidden place in his imagination.

"What is wrong with you," I said, "with people like you, that the human world is not enough?"

"What is wrong with people like you, that is it?" he said, and this time he laughed and raised his eyebrows in a little mockery that shut me out from this place beyond reason, this glittering escape. I knew then that somehow or other, sometime or other, despite all I had said, Keith would go to Dominica.

I poured him another Scotch. As deftly as I could, I led the conversation into other, lighter directions. I asked about his childhood. At first stiffly, then more easily as time and Scotch loosened him, he talked about growing up in the Berkshire Hills. He became more light-hearted, and under my interest turned both shrewd and funny, with a keen sense of humor. His thick brown hair fell over his forehead. I laughed with him, and broke out a bottle of good port. He talked about amateur plays he had acted in; his enthusiasm increased as his coherence decreased. Enthusiasm, humor, thick brown hair. I smoothed the hair back from his forehead. Far into the night I pulled the drapes back from the window and we stood together and looked at the lights of the dying city ten stories below. Fog rolled in from the sea. Keith insisted we open the doors and stand on the balcony; he had never smelled fog tinged with the ocean. We smelled the night, and drank some more, and talked, and laughed.

And then I led him again to the sofa.

"Seena?" Keith said. He covered my hand, laid upon his thigh, with his own, and turned his head to look at me questioningly. I leaned forward and touched my lips to his, barely in contact, for a long moment. He drew back, and his hand tried to lift mine. I tightened my fingers.

"Seena, no . . ."

"Why not?" I put my mouth back on his, very lightly. He had to draw back to answer, and I could feel that he did not want to draw back. Under my lips he frowned slightly; still, despite his drunkenness—so much more than mine—he groped for the word.

"Incest . . ."

"No. We two have never shared a womb."

He frowned again, under my mouth. I drew back to smile at him, and shifted my hand. "It doesn't matter any more, Keith. Not in New York. But even if it did—I am not your sister, not really. You said so yourself—remember? Not a family. Just . . . here."

"Not family," he repeated, and I saw in his eyes the second before he closed them the flash of pain, the greed of a young man's desire, and even the crafty evasions of the good port. Then his arms closed around me.

He was very strong, and more than a little violent. I guessed from what confusions the violence flowed but still I enjoyed it, that overwhelming rush from that beautiful male-Devrie body. I wanted him to be violent with me, as long as I knew there was not real danger. No real danger, no real brother, no real child. Keith was not my child but Devrie was my child-sister, and I had to stop her from destroying herself, no matter how . . . didn't I? "The pull of blood." But this was necessary, was justified . . . was the necessary gamble. For Devrie.

So I told myself. Then I stopped telling myself anything at all, and surrendered to the warm tides of pleasure.

But at dawn I woke and thought—with Keith sleeping heavily across me and the sky cold at the window—*what the hell am I doing*?

When I came out of the shower, Keith was sitting rigidly against the pillows. Sitting next to him on the very edge of the bed, I pulled a sheet around my nakedness and reached for his hand. He snatched it away.

"Keith. It's all right. Truly it is."

"You're my sister."

"But nothing will come of it. No child, no repetitions. It's not all that uncommon, dear heart."

"It is where I come from."

"Yes. I know. But not here."

He didn't answer, his face troubled.

"Do you want breakfast?"

"No. No, thank you."

I could feel his need to get away from me; it was almost palpable. Snatching my bodysuit off the floor, I went into the kitchen, which was chilly. The servant would not arrive for another hour. I turned up the heat, pulled on my bodysuit—standing on the cold floor first on one foot and then on the other, like some extinct species of water fowl—and made coffee. Through the handle of one cup I stuck two folded large bills. He came into the kitchen, dressed even to the torn jacket.

"Coffee."

"Thanks."

His fingers closed on the handle of the cup, and his eyes widened. Pure, naked shock, uncushioned by any defenses whatsoever: the whole soul, betrayed, pinned in the eyes.

"Oh God, no, Keith—how can you even think so? It's for the trip back to Indian Falls! A gift!"

An endless pause, while we stared at each other. Then he said, very low, "I'm sorry. I should have . . . seen what it's for." But his cup trembled in his hand, and a few drops sloshed onto the floor. It was those few drops that undid me, flooding me with shame. Keith had a right to his shock, and to the anguish in his/my/Devrie's face. She wanted him for her mystic purposes, I for their prevention. Fanatic and saboteur, we were both better defended against each other than Keith, without money nor religion nor years, was against either of us. If I could have seen any other way than the gamble I had taken . . . but I could not. Nonetheless, I was ashamed.

"Keith. I'm sorry."

"Why did we? Why did *we*?"

I could have said: *we* didn't; I did. But that might have made it worse for him. He was male, and so young.

Impulsively I blurted, "Don't go to Dominica!" But of course he was beyond listening to me now. His face closed. He set down the coffee cup and looked at me from eyes much harder than they had been a minute ago. Was he thinking that because of our night together I expected to influence him directly? *I* was not that young. He could not foresee that I was trying to guess much farther ahead than that, for which I could not blame him. I could not blame him for anything. But I did regret how clumsily I had handled the money. That had been stupid.

Nonetheless; when he left a few moments later, the handle of the coffee cup was bare. He had taken the money.

The Madagascar exhibits were complete. They opened to much press interest, and there were both favorable reviews and celebrations. I could not bring myself to feel that it mattered. Ten times a day I went through the deadening exercise of willing an interest that had deserted me, and when I looked at the moths, ashy white wings outstretched forever, I could feel my body recoil in a way I could not name.

The image of the moths went home with me. One night in November I actually thought I heard wings beating against the window where I had stood with Keith. I yanked open the drapes and then the doors, but of course there was nothing there. For a long time I stared at the nothingness, smelling the fog, before typing yet another message, urgent-priority personal, to Devrie. The mailnet did not bring any answer.

I contacted the mailnet computer at the college at Indian Falls. My fingers trembled as they typed a request to leave an urgent-priority personal message for a student, Keith Torellen. The mailnet typed back:

> TORELLEN, KEITH ROBERT. 64830016. ON MEDICAL LEAVE OF ABSENCE. TIME OF LEAVE: INDEFINITE. NO FORWARDING MAILNET NUMBER. END.

The sound came again at the window. Whirling, I scanned the dark glass, but there was nothing there, no moths, no wings, just the lights of the decaying city flung randomly across the blackness and the sound, faint and very far away, of a siren wailing out somebody else's disaster.

I shivered. Putting on a sweater and turning up the heat made me no warmer. Then the mail slot chimed softly and I turned in time to see the letter fall from the pneumatic tube from the lobby, the apartment house sticker clearly visible, assuring me that it had been processed and found free of both poison and explosives. Also visible was the envelope's logo: INSTITUTE OF THE BIOLOGICAL HOPE, all the O's radiant golden suns. But Devrie never wrote paper mail. She preferred the mailnet.

The note was from Keith, not Devrie. A short note, scrawled on a torn scrap of paper in nearly indecipherable handwriting. I had seen Keith's handwriting in Indian Falls, across his student notebooks; this was a wildly out-of-control version of it, almost psychotic in the variations of spacing and letter formation that signal identity. I guessed that he had written the note under the influence of a drug, or several drugs, his mind racing much faster than he could write. There was neither punctuation nor paragraphing.

> Dear Seena Im going to do it I have to know my parents are angry but I have to know I have to all the confusion is gone Seena Keith

There was a word crossed out between "gone" and "Seena," scratched out with erratic lines of ink. I held the paper up to the light, tilting it this way and that. The crossed-out word was "mother."

all the confusion is gone mother

Mother.

Slowly I let out the breath I had not known I was holding. The first emotion was pity, for Keith, even though I had intended this. We had done a job on him, Devrie and I. Mother, sister, self. And when he and Devrie artifically drove upward the number and speed of the neuro-transmitters in the brain, generated the twin trance, and then Keith's pre-cloning Freudian-still mind reached for Devrie to add sexual energy to all the other brain energies fueling Bohentin's holotanks—

Mother. Sister. Self.

All was fair in love and war. A voice inside my head jeered: and which is this? But I was ready for the voice. This was both. I didn't think it would be long before Devrie left the Institute to storm to New York.

It was nearly another month, in which the snow began to fall and the city to deck itself in the tired gilt fallacies of Christmas. I felt fine. Humming, I catalogued the Madagascar moths, remounting the best specimens in exhibit cases and sealing them under permaplex, where their fragile wings and delicate antennae could lie safe. The mutant strains had the thinnest wings, unnaturally tenuous and up to twenty-five centimeters each, all of pale ivory, as if a ghostly delicacy were the natural evolutionary response to the glowing landscape of nuclear genocide. I catalogued each carefully.

"Why?" Devrie said. "*Why*?"

"You look like hell."

"Why?"

"I think you already know," I said. She sagged on my white velvet sofa, alone, the PGs that I suspected acted as much as nurses as guards, dismissed from the apartment. Tears of anger and exhaustion collected in her sunken eye sockets but did not fall. Only with effort was she keeping herself in a sitting position, and the effort was costing her energy she did not have. Her skin, except for two red spots of fury high on each cheekbone, was the color of old eggs. Looking at her, I had to keep my hands twisted in my lap to keep myself from weeping.

"Are you telling me you *planned* it, Seena? Are you telling me you located Keith and slept with him because you knew that would make him impotent with me?"

"Of course not. I know sexuality isn't that simple. So do you."

"But you gambled on it. You gambled that it would be one way to ruin the experiment."

"I gambled that it would . . . complicate Keith's responses."

"Complicate them past the point where he knew who the hell he was with!"

"He'd be able to know if you weren't making him glow out of his mind with neurotransmitter kickers! He's not stupid. But he's not ready for whatever mystic hoops you've tried to make him jump through—if anybody ever *can* be said to be ready for that!—and no, I'm not surprised that he can't handle libidinal energies on top of all the other artificial energies you're racing through his brain. Something was bound to snap."

"You caused it, Seena. As cold-bloodedly as that."

A sudden shiver of memory brought the feel of Keith's hands on my breasts. No, not as cold-bloodedly as that. No. But I could not say so to Devrie.

"I trusted you," she said. "'Anything for a sister'—God!"

"You were right to trust me. To trust me to get you out of that place before you're dead."

"Listen to yourself! Smug, all-knowing, self-righteous . . . do you know how *close* we were at the Institute? Do you have any idea what you've destroyed?"

I laughed coldly. I couldn't help it. "If contact with God can be destroyed because one confused kid can't get it up, what does that say about God?"

Devrie stared at me. A long moment passed, and in the moment the two red spots on her cheeks faded and her eyes narrowed. "Why, Seena?"

"I told you. I wanted you safe, out of there. And you are."

"No. No. There's something else, something more going on here. Going on with you."

"Don't make it more complicated than it is, Devrie. You're my sister, and my only family. Is it so odd that I would try to protect you?"

"Keith is your brother."

"Well, then, protect both of you. Whatever derails that experiment protects Keith, too."

She said softly, "Did you want him so much?"

We stared at each other across the living room, sisters, I standing by the mailnet and she supported by the sofa, needing its support, weak and implacable as any legendary martyr to the faith. Her weakness hurt me in some nameless place; as a child Devrie's body had been so strong. The hurt twisted in me, so that I answered her with truth. "Not so much. Not at first, not until we . . . no, that's not true. I wanted him. But that was not the reason, Devrie—it was not a rationalization for lust, nor any lapse in self-control."

She went on staring at me, until I turned to the sideboard and poured myself a Scotch. My hand trembled.

Behind me Devrie said, "Not lust. And not protection either. Something else, Seena. You're afraid."

I turned, smiling tightly. "Of you?"

"No. No, I don't think so."

"What then?"

"I don't know. Do you?"

"This is your theory, not mine."

She closed her eyes. The tears, shining all this time over her anger, finally fell. Head flung back against the pale sofa, arms limp at her side, she looked the picture of desolation, and so weak that I was frightened. I brought her a glass of milk from the kitchen and held it to her mouth, and I was a little surprised when she drank it off without protest.

"Devrie. You can't go on like this. In this physical state."

"No," she agreed, in a voice so firm and prompt that I was startled further. It was the voice of decision, not surrender. She straightened herself on the sofa. "Even Bohentin says I can't go on like this. I weigh less than he wants, and I'm right at the edge of not having the physical resources to control the twin trance. I'm having racking withdrawal symptoms even being on this trip, and at this very minute there is a doctor sitting at Father's desk in your study, in case I need him. Also, I've had my lawyers make over most of my remaining inheritance to Keith. I don't think you knew that. What's left has all been transferred to a bank on Dominica, and if I die it goes to the Institute. You won't be able to touch it, nor touch Keith's portion either, not even if I die. And I will die, Seena, soon, if I don't start eating and stop taking the program's drugs. I'll just burn out body and brain both. You've guessed that I'm close to that, but you haven't guessed how close. Now I'm telling you. I can't handle the stresses of the twin trance much longer."

I just went on holding her glass, arm extended, unable to move.

"You gambled that you could destroy one component in the chain of my experiment at the Institute by confusing my twin sexually. Well, you won. Now *I'm* making a gamble. I'm gambling my life that you can undo what you did with Keith, and without his knowing that I made you. You said he's not stupid and his impotency comes from being unable to handle the drug program; perhaps you're partly right. But he is me—*me*, Seena—and I know you've thought I was stupid all my life, because I wanted things you don't understand. Now Keith wants them, too—it was inevitable that he would—and you're going to undo whatever is standing in his way. I had to fight myself free all my life of your bullying, but Keith doesn't have that kind of time. Because if you don't undo what you cause, I'm going to go ahead with the twin trance anyway—the *twin trance*, Seena—without the sexual component and without letting Bohentin know just how much greater the strain is in trance than he thinks it is. He doesn't know, he doesn't have a twin, and neither do the doctors. But I know, and if I push much farther I'm going to eventually die at it. *Soon* eventually. When I do, all your scheming to get me out of there really will have failed and you'll be alone with whatever it is you're so afraid of. But I don't think you'll let that happen.

"I think that instead you'll undo what you did to Keith, so that the experiment can have one last real chance. And in return, after that one chance, I'll agree to come home, to Boston or here to New York, for one year.

"That's my gamble."

She was looking at me from eyes empty of all tears, a Devrie I had not ever seen before. She meant it, every demented word, and she would do it. I wanted to scream at her, to scream a jumble of suicide and moral blackmail and warped perceptions and outrage, but the words that came out of my mouth came out in a whisper.

"What in God's name is worth *that*?"

Shockingly, she laughed, a laugh of more power than her wasted frame could have contained. Her face glowed, and the glow looked both exalted and insane. "You said it, Seena—in God's name. To finally know. To *know*, beyond the fogginess of faith, that we're not alone in the universe . . . Faith should not mean fogginess." She laughed again, this time defensively, as if she knew how she sounded to me. "You'll do it, Seena." It was not a question. She took my hand.

"You would *kill* yourself?"

"No. I would die trying to reach God. It's not the same thing."

"I never bullied you, Devrie."

She dropped my hand. "All my life, Seena. And on into now. But all of your bullying and your scorn would look rather stupid, wouldn't it, if there really can be proved to exist a rational basis for what you laughed at all those years!"

We looked at each other, sisters, across the abyss of the pale sofa, and then suddenly away. Neither of us dared speak.

My plane landed on Dominica by night. Devrie had gone two days before me, returning with her doctor and guards on the same day she had left, as I had on my previous visit. I had never seen the island at night. The tropical greenery, lush with that faintly menacing suggestion of plant life gone wild, seemed to close in on me. The velvety darkness seemed to smell of ginger, and flowers, and the sea—all too strong, too blandly sensual, like an overdone perfume ad. At the hotel it was better; my room was on the second floor, above the dark foliage, and did not face the sea. Nonetheless, I stayed inside all that evening, all that darkness, until I could go the next day to the Institute of the Biological Hope.

"Hello, Seena."

"Keith. You look—"

"Rotten," he finished, and waited. He did not smile. Although he had lost some weight, he was nowhere near as skeletal as Devrie, and it gave me a pang I did not analyze to see his still-healthy body in the small gray room where last I had seen hers. His head was shaved, and without the curling brown hair he looked sterner, prematurely middle-aged. That, too, gave me a strange emotion, although it was not why he looked rotten. The worst was his eyes. Red-veined, watery, the sockets already a little sunken, they held the sheen of a man who was not forgiving somebody for something. Me? Himself? Devrie? I had lain awake all night, schooling myself for this insane interview, and still I did not know what to say. What does one say to persuade a man to sexual potency with one's sister so that her life might be saved? I felt ridiculous, and frightened, and—I suddenly realized the name of my strange emotion—humiliated. How could I even start to slog towards what I was supposed to reach?

"How goes the Great Experiment?"

"Not as you described it," he said, and we were there already. I looked at him evenly.

"You can't understand why I presented the Institute in the worst possible light."

"I can understand that."

"Then you can't understand why I bedded you, knowing about Bohentin's experiment."

"I can also understand that."

Something was wrong. Keith answered me easily, without restraint, but with conflict gritty beneath his voice, like sand beneath blowing grass. I stepped closer, and he flinched. But his expression did not change.

"Keith. What is this about? What am I doing here? Devrie said you couldn't . . . that you were impotent with her, confused enough about who and what . . ." I trailed off. He still had not changed expression.

I said quietly, "It was a simplistic idea in the first place. Only someone as simplistic as Devrie . . ." Only someone as simplistic as Devrie would think you could straighten out impotency by talking about it for a few hours. I turned to go, and I had gotten as far as laying my hand on the doorknob before Keith grasped my arm. Back to him, I squeezed my eyes shut. What in God would I have *done* if he had not stopped me?

"It's not what Devrie thinks!" With my back to him, not able to see his middle-aged baldness but only to hear the anguish in his voice, he again seemed young, uncertain, the boy I had bought coffee for in Indian Falls. I kept my back to him, and my voice carefully toneless.

"What is it, then, Keith? If not what Devrie thinks?"

"I don't know!"

"But you do know what it's not? It's not being confused about who is your sister and who your mother and who you're willing to have sex with in front of a room full of researchers?"

"No." His voice had gone hard again, but his hand stayed on my arm. "At first, yes. The first time. But, Seena—I *felt* it. *Almost*. I almost felt the presence, and then all the rest of the confusion—it didn't seem as important anymore. Not the confusion between you and Devrie."

I whirled to face him. "You mean God doesn't care whom you fuck if it gets you closer to fucking with Him."

He looked at me hard then—at me, not at his own self-absorption. His reddened eyes widened a little. "Why, Seeny—*you* care. You told me the brother-sister thing didn't matter any-more—but *you* care."

Did I? I didn't even know anymore. I said, "But then, I'm not deluding myself that it's all for the old Kingdom and the Glory."

"Glory," he repeated musingly, and finally let go of my arm. I couldn't tell what he was thinking.

"Keith. This isn't getting us anywhere."

"Where do you want to get?" he said in the same musing tone. "Where did any of you, starting with your father, want to get with me? Glory . . . glory."

Standing this close to him, seeing close up the pupils of his eyes and smelling close up the odor of his sweat, I finally realized what I should have seen all along: he was glowing. He was of course constantly on Bohentin's program of neurotransmitter manipulation, but the same chemicals that made the experiments possible also raised the threshold of both frankness and suggestibility. I guessed it must be a little like the looseness of being drunk, and I wondered if perhaps Bohentin might have deliberately raised the dosage before letting this interview take place. But no, Bohentin wouldn't be aware of the bargain Devrie and I had struck; she would not have told him. The whole bizarre situation was hers alone, and Keith's drugged musings a fortunate side-effect I would have to capitalize on.

"Where do you think my father wanted to get with you?" I asked him gently.

"Immortality. Godhead. The man who created Adam and Eve."

He was becoming maudlin. "Hardly 'the man,'" I pointed out. "My father was only one of a team of researchers. And the same results were being obtained independently in California."

"Results. I am a 'result.' What *do you* think he wanted, Seena?"

"Scientific knowledge of cell development. An objective truth."

"That's all Devrie wants."

"To compare bioengineering to some mystic quest—"

"Ah, but if the mystic quest is given a laboratory answer? Then it, too, becomes a scientific truth. You really hate that idea, don't you, Seena? You hate science validating anything you define as non-science."

I said stiffly, "That's rather an oversimplification."

"Then what do you hate?"

"I hate the risk to human bodies and human minds. To Devrie. To you."

"How nice of you to include me," he said, smiling. "And what do you think Devrie wants?"

"Sensation. Romantic religious emotion. To be all roiled up inside with delicious esoterica."

He considered this. "Maybe."

"And is that what you want as well, Keith? You've asked what everyone else wants. What do you want?"

"I want to feel at home in the universe. As if I belonged in it. And I never have."

He said this simply, without self-consciousness, and the words themselves were predictable enough for his age—even banal. There was nothing in the words that could account for my eyes suddenly filling with tears. "And 'scientifically' reaching God would do that for you?"

"How do I know until I try it? Don't cry, Seena."

"I'm not!"

"All right," he agreed softly. "You're not crying." Then he added, without changing tone, "I am more like you than like Devrie."

"How so?"

"I think that Devrie has always felt that she belongs in the universe. She only wants to find the . . . the coziest corner of it to curl up in. Like a cat. The coziest corner to curl up in is God's lap. Aren't you surprised that I should be more like you than like the person I was cloned from?"

"No," I said. "Harder upbringing than Devrie's. I told you that first day: cloning is only delayed twinning."

He threw back his head and laughed, a sound that chilled my spine. Whatever his conflict was, we were moving closer.

"Oh no, Seena. You're so wrong. It's more than delayed twinning, all right. You can't buy a real twin. You either have one or you don't. But you can buy yourself a clone. Bought, paid for, kept on the books along with all the rest of the glassware and holotanks and electron microscopes. You said so yourself, in your apartment, when you first told me about Devrie and the Institute. 'Money. She'd buy you.' And you were right, of course. Your father bought me, and she did, and you did. But of course you two women couldn't have bought if I hadn't been selling."

He was smiling still. Stupid—we had both been stupid, Devrie and I, we had both been looking in the wrong place, misled by our separate blinders-on training in the laboratory brain. My training had been scientific, hers humanistic, and so I looked at Freud and she looked at Oedipus, and we were equally stupid. How did the world look to a man who did not deal in laboratory brains, a man raised in a grittier world in which limits were not what the mind was capable of but what the bank book would stand? 'Your genes are too expensive for you to claim except as a beggar; your sisters are too expensive for you to claim except as a beggar; God is too expensive for you to claim except as a beggar.' To a less romantic man it would not have mattered, but a less romantic man would not have come to the Institute. What dark humiliations and resentments did Keith feel when he looked at Devrie, the self who was buyer and not bought?

Change the light you shine onto a mind, and you see different neural patterns, different corridors, different forests of trees grown in soil you could not have imagined. Run that soil through your fingers and you discover different pebbles, different sand, different leaf mold from the decay of old growths. Devrie and I had been hacking through the wrong forest.

Not Oedipus, but Marx.

Quick lines of attack came to me. Say: Keith it's a job like any other with high-hazard pay why can't you look at it like that a very dangerous and well-paid job for which you've been hired by just one more eccentric member of the monied class. Say: You're entitled to the wealth you're our biological brother damn it consider it rationally as a kinship entitlement. Say: Don't be so nicey-nice it's a tough world out there and if Devrie's giving it away take it don't be an impractical chump.

I said none of that. Instead I heard myself saying, coolly and with a calm cruelty, "You're quite right. You were bought by Devrie, and she is now using her own purchase for her own ends. You're a piece of equipment bought and paid for. Unfortunately, there's no money in the account. It has all been a grand sham."

Keith jerked me to face him with such violence that my neck cracked. "What are you saying?"

The words came as smoothly, as plausibly, as if I had rehearsed them. I didn't even consciously plan them: how can you plan a lie you do not know you will need? I slashed through this forest blind, but the ground held under my feet.

"Devrie told me that she has signed over most of her inheritance to you. What she didn't know, because I haven't yet told her, is that she doesn't have control of her inheritance any longer. It's not hers. I control it. I had her declared mentally incompetent on the grounds of violent suicidal tendencies and had myself made her legal guardian. She no longer has the legal right to control her fortune. A doctor observed her when she came to visit me in New York. So the transfer of her fortune to you is invalid."

"The lawyers who gave me the papers to sign—"

"Will learn about the New York action this week," I said smoothly. How much inheritance law did Keith know? Probably very little. Neither did I, and I invented furiously; it only needed to *sound* plausible. "The New York courts only handed down their decision recently, and Dominican judicial machinery, like everything else in the tropics, moves slowly. But the ruling will hold, Keith. Devrie does not control her own money, and you're a pauper again. But *I* have something for you. Here. An airline ticket back to Indian Falls. You're a free man. Poor, but free. The ticket is in your name, and there's a check inside it—that's from me. You've earned it, for at least trying to aid poor Devrie. But now you're going to have to leave her to me. I'm now her legal guardian.

I held the ticket out to him. It was wrapped in its airline folder; my own name as passenger was hidden. Keith stared at it, and then at me.

I said softly, "I'm sorry you were cheated. Devrie didn't mean to. But she has no money, now, to offer you. You can go. Devrie's my burden now."

His voice sounded strangled. "To remove from the Institute?"

"I never made any secret of wanting her out. Although the legal papers for that will take a little time to filter through the Dominican courts. She wouldn't go except by force, so force is what I'll get. Here."

I thrust the ticket folder at him. He made no move to take it, and I saw from the hardening of his face—my face, Devrie's face—the moment when Devrie shifted forests in his mind. Now she was without money, without legal control of her life, about to be torn from the passion she loved most. The helpless underdog. The orphaned woman, poor and cast out, in need of protection from the powerful who had seized her fortune.

Not Marx, but Cervantes.

"You would do that? To your own sister?"

Anything for a sister. I said bitterly, "Of course I would."

"She's not mentally imcompetent!"

"Isn't she?"

"No!"

I shrugged. "The courts say she is."

Keith studied me, resolve hardening around him. I thought of certain shining crystals, that will harden around any stray piece of grit. Now that I was succeeding in convincing him, my lies hurt—or perhaps what hurt was how easily he believed them.

"Are you sure, Seena," he said, "that *you* aren't just trying a grab for Devrie's fortune?"

I shrugged again, and tried to make my voice toneless. "I want her out of here. I don't want her to die."

"Die? What makes you think she would die?"

"She looks—"

"She's nowhere near dying," Keith said angrily—his anger a release, so much that it hardly mattered at what. "Don't you think I can tell in twin trance what her exact physical state is? And don't you know how much control the trance gives each twin over the bodily processes of the other? Don't you even know that? Devrie isn't anywhere near dying. And I'd pull her out of trance if she were." He paused, looking hard at me. "Keep your ticket, Seena."

I repeated mechanically, "You can leave now. There's no money." *Devrie had lied to me.*

"That wouldn't leave her with any protection at all, would it?" he said levelly. When he grasped the door knob to leave, the tendons in his wrist stood out clearly, strong and taut. I did not try to stop his going.

Devrie had lied to me. With her lie, she had blackmailed me into yet another lie to Keith. The twin trance granted control, in some unspecified way, to each twin's body; the trance I had pioneered might have resulted in eight deaths unknowingly inflicted on each other out of who knows what dark forests in eight fumbling minds. Lies, blackmail, death, more lies.

Out of these lies they were going to make scientific truth. Through these forests they were going to search for God.

"Final clearance check of holotanks," an assistant said formally. "Faraday cage?"

"Optimum."

"External radiation?"

"Cleared," said the man seated at the console of the first tank.

"Cleared," said the woman seated at the console of the second.

"Microradiation?"

"Cleared."

"Cleared."

"Personnel radiation, Class A?"

"Cleared."

"Cleared."

On it went, the whole tedious and crucial procedure, until both tanks had been cleared and focused, the fluid adjusted, tested, adjusted again, tested again. Bohentin listened patiently, without expression, but I, standing to the side of him and behind the tanks, saw the nerve at the base of his neck and just below the hairline pulse in some irregular rhythm of its own. Each time the nerve pulsed, the skin rose slightly from under his collar. I kept my eyes on that syncopated crawling of flesh, and felt tension prickle over my own skin like heat.

Three-quarters of the lab, the portion where the holotanks and other machinery stood, was softly dark, lit mostly from the glow of console dials and the indirect track lighting focused on the tanks. Standing in the gloom were Bohentin, five other scientists, two medical doctors—and me. Bohentin had fought my being allowed there, but in the end he had had to give in. I had known too many threatening words not in generalities but in specifics: reporter's names, drug names, cloning details, twin trance tragedy, anorexia symptoms, bioengineering amendment. He was not a man who much noticed either public opinion or relatives' threats, but no one else outside his Institute knew so many so specific words—some knew some of the words, but only I had them all. In the end he had focused on me his cold, brilliant eyes, and given permission for me to witness the experiment that involved my sister.

I was going to hold Devrie to her bargain. I was not going to believe anything she told me without witnessing it for myself.

Half the morning passed in technical preparation. Somewhere Devrie and Keith, the human components of this costly detection circuit, were separately being brought to the apex of brain activity. Drugs, biofeedback, tactile and auditory and kinaesthetic stimulation—all carefully calculated for the maximum increase of both the number of neurotransmitters firing signals through the synapses of the brain and of the speed at which the signals raced. The more rapid the transmission through certain pathways, the more intense both perception and feeling. Some neurotransmitters, under this pressure, would alter molecular structure into natural hallucinogens; that reaction had to be controlled. Meanwhile other drugs, other biofeedback techniques, would depress the body's natural enzymes designed to either reabsorb excess transmitters or to reduce the rate at which they fired. The number and speed of neurotransmitters in Keith's and Devrie's brains would mount, and mount, and mount, all natural chemical barriers removed. The two of them would enter the lab with their whole brains—rational cortex, emotional limbic, right and left brain functions—simultaneously aroused to an unimaginable degree. *Simultaneously*. They would be feeling as great a "rush" as a falling skydiver, as great a glow as a cocaine user, as great a mental clarity and receptivity as a da Vinci whose brush is guided by all the integrated visions of his unconscious mind. They would be white-hot.

Then they would hit each other with the twin trance.

The quarter of the lab which Keith and Devrie would use was softly and indirectly lit, though brighter than the rest. It consisted of a raised, luxuriantly padded platform, walls and textured pillows in a pink whose component wavelengths had been carefully calculated, temperature in a complex gradient producing precise convection flows over the skin. The man and woman in that womb-colored, flesh-stimulating environment would be able to see us observers standing in the gloom behind the holotanks only as vague shapes. When the two doors opened and Devrie and Keith moved onto the platform, I knew that they would not even try to distinguish who stood in the lab. Looking at their faces, that looked only at each other, I felt my heart clutch.

They were naked except for the soft helmets that both attached hundreds of needles to nerve clumps just below the skin and also held the earphones through which Bohentin controlled the music that swelled the cathedrals of their skulls. "Cathedrals"—from their faces, transfigured to the ravished ecstasy found in paintings of medieval saints, that was the right word. But here the ecstasy was controlled, understood, and I saw with a sudden rush of pain at old memories that I could recognize the exact moment when Keith and Devrie locked onto each other with the twin trance. I recognized it, with my own more bitter hyperclarity, in their eyes, as I recognized the cast of concentration that came over their features, and the intensity of their absorption. The twin trance. They clutched each other's hands, faces inches apart, and suddenly I had to look away.

Each holotank held two whorls of shifting colors, the outlines clearer and the textures more sharply delineated than any previous holographs in the history of science. Keith's and Devrie's perceptions of each other's presence. The whorls went on clarifying themselves, separating into distinct and mappable layers, as on the platform Keith and Devrie remained frozen, all their energies focused on the telepathic trance. Seconds passed, and then minutes. And still, despite the clarity of the holographs in the tank, a clarity that fifteen years earlier I would have given my right hand for, I sensed that Keith and Devrie were holding back, were deliberately confining their unimaginable perceptiveness to each other's radiant energy, in the same way that water is confined behind a dam to build power.

But how could *I* be sensing that? From a subliminal "reading" of the mapped perceptions in the holotanks? Or from something else?

More minutes passed. Keith and Devrie stayed frozen, facing each other, and over her skeletal body and his stronger one a flush began to spread, rosy and slow, like heat tide rising.

"Jesus H. Christ," said one of the medical doctors, so low that only I, standing directly behind her, could have heard. It was not a curse, nor a prayer, but some third possibility, unnameable.

Keith put one hand on Devrie's thigh. She shuddered. He drew her down to the cushions on the platform and they began to caress each other, not frenzied, not in the exploring way of lovers but with a deliberation I have never experienced outside a research lab, a slow care that implied that worlds of interpretation hung on each movement. Yet the effect was not of coldness nor detachment but of intense involvement, of tremendous energy joyously used, of creating each other's bodies right then, there under each other's hands. They were *working*, and oblivious to all but their work. But if it was a kind of creative work, it was also a kind of primal innocent eroticism, and, watching, I felt my own heat begin to rise. "Innocent"—but if innocence is unknowingness, there was nothing innocent about it at all. Keith and Devrie knew and controlled each heartbeat, and I felt the exact moment, when they let their sexual energies, added to all the other neural energies, burst the dam and flood outward in wave after wave, expanding the scope of each brain's perceptions, inundating the artifically-walled world.

A third whorl formed in holotank.

It formed suddenly: one second nothing, the next brightness. But then it wavered, faded a bit. After a few moments it brightened slightly, a diffused golden haze, before again fading. On the platform Keith gasped, and I guessed he was having to shift his attention between perceiving the third source of radiation and keeping up the erotic version of the twin trance. His biofeedback techniques were less experienced than Devrie's, and the male erection more fragile. But then he caught the rhythm, and the holograph brightened.

It seemed to me that the room brightened as well, although no additional lights came on and the consoles glowed no brighter. Sweat poured off the researchers. Bohentin leaned forward, his neck muscle tautening toward the platform as if it were his will and not Keith/Devrie's that strained to perceive that third presence recorded in the tank. I thought, stupidly, of mythical intermediaries: Merlyn never made king, Moses never reaching the Promised Land. Intermediaries—and then it became impossible to think of anything at all.

Devrie shuddered and cried out. Keith's orgasm came a moment later, and with it a final roil of neural activity so strong the two primary whorls in each holotank swelled to fill the tank and inundate the third. At the moment of break-through Keith screamed, and in memory it seems as if the scream was what tore through the last curtain—that is nonsense. How loud would microbes have to scream to attract the attention of giants? How loud does a knock on the door have to be to pull a sleeper from the alien world of dreams?

The doctor beside me fell to her knees. The third presence—or some part of it—swirled all around us, racing along our own unprepared synapses and neurons, and what swirled and raced was astonishment. A golden, majestic astonishment. We had finally attracted Its attention, finally knocked with enough neural force to be just barely heard—and It was astonished that we could, or did exist. The slow rise of that powerful astonishment within the shielded lab was like the slow swinging around of the head of a great beast to regard some butterfly it has barely glimpsed from the corner of one eye. But this was no beast. As Its attention swung toward us, pain exploded in my skull—the pain of sound too loud, lights too bright, charge too high. My brain was burning on overload. There came one more flash of insight—wordless, pattern without end—and the sound of screaming. Then, abruptly, the energy vanished.

Bohentin, on all fours, crawled toward the holotanks. The doctor lay slumped on the floor; the other doctor had already reached the platform and its two crumpled figures. Someone was crying, someone else shouting. I rose, fell, dragged myself to the side of the platform and then could not climb it. I could not climb the platform. Hanging with two hands on the edge, hearing the voice crying as my own, I watched the doctor bend shakily to Keith, roll him off Devrie to bend over her, turn back to Keith.

Bohentin cried, "The tapes are intact!"

"Oh God oh God oh God oh God oh God," somone moaned, until abruptly she stopped. I grasped the flesh-colored padding on top of the platform and pulled myself up onto it.

Devrie lay unconscious, pulse erratic, face cast in perfect bliss. The doctor breathed into Keith's mouth—what strength could the doctor himself have left?—and pushed on the naked chest. Breathe, push, breathe, push. The whole length of Keith's body shuddered; the doctor rocked back on his heels; Keith breathed.

"It's all on tape!" Bohentin cried. "It's all *on tape*!"

"God damn you to hell," I whispered to Devrie's blissful face. "It didn't even know we were there!"

Her eyes opened. I had to lean close to hear her answer.

"But now . . . we know He . . . is there."

She was too weak to smile. I looked away from her, away from that face, out into the tumultuous emptiness of the lab, anywhere.

They will try again.

Devrie has been asleep, fed by glucose solution through an IV, for fourteen hours. I sit near her bed, frowned at by the nurse, who can see my expression as I stare at my sister. Somewhere in another bed Keith is sleeping yet again. His rest is more fitful than Devrie's; she sinks into sleep as into warm water, but he cannot. Like me, he is afraid of drowning.

An hour ago he came into Devrie's room and grasped my hand.

"How could It—He—It not have been aware that we existed? Not even have *known*?"

I didn't answer him.

"You felt it too, Seena, didn't you? The others say they could, so you must have too. It . . . created us in some way. No, that's wrong. How could It create us and not *know*?"

I said wearily, "Do *we* always know what we've created?" and Keith glanced at me sharply. But I had not been referring to my father's work in cloning.

"Keith. What's a Thysania Africana?"

"A what?"

"Think of us," I said, "as just one more biological side-effect. One type of being acts, and another type of being comes into existence. Man stages something like the African Horror, and in doing so he creates whole new species of moths and doesn't even discover they exist until long afterward. If man can do it, why not God? And why should He be any more aware of it than we are?"

Keith didn't like that. He scowled at me, and then looked at Devrie's sleeping face: Devrie's sleeping bliss.

"Because she is a fool," I said savagely, "and so are you. You won't leave it alone, will you? Having been noticed by It once, you'll try to be noticed by It again. Even though she promised me otherwise, and even if it kills you both."

Keith looked at me a long time, seeing clearly—finally—the nature of the abyss between us, and its dimensions. But I already knew neither of us could cross. When at last he spoke, his voice held so much compassion that I hated him. "Seena. Seena, love. There's no more doubt now, don't you see? Now rational belief is no harder than rational doubt. Why are you so afraid to even believe?"

I left the room. In the corridor I leaned against the wall, palms spread flat against the tile, and closed my eyes. It seemed to me that I could hear wings, pale and fragile, beating against glass.

They will try again. For the sake of sure knowledge that the universe is not empty, Keith and Devrie and all the others like their type of being will go on pushing their human brains beyond what the human brain has evolved to do, go on fluttering their wings against that biological window. For the sake of sure knowledge: belief founded on experiment and not on faith. And the Other: being/alien/God? It, too, may choose to initiate contact, if It can and now that It knows we are here. Perhaps It will seek to know *us*, and even beyond the laboratory Devrie and Keith may find any moment of heightened arousal subtly invaded by a shadowy Third. Will they sense It, hovering just beyond concsciousness, if they argue fiercely or race a sailboat in rough water or make love? How much arousal will it take, now, for them to sense those huge wings beating on the *other* side of the window?

And windows can be broken.

Tomorrow I will fly back to New York. To my museum, to my exhibits, to my moths under permaplex, to my empty apartment, where I will keep the heavy drapes drawn tightly across the glass.

For—oh God—all the rest of my life.

THE BLIND GEOMETER

Kim Stanley Robinson

A. When you are born blind, your development is different from that of sighted infants. (I was born blind, I know.) The reasons for this are fairly obvious. Much normal early infant development, both physical and mental, is linked to vision, which coordinates all sense and action. Without vision reality is . . . (it's hard to describe) a sort of void, in which transitory things come to existence when grasped and mouthed and heard—then when the things fall silent or are dropped, they melt away, they *cease to exist*. (I wonder if I have not kept a bit of that feeling with me always.) It can be shown that this sense of object permanence must be learned by sighted infants as well—move a toy behind a screen and very young babies will assume the toy has ceased to exist—but vision (seeing part of a toy [or a person] behind the screen, etc.) makes their construction of a sense of object permanence fairly rapid and easy. With the blind child it is a much harder task, it takes months, sometimes years. And with no sense of an object world, there can be no complementary concept of self; without this concept, all phenomena can be experienced as part of an extended "body." (Haptic space [or tactile space, the space of the body] expanding to fill visual space . . .) Every blind infant is in danger of autism.

"But we also have, and know that we have the capacity of

complete freedom to transform, in thought and phantasy, our human historical existence . . ."

—Edmund Husserl, *The Origin of Geometry*

C. *Mark point A. Then mark point B. Only one line, AB, can be drawn through these two points.* Say that events, happening hadon by hadon in the unimaginably brief slice of reality that is the present, are points. Connecting these points would then create lines, and the lines figures—figures that would give a shape to our lives, our world. If the world were a Euclidean space, this would make the shapes of our lives comprehensible to us. But the world is not a Euclidean space. And so all our understanding is no more than a reductive mathematics for the world. Language as a kind of geometry.

AB. My first memories are of the Christmas morning when I was some three and a half years old, when one of my gifts was a bag of marbles. I was fascinated by the way the handfuls of marbles felt in my fingers: heavy glass spheres, all so smooth and clickety, all so much the same. I was equally impressed by the leather bag that had contained them. It was so pliable, had such a baggy shape, could be drawn up by such a leathery draw string. (I must tell you, from the viewpoint of tactual aesthetics, there is nothing quite so beautiful as well-oiled leather. My favorite toy was my father's boot.) Anyway, I was rolling on my belly over the marbles spread on the floor (more contact) when I came against the Christmas tree, all prickly and piney. Reaching up to break off some needles to rub between my fingers, I touched an ornament that felt to me, in my excitement, like a lost marble. I yanked on it (and on the branch, no doubt) and—down came the tree.

The alarum afterward is only a blur in my memory, as if it all were on tape, and parts of it forever fast-forwarded to squeaks and trills. Little unspliced snippets of tape: my memory. (My story.)

BA. How often have I searched for snippets before that one, from the long years of my coming to consciousness? How did I first discover the world beyond my body, beyond my searching hands? It was one of my greatest intellectual feats—perhaps the greatest—and yet it is lost to me.

So I read, and learned how other blind infants accomplished the task. I understood better how important my mother had to have been in this process, I began to understand why I felt about her the way I did, why I missed her so.

My own life, known to me through words—the world become a text—this happens to me all the time. It is what T.D. Cutsforth called entering the world of "verbal unreality," and it is part of the fate of the curious blind person.

O. I never did like Jeremy Blasingame. He had been a colleague for a few years, and his office was six doors down from mine. It seemed to me that he was one of those people who are fundamentally uncomfortable around the blind; and it's always the blind person's job to put these people at their ease, which gets to be a pain in the ass. (In fact, I usually ignore the problem.) Jeremy always watched me closely (you can tell this by voice), and it was clear that he found it hard to believe that I was one of the co-editors of *Topological Geometry*, a journal he submitted to occasionally. But he was a good mathematician, and a fair topologist, and we had published some of his submissions, so that he and I remained superficially friendly.

Still, he was always probing, always picking my brains. At this time I was working hard on the geometry of *n*-dimensional manifolds, and some of the latest results from CERN and SLAC and the big new accelerator on Oahu were fitting into the work in an interesting way: it appeared that certain sub-atomic particles were moving as if in a multi-dimensional manifold, and I had Sullivan and Wu and some of the other physicists from these places asking questions about my work in multi-dimensional geometries. With them I was happy to talk, but with Jeremy I couldn't see the point. Certain speculations I once made in conversation with him later showed up in one of his papers; and it just seemed to me that he was looking for help without actually saying so.

And there was the matter of his image. In the sun I perceived him as a shifting, flecked brightness. It's unusual I can see people at all, and as I couldn't really account for this (was it vision, or something else?) it made me uncomfortable.

But no doubt in retrospect I have somewhat exaggerated this uneasiness.

AC. The first event of my life that I recall that has any emotion attached to it (the earlier ones being mere snips of tape that could have come from anyone's life, given how much feeling is associated with them) comes from my eighth year, and has to do, emblematically enough, with math. I was adding columns with my Braille punch, and excited at my new power, I took the bumpy sheet of figures to show my father. He puzzled over it for a while. "Hmm," he said. "Here, you have to make very sure that the columns are in straight vertical rows." His long fingers guided mine down a column. "Twenty-two is off to the left, feel that? You have to keep them all straight."

Impatiently I pulled my hand away, and the flood of frustration began its tidal wash through me (most familiar of sensations, felt scores of times a day); my voice tightened to a high whine: "But *why*? It doesn't *matter*—"

"Yes it does." My father wasn't one for unnecessary neatness, as I already knew well from tripping over his misplaced briefcase, ice skates, shoes . . . "Let's see." He had my fingers again. "You know how numbers work. Here's twenty-two. Now what that means, is two twos, and two tens. This two marks the twenty, this two marks the two, even though they're both just two characters, right? Well, when you're adding, the column to the far right is the column of ones. Next over is the column of tens, and next over is the column of hundreds. Here you've got three hundreds, right? Now if you have the twenty-two over to the left too far, you'll add the twenty in the hundreds column, as if the number were two hundred twenty rather than twenty-two. And that'll be wrong. So you have to keep the columns really straight—"

Understanding, ringing me as if I were a big old church bell, and it the clapper. It's the first time I remember feeling that sensation that has remained one of the enduring joys of my life: *to understand*.

And understanding mathematical concepts quickly led to power (and how I craved that!), power not only in the abstract world of math, but in the real world of father and school. I remember jumping up and down, my dad laughing cheerily, me dashing to my room to stamp out columns as straight as the ruler's edge, to add column after column of figures.

A. Oh yes: Carlos Oleg Nevsky, here. Mother Mexican, father Russian (military advisor). Born in Mexico City in 2018, three months premature, after my mother suffered a bout of German measles during the pregnancy. Result: almost total blindness (I can tell dark from [bright] light.) Lived in Mexico City until father was transferred to Soviet embassy in Washington, D.C., when I was five. Lived in Washington almost continuously since then. My parents divorced when I was ten, and my mother returned to Mexico City when I was thirteen. I never understood that; their whole relationship took place out of earshot, it seemed. But from then on I was wary.

Mathematics professor at George Washington University since 2043.

OA. One cold spring afternoon I encountered Jeremy Blasingame in the faculty lounge as I went to get a coffee refill—in the lounge, where nobody ever hangs out. "Hello, Carlos, how's it going?"

"Fine," I said, reaching about the table for the sugar. "And you?"

"Pretty good. I've got a kind of an interesting problem over at my consulting job, though. It's giving me fits."

Jeremy worked for the Pentagon in military intelligence or something, but he seldom talked about what he did there, and I certainly never asked. "Oh yes?" I said as I found the sugar and spooned some in.

"Yes. They've got a coding problem that I bet would interest you."

"I'm not much for cryptography." Spy games—the math involved is really very limited. Sweet smell of sugar, dissolving in the lounge's bad coffee.

"Yes, I know," Jeremy said. "But—" An edge of frustration in his voice; it's hard to tell when I'm paying attention, I know. (A form of control.) "But this may be a geometer's code. We have a subject, you see, drawing diagrams."

A *subject*. "Hmph," I said. Some poor spy scribbling away in a cell somewhere . . .

"So—I've got one of the drawings here. It reminds me of the theorem in your last article. Some projection, perhaps."

"Yes?" Now what spy would draw something like that?

"Yeah, and it seems to have something to do with her speech, too. Her verbal sequencing is all dislocated—words in strange order, sometimes."

"Yes? What happened to her?"

"Well . . . Here, check out the drawing."

I put out a hand. "I'll take a look."

"And next time you want coffee, come ask me. I do a proper job of it in my office."

"All right."

AB. I suppose I have wondered all my life what it would be like to see. And all my work, no doubt, is an effort to envision things in the inward theater. "I see it *feelingly*." In language, in music, most of all in the laws of geometry, I find the best ways I can to see: by analogy to touch, and to sound, and to abstractions. Understand: to know the geometries fully is to comprehend exactly the physical world that light reveals; in a way one is then perceiving something like the Platonic ideal forms underlying the visible phenomena of the world. Sometimes the great ringing of comprehension fills me so entirely that I feel I *must* be seeing; what more could it be? I believe that I see.

Then comes the problem of crossing the street, of finding my misplaced keys. Geometry is little help; it's back to the hands and ears as eyes, at that point. And then I know that I do not see at all.

BC. Let me put it another way. Projective geometry began in the Renaissance, as an aid to painters newly interested in perspective, in the problems of representing the three-dimensional world on a canvas; it quickly became a mathematics of great power and elegance. The basic procedure can be illustrated quickly.

A geometrical figure is *projected* from one plane to another (as light, they tell me, projects a slide's image onto a wall) (See Figure 1). Note that while certain properties of triangle ABC are changed in triangle A′B′C′ (lengths of sides, measures of angles), other properties are not: points are still points, lines lines, and certain proportions still hold, among other things.

Now imagine that the visual world is triangle ABC (reduction . . .). But then imagine that it has been projected inward onto something different, not onto a plane, but onto a Moebius strip or a Klein bottle say, or really, onto a manifold much more complex and strange than those (you'd be surprised.) Certain features of ABC are gone for good (color, for instance), but other essential features remain. And projective geometry is the art of finding what features or qualities survive the transformations of projection . . .

Do you understand me?

A way into the world, a mode of consciousness, a philosophy, a type of being. A vision. A geometry for the self. Non-Euclidean, of course; in fact, strictly Nevskyan, as it has to be to help me, as I make my projections from visual space to auditive space, to haptic space, to the world inside.

OA. The next time I met Blasingame he was anxious to hear what I thought of his diagram. (There could be an acoustics of emotion, thus a mathematics of emotion; meanwhile the ears of the blind do these calculations every day.)

"One drawing isn't much to go on, Jeremy. I mean, you're right, it looks like a simple projective drawing, but with some odd lines crossing it. Who knows what they mean? The whole thing might be something scribbled by a kid."

"She's not that young. Want to see more?"

"Well . . ." This woman he kept mentioning, some sort of Mata

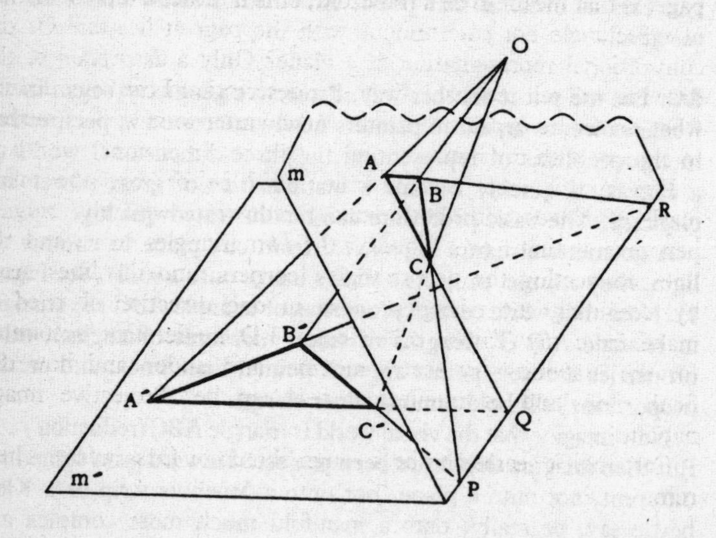

Figure 1

Hari prisoner in the Pentagon, drawing geometrical figures and refusing to speak except in riddles . . . naturally I was intrigued.

"Here, take these anyway. There seems to be a sort of progression."

"It would help if I could talk to this *subject* who's doing all these."

"Actually, I don't think so. But"—(seeing my irritation)—"I can bring her by, I think, if these interest you."

"I'll check them out."

"Good, good." Peculiar edge of excitement in his voice, tension, triumph, fear, the anticipation of . . . something. Frowning, I took the papers from him.

That afternoon I shuffled them into my special xerox machine, and the stiff reproductions rolled out of it heavily ridged. I ran my hands over the raised lines and letters slowly.

Here I must confess to you that most geometrical drawings are almost useless to me. If you consider it you will quickly see why: most drawings are two-dimensional representations of what a three-dimensional construction *looks* like. This does me no good, and in fact is extremely confusing. Say I feel a trapezoid on the page; is that meant to be a trapezoid, or is it rather a representation of a rectangle not coterminous with the page it lies on? Or the conventional representation of a plane? Only a *description* of the drawing will tell me that. Without a description I can only deduce what the figure *appears* to mean. Much easier to have 3-D models to explore with my hands.

But in this case, not possible. So I swept over the mishmash of ridges with both hands, redrew it with my ridging pen several times over, located the two triangles in it, and the lines connecting the two triangles' corners, and the lines made by extending the triangles' sides in one direction. I tried to make from my Taylor collection a 3-D model that accounted for the drawing—try that sometime, and understand how difficult this kind of intellectual feat can be. Projective imagination . . .

Certainly it seemed to be a rough sketch of Desargues's Theorem.

C. Desargues's Theorem was one of the first theorems clearly concerned with projective geometry; it was proposed by Girard

Desargues in the mid-seventeenth century, in between his architectural and engineering efforts, his books on music, etc. It is a relatively simple theorem, in fact in three dimensions it is completely banal. Figure 1 describes it, refer back to it if you want; the theorem states that given the relationships shown in the diagram, points P, Q, and R will be collinear. The proof is simple indeed. By definition P, Q, and R lie on the same plane *m* as triangle ABC, and they lie on the same plane *m′* as A′B′C′. Two planes can only intersect in a line, and as P, Q, and R lie on both *m* and *m′* they must lie on that line of intersection. Therefore P, Q, and R are collinear, as was to be proved.

Obvious, you say, and it is true. But you would be surprised to learn how many proofs in geometry, when taken step by step and reduced to their constituent parts, are just as obvious. With a language so pure, things become clear. Would we had such a language for the heart.

It is also true, by the way, that this theorem is reciprocal: that is, if you postulate two triangles whose extensions of the sides meet at three collinear points, then it is possible to show that lines AA′, BB′, and CC′ meet in a single point. As they say in the textbooks, I leave the proof of this as an exercise for the reader.

AC. But so what? I mean, it is a beautiful theorem, with the sort of purity and elegance characteristic of Renaissance math—but what was it doing in a drawing made by some poor prisoner of the Pentagon?

I considered this as I walked to my health club, Warren's Spa (considered it secondarily, anyway, and no doubt subconsciously; my primary concerns were the streets and the traffic. Washington's streets bear a certain resemblance to one of those confusing geometrical diagrams I described [the state streets crossing diagonally the regular gridwork, creating a variety of intersections]; happily one doesn't have to comprehend all the city at once to walk in it. But it is easy to become lost. So as I walked I concentrated on distances, on the sounds of the streets that tended to remain constant, on smells [the dirt of the park at M and New Hampshire, the hot-dog vendor on Twenty-first and K]; meanwhile my cane established the world directly before my feet, my sonar shades whistled rising or falling notes as objects approached or receded . . . It takes some work just to get from point A to point B without getting disoriented [at which point one has to grind one's teeth and ask for directions] but it can be done, it is one of those small tasks/accomplishments [one chooses which, every time] that the blind cannot escape)—still, I did consider the matter of the drawing as I walked.

On H Street and Twenty-first I was pleased to smell the pretzel cart of my friend Ramon, who is also blind. His cart is the only one where the hot plate hasn't roasted several pretzels to that metallic burnt odor that all the other carts put off; Ramon prefers the clean smell of freshly baked dough, and he claims it brings him more customers, which I certainly believe. "Change only please," he was saying to someone briskly, "there's a change machine on the other side of the cart for your convenience, thanks. Hot pretzels! Hot pretzels, one dollar!"

"Hey there, Superblink!" I called as I approached him.

"Hey yourself, Professor Superblink," he replied. (*Superblink* is a mildly derogatory name used by irritated sighted social service people to describe those of their blind colleagues who are aggressively or ostentatiously competent in getting around, etc., who make a *display* of their competence. Naturally we have appropriated the term for our own use; sometimes it means the same thing for us—when used in the third person, usually—but in the second person it's a term of affection.)

"Want a pretzel?"

"Sure."

"You off to the gym?"

"Yeah, I'm going to throw. Next time we play you're in trouble."

"That'll be the day, when my main mark starts beating me!"

I put four quarters in his callused hand and he gave me a pretzel. "Here's a puzzle for you," I said. "Why would someone try to convey a message by geometrical diagram?"

He laughed. "Don't ask me, that's your department!"

"But the message isn't for me."

"Are you sure about that?"

I frowned.

BC. At the health club I greeted Warren and Amanda at the front desk. They were laughing over a headline in the tabloid newspaper Amanda was shaking; they devoured those things, and pasted the best headlines all over the gym.

"What's the gem of the day?" I asked.

"How about 'Gay Bigfoot Molests Young Boys'?" Warren suggested.

"Or 'Woman Found Guilty of Turning Husband into Bank President,'" Amanda said, giggling. "She drugged him and did bemod to him until he went from teller to president."

Warren said, "I'll have to do that for you, eh Amanda?"

"Make me something better than a bank president."

Warren clicked his tongue. "Entirely too many designer drugs, these days. Come on, Carlos, I'll get the range turned on." I went to the locker room and changed, and when I got to the target room Warren was just done setting it up. "Ready to go," he said cheerily as he rolled past me.

I stepped in, closed the door, and walked out to the center of the room, where a waist-high wire column was filled with baseballs. I pulled out a baseball, hefted it, felt the stitching. A baseball is a beautiful object: nicely flared curves of the seams over the surface of a perfect sphere, an ideal object, exactly the right weight for throwing.

I turned on the range with a flick of a switch, and stepped away from the feeder, a ball in each hand. Now it was quite silent, only the slightest whirr faintly breathing through the soundproofed walls. I did what I could to reduce the sound of my own breathing, heard my heartbeat in my ears.

Then a *beep* behind me to my left, and low; I swirled and threw. Dull thud. "Right . . . low," said the machine voice from above, softly. *Beep* I threw again: "Right . . . high," it said louder, meaning I had missed by more. "Shit," I said as I got another two balls. "Bad start."

Beep—a hard throw to my left—*clang*! "Yeah!" There is very little in life more satisfying than the bell-like clanging of the target circle when hit square. It rings at about middle C with several overtones, like a small thick church bell hit with a hammer. The sound of success.

Seven more throws, four more hits. "Five for ten," the machine voice said. "Average strike time, one-point-three-five seconds. Fastest strike time, point-eight-four seconds."

Ramon sometimes hit the target in half a second or less, but I needed to hear the full beep to keep my average up. I set up for another round, pushed the button, got quiet, *beep* throw, *beep* throw, working to shift my feet faster, to follow through, to use the information from my misses to correct for the next time the target was near the floor, or the ceiling, or behind me (my weakness is the low ones, I can't seem to throw down accurately). And as I warmed up I threw harder and harder. Just throwing a baseball as hard as you can is a joy in itself. And then to set that bell ringing! *Clang*! It chimes every cell of you.

But when I quit and took a shower, and stood before my locker and reached in to free my shirt from a snag on the top of the door, my fingers brushed a small metal buttonlike thing stuck to an upper inside corner, where the door would usually conceal it from both me and my sighted companions; it came away when I pulled on it. I fingered it. The world is full of peculiar things. The cold touch of the unknown, so often felt . . . I am wary, I am always wary, I have to be wary.

I couldn't be certain what it was, but I had my suspicions, so I took it to my friend James Gold, who works in acoustics in the engineering department, and had him take a confidential look at it.

"It's a little remote microphone, all right," he said, and then joked: "Who's bugging you, Carlos?"

He got serious when I asked him where I could get a system like that for myself.

AB."John Metcalf—'Blind Jack of Knaresborough'—(1717–1810). At six he lost his sight through small-pox, at nine he could get on pretty well unaided, at fourteen he announced his intention of disregarding his affliction thenceforward and of behaving in every respect as a normal human being. It is true that immediately on this brave resolve he fell into a gravel pit and received a serious hurt while escaping, under pursuit, from an orchard he was robbing . . . fortunately this did not affect his self-reliance. At twenty he had made a reputation as a pugilist."(!)

—Ernest Bramah, Introduction,
The Eyes of Max Carrados

I have to fight, do you understand? The world wasn't made for me. Every day is fifteen rounds, a scramble to avoid being knocked flat, a counterpunch at every threatening sound.

When I was young I loved to read Ernest Bramah's stories about

Max Carrados, the blind detective. Carrados could hear, smell, and feel with incredible sensitivity, and his ingenious deductions were never short of brilliant; he was fearless in a pinch; also, he was rich, and had a mansion, and a secretary, manservant, and chauffeur who acted as his eyes. All great stuff for the imaginative young reader, as certainly I was. I read every book I could get my hands on; the voice of my reading machine was more familiar to me than any human voice that I knew. Between that reading and my mathematical work, I could have easily withdrawn from the world of my own experience into Cutsforth's "verbal unreality," and babbled on like Helen Keller about the shapes of clouds and the colors of flowers and the like. The world become nothing but a series of texts; sounds kind of like deconstructionism, doesn't it? And of course at an older age I was enamored of the deconstructionists of the last century. The world as text. Husserl's *The Origin of Geometry* is twenty-two pages long, Derrida's *Introduction to the Origin of Geometry* is a hundred and fifty-three pages long—you can see why it would have appealed to me. If, as the deconstructionists seemed to say, the world is nothing but a collection of texts, and I can read, then I am not missing anything by being blind, am I?

The young can be very stubborn, very stupid.

AO. "All right, Jeremy," I said. "Let me meet this mysterious *subject* of yours who draws all this stuff."

"You want to?" he said, trying to conceal his excitement.

"Sure," I replied. "I'm not going to find out any more about all this until I do." My own subtext, yes; but I am better at hiding such things than Jeremy is.

"What have you found out? Do the diagrams mean anything to you?"

"Not much. You know me, Jeremy, drawings are my weakness. I'd rather have her do it in models, or writing, or verbally. You'll have to bring her by if you want me to continue."

"Well, okay. I'll see what I can do. She's not much help, though. You'll find out." But he was pleased.

BA. One time in high school I was walking out of the gym after PE, and I heard one of my coaches (one of the best teachers I have ever had) in his office, speaking to someone (he must have had his back to me)—he said, "You know, it's not the physical handicaps that will be the problem for most of these kids. It's the emotional problems that tend to come with the handicaps that will be the real burden for most of them."

OAA′. I was in my office listening to my reading machine. Its flat, uninflected mechanical voice (almost unintelligible to some of my colleagues) had over the years become a sort of helpless, stupid friend. I called it George, and was always programming into it another pronunciation rule to try to aid its poor speech, but to no avail; George always found new ways to butcher the language. I put the book facedown on the glass; "Finding first line," croaked George as the scanner inside the machine thumped around. Then it read from Roberto Torretti, a philosopher of geometry, quoting and discussing Ernst Mach. (Hear this spoken in the most stilted, awkward, syllable-by-syllable mispronunciation that you can imagine.)

"Mach says that our notions of space are rooted in our *physiological* constitution, and that geometric concepts are the product of the idealization of *physical* experiences of space." (George raises his voice in pitch to indicate italics, which also slow him down considerably.) "But physiological space is quite different from the infinite, isotropic, metric space of classical geometry and physics. It can, at most, be structured as a topological space. When viewed in this way, it naturally falls into several components: visual or optic space, tactile or haptic space, auditive space, etc. Optic space is anisotropic, finite, limited. Haptic space or the space of our skin, Mach says, corresponds to a two-dimensional, finite, unlimited (closed) Riemannian space. This is nonsense, for R-spaces are metric while haptic space is not. I take it that Mach means to say that haptic space can naturally be regarded as a two-dimensional compact connected topological space. But Mach does not emphasize enough the disconnectedness of haptic from optic space—"

There came four quick knocks at my door. I pressed the button on George that stopped him, and said, "Come in!"

The door opened. "Carlos!"

"Jeremy," I said. "How are you."

"Fine. I've brought Mary Unser with me—you know—the one who drew—"

I stood, feeling/hearing the presence of the other in the room. And there are times (like this one) when you *know* the other is in some odd, undefinable way, *different*, or . . . (Our language is not made for the experience of the blind. No words for this feeling, this apprehension.)

"I'm glad to meet you," I said.

I have said that I can tell dark from light, and I can, to an extent, though it is seldom very useful information. In this case, however, I was startled to have my attention drawn to my "sight"—for this woman was darker than other people, she was a sort of bundle of darkness in the room, her face distinctly lighter than the rest of her (or was that her face, exactly?).

A long pause. Then: "On border stand we *n*-dimensional space the," she said. Coming just after George's reading, I was struck by a certain similarity: the mechanical lilt from word to word; the basic incomprehension of a reading machine . . . Goose bumps rose on my forearms.

Her voice itself, on the other hand, had George beat hands down. Fundamentally vibrant under the odd intonation, it was a voice with a very thick timbre, a bassoon or a hurdygurdy of a voice, with the buzz of someone who habitually speaks partly through the sinuses; this combined with overrelaxed vocal cords, what speech pathologists call *glottal fry*. Usually nasal voices are not pleasant, but pitch them low enough . . .

She spoke again, more slowly (definitely glottal fry): "We stand on the border of *n*-dimensional space."

"Hey," Jeremy said. "Pretty good!" He exclaimed: "Her word order isn't usually as . . . ordinary as that."

"So I gathered," I said. "Mary, what do you mean by that?"

"I—*oh*—" A kazoo squeak of distress, pain. I approached her, put out a hand. She took it as if to shake: a hand about the size of mine, narrow, strong fat muscle at base of thumb; trembling distinctly.

"I work on the geometries of topologically complex spaces," I said. "I am more likely than most to understand what you say."

"Are within never see we points us."

"That's true." But there was something wrong here, something I didn't like, though I couldn't tell exactly what it was. Had she spoken toward Jeremy? Speaking to me while she looked at him? The cold touch . . . a bundle of darkness in the dark . . . "But why are your sentences so disordered, Mary? Your words don't come out in the order you thought them. You must know that, since you understand us."

"Folded—*oh*!" Again the double-reed squeak, and suddenly she was weeping, trembling hard; we sat her down on my visitor's couch and Jeremy got her a glass of water, while she quaked in my hands. I stroked her hair (short, loosely curled, wild) and took the opportunity for a quick phrenological check: skull regular and as far as I could tell, undamaged; temples wide, distinct; same for eye sockets; nose a fairly ordinary pyramidal segment, no bridge to speak of; narrow cheeks, wet with tears. She reached up and took my right hand, and her little finger squeezed it hard, three times fast, three times slow, while she sobbed and sort of hiccuped words: "Pain it, station, I, oh, fold end, bright, light, space fold, oh, ohhh . . ."

Well, the direct question is not always the best way. Jeremy returned with a glass of water, and drinking some seemed to calm her. Jeremy said, "Perhaps we could try again later. Although—" He didn't seem very surprised.

"Sure," I said. "Listen, Mary, I'll talk to you again when you're feeling better."

But the language of touch, reduced to a simple code. SO . . . S?

OA. After Jeremy got her out of the office and disposed of her (how? with whom?) he returned to the seventh floor.

"So what the hell happened to her?" I asked angrily. "Why is she like that?"

"We aren't completely sure," he said slowly. "Here's why. She was one of the scientists staffing Tsiolkovsky Base Five, up in the mountains on the back side of the moon, you know. She's an astronomer and cosmologist. Well—I have to ask you to keep this quiet—one day Base Five stopped all broadcasting, and when they went over to see what was wrong, they found only her, wandering the station alone in a sort of catatonic state. No sign of the other scientists or station crew—eighteen people gone without a trace. And nothing much different to explain what had happened, either."

I *hmphed*. "What do they think happened?"

"They're still not sure. Apparently no one else was in the area, or could have been, et cetera. It's been suggested by the Russians, who had ten people there, that this could be first contact—you know, that aliens took the missing ones, and somehow disarranged Mary's thought processes, leaving her behind as a messenger that isn't working. Her brain scans are bizarre. I mean, it doesn't sound very likely—"

"No."

"But it's the only theory that explains everything they found there. Some of which they won't tell me about. So, we're doing what we can to get Mary's testimony, but as you can see, it's hard. She seems most comfortable drawing diagrams."

"Next time we'll start with that."

"Okay. Any other ideas?"

"No," I lied. "When can you bring her back again?"

AO. As if because I was blind I couldn't tell I was being duped!

Alone again, I struck fist into palm angrily. Oh, they were making a mistake, all right. They didn't know how much the voice reveals. The voice's secret expressivity reveals *so much*!—the language really is not adequate to tell it, we need that mathematics of emotion . . . In the high school for the blind that I briefly attended for some of my classes, it often happened that a new teacher was instantly disliked, for some falseness in his or her voice, some quality of condescension or pity or self-congratulation that the teacher (and his or her superiors) thought completely concealed, if they knew of it at all. But it was entirely obvious to the students, because the voice is so utterly revealing, much more so I think than facial expressions; certainly it is less under our control. This is what makes most acting performances unsatisfactory to me; the vocal qualities are so stylized, so removed from those of real life . . .

And here, I thought, I was witnessing a performance.

There is a moment in Olivier Messiaen's *Visions de l'Amen* when one piano is playing a progression of major chords, very traditionally harmonic, while on another piano high pairs of notes plonk down across the other's chords, ruining their harmony, crying out, Something's wrong! Something's wrong!

I sat at my desk and swayed side to side, living just such a moment. Something was wrong. Jeremy and this woman were lying, their voices said it in every intonation.

When I collected myself I called the department secretary, who had a view of the hall to the elevator. "Delphina, did Jeremy just leave?"

"Yes, Carlos. Do you want me to try and catch him?"

"No, I only need a book he left in his office. Can I borrow the master key and get it?"

"Okay."

I got the key, entered Jeremy's office, closed the door. One of the tiny pickups that James Gold had gotten for me fit right under the snap-in plug of the telephone cord. Then a microphone under the desk, behind a drawer. And out. (I have to be bold every day, you see, just to get by. I have to be wary, I have to be *bold*. But they didn't know that.)

Back in my office I closed and locked the door, and began to search. My office is big: two couches, several tall bookcases, my desk, a file cabinet, a coffee table . . . When the partitions on the seventh floor of the Gelman Library were moved around to make more room, Delphina and George Hampton, who was chairman that year, had approached me nervously: "Carlos, you wouldn't mind an office with no windows, would you?"

I laughed. All of the full professors had offices on the outer perimeter of the floor, with windows.

"You see," George said, "since none of the windows in the building opens anyway, you won't be missing out on any breezes. And if you take this room in the inner core of the building, then we'll have enough space for a good faculty lounge."

"Fine," I said, not mentioning that I could see sunlight, distinguish light and dark. It made me angry that they hadn't remembered that, hadn't thought to ask. So I nicknamed my office "The Vault," and I had a lot of room, but no windows. The halls had no windows either, so I was really without sun, but I didn't complain.

Now I got down on hands and knees and continued searching, feeling like it was hopeless. But I found one, on the bottom of the couch. And there was another in the phone. Bugged. I left them in position and went home.

Home was a small top-floor apartment up near Twenty-first and N streets, and I supposed it was bugged too. I turned up Stockhausen's *Telemusik* as loud as I could stand it, hoping to drive my listeners into a suicidal fugal state, or at least give them a headache. Then I slapped together a sandwich, downed it angrily.

I imagined I was captain of a naval sailing ship (like Horatio Hornblower), and that because of my sharp awareness of the wind I was the best captain afloat. They had had to evacuate the city and all the people I knew were aboard, depending on me to save them. But we were caught against a lee shore by two large ships of the line, and in the ensuing broadsides (roar of cannon, smell of gunpowder and blood, screams of wounded like shrieking sea gulls), everyone I knew fell—chopped in half, speared by giant splinters, heads removed by cannonball, you name it. Then when they were all corpses on the sand-strewn splintered decking, I felt a final broadside discharge, every ball converging on me as if I were point O in figure 1. Instant dissolution and death.

I came out of it feeling faintly disgusted with myself. But Cutsforth says that because this type of fantasy in the blind subject actively defends the ego by eradicating those who attack its self-esteem, it is a healthy thing. (At least in fourteen-year-olds.) So be it. Here's to health. Fuck all of you.

C. Geometry is a language, with a vocabulary and syntax as clear and precise as humans can make them. In many cases definitions of terms and operations are explicitly spelled out, to help achieve this clarity. For instance, one could say:

Let (parentheses) designate additional information.

Let [brackets] designate secret causes.

Let {braces} designate . . .

But would it be true, in this other language of the heart?

AB. Next afternoon I played beepball with my team. Sun hot on my face and arms, spring smell of pollen and wet grass. Ramon got six runs in the at-bat before mine (beepball is a sort of cricket/softball mix, played with softball equipment ["It shows you can play cricket blind" one Anglophobe {she was Irish} said to me once]), and when I got up I scratched out two and then struck out. Swinging *too* hard. I decided I liked outfield better. The beepball off in the distance, lofted up in a short arc, smack of bat, follow the ball up and up—out toward me!—drift in its direction, the rush of fear, glove before face as it approaches, stab for it, off after it as it rolls by—pick it up—Ramon's voice calling clearly, "Right here! Right here!"—and letting loose with a throw—really putting everything into it—and then, sometimes, hearing that beepball lance off into the distance and smack into Ramon's glove. It was great. Nothing like outfield.

And next inning I hit one *hard*, and that's great too. A counter-punch. That feeling goes right up your arms and all through you.

Walking home I brooded over Max Carrados, blind detective, and over Horatio Hornblower, sighted naval captain. Over Thomas Gore, blind senator from Oklahoma. As a boy his fantasy was to become a senator. He read the *Congressional Record*, joined the debate team, organized his whole life around the project. And he became senator. I knew that sort of fantasy as well as I knew the vengeful adolescent daydreams: all through my youth I dreamed of being a mathematician. And here I was. So one could do it. One could imagine doing something, and then do it.

But that meant that one had, by definition, imagined something *possible*. And one couldn't always say ahead of the attempt whether one had imagined the possible or the impossible. And even if one had imagined something possible, that didn't guarantee a successful execution of the plan.

The team we had played was called "Helen Keller Jokes" (there are some good ones, too [they come {of course} from Australia] but I won't go into that). It's sad that such an intelligent woman was so miseducated—not so much by Sullivan as by her whole era: all that treacly Victorian sentimentality poured into her, "The fishing villages of Cornwall are very picturesque, seen either from the beaches or the hilltops, with all their boats riding to their moorings or sailing about in the harbor—When the moon, large and serene, floats up the sky, leaving in the water a long track of brightness like a plow breaking up a soil of silver, I can only sigh my ecstasy," come on, Helen. Get off it. Now that is living in a world of texts.

But didn't I live most (all?) of my life in texts as least as unreal to me as moonlight on water was to Helen Keller? These *n*-dimensional manifolds I had explored for so long . . . I suppose the basis for my abilities in them was the lived reality of haptic space, but still, it was many removes from my actual experience. And so was the situation I found myself confronted with now, Jeremy and Mary acting out some drama I did not comprehend. And so was my plan to deal with it. Verbalism, words versus reality . . .

I caressed my glove, refelt the shiver of bat against beepball.

Brooded anxiously over my plan. Under attack, disoriented, frightened. For months after my mother left I made plans to get her back. I invented ailments, I injured myself, I tried to slip away and fly to Mexico. Why had she gone? It was inconceivable. Father didn't want to speak of it. They didn't love each other anymore, he said once. It was hard for her, she didn't speak the language. They wouldn't let her stay as a single person. She couldn't take care of me in Mexico, she had family burdens, things were bad there, and besides he didn't want me to leave, he was my principal teacher now, my caretaker. None of it meant anything to me. I barely even heard him. A whole language of hands, lost. I began to forget and clasped my own hands together and made the words, forefingers for food, the outdoor squeeze, the wanting sweep, the pressure that said I love you. No one heard.

OAA′. The next time Jeremy brought Mary Unser by my office, I said very little. I got out my visitor's supply of paper and pencils, and set her down at the coffee table. I brought over my models: subatomic particles breaking up in a spray of wire lines, like water out of a shower head; strawlike Taylor sticks for model making; polyhedric blocks of every kind. I sat down with the ridged sheets made from her earlier drawings, and the models I had attempted to make of them, and I started asking very limited questions. "What does this line mean? Does it go before or behind? Is this *R* or *R*'? Have I got this right?"

And she would honk a sort of laugh, or say "No, no, no, no," (no problem with sequencing there) and draw furiously. I took the pages as she finished them and put them in my xerox, took out the ridged, bumpy sheets and had her guide my fingers over them. Even so they were difficult, and with a squeak of frustration she went to the straw models, clicking together triangles, parallels, etc. This was easier, but eventually she reached a limit here, too. "Need drawing beyond," she said.

"Fine. Write down whatever you want."

She wrote, and then read aloud to me, or I put it through my xerox machine marked "translation to Braille." And we forged on, with Jeremy looking over our shoulders the whole time.

And eventually we came very close to the edge of my work. (The cold touch.) Following subatomic particles down into the microdimensions where they appeared to make their "jumps." I had proposed an *n*-dimensional topological manifold, where $1<n<$ infinity, so that the continuum being mapped fluctuated between one and some finite number of dimensions, going from a curving line to a sort of *n*-dimensional Swiss cheese, if you like, depending on the amounts of energy displayed in the area in any of the four forms, electromagnetism, gravity, or the strong and weak interactions. The geometry for this manifold pattern (so close to the experience of haptic space) had, as I have said, attracted the attention of physicists at **CERN** and **SLAC**—but there were still unexplained areas, as far as I could tell, and the truth was *I had not published this work*.

So here I was "conversing" with a young woman who in ordinary conversations could not order her words correctly—who in this realm spoke with perfect coherence—who was in fact speaking about (inquiring about?) the edges of my own private work.

The kind of work that Jeremy Blasingame used to ask me about so curiously.

I sighed. We had been going on for two or three hours, and I sat back on the couch. My hand was taken up in Mary's, given a reassuring squeeze. I didn't know what to make of it. "I'm tired," I said.

"I feel better," she said. "Easier to talk way—this way."

"Ah," I said. I took up the model of a positron hitting a "stationary" muon: a wire tree, trunk suddenly bursting into a mass of curling branches . . . So it was here: one set of events, a whole scattering of explanations. Still, the bulk of the particles shot out in a single general direction (the truths of haptic space).

She let go of my hand to make one last diagram. Then she xeroxed it for me, and guided my hands over the ridged copy.

Once again it was Desargues's Theorem: triangles **ABC** and **A′B′C′**, projected from point **O**. Only this time the two triangles were in the same plane, and **AB** and **A′B′** were parallel, as were **BC** and **B′C′**, and **AC** and **A′C′**. **P**, **Q**, and **R** had become ideal points; and she put my finger in the areas marking these ideal points, time after time (Figure 2).

C. Perhaps I should explain a little further, for now we leave the Euclidean world behind.

The geometry of ordinary points and lines (Euclidean geometry) is greatly complicated by the fact that a pair of parallel lines do not meet in a point. Why should this be so? Altering Euclid's fifth axiom concerning parallels led to the first non-Euclidean geometries of Lobachevski and Bolyai and Riemann. To enter this altered world we only need to add to the ordinary points on each line a single "ideal" point. This point belongs to all lines parallel to the given line. Now every pair of lines in the plane will intersect in a single point; lines not parallel will intersect in an ordinary point, and lines parallel will intersect in the ideal point common to the two lines. For intuitive reasons the ideal point is called the *point at infinity* on the line.

(This notion of ideality can be extended to other geometrical figures: all the points at infinity in a plane lie on a *line at infinity*; all the lines at infinity lie on the *plane at infinity*, the ideal plane in space, out beyond the rest; and all ideal planes lie in the *space at infinity*, in the next dimension over; and so on, unto *n* dimensions. [In the haptic space of Nevskyan geometry I can feel the presence of these ideal realms, for beyond certain ideal planes {membranes just beyond my touch} there are ideal activities that I can only imagine, can only yearn for. . . .])

Note, by the way, that with the concept of ideal points we can

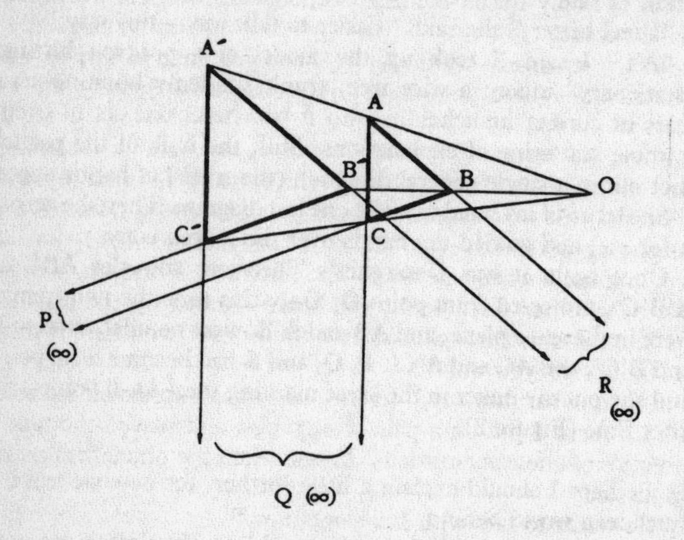

Figure 2

prove Desargues's Theorem in a single plane. Remember that to prove a theorem in general it suffices to prove it in a special case, as here, where AB and A′B′ are parallel, and the same for BC and B′C′, and AC and A′C′. As these pairs of lines are parallel, they intersect at their ideal points—call them P, Q, and R again for familiarity. And since all ideal points in a plane lie on the line at infinity, then P, Q, and R are collinear. Simple. And this proves not only the specific case when the sides of the triangles are parallel, but all the other cases, when they are not.

If only the world conformed to this rigorous logic!

A′AO. At this point Mary said, "Mr. Blasingame, I need a drink of water." He went out to the hall water dispenser, and she quickly took my forefinger between her finger and thumb (pads flattening with an inappropriate pressure, until my finger ached)—squeezed twice, and jabbed my finger first onto her leg, then onto the diagram, tracing out one of the triangles. She repeated the movements, then poked my leg and traced out the other triangle. Fine; she was one, I was the other. We were parallel, and in projection from point O, which was . . .

But she only traced the lines to point O, over and over. What did she mean?

Jeremy returned, and she let my hand go. Then in a while, after the amenities (hard handshake, quivering hand) Jeremy whisked her off.

When he returned, I said, "Jeremy, is there any chance I can talk to her alone? I think she's made nervous by your presence—the associations, you know. She really does have an interesting perspective on the *n*-dimensional manifold, but she gets confused when she stops and interacts with you. I'd just like to take her for a walk, you know—down by the canal, or the Tidal Basin, perhaps, and talk things over with her. It might get the results you want."

"I'll see what they say," Jeremy said in an expressionless voice.

That night I put on a pair of earplugs, and played the tape of Jeremy's phone conversations. In one when the phone was picked up he said:

"He wants to talk with her alone now."

"Fine," said a tenor voice. "She's prepared for that."

"This weekend?"

"If he agrees." *Click.*

BA. I listen to music. I listen to twentieth-century composers the most, because many of them made their music out of the sounds of the world we live in now, the world of jets and sirens and industrial machinery, as well as bird song and wood block and the human voice. Messiaen, Partch, Reich, Glass, Shapiro, Subotnik, Ligeti, Penderecki—these first explorers away from the orchestra and the classical tradition remain for me the voices of our age. They speak to me. In fact they speak for me; in their dissonance and confusion and anger I hear myself being expressed, I hear the loss and feel its transformation into something else, into something less painful. And so I listen to their difficult, complex music because I understand it, which gives me pleasure, and because while doing I am participating fully, I am excelling. No one can bring more to the act than I. I am *in control.*

I listened to music.

O. You see, these *n*-dimensional manifolds . . . if we understood them well enough to manipulate them, to tap their energy . . . well, there is a tremendous amount of energy contained there. That kind of energy means power, and power . . . draws the powerful. Or those seeking power, fighting for it. I began to feel the extent of the danger.

BB′. She was quiet as we walked across the Mall toward the Lincoln Monument. I think she would have stopped me if I had spoken about anything important. But I knew enough to say nothing, and I think she guessed I knew she was bugged. I held the back of her upper arm loosely in my left hand, and let her guide us. A sunny, windy day, with occasional clouds obscuring the sun for a minute or two. Down by the Mall's lake the slightly stagnant smell of wet algae tinged all the other scents: grass, dust, the double strand of lighter fluid and cooking meat. . . . The sink of darkness swirling around the Vietnam Memorial. Pigeons cooed their weird, larger-than-life coos, and flapped away noisily as we walked through their affairs. We sat on grass that had been recently cut, and I brushed a hand over the stiff blades.

A curious procedure, this conversation. No visuals, for me; and perhaps we were being watched, as well. (Such a common anxiety of the blind, the fear of being watched—and here it was true.) And we couldn't talk freely, even though at the same time we had to say something, to keep Blasingame and friends from thinking I was aware of anything wrong. "Nice day." "Yeah. I'd love to be out on the water on a day like this." "Really?" "Yeah."

And all the while two fingers held one finger. My hands are my eyes, and always have been. Now they were as expressive as voice, as receptive as ever touch can be, and into haptic space we projected a conversation of rare urgency. Are you okay? I'm okay. Do you know what's going on? Not entirely, can't explain.

"Let's walk down to the paddle boats and go out on the Basin, then."

I said, "Your speech is much better today."

She squeezed my hand thrice, hard. False information? "I . . . had . . . electroshock." Her voice slid, slurred; it wasn't entirely under control.

"It seems to have helped."

"Yes. Sometimes."

"And the ordering of your mathematical thought?"

Buzzing laugh, hurdy-gurdy voice: "I don't know—more disarranged, perhaps—complementary procedure? You'll have to tell me."

"As a cosmologist did you work in this area?"

"The topology of the microdimensions apparently determines both gravity and the weak interaction, wouldn't you agree?"

"I couldn't say. I'm not much of a physicist."

Three squeezes again. "But you must have an idea or two about it?"

"Not really? You?"

"Perhaps . . . once. But it seems to me your work is directly concerned with it."

"Not that I know of."

Stalemate. Was that right? I was becoming more and more curious about this woman, whose signals to me were so mixed. . . . Once again she seemed a bundling of darkness in the day, a whirlpool where all lightness disappeared, except for around her head. (I suppose I imagine all that I "see," I suppose they are always haptic visions.)

"Are you wearing dark clothes?"

"Not really. Red, beige . . ."

As we walked I held her arm more tightly. She was about my height. Her arm muscles were distinct, and her lats pushed out from her ribs. "You must swim."

"Weight lifting, I'm afraid. They made us on Luna."

"On Luna," I repeated.

"Yes," and she fell silent.

This really was impossible. I didn't think she was completely an ally—in fact I thought she was lying—but I felt an underlying sympathy from her, and a sense of conspiracy with her, that grew more powerful the longer we were together. The problem was, what did that feeling mean? Without the ability to converse freely, I was stymied in my attempts to learn more; pushed this way and that in the cross-currents of her behavior, I could only wonder what she was thinking. And what our listeners made of this mostly silent day in the sun.

So we paddled out onto the Tidal Basin, and talked from time to time about the scene around us. I love the feel of being on water—the gentle rocking over other boats' wakes, the wet stale smell. . . . "Are the cherry trees blossoming still?"

"Oh yes. Not quite at the peak, but just past. It's beautiful. Here—" she leaned out—"here's one about to drown." She put it in my hand. I sniffed at it. "Do they smell?"

"No, not much," I said. "The prettier people say flowers are, the less scent they seem to have. Did you ever notice that?"

"I guess. I like the scent of roses."

"It's faint, though. These blossoms must be very beautiful—they smell hardly at all."

"En masse they are lovely. I wish you could see them."

I shrugged. "And I wish you could touch their petals, or feel us bouncing about as I do. I have enough sense data to keep entertained."

"Yes . . . I suppose you do." She left her hand covering mine. "I suppose we're out quite a ways," I said. So that we couldn't be seen well from the shore, I meant.

"From the dock, anyway. We're actually almost across the Basin."

I moved my hand from under hers, and held her shoulder. Deep hollow behind her collarbone. This contact, this conversation of touch . . . it was most expressive hand to hand, and so I took her hand again, and our fingers made random entanglements, explorations. Children shouting, then laughing in boats to our left, voices charged with excitement. How to speak in this language of touch?

Well, we all know that. Fingertips, brushing lines of the palm; ruffling the fine hair at the back of the wrist; fingers pressing each other back: these are sentences, certainly. And it is a difficult language to lie in. That catlike sensuous stretch, under my stroking fingertips . . .

"We've got a clear run ahead of us," she said after a time, voice charged with humming overtones.

"Stoke the furnaces," I cried. "Damn the torpedoes!" And with a gurgling *clug-clug-clug-clug* we paddle-wheeled over the Basin into the fresh wet wind, sun on our faces, laughing at the release from tension (bassoon and baritone), crying out "Mark twain!" or "Snag dead ahead" in jocular tones, entwined hands crushing the other as we pedaled harder and harder . . . "Down the Potomac!" "Across the sea!" and the spray cold on the breeze—

She stopped pedaling, and we swerved left.

"We're almost back," she said quietly.

We let the boat drift in, without a word.

OA. My bugs told me that my office had been broken into, by two, possibly three people, only one of whom spoke—a man, in an undertone: "Try the file cabinet." The cabinet drawers were rolled out (familiar clicking of the runners over the ball bearings), and the desk drawers, too, and then there was the sound of paper shuffling, of things being knocked about.

I also got an interesting phone conversation over Jeremy's phone. The call was incoming; Jeremy said "Yes?" and a male voice—the same one Jeremy had called earlier—said, "She says he's unwilling to go into any detail."

"That doesn't surprise me," Jeremy said. "But I'm sure he's got—"

"Yes, I know. Go ahead and try what we discussed."

The break-in, I supposed.

"Okay." *Click*.

AO. No doubt it never even occurred to them that I might turn the tables on them, or act against them in any way, or even figure out that something was strange. It made me furious.

OA. At the same time I was frightened. You feel the lines of force, living in Washington, D.C.; feel the struggle for power among the shadowy manifolds surrounding the official government space; read of the unsolved murders, of shadowy people whose jobs are not made clear. . . . As a blind person one feels apart from that nebulous world of intrigue and hidden force, on the edge by reason of disability. ("No one harms a blind man.") Now I knew I was part of it, pulled in, on my own. It was frightening.

But they didn't know how much I knew. Snuffle of an approaching boxer, counterpunch right in the face. I have to be bold just to cross the street!

AA'. One night I was immersed in Harry Partch's *Cloud Chamber Music*, floating in those big glassy notes, when my doorbell rang. I picked up the phone. "Hello?"

"It's Mary Unser. May I come up?"

"Sure." I pushed the button and walked onto the landing.

She came up the stairs alone. "Sorry to bother you at home," she buzzed, out of breath. Such a voice. "I looked up your address in the phone book. I'm not supposed . . ."

She stood before me, touched my right arm. I lifted my hand and held her elbow. "Yes?"

Nervous, resonant laugh. "I'm not supposed to be here."

Then you'll soon be in trouble, I wanted to say. But surely she knew my apartment would be bugged? Surely she *was* supposed to be here? She was trembling violently, enough so that I put up my other hand and held her by the shoulders. "Are you all right?"

"Yes. No." Falling oboe tones, laugh that was not a laugh . . . She seemed frightened, very frightened. I thought, if she is acting she is *very* good.

"Come on in," I said, and led her inside. I went to the stereo and turned down the Partch—then reconsidered, and turned it back up. "Have a seat—the couch is nice." I was nervous myself. "Would you like something to drink?" Quite suddenly it all seemed unreal, a dream, one of my fantasies. Phantasmagoric cloud chamber ringing to things, how did I know what was real? Those membranes. Beyond the plane at infinity, what?

"No. Or yes." She laughed again, that laugh that was not a laugh.

"I've got some beer." I went to the refrigerator, got a couple of bottles, opened them.

"So what's going on?" I said as I sat down beside her. As she spoke I drank from my beer, and she stopped from time to time to take long swallows.

"Well, I feel that the more I understand what you're saying about the transfer of energies between *n*-dimensional manifolds, the better I understand what . . . happened to me." But now there was a different sound to her voice—an overtone was gone, it was less resonant, less nasal.

I said, "I don't know what I can tell you. It's not something I can talk about, or even write down. What I can express, I have, you know. In papers." This a bit louder, for the benefit of our audience. (If there was one?)

"Well . . ." and her hand, under mine, began to tremble again.

We sat there for a very long time, and all during that time we conversed through those two hands, saying things I can scarcely recall now, because we have no language for that sort of thing. But they were important things nevertheless, and after a while I said, "Here. Come with me. I'm on the top floor, so I have a sort of a porch on the roof. Finish your beer. It's a pleasant night out, you'll feel better outside." I led her through the kitchen to the pantry, where the door to the backstairs was. "Go on up." I went back to the stereo and put on Jarrett's *Köln Concert*, loud enough so we'd be able to hear it. Then I went up the stairs onto the roof, and crunched over the tarred gravel.

This was one of my favorite places. The sides of the building came up to the chest around the edge of the roof, and on two sides large willows draped their branches over it, making it a sort of haven. I had set a big old wreck of a couch out there, and on certain nights when the wind was up and the air was cool, I would lie back on it with a bumpy Braille planisphere in my hands, listening to Scholz's *Starcharts* and feeling that with those projections I knew what it was to see the night sky.

"This is nice," she said.

"Isn't it?" I pulled the plastic sheet from the couch, and we sat.

"Carlos?"

"Yes?"

"I—I—" That double-reed squeak—

I put an arm around her. "Please," I said, suddenly upset myself. "Not now. Not now. Just relax. Please." And she turned into me, her head rested on my shoulder; she trembled. I dug my fingers into her hair and slowly pulled them through the tangles. Shoulder length, no more. I cupped her ears, stroked her neck. She calmed.

Time passed, and I only caressed. No other thought, no other perception. How long this went on I couldn't say—perhaps a half hour? Perhaps longer. She made a sort of purring kazoo sound, and I leaned forward and kissed her. Jarrett's voice, crying out briefly over a fluid run of piano notes. She pulled me to her, her breath caught, rushed out of her. The kiss became intense, tongues dancing together in a whole intercourse of their own, which I felt all through me in that *chakra* way, neck, spine, belly, groin, nothing but kiss. And without the slightest bit of either intention or resistance, I fell into it.

I remember a college friend once asked me, hesitantly, if I didn't have trouble with my love life. "Isn't it hard to tell when they . . . want to?" I had laughed. The whole process, I had wanted to say, was amazingly easy. The blind's dependence on touch puts them in an advance position, so to speak: using hands to see faces, being led by the hand (being dependent), one has already crossed what Russ calls the border between the world of not-sex and the world of sex; once over that border (with an other feeling protective) . . .

My hands explored her body, discovering it then and there for the first time: as intensely exciting a moment as there is, in the whole process. I suppose I expect narrow-cheeked people to be narrow-hipped (it's mostly true, you'll find), but it wasn't so, in this case—her hips flared in those feminine curves that one can only hold, without ever getting used to (without ever [the otherness of the other] quite believing). On their own my fingers slipped under clothes, between buttons, as adroit as little mice, clever lusty little creatures, unbuttoning blouse, reaching behind to undo bra with a twist. She shrugged out of them both and I felt the softness of her breasts while she tugged at my belt. I shifted, rolled, put my ear to her hard sternum, kissing the inside of one breast as it pressed against my face, feeling that quick heartbeat speak to me. . . . She moved me back, got me unzipped, we paused for a speedy moment and got the rest of our clothes off, fumbling at our own and each other's until they were clear. Then it was flesh to flesh, skin to skin, in a single haptic space jumping with energy, with the insistent *yes* of caresses, mouth to mouth, four hands full, body to body, with breasts and erect penis crushed, as it were, between two pulsing walls of muscle.

The skin is the ultimate voice.

So we made love. As we did (my feet jabbing the end of the couch, which was quite broad enough, but a little too short) I arched up and let the breeze between us (cool on our sweat), leaned down and sucked on first one nipple and then the other—

(thus becoming helpless in a sense, a needy infant, completely dependent [because for the blind from birth, mother love is even more crucial than for the rest of us—the blind depend on their mothers for almost *everything*, for the sense of object permanence, for the education that makes the distinction between self and world, for the beginning of language, and also for the establishment of a private language that compensates for the lack of sight {if your mother doesn't know that a sweeping hand means "*I want!*"} and bridges the way to the common tongue—without all that, which only a mother can give, the blind infant is lost—without mother love beyond mother love, the blind child will very likely go mad] so that [for any of us] to suck on a lover's nipple brings back that primal world of trust and need, I am sure of it)

—I was sure of it even then, as I made love to this strange other Mary Unser, a woman as unknown to me as any I had ever spoken with. At least until now. Now with each plunge into her (cylinder capped by cone, sliding through cylinder into rough sphere, neuron to neuron, millions of them fusing across, so that I could not tell where I stopped and she began) I learned more about her, the shape of her, her rhythms, her whole nerve-reality, spoken to me in movement and touch (spread hands holding my back, flanks, bottom) and in those broken bassoon tones that were like someone humming, briefly, involuntarily. "Ah," I said happily at all this sensation, all this new knowledge, feeling all my skin and all my nerves swirl up like a gust of wind into my spine, the back of my balls, to pitch into her all my self—

When we were done (oboe squeaks) I slid down, bending my knees so my feet stuck up in the air. I wiggled my toes in the breeze. Faint traffic noises played a sort of city music to accompany the piano in the apartment. From the airshaft came the sound of a chorus of pigeons, sounding like monkeys with their jaws wired shut, trying to chatter. Mary's skin was damp and I licked it, loving the salt. Patch of darkness in my blur of vision, darkness bundling in it. . . . She rolled onto her side and my hands played over her. Her biceps made a smooth hard bulge. There were several moles on her back, like little raisins half-buried in her skin. I pushed them down, fingered the knobs of her spine. The muscles of her back put her spine in a deep trough of flesh. Women are so bifurcated that way: between the shoulder blades the spine drops into a valley between two ridges of muscle, then dives even deeper between the halves of the butt, past the curl of the coccyx, past anus and vagina and the split nest of pubic hair and over the pubic bone, a sort of low pass; then on most women the valley begins again, as a broad depression up to belly button and up to sternum, and between breasts, and all the way up to the hollow between the collarbones, so that their whole torso is divided this way, into left and right. I explored this valley in Mary's body and she shifted, threw her top leg over mine. My head rested on her biceps, snuggled against her side.

I remembered a day my blind science class was taken to a museum, where we were allowed to feel a skeleton. All those hard bones, in just the right places; it made perfect sense, it was exactly as it felt under skin, really—there were no big surprises. But I remember being so upset by the experience of feeling the skeleton that I had to go outside and sit down on the museum steps. I don't know to this day exactly why I was so shaken, but I suppose (all those hard things left behind) it was something like this: it was frightening to know how *real* we were!

Now I tugged at her, gently. "Who are you, then."

"Not now." And as I started to speak again she put a finger to my mouth (scent of us): "A friend." Buzzing nasal whisper, like a tuning fork, like a voice I was beginning (and this scared me, for I knew I did not know her) to love: "A friend . . ."

C. At a certain point in geometrical thinking vision becomes only an obstruction. Those used to visualizing theorems (as in Euclidean geometry) reach a point, in the *n*-dimensional manifolds or elsewhere, where the concepts simply *can't* be visualized; and the attempt to do so only leads to confusion and misunderstanding. Beyond that point an interior geometry, a haptic geometry, guided by a kinetic aesthetics, is probably the best sensory analogy we have; and so I have my advantage.

But in the real world, in the geometries of the heart, do I ever have any comparable advantage? Are there things we feel that can never be seen?

OA. The central problem for everyone concerned with the relationship between geometry and the real world is the question of how one moves from the incommunicable impressions of the sensory world (vague fields of force, of danger), to the generally agreed-upon abstractions of the math (the explanation). Or, as Edmund Husserl puts it in *The Origin of Geometry* (and on this particular morning George was enunciating this passage for me with the utmost awkwardness): "How does geometrical ideality (just like that of all the sciences) proceed from its primary intrapersonal origin, where it is a structure within the conscious space of the first inventor's soul, to its ideal objectivity?"

At this point Jeremy knocked at my door: four quick raps. "Come in, Jeremy," I said, my pulse quickening.

He opened the door and looked in. "I have a pot of coffee just ready to go," he said. "Come on down and have some."

So I joined him in his office, which smelled wonderfully of strong French roast. I sat in one of the plush armchairs that circled Jeremy's desk, accepted a small glazed cup, sipped from it. Jeremy moved about the room restlessly as he chattered about one minor matter after another, obviously avoiding the topic of Mary, and all that she represented. The coffee sent a warm flush through me—even the flesh of my feet buzzed with heat, though in the blast of air-conditioned air from the ceiling vent I didn't start to sweat. At first it was a comfortable, even pleasant sensation. The bitter, murky taste of the coffee washed over my palate, through the roof of my mouth into my sinuses, from there up behind my eyes, through my brain, all the way down my throat, into my lungs: I breathed coffee, my blood singing with warmth.

. . . I had been talking about something. Jeremy's voice came from directly above and before me, and it had a crackly, tinny quality to it, as if made by an old carbon microphone: "And what would happen if the Q energy from this manifold were directed through these vectored dimensions into the macrodimensional manifold?"

Happily I babbled, "Well, provide each point P of an *n*-dimensional differentiable manifold M with the analogue of a tangent plane, an *n*-dimensional vector space Tp(M), called the tangent space at P. Now we can define a *path* in manifold M as a differentiable mapping of an open interval of R into M. And along this path we can fit the *whole* of the forces defining K the submanifold of M, a lot of energy to be sure," oh, yes, a lot of energy, and I was writing it all down, when the somatic effect of the drug caught up with the mental effect, and I recognized what was happening. ("Entirely too many new designer drugs these days. . . .")

Jeremy's breathing snagged as he looked up to see what had stopped me; meanwhile I struggled with a slight wave of nausea, caused more by the realization that I had been drugged than by the chemicals themselves, which had very little noise. What had I told him? And why, for God's sake, did it matter so much?

"Sorry," I muttered through the roar of the ventilator. "Bit of a headache."

"Sorry to hear that," Jeremy said, in a voice exactly like George's. "You look a little pale."

"Yes," I said, trying to conceal my anger. (Later, listening to the tape of the conversation, I thought I only sounded confused.) (And I hadn't said much about my work, either—mostly definitions.) "Sorry to run out on you, but it really is bothering me."

I stood, and for a moment I panicked; the location of the room's door—the most fundamental point of orientation, remembered without effort in every circumstance—wouldn't come to me. I was damned if I would ask Jeremy Blasingame about such a thing, or stumble about in front of him. I consciously fought to remember: desk faces door, chair faces desk, door therefore behind you. . . .

"Let me walk you to your office," Jeremy said, taking me by the arm. "Listen, maybe I can give you a lift home?"

"That's all right," I said, shrugging him off. I found the door by accident, it seemed, and left him. Down to my office, wondering if I would get the right door. My blood was hot Turkish coffee. My head spun. The key worked, so I had found the right door. Locked in I went to my couch and lay down. I was as dizzy there as standing, but found I couldn't move again. I spun in place helplessly. I had read that the drugs used for such purposes had almost no somatic effect, but perhaps this was true only for subjects less sensitive to their kinetic reality—otherwise, why was I reacting so? Fear. Or Jeremy had put something beyond the truth drug in me. A warning? Against? Suddenly I was aware of the tight boundaries of my comprehension, beyond it the wide manifold of action I did not understand—and the latter threatened to completely flood the former, so that there would be left nothing at all that I understood about this matter. Drowned in the unknown, ah, God, such a prospect terrified me!

Sometime later—perhaps as much as an hour—I felt I had to get home. Physically I felt much better, and it was only when I got outside in the wind that I realized that the psychological effects of the drug were still having their way with me. Rare, heavy waft of diesel exhaust, a person wearing clothes rank with old sweat: these smells overwhelmed any chance I had of locating Ramon's cart by nose. My cane felt unusually long, and the rising and falling whistles of my sonar glasses made a musical composition like something out of Messiaen's *Catalogue d'Oiseaux*. I stood entranced by the effect. Cars zoomed past with their electric whirrs, the wind made more sound than I could process. I couldn't find Ramon and decided to give up trying; it would be bad to get him mixed up in any of this anyway. Ramon was my best friend. All those hours at Warren's throwing together, and when we played beeper Ping-Pong at his apartment we sometimes got to laughing so hard we couldn't stand—and what else is friendship than that, after all?

Distracted by thoughts such as these, and by the bizarre music of wind and traffic, I lost track of which street I was crossing. The *whoosh* of a car nearly brushing me as I stepped up from a curb. Lost! "Excuse me, is this Pennsylvania or K?" Fuckyouverymuch. Threading my way fearfully between broken bottles, punji-stick nails poking up out of boards on the sidewalk, low-hanging wires holding up tree branch or street sign, dogshit on the curb waiting like banana peel to skid me into the street under a bus, speeding cars with completely silent electric motors careening around the corner, muggers who didn't care if I was blind or paraplegic or whatever, open manholes in the crosswalks, rabid dogs with their toothy jaws stuck out between the rails of a fence, ready to bite . . . Oh yes, I fought off all these dangers and more, and I must have looked mad tiptoeing down the sidewalk, whapping my cane about like a man beating off devils.

* * *

AO. By the time I got into my apartment I was shaking with fury. I turned on Steve Reich's *Come Out* (in which the phrase "Come out to show them" is looped countless times) as loud as I could stand it, and barged around my place alternately cursing and crying (that stinging of the eyes), all under the sound of the music. I formulated a hundred impossible plans of revenge against Jeremy Blasingame and his shadowy employers, brushed my teeth for fifteen minutes to get the taste of coffee out of my mouth.

By the next morning I had a plan: it was time for some confrontation. It was a Saturday and I was able to work in my office without interruption. I entered the office and unlocked a briefcase, opened my file cabinet and made sounds of moving papers from briefcase to cabinet. Much more silently I got out a big mousetrap that I had bought that morning. On the back of it I wrote, *You're caught. The next trap kills.* I set the trap and placed it carefully behind the new file I had added to the cabinet. This was straight out of one of my adolescent rage fantasies, of course, but I didn't care, it was the best way I could think of to both punish them and warn them from a distance. When the file was pulled from the cabinet, the trap would release onto the hand pulling the file out, and it would also break tape set in a pattern only I would be able to feel. So if the trap went off, I would know.

The first step was ready.

CA. In Penderecki's *Threnody for the Victims of Hiroshima*, a moment of deadly stillness, strings humming dissonant strokes as the whole world waits.

Cut shaving; the smell of blood.

Across the road, a carpenter hammering nails on a roof, each set of seven strokes a crescendo: *tap-tap-tap-tap-tap-tap-TAP*! *Tap-tap-tap-tap-tap-tap-TAP*!

In that mathematics of emotion, stress calculations to measure one's tension: already there for us to use. Perhaps all of math already charts states of consciousness, moments of being.

CC′. She came to me again late at night, with the wind swirling by her through the doorway. It was late, the wind was chill and blustery, the barometer was falling. Storm coming.

"I wanted to see you," she said.

I felt a great thrill of fear, and another of pleasure, and

I could not tell which was stronger or, after a time, which was which.

"Good." We entered the kitchen, I served her water, circled her unsteadily, my voice calm as we discussed trivia in fits and starts. After many minutes of this I very firmly took her by the hand. "Come along." I led her into the pantry, up the narrow musty stairs, out the roof door into the wind. A spattering of big raindrops hit us. "Carlos—" "Never mind that!" The *whoosh* of the wind was accompanied by the rain smell of wet dust and hot asphalt, and a certain electricity in the air. Off in the distance, to the south, a low rumble of thunder shook the air.

"It's going to rain," she ventured, shouting a bit over the wind.

"Quiet," I told her, and kept her hand crushed in mine. The wind gusted through our clothes, and mixed with my anger and my fear I felt rising the electric elation that storms evoke in me. Face to the wind, hair pulled back from my scalp, I held her hand and waited: "Listen," I said, "watch, feel the storm." And after a time I felt—no, I saw, I *saw*—the sudden jerk of lightness that marked lightning. "Ah," I said aloud, counting to myself. The thunder pushed us about ten seconds later. Just a couple of miles away.

"Tell me what you see," I commanded, and heard in my own voice a vibrancy that could not be denied. Punching through the membranes . . .

"It's—it's a thunderstorm," she replied, uncertain of me in this new mood. "The clouds are very dark, and fairly low at their bottoms, but broken up in places by some largish gaps. Kind of like immense boulders rolling overhead. The lightning—there! You noticed that?"

I had jumped. "I can see lightning," I said, grinning. "I have a basic perception of light and darkness, and everything flashes to lightness for a moment. As if the sun had turned on and then off."

"Yes. It's sort of like that, only the light is shaped in jagged white lines, extending from cloud to ground. Like that model you have of subatomic particles breaking up—a sort of broken wire sculpture, white as the sun, forking the earth for just an instant, as bright as the thunder is loud." Her voice rasped with an excitement that had sparked across our hands—also with apprehension, curiosity, I didn't know what. *Light* . . . *Blam*, the thunder struck us like a fist and she jumped. I laughed. "That was off to the side!" she said fearfully. "We're in the middle of it!"

I couldn't control a laugh. "More!" I shouted. "Pick up the pace!" And as if I were a weathermonger the lightning snapped away the darkness around us, flash-*blam* . . . flash-*blam* . . . flash-*BLAM*!

"We should get down!" Mary shouted over the wind's ripping, over the reverberating crashes of thunder. I shook my head back and forth and back and forth, gripped her by the arm so hard it must have hurt.

"*No*! This is *my* visual world, do you understand? This is as beautiful as it ever—" flash-*crack-blam*.

"*Carlos*—"

"No! Shut up!" Flash-flash-flash-*BOOM*! Rolling thunder, now, hollow casks the size of mountains, rolling across a concrete floor.

"I'm afraid," she said miserably, tugging away from me.

"You feel the exposure, eh?" I shouted at her, as lightning flashed and the wind tore at us, and rain drops pummeled the roof, throwing up a tarry smell to mix with the lightning's ozone. "You feel what it's like to stand helpless before a power that can kill you, is that right?"

Between thunderclaps she said, desperately, "Yes!"

"Now you know how I've felt around you people!" I shouted. *BLAM*! *BLAM*! "God damn it," I said, pain searing my voice as the lightning seared the air, "I can go sit in the corner park with the drug dealers and the bums and the crazies and I *know* I'll be safe, because even those people still have the idea that it isn't right to hurt a blind man. But you people!" I couldn't go on. I shoved her away from me and staggered back, remembering it all. Flash-*blam*! Flash-*blam*!

"Carlos—" Hands pulling me around.

"What."

"I didn't—"

"The hell you didn't! You came in and gave me that story about the moon, and talked backward, and drew stuff, and all to steal my work—how could you do it? How could you do it."

"I *didn't*, Carlos, I didn't!" I batted her hands away, but it was as if a dam had burst, as if only now, charged to it in the storm, was she able to speak and it all came pouring out of her, "*Listen to me*!" Flash-*blam*. "*I'm just like you*. They made me do it. They took me because I have some math background, I guess, and they ran me through more memory implants than I can even count!" Now the charged buzzing timbre of her desperate voice scraped directly across my nervous system: "You know what they can do with those drugs and implants. They can program you just like a machine. You walk through your paces and watch yourself and can't do a thing about it." *Blam.* "And they programmed me and I went in there and spouted it all off to you on cue. But you *know*"—*blam*— "was trying, you know there's the parts of the mind they can't touch—I fought them as hard as I could, don't you see?"

Flash-*blam*. Sizzle of scorched air, ozone, ringing eardrums. That one was close.

"I took TNPP-50," she said, calmer now. "That and MDMA. I just *made* myself duck into a pharmacy on my way to meet you alone, and I used a blank prescription pad I keep, and got them. I was so drugged up when we went to the Tidal Basin that I could barely walk. But it helped me to speak, helped me to fight the programming."

"You were drugged?" I said, amazed. (I know—Max Carrados would have figured it out. But me—)

"Yes!" *Boom.* "Every time I saw you after that time. And it's worked better every time. But I've had to pretend I was still working on you, to protect us both. The last time we were up here"—*boom*—"you *know* I'm with you, Carlos, do you think I would have faked that?"

Bassoon voice, hoarse with pain. Low rumble of thunder, in the distance. Flickers in the darkness, no longer as distinct as before: my moments of vision were coming to an end. "But what do they *want*?" I cried.

"Blasingame thinks your work will solve the problems they're having getting sufficient power into a particle-beam weapon. They think they can channel energy out of the microdimensions you've been studying." *Blam.* "Or so I guess, from what I've overheard."

"Those fools." Although to an extent there might be something to the idea. I had almost guessed it, in fact. So much energy . . . "Blasingame is such a *fool*. He and his stupid Pentagon bosses—"

"*Pentagon*!" Mary exclaimed. "Carlos, these people are *not* with the Pentagon! I don't know who they are—a group from West

Germany, I think. But they kidnapped me right out of my apartment, and I'm a statistician for the Defense Department! The Pentagon has nothing to do with it!"

Blam. "But Jeremy . . ." My stomach was falling.

"I don't know how he got into it. But whoever they are, they're dangerous. I've been afraid they'll kill us both. I know they've discussed killing you, I've heard them. They think you're onto them. Ever since the Tidal Basin I've been injecting myself with Fifty and MDMA, a lot of it, and telling them you don't know a thing, that you just haven't *got* the formula yet. But if they were to find out you know about them . . ."

"God I hate this spy shit!" I exclaimed bitterly. And the oh-so-clever trap in my office, warning Jeremy off . . .

It started to rain hard. I let Mary lead me down into my apartment. No time to lose, I thought. I had to get to my office and remove the trap. But I didn't want her at risk, I was suddenly frightened more for this newly revealed ally than for myself—

"Listen, Mary," I said when we were inside. Then I remembered, and whispered in her ear. "Is this room bugged?"

"No."

"For God's sake"—all those silences—she must have thought me deranged! "All right. I want to make some calls, and I'm sure my phones are bugged. I'm going to go out for a bit, but I want you to stay right here. All right?" She started to protest and I stopped her. "Please! *Stay right here*, I'll be right back. Just stay here and wait for me, *please*."

"Okay, okay. I'll stay."

"You promise?"

"I promise."

OA. Down on the street I turned left and took off for my offices. Rain struck my face and I automatically thought to return for an umbrella, then angrily shook the thought away. Thunder still rumbled overhead from time to time, but the brilliant ("brilliant!" I say—meaning I saw a certain lightness in the midst of a certain darkness)—the brilliant flashes that had given me a momentary taste of vision were gone.

Repeatedly I cursed myself, my stupidity, my presumption. I had made axioms out of theorems (humanity's most common logical-syntactic flaw?), never pausing to consider that my whole edifice of subsequent reasoning rested on them. And now, having presumed to challenge a force I didn't understand, I was in real danger, no doubt about it; and no doubt (as corollary) Mary was as well. The more I thought of it the more frightened I became, until finally I was as scared as I should have been all along.

The rain shifted to an irregular drizzle. The air was cooled, the wind had dropped to an occasional gust. Cars hissed by over wet Twenty-first Street, humming like Mary's voice, and everywhere water sounded, squishing and splashing and dripping. I passed Twenty-first and K, where Ramon usually set up his cart; I was glad that he wouldn't be there, that I wouldn't have to walk by him in silence, perhaps ignoring his cheerful invitation to buy, or even his specific hello. I would have hated to fool him so. Yet if I had wanted to, how easy it would have been! Just walk on by, he would have had no way of knowing.

A sickening sensation of my disability swept over me, all the small frustrations and occasional hard-learned limits of my entire life balling up and washing through me in a great wave of fear and apprehension, like the flash-*boom* of the lightning and thunder, the drenching of the downpour: where was I, where was I going, how could I take even one step more?

It is important to split the great fear into component parts, because if ever they all coalesce—paralysis. I was paralyzed by fear, I felt as though I had never come down from the drugs Jeremy had given me, as though I struggled under their hallucinatory influence still. I literally had to stop walking, had to lean on my cane.

And so I heard their footsteps. Henry Cowell's *The Banshee* begins with fingernails scraping repeatedly up the high wires of an open piano; the same music played my nervous system. Behind me three or four sets of footsteps had come to a halt, just a moment after I myself had stopped.

For a while my heart hammered so hard within me that I could hear nothing else. I forced it to slow, took a deep breath. Of course I was being followed. It made perfect sense. And ahead, at my office . . .

I started walking again. The rain picked up on a gust of wind, and silently I cursed it; it is difficult to hear well when rain is pouring down everywhere, so that one stands at the center of a universal *puh-puh-puh-puh*. But attuned now to their presence, I could hear them behind me, three or four (likely three) people walking, walking at just my pace.

Detour time. Instead of continuing down Twenty-first Street I decided to go west on Pennsylvania, and see what they did. No sound of nearby cars as I stood still; I crossed swiftly, nearly losing my cane as it struck the curb. As casually, as "accidentally" as I could, I turned and faced the street; the sonar glasses whistled up at me, and I knew people were approaching, though I could not hear their footsteps in the rain. More fervently than ever before I blessed the glasses, turned and struck off again, hurrying as much as seemed natural.

Wind and rain, the electric hum and tire hiss of a passing car. Washington late on a stormy spring night, unusually quiet and empty. Behind me the wet footsteps were audible again. I forced myself to keep a steady pace, to avoid giving away the fact that I was aware of their presence. Just a late-night stroll to the office . . .

At Twenty-second I turned south again. Ordinarily no one would have backtracked on Pennsylvania like that, but these people followed me. Now we approached the university hospital, and there was a bit more activity, people passing to left and right, voices across the street discussing a movie, an umbrella being shaken out and folded, cars passing . . . still the footsteps were back there, farther away now, almost out of earshot.

As I approached Gelman Library my pulse picked up again, my mind raced through a network of plans, all unsatisfactory in different ways. . . . Outdoors I couldn't evade pursuit. Given. In the building—

My sonar whistled up as Gelman loomed over me, and I hurried down the steps from the sidewalk to the foyer containing the elevator to the sixth and seventh floors. I missed the door and adrenaline flooded me, then there it was just to my left. The footsteps behind me hurried down the sidewalk steps as I slipped inside and stepped left into the single elevator, punched the button for the seventh floor. The doors stood open, waiting . . . then mercifully they slid together, and I was off alone.

A curious feature of Gelman Library is that there are no stairways to the sixth and seventh floors (the offices above the library proper) that are not fire escapes, locked on the outside. To get to the offices you are forced to take the single elevator, a fact I had complained about many times before—I liked to walk. Now I was thankful, as the arrangement would give me some time. When the elevator opened at the seventh floor, I stepped out, reached back in and punched the buttons for all seven floors. Only when the door closed did it occur to me that I could have tried to find and hit the emergency-stop button, putting the elevator out of action. "Damn!" I cried. Biting my lip, I ran for my office. I started jangling through my keys for the right one, rattled by a mistake as foolish as that.

I couldn't find the key.

I slowed down. Went through them one by one. I found the key, opened my door, propped it wide with the stopper at its base. Over to the file cabinet, where I opened the middle drawer and very carefully slid one hand down the side of the correct file.

The mousetrap was gone. They knew that I knew.

AO. I don't know how long I stood there thinking; it couldn't have been long, though my thoughts spun madly through scores of plans. Then I went to my desk and got the scissors from the top drawer. I followed the power cord of the desk computer to its wall socket beside the file cabinet. I pulled out the plugs there, opened the scissors wide, fitted one point into a socket, jammed it in and twisted it hard.

Crack. The current held me cramped down for a moment—intense pain pulsed through me—I was knocked away, found myself on my knees, slumping against the file cabinets.

(For a while when I was young I fancied I was allergic to novocaine, and my dentist drilled my teeth without anesthetic. It was horribly uncomfortable, but tangent to normal pain: pain beyond pain. So it was with the shock that coursed through me. Later I asked my brother, who is an electrician, about it, and he said that the nervous system was indeed capable of feeling the sixty cycles per second of the alternating current: "When you get bit, you always feel it pumping like that, very fast but distinct." He also said that with my wet shoes I could have been killed. "The current cramps the muscles down so that you're latched on to the source, and that can kill you. You were lucky. Did you find blisters on the bottoms of your feet?" I had.)

Now I struggled up, with my left arm aching fiercely, and a loud hum in my ears. I went to my couch end table, turned on a desk lamp left there for guests, put my face to it. Light. The lights were still working, it seemed; jamming scissors into the wall socket had done nothing but destroy my hearing. Feeling panicky I ran around the corner and down to Delphina's office, remembering a day long before when the lights on the floor had gone out and I had had an opportunity to superblink around for a while, the blind leading the sightless. Somewhere behind her desk, a panel—flush with the wall, how to get it open—a wire handle, open the panel. Circuit breakers in a long vertical row. I clacked them all from left to right and ran back to my office. Face in the lamp. No sensation of light. Heat receding from the bulb. Lights out on the seventh floor.

I took a big breath. Stopped to listen. My glasses beeped fairly loudly, so I took them off and put them on a bookshelf facing the door. I tested the radio, still unsure if the floor had lost all power or not. No sound from the radio. I went into the hall briefly to look into a ceiling light. Nothing, but would I have been able to see if it were on?

Had to assume all power was gone. Back at my desk I took stapler and water tumbler, put them beside the file cabinet. I went to the bookshelves and gathered all the plastic polyhedral shapes (the sphere was just like a big cue ball), and took them to the file cabinet as well. Then I relocated the scissors on the floor.

Out in the hall the elevator doors opened.

"It's dark—"

"Shh."

Hesitant steps, into the hall.

I tiptoed to the doorway. Here it was possible to tell for sure that there were only three of them. There would be light from the elevator, I recalled suddenly, and stepped back into my room.

(Once Max Carrados was caught in a situation similar to mine, and he simply announced to his assailants that he had a gun on them, and would shoot the first person to move. In his case it had worked. But now I saw clearly that the plan was insanely risky. More verbal unreality . . .)

"Down here," one whispered. "Spread out, and be quiet."

Rustling, quiet footsteps, three small clicks (gun safeties?).

I retreated into the office, behind the side of the file cabinet. Stilled my breathing, and was silent in a way they'd never be able to achieve. If they heard anything, it would be my glasses. . . .

"It's here," the first voice whispered. "Door's open, watch it." Their breathing was quick. They were bunched up outside the door, and one said, “Hey, I’ve got a lighter,” so I threw the pulled-open scissors overhand.

“*Ah*! Ah—” Clatter, hard bump against the hall wall, voices clashing, “What”—“threw a knife”—“*ah*”—

I threw the stapler as hard as I could, *wham*—the wall above, I guessed, and threw the dodecahedron as they leaped back. I don’t know what I hit. I jumped almost to the doorway, and heard a voice whisper, “Hey.” I threw the cue-ball sphere right at the voice. *Ponk*. It sounded like—like nothing else I have ever heard. (Although every once in a while some outfielder takes a beepball in the head, and it sounded something like that, wooden and hollow). The victim fell right to the hall floor, making a heavy sound like a car door closing; a metallic clatter marked his gun skidding across the floor. Then CRACK! CRACK! CRACK! another of them shot into the office. I cowered on the floor and crawled swiftly back to the file cabinet, ears ringing painfully, hearing wiped out, fear filling me like the smell of cordite leaking into the room. No way of telling what they were doing. The floor was carpet on concrete, with no vibrations to speak of. I hung my mouth open, trying to focus my hearing on the sound of my glasses. They would whistle up if people entered the room quickly, perhaps (again) more loudly than the people would be on their own. The glasses were still emitting their little beep, now heard through the pulsing wash of noise the gunshots had set off in my ears.

I hefted the water tumbler—it was a fat glass cylinder, with a heavy bottom. A rising whistle—and then, in the hall, the rasp of a lighter flint being sparked—

I threw the tumbler. *Crash*, tinkle of glass falling. A man entered the office. I picked up the pentahedron and threw it. Thump of it against the far wall. I couldn’t find any of the other polyhedrons, somehow they weren’t there besides the cabinet. I crouched and pulled off a shoe—

He swept my glasses aside and I threw the shoe. I think it hit him, but nothing happened. And there I was, without a weapon, utterly vulnerable, curled over waiting to be killed, revealed in the glow of a damned cigarette lighter. . . .

When the shots came I thought they had missed, or that I was hit and couldn’t feel it. Then I realized some of the shots had come from the doorway, others from the bookcase. Sounds of bodies hit, staggering, exhaling, falling, writhing—and all the while I cowered in my corner, trembling.

Then I heard a nasal groan from the hall, a groan like a viola bowed by a rasp. "Mary," I cried, and ran into the hallway to her, tripped on her. She was sitting against the wall—"Mary!" Blood on her—"Carlos," she squeaked painfully, sounding surprised.

A′. Endless moments of fear beyond fear. I had never felt anything like it. Ears ringing, hands exploring her, saying her name over and over, feeling the blood seep out of her shoulder. Feeling her harsh breath. I was bent over my stomach, sick with fear. Under my hands lay the only person I had been bold enough to love in years and years and years, and she was hurt beyond speech, barely conscious, her blood ran over my hands. If she were to die! If I were to lose her, after all that time . . .

I know, I know. That I could be so selfish in such a moment as that. The first axiom. But I barely knew her, I only knew us, I only knew what I felt. We only know what we feel.

There are eons in every hadon, when you are afraid enough. I learned that then.

Finally I gathered the courage to leave her long enough to make a call. Phones still working. 911, our number code for a scream of fear, a desperate cry for help.

And then I waited, in darkness so far beyond my daily darkness I was shocked to awareness of it. Suddenly aware that in ordinary life I walked sightless in sunlight.

And then help came.

AA′. Fortunately, it turned out that she had only been wounded. The bullet had entered just beside the shoulder, wrecking it for a long time after. But no fatal damage.

I learned this later, at the hospital. More than an hour after our arrival a doctor came out and told me, and the sickening knot of tension in my diaphragm untied all at once, making me feel sick in another way, dizzy and nauseous with relief. Unbelievably intense relief. Time lurched back to its ordinary rate of speed.

After that I went through a session with the police. Later Mary talked a lot with her employers, and we both answered a lot of questions from the FBI. (In fact, that process took days.) Two of our assailants were dead (one shot, another hit in the temple with a sphere) and the third had been stabbed: what had happened? I stayed up all through that first night explaining, retrieving and playing my tapes, and so on, and still they didn't go for Jeremy until dawn; by that time he was nowhere to be found.

Eventually I got a moment alone with Mary, about ten the following morning.

"You didn't stay at my place," I said.

"No. I thought you were headed for Blasingame's apartment, and I drove there, but it was empty. So I drove to your office and came upstairs. The elevator opened just as shots were being fired, so I hit the deck and crawled right over a gun. But then I had a hell of a time figuring out who was where. I don't know how you do it."

"Ah."

"So I broke my promise."

"I'm glad."

"Me too."

Our hands found each other and embraced, and I leaned forward until my forehead touched her shoulder (the good one), and rested.

CC′. A couple of days later I said to her, "But what were all those diagrams of Desargues's Theorem about?"

She laughed, and the rich timbre of it cut through me like a miniature of the current from my wall socket. "Well, they programmed me with all those geometrical questions for you, and I was roboting through all that, you know, and struggling underneath it all to understand what was going on, what they wanted. And later, how I could alert you. And really, Desargues's Theorem was the only geometry of my own that I could remember from school. I'm a statistician, you know, most of my training is in that and analysis. . . . So I kept drawing it to try to get your attention to *me*. I had a message in it, you see. You were the triangle in the first plane, and I was the triangle in the second plane, but we were both controlled by the point of projection—"

"But I knew that already!" I exclaimed.

"Did you? But also I marked a little *J* with my thumbnail by the point of projection, so you would know Jeremy was doing it. Did you feel that?"

"No. I xeroxed your drawings, and an impression like that

wouldn't show up." So my indented copy had not included the crucial indentation. . . .

"I know, but I was hoping you would brush it or something. Stupid. Well, anyway, between us all we were making the three collinear points off to the side, which is what they were after, you see."

I laughed. "It never occurred to me," I said, and laughed again, "but I sure do like your way of thinking!"

C. I saw, however, that the diagram had a clearer symbolism than that. Points (events) determine what we are. The essential self, the disabilities, the compensations: isosceles characters projecting onto each other, distorting some features, clarifying others . . . Ah yes. A fantastically complex topology, reduced to stark Euclidean triangles. Lovely.

CBA. When I told Ramon about it, he laughed too. "Here you're the mathematician and you never got it! It was too simple for you!"

"I don't know if I'd call it *too simple*—"

"And wait—wait—you say you told this here girlfriend of yours to stay behind at your house, when you knew you were going to run into those thugs at your office?"

"Well, I didn't *know* they'd be there right then. But . . ."

"Now *that* was superblink."

"Yeah."

I had to admit it; I had been stupid. I had gone too far. And it occurred to me then that in the realm of thought, of analysis and planning—in the realm where I might be most expected to deal competently with the problem—I had consistently and spectacularly failed. Whereas in the physical continuum of action, I had (up to a point) (a point that I didn't like to remember [*ponk* of sphere breaking skull, cowering revealed in a lighter's glare]) done pretty well. Though it was disturbing, in the end this reflection pleased me. For a while there, anyway, I had been almost free of the world of texts.

PQR. *Take two parallel lines*, and slide down them to their intersection, to the point at infinity. To a new haptic space:

Naturally it took a while for Mary to regain her health. The kidnapping, the behavior programming, the shooting, and most of all the repeated druggings her captors and she had subjected herself to, had left her quite sick, and she was in the hospital for some weeks. I visited every day; we talked for hours.

And naturally, it took quite a while for us to sort things out. Not only with the authorities, but with each other. What was real and permanent between us, and what was a product of the strange circumstances of our meeting—no one could say for sure which was which, there.

And maybe we never did disentangle those strands. The start of a relationship remains a part of it forever; and in our case, we had seen things in each other that we might never have otherwise, to our own great good. I know that years later, sometimes, when her hand touched mine I would feel that primal thrill of fear and exhilaration that her first touches had caused in me, and I would shiver again under the mysterious impact of the unknown other. . . . And sometimes, arm in arm, the feeling floods me that we are teamed together in an immense storm of trouble that cracks and thunders all around us, threatening every moment of our lives. So that it seems clear to me, now, that loves forged in the smithy of intense and dangerous circumstances are surely the strongest loves of all.

I leave the proof of this as an exercise for the reader.

SURFACING

Walter Jon Williams

There was an alien on the surface of the planet. A Kyklops had teleported into Overlook Station, and then flown down on the shuttle. Since, unlike humans, it could teleport without apparatus, presumably it took the shuttle just for the ride. The Kyklops wore a human body, controlled through an *n*-dimensional interface, and took its pleasures in the human fashion.

The Kyklops expressed an interest in Anthony's work, but Anthony avoided it: he stayed at sea and listened to aliens of another kind.

Anthony wasn't interested in meeting aliens who knew more than he did.

The boat drifted in a cold current and listened to the cries of the sea. A tall grey swell was rolling in from the southwest, crossing with a wind-driven easterly chop. The boat tossed, caught in the confusion of wave patterns.

It was a sloppy ocean, somehow unsatisfactory. Marking a sloppy day.

Anthony felt a thing twist in his mind. Something that, in its own time, would lead to anger.

The boat had been out here, both in the warm current and then in the cold, for three days. Each more unsatisfactory than the last.

The growing swell was being driven toward land by a storm

that was breaking up fifty miles out to sea: the remnants of the storm itself would arrive by midnight and make things even more unpleasant. Spray feathered across the tops of the waves. The day was growing cold.

Spindrift pattered across Anthony's shoulders. He ignored it, concentrated instead on the long, grating harmonic moan picked up by the microphones his boat dangled into the chill current. The moan ended on a series of clicks and trailed off. Anthony tapped his computer deck. A resolution appeared on the screen. Anthony shaded his eyes from the pale sun and looked at it.

Anthony gazed stonily at the translation tree. "I am rising toward and thinking hungrily about the slippery-tasting coordinates" actually made the most objective sense, but the right-hand branch of the tree was the most literal and most of what Anthony suspected was context had been lost. "I and the oily current are in a state of motion toward one another" was perhaps more literal, but "We (the oily deep and I) are in a cold state of mind" was perhaps equally valid.

The boat gave a corkscrew lurch, dropped down the face of a swell, came to an abrupt halt at the end of its drogue. Water slapped against the stern. A mounting screw, come loose from a bracket on the bridge, fell and danced brightly across the deck.

The screw and the deck are in a state of relative motion, Anthony thought. The screw and the deck are in a motion state of mind.

Wrong, he thought, there is no Other in the Dwellers' speech.

We, I and the screw and the deck, are feeling cold.

We, I and the Dweller below, are in a state of mutual incomprehension.

A bad day, Anthony thought.

Inchoate anger burned deep inside him.

Anthony saved the translation and got up from his seat. He went to the bridge and told the boat to retrieve the drogue and head for Cabo Santa Pola at flank speed. He then went below and found a bottle of bourbon that had three good swallows left.

The trailing microphones continued to record the sonorous moans from below, the sound now mingled with the thrash of the boat's propellers.

The screw danced on the deck as the engines built up speed. Its state of mind was not recorded.

* * *

The video news, displayed above the bar, showed the Kyklops making his tour of the planet. The Kyklops' human body, male, was tall and blue-eyed and elegant. He made witty conversation and showed off his naked chest as if he were proud of it. His name was Telamon.

His real body, Anthony knew, was a tenuous uncorporeal mass somewhere in *n*-dimensional space. The human body had been grown for it to wear, to move like a puppet. The *n*th dimension was interesting only to a mathematician: its inhabitants preferred wearing flesh.

Anthony asked the bartender to turn off the vid.

The yacht club bar was called the Leviathan, and Anthony hated the name. His creatures were too important, too much themselves, to be awarded a name that stank of human myth, of human resonance that had nothing to do with the creatures themselves. Anthony never called them Leviathans himself. They were Deep Dwellers.

There was a picture of a presumed Leviathan above the bar. Sometimes bits of matter were washed up on shore, thin tenuous membranes, long tentacles, bits of phosphorescence, all encrusted with the local equivalent of barnacles and infested with parasites.

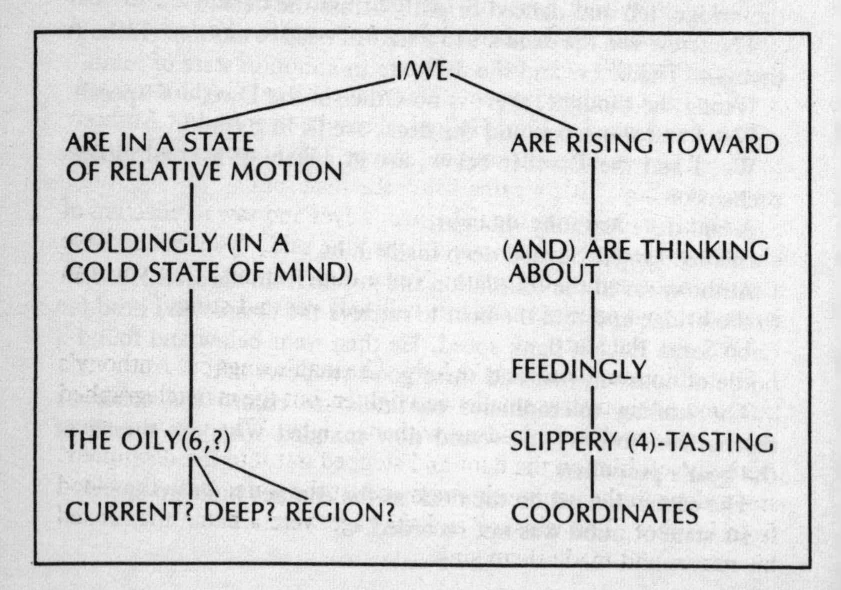

It was assumed the stuff had broken loose from the larger Dweller, or were bits of one that had died. The artist had done his best and painted something that looked like a whale covered with tentacles and seaweed.

The place had fake-nautical decor, nets, harpoons, flashing rods, and knicknacks made from driftwood, and the bar was regularly infested by tourists: that made it even worse. But the regular bartender and the divemaster and the steward were real sailors, and that made the yacht club bearable, gave him some company. His mail was delivered here as well.

Tonight the bartender was a substitute named Christopher: he was married to the owner's daughter and got his job that way. He was a fleshy, sullen man and no company.

We, thought Anthony, the world and I, are drinking alone. Anger burned in him, anger at the quality of the day and the opacity of the Dwellers and the storm that beat brainlessly at the windows.

"*Got* the bastard!" A man was pounding the bar. "Drinks on me." He was talking loudly, and he wore gold rings on his fingers. Raindrops sparkled in his hair. He wore a flashing harness, just in case anyone missed why he was here. Hatred settled in Anthony like poison in his belly.

"Got a thirty-foot flasher," the man said. He pounded the bar again. "Me and Nick got it hung up outside. Four hours. A four-hour fight!"

"Why have a fight with something you can't eat?" Anthony said.

The man looked at him. He looked maybe twenty, but Anthony could tell he was old, centuries old maybe. Old and vain and stupid, stupid as a boy. "It's a game fish," the man said.

Anthony looked into the fisherman's eyes and saw a reflection of his own contempt. "You wanna fight," he said, "you wanna have a *game*, fight something *smart*. Not a dumb animal that you can outsmart, that once you catch it will only rot and stink."

That was the start.

Once it began, it didn't take long. The man's rings cut Anthony's face, and Anthony was smaller and lighter, but the man telegraphed every move and kept leading with his right. When it was over, Anthony left him on the floor and stepped out into the downpour, stood alone in the hammering rain and let the water wash the blood from his face. The whiskey and the rage were a flame that licked his nerves and made them sing.

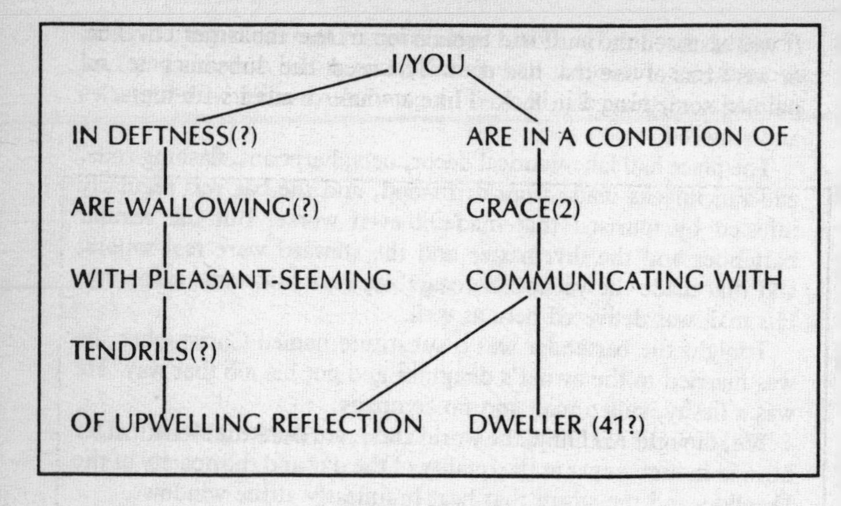

He began walking down the street. Heading for another bar.

GRACE(2) meant grace in the sense of physical grace, dexterity, harmony of motion, as opposed to spiritual grace, which was GRACE(1). The Dweller that Anthony was listening to was engaged in a dialogue with another, possibly the same known to the computer as 41, who might be named "Upwelling Reflection," but Deep Dweller naming systems seemed inconsistent, depending largely on a context that was as yet opaque, and "upwelling reflection" might have to do with something else entirely.

Anthony suspected the Dweller had just said hello.

Salt water smarted on the cuts on Anthony's face. His swollen knuckles pained him as he tapped the keys of his computer deck. He never suffered from hangover, and his mind seemed filled with an exemplary clarity; he worked rapidly, with burning efficiency. His body felt energized.

He was out of the cold Kirst Current today, in a warm, calm subtropical sea on the other side of the Las Madres archipelago. The difference of forty nautical miles was astonishing.

The sun warmed his back. Sweat prickled on his scalp. The sea sparkled under a violet sky.

The other Dweller answered.

Through his bare feet, Anthony could feel the subsonic overtones vibrating through the boat. Something in the cabin rattled. The microphones recorded the sounds, raised the subsonics to an audible level, played it back. The computer made its attempt.

I/YOU

A9140

OILY(5)

TOTALITY OF FEEDING

HAPPY TENDRILITY

IN WARMNESS(3)

A9140 was a phrase that, as yet, had no translation.

The Dweller language, Anthony had discovered, had no separation of subject and object; it was a trait in common with the Earth cetaceans whose languages Anthony had first learned. "I swim toward the island" was not a grammatical possibility: "I and the island are in a condition of swimming toward one another" was the nearest possible approximation.

The Dwellers lived in darkness, and, like Earth's cetaceans, in a liquid medium. Perhaps they were psychologically unable to separate themselves from their environment, from their fluid surroundings. Never approaching the surface—it was presumed they could not survive in a nonpressurized environment—they had no idea of the upper limit of their world.

They were surrounded by a liquid three-dimensional wholeness, not an air-earth-sky environment from which they could consider themselves separate.

A high-pitched whooping came over the speakers, and Anthony smiled as he listened. The singer was one of the humpbacks that he had imported to this planet, a male called The One with Two Notches on His Starboard Fluke.

Two Notches was one of the brighter whales, and also the most playful. Anthony ordered his computer to translate the humpback speech.

Anthony, I and a place of bad smells have found one another, but this has not deterred our hunger.

The computer played back the message as it displayed the translation, and Anthony could understand more context from the sound of the original speech: that Two Notches was floating in a cold layer beneath the bad smell, and that the bad smell was methane or something like it—humans couldn't smell methane, but whales could. The overliteral translation was an aid only, to remind Anthony of idioms he might have forgotten.

Anthony's name in humpback was actually He Who Has Brought Us to the Sea of Rich Strangeness, but the computer translated it simply. Anthony tapped his reply.

What is it that stinks, Two Notches?

Some kind of horrid jellyfish. Were they-and-I feeding, they-and-I would spit one another out. I/They will give them/me a name: they/me are the jellyfish that smell like indigestion.

That is a good name, Two Notches.

I and a small boat discovered each other earlier today. We itched, so we scratched our back on the boat. The humans and I were startled. We had a good laugh together in spite of our hunger.

Meaning that Two Notches had risen under the boat, scratched his back on it, and terrified the passengers witless. Anthony remembered the first time this had happened to him back on Earth, a vast female humpback rising up without warning, one long scalloped fin breaking the water to port, the rest of the whale to starboard, thrashing in cetacean delight as it rubbed itself against a boat half its length. Anthony had clung to the gunwale, horrified by what the whale could do to his boat, but still exhilarated, delighted at the sight of the creature and its glorious joy.

Still, Two Notches ought not to play too many pranks on the tourists.

We should be careful, Two Notches. Not all humans possess our sense of humor especially if they are hungry.

We were bored, Anthony. Mating is over, feeding has not begun. Also, it was Nick's boat that got scratched. In our opinion Nick and I enjoyed ourselves, **even though we were hungry.**

Hunger and food seemed to be the humpback subtheme of the day. Humpback songs, like the human, were made up of text and chorus, the chorus repeating itself, with variations, through the message.

I and Nick will ask each other and find out, as we feed.

Anthony tried to participate in the chorus/response about food, but he found himself continually frustrated at his clumsy phrasing. Fortunately the whales were tolerant of his efforts.

Have we learned anything about the ones that swim deep and do not breathe and feed on obscure things?

Not yet, Two Notches. Something has interrupted us in our hungry quest.

A condition of misfortune exists, like unto hunger. We must learn to be quicker.

We will try, Two Notches. After we eat.

We would like to speak to the Deep Dwellers now, and feed with them, but we must breathe.

We will speak to ourselves another time after feeding.

We are in a condition of hunger, Anthony. We must eat soon.

We will remember our hunger and make plans.

The mating and calving season for the humpbacks was over. Most of the whales were already heading north to their summer feeding grounds, where they would do little but eat for six months. Two Notches and one of the other males had remained in the vicinity of Las Madres as a favor to Anthony, who used them to assist in locating the Deep Dwellers, but soon—in a matter of days—the pair would have to head north. They hadn't eaten anything for nearly half a year; Anthony didn't want to starve them.

But when the whales left, Anthony would be alone—again—with the Deep Dwellers. He didn't want to think about that.

The system's second sun winked across the waves, rising now. It was a white dwarf and emitted dangerous amounts of X-rays. The boat's falkner generator, triggered by the computer, snapped on a field that surrounded the boat and guarded it from energetic radiation. Anthony felt the warmth on his shoulders decrease. He turned his attention back to the Deep Dwellers.

A blaze of delight rose in Anthony. The Dwellers, he realized, had overheard his conversation with Two Notches, and were commenting on it. Furthermore, he knew, A9140 probably was

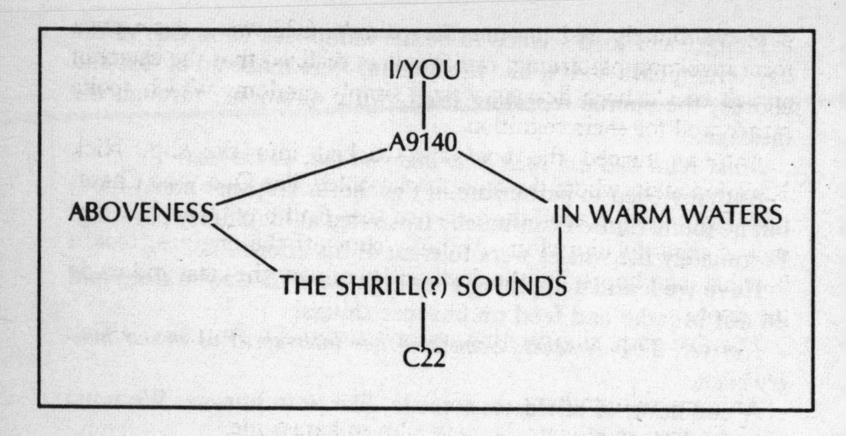

a verb form having to do with hearing—the Dwellers had a lot of them. "I/You hear the shrill sounds from above" might do as a working translation, and although he had no idea how to translate C22, he suspected it was a comment on the sounds. In a fever, Anthony began to work. As he bent over his keys he heard, through water and bone, the sound of Two Notches singing.

The Milky Way was a dim watercolor wash overhead. An odd twilight hung over Las Madres, a near-darkness that marked the hours when only the dwarf star was in the sky, providing little visible light but still pouring out X-rays. Cabo Santa Pola lay in a bright glowing crescent across the boat's path. Music drifted from a waterfront tavern, providing a counterpoint to the Deep Dweller speech that still rang in Anthony's head. A familiar figure waited on the dock, standing beneath the yellow lamp that marked Anthony's slip. Anthony waved and throttled the boat back.

A good day. Even after the yellow sun had set, Anthony still felt in a sunny mood. A9140 had been codified as "listen(14)," meaning listen solely in the sense of listening to a sound that originated from far outside the Dwellers' normal sphere—from outside their entire universe, in fact, which spoke volumes for the way the Dwellers saw themselves in relation to their world. They knew something else was up there, and their speech could make careful distinction between the world they knew and could perceive directly and the one they didn't. C22 was a descriptive term involving patterning: the Dwellers realized that the cetacean speech they'd been hearing wasn't simply random. Which spoke rather well for their cognition.

Anthony turned the boat and backed into the slip. Nick Kanellopoulos, whom the humpbacks called The One Who Chases Bad-Tasting Fish, took the sternline that Anthony threw him and tied it expertly to a cleat. Anthony shut off the engines, took a bowline, and hopped to the dock. He bent over the cleat and made his knot.

"You've gotta stop beating up my customers, Anthony," Nick said.

Anthony said nothing.

"You even send your damn whales to harass me."

Anthony jumped back into the boat and stepped into the cabin for a small canvas bag that held his gear and the data cubes containing the Dwellers' conversation. When he stepped back out of the cabin, he saw Nick standing on one foot, the other poised to step into the boat. Anthony gave Nick a look and Nick pulled his foot back. Anthony smiled. He didn't like people on his boat.

"Dinner?" he asked.

Nick gazed at him. A muscle moved in the man's cheek. He was dapper, olive-skinned, about a century old, the second-youngest human on the planet. He looked in his late teens. He wore a personal falkner generator on his belt that protected him from the dwarf's X-rays.

"Dinner. Fine." His brown eyes were concerned. "You look like hell, Anthony."

Anthony rubbed the stubble on his cheeks. "I feel on top of the world," he said.

"Half the time you don't even talk to me. I don't know why I'm eating supper with you."

"Let me clean up. Then we can go to the Villa Mary."

Nick shook his head. "Okay," he said. "But you're buying. You cost me a customer last night."

Anthony slapped him on the shoulder. "Least I can do, I guess."

A good day.

Near midnight. Winds beat at the island's old volcanic cone, pushed down the crowns of trees. A shuttle, black against the darkness of the sky, rose in absolute silence from the port on the other side of the island, heading toward the bright fixed star that was Overlook Station. The alien, Telamon, was aboard, or so the newscasts reported.

Deep Dwellers still sang in Anthony's head. Mail in hand, he let himself in through the marina gate and walked toward his slip. The smell of the sea rose around him. He stretched, yawned. Belched up a bit of the tequila he'd been drinking with Nick. He intended to get an early start and head back to sea before dawn.

Anthony paused beneath a light and opened the large envelope, pulled out page proofs that had been mailed, at a high cost, from the offices of the *Xenobiology Review* on Kemps. Discontent scratched at his nerves. He frowned as he glanced through the pages. He'd written the article over a year before, at the end of the first spring he'd spent here, and just glancing through it he now found the article overtentative, overformal, and, worse, almost pleading in its attempt to justify his decision to move himself and the whales here. The palpable defensiveness made him want to squirm.

Disgust filled him. His fingers clutched at the pages, then tore the proofs across. His body spun full circle as he scaled the proofs out to the sea. The wind scattered thick chunks of paper across the dark waters of the marina.

He stalked toward his boat. Bile rose in his throat. He wished he had a bottle of tequila with him. He almost went back for one before he realized the liquor stores were closed.

"Anthony Maldalena?"

She was a little gawky, and her skin was pale. Dark hair in a single long braid, deep eyes, a bit of an overbite. She was waiting for him at the end of his slip, under the light. She had a bag over one shoulder.

Anthony stopped. Dull anger flickered in his belly. He didn't want anyone taking notice of the bruises and cuts on his face. He turned his head away as he stepped into his boat, dropped his bag on a seat.

"Mr. Maldalena. My name is Philana Telander. I came here to see you."

"How'd you get in?"

She gestured to the boat two slips down, a tall FPS-powered yacht shaped like a flat oval with a tall flybridge jutting from its center so that the pilot could see over wavetops. It would fly from place to place, but she could put it down in the water if she wanted. No doubt she'd bought a temporary membership at the yacht club.

"Nice boat," said Anthony. It would have cost her a fair bit to have it gated here. He opened the hatch to his forward cabin, tossed his bag onto the long couch inside.

"I meant," she said, "I came to this *planet* to see you."

Anthony didn't say anything, just straightened from his stoop by the hatch and looked at her. She shifted from one foot to another. Her skin was yellow in the light of the lamp. She reached into her bag and fumbled with something.

Anthony waited.

The clicks and sobs of whales sounded from the recorder in her hand.

"I wanted to show you what I've been able to do with your work. I have some articles coming up in *Cetology Journal* but they won't be out for a while."

"You've done very well," said Anthony. Tequila swirled in his head. He was having a hard time concentrating on a subject as difficult as whale speech.

Philana had specialized in communication with female humpbacks. It was harder to talk with the females: although they were curious and playful, they weren't vocal like the bulls; their language was deeper, briefer, more personal. They made no songs. It was almost as if, solely in the realm of speech, the cows were autistic. Their psychology was different and complicated, and Anthony had had little success in establishing any lasting communication. The cows, he had realized, were speaking a second tongue: the humpbacks were essentially bilingual, and Anthony had only learned one of their languages.

Philana had succeeded where Anthony had found only frustration. She had built from his work, established a structure and basis for communication. She still wasn't as easy in her speech with the cows as Anthony was with a bull like Two Notches, but she was far closer than Anthony had ever been.

Steam rose from the coffee cup in Philana's hand as she poured from Anthony's vacuum flask. She and Anthony sat on the cushioned benches in the stern of Anthony's boat. Tequila still buzzed in Anthony's head. Conflicting urges warred in him. He didn't want anyone else here, on his boat, this close to his work; but

Philana's discoveries were too interesting to shut her our entirely. He swallowed more coffee.

"Listen to this," Philana said. "It's fascinating. A cow teaching her calf about life." She touched the recorder, and muttering filled the air. Anthony had difficulty understanding: the cow's idiom was complex, and bore none of the poetic repetition that made the males' language easier to follow. Finally he shook his head.

"Go ahead and turn it off," he said. "I'm picking up only one phrase in five. I can't follow it."

Philana seemed startled. "Oh, I'm sorry. I thought—"

Anthony twisted uncomfortably in his seat. "I don't know every goddamn thing about whales," he said.

The recorder fell silent. Wind rattled the canvas awning over the flybridge. Savage discontent settled into Anthony's mind. Suddenly he needed to get rid of this woman, get her off his boat and head to sea right now, away from all the things on land that could trip him up.

He thought of his father upside down in the smokehouse. Not moving, arms dangling.

He should apologize, he realized. We are, he thought, in a condition of permanent apology.

"I'm sorry," he said. "I'm just . . . not used to dealing with people."

"Sometimes I wonder," she said. "I'm only twenty-one, and . . ."

"Yes?" Blurted suddenly, the tequila talking. Anthony felt disgust at his own awkwardness.

Philana looked at the planks. "Yes. Truly. I'm twenty-one, and sometimes people get impatient with me for reasons I don't understand."

Anthony's voice was quiet. "I'm twenty-six."

Philana was surprised. "But, I thought." She thought for a long moment. "It seems I've been reading your papers for . . ."

"I was first published at twenty," he said. "The finback article."

Philana shook her head. "I'd never have guessed. Particularly after what I saw in your new *XR* paper."

Anthony's reaction was instant. "You saw that?" Another spasm of disgust touched him. Tequila burned in his veins. His stomach turned over. For some reason his arms were trembling.

"A friend on Kemps sent me an advance copy. I thought it was brilliant. The way you were able to codify your conceptions about a race of which you could really know nothing, and have it all pan out when you began to understand them. That's an incredible achievement."

"It's a piece of crap." Anthony wanted more tequila badly. His body was shaking. He tossed the remains of his coffee over his shoulder into the sea. "I've learned so much since. I've given up even trying to publish it. The delays are too long. Even if I put it on the nets, I'd still have to take the time to write it, and I'd rather spend my time working."

"I'd like to see it."

He turned away from her. "I don't show my work till it's finished."

"I . . . didn't mean to intrude."

Apology. He could feel a knife twisting in his belly. He spoke quickly. "I'm sorry, Miss Telander. It's late, and I'm not used to company. I'm not entirely well." He stood, took her arm. Ignoring her surprise, he almost pulled her to her feet. "Maybe tomorrow. We'll talk again."

She blinked up at him. "Yes. I'd like that."

"Good night." He rushed her off the boat and stepped below to the head. He didn't want her to hear what was going to happen next. Acid rose in his throat. He clutched his middle and bent over the small toilet and let the spasms take him. The convulsions wracked him long after he was dry. After it was over he stood shakily, staggered to the sink, washed his face. His sinuses burned and brought tears to his eyes. He threw himself on the couch.

In the morning, before dawn, he cast off and motored out into the quiet sea.

The other male, The One Who Sings of Others, found a pair of Dwellers engaged in a long conversation and hovered above them. His transponder led Anthony to the place, fifty miles south into the bottomless tropical ocean. The Dwellers' conversation was dense. Anthony understood perhaps one word-phrase in ten. Sings of Others interrupted from time to time to tell Anthony how hungry he was.

The recordings would require days of work before Anthony could even begin to make sense of them. He wanted to stay on the site, but the Dwellers fell silent, neither Anthony nor Sings of Others could find another conversation, and Anthony was near out of supplies. He'd been working so intently he'd never got around to buying food.

The white dwarf had set by the time Anthony motored into harbor. Dweller mutterings did a chaotic dance in his mind. He felt a twist of annoyance at the sight of Philana Telander jumping from her big air yacht to the pier. She had obviously been waiting for him.

He threw her the bowline and she made fast. As he stepped onto the dock and fastened the sternline, he noticed sunburn reddening her cheeks. She'd spent the day on the ocean.

"Sorry I left so early," he said. "One of the humpbacks found some Dwellers, and their conversation sounded interesting."

She looked from Anthony to his boat and back. "That's all right," she said. "I shouldn't have talked to you last night. Not when you were ill."

Anger flickered in his mind. She'd heard him being sick, then.

"Too much to drink," he said. He jumped back into the boat and got his gear.

"Have you eaten?" she asked. "Somebody told me about a place called the Villa Mary."

He threw his bag over one shoulder. Dinner would be his penance. "I'll show you," he said.

"Mary was a woman who died," Anthony said. "One of the original Knight's Move people. She chose to die, refused the treatments. She didn't believe in living forever." He looked up at the arched ceiling, the moldings on walls and ceiling, the initials ML worked into the decoration. "Brian McGivern built this place in her memory," Anthony said. "He's built a lot of places like this, on different worlds."

Philana was looking at her plate. She nudged an ichthyoid exomembrane with her fork. "I know," she said. "I've been in a few of them."

Anthony reached for his glass, took a drink, then stopped himself from taking a second swallow. He realized that he'd drunk most of a bottle of wine. He didn't want a repetition of last night.

With an effort he put the glass down.

"She's someone I think about, sometimes," Philana said. "About the choice she made."

"Yes?" Anthony shook his head. "Not me. I don't want to spend a hundred years dying. If I ever decide to die, I'll do it quick."

"That's what people say. But they never do it. They just get older and older. Stranger and stranger." She raised her hands, made a gesture that took in the room, the decorations, the entire white building on its cliff overlooking the sea. "Get old enough, you start doing things like building Villa Marys all over the galaxy. McGivern's an oldest-generation immortal, you know. Maybe the wealthiest human anywhere, and he spends his time immortalizing someone who didn't want immortality of any kind."

Anthony laughed. "Sounds like you're thinking of becoming a Diehard."

She looked at him steadily. "Yes."

Anthony's laughter froze abruptly. A cool shock passed through him. He had never spoken to a Diehard before: the only ones he'd met were people who mumbled at him on street corners and passed out incoherent religious tracts.

Philana looked at her plate. "I'm sorry," she said.

"Why sorry?"

"I shouldn't have brought it up."

Anthony reached for his wine glass, stopped himself, put his hand down. "I'm curious."

She gave a little, apologetic laugh. "I may not go through with it."

"Why even think about it?"

Philana thought a long time before answering. "I've seen how the whales accept death. So graceful about it, so matter-of-fact—and they don't even have the myth of an afterlife to comfort them. If they get sick, they just beach themselves; and their friends try to keep them company. And when I try to give myself a reason for living beyond my natural span, I can't think of any. All I can think of is the whales."

Anthony saw the smokehouse in his mind, his father with his arms hanging, the fingers touching the dusty floor. "Death isn't nice."

Philana gave him a skeletal grin and took a quick drink of wine. "With any luck," she said, "death isn't anything at all."

Wind chilled the night, pouring upon the town through a slot in the island's volcanic cone. Anthony watched a streamlined head as it moved in the dark wind-washed water of the marina. The head belonged to a cold-blooded amphibian that lived in the warm surf of the Las Madres; the creature was known misleadingly as a Las Madres seal. They had little fear of humanity and were curious about the new arrivals. Anthony stamped a foot on the slip. Planks boomed. The seal's head disappeared with a soft splash. Ripples spread in starlight, and Anthony smiled.

Philana had stepped into her yacht for a sweater. She returned, cast a glance at the water, saw nothing.

"Can I listen to the Dwellers?" she asked. "I'd like to hear them."

Despite his resentment at her imposition, Anthony appreciated her being careful with the term: she hadn't called them Leviathans once. He thought about her request, could think of no reason to refuse save his own stubborn reluctance. The Dweller sounds were just background noise, meaningless to her. He stepped onto his boat, took a cube from his pocket, put it in the trapdoor, pressed the PLAY button. Dweller murmurings filled the cockpit. Philana stepped from the dock to the boat. She shivered in the wind. Her eyes were pools of dark wonder.

"So different."

"Are you surprised?"

"I suppose not."

"This isn't really what they sound like. What you're hearing is a computer-generated metaphor for the real thing. Much of their communication is subsonic, and the computer raises the sound to levels we can hear, and also speeds it up. Sometimes the Dwellers take three or four minutes to speak what seems to be a simple sentence."

"We would never have noticed them except for an accident," Philana said. "That's how alien they are."

"Yes."

Humanity wouldn't know of the Dwellers' existence at all if it weren't for the subsonics confusing some automated sonar buoys, followed by an idiot computer assuming the sounds were deliberate interference and initiating an ET scan. Any human would have looked at the data, concluded it was some kind of seismic interference, and programmed the buoys to ignore it.

"They've noticed *us*," Anthony said. "The other day I heard them discussing a conversation I had with one of the humpbacks."

Philana straightened. Excitement was plain in her voice. "They can conceptualize something alien to them."

"Yes."

Her response was instant, stepping on the last sibilant of his answer. "And theorize about our existence."

Anthony smiled at her eagerness. "I . . . don't think they've got around to that yet."

"But they are intelligent."

"Yes."

"Maybe more intelligent than the whales. From what you say, they seem quicker to conceptualize."

"Intelligent in certain ways, perhaps. There's still very little I understand about them."

"Can you teach me to talk to them?"

The wind blew chill between them. "I don't," he said, "talk to them."

She seemed not to notice his change of mood, stepped closer. "You haven't tried that yet? That would seem to be reasonable, considering they've already noticed us."

He could feel his hackles rising, mental defenses sliding into place. "I'm not proficient enough," he said.

"If you could attract their attention, they could teach you." Reasonably.

"No. Not yet." Rage exploded in Anthony's mind. He wanted her off his boat, away from his work, his existence. He wanted to be alone again with his creatures, solitary witness to the lonely and wonderful interplay of alien minds.

"I never told you," Philana said, "why I'm here."

"No. You didn't."

"I want to do some work with the humpback cows."

"Why?"

Her eyes widened slightly. She had detected the hostility in his tone. "I want to chart any linguistic changes that may occur as a result of their move to another environment."

Through clouds of blinding resentment Anthony considered her plan. He couldn't stop her, he knew: anyone could talk to the whales if they knew how to do it. It might keep her away from the Dwellers. "Fine," he said. "Do it."

Her look was challenging. "I don't need your permission."

"I know that."

"You don't own them."

"I know that, too."

There was a splash far out in the marina. The Las Madres seal chasing a fish. Philana was still staring at him. He looked back.

"Why are you afraid of my getting close to the Dwellers?" she asked.

"You've been here two days. You don't know them. You're making all manner of assumptions about what they're like, and all you've read is one obsolete article."

"You're the expert. If my assumptions are wrong, you're free to tell me."

"Humans interacted with whales for centuries before they learned to speak with them, and even now the speech is limited and often confused. I've only been here two and a half years."

"Perhaps," she said, "you could use some help. Write those papers of yours. Publish the data."

He turned away. "I'm doing fine," he said.

"Glad to hear it." She took a long breath. "What did I *do*, Anthony? Tell me."

"Nothing," he said. Anthony watched the marina waters, saw the amphibian surface, its head pulled back to help slide a fish down its gullet. Philana was just standing there. We, thought Anthony, are in a condition of nonresolution.

"I work alone," he said. "I immerse myself in their speech, in their environment, for months at a time. Talking to a human breaks my concentration. I don't know *how* to talk to a person right now. After the Dwellers, you seem perfectly . . ."

"Alien?" she said. Anthony didn't answer. The amphibian slid through the water, its head leaving a short, silver wake.

The boat rocked as Philana stepped from it to the dock. "Maybe we can talk later," she said. "Exchange data or something."

"Yes," Anthony said. "We'll do that." His eyes were still on the seal.

Later, before he went to bed, he told the computer to play Dweller speech all night long.

Lying in his bunk the next morning, Anthony heard Philana cast off her yacht. He felt a compulsion to talk to her, apologize again, but in the end he stayed in his rack, tried to concentrate on Dweller sounds. I/We remain in a condition of solitude, he thought, the

Dweller phrases coming easily to his mind. There was a brief shadow cast on the port beside him as the big flying boat rose into the sky, then nothing but sunlight and the slap of water on the pier supports. Anthony climbed out of his sleeping bag and went into town, provisioned the boat for a week. He had been too close to land for too long: a trip into the sea, surrounded by nothing but whales and Dweller speech, should cure him of his unease.

Two Notches had switched on his transponder: Anthony followed the beacon north, the boat rising easily over deep blue rollers. Desiring sun, Anthony climbed to the flybridge and lowered the canvas cover. Fifty miles north of Cabo Santa Pola there was a clear dividing line in the water, a line as clear as a meridian on a chart, beyond which the sea was a deeper, purer blue. The line marked the boundary of the cold Kirst current that had journeyed, wreathed in mist from contact with the warmer air, a full three thousand nautical miles from the region of the South Pole. Anthony crossed the line and rolled down his sleeves as the temperature of the air fell.

He heard the first whale speech through his microphones as he entered the cold current: the sound hadn't carried across the turbulent frontier of warm water and cold. The whales were unclear, distant and mixed with the sound of the screws, but he could tell from the rhythm that he was overhearing a dialogue. Apparently Sings of Others had joined Two Notches north of Las Madres. It was a long journey to make overnight, but not impossible.

The cooler air was invigorating. The boat plowed a straight, efficient wake through the deep blue sea. Anthony's spirits rose. This was where he belonged, away from the clutter and complication of humanity. Doing what he did best.

He heard something odd in the rhythm of the whalespeech; he frowned and listened more closely. One of the whales was Two Notches: Anthony recognized his speech patterns easily after all this time; but the other wasn't Sings of Others. There was a clumsiness in its pattern of chorus and response.

The other was a human. Annoyance hummed in Anthony's nerves. Back on Earth, tourists or eager amateur explorers sometimes bought cheap translation programs and tried to talk to the whales, but this was no tourist program: it was too eloquent, too knowing. Philana, of course. She'd followed the transponder signal and was busy gathering data about the humpback females. Anthony cut his engines and let the boat drift slowly to put its bow into the wind; he deployed the microphones from their wells in the hull and listened. The song was bouncing off a colder layer below, and it echoed confusingly.

Deep Swimmer and her calf, called The One That Nudges, are possessed of one another. I and that one am the father. We hunger for one another's presence.

Apparently hunger was once again the subtheme of the day. The context told Anthony that Two Notches was swimming in cool water beneath a boat. Anthony turned the volume up:

We hunger to hear of Deep Swimmer and our calf.

That was the human response: limited in its phrasing and context, direct and to the point.

I and Deep Swimmer are shy. We will not play with humans. Instead we will pretend we are hungry and vanish into deep waters.

The boat lurched as a swell caught it at an awkward angle. Water splashed over the bow. Anthony deployed the drogue and dropped from the flybridge to the cockpit. He tapped a message into the computer and relayed it.

I and Two Notches are pleased to greet ourselves. I and Two Notches hope we are not too hungry.

The whale's reply was shaded with delight. **Hungrily I and Anthony greet ourselves. We and Anthony's friend, Air Human, have been in a condition of conversation.**

Air Human, from the flying yacht. Two Notches went on.

We had found ourselves some Deep Dwellers, but some moments ago we and they moved beneath a cold layer and our conversation is lost. I starve for its return.

The words echoed off the cold layer that stood like a wall between Anthony and the Dwellers. The humpback inflections were steeped in annoyance.

Our hunger is unabated, Anthony typed. *But we will wait for the nonbreathers' return.*

We cannot wait long. Tonight we and the north must begin the journey to our feeding time.

The voice of Air Human rumbled through the water. It sounded like a distant, throbbing engine. **Our finest greetings, Anthony. I and Two Notches will travel north together. Then we and the others will feed.**

Annoyance slammed into Anthony. Philana had abducted his whale. Clenching his teeth, he typed a civil reply:

Please give our kindest greetings to our hungry brothers and sisters in the north.

By the time he transmitted his speech his anger had faded. Two Notches' departure was inevitable in the next few days, and he'd known that. Still, a residue of jealousy burned in him. Philana would have the whale's company on its journey north: he would be stuck here by Las Madres without the keen whale ears that helped him find the Dwellers.

Two Notches' reply came simultaneously with a programmed reply from Philana. Lyrics about greetings, hunger, feeding, calves, and joy whined through the water, bounced from the cold layer. Anthony looked at the hash his computer made of the translation and laughed. He decided he might as well enjoy Two Notches' company while it lasted.

That was a strange message to hear from our friend, Two Mouths, he typed. "Notch" and "mouth" were almost the same phrase: Anthony had just made a pun.

Whale amusement bubbled through the water. **Two Mouths and I belong to the most unusual family between surface and cold water. We-All and air breathe each other, but some of us have the bad fortune to live in it.**

The sun warmed Anthony's shoulders in spite of the cool air. He decided to leave off the pursuit of the Dwellers and spend the day with his humpback.

He kicked off his shoes, then stepped down to his cooler and made himself a sandwich.

The Dwellers never came out from beneath the cold layer. Anthony spent the afternoon listening to Two Notches tell stories about his family. Now that the issue of hunger was resolved by the whale's decision to migrate, the cold layer beneath them became the new topic of conversation, and Two Notches amused himself by harmonizing with his own echo. Sings of Others arrived in late afternoon and announced he had already begun his journey: he and Two Notches decided to travel in company.

Northward homing! Cold watering! Reunion joyous! The phrases dopplered closer to Anthony's boat, and then Two Notches broke the water thirty feet off the port beam, salt water pouring like Niagara from his black jaw, his scalloped fins spread like wings eager to take the air . . . Anthony's breath went out of him in surprise. He turned in his chair and leaned away from the sight, half in fear and half in awe . . . Even though he was used to the whales, the sight never failed to stun him, thrill him, freeze him in his tracks.

Two Notches toppled over backward, one clear brown eye fixed on Anthony. Anthony raised an arm and waved, and he thought he saw amusement in Two Notches' glance, perhaps the beginning of an answering wave in the gesture of a fin. A living creature the size of a bus, the whale struck the water not with a smack, but with a roar, a sustained outpour of thunder. Anthony braced himself for what was coming. Salt water flung itself over the gunwale, struck him like a blow. The cold was shocking: his heart lurched. The boat was flung high on the wave, dropped down its face with a jarring thud. Two Notches' flukes tossed high and Anthony could see the mottled pattern, grey and white, on the underside, distinctive as a fingerprint . . . and then the flukes were gone, leaving behind a rolling boat and a boiling sea.

Anthony wiped the ocean from his face, then from his computer. The boat's auto-bailing mechanism began to throb. Two Notches surfaced a hundred yards off, spouted a round cloud of steam, submerged again. The whale's amusement stung the water. Anthony's surprise turned to joy, and he echoed the sound of laughter.

I'm going to run my boat up your backside, Anthony promised; he splashed to the controls in his bare feet, withdrew the drogue and threw his engines into gear. Props thrashed the sea into foam. Anthony drew the microphones up into their wells, heard them thud along the hull as the boat gained way. Humpbacks usually took breath in a series of three: Anthony aimed ahead for Two Notches' second rising. Two Notches rose just ahead, spouted, and dove before Anthony could catch him. A cold wind cut through Anthony's wet shirt, raised bumps on his flesh. The boat increased speed, tossing its head on the face of a wave, and Anthony raced ahead, aiming for where Two Notches would rise for the third time.

The whale knew where the boat was and was able to avoid him easily; there was no danger in the game. Anthony won the race: Two Notches surfaced just aft of the boat, and Anthony grinned as he gunned his propellers and wrenched the rudder from side to side while the boat spewed foam into the whale's face. Two Notches gave a grunt of disappointment and sounded, tossing his flukes high. Unless he chose to rise early, Two Notches would be down for five minutes or more. Anthony raced the boat in circles, waiting. Two Notches' taunts rose in the cool water. The wind was cutting Anthony to the quick. He reached into the cabin for a sweater, pulled it on, ran up to the flybridge just in time to see Two Notches leap again half a mile away, the vast dark body silhouetted for a moment against the setting sun before it fell again into the welcoming sea.

Goodbye, goodbye. I and Anthony send fragrant farewells to one another.

White foam surrounded the slick, still place where Two Notches had fallen into the water. Suddenly the flybridge was very cold. Anthony's heart sank. He cut speed and put the wheel amidships. The boat slowed reluctantly, as if it, too, had been enjoying the game. Anthony dropped down the ladder to his computer.

Through the spattered windscreen, Anthony could see Two Notches leaping again, his long wings beating air, his silhouette refracted through seawater and rainbows. Anthony tried to share the whale's exuberance, his joy, but the thought of another long summer alone on his boat, beating his head against the enigma of the Dwellers, turned his mind to ice.

He ordered an infinite repeat of Two Notches' last phrase and stepped below to change into dry clothes. The cold layer echoed his farewells. He bent almost double and began pulling the sweater over his head.

Suddenly he straightened. An idea was chattering at him. He yanked the sweater back down over his trunk, rushed to his computer, tapped another message.

Our farewells need not be said just yet. You and I can follow one another for a few days before I must return. Perhaps you and the nonbreathers can find one another for conversation.

Anthony is in a condition of migration. Welcome, welcome. Two Notches' reply was jubilant.

For a few days, Anthony qualified. Before too long he would have to return to port for supplies. Annoyed at himself, he realized he could as easily have victualed for weeks.

Another voice called through the water, sounded faintly through the speakers. *Air Human and Anthony are in a state of tastiest welcome*.

In the middle of Anthony's reply, his fingers paused at the keys. Surprise rose quietly to the surface of his mind.

After the long day of talking in humpback speech, he had forgotten that Air Human was not a humpback. That she was, in fact, another human being sitting on a boat just over the horizon.

Anthony continued his message. His fingers were clumsy now, and he had to go back twice to correct mistakes. He wondered why it was harder to talk to Philana, now that he remembered she wasn't an alien.

He asked Two Notches to turn on his transponder, and, all through the deep shadow twilight when the white dwarf was in the sky, the boat followed the whale at a half-mile's distance. The current was cooperative, but in a few days a new set of northwest trade winds would push the current off on a curve toward the equator and the whales would lose its assistance.

Anthony didn't see Philana's boat that first day: just before dawn, Sings of Others heard a distant Dweller conversation to starboard. Anthony told his boat to strike off in that direction and spent most of the day listening. When the Dwellers fell silent, he headed for the whales' transponders again. There was a lively conversation in progress between Air Human and the whales, but Anthony's mind was still on Dwellers. He put on headphones and worked far into the night.

The next morning was filled with chill mist. Anthony awoke to the whooping cries of the humpbacks. He looked at his computer to see if it had recorded any announcement of Dwellers, and there was none. The whales' interrogation by Air Human continued. Anthony's toes curled on the cold, damp planks as he stepped on deck and saw Philana's yacht two hundred yards to port, floating three feet over the tallest swells. Cables trailed from the stern, pulling hydrophones and speakers on a subaquatic sled. Anthony grinned at the sight of the elaborate store-bought rig. He suspected that he got better acoustics with his homebuilt equipment, the translation softwear he'd programmed himself, and his hopelessly old-fashioned boat that couldn't even rise out of the water, but that he'd equipped with the latest-generation silent propellers.

He turned on his hydrophones. Sure enough, he got more

audio interference from Philana's sled than he received from his entire boat.

While making coffee and an omelette of mossmoon eggs Anthony listened to the whales gurgle about their grandparents. He put on a down jacket and stepped onto the boat's stern and ate breakfast, watching the humpbacks as they occasionally broke surface, puffed out clouds of spray, sounded again with a careless, vast toss of their flukes. Their bodies were smooth and black: the barnacles that pebbled their skin on Earth had been removed before they gated to their new home.

Their song could be heard clearly even without the amplifiers. That was one change the contact with humans had brought: the males were a lot more vocal than once they had been, as if they were responding to human encouragement—or perhaps they now had more worth talking about. Their speech was also more terse than before, less overtly poetic; the humans' directness and compactness of speech, caused mainly by their lack of fluency, had influenced the whales to a degree.

The whales were adapting to communication with humans more easily than the humans were adapting to them. It was important to chart that change, be able to say how the whales had evolved, accommodated. They were on an entire new planet now, explorers, and the change was going to come fast. The whales were good at remembering, but artificial intelligences were better. Anthony was suddenly glad that Philana was here, doing her work.

As if on cue she appeared on deck, one hand pressed to her head, holding an earphone: she was listening intently to whalesong. She was bundled up against the chill, and gave a brief wave as she noticed him. Anthony waved back. She paused, beating time with one hand to the rhythm of whalespeech, then waved again and stepped back to her work.

Anthony finished breakfast and cleaned the dishes. He decided to say good morning to the whales, then work on some of the Dweller speech he'd recorded the day before. He turned on his computer, sat down at the console, typed his greetings. He waited for a pause in the conversation, then transmitted. The answer came back sounding like a distant buzzsaw.

We and Anthony wish one another a passage filled with splendid odors. We and Air Human have been scenting one another's families this morning.

We wish each other the joy of converse, Anthony typed.

We have been wondering, Two Notches said, **if we can scent whether we and Anthony and Air Human are in a condition of rut.**

Anthony gave a laugh. Humpbacks enjoyed trying to figure out human relationships: they were promiscuous themselves, and intrigued by ways different from their own.

Anthony wondered, sitting in his cockpit, if Philana was looking at him.

Air Human and I smell of aloneness, unpairness, he typed, and he transmitted the message at the same time that Philana entered the even more direct, **We are not.**

The state is not rut, apartness is the smell, Two Notches agreed readily—it was all one to him—and the lyrics echoed each other for a long moment, *aloneness, not, unpairness, not. Not.* Anthony felt a chill.

I and the Dwellers' speech are going to try to scent one another's natures, he typed hastily, and turned off the speakers. He opened his case and took out one of the cubes he'd recorded the day before.

Work went slowly.

By noon the mist had burned off the water. His head buzzing with Dweller sounds, Anthony stepped below for a sandwich. The message light was blinking on his telephone. He turned to it, pressed the play button.

"May I speak with you briefly?" Philana's voice. "I'd like to get some data, at your convenience." Her tone shifted to one of amusement. "The condition," she added, "is not that of rut."

Anthony grinned. Philana had been considerate enough not to interrupt him, just to leave the message for whenever he wanted it. He picked up the telephone, connected directory assistance in Cabo Santa Pola, and asked it to route a call to the phone on Philana's yacht. She answered.

"Message received," he said. "Would you join me for lunch?"

"In an hour or so," she said. Her voice was abstracted. "I'm in the middle of something."

"When you're ready. Bye." He rang off, decided to make a fish chowder instead of sandwiches, and drank a beer while preparing it. He began to feel buoyant, cheerful. Siren wailing sounded through the water.

Philana's yacht maneuvered over to his boat just as Anthony finished his second beer. Philana stood on the gunwale, wearing a pale sweater with brown zigzags on it. Her braid was undone, and her brown hair fell around her shoulders. She jumped easily from her gunwale to the flybridge, then came down the ladder. The yacht moved away as soon as it felt her weight leave. She smiled uncertainly as she stepped to the deck.

"I'm sorry to have to bother you," she said.

He offered a grin. "That's okay. I'm between projects right now."

She looked toward the cabin. "Lunch smells good." Perhaps, he thought, food equaled apology.

"Fish chowder. Would you like a beer? Coffee?"

"Beer. Thanks."

They stepped below and Anthony served lunch on the small foldout table. He opened another beer and put it by her place.

"Delicious. I never really learned to cook."

"Cooking was something I learned young."

Her eyes were curious. "Where was that?"

"Lees." Shortly. He put a spoonful of chowder in his mouth so that his terseness would be more understandable.

"I never heard the name."

"It's a planet." Mumbling through chowder. "Pretty obscure." He didn't want to talk about it.

"I'm from Earth."

He looked at her. "Really? Originally? Not just a habitat in the Sol system?"

"Yes. Truly. One of the few. The one and only Earth."

"Is that what got you interested in whales?"

"I've *always* been interested in whales. As far back as I can remember. Long before I ever saw one."

"It was the same with me. I grew up near an ocean, built a boat when I was a boy and went exploring. I've never felt more at home than when I'm on the ocean."

"Some people live on the sea all the time."

"In floating habitats. That's just moving a city out onto the ocean. The worst of both worlds, if you ask me."

He realized the beer was making him expansive, that he was declaiming and waving his free hand. He pulled his hand in.

"I'm sorry," he said, "about the last time we talked."

She looked away. "My fault," she said. "I shouldn't have—"

"You didn't do anything wrong." He realized he had almost shouted that, and could feel himself flushing. He lowered his voice. "Once I got out here I realized . . ." This was really hopeless. He plunged on. "I'm not used to dealing with people. There were just a few people on Lees and they were all . . . eccentric. And everyone I've met since I left seems at least five hundred years old. Their attitudes are so . . ." He shrugged.

"Alien." She was grinning.

"Yes."

"I feel the same way. Everyone's so much older, so much more . . . sophisticated, I suppose." She thought about it for a moment. "I *guess* it's sophistication."

"*They* like to think so."

"I can feel their pity sometimes." She toyed with her spoon, looked down at her bowl.

"And condescension." Bitterness striped Anthony's tongue. "The attitude of, oh, we went through that once, poor darling, but now we know better."

"Yes." Tiredly. "I know what you mean. Like we're not really people yet."

"At least my father wasn't like that. He was crazy, but he let me be a person. He—"

His tongue stumbled. He was not drunk enough to tell this story, and he didn't think he wanted to anyway.

"Go ahead," said Philana. She was collecting data, Anthony remembered, on families.

He pushed back from the table, went to the fridge for another beer. "Maybe later," he said. "It's a long story."

Philana's look was steady. "You're not the only one who knows about crazy fathers."

Then you tell me about yours, he wanted to say. Anthony opened the beer, took a deep swallow. The liquid rose again, acid in his throat, and he forced it down. Memories rose with the fire in Anthony's throat, burning him. His father's fine madness whirled in his mind like leaves in a hurricane. We are, he thought, in a condition of mutual distrust and permanent antagonism. Something therefore must be done.

"All right." He put the beer on the top of the fridge and returned to his seat. He spoke rapidly, just letting the story come. His throat burned. "My father started life with money. He became a psychologist and then a fundamentalist Catholic lay preacher, kind of an unlicensed messiah. He ended up a psychotic. Dad concluded that civilization was too stupid and corrupt to survive, and he decided to start over. He initiated an unauthorized planetary scan through a transporter gate, found a world that he liked, and moved his family there. There were just four of us at the time, dad and my mother, my little brother, and me. My mother was—is—she's not really her own person. There's a vacancy there. If you're around psychotics a lot, and you don't have a strong sense of self, you can get submerged in their delusions. My mother didn't have a chance of standing up to a full-blooded lunatic like my dad, and I doubt she tried. She just let him run things.

"I was six when we moved to Lees, and my brother was two. We were—" Anthony waved an arm in the general direction of the invisible Milky Way overhead. "—we were half the galaxy away. Clean on the other side of the hub. We didn't take a gate with us, or even instructions and equipment for building one. My father cut us off entirely from everything he hated."

Anthony looked at Philana's shocked face and laughed. "It wasn't so bad. We had everything but a way off the planet. Cube readers, building supplies, preserved food, tools, medical gear, wind and solar generators—Dad thought falkner generators were the cause of the rot, so he didn't bring any with him. My mother pretty much stayed pregnant for the next decade, but luckily the planet was benign. We settled down in a protected bay where there was a lot of food, both on land and in the water. We had a smokehouse to preserve the meat. My father and mother educated me pretty well. I grew up an aquatic animal. Built a sailboat, learned how to navigate. By the time I was fifteen I had charted two thousand miles of coast. I spent more than half my time at sea, the last few years. Trying to get away from my dad, mostly. He kept getting stranger. He promised me in marriage to my oldest sister after my eighteenth birthday." Memory swelled in Anthony like a tide, calm green water rising over the flat, soon to whiten and boil.

"There were some whale-sized fish on Lees, but they weren't intelligent. I'd seen recordings of whales, heard the sounds they made. On my long trips I'd imagine I was seeing whales, imagine myself talking to them."

"How did you get away?"

Anthony barked a laugh. "My dad wasn't the only one who could initiate a planetary scan. Seven or eight years after we landed some resort developers found our planet and put up a hotel about two hundred miles to the south of our settlement." Anthony shook his head. "Hell of a coincidence. The odds against it must have been incredible. My father frothed at the mouth when we started seeing their flyers and boats. My father decided our little settlement was too exposed and we moved farther inland to a place where we could hide better. Everything was camouflaged. He'd hold drills in which we were all supposed to grab necessary supplies and run off into the forest."

"They never found you?"

"If they saw us, they thought we were people on holiday."

"Did you approach them?"

Anthony shook his head. "No. I don't really know why."

"Well. Your father."

"I didn't care much about his opinions by that point. It was so *obvious* he was cracked. I think, by then, I had all I wanted just living on my boat. I didn't see any reason to change it." He thought for a moment. "If he actually tried to marry me off to my sister, maybe I would have run for it."

"But they found you anyway."

"No. Something else happened. The water supply for the new settlement was unreliable, so we decided to build a viaduct from a spring nearby. We had to get our hollow-log pipe over a little chasm, and my father got careless and had an accident. The viaduct fell on him. Really smashed him up, caused all sorts of internal injuries. It was very obvious that if he didn't get help, he'd die. My mother and I took my boat and sailed for the resort."

The words dried up. This was where things got ugly. Anthony decided he really couldn't trust Philana with it, and that he wanted his beer after all. He got up and took the bottle and drank.

"Did your father live?"

"No." He'd keep this as brief as he could. "When my mother and I got back, we found that he'd died two days before. My brothers and sisters gutted him and hung him upside down in the smokehouse." He stared dully into Philana's horrified face. "It's what they did to any large animal. My mother and I were the only ones who remembered what to do with a dead person, and we weren't there."

"My God. Anthony." Her hands clasped below her face.

"And then—" He waved his hands, taking in everything, the boat's comforts, Overlook, life over the horizon. "Civilization. I was the only one of the children who could remember anything but Lees. I got off the planet and got into marine biology. That's been my life ever since. I was amazed to discover that I and the family were rich—my dad didn't tell me he'd left tons of investments behind. The rest of the family's still on Lees, still living in the old settlement. It's all they know." He shrugged. "They're rich, too, of course, which helps. So they're all right."

He leaned back on the fridge and took another long drink. The ocean swell tilted the boat and rolled the liquid down his throat. Whale harmonics made the bottle cap dance on the smooth alloy surface of the refrigerator.

Philana stood. Her words seemed small after the long silence. "Can I have some coffee? I'll make it."

"I'll do it."

They both went for the coffee and banged heads. Reeling back, the expression on Philana's face was wide-eyed, startled, fawnlike, as if he'd caught her at something she should be ashamed of. Anthony tried to laugh out an apology, but just then the white dwarf came up above the horizon and the quality of light changed as the screens went up, and with the light her look somehow changed. Anthony gazed at her for a moment and fire began to lap at his nerves. In his head the whales seemed to urge him to make his move.

He put his beer down and grabbed her with an intensity that was made ferocious largely by Anthony's fear that this was entirely the wrong thing, that he was committing an outrage that would compel her shortly to clout him over the head with the coffee pot and drop him in his tracks. Whalesong rang frantic chimes in his head. She gave a strangled cry as he tried to kiss her and thereby confirmed his own worst suspicions about this behavior.

Philana tried to push him away. He let go of her and stepped back, standing stupidly with his hands at his sides. A raging pain in his chest prevented him from saying a word. Philana surprised him by stepping forward and putting her hands on his shoulders.

"Easy," she said. "It's all right, just take it easy."

Anthony kissed her once more, and was somehow able to restrain himself from grabbing her again out of sheer panic and desperation.

By and by, as the kiss continued, his anxiety level decreased. I/You, he thought, are rising in warmness, in happy tendrils.

He and Philana began to take their clothes off. He realized this was the first time he had made love to anyone under two hundred years of age.

Dweller sounds murmured in Anthony's mind. He descended into Philana as if she were a midnight ocean, something that on first contact with his flesh shocked him into wakefulness, then relaxed around him, became a taste of brine, a sting in the eyes, a fluid vagueness. Her hair brushed against his skin like seagrass. She surrounded him, buoyed him up. Her cries came up to him as over a great distance, like the faraway moans of a lonely whale in love. He wanted to call out in answer. Eventually he did.

Grace(1), he thought hopefully. Grace(1).

Anthony had an attack of giddiness after Philana returned to her flying yacht and her work. His mad father gibbered in his memory, mocked him and offered dire warnings. He washed the dishes and cleaned the rattling bottle cap off the fridge, then he listened to recordings of Dwellers and eventually the panic went away. He had not, it seemed, lost anything.

He went to the double bed in the forepeak, which was piled high with boxes of food, a spool of cable, a couple spare microphones, and a pair of rusting Danforth anchors. He stowed the food in the hold, put the electronics in the compartment under the mattress, jammed the Danforths farther into the peak on top of the anchor chain where they belonged. He wiped the grime and rust off the mattress and realized he had neither sheets nor a second pillow. He would need to purchase supplies on the next trip to town.

The peak didn't smell good. He opened the forehatch and tried to air the place out. Slowly he became aware that the whales were trying to talk to him. **Odd scentings**, they said, **Things that stand in water**. Anthony knew what they meant. He went up on the flybridge and scanned the horizon. He saw nothing.

The taste is distant, he wrote. *But we must be careful in our movement*. After that he scanned the horizon every half hour.

He cooked supper during the white dwarf's odd half-twilight and resisted the urge to drink both the bottles of bourbon that were waiting in their rack. Philana dropped onto the flybridge with a small rucksack. She kissed him hastily, as if to get it over with.

"I'm scared," she said.
"So am I."
"I don't know why."
He kissed her again. "I do," he said. She laid her cheek against his woolen shoulder. Blind with terror, Anthony held on to her, unable to see the future.

After midnight Anthony stood unclothed on the flybridge as he scanned the horizon one more time. Seeing nothing, he nevertheless reduced speed to three knots and rejoined Philana in the forepeak. She was already asleep with his open sleeping bag thrown over her like a blanket. He raised a corner of the sleeping bag and slipped beneath it. Philana turned away from him and pillowed her cheek on her fist. Whale music echoed from a cold layer beneath. He slept.

Movement elsewhere in the boat woke him. Anthony found himself alone in the peak, frigid air drifting over him from the forward hatch. He stepped into the cabin and saw Philana's bare legs ascending the companion to the flybridge. He followed. He shivered in the cold wind.

Philana stood before the controls, looking at them with a peculiar intensity, as though she were trying to figure out which switch to throw. Her hands flexed as if to take the wheel. There was gooseflesh on her shoulders and the wind tore her hair around her face like a fluttering curtain. She looked at him. Her eyes were hard, her voice disdainful.

"Are we lovers?" she asked. "Is that what's going on here?" His skin prickled at her tone.

Her stiff-spined stance challenged him. He was afraid to touch her.

"The condition is that of rut," he said, and tried to laugh.

Her posture, one leg cocked out front, reminded him of a haughty water bird. She looked at the controls again, then looked aft, lifting up on her toes to gaze at the horizon. Her nostrils flared, tasted the wind. Clouds scudded across the sky. She looked at him again. The white dwarf gleamed off her pebble eyes.

"Very well," she said, as if this was news. "Acceptable." She took his hand and led him below. Anthony's hackles rose. On her way to the forepeak Philana saw one of the bottles of bourbon in its rack and reached for it. She raised the bottle to her lips and drank from the neck. Whiskey coursed down her throat. She lowered the bottle and wiped her mouth with the back of her hand. She looked at him as if he were something worthy of dissection.

"Let's make love," she said.

Anthony was afraid not to. He went with her to the forepeak. Her skin was cold. Lying next to him on the mattress she touched his chest as if she were unused to the feel of male bodies. "What's your name?" she asked. He told her. "Acceptable," she said again, and with a sudden taut grin raked his chest with her nails. He knocked her hands away. She laughed and came after him with the bottle. He parried the blow in time and they wrestled for possession, bourbon splashing everywhere. Anthony was surprised at her strength. She fastened teeth in his arm. He hit her in the face with a closed fist. She gave the bottle up and laughed in a cold metallic way and put her arms around him. Anthony threw the bottle through the door into the cabin. It thudded somewhere but didn't break. Philana drew him on top of her, her laugh brittle, her legs opening around him.

Her dead eyes were like stones.

In the morning Anthony found the bottle lying in the main cabin. Red clawmarks covered his body, and the reek of liquor caught at the back of his throat. The scend of the ocean had distributed the bourbon puddle evenly over the teak deck. There was still about a third of the whiskey left in the bottle. Anthony rescued it and swabbed the deck. His mind was full of cotton wool, cushioning any bruises. He was working hard at not feeling anything at all.

He put on clothes and began to work. After a while Philana unsteadily groped her way from the forepeak, the sleeping bag draped around her shoulders. There was a stunned look on her face and a livid bruise on one cheek. Anthony could feel his body tautening, ready to repel assault.

"Was I odd last night?" she asked.

He looked at her. Her face crumbled. "Oh no." She passed a hand over her eyes and turned away, leaning on the side of the hatchway. "You shouldn't let me drink," she said.

"You hadn't made that fact clear."

"I don't remember any of it," she said. "I'm sick." She pressed her stomach with her hands and bent over. Anthony narrowly watched her pale buttocks as she groped her way to the head. The door shut behind her.

Anthony decided to make coffee. As the scent of the coffee began to fill the boat, he heard the sounds of her weeping. The long keening sounds, desperate throat-tearing noises, sounded like a pinioned whale writhing helplessly on the gaff.

A vast flock of birds wheeled on the cold horizon, marking a colony of drift creatures. Anthony informed the whales of the creatures' presence, but the humpbacks already knew and were staying well clear. The drift colony was what they had been smelling for hours.

While Anthony talked with the whales, Philana left the head and drew on her clothes. Her movements were tentative. She approached him with a cup of coffee in her hand. Her eyes and nostrils were rimmed with red.

"I'm sorry," she said. "Sometimes that happens."

He looked at his computer console. "Jesus, Philana."

"It's something wrong with me. I can't control it." She raised a hand to her bruised cheek. The hand came away wet.

"There's medication for that sort of thing," Anthony said. He remembered she had a mad father, or thought she did.

"Not for this. It's something different."

"I don't know what to do."

"I need your help."

Anthony recalled his father's body twisting on the end of its rope, fingertips trailing in the dust. Words came reluctantly to his throat.

"I'll give what help I can." The words were hollow: any real resolution had long since gone. He had no clear notion to whom he was giving this message, the Philana of the previous night or this Philana or his father or himself.

Philana hugged him, kissed his cheek. She was excited.

"Shall we go see the drifters?" she asked. "We can take my boat."

Anthony envisioned himself and Philana tumbling through space. He had jumped off a precipice, just now. The two children of mad fathers were spinning in the updraft, waiting for the impact.

He said yes. He ordered his boat to circle while she summoned her yacht. She held his hand while they waited for the flying yacht to drift toward them. Philana kept laughing, touching him, stropping her cheek on his shoulder like a cat. They jumped from the flybridge to her yacht and rose smoothly into the sky. Bright sun warmed Anthony's shoulders. He took off his sweater and felt warning pain from the marks of her nails.

The drifters were colony creatures that looked like miniature mountains twenty feet or so high, complete with a white snowcap of guano. They were highly organized but unintelligent, their underwater parts sifting the ocean for nutrients or reaching out to capture prey: the longest of their gossamer stinging tentacles was up to two miles in length, and though they couldn't kill or capture a humpback, they were hard for the whale to detect and could cause a lot of stinging wounds before the whale noticed them and made its escape. Perhaps they were unintelligent, distant relatives of the Deep Dwellers, whose tenuous character they resembled. Many different species of sea birds lived in permanent colonies atop the floating islands, thousands of them, and the drifters processed their guano and other waste. Above the water, the drifters' bodies were shaped like a convex lens set on edge, an aerodynamic shape, and they could clumsily tack into the wind if they needed to. For the most part, however, they drifted on the currents, a giant circular circumnavigation of the ocean that could take centuries.

Screaming sea birds rose in clouds as Philana's yacht moved silently toward their homes. Philana cocked her head back, laughed into the open sky, and flew closer. Birds hurtled around them in an overwhelming roar of wings. Whistlelike cries issued from peg-toothed beaks. Anthony watched in awe at the profusion of colors, the chromatic brilliance of the evolved featherlike scales.

The flying boat passed slowly through the drifter colony. Birds roared and whistled, some of them landing on the boat in apparent hopes of taking up lodging. Feathers drifted down; birdshit spattered the windscreen. Philana ran below for a camera and used up several data cubes taking pictures. A trickle of optimism began to ease into Anthony at the sight of Philana in the bright morning sun, a broad smile gracing her face as she worked the camera and took picture after picture. He put an arm around Philana's waist and kissed her ear. She smiled and took his hand in her own. In the bright daylight the personality she'd acquired the previous night seemed to gather unto itself the tenebrous, unreal quality of a nightmare. The current Philana seemed far more tangible.

Philana returned to the controls; the yacht banked and increased speed. Birds issued startled cries as they got out of the way. Wind tugged at Philana's hair. Anthony decided not to let Philana near his liquor again.

After breakfast, Anthony found both whales had set their transponders. He had to detour around the drifters—their insubstantial, featherlike tentacles could foul his state-of-the-art silent props—but when he neared the whales and slowed, he could hear the deep murmurings of Dwellers rising from beneath the cold current. There were half a dozen of them engaged in conversation, and Anthony worked the day and far into the night, transcribing, making hesitant attempts at translation. The Dweller speech was more opaque than usual, depending on a context that was unstated and elusive. Comprehension eluded Anthony; but he had the feeling that the key was within his reach.

Philana waited for the Dwellers to end their converse before she brought her yacht near him. She had heated some prepared dinners and carried them to the flybridge in an insulated pouch. Her grin was broad. She put her pouch down and embraced him. Abstracted Dweller subsonics rolled away from Anthony's mind. He was surprised at how glad he was to see her.

With dinner they drank coffee. Philana chattered bravely throughout the meal. While Anthony cleaned the dishes, she embraced him from behind. A memory of the other Philana flickered in his mind, disdainful, contemptuous, cold. Her father was crazy, he remembered again.

He buried the memory deliberately and turned to her. He kissed her and thought, I/We deny the Other. The Other, he decided, would cease to exist by a common act of will.

It seemed to work. At night his dreams filled with Dwellers crying in joy, his father warning darkly, the touch of Philana's flesh, breath, hands. He awoke hungry to get to work.

The next two days a furious blaze of concentration burned in Anthony's mind. Things fell into place. He found a word that, in its context, could mean nothing but light, as opposed to fluorescence—he was excited to find out the Dwellers knew about the sun. He also found new words for darkness, for emotions that seemed to have no human equivalents, but which he seemed nevertheless to comprehend. One afternoon a squall dumped a gallon of cold water down his collar and he looked up in surprise: he hadn't been aware of its slow approach. He moved his computer deck to the cabin and kept working. When not at the controls he moved dazedly over the boat, drinking coffee, eating what was at hand without tasting it. Philana was amused and tolerant; she buried herself in her own work.

On preparing breakfast the morning of the third day, Anthony realized he was running out of food. He was farther from the archipelago than he'd planned on going, and he had about two days' supply left; he'd have to return at flank speed, buy provisions, and then run out again. A sudden hot fury gripped him. He clenched his fists. He could have provisioned for two or three months—why hadn't he done it when he had the chance?

Philana tolerantly sipped her coffee. "Tonight I'll fly you into Cabo Santa Pola. We can buy a ton of provisions, have dinner at Villa Mary, and be back by midnight."

Anthony's anger floundered uselessly, looking for a target, then gave up. "Fine," he said.

She looked at him. "Are you ever going to talk to them? You must have built your speakers to handle it."

Now the anger had finally found a home. "Not yet," he said.

In late afternoon, Anthony set out his drogue and a homing transponder, then boarded Philana's yacht. He watched while she hauled up her aquasled and programmed the navigation computer. The world dimmed as the falkner field increased in strength. The transition to full speed was almost instantaneous. Waves blurred silently past, providing the only sensation of motion—the field cut out both wind and inertia. The green-walled volcanic islands of the Las Madres archipelago rolled over the horizon in minutes. Traffic over Cabo Santa Pola complicated the approach somewhat; it was all of six minutes before Philana could set the machine down in her slip.

A bright, hot sun brightened the white-and-turquoise waterfront. From a cold Kirst current to the tropics in less than half an hour.

Anthony felt vaguely resentful at this blinding efficiency. He could have easily equipped his own boat with flight capability, but he hadn't cared about speed when he'd set out, only the opportunity to be alone on the ocean with his whales and the Dwellers. Now the very tempo of his existence had changed. He was moving at unaccustomed velocity, and the destination was still unclear.

After giving him her spare key, Philana went to do laundry—when one lived on small boats, laundry was done whenever the opportunity arose. Anthony bought supplies. He filled the yacht's forecabin with crates of food, then changed clothes and walked to the Villa Mary.

Anthony got a table for two and ordered a drink. The first drink went quickly and he ordered a second. Philana didn't appear. Anthony didn't like the way the waiter was looking at him. He heard his father's mocking laugh as he munched the last bread stick. He waited for three hours before he paid and left.

There was no sign of Philana at the laundry or on the yacht. He left a note on the computer expressing what he considered a contained disappointment, then headed into town. A brilliant sign that featured aquatic motifs called him to a cool, dark bar filled with bright green aquaria. Native fish gaped at him blindly while he drank something tall and cool. He decided he didn't like the way the fish looked at him and left.

He found Philana in his third bar of the evening. She was with two men, one of whom Anthony knew slightly as a charter boat skipper whom he didn't much like. He had his hand on her knee; the other man's arm was around her. Empty drinks and forsaken hors d'oeuvres lay on a table in front of them.

Anthony realized, as he approached, that his own arrival could only make things worse. Her eyes turned to him as he approached; her neck arched in a peculiar, balletic way that he had seen only once before. He recognized the quick, carnivorous smile, and a wash of fear turned his skin cold. The stranger whispered into her ear.

"What's your name again?" she asked.

Anthony wondered what to do with his hands. "We were supposed to meet."

Her eyes glittered as her head cocked, considering him. Perhaps what frightened him most of all was the fact there was no hostility in her look, nothing but calculation. There was a cigarette in her hand; he hadn't seen her smoke before.

"Do we have business?"

Anthony thought about this. He had jumped into space with this woman, and now he suspected he'd just hit the ground. "I guess not," he said, and turned.

"Qué pasó, hombre?"

"Nada."

Pablo, the Leviathan's regular bartender, was one of the planet's original Latino inhabitants, a group rapidly being submerged by newcomers. Pablo took Anthony's order for a double bourbon and also brought him his mail, which consisted of an inquiry from *Xenobiology Review* wondering what had become of their galley proofs. Anthony crumpled the note and left it in an ashtray.

A party of drunken fishermen staggered in, still in their flashing harnesses. Triumphant whoops assaulted Anthony's ears. His fingers tightened on his glass.

"Careful, Anthony," said Pablo. He poured another double bourbon. "On the house," he said.

One of the fishermen stepped to the bar, put a heavy hand on Anthony's shoulder. "Drinks on me," he said. "Caught a twelve-meter flasher today." Anthony threw the bourbon in his face.

He got in a few good licks, but in the end the pack of fishermen beat him severely and threw him through the front window. Lying breathless on broken glass, Anthony brooded on the injustice of his position and decided to rectify matters. He lurched back into the bar and knocked down the first person he saw.

Small consolation. This time they went after him with the flashing poles that were hanging on the walls, beating him senseless and once more heaving him out the window. When Anthony recovered consciousness he staggered to his feet, intending to have another go, but the pole butts had hit him in the face too many times and his eyes were swollen shut. He staggered down the street, ran face-first into a building, and sat down.

"You finished there, cowboy?" It was Nick's voice.

Anthony spat blood. "Hi, Nick," he said. "Bring them here one at a time, will you? I can't lose one-on-one."

"Jesus, Anthony. You're such an asshole."

Anthony found himself in an inexplicably cheerful mood. "You're lucky you're a sailor. Only a sailor can call me an asshole."

"Can you stand? Let's get to the marina before the cops show up."

"My boat's hundreds of miles away. I'll have to swim."

"I'll take you to my place, then."

With Nick's assistance Anthony managed to stand. He was still too drunk to feel pain, and ambled through the streets in a contented mood. "How did you happen to be at the Leviathan, Nick?"

There was weariness in Nick's voice. "They always call me, Anthony, when you fuck up."

Drunken melancholy poured into Anthony like a sudden cold squall of rain. "I'm sorry," he said.

Nick's answer was almost cheerful. "You'll be sorrier in the morning."

Anthony reflected that this was very likely true.

Nick gave him some pills that, by morning, reduced the swelling. When Anthony awoke he was able to see. Agony flared in his body as he staggered out of bed. It was still twilight. Anthony pulled on his bloody clothes and wrote an incoherent note of thanks on Nick's computer.

Fishing boats were floating out of harbor into the bright dawn. Probably Nick's was among them. The volcano above the town was a contrast in black stone and green vegetation. Pain beat at Anthony's bones like a rain of fists.

Philana's boat was still in its slip. Apprehension tautened Anthony's nerves as he put a tentative foot on the gunwale. The hatch to the cabin was still locked. Philana wasn't aboard. Anthony opened the hatch and went into the cabin just to be sure. It was empty.

He programmed the computer to pursue the transponder signal on Anthony's boat, then as the yacht rose into the sky and arrowed over the ocean, Anthony went into Philana's cabin and fell asleep on a pillow that smelled of her hair.

He awoke around noon to find the yacht patiently circling his boat. He dropped the yacht into the water, tied the two craft together, and spent half the afternoon transferring his supplies to his own boat. He programmed the yacht to return to Las Madres and orbit the volcanic spire until it was summoned by its owner or the police.

I and the sea greet one another, he tapped into his console, and as the call wailed out from his boat he hauled in the drogue and set off after the humpbacks. Apartness is the smell, he thought, aloneness is the condition. Spray shot aboard and spattered Anthony, and salt pain flickered from the cuts on his face. He climbed to the flybridge and hoped for healing from the sun and the glittering sea.

The whales left the cold current and suddenly the world was filled with tropic sunshine and bright water. Anthony made light conversation with the humpbacks and spent the rest of his time working on Dweller speech. Despite hours of concentrated endeavor he made little progress. The sensation was akin to that of smashing his head against a stone wall over and over, an act that was, on consideration, not unlike the rest of his life.

After his third day at sea his boat's computer began signaling him that he was receiving messages. He ignored this and concentrated on work.

Two days later he was cruising north with a whale on either beam when a shadow moved across his boat. Anthony looked up from his console and saw without surprise that Philana's yacht was eclipsing the sun. Philana, dark glasses over her deep eyes and a floppy hat over her hair, was peering down from the starboard bow.

"We have to talk," she said.

Joyously we greet Air Human, whooped Sings of Others.

I and Air Human are pleased to detect one another's presence, called Two Notches.

Anthony went to the controls and throttled up. Microphones slammed at the bottom of his boat. Two Notches poked one large brown eye above the waves to see what was happening, then cheerfully set off in pursuit.

Anthony and Air Human are in a state of excitement, he chattered. **I/We are pleased to join our race**.

The flying yacht hung off Anthony's stern. Philana shouted through cupped hands. "Talk to me, Anthony!"

Anthony remained silent and twisted the wheel into a fast left turn. His wake foamed over Two Notches' face and the humpback burbled a protest. The air yacht seemed to have little trouble following the turn. Anthony was beginning to have the sense of that stone wall coming up again, but he tried a few more maneuvers just in case one of them worked. Nothing succeeded. Finally he cut the throttle and let the boat slow on the long blue swells.

The trade winds had taken Philana's hat and carried it away. She ignored it and looked down at him. Her face was pale and beneath the dark glasses she looked drawn and ill.

"I'm not human, Anthony," she said. "I'm a Kyklops. That's what's really wrong with me."

Anthony looked at her. Anger danced in his veins. "You really are full of surprises."

"I'm Telamon's other body," she said. "Sometimes he inhabits me."

Whalesong rolled up from the sea. **We and Air Human send one another cheerful salutations and expressions of good will.**

"Talk to the whales first," said Anthony.

"Telamon's a scientist," Philana said. "He's impatient, that's his problem."

The boat heaved on an ocean swell. The trade wind moaned through the flybridge. "He's got a few more problems than that," Anthony said.

"He wanted me for a purpose but sometimes he forgets." A tremor of pain crossed Philana's face. She was deeply hung over. Her voice was ragged: Telamon had been smoking like a chimney and Philana wasn't used to it.

"He wanted to do an experiment on human psychology. He wanted to arrange a method of recording a person's memories, then transferring them to his own . . . sphere. He got my parents to agree to having the appropriate devices implanted, but the only apparatus that existed for the connection of human and Kyklops was the one the Kyklopes use to manipulate the human bodies that they wear when they want to enjoy the pleasures of the flesh. And Telamon is . . ." She waved a dismissive arm. "He's a decadent, the way a lot of the Kyklopes turn once they discover how much fun it is to be a human and that their real self doesn't get hurt no matter what they do to their clone bodies. Telamon likes his pleasures, and he likes to interfere. Sometimes, when he dumped my memory into the *n*th dimension and had a look at it, he couldn't resist the temptation to take over my body and rectify what he considered my errors. And occasionally, when he's in the middle of one of his binges, and his other body gives out on him, he takes me over and starts a party wherever I am."

"Some scientist," Anthony said.

"The Kyklopes are used to experimenting on pieces of themselves," Philana said. "Their own beings are tenuous and rather . . . detachable. Their ethics aren't against it. And he doesn't do it very often. He must be bored wherever he is—he's taken me over twice in a week." She raised her fist to her face and began to cough, a real smoker's hack. Anthony fidgeted and wondered whether to offer her a glass of water. Philana bent double and the coughs turned to cries of pain. A tear pattered on the teak.

A knot twisted in Anthony's throat. He left his chair and held Philana in his arms. "I've never told anyone," she said.

Anthony realized to his transient alarm that once again he'd jumped off a cliff without looking. He had no more idea of where he would land than last time.

Philana, Anthony was given to understand, was Greek for "lover of humanity." The Kyklopes, after being saddled with a mythological name by the first humans who had contacted them, had gone in for classical allusion in a big way. Telamon, Anthony learned, meant (among other things) "the supporter." After learning this, Anthony referred to the alien as Jockstrap.

"We should do something about him," Anthony said. It was late—the white dwarf had just set—but neither of them had any desire to sleep. He and Philana were standing on the flybridge. The falkner shield was off and above their heads the uninhibited stars seemed almost within reach of their questing fingertips. Overlook Station, fixed almost overhead, was bright as a burning brand.

Philana shook her head. "He's got access to my memory. Any plans we make, he can know in an instant." She thought for a moment. "If he bothers to look. He doesn't always."

"I'll make the plans without telling you what they are."

"It will take forever. I've thought about it. You're talking court case. He can sue me for breach of contract."

"It's your parents who signed the contract, not you. You're an adult now."

She turned away. Anthony looked at her for a long moment, a cold foreboding hand around his throat. "I hope," he said, "you're going to tell me that you signed that contract while Jockstrap was riding you."

Philana shook her head silently. Anthony looked up into the Milky Way and imagined the stone wall falling from the void, aimed right between his eyes, spinning slightly as it grew ever larger in his vision. Smashing him again.

"All we have to do is get the thing out of your head," Anthony said. "After that, let him sue you. You'll be free, whatever happens." His tone reflected a resolve that was absent entirely from his heart.

"He'll sue you, too, if you have any part of this." She turned to face him again. Her face pale and taut in the starlight. "All my money comes from him—how else do you think I could afford the yacht? I owe everything to him."

Bitterness sped through Anthony's veins. He could feel his voice turning harsh. "Do you want to get rid of him or not? Yes or no."

"He's not entirely evil."

"Yes or no, Philana."

"It'll take years before he's done with you. And he could kill you. Just transport you to deep space somewhere and let you drift. Or he could simply teleport me away from you."

The bright stars poured down rage. Anthony knew himself seconds away from violence. There were two people on this boat and one of them was about to get hurt. "*Yes or no*!" he shouted.

Philana's face contorted. She put her hands over her ears. Hair fell across her face. "Don't shout," she said.

Anthony turned and smashed his forehead against the control panel of the flybridge. Philana gave a cry of surprise and fear. Anthony drove himself against the panel again. Philana's fingers clutched at his shoulders. Anthony could feel blood running from his scalp. The pain drained his anger, brought a cold, brilliant clarity to his mind. He smashed himself a third time. Philana cried out. He turned to her. He felt a savage, exemplary satisfaction. If one were going to drive oneself against stone walls, one should at least take a choice of the walls available.

"Ask me," Anthony panted, "if I care what happens to me."

Philana's face was a mask of terror. She said his name.

"I need to know where you stand," said Anthony. Blood drooled from his scalp, and he suppressed the unwelcome thought that he had just made himself look ridiculous.

Her look of fear broadened.

"Am I going to jump off this cliff by myself, or what?" Anthony demanded.

"I want to get rid of him," she said.

Anthony wished her voice had contained more determination, even if it were patently false. He spat salt and went in search of his first aid kit. We are in a condition of slow movement through deep currents, he thought.

In the morning he got the keys to Philana's yacht and changed the passwords on the falkner controls and navigation comp. He threw all his liquor overboard. He figured that if Jockstrap appeared and discovered that he couldn't leave the middle of the ocean, and he couldn't have a party where he was, he'd get bored and wouldn't hang around for long.

From Philana's cabin he called an attorney who informed him that the case was complex but not impossible, and furthermore that it would take a small fortune to resolve. Anthony told him to get to work on it. In the meantime he told the lawyer to start calling neurosurgeons. Unfortunately there were few neurosurgeons capable of implanting, let alone removing, the rider device. The operation wasn't performed that often.

Days passed. A discouraging list of neurosurgeons either turned him down flat or wanted the legal situation clarified first. Anthony told the lawyer to start calling *rich* neurosurgeons who might be able to ride out a lawsuit.

Philana transferred most of her data to Anthony's computer and worked with the whales from the smaller boat. Anthony used her yacht and aquasled and cursed the bad sound quality. At least the yacht's flight capability allowed him to find the Dwellers faster.

As far as the Dwellers went, he had run all at once into a dozen blind alleys. Progress seemed measured in microns.

"What's B 1971?" Philana asked once, looking over his shoulder as he typed in data.

"A taste. Perhaps a taste associated with a particular temperature striation. Perhaps an emotion." He shrugged. "Maybe just a metaphor."

"You could ask them."

His soul hardened. "Not yet." Which ended the conversation.

Anthony wasn't sure whether or not he wanted to touch her. He and Jockstrap were at war and Philana seemed not to have entirely made up her mind which side she was on. Anthony slept with Philana on the double mattress in the peak, but they avoided sex. He didn't know whether he was helping her out of love or something else, and while he figured things out, desire was on hold, waiting.

Anthony's time with Philana was occupied mainly by his attempt to teach her to cook. Anything else waited for the situation to grow less opaque. Anthony figured Jockstrap would clarify matters fairly soon.

Anthony's heart lurched as he looked up from lunch to see the taut, challenging grin on Philana's face. Anthony realized he'd been foolish to expect Telamon to show up only at night, as he always had before.

Anthony drew his lips into an answering grin. He was ready, no matter what the hour.

"Do I know you?" Anthony mocked. "Do we have business?"

Philana's appraisal was cold. "I've been called Jockstrap before," Telamon said.

"With good reason, I'm sure."

Telamon lurched to his feet and walked aft. He seemed not to have his sea legs yet. Anthony followed, his nerves dancing. Telamon looked out at the sea and curled Philana's lip as if to say that the water held nothing of interest.

"I want to talk about Philana," Telamon said. "You're keeping her prisoner here."

"She can leave me anytime she wants. Which is more than she can say about you."

"I want the codes to the yacht."

Anthony stepped up to Telamon, held Philana's cold gaze. "You're hurting her," he said.

Telamon stared at him with eyes like obsidian chips. He pushed Philana's long hair out of his face with an unaccustomed gesture. "I'm not the only one, Maldalena. I've got access to her mind, remember."

"Then look in her mind and see what she thinks of you."

A contemptuous smile played about Philana's lips. "I know very well what she thinks of me, and it's probably not what she's told you. Philana is a very sad and complex person, and she is not always truthful."

"She's what you made her."

"Precisely my next point." He waved his arm stiffly, unnaturally. The gesture brought him off balance, and Philana's body swayed for a moment as Telamon adjusted to the tossing of the boat. "I gave her money, education, knowledge of the world. I have corrected her errors, taught her much. She is, in many ways, my creation. Her feelings toward me are ambiguous, as any child's feelings would be toward her father."

"Daddy Jockstrap." Anthony laughed. "Do we have business, Daddy? Or are you going to take your daughter's body to a party first?"

Anthony jumped backward, arms flailing, as Philana disappeared, her place taken by a young man with curly dark hair and bright blue eyes. The stranger was dressed in a white cotton shirt unbuttoned to the navel and a pair of navy blue swimming trunks. He had seen the man before on vid, showing off his chest hairs. The grin stayed the same from one body to the next.

"She's gone, Maldalena. I teleported her to someplace safe." He laughed. "I'll buy her a new boat. Do what you like with the old one."

Anthony's heart hammered. He had forgotten the Kyklopes could do that, just teleport without the apparatus required by humans. And teleport other things as well.

He wondered how many centuries old the Kyklops' body was. He knew the mind's age was measured in eons.

"This doesn't end it," Anthony said.

Telamon's tone was mild. "Perhaps I'll find a nice planet for you somewhere, Maldalena. Let you play Robinson Crusoe, just as you did when you were young."

"That will only get you in trouble. Too many people know about this situation by now. And it won't be much fun holding Philana wherever you've got her."

Telamon stepped toward the stern, sat on the taffrail. His movements were fluid, far more confident than they had been when he was wearing the other, unaccustomed body. For a moment Anthony considered kicking Telamon into the drink, then decided against it. The possible repercussions had a cosmic dimension that Anthony preferred not to contemplate.

"I don't dislike you, Maldalena," the alien said. "I truly don't. You're an alcoholic, violent lout, but at least you have proven intelligence, perhaps a kind of genius."

"Call the kettle black again. I liked that part."

Two Notches' smooth body rose a cable's length to starboard. He exhaled with an audible hiss, mist drifting over his back. Telamon gave the whale a disinterested look, then turned back to Anthony.

"Being the nearest thing to a parent on the planet," he said, "I must say that I disapprove of you as a partner for Philana. However—" He gave a shrug. "Parents must know when to compromise in these matters." He looked up at Anthony with his blue eyes. "I propose we share her, Anthony. Formalize the arrangement we already seem to possess. I'll only occupy a little of her time, and for all the rest, the two of you can live out your lives with whatever sad domestic bliss you can summon. Till she gets tired of you, anyway."

Two Notches rolled under the waves. A cetacean murmur echoed off the boat's bottom. Anthony's mind flailed for an answer. He felt sweat prickling his scalp. He shook his head in feigned disbelief.

"Listen to yourself, Telamon. Is this supposed to be a scientist talking? A researcher?"

"You don't want to share?" The young man's face curled in disdain. "You want everything for yourself—the whole planet, I suppose, like your father."

"Don't be ridiculous."

"I know what Philana knows about you, and I've done some checking on my own. You brought the humpbacks here because you needed them. Away from *their* home, *their* kind. You *asked* them, I'm sure; but there's no way they could make an informed decision about this planet, about what they were doing. You needed them for your Dweller study, so you took them."

As if on cue, Two Notches rose from the water to take a breath. Telamon favored the whale with his taut smile. Anthony floundered for an answer while the alien spoke on.

"You've got data galore on the Dwellers, but do you publish? Do you share it with anybody, even with Philana? You hoard it all for yourself, all your specialized knowledge. You don't even talk to the Dwellers!" Telamon gave a scornful laugh. "You don't even want the *Dwellers* to know what Anthony knows!"

Anger poured through Anthony's veins like a scalding fire. He clenched his fists, considered launching himself at Telamon. Something held him back.

The alien stood, walked to Anthony, looked him up and down. "We're not so different," he said. "We both want what's ours. But *I'm* willing to share. Philana can be our common pool of data, if you like. Think about it."

Anthony swung, and in that instant Philana was back, horror in her eyes. Anthony's fist, aimed for the taller Telamon's chin, clipped Philana's temple and she fell back, flailing. Anthony caught her.

"It just happened, didn't it?" Her voice was woeful.

"You don't remember?"

Philana's face crumpled. She swayed and touched her temple. "I never do. The times when he's running me are just blank spots."

Anthony seated her on the port bench. He was feeling queasy at having hit her. She put her face in her hands. "I hate when that happens in front of people I know," she said.

"He's using you to hide behind. He was here in person, the son of a bitch." He took her hands in his own and kissed her. Purest desire flamed through him. He wanted to commit an act of defiance, make a statement of the nature of things. He put his arms around her and kissed her nape. She smelled faintly of pine, and there were needles in her hair. Telamon had put her on Earth, then, in a forest somewhere.

She strained against his tight embrace. "I don't know if this is a good idea," she said.

"I want to send a message to Telamon," Anthony said.

They made love under the sun, lying on the deck in Anthony's cockpit. Clear as a bell, Anthony heard Dweller sounds rumbling up the boat. Somewhere in the boat a metal mounting bracket rang to the subsonics. Philana clutched at him. There was desperation in her look, a search for affirmation, despair at finding none. The teak punished Anthony's palms. He wondered if Telamon had ever possessed her thus, took over her mind so that he could fuck her in his own body, commit incest with himself. He found the idea exciting.

His orgasm poured out, stunning him with its intensity. He kissed the moist juncture of Philana's neck and shoulder, and rose on his hands to stare down into Telamon's brittle grin and cold, knowing eyes.

"Message received, Anthony." Philana's throat convulsed in laughter. "You're taking possession. Showing everyone who's boss."

Horror galvanized Anthony. He jumped to his feet and backed away, heart pounding. He took a deep breath and mastered himself, strove for words of denial and could not find them. "You're sad, Telamon," he said.

Telamon threw Philana's arms over her head, parted her legs. "Let's do it again, Anthony." Taunting. "You're so masterful."

Anthony turned away. "Piss off, Telamon, you sick fuck." Bile rose in his throat.

"What happened?" Anthony knew Philana was back. He turned and saw her face crumple. "We were making love!" she wailed.

"A cheap trick. He's getting desperate." He squatted by her and tried to take her in his arms. She turned away from him.

"Let me alone for a while," she said. Bright tears filled her eyes.

Misplaced adrenaline ran charges through Anthony's body—no one to fight, no place to run. He picked up his clothes and went below to the main cabin. He drew on his clothing and sat on one of the berths, hands helpless on the seat beside him. He wanted to get blind drunk.

Half an hour later Philana entered the cabin. She'd braided her hair, drawn it back so tight from her temples it must have been painful. Her movements were slow, as if suddenly she'd lost her sea legs. She sat down at the little kitchen table, pushed away her half-eaten lunch.

"We can't win," she said.

"There's got to be some way," Anthony said tonelessly. He was clean out of ideas.

Philana looked at Anthony from reddened eyes. "We can give him what he wants," she said.

"No."

Her voice turned to a shout. "It's not *you* he does this to! It's not you who winks out of existence in the middle of doing laundry or making love, and wakes up somewhere else." Her knuckles were white as they gripped the table edge. "I don't know how long I can take this."

"All your life," said Anthony, "if you give him what he wants."

"At least then he wouldn't use it as a *weapon*!" Her voice was a shout. She turned away.

Anthony looked at her, wondered if he should go to her. He decided not to. He was out of comfort for the present.

"You see," Philana said, her head still turned away, "why I don't want to live forever."

"Don't let him beat you."

"It's not that. I'm afraid . . ." Her voice trembled. "I'm afraid that if I got old I'd *become* him. The Kyklopes are the oldest living things ever discovered. And a lot of the oldest immortals are a lot like them. Getting crazier, getting . . ." She shook her head. "Getting less human all the time."

Anthony saw a body swaying in the smokehouse. Philana's body, her fingernails trailing in the dust. Pain throbbed in his chest. He stood up, swayed as he was caught by a slow wave of vertigo. Somewhere his father was laughing, telling him he should have stayed on Lees for a life of pastoral incest.

"I want to think," he said. He stepped past her on the way to his computer. He didn't reach out to touch her as he passed. She didn't reach for him, either.

He put on the headphones and listened to the Dwellers. Their speech rolled up from the deep. Anthony sat unable to comprehend, his mind frozen. He was helpless as Philana. Whose was the next move? he wondered. His? Philana's?

Whoever made the next move, Anthony knew, the game was Telamon's.

At dinnertime Philana made a pair of sandwiches for Anthony, then returned to the cabin and ate nothing herself. Anthony ate one sandwich without tasting it, gave the second to the fish. The Dweller speech had faded out. He left his computer and stepped into the cabin. Philana was stretched out on one of the side berths, her eyes closed. One arm was thrown over her forehead.

Her body, Anthony decided, was too tense for this to be sleep. He sat on the berth opposite.

"He said you haven't told the truth," Anthony said.

Anthony could see Philana's eyes moving under translucent lids as she evaluated this statement, scanning for meaning. "About what," she said.

"About your relationship to him."

Her lips drew back, revealing teeth. Perhaps it was a smile.

"I've known him all my life. I gave you the condensed version."

"Is there more I should know?"

There was another pause. "He saved my life."

"Good for him."

"I got involved with this man. Three or four hundred years old, one of my professors in school. He was going through a crisis—he was a mess, really. I thought I could do him some good. Telamon disagreed, said the relationship was sick." Philana licked her lips. "He was right," she said.

Anthony didn't know if he really wanted to hear about this.

"The guy started making demands. Wanted to get married, leave Earth, start over again."

"What did you want?"

Philana shrugged. "I don't know. I hadn't made up my mind. But Telamon went into my head and confronted the guy and told him to get lost. Then he just took me out of there. My body was half the galaxy away, all alone on an undeveloped world. There were supplies, but no gates out."

Anthony gnawed his lip. This was how Telamon operated.

"Telamon kept me there for a couple weeks till I calmed down. He took me back to Earth. The professor had taken up with someone else, another one of his students. He married her, and six weeks later she walked out on him. He killed her, then killed himself."

Philana sighed, drew her hand over her forehead. She opened her eyes and sat up, swinging her legs off the berth. "So," she said. "That's one Telamon story. I've got more."

"When did this happen?"

"I'd just turned eighteen." She shook her head. "That's when I signed the contract that keeps him in my head. I decided that I couldn't trust my judgment about people. And Telamon's judgment of people is, well, quite good."

Resentment flamed in Anthony at this notion. Telamon had made his judgment of Anthony clear, and Anthony didn't want it to become a subject for debate. "You're older now," he said. "He can't have a veto on your life forever."

Philana drew up her legs and circled her knees with her arms. "You're violent, Anthony."

Anthony looked at her for a long moment of cold anger. "I hit you by accident. I was aiming at *him*, damn it."

Philana's jaw worked as she returned his stare. "How long before you aim at *me*?"

"I wouldn't."

"That's what my old professor said."

Anthony turned away, fury running through him like chill fire. Philana looked at him levelly for a moment, then dropped her forehead to her knees. She sighed. "I don't know, Anthony. I don't know anymore. If I ever did."

Anthony stared fixedly at the distant white dwarf, just arrived above the horizon and visible through the hatch. We are, he thought, in a condition of permanent bafflement. "What do you want, Philana?" he asked.

Her head came up, looked at him. "I want not to be a tennis ball in your game with Telamon, Anthony. I want to know I'm not just the prize given the winner."

"I wanted you before I ever met Telamon, Philana."

"Telamon changed a few things." Her voice was cold. "Before you met him, you didn't use my body to send messages to people."

Anthony's fists clenched. He forced them to relax.

Philana's voice was bitter. "Seems to me, Anthony, that's one of Telamon's habits you're all too eager to adopt."

Anthony's chest ached. He didn't seem able to breathe in enough air. He took a long breath and hoped his tension would ease. It didn't. "I'm sorry," he said. "It's not . . . a normal situation."

"For you, maybe."

Silence hung in the room, broken only by the whale clicks and mutters rising through the boat. Anthony shook his head. "What do we do, then?" he asked. "Surrender?"

"If we have to." She looked at him. "I'm willing to fight Telamon, but not to the point where one of us is destroyed." She leaned toward him, her expression intent. "And if Telamon wins, could you live with it?" she asked. "With surrender? If we had to give him what he wanted?"

"I don't know."

"I *have* to live with it. You don't. That's the difference."

"That's *one* difference." He took a breath, then rose from his place. "I have to think," he said.

He climbed into the cockpit. Red sunset was splattered like blood across the windscreen. He tried to breathe the sea air, clear the heaviness he felt in his chest, but it didn't work. Anthony went up onto the flybridge and stared forward. His eyes burned as the sun went down in flames.

The white dwarf was high overhead when Anthony came down. Philana was lying in the forepeak, covered with a sheet, her eyes staring sightlessly out the open hatch. Anthony took his clothes off and crawled in beside her.

"I'll surrender," he said. "If I have to, I'll surrender." She turned to him and put her arms around him. Hopeless desire burned in his belly.

He made love to Philana, his nerves numb to the possibility that Telamon might reappear. Her hungry mouth drank in his pain. He didn't know whether this was affirmation or not, whether this meant anything other than the fact there was nothing left to do at this point than stagger blindly into one another's embrace.

A Dweller soloed from below, the clearest Anthony had ever heard one. **We call to ourselves**, the Dweller said, **We speak of things as they are**. Anthony rose from bed and set his computer to record. Sings of Others, rising alongside to breathe, called a hello. Anthony tapped his keys, hit TRANSMIT.

Air Human and I are in a condition of rut, he said.

We congratulate Anthony and Air Human on our condition of rut, Sings of Others responded. The whooping whale cries layered atop the thundering Dweller noises. **We wish ourselves many happy copulations.**

Happy copulations, happy copulations, echoed Two Notches.

A pointless optimism began to resonate in Anthony's mind. He sat before the computer and listened to the sounds of the Deep Dwellers as they rumbled up his spine.

Philana appeared at the hatch. She was buttoning her shirt. "You told the whales about us?" she said.

"Why not?"

She grinned faintly. "I guess there's no reason not to."

Two Notches wailed a question. **Are Anthony and Air Human copulating now**?

Not at present, Anthony replied.

We hope you will copulate often.

Philana, translating the speech on her own, laughed. "Tell them we hope so, too," she said.

And then she stiffened. Anthony's nerves poured fire. Philana turned to him and regarded him with Telamon's eyes.

"I thought you'd see reason," Telamon said. "*I'll surrender*. I like that."

Anthony looked at the possessed woman and groped for a vehicle for his message. Words seemed inadequate, he decided, but would have to do. "You haven't won yet," he said.

Philana's head cocked to one side as Telamon viewed him. "Has it occurred to you," Telamon said, "that if she's free of me, she won't need you at all?"

"You forget something. I'll be rid of *you* as well."

"You can be rid of me any time."

Anthony stared at Telamon for a moment, then suddenly he laughed. He had just realized how to send his message. Telamon looked at him curiously. Anthony turned to his computer deck and flipped to the Dweller translation file.

I/We, he typed, *live in the warm brightness above. We are new to this world, and send good wishes to the Dwellers below.*

Anthony pressed TRANSMIT. Rolling thunder boomed from the boat's speakers. The grammar was probably awful, Anthony knew, but he was fairly certain of the words, and he thought the meaning would be clear.

Telamon frowned, stepped to gaze over Anthony's shoulder.

Calls came from below. A translation tree appeared on the screen.

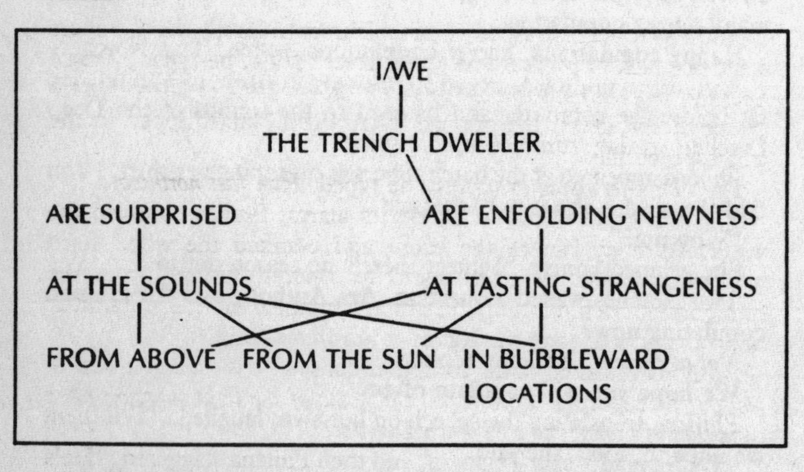

"Trench Dweller" was probably one of the Dwellers' names. "Bubbleward" was a phrase for "up," since bubbles rose to the surface. Anthony tapped the keys.

We are from far away, recently arrived. We are small and foreign to the world. We wish to brush the Dwellers with our thoughts. We regret our lack of clarity in diction.

"I wonder if you've thought this through," Telamon said.

Anthony hit TRANSMIT. Speakers boomed. The subsonics were like a punch in the gut.

"Go jump off a cliff," Anthony said.

"You're making a mistake," said Telamon.

The Dweller's answer was surprisingly direct.

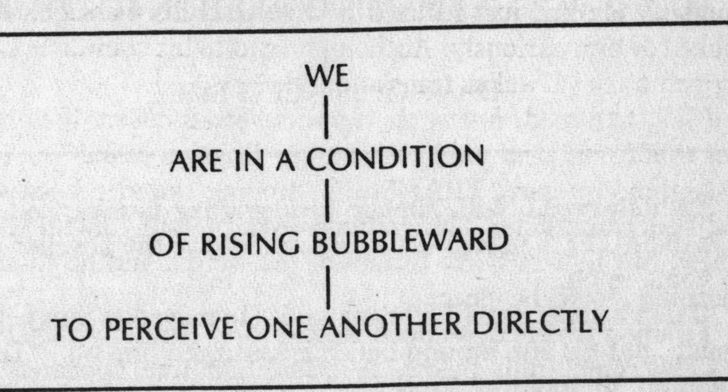

Anthony's heart crashed in astonishment. Could the Dwellers stand the lack of pressure on the surface? *I/We*, he typed, *Trench Dweller, proceed with consideration for safety. I/We recollect that we are small and weak*. He pressed TRANSMIT and flipped to the whalespeech file.

Deep Dweller rising to surface, he typed. *Run fast northward*.

The whales answered with cries of alarm. Flukes pounded the water. Anthony ran to the cabin and cranked the wheel hard to starboard. He increased speed to separate himself from the humpbacks. Behind him, Telamon stumbled in his unfamiliar body as the boat took the waves at a different angle.

Anthony returned to his computer console. *I/We are in a state of motion*, he reported. *Is living in the home of the light occasion for a condition of damage to us/Trench Dweller*?

"You're mad," said Telamon, and then Philana staggered. "He's done it *again*," she said in a stunned voice. She stepped to the starboard bench and sat down. "What's happening?" she asked.

"I'm talking to the Dwellers. One of them is rising to say hello."

"*Now?*"

He gave her a skeletal grin. "It's what you wanted, yes?" She stared at him.

I'm going over cliffs, he thought. One after another.

That, Anthony concluded, is the condition of existence.

Subsonics rattled crockery in the kitchen.

BUBBLEWARD PLATEAU IS CONDITION FOR DAMAGE

|

DAMAGE IS ACCEPTABLE

Anthony typed, *I/We happily await greeting ourselves* and pressed TRANSMIT, then REPEAT. He would give the Dweller a sound to home in on.

"I don't understand," Philana said. He moved to join her on the bench, put his arm around her. She shrugged him off. "Tell me," she said. He took her hand.

"We're going to win."

"How?"

"I don't know yet."

She was too shaken to argue. "It's going to be a long fight," she said.

"I don't care."

Philana took a breath. "I'm scared."

"So am I," said Anthony.

The boat beat itself against the waves. The flying yacht followed, a silent shadow.

Anthony and Philana waited in silence until the Dweller rose, a green-grey mass that looked as if a grassy reef had just calved. Foam roared from its back as it broke water, half an ocean running down its sides. Anthony's boat danced in the sudden white tide, and then the ocean stilled. Bits of the Dweller were all around, spread over the water for leagues—tentacles, filters, membranes. The Dweller's very mass had calmed the sea. The Dweller was so big, Anthony saw, it constituted an entire ecosystem. Sea creatures lived among its folds and tendrils: some had died as they rose, their swim bladders exploding in the release of pressure; others leaped and spun and shrank from the brightness above.

Sunlight shone from the Dweller's form, and the creature pulsed with life.

Terrified, elated, Philana and Anthony rose to say hello.

DATE DUE